To my friend, Jalena Bowling,
Enjoy your journey into the world
of Susie & Simon.
Love + Best Wishes Always,
Karen
(Jn 17:3)
12/11/2015

The Adventures of
Susie & Simon

IN THE SECRET OF GLEN HOLLOW

Karen S. Putnam

ISBN: 1503091058
ISBN 13: 9781503091054
Library of Congress Catalogue Number: 2014919801
CreateSpace Independent Publishing Platform
North Charleston, South Carolina

First Edition

DEDICATION

To Sarah Vickers & Stevie Vickers, two of the neatest, greatest souls one could ever hope to know, and have the privilege of knowing. Watching you interact with each other and seeing the strong bond that has developed between the two of you has been a wondrous sight to see. It has also served to resurrect long-forgotten memories in me.

To Jackie Worman, my closest and dearest friend of nearly four decades. Thank you for reading my first attempt at writing this book while it was still in its infancy, and for also encouraging me to go forward with it. Thank you for allowing me to hide at your home, granting me the seclusion needed to write the last ten chapters. Thank you, also, for giving of your time and energy to read and proofread what I wrote. And thank you for creating for me a synopsis of the book.

To my wonderful husband, Philip Putnam: without you this book would never have been written. Your insistence that the dream I had that forms the foundation of this story needed to be written. Your faith in me and your encouragement gave me the confidence to put my dreams, my thoughts and my imaginations onto paper. Thank you for believing in me – not just in words to me, but in action as you enthusiastically told everyone about the book I was writing. Thank you for all of your hard work in reading and proofreading my manuscript, time and time again. Thank you for all that you have done to help bring this story to fruition; your dedication to it and to me is amazing.

To my little brother, Curtis, who was my Simon.

And to my mother, Myrtle Lee Roy Schultz, who taught me to read and to love reading.

THINGS TO PONDER

"When you were born, you cried and the world rejoiced. Live your life so that when you die, the world cries and you rejoice." - White Elk; a chief of the Oto Nation

Many and Great, O God   (Wakantanka Taku Nitawa)
Many and great, O God, are Thy things,
Maker of earth and sky;
Thy hands have set the heavens with stars;
Thy fingers spread the mountains and plains.
Lo, at Thy Word the waters were formed;
Deep seas obey Thy Voice.
Grant unto us communion with Thee,
Thou star abiding One;
Come unto us and dwell with us;
With Thee are found the gifts of life,
Bless us with life that has no end,
Eternal life with Thee.
- Joseph R. Renville 1779 – 1846; French-Indian fur trader, guide, interpreter, translator, businessman, and an elder of the Dakota (1841 – 1846).

TABLE OF CONTENTS

Chapter 1

JOURNEY TO GLEN HOLLOW

The old, black sedan slowly lumbered its way down the narrow dirt road, missing very few of the holes and ruts that had been carved into it. Nine days earlier a violent thunderstorm, unseasonable for late November, had swept through the peaceful countryside. It left a trail of destruction as if a mighty giant had wantonly stomped and smashed his way throughout the area. Many trees, both large and small, had been damaged or destroyed. Some had been split by lightning; some had lost branches while others were completely uprooted, tossed around like they were merely toothpicks. Several times the driver was required to stop and remove debris from the dirt road before they could continue their journey.

The rain that fell during the storm had been more akin to that of a deluge. The effect of such a torrent gives rise to the image of a dam in the heavens that had suddenly burst, sending forth an avalanche of water down upon the land. The water had descended so fast and so furious that it flowed like a river across the little road, forging crevices and craters of various sizes and depths. With each bump and jolt the driver frowned and muttered. Tightly grasping the steering wheel, his large, beefy hands struggled to maintain control of the sedan as it jerked and swayed.

Occasionally he would peer at them in the rearview mirror. The only visible portion of his face was his squinty brown eyes and shaggy eyebrows. Susie didn't understand why he kept darting glances at them – it wasn't as if they were going to disappear. Perhaps he thought they would jump out and run away. "As if he would care," she mumbled to herself.

Susie was very much aware that the driver was not particularly fond of the fact that he had been assigned the task to take them to Glen Hollow. He had grumbled many times, quite loudly, about the long drive during the first few hours after their departure from the Willington Child Services Office. But take them he did.

Because the trip to Glen Hollow was a long one (Mrs. Crenshaw had said about eight hours, give or take an hour), Mrs. Crenshaw had packed a snack basket of biscuits and a small thermos of milk for them. They had eaten the last of the biscuits and shared the remaining milk a little more than an hour ago, shortly before turning onto this road. Simon's appetite was so voracious that Susie had given him her biscuit and the majority of the milk. Her abdomen had begun growling now, reminding her it was empty and in need of food. She pressed in on her stomach in an attempt to quiet its rumblings.

Mrs. Crenshaw had awakened her entire household at four o'clock in order to allow them time to properly eat and say their goodbyes. To Simon's delight, she had prepared for them a hearty breakfast of scrambled eggs, bacon, crispy fried potatoes and Simon's all-time favorite - pancakes with lots of butter and warm maple syrup. The milk was fresh from the dairy (just delivered that morning), and there was even fresh-squeezed orange juice prepared by Darcy, Mrs. Crenshaw's daughter.

The early rising made for a very long and wearisome day. They had been traveling now for over ten hours; the past hour had been on this awful road called Glen Hollow Road. The sun was low in the sky, getting ready to set. Soon it would be dark, and Simon would be upset. He hated the dark.

Susie closed her eyes and rested her head against the seat. She felt very tired as she thought back on the events of the morning. They had left Willington at six in order to arrive at Glen Hollow by two o'clock that afternoon. No one could have foreseen the problems they had encountered along the way.

The first two hours of their journey was on the expressway; it was uneventful even though it was crowded with vehicles of all types and sizes. Simon, her four year old brother, slept most of the way curled up beside her with his head in her lap.

Leaving the expressway, they entered State Highway 135 North. Though it was a main road and heavily traveled, it only had one wide lane for each direction. They had scarcely traveled more than twenty minutes when traffic had come to a halt. Mr. Warbly followed suit, of course, and eased the clunky, old sedan to a stop. Five cars ahead, a small group of people were gathered together, standing around and talking. Like smoke signals, each time they spoke their breaths rose up in little puffs as the warmth collided with the frosty air.

Mr. Warbly got out of the sedan, poked his head back in through the open door and gruffly told Susie that she and Simon were to "stay put". As an apparent afterthought, he reached over the steering column and shut off the ignition, removed the keys and shoved them into his coat pocket. He shut his door and turned his collar up to shield his neck from the chilly air, thrusting his hands into his pockets as he trudged over to the small gathering.

The frigid December air quickly penetrated the sedan, dissipating the fragile remains of heated air without much effort. The rapidly falling temperature awakened Simon. He sat up, shivered, and looked around.

"What happened?" he asked.

"I don't know. There's probably an accident up ahead," Susie answered.

"Can we see?"

"No, it's too far up ahead."

"I'm cold," Simon declared as he hunched his shoulders, pressing his arms up against his chest in an attempt to gain warmth.

Susie unbuttoned her coat and removed it. "Come, sit on my lap, and I'll share my coat with you. That way, you'll have two coats to help keep you warm," she offered, smiling at him while mentally bracing herself in an attempt to prevent the shivers from starting.

Without hesitation Simon slid over and climbed into her lap, snuggling up against her. She wrapped her coat around him, turning the collar up so that it would help keep his neck warm. Deftly she pulled his knit hat further down on his head so that his ears were completely covered. She smiled sadly as a memory of Nana surfaced. Nana knitted the hat for Simon last Christmas. It was a bright purple and had white snowflakes and lime green dinosaurs with purple spots (Simon's favorite color combination, as it pertains to dinosaurs). The pompom at the tip of the hat was fat and fluffy, with all three colors in equal proportions.

"Are we almost there?" he asked amid a yawn.

"It'll be a little while yet," she answered. "Why don't you go back to sleep?"

"Okay," he mumbled. He closed his eyes, drifting off to sleep as Susie gently rubbed his back.

Several minutes passed before Mr. Warbly returned; his face was quite red from the bitterly cold air. Quickly he started the car and ramped up the heat, holding his hands up against the vents in order to warm them. He told her that there had been a collision a mile or so up the road involving several vehicles; all but one of the damaged vehicles had been removed, and the tow truck was currently in the process of removing it. Susie asked if anyone had been hurt. He shrugged and said two ambulances had each taken a person; but their injuries were minor, according to the group he had joined.

After the heat had been sufficiently restored in the old car, Susie removed her coat from around Simon and gently shifted him onto the seat. She put her coat back on, repositioned herself and then laid his head back in her lap. He slept soundly through it all. Thirty minutes later traffic was once again moving.

Mr. Warbly was very unhappy about the loss of time and proceeded to make up for it. Rapidly he would approach a car, or a small line of cars, traveling the speed limit. He would mumble something about "slow-pokes" and "Sunday drivers". Every time there was even the slightest break in the string of oncoming cars, he would gun the engine, darting around the vehicles that were in his way. Each time Susie would hold her breath, praying they would safely make it back to their own lane. Several times the traffic was so heavy, both in their lane and in the oncoming traffic lane, he could only pass the cars one at a time, playing vehicle leap frog. And every time he broke free from the pack, the old sedan's engine would roar, sounding like thunder as they flew down the road.

They sped along in this manner toward Foxboro Station for just over two hours. Dozens of isolated towns and villages dotted the landscape along the main road, none being a size of any consequence. Susie noticed that few had more than a general store, an occasional gas station and a scattering of houses.

Not too far from the outskirts of Foxboro Station they heard the wail of a siren. Simon's head popped up like a gopher exiting its burrow. Susie turned and looked out the rear window. Several hundred yards behind them a police car was rapidly approaching, lights flashing and siren blaring. It quickly caught up to their old sedan.

"Good grief," Mr. Warbly muttered, turning on his signal light and maneuvering his car onto the shoulder of the road.

After stopping the car, he reached over, opened the glove box and removed the vehicle registration and proof of insurance. Next he pulled his wallet from his back pocket and removed his driver's license. The police officer approached his car door just as he rolled down the window.

"License, registration and proof of insurance, please," the officer requested.

Mr. Warbly handed them to the officer. "I know I was speedin', off'cer; but, you see, I'm t' deliver these two kids t' Glen Hollow Orphanage by two o'clock. We're runnin' late 'cause there was an accident that delayed us; 'n I was just tryin' t' make up the time."

The officer peered inside the sedan at Susie and Simon. He smiled at them both, giving them a polite nod of his head in response to Susie's smile and Simon's big grin. He then turned his attention to Mr. Warbly as he opened his ticket book and began writing.

"Sir, there's no excuse for speeding. You were doing seventy-five in a fifty-five zone. It's better to arrive at your destination safe, and a little late, than not at all," he remarked in a firm but courteous manner.

"Yes, sir," Mr. Warbly responded meekly.

He removed the ticket from his book and handed it to Mr. Warbly. He had written in large letters the word 'WARNING' diagonally across the ticket.

"I'm giving you a warning this time, Mr. Warbly. Slow it down, sir." He returned to Mr. Warbly his license, registration and proof of insurance. Cordially he said, "You have a nice day, sir."

"Thank you," Mr. Warbly responded, a hint of surprise surfacing in his tone.

The officer turned to leave and, as he did so, smiled at Simon and returned Simon's wave, thoroughly delighting Simon. He proceeded to his vehicle and got back into his car.

Mr. Warbly returned his license to his wallet before shoving the wallet into his back pocket. Hastily he tossed the registration and proof of insurance back into the glove box and slammed its door shut. Turning on the signal indicator, he checked to see that the coast was clear, then eased the old sedan back onto the road. The police car followed them, and continued to do so the remaining thirty miles to Foxboro Station. Upon entering the outskirts of town, the police officer turned onto the first side street, disappearing from their view.

They had arrived at Foxboro Station just past the noon hour, and Mr. Warbly stopped to refuel at the first place he saw. In addition to being a gas station, a tow company and a mechanic shop, it also housed a small diner. To save time, Mr. Warbly decided that they would have a sandwich in the diner instead of finding a restaurant elsewhere in town.

As they exited the sedan, he granted them a grand total of fifteen minutes to eat and use the facilities. Susie took Simon by the hand, race-walking to the restroom doors. After making certain it was clean (it was sparkling clean), she left Simon in the men's room and hastened to the ladies room.

When she exited, Simon was outside the door, quietly waiting for her. Together they walked back to the sedan and waited for Mr. Warbly to finish paying for the fuel. They had a very short wait before he burst through the station door and proceeded toward the glass door of the diner.

"Come on," he huffed; "ain't got all day."

They ran and quickly caught up to him; Simon was practically stepping on his heels. As they entered the diner, they were cheerfully greeted by a lady who was standing behind the counter.

Her name, according to her name tag, was Annie, and she was really pretty. She had short-cut, flaming red hair, milky-white skin and large, cat-green eyes that had the most thick, sweeping black eyelashes Susie had ever seen. Annie wore a short-sleeve, hot pink uniform trimmed in white. Its lace overlay collar, white pearl buttons and wide, flared sleeve cuffs smartly set off the pink color.

Annie's perky demeanor and dazzling smile amused Simon. He returned her smile with his own cheery grin as he waved 'hello.' Susie, too, was intrigued by Annie; she looked like a delicate porcelain doll that you see as a collector's edition. To her own surprise, Susie suddenly realized that the dismal cloud that had hung over their journey thus far had now miraculously evaporated. She smiled back at Annie, and softly said 'hello'.

"Three in your party?" she inquired of Mr. Warbly as she winked at Simon.

"Yes, ma'am," Mr. Warbly responded crustily as Annie walked toward the end of the counter.

Susie noticed that she and Annie were about the same height (five foot); that is, until Annie came out from behind the counter. She was wearing six-inch pink stilettos!

'She's like a living doll,' Susie thought with an amused chuckle.

Watching the diminutive Annie as she sauntered toward the tables caused another thought to flash into Susie's mind; 'Or like a pixie from Nana's stories'.

As soon as that thought popped into Susie's mind, Annie turned her head. From over her shoulder, she looked directly at Susie, their eyes locking. Annie's eyes were twinkling; she smiled playfully and then… she winked! Suddenly, Annie's ears were elongated and pointy at the top; and, for a fleeting second, Susie was positive she saw sheer butterfly wings protruding from Annie's back. And just as quickly as it all started, it was over.

Neither Mr. Warbly nor Simon appeared to have seen anything, even though they were immediately behind Annie and couldn't possibly have missed it.

"I must really be tired," Susie muttered softly; "I'm starting to hallucinate."

Annie escorted them to a booth, patiently waiting while Susie assisted Simon in removing his coat and then her own. Simon insisted that he sit on the aisle and not next to the wall as Susie suggested. After biting her lower lip momentarily, she smiled and said he could, but that he would have to behave like a big boy. Giving her a very animated agreement to do just that, Susie accepted his promise and folded their coats neatly. Sliding into the booth, she placed the coats between herself and the wall. Simon scampered up onto the seat next to her and plopped down. His eyes were level with the table.

"I think you need a booster seat," Annie commented with a cheery smile. "Allow me," she said, scurrying away to the stack of booster seats that were leaning precariously in the corner against the back wall.

She was back seconds later with the booster seat and assisted Simon in reseating himself. After that task was accomplished, she attempted to give Mr. Warbly a menu.

He shook his head 'no' and curtly said, "don't need it". He ordered grill cheese sandwiches and potato chips all around, with a small glass of milk each for Susie and Simon and a cup of coffee for himself. Simon protested, a little ardently, that he wanted a cheeseburger. Regrettably for Simon, Mr. Warbly was unimpressed with his pleas, stating they didn't have time to wait for a cheeseburger to cook.

Annie gave Simon a conciliatory smile, telling him that she'd make his sandwich with extra cheese. He grinned, flashing her one of his best smiles, and told her "thank you".

Mr. Warbly scowled and grumbled, "No ma'am; I ain't payin' for extra cheese."

Annie eyed him and replied tartly, "No extra charge, sir."

"Well, all right then; he can have it," he huffed, turning his attention to the road map he had purchased in the gas station.

Five minutes later, Annie brought their order. Her friendliness and cheerful voice was a most welcome change from the surly attitude of Mr. Warbly. And although he dismissed Annie abruptly, Annie's demeanor was just as sunny as when they first met her. She winked at Simon as she turned to leave; Simon giggled.

Gruffly, Mr. Warbly ordered Susie and Simon to "eat 'n be quick 'bout it".

Simon wasn't exactly co-operative, and was completely undeterred by Mr. Warbly's constant urging to hurry. In his impish voice and with gleeful smiles, Simon kept repeating to Mr. Warbly that "Nana said it was bad for the tummy to eat fast".

Mr. Warbly had finished his lunch before Susie was even half finished, and Simon … well, Simon had taken just two bites of his sandwich and had eaten only three potato chips. It was difficult for Susie not to laugh, but she managed to contain her mirth. She knew Simon well, and to do otherwise would only encourage him to continue his antics.

Unfortunately, Annie did laugh. To add insult to injury, she also told Simon he was right. That was all the encouragement Simon needed; he slowly chewed, counting each deliberate bite to make certain he chewed the minimum required times.

Mr. Warbly was livid. He got out of the booth and began furiously pacing, muttering something about a schedule to keep. He'd stop every few passes, glare at Simon and try his best to get Simon to hurry. The more Simon ignored him, the angrier Mr. Warbly grew; and the angrier he became, the redder his face turned. Finally, after several minutes of this dance of wills, his bulbous nose was a much deeper red than his face.

Simon, giggling, leaned over to Susie and whispered in her ear. Susie stifled her laughter (although a couple of chuckles did escape) and told him to eat. Mr. Warbly stormed over, demanding to know what was so funny.

Susie responded calmly, "Nothing; Simon is just being Simon. He's almost finished with his lunch."

Simon, in all innocence, spoke up, "I didn't say 'nothing', Susie. Didn't you hear me?"

Leaning toward her, he looked intently at Susie as he placed his hand on her shoulder in an attempt to garner her attention. Susie promptly shushed him, but Mr. Warbly wouldn't let it go.

With his large hands placed solidly on the table, he leaned down toward Simon. Looking squarely at Simon, Mr. Warbly said, "Why don't you just tell us both?"

Simon nodded as he swallowed the morsel he had been chewing.

As she began to protest, Mr. Warbly cut her off, saying, "Quiet, missy!" rather harshly.

Simon, puzzled by his reaction, looked at Susie. She shrugged. With his usual effervescence, Simon repeated what he had whispered to Susie. "When you were walking so fast and your face was so red, I told Susie that your nose looked like Rudolph the Red Nosed Reindeer."

He giggled gleefully and nodded. "And it did," he proclaimed exuberantly. His bright, blue eyes sparkled with delight at the image of Mr. Warbly as Rudolph the Red Nosed Reindeer, expressing the childlike joy of his young age.

"That's 'nough," Mr. Warbly barked. "We're leavin' now!" he ordered, grabbing Simon's arm.

Simon desperately held onto Susie, crying out her name. Susie wrapped her arms around Simon, struggling with all her might to keep Simon with her while yelling at Mr. Warbly to "leave him alone".

Seemingly out of nowhere Annie appeared, furious with Mr. Warbly and attempted to intervene. Mr. Warbly angrily pushed her away, so she yelled for someone named Ed to "get out here now".

A big, burly man with broad shoulders came out of the kitchen, pushing the heavy, swinging doors as if they were made of paper. He strode over to Mr. Warbly, his long stride closing the distance with relative ease and in a very short amount of time. Stopping a few feet in front of Mr. Warbly, he politely asked if there was a problem. His voice was a deep bass, echoing like rolling thunder. Mr. Warbly released Simon, glared at the man and told him to mind his own business.

Ed, who was at least two feet taller and a hundred pounds heavier than Mr. Warbly, chuckled as he crossed his muscular arms across his barrel chest. Staring down at Mr. Warbly, he said, "This *is* my business; I own it, and what happens in here is of my concern. So, you want to explain your behavior?"

Mr. Warbly was flabbergasted; and apparently a little anxious, realizing that perhaps he was no match for this man. He began to stutter and stammer. "Well, uh... I... uh... I've been hired t' drive these two kids t' Glen Hollow. I have a schedule t' keep, 'n they're wastin' time."

"You've been here all of twenty minutes; I hardly think that constitutes time wasted," he retorted sharply. Ed turned to Simon, smiled and kindly said, "Finish your sandwich, little man; you can't have dessert until your plate's clean."

Simon's countenance lit up; he quickly took another bite, chewing rapidly.

Mr. Warbly glared at Ed, squinting his beady, little eyes and jutting out his chin. "There'll be no dessert; Child Services didn't give me 'nough for that," he groused.

"It's on the house," Ed responded cheerfully, winking at both Susie and Simon. "Whatever you want, just tell Annie."

"Thank you," Susie and Simon said in unison, truly grateful for his kindness.

"It's my pleasure. Here's my card," he said, handing a business card to each of them. "If either of you should ever need anything, just give me or Annie a call." He smiled and added, "Any time, day or night."

Susie nodded and again thanked him. He gave her a slight nod. Briefly he turned to face Mr. Warbly, giving him a warning look before returning to his kitchen.

Simon wolfed down the last portion of his sandwich while Annie took their dessert orders. Simon, of course, ordered his favorite – a banana split; Susie ordered a piece of peach pie a la mode. Mr. Warbly, with a sour look, shook his head when Annie asked for his order.

"You sure?" she asked. "It's on the house," she added persuasively.

Mr. Warbly looked up at her, and then sheepishly requested a piece of apple pie and another cup of coffee.

Annie smiled at him and replied, "Coming right up", as she hurriedly left for the kitchen.

Minutes later Annie returned with their desserts, two more small glasses of milk and poured Mr. Warbly another cup of coffee. "If you have a thermos, I'll fill it free of charge," she offered sweetly. "It's fresh brewed," she said as an additional inducement.

Mr. Warbly slowly nodded and said, "Thank you, Miss; but it's in the sedan."

Smiling, ever so graciously, she told him, "You're welcome to go get it."

He actually smiled… and smiled *at* her. He nodded and said, "I'll do that. Thank you."

Annie returned his smile with one of her own. Then she smiled and winked at Simon before disappearing into the kitchen.

Mr. Warbly looked at Susie and said gruffly, "Be right back."

He slid out of the booth and was out the door faster than Susie would have thought possible. True to his word, he was right back; it took him about two minutes to return with the thermos. Susie watched as he approached the counter. To her surprise, he seemed a little nervous. He handed Annie the thermos and politely asked her to total up the bill so he could pay it. Smiling courteously, she told him she would as soon as she filled his thermos.

Annie went into the kitchen and returned a few minutes later. Handing him his thermos, she pleasantly said, "I rinsed it out with hot water first so the coffee will stay hot longer. I hope you have a safe journey."

He gave her a crooked, little smile as if this had been the first time anyone had done anything, or said anything, nice to him. "Thank you, Miss. Now if my bill is ready, I'd like t' pay so we can be on our way."

"Certainly," she responded as she began tallying up the order ticket.

Mr. Warbly turned to Susie and Simon who were still sitting in the booth. Simon, with a very contented look on his face, had just swallowed the last bite of his banana split. Competing for space on his little face were the remnants of chocolate syrup, butterscotch syrup, cherry syrup, vanilla, chocolate and strawberry ice creams and a little whip cream.

"Susie, take Simon t' the bathroom 'n wash his face. Be quick 'bout it," he snapped.

"No need for that," Annie countered. "Use one of these wet cloths, Susie." She held up a container for Susie and Mr. Warbly to see.

Susie smiled at Annie as she guided Simon up to the counter and took a cloth from the container. Holding him steady, her right hand firmly on his shoulder, she began cleaning Simon's face and hands, removing the last vestiges of his treat.

Just as she finished her task, Ed came out through the swinging doors. He took the order ticket from Annie, tore it up and extended his right hand to Mr. Warbly. "I've decided the whole meal is on the house. The same will be true for your meal on your return trip if you have a mind to eat here."

Mr. Warbly was dumbfounded. As if in a trance, he slowly put his right hand into Ed's and shook hands with him. "Thank you," he stammered.

"You're welcome," Ed responded cordially. With a conspiratorial wink at Susie and Simon, he quickly disappeared behind the metal and glass swinging doors of the kitchen.

They said their goodbyes to Annie as Mr. Warbly ushered them out the door and into the sedan. Susie felt a little saddened about leaving; Simon was too. But Annie had assured them both that she and Ed were just a phone call away. She waved to them as the old sedan pulled away from the Diner and back onto the highway.

Lunch had taken a total of forty-five minutes; Mr. Warbly was not happy that his schedule had been so terribly disrupted. He groused to Susie and Simon how he had been inconvenienced enough as it is, what with having to drive to Glen Hollow on what should have been his day off. Therefore, he announced, there would be no stopping until they arrived at Glen Hollow. (However, two hours later, Simon did convince him that a quick bathroom stop was *very* necessary.)

An hour out of Foxboro Station, they turned onto County Road 24 East which would take them to the turnoff for Glen Hollow, aptly named Glen Hollow Road. They sped along the wide paved road, flying past a multitude of small farms. Thirty minutes later their journey was again interrupted – this time it was the bridge. Up ahead, near the bridge, were barricades with flashing yellow lights. Mr. Warbly slowed the sedan to a stop. The sign read 'Bridge Out'. He began shaking his head and muttering.

He turned the car around and returned to the main road. Once there, he turned right and headed for Rosemont, a little village fifty miles further north of Foxboro Station. Just outside of Rosemont, Mr. Warbly eased the cumbersome sedan onto County Road 4 East, and they hastily and precariously continued their journey. Hastily because Mr. Warbly ignored the posted 35 mile-an-hour speed-limit sign. Precariously because the road had once been an old stagecoach road; its curving pavement held many dips and hills, and was extremely narrow with barely enough room for one small vehicle in each lane. This particular, ancient sedan was too wide, claiming half of the other lane in addition to its own.

Nearly another hour passed before they reached and crossed the old, masonry seven-arch bridge spanning the mighty Anicaw River. A large river under normal circumstances, the Anicaw was swollen with the recent flush of rainwater. Its waves were nearly lapping the underside of the bridge.

Susie was thankful that Simon was asleep. When Simon was barely six weeks old, they had been left with Nana so that Mommy and Daddy could go out to dinner. On their way back from dinner, a freakish storm caused their car to skid off the road and into the Miramahonni River, just on the outskirts of Stonebridge. It was in the dead of night; no one was there to help. They drowned. It was only last year that Simon learned how they had died. Deep water terrified him ever since. His nightmares about drowning had just recently ceased; but with this bridge being so close to the water, Susie feared it would trigger those dreams anew if he awakened and saw the river. She breathed a sigh of relief once they had reached the other side.

Shortly after crossing the Anicaw, they connected with County Road 15 South, quickly traveling the short distance to County Road 24 East on this side of the river. Fifteen minutes later, they had reached Glen Hollow Road.

Well, Susie really didn't think you could call it 'a road' considering it was more like an obstacle course or a roller-coaster. They had been bouncing down this road for an hour, and Susie silently prayed they would soon arrive at the orphanage.

'Hopefully in one piece', she thought as the sedan hit another large hole, bouncing both she and Simon around like marbles in a bag.

Carefully so as not to wake him, Susie gently moved Simon's head from her lap onto the seat. She slid forward and lightly tapped the driver on his shoulder. "Mr. Warbly, are we almost there?" she asked.

"Don't rightly know; never been t' Glen Hollow," he responded irritably. "Accordin' t' the directions Mrs. Crenshaw gave me, this road only goes t' Glen Hollow; 'n it's 'bout a half hour or so from the main road. I guess that doesn't account for the current road condition."

He narrowed his eyes as if to discourage any more questions and continued, "Don't fret yourself, missy. It's my guess Glen Hollow's 'bout twenty miles from the main road." He shrugged. "We've been averagin' 'bout ten mile-'n-hour, so I figure we should be there in about an hour." Mr. Warbly gave her a dismissive nod, and then returned his full attention to navigating the treacherous slip of a road.

Susie gently lifted Simon's head, placing it onto her lap as she settled back into the worn seat of the aging sedan. There was nothing to see along this little road except an occasional clearing that might contain a few horses or cows. She smiled. She loved horses; they are such noble creatures. And she loved cows, too, for they seemed to be gentle giants, like elephants. She closed her eyes, and her thoughts drifted back to yesterday.

Mrs. Crenshaw, the director of the Child Services Office in Willington, had come home from her office early. She was excited and yet a little sad.

"A private orphanage called Glen Hollow," she said; "will take both of you immediately."

She had been kind enough to allow them to stay with her until she could locate a place or a family that would accept both of them. That process had taken a little more than three months. Mrs. Crenshaw's eyes had welled with tears as she hugged them both.

"If it were even remotely possible, I would keep you. But, as a widow with four children at home," she sighed; "well, you know firsthand that I can't."

Mrs. Crenshaw's tiny, two-bedroom home just couldn't expand to permanently house two more people no matter how much they wished it could. Susie merely nodded, struggling not to show her disappointment in being sent to an orphanage.

Simon kept his eyes focused onto his shoes, his hands thrust deep in his pockets. He bit down on his lower lip, attempting to still its quivering. He had allowed himself to hope, to believe, that they would stay forever with Mrs. C (that's what he called her). He liked Mrs. C; she was nice, and so were her children. It was fun having three older brothers and another sister. Sure, he knew it was crowded with so many people living here; but he *liked* Mrs. C. He thought she liked him. And now she was sending him away to an orphanage; not even to a family. Though he struggled hard not to cry, tears began filling his eyes.

In contrast, Susie's face became as hard and as vacant as that of a stone statue upon hearing the news. She didn't want Mrs. Crenshaw to know the depth of her disappointment. Contrary to what Simon had come to believe, Susie had always known that they would inevitably leave Mrs. Crenshaw's home; but she had hoped that a family would be found to take them both. Now she knew that would not happen. Instinctively she put her arm around Simon and drew him close.

"Come," Mrs. Crenshaw had said as she shepherded Susie and Simon to the couch and sat them down.

She gracefully slipped around the coffee table and into the chair opposite them, perching on the edge of the seat. Smiling encouragingly, she reached over and clasped their small hands into hers.

Giving their hands an affectionate squeeze, she softly said, "Please allow me to tell you what I know of Glen Hollow."

The children meekly nodded their assent.

Mrs. Crenshaw smiled and said, "Thank you", releasing their hands as she gracefully slid back into the depths of her chair.

"Glen Hollow," she began; "is the ancestral home of the Evermore family, and has been for hundreds of years. Many, many years ago it was quite the showplace. It had all manner of livestock, orchards and produce. They also had a stable of the most beautiful horses and were quite famous for their horses. It is a very large estate – thousands and thousands of acres - and has many trees and meadows, ponds and streams. The Anicaw River even flows through a portion of it. It's because of the Anicaw River they were able to harvest their forest timber and to mill the lumber on the estate. But that old mill hasn't been used in decades."

"How do they do it now?" Susie asked.

"The past fifty or so years, they have contracted a company in Foxboro Station to handle it. The company hires the lumberjacks to harvest the trees, and the logs are transported to mills in Rosemont and Eagles Ridge. Both are small towns, and they depend on the mills for jobs. The Evermore's gristmill has also been closed for about the same amount of time."

"What's a gristmill?" Simon interrupted.

"A gristmill, Simon, such as the one on the Evermore Estate," Mrs. Crenshaw patiently explained; "is a building that has grinding stones used to grind grain. The water flows over the water wheel, turning the wheel which then turns the grinding stones. After harvest, the various grains were ground into flour, or meal or into feed for the animals."

Simon's eyes sparkled with the revelation. "That's where the flour comes from in the grocery store," he said.

"Not exactly, Simon," she chuckled. "The modern process doesn't use stones. Some people prefer the course texture of stone ground flour or meal, so there are a few old mills still operating. I think both Morton's Cove and Black Rock have one. Rosemont did, but it closed about three years ago."

Simon just nodded his head as he absorbed this tidbit of information.

"Anyway," Mrs. Crenshaw continued her story; "before Miss Pritchett's mother died, there were several lovely gardens and fountains all throughout the estate. For as long as anyone can remember, the Evermores hosted garden festivals. People came from *everywhere* to join in the festivities."

She smiled and her eyes sparkled as images were recalled from deep within her memory. "My parents lived nearby in Rosemont, so I attended the festivals from the time I was born. I actually remember a little of one festival. Most of my memories stem from pictures and from stories told by my parents, my grandparents and other relatives."

"Tell us about it," Susie and Simon begged her as they leaned forward, anxiously awaiting her story.

She smiled at their love of a good story.

"Well," she said slowly, recalling the faded memories; "the festivals were a three day affair and were held each season. It was a way for neighbors to get together, catch up on news and to just celebrate life. It was like a carnival or a fair, only better. Everywhere you looked, they had decorated the grounds with streamers, and balloons and pretty lanterns. It was truly amazing; a wonderland for both children and adults."

"Some of the meadows were used for camping because most people had traveled a considerable distance to Glen Hollow. But the meadow directly in front of the manor was where they erected the big tent pavilions. Some of the pavilions were where the food was cooked, some were for dining and others were for resting or just visiting. Oh, and a small one served as the first aid station."

Lost in the distant memories, Mrs. Crenshaw's face took on the starry gaze of a dreamer. She spoke softly as if the magical memories might flee at any moment. "And the food…. there were so many tables of food and drink. Everything you could imagine and more. There was such a variety of meats and cheeses, fruits and vegetables, breads, puddings, pies, cakes and a wide assortment of pastries like you've never seen. There were bowls of nuts and berries; platters of caramel apples, popcorn balls and so many different types of homemade candy. To drink, they had fresh milk, fruit punch, apple cider, lemonade, coffee and tea."

Her smile was tender and soft as the memories replayed in her mind, as vibrant as if it were only yesterday. "Several groups of musicians wandered all around playing songs."

With a brief pause, she gave a nod to Simon since he loved sing-alongs. "And they'd even take requests. I remember one such man repeatedly playing for me 'Old MacDonald Had a Farm.'"

She laughed lightheartedly. "Now that was a patient soul if there ever was one." Smiling, she continued; "There were jugglers, and clowns and magicians. They also had games…."

"What kind of games?" Simon interrupted again, his curiosity piqued.

"Well, let's see." Mrs. Crenshaw bit her lower lip slightly as she concentrated, searching her memories. "I believe they had croquet, horseshoes, lawn darts, badminton and lawn hopscotch. They even had horse rides."

"Wow-wee," Simon exclaimed as Susie asked, "Really?"

"Oh, yes," Mrs. Crenshaw nodded. "It was a great time of fun and fellowship. But the winter festivals weren't quite as elaborate, I'm told, since they were held inside the manor."

"Why?" Simon asked.

"The weather, dear; it's far too cold to be outside. Anyway, the festivals would begin each day at sunrise and ended at sunset. The grand finale was always a fireworks display on the last night. My mother has many, many albums full of pictures of the festivals. My favorite picture is of me when I was just five years old. It was the September 1956 festival; I was sitting with Miss Murielle on a very large, white stallion."

"Do they still have the festivals?" Susie asked, optimistically, while simultaneously Simon burst out with, "Can I see the pictures?"

Mrs. Crenshaw laughed and nodded. "I'm sure my mother wouldn't mind, Simon. I'll bring some to you."

"When?" Simon pressed.

"Next weekend I'll be visiting my mother, so I'll visit you at Glen Hollow about three o'clock on Sunday afternoon," she responded, grinning at him.

"All right!" he exclaimed exuberantly, bobbing his head and pumping his arm in a triumphant gesture.

"As to the festivals, Susie, I'm sorry to say they no longer have them." There was a hint of sadness in her voice and in her eyes.

"Why?" both children chimed in unison.

Mrs. Crenshaw slowly exhaled. "Miss Murielle died just before the Winter Festival in 1956, and Mr. Pritchett didn't continue them. Over the years, he allowed the gardens to fall into considerable disrepair."

Both Susie and Simon registered surprise and curiosity as they again asked, "Why?"

Mrs. Crenshaw shrugged, attempting to deflect the question. "Perhaps they reminded him too much of her. No one really knows."

She emitted a small sigh, more of an effort to collect her thoughts than anything else. "Anyway, the current owner, Miss Eloise Pritchett, inherited the property sometime after her father died." Her eyes narrowed as she reflected, thinking of the timeframe. "That was a little more than forty years ago," she added.

Smiling tenderly at Susie, she nodded her head ever so briefly. "Like you Susie, Miss Pritchett was seven when her mother died. Her father never remarried."

"Why not?" Susie asked, a little curious.

Mrs. Crenshaw shrugged and shook her head. "Everyone said that he missed his wife so much."

Silence ensued as the somber news wove its way into their minds.

After a few seconds had passed, Mrs. Crenshaw cleared her throat and continued. "A few years after she inherited Glen Hollow, Miss Pritchett decided to turn it into a private orphanage."

Simon's bright, blue eyes flashed with a quizzical gleam as he asked, "Does Miss Pritchett have children?"

Mrs. Crenshaw, surprised by his question, inhaled sharply. Her response was cautious. "Yes, she did. She had a child many years ago, a baby girl. Her husband left one night and took the baby with him. The police were never able to find them. She hired private investigators, but they also couldn't find them. It was a very sad time for her, and for the surrounding communities. Everyone pitched in and helped search for them, but no one had any luck in finding them."

"Why did he do it?" Simon asked, his voice beginning to tremble. "Was she bad?"

"No, Simon," Mrs. Crenshaw was quick to reassure him. "Miss Pritchett is a very nice lady. No one knows why he did what he did; but it broke her heart."

"Is that why she started the orphanage?" Susie asked softly.

"Possibly; but whatever her reason, she has helped many children over the years. She limits the number of children to twelve; probably because she has a small staff. The majority of their food is raised on the estate; it's still a working farm. In addition to the herb and vegetable gardens, there are chickens, pigs, a few horses and, I do believe, milk cows."

Simon's face brightened, and he asked, "Can I pet them?"

"It's 'may I', and I don't know, Simon," she answered, smiling at him. "But I'm certain Miss Pritchett will tell you what is allowed."

She would truly miss them both, and it saddened her greatly that she could not keep them with her. She inhaled deeply and softly released it, forcing herself to remain cheerful.

"Now as to the staff," she continued; "Miss Pritchett does employ some seasonal staff to help with the fields, but her permanent staff consists of eighteen people. There are four men that take care of the animals and fields, four men that handle the general repairs and maintenance, a Head Housemistress, three maids, one cook, a cook's assistant, two general duty assistants, a nurse and a teacher."

"Why a nurse and a teacher?" Simon queried, his expression a cross between puzzlement and curiosity.

"That's because Glen Hollow is a long way into the countryside." she patiently explained. "The closest town is called Foxboro Station, and it's about two hours from Glen Hollow. It's too far to attend school in Foxboro Station, so it's necessary to have a teacher on staff. She employs a nurse just in case there are any minor illnesses or injuries."

"What happens if I get really, *really* sick?" Simon asked.

Mrs. Crenshaw smiled at Simon, affectionately tapping the tip of his nose with her index finger. "I doubt you will, Simon; but if you do, they will take you to Foxboro Station. There is a small hospital there."

"What's a general duty assistant?" Susie's asked.

Mrs. Crenshaw slightly shrugged her shoulders as she slowly shook her head. "I'm not certain, Susie; I think the assistants supervise the children for the most part. It's my guess they also help with other duties wherever they are needed because the manor is quite large. It has three stories and some areas also have an attic."

"Wow," both children replied.

"Do we have our own rooms?" Susie asked, hopeful.

"I don't believe so," Mrs. Crenshaw responded tentatively. "From what I understand, the rooms are quite spacious and are designed for room-mates; but I don't know the specific number per room."

Simon's face registered the panic he felt, and he shook his head vigor-ously. "No, I want Susie," he cried.

Quickly Mrs. Crenshaw arose from her chair and sat on the edge of the coffee table, across from Simon. Pulling him to her, Mrs. Crenshaw hugged Simon and gently rocked him several times. She kissed the top of his head and then released him, her forehead touching his.

"Simon, I have given instruction to Miss Pritchett that you and Susie will room together until such time as you, Simon, decide you are ready to share a room with the other boys."

She sat back and looked directly into his eyes. "Please don't worry Simon. Miss Pritchett will follow my instructions. Okay?"

Simon nodded as he sat against the back of the couch, snuggling up to Susie.

"If they only accept twelve, are there ten now?" Susie softly asked.

"No," Mrs. Crenshaw replied. "There are eight currently. Simon will be the youngest; however, I think one boy is only a few months older than Simon. And you will be the oldest, Susie, but not by much."

"Did you send those children there, too?" Susie asked, her voice tinged with sadness.

Mrs. Crenshaw responded gently, her eyes filled with compassion. "No, dear; you and Simon are the first. I've heard good reports about Glen Hollow over the years. I've never placed anyone there because it's so far away. I wouldn't have this time if anything nearby had been available."

She leaned forward, gently cradled their faces in her hands and said, "I promise you that I will not stop looking for a good family that will adopt both of you. In the meantime, I will visit you regularly at Glen Hollow.

Should there be any problems, I will bring you back here; and we will search again. But please give Glen Hollow an honest try."

"We will, Mrs. Crenshaw," Susie spoke in a voice far more mature than her young age. Simon had echoed Susie's words with the animated nodding of his head.

The sedan swerved hard to the left, lurching Susie sideways against the car door, jarring her from her thoughts. A weary sigh escaped from her lips, one that found its roots in the deep sorrow that filled her heart. With a staunch effort, she subdued the tears that began to fall.

'I have to be strong for Simon', she told herself; 'he needs me. It's just the two of us now.'

Susie looked fondly at Simon, amused and amazed at his ability to sleep through anything. Her fingers lightly moved his curls away from his face as her thoughts drifted back to Nana. Every Sunday had been family day in the Howard family. They had always spent it together with Sophie Tremont, their mother's grandmother, and whom they called Nana.

They went on picnics to the city park or at the lake, and sometimes to the park at the Miramahonni River. Occasionally they went to the zoo, or to the aquarium and even to the amusement park. And every so often they just stayed at home, or at Nana's house, and played games and had a backyard cookout. They had a lot of fun, or so the pictures in Nana's albums reflected. Susie really didn't remember much about her parents of her own accord; the bulk of her memories stemmed from Nana's stories, and from the many, many photos in her albums.

She smiled fondly as she thought of Nana. Though Nana was quite elderly (eighty-two when Susie was born), she was spry and sharp witted. She had a zest for life that rivaled even the youngest of folks. Nana became their guardian the day their parents died; she was seven and Simon was just a baby, barely six weeks old. Though Nana took great care of them, Susie still made it her mission to always look out for Simon.

Tenderly she stroked his hair, then gently began rubbing his back. She smiled at how peaceful he looked – he always did fall fast asleep when she rubbed his back. Susie closed her eyes again and rested her head once more against the seat. Reflexively she raised her left hand and clasped the silver filigree pendant she wore, her fingers gently caressing it. Nana had given it to her on her tenth birthday. Her face brightened at the memory.

Nana had made such a to-do about her tenth birthday. Nana's eyes had sparkled with joy, even more so than usual; and Nana's exuberance was quite contagious that day. Both she and Simon found themselves giggling and frolicking along with Nana. After the traditional birthday song and birthday cake, Susie had opened her presents - Simon's first and then Nana's. Simon could hardly contain his enthusiasm as he watched her open the oddly wrapped package that he had wrapped "all by himself", as he had so proudly announced.

He had made her a beaded bracelet (with a great deal of help from Nana). Each perfectly round crystal was a different color. He excitedly bounced up and down, clapping his hands as Susie held it up, admiring it.

"It's Noah's rainbow," he told her. "It stands for …" he looked at Nana for assistance.

"God's promises," she finished for him.

He nodded vigorously, grinning like the Cheshire cat, as he repeated, "Yeah, God's promises."

Susie gave him a big hug and thanked him. He giggled and squealed, then confessed that "Nana helped a little". Nana was quick to point out that the bracelet was entirely Simon's idea. He had also selected the beads and threaded them; she only helped with the knotting of the elastic thread between each bead. As the memories flooded her, Susie chuckled softly, and she smiled at her little brother. She closed her eyes, allowing herself to drift back into the memories.

Next she had opened Nana's present, a beautiful cloisonné brooch. It was three inches in diameter and overlaid onto a sterling silver base. Its clasp was thick and sturdy. The brooch portrayed a meadow scene with a lady and a white unicorn standing near an oak tree. Little acorns and oak leaves adorned the tree and were also scattered on the ground. Above them, the sun (or perhaps the moon) was depicted by the insertion of a small, round diamond.

The lady was dressed in a long, dark purple gown, decorated with a gold and silver braid around her waist. Concealing her hair was a veil of a lighter purple that cascaded behind her, flowing down to the ground. Encircling her head was a dazzling array of white, purple and pink wildflowers, adorning the lady's veil and head as if the flowers were a crown.

The noble creature had lowered its head so that their eyes met, gazing at each other. Her left hand gently cradled the muzzle of the unicorn while her right hand was placed on its neck. The scene conveyed the feeling of mutual trust and affection.

Susie's eyes had filled with tears; she looked up at Nana. "It's so beautiful," she whispered.

Nana had smiled and nodded, her own eyes welling with tears. "Yes it is," she said softly.

"I want to see," Simon insisted, reaching for it.

"You may look at it, Simon," Nana spoke firmly; "but it isn't a toy. You may not play with it. Okay?"

"Okay," he agreed, accentuating his agreement with the rapid nodding of his head.

Susie had held it out to him, carefully placing it in his tiny hands.

"Wooow-weee," he whispered admiringly.

Nana held out her hand, signaling Simon to hand it to her. He complied, cautiously placing the item into her hand. After thanking him, she pinned the brooch onto Susie's blouse, centered over her heart.

Nana's face glowed with a sweet joy and a sense of fulfillment. "This brooch has been in our family for many, many generations. It has been handed down from mother to eldest daughter. Your mother, had she lived, would have given this to you today, just as her mother, Arielle, gave it to her; and I gave it to Arielle, for whom you are named."

Pausing momentarily, Nana's smile was bittersweet. "It seems like only yesterday that I received it from my mother."

Gazing lovingly upon Susie, Nana's fingers gently touched the brooch. "You must wear it on your birthday, every birthday and only on your birthdays, from now until your first born daughter is ten years of age. On that day, you will present it to her; and so the cycle continues."

"Is there one for me when I'm ten?" Simon asked a little petulantly, unhappy to be left out of such grand tradition.

Nana chuckled and smiled as she tousled his hair. "Yes, my angel, but it's a little different than Susie's."

Simon beamed at her. "Can I see it?"

"It's 'may I'," she corrected him.

He sighed, slightly exasperated at always being corrected. "May I see it?" he asked.

"No, dear," she said with great affection. "You must wait until you are ten."

Nana kissed each of them on their cheek, stepped back and clapped her hands. "We have two more traditions to honor today," she said cheerfully. "First we sing the 'Song of Joy'."

Susie and Simon looked at each other, their expressions fully revealing they had no idea what she meant. Nana chuckled and told them it was a simple, little song that their people had been singing for ages. Most people ignore tradition these days, she had said, but it didn't hurt to revive it. Then she taught them the song as well as the dance that went with it. After many dismal attempts, they finally had what could pass as a successful performance. Nana declared they were indeed victorious in their endeavor and could now proceed to the next tradition.

From the top shelf of the china cupboard she removed an ornately carved box, placed it on the table and opened it. Its aromatic fragrance lightly wafted out, perfuming the air. She removed a small satin pillow, approximately three inches square. It was dark purple, and embellishing its edges was a braided cord of purple, silver and gold threads. A tassel, made with the same threads as the braided cord, hung from each corner of the pillow. Attached to each tassel was a silver charm, each one different. There was a wolf, a tiger, an eagle and a dolphin.

Centered, and covering most of the small pillow, was a magnificent unicorn; it was embroidered onto the pillow with white silk thread. Surrounding the unicorn was a circle of intertwining purple, silver and gold threads. Culminating at the top, the circle formed a tri-pointed crown; its center point was slightly taller than the other two and had a white star embroidered at its tip. At the feet of the unicorn was a lovely, silver filigree pendant dangling on a braided silver chain. The pendant was slender, cylindrical in shape, and about an inch in length.

With a great dramatic flourish, Nana eloquently curtsied as she proffered the pillow to her. Susie chuckled as she remembered Nana's theatrics – 'it's probably where Simon gets his dramatic flair,' she mused silently.

Susie sighed deeply. It had been a very special day, nearly two years ago now. The fact that Nana made every day special was true, for she firmly believed that each day was a gift from God and that life should be celebrated. But Susie's tenth birthday was very different from all the others.

Nana had told her it was also a tradition that upon her tenth birthday, the eldest daughter would receive this very special pendant. "Never take it off," Nana instructed her. "It is a talisman, an amulet of protection. It will reveal many truths to you at the proper time."

"What truths?" Susie had asked, perplexed and curious.

"Not now, child," Nana had answered softly. "In due time, I will tell you many things you need to know." She smiled and hugged Susie. "For now, just enjoy your day."

The sedan swerved sharply as the driver attempted to avoid another major hole in the dirt road. Susie was slammed hard against the window, and this time she was certain she would end up with a lump the size of the proverbial goose egg. Instinctively she gently rubbed the area as its throbbing increased. Simon momentarily awakened, shifted his position and then dropped back off to sleep. Susie slowly rubbed his back, assisting his effort to return to Dreamland.

Her thoughts shifted back to the day Nana had died three months earlier. Tears stung her eyes, and she quickly brushed them away. She had awakened that morning to discover that Nana was not yet up and about.... Very unusual..... She knocked on Nana's door and called out to her.... No response.

Hesitantly she had opened the door and entered the room. Nana had a peaceful smile on her face as if she were dreaming a very pleasant dream. Susie approached her bedside; and, as she neared Nana, Susie knew Nana had died quietly in her sleep.

In the past year, she and Nana had had several discussions about death. It started when she had a dream very similar to the way she actually found Nana. The dream had upset her greatly; she told Nana about it. Nana assured her that everyone passes over; some sooner than others, but everyone does. She remembered how Nana had held her for the longest time, gently stroking her hair as Susie cried and cried.

When finally her sobs had ceased, Nana gently wiped away her tears and kissed Susie on her forehead. Nana smiled and said, "Remember, love, that when it's my time, I'll be with your Mom and Dad, and our family and friends. And many, many years from now, when you've lived a long, full life, your time, too, will come. And when it does, I and your parents will be there to meet you; and we'll be together forever. So no more crying; I look forward to the day when we'll all be together."

Susie wasn't certain she'd ever stop crying when it was Nana's time, and she said so. Nana chuckled lightheartedly. "There'll always be some tears, little one," she said comfortingly as she kissed Susie's forehead. "The grief and sadness gives way in time to understanding, and then eventually to tears of joy. For when you truly understand that we go to a better place where we're with our loved ones for all eternity, you cannot help but be glad for those who are already there."

"Then why should we stay here? Why can't we go when you do?" Susie asked earnestly.

"Because, child, there is a time for everyone. Until that time, we have a purpose here to fulfill," Nana answered, cupping Susie's face in her hands.

"What's my purpose?" Susie countered snappishly.

Nana grinned, laughing with delight. "That, my precious, little one, is part of the mystery that is your life path. The fun of discovering just where you fit in the Tapestry of Life is an amazing adventure. Knowledge and Wisdom come from learning and experience. You will discover what your purpose is; and, once you have, that is an exhilarating feeling. Perhaps you will be a doctor, a teacher, or a musician. Perhaps your purpose will be in ministry or perhaps it is to raise a family. There is a multitude of directions, and there may be more than one, simultaneously or even consecutively."

Nana paused for a minute, studying Susie. She tilted her head slightly to the right as she leveled her gaze upon Susie. Her voice, though soft, was strong with conviction. "Whatever your purpose, Susie; it will be revealed to you if you listen with your heart, your spirit," she said as she tapped her own chest and then Susie's for emphasis.

Afterwards, the conversations about death were not as heart-wrenching for Susie. As they talked more about the family members waiting for them, Susie found herself not dreading the inevitable. True, she would prefer it if Nana, and she and Simon could remain here forever and somehow her parents re-join them here; but she was coming to terms with it.

Nana began telling her stories about all their relatives that were now waiting for them. Simon overheard one such story and decided he wanted to hear more. So every afternoon, at four o'clock, they had a family story time, complete with pictures from Nana's many picture albums. It was fascinating to see what they looked like, what they wore, where they lived and the times in which they lived. On some pages, Nana had newspaper clippings that recorded important events: births, christenings, baptisms, weddings, graduations, businesses, military service and, of course, funerals.

Three weeks before Nana's time had come, she handed Susie an envelope. She instructed Susie that when her time came, Susie was to call the authorities and give them the envelope. Susie began to panic, and her face very much registered that feeling. Nana smiled, hugged Susie and told her "not to worry; that this was just a precaution". She had explained to Susie that because they had no other relatives, the authorities would place them in the care of Child Services. Since Nana wanted to be certain they were well cared for, she had already made arrangements with a lady named Mrs. Crenshaw in Willington. She then gave Susie Mrs. Crenshaw's business card, telling her to "keep it safe, just in case".

And that is how they met Mrs. Crenshaw – she came to collect them at their local precinct in Stonebridge. She had such a kind face and gentle way that even Simon warmed up to her immediately. She reminded them a little of Nana, only a much younger version. Though her hair wasn't snowy white, it was heavily streaked with gray, contrasting sharply with the remaining ebony color of her hair. She was tall and thin like Nana, but her face had very few wrinkles.

When they had arrived at the Boy's Facility in Willington, Simon wouldn't get out of her car. Mrs. Crenshaw kept trying to reassure him that it was only temporary. She repeatedly told him that, come morning, she would find a foster home for the two of them until she could find a permanent home. He held tightly to Susie, pleading hysterically. Mrs.

Crenshaw relented, taking them home with her instead. Susie smiled at the memory of the following day when Mrs. Crenshaw hugged them and said the judge had agreed to allow them to stay with her while she located a family that would take them both.

Susie softly sighed; she missed her parents, and she really missed Nana. She had few memories of her Mom and Dad compared to the memories she had of Nana. She missed Nana's laughter, her smiles, her hugs and, especially, her stories. Nana always told the best stories.

Nana had always made them feel loved and special every moment of every day. Two days after they came to live with Nana, Willie - the mean, older boy who lived next door - taunted and teased her about the faint purple birthmark on her right cheek.

Nana pointed to her own birthmark and told her all their family had one. Nana held her index finger to her lips and slowly looked to her right, and then to her left. As if they were conspirators, Nana leaned close to Susie's ear and whispered, "You were kissed by an angel the day you were born, as was Simon."

She moved her face, nose to nose with Susie, gave a slight nod and added, "The mark was left by the angel's kiss." (It did slightly resemble a tiny lip print, sort of.)

Susie missed the way Nana made ordinary, everyday things seem extraordinary; the way she made everything special. Whether baking cookies, or sweeping the floor, cleaning her room, picking flowers from Nana's garden or with any number of daily things, Nana had a story for everything that made the ordinary seem spectacular.

Just like the time, a few months before Nana died, when she and Nana were sitting on the porch after dinner. Simon had been playing in the yard with his Tonka trucks. Suddenly he ran to the oak tree and started climbing the tree. Though Nana had repeatedly told him to stop, he ignored her. (Simon does love his trees, Susie chuckled at the thought).

In retrospect, it was more of an attempt to climb rather than actually climbing. He had shinnied his way up the tree trunk (much like a monkey, Susie had noted at the time). He fell off the first branch; albeit the branch was only about five feet off the ground, but still a considerable distance if you're the one that's falling and happen to be as small a person as Simon.

He had been standing on the first branch, tippy-toed, with his little hands grasping as much as possible of the thick branch directly above him. In an attempt to swing up to the next branch, he fell out of the tree and knocked out a front tooth. They ran to him, fearing the worst; but he was already sitting up and laughing when they reached him. His mouth was bloody, both from the split upper lip and from the hole where his tooth had been. Proudly he held open his hand showcasing the missing tooth, both hand and tooth speckled with blood.

After reassuring herself that Simon was all right, Nana had asked why he didn't climb it by hanging onto the tree trunk, using the branches as steps. Simon's expression was one of incredulity at such a silly question.

He responded with, "Where's the fun in that? *Anybody* can do it that way."

They quickly shuffled him inside the kitchen, and Nana swiftly prepared a tepid salt water rinse. After she was certain his mouth was properly rinsed, she had him open wide, which he was all too glad to oblige. The bleeding from the gaping hole had completely stopped. She checked for any other damages, clucking the whole time about it being a wonder that Simon had managed to live this long. She found no other damage, but sharply informed Simon that he would still have to see the dentist the next day. Simon had pouted until Nana told him about the Tooth Fairy.

That night he had placed the tooth under his pillow, as Nana instructed, and the next morning it was gone; a shiny quarter was in its place. Simon was ecstatic and was jumping around as if he had ants in his pants. Nana had laughed at his gleeful antics. She reminded him that the Tooth Fairy had left it, and he needed to thank her come bedtime when he said his prayers. Susie blurted out that it wasn't the Tooth Fairy, that she had seen Nana do it.

Nana smiled patiently at her and said, "Every act of kindness puts a little magic in the heart of the receiver, and in the heart of the giver. Just because I put it there doesn't change the fact that the Tooth Fairy gave it to me to give to Simon. Someday you'll understand."

The trip to the dentist later that morning found Simon much less gleeful. However, Nana did manage to convince him that it was very necessary to allow Dr. Charles to fix his problem. And he did. Simon displayed his "new tooth" (a space maintainer), and Susie was amazed that it looked so much like a real tooth.

Susie looked at Simon sleeping so peacefully and smiled fondly at him. Her eyes misted slightly; she turned her attention to the trees and meadows they were slowly passing. She sighed as memories of their life with Nana flooded her, stirring the deep emotions of loss and of fear – fear of the uncertainty of what was to become of them.

Closing her eyes, her thoughts drifted to home; Nana's cottage would always be home to her. She missed the wonderful aromas that always seemed to fill the little cottage. There was the smell of bread baking, or cookies, or cakes, or pies; not to ignore the delicious smells from the meals that Nana prepared. And who could forget the heavenly scents from the multitude of flowers in Nana's garden; they kept her cottage fragrant as their varied perfumes wafted in through her open windows.

But most of all, Susie missed Nana's stories – she told awesome tales. There were all sorts of stories about pixies and fairies, dragons and unicorns, angels and demons, witches and warlocks and a host of magical creatures and mystical places. Susie treasured her memories of Story Time; it was a wondrous time that they shared. Every night, an hour before bedtime, they would sit with Nana in their comfortable parlor. The small fire in the fireplace would crackle and pop, gently warming the room, making them feel safe and secure there in that little cottage with Nana.

Although most of Nana's stories required a couple of nights to complete, there were a few that were woven over the course of weeks, even months. Nana would spin her chosen tale with the greatest of detail; she included the names of the people, animals and places. It was fantastic how she could remember all the different names, never confusing them or forgetting them. The way she spoke of these people and places, with the elaborate descriptions she gave, well, it was as if she'd been there, seen them, *knew* them. Her facial expressions, gestures and her voice impersonations all worked in perfect harmony to create these amazing, wonderful worlds that she brought so vividly to life. Nana made it all so real and so vibrant; you just *knew* the stories were true.

As Nana would regale them with her stories, her bright, blue eyes would sparkle. A big smile would fill her weathered face; she'd cross her heart and swear she was telling the truth. With a smile and a wink, she'd say, "One thing I do know for certain is that there are more things, seen and unseen, that are true, in the heavens and on earth, than we can ever know or hope to know."

At the end of each story Nana would say, "And to be sure, you cannot believe everything that you see or hear, for there are tricksters everywhere. You must be wise in order to know what is true."

And Susie would know it was only a story. But secretly, in her innermost heart, Susie still hoped that the wondrous tales might just be true.

Chapter 2

ARRIVAL AT LAST

Susie was jolted from her reverie as the old sedan bounced and swayed, dropping hard into one of the deep holes that so profusely scarred the road. The sunlight had dissipated to the point of turning the sky into beautiful hues of blue and red, pink and purple, yellow and orange.

At long last they came to the end of the road. An old iron gate, chained and locked, prevented anyone from continuing further on down the rugged country road. Travelers were forced to turn back or maneuver their way onto the tiny lane to their right. Mr. Warbly cautiously made the sharp right turn onto the lane, the condition of which wasn't much better (or worse for that matter) than the road they just left.

Enormous oak trees lined both sides of the lane such that the leaves would create a canopy, casting the entire lane in shade and shadow through the spring, summer and fall. Their gnarled and scarred trunks rose skyward; their empty branches reached out and upward like a Titan, rising and stretching after a long sleep. Their large, ancient roots ran along the ground, intertwining with each other until it was no longer possible to distinguish the origin of any one particular root.

Beyond the oak trees were vast meadows, their tall winter grasses gently swaying back and forth in the light breeze. Further still, beyond the meadows, were the dense, dark forests where Susie imagined lived all manner of animals, friendly and the not so friendly.

Much like a slithering snake, the lane meandered repeatedly to the left and then to the right as it coiled its way up and down the rolling hills. Finally, Glen Hollow came into view as the old sedan reached the top of a tall hill.

Mr. Warbly stopped the car. "There it is," he said brusquely, pointing at the manor; "your new home."

Deftly moving her little brother to the seat, Susie slid forward and to the center of the seat in order to gain a better view. She could see several small streams that wound their way through the valley; a few of which they had crossed on the small bridges as the lane carved its serpentine route through the land. Far to the southeast corner of the valley, she could barely see a portion of the Anicaw River, coursing through the estate on its way down to the southern coast. Quite a distance behind the old manor was another patch of fields and beyond that another dense grove of forest. With the northern mountains high in the background behind her, it made for an idyllic scene. However, what captured Susie's attention the most was Glen Hollow manor itself.

"Like something out of Nana's stories," Susie whispered. The thought of Nana caused a smile to grace her lips.

Sitting high on a large, flat knoll in the middle of an enormous valley, it loomed over the land below it. Like a dark knight presiding over his territory, it stood guard, ever silent, ever vigilant. The immense size of the building with its dark gray stones seemed to convey a sense of isolation and loneliness, almost a feeling of foreboding. Susie shuddered as a creepy-crawly tingle inched its way down her spine.

Slowly they began their final descent toward the old manor, swaying and bumping along as the old sedan found more holes than it missed.

A considerable distance from the manor, to the east and just slightly to the north, was a group of large buildings. Some were obviously barns that were currently in use; the outside lights were on and brightly shining. Three large buildings farthest away from the main group appeared to no longer be in use. There were no outside lights burning, and Susie could see no visible trail to them. But then, Susie knew, the light of day could change everything; paths not visible at night could be quite visible in the day.

Between the manor and the barns were eight, picturesque cottages arranged to form a half circle. 'Actually,' Susie thought; 'with the two end cottages inset like that, it looks more like a horseshoe than a half circle.'

Tall, antique-style lampposts alternated along the sides of the main path that led to the cottages. Their old-world charm as well as their bright light helped to dispel the encroaching darkness of night.

The cottages were painted an eggshell color, each having a different color trim; blue, purple, yellow, pink, red, orange, green and brown. Window boxes adorned each of the cottages, and the decorative cutouts of the boxes were different with each one. The perfect finishing touches to the quaint cottages were the gingerbread trim and the scalloped roof lines. Only four of the cottages had porch lights shining, each faintly lighting the small patch of walkway within their immediate realm.

On a slight rise, several hundred yards front and center of the manor, a magnificent, old oak tree stood, proud and glorious in its beauty. Stretching high into the sky, it was taller than any tree Susie could ever remember seeing. "It must be nearly three hundred feet tall," she whispered reverently. Its branches spread outward nearly as wide as it was tall, and the lower branches were within easy climbing reach. 'Even for Simon', Susie noted to herself; 'I'll have to really watch him.'

Along the ground and encircling the tree was a group of small, white stones that appeared to have been placed about thirty feet from the tree trunk. Susie strained and squinted, trying to see if there were any benches around the tree or within the stone circle. She didn't see any; however, in this fading light, she knew it was possible that they were there. It would be a great place to read or to draw, with or without benches, she decided.

As they drew closer to the manor, a tingling sensation ran down Susie's back causing her to shiver. It gave her an eerie feeling. She shrugged her shoulders, attempting to rid herself of negative thoughts. 'I'm just tired,' she reminded herself.

Susie smiled when she saw that the windows of the manor were tall and plentiful, each having wooden shutters that would protect the glass during the area's frequent storms. With so many windows, the manor would have plenty of light in the day. It was a comforting thought, and Susie wondered why it comforted her. Chiding herself for being so silly, she forced her attention onto her surroundings, believing that to be the cure for her imagination.

Holly bushes, well-trimmed and evenly spaced, were planted all along the front of the manor. Rising heavenward, and adorning each end of the front of the manor house, was a tall cedar tree. The tips of their slender, triangular shape did not quite reach the sharply pitched roof top. Though the cedars gave the old manor somewhat of a stately appearance, Susie was certain it was nowhere near its former glory.

There were no flowerbeds like at Nana's cottage, but Susie thought she could identify several areas that must be the old gardens Mrs. Crenshaw had mentioned. Areas, once lush and vibrant with color, were now overgrown with grasses.

Overall, the manor appeared to be rectangular in shape except for its center section; it was circular and soared well above what Susie surmised as being the attic portion of the manor. Made of large, granite stones, flat with rounded edges, the stones of the center section were a lighter gray than the manor's square granite blocks, but not by much. The center section extended out from the manor front, giving it a tower-like appearance. 'Like the castles in Nana's stories,' Susie thought.

The arched front door was in the center of the circular section. Leading to it was a large, stone staircase. The staircase, with its stone balustrades and rails, gracefully flared outward at the bottom. Its color suggested it was made of the same stone as the center section of the manor.

The stone posts at the bottom of the stairway were capped with a round, thick slab of dark-gray granite, identical to the stone posts at the top of the landing. In the center of each of the capstones was a black wrought-iron lamp with a matching (though much larger) lamp bolted onto each side of the front door. The light emitted from all the lamps kept the steps and the entrance brightly lit.

"It's still awesome," she whispered, admiring the grandeur of the old manor.

From this angle of their final approach, Susie could see that the west side of the manor had a south wing. It wasn't quite as tall as the main section. Susie noticed, too, that the wing was built on the diagonal, angled slightly inward toward the back center of the structure. She wondered if the same would be true for the east side, or if the manor was built in a lopsided "L" shape.

'I'll know soon enough,' she cheerfully told herself, looking forward to exploring the manor.

The lane came to an end, becoming the driveway as the sedan drove across octagon-shaped paver stones. The driveway coursed along in front of the manor and on past it; 'to the garage or those buildings,' Susie surmised.

As they entered the driveway, Susie gently shook Simon. "Wake up, Simon," she told him; "we're here."

Simon opened his eyes, stretched and yawned. He sat up just as Mr. Warbly brought the sedan to a stop.

"Wo-o-o-o-o-w; whee-eee." His protracted utterance clearly revealed his amazement as he stared up at the colossal front door. It was a little intimidating, reminiscent of a castle door with its arched doorway, thick wooden door and black wrought-iron hinges.

"All right you kids, we're here. Stay in the car 'til I get your bags unloaded. I don't need you wanderin' off 'n gettin' lost," Mr. Warbly said curtly. Before she could respond, Mr. Warbly exited the sedan, slamming the door closed.

Simon busied himself looking out the windows, straining to see in the remaining vestiges of light. His darting and hopping from window to window, nearly standing on his head while angling for a better view, reminded Susie of a chimpanzee. She giggled.

The setting sun was now gone, and dusk had fully fallen. All that remained was a faint reddish-orange glow that filtered slightly between the distant trees. Simon jumped back down onto the seat next to Susie causing the seat to jostle her. He laughed with glee, and his eyes twinkled with delight.

"Look at all the *trees*, Susie, and lots of places to play. Maybe it'll be fun here."

She couldn't help but smile at his exuberance, and nodded in a resigned agreement.

"That's *my* tree," he announced, pointing at the massive, old oak tree. "I can't wait to climb it," he added. Pressing his nose against the cold glass, his breath created a fog that resembled a snow cloud. Softly he whispered, "Will it be okay?"

Susie wasn't certain if he was asking her or the tree. As she began to respond, a chill crept its way through her causing her to shudder. Silently she prayed that all would be okay, that this would be a good place for them until Mrs. Crenshaw could find them a real family.

'If ever,' she thought dismally, looking out the window. She sighed heavily and shook her head ever so slightly, attempting to dispel the negative thought. It was important that she remain positive for Simon. He needed her, and needed her to be strong.

She took a deep breath and softly exhaled. 'I won't let him down,' she promised herself.

Mr. Warbly opened Simon's door, barking at them to 'fall out'. He had already carried his overnight case and their suitcases up to the landing. Now he was hastily ushering them up the steps as well.

Upon reaching the door, he raised the weather-worn iron ring and loudly banged it several times onto the much used iron plate behind it. The sound echoed eerily as each contact reverberated in the bleak December night.

Simon quickly slid his hand into Susie's as he pressed up against her. She gave him an encouraging smile and gently squeezed his hand.

Several minutes later the massive oak door slowly opened, groaning on its hinges, to reveal an elderly woman dressed in a dark-gray tweed suit, a black blouse and an elegant, silver pendant watch fastened to her suit lapel. Her silvery, white hair was fashioned loosely into a bun at the nape of her neck. She wore half glasses, for reading purposes, and they were perched toward the end of her nose.

"I'm Joe Warbly, Ma'am. These are the children from the Willington Child Services I'm t' deliver t' you," Mr. Warbly spoke respectfully.

She peered at the children briefly, her pea-green eyes quickly assessing them. She then turned her full attention to Mr. Warbly. "Where have you been, man? You're nearly four hours late. We've been worried sick." She registered the proper mix of concern and agitation as she admonished him.

"I'm sorry Miss Pritchett, but the roads--", he began, removing his cap and clutching it in front of him.

She raised her hand and quickly cut him off. "I am not Miss Pritchett," she corrected him. "I am Hilda McKinley, the Head Housemistress. You may address me as Miss Hilda."

She moved back, opened the door wide, inviting them in. "Do come in before you children catch your death of cold."

She pulled Susie, with Simon in tow, into the foyer, and Mr. Warbly followed close behind the children. Miss Hilda shut the door and turned to properly greet them.

Her smile was genuine, and it filled her round face. "Well, let's have a look at you. You must be Susie and are, I must say, quite a lovely young lady."

Susie smiled and responded with a quick "Thank you."

Miss Hilda stooped down to face level with Simon, tousling his short, blond ringlets. "And you must be Simon." She straightened and smiled at him, "You're a handsome young man, but you are in need of a haircut, dear."

Simon drew closer to Susie, partially hiding behind her.

"Our Nana liked his hair this way. Any shorter and it won't curl properly," Susie spoke tersely, defending Simon's locks.

"Well, he does have the face of a cherub," Miss Hilda said conciliatorily; "so perhaps we can allow his hair to look like it belongs to one, too." She patted his head, smiled at him and added, "At least for a little while longer."

Miss Hilda knelt down and began unbuttoning Simon's coat. "Give me your coats," she instructed; "and we'll hang them in the Cloak Room on our way to the Lavatory."

Susie quickly shed her coat and handed it to Miss Hilda at about the same time as Simon slid out of his. Miss Hilda stood and folded their coats over her arm.

"As I was saying, Miss Hilda," Mr. Warbly began and was once again interrupted.

"There's no time for explanations," she intoned, taking Mr. Warbly's coat and placing it atop Susie's. "Dinner is served promptly at six p.m. and," she checked her pendant watch, "that is in fifteen minutes. Miss Pritchett is very strict regarding punctuality. Leave your bags here in the foyer; after dinner you'll be shown to your rooms. If you'll follow me, I'll take you to the lavatory where you may quickly freshen up before we proceed to the Dining Hall."

She turned and briskly headed toward the back corridor with Mr. Warbly barely a step behind her. Susie and Simon were far more interested in their surroundings. The foyer in which they entered the manor was the circular section seen from the outside. The walls were gray stone, just like the exterior, and held no decorations other than black, wrought-iron light sconces. They were evenly spaced around the foyer walls on all three levels, emitting a soft, bright light.

Three corridors led out of the foyer into the manor; one to the left, one to the right and one at the end opposite from the door, past the staircase entrance. The left corridor doors were closed; the doors were fully opened to the other two corridors.

Covering most of the foyer's granite flooring was a very large carpet, round and plush. Susie pulled off her right shoe and pressed her foot down into its pillow like softness. "Wow," she whispered appreciatively. Susie put her shoe back on and followed Simon as he ran to the oak table positioned in the center of the carpet.

The round table was quite large and had four, gigantic claw-foot pedestals that supported it. Simon was already under the table. He grinned up at Susie and then slid under the bar connecting the pedestals.

"Help me; I've been caught by a dragon," he called out, pretending to be terrified of the dreaded beast.

Susie laughed. "Come out of there, Simon; and be careful," she told him.

Her attention was drawn to the delicate lace runner elegantly draped across the table. She could just envision Simon entangling himself in it, crashing to the floor with it and with the floral arrangement as well. The tall, crystal vase was filled with beautiful, white calla lilies, what Nana had called 'giant whites'.

Susie felt a little sad as the thought of Nana had popped into her mind. She missed Nana more and more every day. Everything seemed to remind her of Nana. Distracted by her thoughts, her hand reached out and gently touched one of the flowers. She let out a little sigh, forcing herself to face the current situation.

Turning to look for Simon, she noticed that the granite flooring seemed a little odd. The large squares were made of different color tiles except for the outer rings. The ones adjacent to the walls were black; next was a ring that comprised a double row of tiles and was a bright, cobalt blue followed by another black ring. Alternating tiles in the two black rings held a silver symbol, some Susie recognized and some she didn't. She stepped off the measurement of the blue ring; it was wider than she was tall!

Susie stood and stared at what little was visible of the floor between the inner black ring and the carpet, trying to figure out what it was meant to be. Hard as she tried, she just couldn't see a pattern. Its tile arrangement appeared to be random; much like an artist's brush had been saturated with a multitude of paint colors and then flung haphazardly back and forth over the floor.

"Hmm," she pondered. "You'd have to roll up the carpet to know what it is," Susie concluded.

"Susie, look at me!" Simon called out, breaking her concentration.

She turned and looked; sure enough, he was proud of his accomplishment. Simon had managed to climb up onto the banister and was holding onto the large acorn finial. He was just sitting there, his face radiant with one of his famous Cheshire cat grins.

"This is great. I bet I can slide all the way down from the top!" he excitedly exclaimed. "Want to see?"

"No," Susie said as authoritatively as she could muster. "Come back here. ...Now!"

His face became sullen as he climbed down. "Fine," he muttered, shuffling his feet as he slowly walked back to her.

Susie's gaze was now fixed on the foyer's main attraction; the grand staircase which wound its way up the three stories, an awesome sight. It was made of carved oak, and was so highly polished that it gleamed in the foyer's light. She guessed it was at least ninety feet to the third floor landing. It was another thirty or so feet beyond that to the foyer's ceiling, a ceiling which was completely covered in a beautiful mural.

"What are you looking at?" he asked petulantly. (She was still staring at it.)

Though somewhat faded, Susie could still see the images. It was a collage of several different scenes, interwoven in such a way as to form a picture story.

"Isn't it amazing?" she said to Simon. Susie began pointing out to Simon the different animals she saw and he joined in, making it a contest to see who could name the most animals.

"Children!" Miss Hilda's voice sharply called out as she reentered the foyer. "Come here now. There'll be plenty of time later for gawking and exploring."

They quickly complied and ran to her.

"And remember, there's no running in the house," she reminded them when they reached her. Her voice had softened, and her smile was big and kind. Simon stood in his Peter Pan pose, grinning back at her.

Dutifully they followed Miss Hilda down the corridor, glancing quickly at their surroundings as they passed. There was a variety of paintings of still life, waterscapes and landscapes.

Upon arrival at the lavatory, Mr. Warbly was still patiently waiting by the door. He had dampened and combed his hair in an attempt to control his unruly cowlick. It was obvious that he had also washed his face and neck - they were quite red from the scrubbing received.

Graciously he held the door open for them as they approached.

"Thank you," Susie said politely as she entered.

But she wasn't fast enough to suit Simon. In his haste to get past her, he stepped on the back of her shoe, causing it to fall off of her foot. "Simon!" she fumed.

"That'll be enough, children," Miss Hilda said admonishing them. "There's no time for horseplay or for quarrelling. Susie dear, fix your shoe and wash your hands," she instructed as she tested the water temperature. "Come, Simon; let's get your hands washed."

Simon marched up to the sink, stepping up onto the stepstool Miss Hilda had placed in front of the sink and thrust his hands under the running water. Miss Hilda soaped his hands well, assisting in the rinsing process as Susie began washing her hands at the next sink.

Miss Hilda handed Simon a towel. As he made great sport of drying his hands, Miss Hilda wiped his face with a damp cloth. "There now, don't you look handsome," she said approvingly. He grinned, gave a royal nod of agreement, then impishly turned to Susie and stuck his tongue out at her.

"Simon, that's bad behavior," Susie retorted hotly. "You know better." She was very tired, and her patience was wearing a bit thin.

Miss Hilda intervened, quickly giving Simon one of her best '*I'm disappointed*' looks. "Simon, this behavior is unacceptable, and is absolutely unsuitable for a nice young man such as you. Please apologize to your sister."

Simon hung his head and crossed his arms over his chest. Furrowing his brow and pursing his lips in an exaggerated pout, he whined, "I was only playing."

"Be that as it may, your behavior was rude," Miss Hilda told him, unrelenting. "Please apologize so that we may go to dinner. Miss Pritchett will not allow anyone to be seated if they are late. We barely have five minutes to get to the Dining Hall, or we'll all be doing without dinner tonight."

"I'm sorry Susie," Simon complied with a great sigh.

"Apology accepted," she responded and gave him a hug.

To Miss Hilda's surprise, Simon quite enthusiastically returned her hug, and did so amid a stream of giggles.

"You can be so silly sometimes, Simon." Susie smiled at him as she extricated herself from his grasp.

Miss Hilda quickly herded them out the door and back into the corridor where poor Mr. Warbly was still waiting. "Come now," she dictated; "we've no time to waste."

With one child firmly grasped in each hand, she headed down the corridor at a very brisk pace. Both Susie and Simon were practically running to keep up with her. Simon looked back at Mr. Warbly – he too seemed to be out of breath, huffing and puffing as he attempted to keep pace with Miss Hilda.

They arrived at the Dining Hall with barely a minute to spare.

Chapter 3

GETTING ACQUAINTED

"Wow-wee," Simon whispered.

Susie merely nodded. She, too, was astounded at the grandeur of which her eyes beheld.

They entered the Dining Hall through the double door entrance on its south wall, and stopped in the middle of its wide threshold. Miss Hilda had released their hands as soon as they reached the Dining Hall, slowing her pace as she entered. Pushing past Susie and Simon, Mr. Warbly hurriedly caught up to Miss Hilda.

Susie reached down and gently clasped Simon's small hand into hers, giving it a little squeeze of reassurance. They slowly walked into the Hall, gazing all around at the immense room. Painted a bright tomato red, the upper half of the walls complemented the glossy, honey oak paneling of the lower half. The vivid colors gave the room a warm feeling, cheerful and lively in spite of the dim lighting.

Suspended from the ceiling were a series of seven-tiered, crystal chandeliers, fourteen in total. Only four were lit, casting the majority of the Hall in varying degrees of shadows and darkness. On the far wall to her right, the flickering light from the fireplace dispersed a good deal of the darkness in its immediate vicinity. The way the firelight danced through the gloom looked eerily like something out of a horror film. It gave the illusion that some creature was striving to enter this world, twisting and contorting, trying to pull free from whatever held it on the other side and not quite able to free itself.

On the north wall, opposite from where they were standing, were seven, tall windows that nearly reached to the ceiling. Each window culminated at its top into an arched crown, as if the glass under the crown portion was royalty and it the symbol of said privilege and position. The beveled glass of the lower portion ran to within a foot from the floor and was crystal clear, whereas the crown portion of each window was made with stained glass. The lighting wasn't bright enough for Susie to ascertain any image they might convey, just some of the colors.

Susie smiled, and could hardly wait for morning. She knew that the morning light would reveal the images now hidden. Not to mention the kaleidoscope of colors the daylight would expose when its rays began streaming through the colored glass, scattering its dazzling jewel tones along the pale gray color of the stone floor.

With just a quick, precursory glance, Susie could see that just like the foyer ceiling, this ceiling was also meticulously painted, displaying a variety of scenes. Of what she could see, some scenes were of the forest and its myriad of animals while some were of the lakes and rivers with their vast aquatic life. Others held images of the plains and the various animals that called it home, while others still were scenes of farm life and all its creatures, both great and small. There were orchards and vines, flowers and trees, cornucopia baskets and also bushels of many types of produce. Nesting birds, birds in flight, butterflies and bees and a host of other creatures also graced the collage.

A loud pop emanating to her left drew her attention to the fireplaces. There were two white marble fireplaces in the Dining Hall, one on the east wall and one on the west wall (next to the table in use) and were perfectly centered across from each other. Their size was huge (cavernous really, Susie thought) for the firebox inserts appeared to be at least eighteen feet long, six feet high and at least six feet deep. The hearths were raised about three feet off the floor. Both had fires that were roaring, huge logs blazing away, keeping the Hall quite warm in spite of the early December chill.

The fireplaces, with the gleaming white of their marble, beautifully accentuated the red walls and its honey-colored wainscoting. Fluted columns, rising to the ceiling, graced each end of the fireplaces. Niches, carved into the marble columns, held a variety of small porcelain statuettes. Connecting the fluted columns of the fireplaces were thick marble mantelpieces. The crowning touch to each fireplace was the gleaming silver candelabras, resting upon each mantle.

The only furnishings, other than the tables and chairs, were large service cabinets, called sideboards. Made of solid oak, they were placed on the south wall, each one being positioned in line with a table. Very old, they looked to be quite sturdy and appeared to be able to hold a number of items. They each had two center doors, four short drawers on each side of the doors with one long drawer above the doors.

On either side of the service cabinets stood tall, black, wrought-iron torchieres, matching the ones positioned in the corners of the Hall. To Susie, they looked to be extremely heavy – she pitied the poor person assigned to dust it, and especially the one who had to move it. The stick portion of the torchieres had as large a circumference as that of a young tree. Susie couldn't be certain from this distance, but it appeared as if the torchieres had a vine pattern weaving its way up the shaft toward the top. As none of the candles (nine fat ones per candelabra) were lit, it was apparent that they were used only when the electricity was out due to the violent storms that the area suffered each spring and fall.

Prominently filling the center of the room were seven tables, long and narrow, and strategically aligned with the windows. Only one was in use; the one on her far left, nearest to the west wall (about twelve feet from the fireplace, Susie guessed). Quickly counting the chairs, Susie knew each table accommodated thirty-six people. She thought it strange to have so many tables and chairs and so few people that actually use them.

Her swift critique lasted barely a minute or two before the wafting aromas from the table captured her full attention. The dinner fare was abundant, and Susie was nearly ecstatic. She was absolutely famished.

The table was laden with platters of roasted chicken and steaming bowls of sweet peas, mashed potatoes, carrots, gravy and dinner rolls. It looked and smelled delicious, causing her mouth to water in anticipation of the feast in which she was about to partake. But then Susie hadn't eaten much all day and, to her growling stomach, even a piece of bread would be a feast. While scrutinizing the dinner fare, Susie noticed that the food dishes and pitchers of milk were identically arranged four times, dividing the long table into four sections.

After their hurried arrival, they had but a few minutes to absorb the room, its contents and its people while Miss Hilda caught her breath. As soon as Miss Hilda's breaths had become less gasping, the elegant woman at the far end of the table gracefully rose from her chair. Her eyes sparkled with amusement as she observed their rushed entrance.

She was slender, of medium height, and her short, curly hair was as white as snow. Black lashes framed eyes that were indigo blue in color. Her alabaster skin was flawless except for a small, reddish scar on her upper right cheek. Its jagged edges gave it a puckered look even from this distance, causing Susie to wonder if the lady had been in an accident like her parents had been. Tears began to sting her eyes at the memory, and she struggled to keep the tears at bay.

"Miss Hilda, we're delighted that you've decided to join us for dinner," the lady said with a cheerful smile and with an amused lilt in her voice. "Please introduce your companions."

With her breathing still quite laborious, and her face as red as a sugar beet from her near Olympic sprint down the corridor, Miss Hilda very calmly wheezed, "It'd be my pleasure, Miss Pritchett."

She turned to the driver (his cap still clutched tightly in his hands), "Mr. Warbly, may I present Miss Pritchett, Head Mistress and owner of Glen Hollow."

To which he responded (with a slight nod of his head), "G'evenin', Miss Pritchett."

Miss Hilda turned to Miss Pritchett and continued. "Miss Pritchett, allow me to present Mr. Warbly from Willington Child Services, and our two new residents, Susie Howard and Simon Howard."

To the children she simply stated, "Children, this is Miss Pritchett."

Suddenly aware that everyone in the room was staring at them, Susie responded with a 'hello' that was just a little on the quiet side while Simon merely waved.

"Good evening," the lady said vibrantly; "and welcome to Glen Hollow."

"Mr. Warbly," she continued, gracefully extending her hand toward a young lady with short black hair; "please be seated next to Miss Emma (who now raised her hand and gave a little wave), and Miss Hilda will seat the children."

Mr. Warbly nodded to Miss Pritchett, folding his cap and stuffing it into his back pocket. He quickly took his seat as Miss Hilda ushered Susie and Simon to the opposite side of the table.

Lightly tapping Susie on her shoulder, Miss Hilda gestured to the second chair. In one fluid motion, she slid the first chair away from the table, lifted Simon up and into the booster seat and gently eased the chair back to the table. She then took her place at the end of the table, next to Simon.

After everyone was seated, Miss Pritchett sat back down in her chair. With a cheerful smile, she looked to her left at a young lady seated midway down the table from her. Though soft spoken, Miss Pritchett's voice projected well. "I believe we're ready to begin. Cora, please ask the Blessing."

Nodding, the young lady said, "Shall we," as she placed her hands together in a prayer pose. Everyone was quick to follow her lead. Everyone, that is, except Simon. He was far too busy checking out the food.

Miss Cora loudly cleared her throat, garnering everybody's attention including Simon's. Leveling her gaze at him, she tilted her head to the right ever so slightly, raised her left eyebrow and slightly moved her hands up and down.

Susie leaned over to Simon and whispered, "Close your eyes, bow your head and fold your hands."

Simon complied, and Susie stole a quick glance at Miss Pritchett. With eyes still closed, she was grinning and attempting to suppress a laugh.

As it turned out, Miss Cora was a little windy when it came to prayers. Simon began swinging his legs; he was bored, a little tired and hungry. Susie reached over and squeezed his thigh gently. He got the message and sat still. Finally, Miss Cora said "Amen", and everyone echoed with their own enthusiastic "Amen".

When the adults began the process of serving the food, Susie realized that the seating arrangement was not by chance but by design. They would first fill the plate of the child seated next to them, then their own plate before passing the serving dish on to the next adult in their group. This process repeated itself with each of the heavy bowls and the large platters until all had been served. Once accomplished, Miss Pritchett gave a slight nod and simply stated, "Please begin" - and everyone did.

"I think this is a good time for us to introduce ourselves to our new arrivals, and them to us," Miss Pritchett said, her voice carrying above the din. "Miss Hilda, would you be so kind as to begin; we'll proceed to your right and end with Simon."

"Certainly," Miss Hilda agreed, placing her fork down on her plate. "I am Hilda Lynn McKinley. I have one child, a son, who lives in Fairview and –"

"How old is he?" Simon asked, interrupting her.

"Simon, don't interrupt when someone is talking," Susie admonished.

"Thank you, Susie," Miss Hilda said with a smile. "Simon, it isn't polite to interrupt. You must wait until the person has finished speaking."

His pouty frown turned into a grin when she added with a wink, "Kyle is a dentist and is married to a lovely, young lady named Alice. They have two children, Grant and Mary. You'll get to meet them in a couple of weeks when they visit for Christmas."

This revelation brought an excited round of chatter as all the adults seemed very pleased at the news. The other children remained silent. That struck Susie as just a little odd.

"How old are they?" Simon loudly persisted over the noise.

Miss Hilda chuckled. "Grant is ten, and Mary is eight." She patted him lightly on his shoulder and continued. "As to my duties here, I assist Miss Pritchett in the managing of Glen Hollow. I am a licensed teacher; and, whenever necessary, I substitute for Miss Emma. When I was three, my father accepted the position as general manager of the farming operations here. That was sixty-one years ago this past June. Many people, staff and children, have come and gone through the years, but we're all family. It makes for great fun and great memories at our reunion every June."

She paused a moment and smiled fondly at the faces around the table and then directed her attention to Susie and Simon. "I am a little biased, I know; but you'll see that Glen Hollow is a great place to live and an even greater place in which to grow up."

"Where's Mr. Hilda?" Simon asked, his big, blue eyes innocent in their curiosity. (He had noticed the ring on her left finger.)

Miss Hilda's eyes misted, but she didn't miss a step. "That would be Mr. Eric, dear. He passed on two years ago, this past October first," she said with a sad smile.

"Like Nana," Simon commiserated, his own eyes beginning to tear. Miss Hilda patted his back and nodded. A new concept flashed into his

49

mind, and he blurted out, "Maybe Nana and Mr. Eric will meet and be friends just like us."

His buoyant enthusiasm caused everyone to chuckle, and Miss Hilda told him "maybe so". His blue eyes sparkled, his countenance changing to joy at the thought of Nana making new friends.

Miss Pritchett said gently, "Thank you, Hilda, Simon. Now, Miss Emma, if you please."

The young lady in question was slight of build with straight, black hair cut at chin level. Her dark brown eyes were fringed with short, black lashes. The red, square-framed glasses slightly overpowered her small, thin face. When she spoke, her voice was not what Susie had expected. Based on her appearance, Susie thought Miss Emma would have a meek, little, mousy voice. Instead, it was loud and robust.

"I'm Emma Rose Wilson," she said with a perky smile. "I was born and raised in Brinkston, and I taught there for three years. I've only been here since August. I have a master's degree in early childhood education and one also in secondary childhood education."

Noticing the bewilderment on Simon's face, she grinned and chuckled, then explained. "That means, Simon, I'm qualified to teach grades kindergarten through twelve." She laughed softly in response to the rapid bobbing of his head, signifying that he understood. "I was fortunate," she continued, "to hear of this position in May. I applied and was very thrilled to have been accepted." To Simon, she added with a wink and a smile, "And I'm not married." Simon giggled at her remark, tilting his head slightly downward, feigning shyness.

A silence ensued as everyone waited for Mr. Warbly to introduce himself; he was busy wolfing down his food. Slowly it dawned on him that no one was speaking. He looked up, his eyes darting around the table and eventually focusing on Miss Pritchett. She smiled at him. "If you please, Mr. Warbly, tell us about yourself."

"O-o-oh," he stammered, "I thought it was just for folks livin' here." He wiped his mouth with his napkin and nervously cleared his throat. "Okay, then. Well, I'm Joe Warbly, 'n I'm a driver for Child Services. Been doin' it for 'bout thirty years now." He paused and then added, "'n I live just outside Willington in a little place called Pottsville. I have a wife 'n six kids; oldest four are married with kids of their own. Guess that's it."

"Thank you, Mr. Warbly," Miss Pritchett said appreciatively.

"Oh, uhh," Mr. Warbly hastily added. "Miss Pritchett, I just wanted t' apologize for bein' so late deliverin' the kids." With a jerk of his head, he gave a slight nod toward Susie and Simon. "Just wanted you t' know t'wernt my fault. I did the best I could, Miss Pritchett; I did. You see, the bridge was out on County Road 24; 'n I had t' go all the way back t' 135 North, pert' near t' Foxboro Station, 'n then come 'cross the bridge on County Road 4. Then that turn-off road t' come here was in real bad shape. I couldn't do more 'n ten mile 'n hour the whole rest of the way, 'n that's why we were so late. Again I'm real sorry, but the county needs t' grade that turn-off road; 'n, beggin' your pardon, your lane needs gradin' too."

"There isn't any need to apologize, Mr. Warbly," she responded with a warm smile. "I am aware that both the road and the lane are in terrible condition. The recent storm nearly washed them away; and since both roads are the property of Glen Hollow and not the county, it is my responsibility to repair and maintain them. The men have been rather busy repairing the buildings and the fences. It is, however, my understanding that they will grade both roads on Monday. I do apologize for the inconvenience caused to you."

"Thank you, Ma'am," he said softly, bobbing his head up and down like it was a bobble-headed toy; "'t'wernt no problem at all, Ma'am."

She gave him a slight nod, acknowledging his statement, turned to the man seated next to Mr. Warbly and said, "Henry, I believe you're next."

Mr. Henry David Canton, a tall, willowy man, appeared to be in his mid-fifties. His dark brown hair was graying at the temples, and his brown eyes had a kind look to them. He had a jovial smile and a deep bass voice. He was in charge of the maintenance and repairs of the out buildings and of the manor. A master carpenter, he had been at Glen Hollow for fifteen years, becoming the supervisor of repairs and maintenance five years ago.

Seated next to him was his wife, Thelma June. She was a stout woman with light brown hair that she wore braided and pinned behind her head like a big cinnamon bun. Her rounded face overwhelmed her small brown eyes and her round, little nose. She was one of the three maids. She and Mr. Canton had been married for twenty-five years. Their only child, Jason, was attending college in another state. Excitedly she announced that Jason would be spending his winter break with them this year, and would be arriving at the Willington airport on the twentieth. Everyone seemed to be glad to hear the news; everyone, that is, except the other children. Again, none of them said anything, and Susie couldn't help but wonder why. (Later she learned that they were new to Glen Hollow, just as she and Simon were.)

"Please, everyone, be quite," Miss Pritchett spoke firmly, quelling the roar of voices like a dissipating storm. "Jose, please tell us your name, your age, when you arrived here and something about yourself."

"Like what?" he asked.

She chuckled slightly, "Perhaps your favorite school subject or a hobby."

Jose bobbed his head slowly as he contemplated what he would say. He had wavy, dark brown hair with just a hint of amber highlights. He sported small, rectangular glasses that had a tortoise-shell colored frame, perfectly complementing his hazel eyes. "My name is Jose Ramon Santos, and I'm nine. My first day here was August 28th of this year."

He paused. Tentatively, he asked, "Miss Pritchett, do I have to say why I'm here?"

"No, Jose;" she answered. "That is entirely your decision. It would be nice, though, to at least say what your favorite subject is in school or your hobbies."

Jose nodded. "I love to read and to play chess. And I really love Dragon Lore. I watch it every Saturday, and I have all of the collector cards. The movie's coming to the theater next month, and we're all going."

Although the same excited sentiment was echoed by several of the other children, Simon turned to Susie and gave her a puzzled look. Silently he mouthed, "What's that"? Susie gave a fast, little shrug, telling him she didn't know.

Jose caught their exchange. "You don't know about Dragon Lore?" he asked incredulously.

"No," Susie and Simon answered simultaneously. A few of the other children snickered, amused at the newcomers' ignorance.

Jose, however, smiled kindly as he explained. "Dragon Lore is really neat," he began enthusiastically. "The story is about these five kids who fight evil with the help of this magical dragon. He's really old, like millions and millions of years old; and he's super wise and knows everything. He's real powerful and can do anything. In today's episode, the evil sorcerer found the place where Niku Nasha, that's the good dragon, imprisoned the evil dragon, Zi Chong, thousands of years ago. And..,"

"That's enough, Jose," Miss Pritchett interrupted good-naturedly. "Perhaps you can catch them up on the storyline later. Is there anything else you would like to share with us about yourself?"

Jose grinned. "My favorite school subject is languages. I know six now, and am learning another one; but I want to learn more."

Amazed, Susie asked, "You're fluent in six languages?"

Jose merely nodded, but the adults echoed, "Oh yes."

"That's incredible," Susie said in admiration.

Jose shrugged his shoulders as if it was no big deal, but his grin said otherwise. "It's nothing. My mother was a nurse, and she spoke three languages. She taught me English and Spanish, of course, but also French by the time I was three. When I was four, Mama asked our priest if he would teach me Latin, Hebrew and Greek. So I started lessons with him every day. When I was five, he arranged for me to attend a private school."

He paused and grinned at Miss Emma. "I'm learning German now."

"Yes, and he's a very quick study," Miss Emma vouched appreciatively.

"Thank you, Jose; now...." Miss Pritchett stopped in mid-sentence for she noticed Jose had raised his hand. "Yes, Jose?"

Though his countenance was sad, his voice was steady and calm. "Miss Pritchett, I don't mind telling why I'm here."

She smiled fondly. Softly she said, "It's your choice, Jose. You may if you wish."

He nodded. "My mother was a Nurse Practitioner, like Miss Bettye," he smiled at her. "Mama worked at the Fairview Trauma Center. It's a Level One Center; that means they handle the most severe cases. She worked a lot, but not on Saturdays because that was our special day. We would get a burger or a pizza, and sometimes we'd have a picnic in the park. Then afterwards, we always went to a movie. She had to work late Friday night and didn't come home until noon on Saturday. She said she needed to sleep, and we'd make Sunday our day just this once."

He shrugged. "I could see how tired she was, so I didn't mind.... Now I wish we didn't go at all ...."

His voice trailed off for a moment. He emitted a deep sigh and then continued. "We were coming home from a movie on Sunday afternoon. A drunk driver smashed into our car on her side. Later, they told me the driver died immediately because he wasn't wearing a seat belt. ... My mother died in the ambulance on the way to the hospital... I was in the hospital for two months. Both of my legs were broken, my right arm was broken, my collar bone was broken, and I had a concussion."

He dropped his gaze. "I never knew my father; he was a pilot and died when I was just a baby," he continued in a hushed tone. "Mama was an orphan, too, so there was no family to take me when she died."

He paused, his gaze now firmly fixed on his dinner plate. He swallowed hard several times before continuing. "So Child Services assigned me a case worker. When I was released from the hospital, I went to live at the Boy's Home. Somehow Miss Pritchett found out about me, and I came here."

Tears had begun rolling down his cheeks. Miss Thelma placed her arm around him, giving him a hug. "That was very brave of you," she whispered. He nodded, wiping the tears from his face.

Miss Pritchett lightly cleared her throat. "Thank you. Jose," she spoke fondly. "We are very glad that you came to live with us. You are a wonderful part of our family."

Jose looked up at her and smiled. Affectionately she returned his smile and then directed her gaze to the next person. With a nod so brief that it was nearly imperceptible, Miss Pritchett signaled him to begin.

The man had an affable air to his mannerisms and to his voice. In a pleasant baritone, he introduced himself. "I'm Joel Travis Casey; but I've always been called JT, so I'd appreciate if you also call me JT," he said, nodding at Susie and Simon.

His thick, wavy hair was sable brown in color and looked to be as soft and silky as a mink. His large eyes were hazel, deep-set and had short black lashes. Based on his seated height, Susie figured JT has to be well over six feet tall. His narrow shoulders and thin body frame also added to that appearance.

"I'm a master plumber, so I take care of the plumbing issues for the manor and the farm. Cora Jane and I have been here just over a year, and we love it here."

"So you fix the toilets," Simon blurted; "I bet this place has a lot of them."

JT laughed. "There's a few," he acknowledged, amused at Simon's boisterous energy; "but there's a little more to it than fixing toilets."

"Like the sinks? Nana had a real bad leak in her kitchen sink, and she had to call a plumber because she couldn't get it to stop," Simon volunteered.

"Did the plumber fix the leak?" JT asked with a grin.

Simon bobbed his head rapidly. "Yeah and fast, too; Nana said he was faster than greased lightning."

JT chuckled, "That's pretty fast, all right," he agreed. "Well, I fix leaks in sinks, tubs, showers and such; but I also maintain all the plumbing, which includes the plumbing for the radiant heating system."

"What's that?" both Susie and Simon asked.

He grinned. "You see how big the manor is?" (They nodded.) "It's kind of like a castle with all the stone and wood; and since it is so large, it is a little difficult to heat. It stayed fairly cold in the winter, even with all of the fireplaces blazing away night and day. About seventy years ago, they hired a master plumber and an engineer to plan a heating system that would use hot water. They did, and the system was installed. The hot water flows through the pipes under the floors and circulates back to the furnace that heats it. The floors absorb the heat from the hot pipes; the heat rises up from the floor, providing a warmer house."

"Wow," Simon responded; "that a lot of pipes."

"Yes it is," JT agreed; "and it works rather well."

"What if it's below freezing outside?" Susie asked.

"Doesn't matter because I can increase the temperature setting of the furnace if we need more heat," he patiently explained. "If you're interested, I'll show you the furnace."

Simon's face brightened, and his eyes flashed with glee. "Yeah!" he answered.

Chuckling lightly, he responded, "Maybe Monday afternoon. Well, I guess that's more than enough about what I do."

Turning to the lady seated beside him, he smiled as he placed his arm around her and said, "This is my wife, Cora Jane. You're up," he told her, removing his arm after giving her a small hug.

Cora Jane appeared to be in her mid-twenties. She was an enthusiastic young lady with an abundance of energy, which was really a good thing since she was one of the general duty assistants. (Keeping pace with all of the children would definitely require energy, Susie noted to herself, and lots of it.)

Miss Cora's pale blond hair was short, layered so that the back barely touched the nape of her neck while the sides angled gently toward her chin. Her eyes were light green, like the warm sea waters near the shore as the light from the sun brightens it, turning it from a deep, turquoise green to a sparkly, light green. She wore no makeup, and her eyelashes were so blond that, unless you were close to her, it looked as if she didn't have any eyelashes. Her complexion was fair, and her rosy cheeks looked as if she had just come in from the cold.

Rambling on and on, Miss Cora seemed to flit like a hummingbird from one subject to the next. She prattled about how they learned of Glen Hollow, and its need for a master plumber; how much she and JT loved it here, loved the farm life, and loved the people here, the children and especially how much she felt like they were all one, big family. She had a master's degree, although Susie wasn't certain as to what field. Susie had tuned Miss Cora out several minutes ago, just drifting back when she heard Miss Cora say that she had received her master's degree in August. (Later, Susie learned that it was in music.)

Miss Cora barely had finished that sentence when the little boy next to her blurted out rather loudly, "Are you *done* yet?"

With a little giggle, Miss Cora patted him on the back and replied, "Sure, sweetie. You go right ahead."

Susie stifled a laugh; he was so cute. He had the chubbiest cheeks (like a Valentine cherub) and the biggest, golden brown eyes framed with long, black lashes that touched his cheeks whenever he looked down. His short afro with its golden brown color perfected the cherub look. His eyes sparkled and danced with the energy and cleverness of a rascal; it was easy for Susie to determine that he and Simon were certainly two peas in a pod. They would get along great.

"My name is Timothy, but everybody calls me Timmy," he announced proudly. "I'm five years old," he proclaimed, holding his right hand up with his fingers splayed open for ease in counting. "My brother, Aaron, (he pointed to the older boy sitting to his right) and me have been here fourteen days."

He paused and giggled. "That's *two* weeks in case you don't know." ('Gregarious is definitely the word that describes him', Susie thought.)

"Tell them what you like to do," Aaron prompted patiently.

"I like lots of things," he stated as he threw his arms outward in an exaggerated gesture. "I like stories, and I like coloring, and I like puzzles and I like to play outside. And I love to build trains with Legos. They're not as good as a real train set," he confessed; "but they're still fun."

His eyes flashed with boyish glee as he added with a giggle, "But what I really like the most is to climb trees, even though we're not supposed to."

"Thank you Timmy," Miss Pritchett quickly interrupted. "Aaron, you're next."

Susie studied the expression (or the lack thereof would be more accurate) on Aaron's face. He was really distant, stoic even. Susie understood – he was trying to remain strong for Timmy the way she did for Simon. Aaron's wavy hair was medium short and a rich, chestnut brown in color. He parted his hair on the left, allowing an unruly curl to drop like a coiled spring in the center of his forehead. His eyes were expressive and soulful; they could draw you in, or just as easily cut you to the quick. Susie recalled Nana's friend, Amelia, a poet whose eyes had the same quality.

Aaron released a heavy sigh. It was obvious he didn't want to participate, but he did. "My name is Aaron Sutton, and I'm ten."

Timmy rapidly shook his head back and forth, obviously disagreeing. He leaned toward his big brother and said, "Na-uh; your first name is *Alvin.*" Giggling profusely, he began bouncing side to side in his booster seat, delighting in outing his big brother.

Aaron was not amused. He glowered at Timmy. "I don't like my first name any more than you like to be called Timothy or Ryan," he retorted with a slight growl to his tone.

Timmy ceased his little dance, began rolling his eyes, and had just a hint of a smirk on his face.

Aaron exhaled a little forcefully, revealing the depth of his irritation before continuing his narrative. "My favorite subjects are math and science. I like mystery books, and I like to design aircraft and spacecraft."

"You forgot to say when we came here," Timmy chided, pushing gently on Aaron's shoulder several times.

"I didn't need to because you already told them," Aaron snapped, annoyed with his little brother.

"Oh … you could say why we came here, like Jose did. I didn't tell that," he offered, sincerely attempting to be helpful. Aaron shook his head and focused his attention on his food, pushing it around the plate with his fork.

"It's all right, Timmy, if Aaron doesn't wish to share at this time," Miss Pritchett intervened. "Allan, I believe you're next."

"Wait, Miss Pritchett," Timmy interrupted; "I'll tell. I don't know as much as Aaron, but I know some."

Aaron scowled, and his jaw set tight.

"Very well, Timmy," she agreed, smiling encouragingly; "you may share your story of how you came to live with us."

Timmy straightened and sat up tall in his booster seat. He looked first to his left and then to his right, making certain everyone was paying attention. "Mommy had cancer and was real, real sick for a very lo-o--ng, lo-o-ng time; so Mommy, me and Aaron all lived with Grammy. Grammy is my Mommy's Mommy." He accentuated this last sentence with a sharp nod of his head.

Taking in a deep breath, Timmy exhaled with a big sigh as his face saddened. "Mommy got worse, and worse and went to the hospital. Then she went to Heaven. That's when I was three. We stayed with Grammy, and then *Grammy* got sick."

Slowly moving his head from side to side, his face was the epitome of sorrow. "She couldn't walk or talk, so we had to go to a foster home."

Timmy exhaled a short, little burst of breath, a cross between a sigh of relief and one of sadness. "Grammy got better, but she couldn't take care of us. Then we came here." He shrugged his shoulders. "That's all I know."

"Thank you, Timmy, for sharing," Miss Pritchett said encouragingly as she watched Aaron's reaction. He was guarded, but it was still very much evident he wasn't happy with Timmy for sharing. Again Miss Pritchett signaled to the man sitting next to Aaron to begin his introduction.

He had sandy blonde hair, sky blue eyes, high cheekbones and a slender nose. His demeanor was easygoing, and his voice was definitely that of a tenor. "I'm Allan Roy Stovall; just call me Allan Roy. Folks have always used both my names. I guess it was to differentiate me from my cousin Allan; he's Allan James. Anyway, I was born and raised in Rosemont."

(Susie's memory flashed to Mrs. Crenshaw – she was from Rosemont, too. Maybe she and Allan Roy know each other, she thought.)

"Ginger and I met in high school, in our junior year, a week before homecoming. Her family had just moved to Rosemont from Eagle Ridge."

He grinned at his wife, his eyes crinkling with delight as he remembered that day. "She was the prettiest girl I had ever seen." He winked at her and added, "Still is. I decided that very day I was going to marry her. And five years later, I did. It's been sheer heaven ever since."

He chuckled lightly, giving his wife a nudge with his elbow. "Anyhow, I'm an electrical engineer, so I mainly handle the electric issues for Glen Hollow. We installed a solar panel system last year so we would have a better, more stable source of electricity."

Grinning at Simon's puzzled look, he winked at Simon and explained, "That means we capture the sunlight for our use. We shouldn't have as many black outs due to storms or winter weather, and hopefully not any. All of our power lines are buried deep and are well insulated."

Simon grinned at him, his eyes twinkling mischievously. "What if it rains, or it's cloudy for days and days?"

Allan Roy laughed, delighted with the way Simon's mind worked. "That's why we have a back-up system that stores electricity for just those days. The solar panels still absorb whatever light there is and sends it to the system's hub. From there, whatever is needed is drawn from the hub or the backup system.

He smiled warmly at Simon. "If you're interested, I'll be glad to show you our system and explain it to you."

"Okay," Simon quickly agreed.

"Me, too," Timmy popped off; "I want to see it."

"That's fine with me, Timmy. Would Monday, after your naptime, be good with you guys?"

Both boys animatedly nodded, chorusing their approval with "You bet" and "Yes".

Allan Roy laughed softly. "Good; I'll come get you right after your nap on Monday."

"Wait," Simon barked; "I can't. I'm going to see the furnace!"

"Me, too," Timmy piped up; "I want to see the furnace, too."

"No problem, boys," JT answered. "You can go with Allan Roy right after nap time, and afterwards you can come with me."

"Works for me," Allan Roy said.

"Okay!" Simon agreed as Timmy added, "Me too!"

Continuing with his narrative, Allan Roy turned to his wife and said, "We came here about twenty years ago, is that right?"

"Twenty-four years actually," Miss Ginger said, correcting him. "Zoe was a year old, and I was three months pregnant with Chad."

Miss Ginger, Allan Roy's wife, was appropriately named for her hair was a bright auburn color, definitely more red than brown. Her eyes were dark blue, like the deepest ocean, and were fringed with short, reddish-brown lashes. There was a light in her eyes that portrayed a joy that resided deep within her soul. Like Miss Cora, she was also a general duty assistant.

It was fairly apparent that Miss Ginger's temperament and disposition were not nearly as hyper as Miss Cora's. However, Miss Ginger did possess an effervescent quality that seemed to permeate those around her, infusing them with a sense of peace and joy. That quality, combined with her melodic voice, brought a sense of calm to those around her.

Miss Ginger loved to talk about her two children, both of whom are grown and live elsewhere. Their daughter, Zoe, is an RN and is married to a doctor whose practice is in Shiloh Creek. Whereas their son, Chad, is currently single and is a pilot for a commercial airliner whose hub is in Willington.

She finished her introduction and turned to the person on her right. "Your turn," she said pleasantly.

The young girl ignored her and continued playing with the food on her plate.

"Kat, please introduce yourself," Miss Pritchett prodded.

The young girl in question had built a tall reservoir with her mashed potatoes, filled it with gravy and painstakingly lined up the peas, carrots and bits of biscuits and meat as if they were a miniature village.

"I don't want to," she said coolly, still fixated on her creation. And then, she slowly raised her fork and smashed the dam, allowing the gravy to flow down, drowning the make-believe village.

Patiently, but firmly, Miss Pritchett responded, "It isn't a matter of what you want to do; it is a matter of common courtesy, and you will be courteous."

Staring defiantly at Miss Pritchett, the girl released her fork, mid-air, and it dropped with a clatter onto her plate.

"Fine," she said icily. Tossing her hair back from her face, she turned and glared at Susie. Susie caught her breath and subconsciously held it for several seconds, startled by the girl's appearance.

The girl called Kat was incredibly beautiful. Her long, ebony hair, with its blue-black sheen, glimmered like silk; her skin was as white as new-fallen snow. She had a slender, tiny nose and high cheekbones. But most striking of all were her eyes. They were the palest gray! So pale in fact, they were nearly colorless. It was a little unsettling to have those eyes fixated on her, but Susie didn't avert her gaze. Neither did the girl.

"My name is Kat; Katherine Peters actually, but *no one* calls me Katherine. My name is Kat." ('Appropriate,' Susie thought, 'since she looks like the panther we saw last year at the zoo.')

"I'm nine, and I arrived here six months ago today. That's June 6th, in case you're not proficient in math," she continued a little caustically. "My favorite subjects are art and history. I love to draw, and I love to read."

"What do you draw?" Simon asked, for he too loved to draw although his creations were mostly stick figures drawn with crayons and markers.

Kat smiled slyly as she focused her attention on Simon. "Everything; I'll even draw a picture of you, if you like."

Grinning, Simon nodded vigorously and said, "Yes, please."

"Thank you, Kat. Mrs. Copp - -", Miss Pritchett began.

"I'm not finished, Miss Pritchett," Kat coolly piped up, interrupting her. "May I please continue?"

Miss Pritchett eyed her warily. Although Kat's expression appeared benign, she knew all too well the cunning that Kat possessed. Kat was not one to "share" anything, especially any information regarding her own self. She was most adept at evading and blocking inquiries, more so than most adults

"Certainly, please do," she answered cautiously. Miss Pritchett's intense gaze was intended to remind Kat to mind her manners; however, Kat had other plans.

Kat slowly turned her head, focusing her attention once again on Susie. That slow, deliberate movement caused an uneasy feeling to arise in Susie. It was nothing compared to the tremor that ran through her when Kat smiled. It wasn't really a smile, more like a sneer that had just a hint of an ominous undercurrent.

An image of a jungle panther stalking its prey flashed into Susie's mind, and she shuddered. She pushed the image away and returned Kat's stare. Surprisingly, Kat chuckled and then gave Susie a genuine smile.

Her voice was soft, almost like a whisper, yet it carried well throughout the room. Everyone had stopped talking to listen.

"My parents died in a boating accident," she announced and then paused for a few moments before continuing. "I lived with my Mom's sister and her husband for four months afterwards."

Her smile became wicked again. "They tried to "cure" me, but the neighbors and police didn't approve of their methods."

Simon blurted out "What was wrong?" as Timmy asked, "Did you have cancer?"

Miss Pritchett, however, calmly stated, "I think that's enough for now, Kat."

Kat's eyes narrowed as she glared at Miss Pritchett. "Why? Jose and Timmy shared their stories. Why can't I?" she asked, her voice having just a tinge of an insidious tone.

Miss Pritchett's gaze never wavered from Kat's face as she studied Kat. After a few seconds had passed, she smiled. "Very well, Kat, if you insist; please proceed."

Kat did not expect that reaction from Miss Pritchett. She had been certain Miss Pritchett would refuse her request, thus giving Kat the perfect reason to storm out of the Dining Hall. The look of surprise on Kat's face was fleeting, but it had been there nonetheless. Momentarily pressing her lips together, she tilted her head slightly, contemplating her next move. It was done in a fraction of second; she turned her attention to Simon and Timmy.

"No, Timmy, I didn't, and don't, have cancer. And nothing is wrong with me, Simon. ..."

Hesitating, she bit her lower lip and changed her focus to Susie. "My aunt and uncle first punished me. ...until what I said came true; then they thought I was possessed. They hired a man to get rid of the demons."

She fell quiet for a moment. She saw the bewilderment on Simon's face and the concern on Susie's. Her own expression changed; it became as one who desperately needed someone to understand, to accept her experiences as valid and not the raving of a deranged mind.

"I see spirit people; some are good and some aren't. I've seen them since I was three," she stated as calmly as if she were reciting the alphabet.

There were mixed reactions ranging from gasps, to 'don't be silly', and 'preposterous' remarks from nearly everyone. A few of the adults did not seem surprised, just wary. While both Miss Pritchett's and Miss Hilda's faces displayed compassion, Simon's eyes were wide open with his "deer caught in headlights" look; and Susie, well, she knew Kat was telling the truth; at least, the truth that Kat perceived.

Until a few months ago, Simon often spoke of his "imaginary" people; the bad ones terrified him. He had always slept either with her or Nana, insisting it was the only way the bad ones would leave him alone. Susie had always thought it was because he was afraid of the dark and had invented the stories about the imaginary people so he wouldn't have to sleep alone. Just before Nana had passed, Simon had told Susie that they were all gone. He didn't know why; he missed the good ones because they were friends, but he was glad the bad ones were gone. The recollection caused a shiver to creep its way down Susie's spine.

Emphatically Kat continued, having to nearly shout above the various voices and their opinions. "I'm not crazy, and I'm not lying!" she insisted.

One by one they began to be quiet as they noticed Miss Pritchett's hand motioning them to be silent. "We apologize for the rudeness shown to you," she said softly to Kat. "Please continue, if you wish."

"I'm not crazy and I'm not lying," she repeated. Her voice now a little less harsh than it had been as she continued; "My parents didn't believe me; they thought I had an overly active imagination."

Her voice now softened, sadness filling it as she continued. "They died because they didn't listen to me ... I told them not to go in that boat. I told them the spirit people told me it would explode. .... I tried... I tried to tell them, but they wouldn't listen."

She paused slightly, her voice and her expression becoming hard with anger. "I had to stay with my Mom's sister. My aunt and uncle didn't believe me either. Every day they punished me for lying. They tried to make me say I lied. I wouldn't ... they decided I was crazy, and took me to a lot of doctors. Then they noticed that what I told them came true."

Kat closed her eyes for a moment. When she opened them, she looked directly at Susie.

"They were scared," she intoned, her voice flat and empty. "A friend of my uncle's said it was demons. He told them to lock me in my room. So they did; they took me out of school and kept me locked up. They put bars on the window after I broke the window and escaped. A week later they brought this man to see me because he said he could get rid of the demons. I still have the scars." She shrugged as if that simple movement could dispel all of the heartache she had suffered.

She sighed deeply. "The neighbors called the police. They came and took me away." The old Kat was now back; her smile once again was unnerving.

Kat's voice rang with bitterness. "None of my foster parents believed me either; although some probably wish they had." Her face hardened, and her eyes narrowed in anger as she stared defiantly at Susie.

"Anyway," she continued after taking in a deep breath to calm herself. "All of the foster parents kept returning me to the State Home until no one would take me. A judge sent me to visit Glen Hollow for a weekend."

Her smile was as dismissive as her tone. "I decided to stay because the bad ones don't bother me here."

"Perhaps the reason you don't see them anymore is due to the progress you've made in counseling," Miss Pritchett suggested, the tenderness and compassion she felt toward Kat well displayed in her voice, her eyes and her face.

Kat's face lit up as she rolled her eyes and laughed. "No way! I didn't say 'I don't *see* them anymore'; I said they don't *bother* me here."

She released a heavy sigh showing her frustration with non-believers. "Counseling has helped me deal with my anger," she admitted; "but it isn't the reason they won't come here."

She paused, attempting to calm herself before continuing. "Why do you think I stay here and don't go to town anymore with everyone else?" she hotly retorted.

"I don't know, Kat; why do you remain here?" Miss Pritchett asked gently.

Kat drew in her breath sharply and released it slowly. Quietly, with practiced control, she responded, "I don't go because they're out there, waiting. If I leave here, they surround me and talk to me all the time. Sometimes the good ones come and make them leave, but they always come back. The bad ones won't come any closer than the oak tree out front; but they're still there. ..."

Her voice trailed off, and she was quiet for a few moments. Slowly she shook her head, contemplating and searching for just the right words. "When I'm inside I can't hear or see them, so I spend most of my time inside. Outside, I can see them and hear them, but they don't come closer than the tree... I don't know why." She looked at Susie as if she expected an explanation from her. It wasn't forthcoming.

"Perhaps we should ask Reverend Tillman tomorrow," Miss Hilda suggested softly, concern for Kat fully displayed on her face as she and Miss Pritchett exchanged a quick glance.

"No!" Kat responded forcefully.

"As you wish," Miss Hilda replied; "however, if it were me, he would be a person I would be able to trust with any spiritual problem." Giving Kat a fond look and a kind smile, she added, "You know him well enough to know that's true."

Kat said nothing and returned to staring at her plate, a sullen expression clouding her face.

Miss Pritchett lightly tapped the table next to Mrs. Coppersmith. They exchanged a brief glance after which Mrs. Coppersmith cleared her throat.

Mrs. Coppersmith's voice matched what Susie had expected; a no-nonsense, practical drill sergeant. She was thin but wiry. Her short brown hair was graying, sort of a salt and pepper effect; and it curled naturally into little pin curls. Her large, brown eyes seem to protrude just a smidge, giving her the appearance of a hawk. Her nose did little to diminish that effect.

Although her name is Bernice Coppersmith, she unequivocally stated, she preferred to be called Mrs. Coppersmith and would be so addressed. She had been chief cook and bottle washer at Glen Hollow for twenty-four years. Both she and her husband, Edward Marvin Coppersmith (May he rest in Peace), were born and raised in Foxboro Station. They were never blessed with any little ones of their own, and Mr. Coppersmith passed on to his eternal reward August Fifth, 1993. With an air of finality, Mrs. Coppersmith gave a slight nod to Miss Pritchett, signaling she had ended her brief discourse.

"I am Eloise Pritchett," she began, her voice light and soft. "Glen Hollow is my ancestral home through my mother's family. In 1974, I decided that it could be put to better use than just to serve as my home, so I started Glen Hollow Orphanage. Through the years we've been the home and family to many children, just like the ten of you. Some were with us just a few days, while others were here until they were grown. I hope you will consider this your home and that we are your family, whether you're here one day or until you're eighteen."

"Megan, please tell us your name and something about yourself," Miss Pritchett gently instructed the cute, little girl to her right.

She had sandy blonde hair, curled into little ringlets that bounced like crazy with every move she made. Her eyes were the color of blue that most would call Robin's Egg blue, and framing them were a double row of thick, black lashes. With her round face, button nose, chubby, dimpled cheeks, and her dazzling white, baby teeth, she looked like a porcelain doll that had magically come to life.

"My name is Megan Sinclair; and my birthday is October eleventh, so I just turned five," the little girl proudly stated in a voice sweet and light. "I love to color; and I have lots and lots of color books, and crayons and markers," she confided with a giggle.

"Oh! And I *love* tea parties," she informed them joyfully. Her eyes sparkled as she added, "I have one every day and sometimes two." She grinned and coyly tilted her head as she made that last admission.

Smiling at Miss Pritchett, she continued. "I love to read, but mostly with Miss Pritchett." Her curls bounced like coiled springs as she nodded her head. "She reads the best stories."

Miss Pritchett smiled at her and thanked her. She looked at the lady sitting next to Megan; however, before she could speak, Simon interrupted.

"How come you're here?" Simon asked Megan inquisitively.

Frowning fiercely at Simon, Megan spouted angrily, "I don't have to tell!" She crossed her arms and sat with her shoulders hunched as she furled her eyebrows, puckering her mouth into a hostile pout.

"That's correct, Megan. We share our stories only when we want to share," Miss Pritchett agreed soothingly.

Simon leaned forward so that Megan would have a better view of him. "I'm sorry, Megan," he sincerely apologized. "I just wanted to know if you lost your Mommy and Daddy like Susie and me."

Megan's face brightened for suddenly she realized that she was currently the center of attention. Everyone was looking at her. The dimples in her cheeks deepened as she grinned, relishing the attention.

"You could tell Simon when you arrived here," Miss Pritchett gently prompted.

"I think it was June," she responded.

"That's correct," Miss Pritchett agreed. "Is there anything else you would like to share?"

Megan's brow furrowed slightly. "I told you I don't remember much." Her tone was slightly agitated.

Miss Pritchett reached over and lightly patted her hand. "It's okay if you don't remember; or even if you do, and don't want to share." She smiled tenderly at Megan. "I thought perhaps you may have remembered something by now."

Miss Pritchett looked to the lady next to Megan. "Fiona, I believe you're next."

"Wait," Megan blurted, not wanting the attention to shift away from her so soon. "I remember a little," she confessed; "but I was afraid to say because I didn't think anyone would believe me."

"I'm certain we will believe you," Miss Pritchett assured her.

"Okay! ... I remember I was on a train with Mommy and Daddy. We were going on a vacation."

Megan paused slightly. Her voice was soft and expressive when she continued her narrative. "It was really cold; there was snow everywhere. But we always have a lot of snow. Daddy said it was because Angels Crest is the highest peak in the mountains."

Her face clouded a little as she thought back on that day. "I remember the train going faster and faster downhill. It was moving funny, not like it's supposed to – it wiggled kind of side to side. And it made a lot of loud noises, and it was real bumpy. Then the noises all stopped, and it was just going downhill. ... and it wasn't bumpy anymore."

Her face brightened a little, and her mouth curled upwards into a warm smile. "Daddy told me to sit with him, so I sat in Daddy's lap. Mommy looked so sad. She came and sat by Daddy and me, and put her arms around us. It was real quiet, and all I could hear was Mommy and Daddy whispering their prayers."

Tears stung her eyes as she slowly moved her head back and forth. "Daddy held me real tight and whispered that everything would be okay; but it wasn't."

Megan shrugged her shoulders. "Then I wasn't in the train, and I saw it fall way down into the river. An angel was holding me; we were floating in the sky."

A sad smile formed on her lips. "My angel told me Mommy and Daddy went to Heaven. I miss them lots, but I'm happy they're in Heaven."

Pausing briefly, she swallowed hard a couple of times before continuing her tale. "It was so cold I could see my breath make clouds. But I wasn't cold because my angel kept me warm. She took me real close to where the train fell, and stayed with me until the police came. The policeman put a blanket around me. I told him about my angel, but he didn't believe me."

She giggled and grinned, confiding, "He couldn't see her." Her eyes flashed with glee as she added, "My angel told me I was special, and that's why I could see her."

Megan paused for a moment as the memories of that night resurfaced in her mind. Her little face filled with sadness as she continued her story. "Lots and lots of people came. And there were lots of ambulances, and police cars and fire trucks. The policeman told them what I said."

She frowned. "Everybody said I dreamed it because it was so cold outside, and I didn't have a coat. So I wouldn't talk to them because they didn't believe me."

A small sigh escaped as she shrugged. "I was holding my storybook. A lady asked to see it so I showed it to her. It had my name on the front, 'Megan, The Fairy Princess of Nightingale Forest'."

She began to grin, and her dimples deepened as her eyes flashed with delight. "Daddy gave it to me when we got on the train. Daddy had it made just for me! Daddy said I'm his fairy princess, and the story is about me. And it is, because the fairy princess has my face, and her name is Megan. I live in a beautiful forest with lots of flowers, and trees, and lakes, and rivers, and lots of fairy people, and other people and all kinds of animals. And they are all my friends. I have magical powers; and I can fly and disappear, and do all kinds of things. I even help people who are lost or hurt. It's a really neat book; I love it!"

"Do you still have the book?" Susie asked.

Megan grinned and slowly nodded. "Yes, but I keep it in a secret place."

"That's good," Susie told her, smiling. "That way you'll always have it."

"Is that when you came here?" Simon asked.

Megan scowled. "No! They made me go to lots of places. I didn't like any of them because they didn't believe me. They weren't nice, so I wasn't nice."

Megan fell silent for a moment; slowly a smile crept onto her face. Looking up at Miss Pritchett, Megan's face became joyful. "Miss Pritchett found me and brought me to live with her."

Megan tossed her head playfully and smiled at Simon. "That's all," she announced.

"Thank you, Megan, for sharing with us," Miss Pritchett said, affectionately squeezing Megan's hand. "We appreciate very much you choosing to share. Now, I believe it is Miss Fiona's turn."

The lady in question had flaming red hair that was quite long, cascading well below the arm of her chair. The golden highlights gave it the illusion of having a ring of golden fire surrounding her head. Her hair was thick and wavy with little tendrils that spiraled around her face, mimicking the longer strands that formed spirals only toward their ends.

She had the most intriguing and beguiling eyes, large and cat-like in shape. Susie was dazzled by the unique color; she had never seen eyes that color. They were the palest shade of sea green – reminiscent of when the sea is turbulent and churning, all frothy with just a hint of green in the foamy, white color. It bestowed upon Miss Fiona an ethereal quality, as if in any second she would vanish, a mere illusion and nothing more.

A light scattering of tiny, pinkish-red freckles were present on her face and on her arms. Against her alabaster skin, they were like little neon signs. Her smile seemed to brighten the room as much as did the sunny quality to her voice.

"My name is Fiona Fey Morgan," she began; "and I've been here for nearly three years now. Glen Hollow is a grand old place, full of wonder and mystery."

She winked at Simon, followed by a playful smile at both Susie and Simon. "I think you'll find the wonder and mystery is there are so many people here who care, and want to give you the best possible life that they can. It's up to you to accept that gift, and I hope you do."

Maintaining eye contact with Susie, Miss Fiona gave a brief nod to Susie and added, "I believe that'll be all I have to say for now."

Gently nudging the boy next to her, she said teasingly, "That was your cue, in case you missed it."

The boy next to her couldn't have grinned any bigger if he had tried. He obviously liked Miss Fiona; some might even say he was smitten with her. He could have been a relative of hers, though, what with his fire-engine red hair and emerald green eyes. His freckles were larger and a deeper red in color than hers, and he seemed to have considerably more of them than she.

He wore gold, wire-rimmed glasses that looked similar to what Ben Franklin had worn. He was big for his age, tall and broad shouldered. Easily, he could have been on a football team had he lived anywhere other than Glen Hollow. He seemed to have a quiet nature, further accentuated by his soft-spoken voice.

"My name is Jared Montgomery. I'm eleven. Chemistry and physics are my favorite subjects in school, and I'm into martial arts. I study several disciplines, and have been taking lessons since I was three."

He smiled at Miss Pritchett. "Miss Pritchett set up lessons for me via the satellite so I can continue my training."

Looking at the girl sitting to his right, he asked, "Do you want to tell why we're here?"

Her response was to roll her eyes and shrug.

Raising his eyebrow slightly at his sister, he waited briefly before continuing. "We came here in August. There was a really, bad lightning storm two years ago. It caused our house to catch fire."

His words caught in his throat as he remembered that night. He stared at his plate, regulating his breathing. Susie didn't know if anyone else noticed, but she did - she used that technique herself.

After a few seconds he apparently felt calm enough to continue. "I woke up coughing and couldn't breathe. I found Juls and got her outside. But it was too late to go back inside to get Mom and Dad. The firemen and police were there; they made us stay with the ambulances. After they released us from the hospital, we were sent to different foster homes. We got to see each other only one Saturday a month. Miss Pritchett heard about us, and we came here in August."

He smiled fondly at the girl next to him. He chuckled and added, "Oh, I almost forgot. This is my twin sister, Juls. I'm older by seven minutes."

The girl in question looked nothing like her brother; but then she and Simon didn't look anything alike either, Susie acknowledged silently. Juls had long, chocolate brown hair that she wore pulled back into a pony-tail. Physically she was her brother's opposite; she was slender, small boned, and had a slight olive tone to her complexion. Her soft, brown eyes were large like a doe's, fringed with short, dark brown lashes.

She smiled at her brother as she shook her head in a disapproving manner. "Seven minutes is no big deal," she unequivocally stated. "We're still the same age." Her tone revealed that she was teasing, irrespective of her words.

"Jared's already told you my name, why and when we arrived." She sighed dramatically. "My only interest is ballet. I love everything about it, and someday I'll be a prima ballerina. I've been studying ballet since I was two. Miss Pritchett arranged for me to have personal instruction from the foremost prima ballerina, Bethany Kessler. We went to New York to see her, and I had a private audition. I have lessons with her via the satellite three times a week, and I practice every day."

"Is she good?" Simon inquisitively asked. Timmy and Megan laughed loudly while several of the other children snickered.

Juls' eyes widened at the very idea that he would ask such a boorish question. "Only the most perfect ballerina of all time," she informed him acidly.

Simon shrugged and tossed his head from side to side, serving only to fuel Juls' anger.

With an amused smile, Miss Pritchett intervened before Juls could castigate him. "Bethany is very good and very famous, Simon. She's a longtime friend of mine, and that is why I took Juls to see her. Bethany believes that Juls has a rare gift for ballet, not just a talent. That is why she is training Juls. We hope that Juls will be able to dance wherever she chooses when she is of age."

"Why did your Mommy and Daddy name you 'jewels'?" Simon asked.

"Not jew-els," Juls retorted haughtily. "It's Juls: J - u - l - s; it's short for Julia."

"Oh," Simon responded, unimpressed. "Did you pick that nickname?"

She glowered at him. "Yes."

Simon giggled and rolled his eyes. His reaction was mimicked by Timmy and by Megan.

"Settled down, children," Miss Pritchett lightly reprimanded them. She had seen the anger building in Juls, and thus now thwarted any volcanic response from her. Miss Pritchett smiled at the lady next to Juls, giving her a brief nod.

The petite lady quietly placed her fork onto the rim of her dinner plate. Daintily raising her napkin to her lips, she gently touched it to first one corner of her mouth and then to the other. Gracefully she returned the napkin to her lap and then laid her hands atop it. She was fairly young, not yet forty (Susie estimated) and had perfect posture which went well with her immaculate, elegant attire and jewelry. Her ebony hair cascaded softly around her face, falling to her shoulders where it gently rolled under, ever so slightly, and the front tips curled in toward her neck. She had beautiful, turquoise green eyes which she had lightly accentuated with cosmetics. With her high cheekbones and delicate porcelain features, Susie could easily envision her being a model.

When she spoke, her voice was soft, and unmistakable was her accent. She sounded as if she had just arrived from France. "Bonsoir; I am Mrs. Claire Lisette DuBois McKay. You may address me as Miss Claire. I am Taryn's Mama."

Smiling lovingly, she looked at her daughter, seated to her right, and continued. "I have just arrived from New Orleans earlier this afternoon."

"How come you talk funny?" Timmy asked, genuinely curious.

With a light-hearted laugh, she smiled at him and answered him graciously. "My parents were French and immigrated to America with their families when they were very young. French was spoken exclusively in their homes. Eventually they did learn to speak English; however, French was still their first language. I learned French along with English, but French was also my first language when I was a child. Even today, French is still spoken as a first language in their home; it is the natural thing for them to do."

"Why?" Timmy persisted.

"Because, ma petit chèr, they think in French, and must translate their thoughts to English and then speak English. That is difficult to do. So, when one is at home, one does what is easiest." She smiled warmly at him. "Understand?"

He nodded and said," I guess so."

73

Grinning, she gave him a slight nod of acknowledgement and said, "Bon." Turning to her daughter she said, "Your turn, chère."

"Why are you here?" Megan asked Miss Claire before Miss Taryn had a chance to speak.

"My Taryn is getting married in February, so I am here to assist her in her wedding plans," she responded graciously. With a coy grin at Taryn and Joe she added; "I am also making a photo journal of this time for them, so you will see me taking pictures of them and also of everyone here."

"She's too young to get married," Simon blurted out, pointing at Miss Taryn. "She's just a little girl."

Megan and Timmy howled with laughter, agreeing with Simon. The adults chuckled, but also attempted to quell the rising tide of laughter that was beginning to develop. They had no success initially, and it was several minutes before order was restored. Simon's comments and the ensuing laughter generated a hot rebuttal from Miss Taryn, declaring that she was eighteen, legally an adult, and not a child. Miss Claire attempted to quiet her, but was the recipient of an icy rebuff.

Joe, Taryn's fiancé, took it good naturedly. He laughed and agreed that it appeared he was robbing the cradle; but, he said, Taryn couldn't help looking so young with her angel face, big bunny eyes and her waist-length, honey-brown hair that hung in little-girl spirals. He winked at Simon and added that Taryn had one of those baby faces and always would. Simon giggled, and Miss Taryn blushed deeply; she was not amused.

"Why are you getting married in winter?" Susie asked inquisitively of Miss Taryn. "Wouldn't summer be better?"

"No," Miss Taryn replied with a petulant tone; "it would not."

Miss Claire patted her daughter's arm lightly just as Mr. Joe nudged Taryn gently with his elbow. Taryn sighed lightly, and her voice had less of an edge to it when she continued. "February second is the beginning of the spring season, symbolizing new life just as marriage does."

"Nu-uh," Timmy spouted informatively. "*Everybody* knows that spring is at *Easter*. The Easter Bunny comes when the spring flowers start blooming, and he brings us Easter eggs and candy."

The other children began laughing as they touted their own opinions as to when spring began. In response to the marriage analogy, there were a few "yuchs, I'm trying to eat" from some of the boys. The adults chuckled and smiled, some agreeing with the analogy that Miss Taryn had stated. The noise level rose once again to just shy of a deafening roar.

Finally Miss Pritchett restored order, and all was relatively quiet. Though her eyes were definitely twinkling, Miss Pritchett successfully suppressed her own urge to laugh. "Actually, children, Miss Taryn is correct. March twentieth is the Spring Equinox, which is the mid-point of the spring season. The season begins February second and ends April thirtieth. I also agree with Miss Taryn that to have a wedding on the first day of the spring season is a lovely sentiment."

Again, most of the children wrinkled their noses at such a thought and loudly proclaimed their disgust for what, in their minds, was a thorough trashing of a great time of year whether it was the warm spring days, or baseball, basketball or Easter time and the Easter Bunny.

Miss Pritchett raised her right hand and quickly snapped her fingers three times. The children fell silent. "It would be in your best interest to mind your manners," she reminded them. Looking affectionately at Taryn, she smiled warmly and said, "Taryn, if you please, give your introduction."

Scowling first at Simon, then at Timothy and finally at Megan, Miss Taryn launched into her story. "I am Taryn McKay, and I'm engaged to Joe." She turned to him as she spoke, placing her right hand gently on top of his left hand. "I am Mrs. Coppersmith's assistant and have been since June, although I grew up here. My mother worked here until she left in March to help take care of my great-great grandmother."

Again Miss Taryn was interrupted, only this time it was Aaron. "You worked here?" he asked Miss Claire.

"Oui, I did; however, chèr, it isn't polite to interrupt. Taryn…" she began, but now she was also interrupted.

Simultaneously the questions were asked, popping like a pack of firecrackers. "Where's your Dad?" Timmy asked Miss Taryn; "When did you come here?" Megan asked of Miss Claire; Simon asked Miss Claire, "What did you do here?", and Jose asked of Miss Taryn, "What did your Dad do here?"

"Please," Miss Claire intervened for a flustered Miss Taryn. "Please, ma petit chèrs; these are all questions best left to another time." She smiled slightly, patted her daughter lightly on her shoulder and then softly said, "Ma chère, please continue."

Miss Taryn shrugged and, in a somewhat pouty tone, said, "I'm finished."

Joe reached his long arm around her, giving her a conciliatory hug and grinned. He was amused. "I guess I'm next," he quickly stated, giving a brief glance and nod to Miss Pritchett. "I'm Joe Johnson. Well, actually my name is Gordon Joseph, but everyone calls me Joe."

His smile was warm and friendly, and so was his deep, baritone voice. His chestnut brown hair was cut short, almost a crew cut. He glanced up and down the table, giving each person a look and a nod. When it was Susie's turn to receive his glance, she marveled at his eyes. They were the darkest, deepest green she'd ever seen, with a hint of a smoldering, smoky cast around the edge.

Suddenly she realized that she was staring at him and, worse yet, with a goofy grin on her face. Unfortunately, by the angry glare Miss Taryn was giving her, she had noticed Susie staring at Joe. More unfortunate was the fact that Joe had noticed both her stare and her grin; he winked at Susie. Susie quickly averted her eyes; she could feel her face flushing, all the while praying the ground would open up and swallow her.

Joe chuckled good-naturedly at her reaction and continued his intro-duction. "I'm one of the farm hands, and I also grew up here. I was abandoned when I was two years old. I was left at the Riverside Park in Micah's Landing with a note pinned to my shirt pocket."

Smiling fondly, he nodded at Miss Pritchett and added, "I wish I could thank my birth mother. What she did was wrong; but having done so, it actually turned out to be the best thing for me. The police called Reverend Tillman, who called Miss Pritchett, and I've been here ever since. Miss Pritchett was granted custody, and I couldn't have been placed in a better home. I graduated from Willington University with a degree in Agriculture, and then got my master's degree in farm management this past May. But the best education I ever received was from Miss Hilda's Dad and from Mr. Sean." He nodded to Miss Hilda, and then to Mr. Sean.

He grinned and tightened his grip around Miss Taryn, pulling her toward him. "Oh, and I plan to marry this little filly in February."

He turned to the young girl next to him and smiled. Leaning toward her, he said teasingly, "You're next, sweet pea."

The young girl in question gave him a sideways glance and rolled her eyes, pretending to be annoyed by his attention. She had raven black, chin-length hair. It was thick and straight, and blunt-cut just like her bangs. Her eyes were nearly as black as her hair and were quite large, making them appear like they belonged to a cartoon character. She was small boned and short for her age, and could have benefited from a booster seat. Although she had delicate features, her voice was anything but delicate. It was forceful enough to be heard over just about anything.

She had an air of haughtiness when she spoke. "My name is Danielle Hobson. I prefer my nickname, which is Dani. I'm eight and a half years old. I came here in July. I like music, and I like to read." She shrugged her shoulders with a dismissive quality and flippantly stated, "I'm done."

"Thank you, Dani," Miss Pritchett responded.

"Actually, your first name is Sakura," Kat interjected with a smirking chuckle.

"Shut up!" Dani yelled at her.

"Dani," Miss Pritchett quickly admonished. "We do not use that phrase, nor do we use our outside voice when we are indoors."

Miss Pritchett turned to Kat, her expression one of austerity. With a firm tone, she stated, "Kat, please mind your manners."

Kat shrugged, feigning innocence. "What did I do wrong? Isn't her first name Sakura?"

Miss Pritchett, obviously annoyed, answered, "Yes, it is; however, she prefers to be called Dani just as you prefer to be called Kat. I suppose we could start calling you by your given name, Katherine, or perhaps by your middle name of Annette. What do you think?"

With eyes blazing hostility at Miss Pritchett, Kat snarled her response. "If you did, I wouldn't answer."

"Precisely," Miss Pritchett replied, just a hint of a smile gracing her lips.

Susie smiled at Dani and told her, "I think Sakura sounds pretty. What language is it?"

Dani smiled feebly at Susie and then looked down at her plate. "It's Japanese. It means cherry blossom. It's supposed to be a symbol of love, of good fortune and of spring."

"That sounds really nice," Susie commented. Dani looked up at her; when she realized Susie meant what she said, Dani beamed.

The lady sitting to Dani's right smiled at her affectionately and asked, "Do you want to share how you came to live here?"

Dani's eyebrows furled, forming a deep crease in the center of her forehead. She scowled at the lady, crossed her arms over her chest and emphatically said, "No!"

"I know why she's here," Kat wickedly intoned. She grinned mischievously at Dani.

"That will be enough, Kat," Miss Pritchett cautioned her, then smiled at Dani. "That's quite all right, Dani. Perhaps you will choose to share at another time," Miss Pritchett said encouragingly, then spoke to the woman sitting to the right of Dani. "Elsa, if you please."

"Certainly; I am Elsa Jean Burgess. I am married to Samuel," she said grinning as she looked at the man seated to her right. "We were married here in the Chapel three years ago. I also grew up here at Glen Hollow."

She paused momentarily, gathering her thoughts. As she did so, her naturally pale complexion paled even further, a condition which Susie wouldn't have thought possible. Her flaxen colored hair had a whitish hue, bordering on the level of the paleness of the midnight sun. Her eyes were an unusual color, ice blue with just a hint of green around the rim of the iris.

"I, too, was abandoned as a child," she began softly, her voice just barely above that of a whisper. "I was nearly three when I was left at the doorstep of a church in Micah's Landing, dehydrated and starving. Reverend Tillman took me to the hospital. After I was released, I was brought here. Miss Pritchett and our wonderful family here at Glen Hollow gave me my life. I love it here," she said smiling, tears glistening in her eyes as she leaned forward to make eye contact with Susie and Simon; "and I know you will also."

She gave them both a brief nod as if to stress that her prophecy would come true. She sat back in her chair and dabbed the tears away with her napkin.

Her husband, Samuel, cleared his throat, graciously shifting the attention away from his wife. He was a big man, well over six feet tall, with broad shoulders and a muscular build. He had short, light brown hair, high cheekbones, a long angular nose and a strong, square chin. His eyes were deep-set and were light brown with green and gold flecks. His voice was a deep, robust bass.

"I'm Samuel Burgess and, as Elsa said, we're married. I started working here during summers when I was fourteen. I enjoyed working with Miss Hilda's Dad, and with Mr. Sean. I decided that I wanted to work here permanently; when Miss Pritchett offered me a full-time position here, I accepted. Besides, I'd already met and fallen in love with Elsa," he nudged his shoulder against hers; "and I knew I'd never get her to leave this place."

He turned to the man seated next to him and said, "You're next." Before the man could begin, Samuel added, "Oh, and this dude is my little cousin."

The man in question chuckled affably, reached over and good-naturedly clapped Samuel on the back several times. "Little?" he retorted in mock disagreement. "You're older by only five weeks."

"Five and half," Samuel jokingly corrected; "which still makes you my *little* cousin."

The man's laugh was hearty, and his voice was a pleasant baritone. His thick, black hair had a glossy sheen and was tied back just below his shirt collar with what appeared to be a shoestring. (Later Susie learned it was a strip of rawhide.) His dark brown eyes were nearly black in color, and his skin held a reddish-bronze tone to it. With his prominent cheekbones and high-bridged nose, he could easily have portrayed a tribal chief in any movie or documentary. He was tall, but not quite as tall as his cousin. He was broad shouldered and had a lean, muscular physique.

"I'm Kevin Yashta. Yashta in the Icori language means wolf in English. As you've already guessed, I'm Icori... well, three quarters, anyway. My father is full Icori. My mother is half Icori and half Irish. My mother and Sam's mother are sisters."

"I grew up in Spirit Canyon. So did Sam until he was thirteen – that's when his Dad bought a coffee house in Micah's Landing, and they moved away. But before they moved away, Sam and I hunted and fished all over Spirit Canyon and the surrounding areas. By the time I was fifteen, I loved tinkering with engines; in high school I took shop classes and earned a scholarship to Huntington Vo-Tech College in Willington. After I graduated, I went to work for a freight company. A few years later, I married the boss's daughter."

His voice was tinged with sadness as he continued. "We visited here often, and I thought she liked it here. When a position opened, I applied and was hired. She wasn't real thrilled about it. She did try living here for a while, but decided she didn't like it. Or to use her phraseology, she didn't like living in the boonies."

He paused for a moment, attempting to stifle the pain the memories still caused. Then he added with a shrug, "I wouldn't quit, so she left last year and filed for divorce…. I can understand it. I was a fish out of water in the big city, and she was one here."

As fast as a rabbit changes direction, Kevin's mood elevated. Grinning at Mr. Henry, he said, "Henry is a cousin of ours. He and our mothers are first cousins."

Mr. Henry smiled and nodded. "That's a fact," he said. "I've known both Kevin and Sam since they were born." A teasing grin spread across his face as he added, "They turned out fine; but, I tell you, there for a while, they had us all worried."

Sam and Kevin laughed, exchanging glances that shouted they held secrets not even Mr. Henry knew.

"No, I'm just teasing. They were both good boys; still are," Mr. Henry added sincerely.

"Dale, if you please," Miss Pritchett instructed. Though amused by the banter between the cousins, she wanted to keep the introductions flowing as it was already seven o'clock.

The young man gave her a nod and turned toward Susie. He smiled, but his smile wasn't genuine; or, at least, that was Susie's intuition. Deep-set and small, his eyes were close together creating a pinched appearance. They had a coldness to them that had nothing to do with their dark brown color. His build was small, and he didn't appear to be but of medium height. He reminded her of a weasel with his pointy nose, beady eyes and thin face. His voice was high pitched for a man, probably an upper range tenor, Susie guessed. When he spoke, the undercurrent in his tone did not do anything to change her first impression of him. She didn't like him.

"I'm Dale Thomas," he stated, staring off into space. "I've been working here for a year and a half. I was born and raised in Willow Creek. It's barely a spot along the road. It has all of forty-two people, and one general store that's also the post office."

He gave a derisive, little snort. "I couldn't wait to leave that place. I went to Oakmont right after high school, and stayed there about a month. I couldn't find any work, so I went back home. Then I heard Glen Hollow needed a groundskeeper, so I applied and was hired."

He fixed his cold stare onto Susie. "I guess this is just as good a place as any to land. You could do worse." He returned his focus to his plate, resuming his meal.

There was an awkward silence, but only for a fleeting moment. The man seated next to him quickly spoke, his rich baritone voice projecting well throughout the Hall.

"I'm Sean Callaway, and I head the farming operations for Glen Hollow. I had worked two years in the Peace Corps after getting my Master's Degree in Ag Science. I began working here in 1978. Miss Hilda's Dad was the head of farming then."

"I met, Bettye, (he grinned as he gently nudged her) when she came to work here in 1980. I knew she was the one, but it took her a little while to figure it out."

His laughter was light-hearted, matching hers. His blue eyes twinkled and danced, and were very much alive with an impish type of joy. Slightly salt and pepper, his black hair was kept cropped much like a military cut. Although he appeared to be short, his frame was sturdy, having broad shoulders and a muscular build. He reminded Susie of the old pictures of Nana's Dad. He had been a boxer in his youth. Mr. Sean had that same type of stance and build. It made her wonder if Mr. Sean had ever been a boxer.

"I think you'll come to love it here as we have," Mr. Sean was saying, breaking Susie's reverie. "Like Miss Pritchett said, whether you're here a

81

day or until you're an adult, you're family; and this is home." He smiled at her and then Simon before surrendering the floor to his wife.

Miss Bettye was taller than her husband by at least five inches, Susie guessed from the difference in their seated heights. Miss Bettye had ash brown hair and wore it cut into a short, layered style that neatly framed her face. Her golden brown eyes flashed and sparkled with a youthful vibrancy. She had an easy-going laugh, and a calming demeanor. But then, Susie reasoned, she's a nurse so it made sense.

Playfully Miss Bettye tweaked her husband's ear. "Well, it's true he did pursue me for nearly four years. I just had to be certain that he would stick around and not decide to move elsewhere."

She laughed affectionately and added, "Seriously, I knew he was the one; I just needed to wait for the right time. We also were married here in the Chapel. That was in 1985. I've been here since September of 1980, which was two years after I graduated as a Nurse Practitioner. We have one child, Erin Elise. She owns The Oasis in Willington. It's a Day Spa. She has several licenses; beautician, cosmetologist and massage therapy, just to name a few. She comes here one weekend a month to visit, but she also provides free haircuts to anyone who is so inclined."

Winking at Susie, she grinned. "And, occasionally, we also get a day of beauty at her salon. It's always nice to have a day that you're pampered, don't you think?"

Miss Bettye, patted Susie's shoulder lightly, her voice softened to nearly a whisper when she continued. "Erin really loved growing up here. Sure, the buildings are old and sometimes spooky with their creaking noises and drafts, but that's just part of any old building. The real beauty of Glen Hollow is the people; and if you choose to, I think you'll see that that is true." Her smile was as warm and as kind as the expression in her eyes. She gave Susie an encouraging nod to start her own introduction. Susie decided she liked Miss Bettye.

Heavily fringed with thick, black lashes, Susie's cornflower blue eyes had a quality so translucent it seemed as if they could pierce through the hardest of souls, capturing and captivating at will. Adding to that effect were the intermittent streaks of cobalt blue, creating the look of a cats-eye marble. Her dark brown hair shimmered in the light emanating from the fireplace behind her. The soft light of its flames illuminated the auburn and gold highlights in her hair, creating the illusion of a golden, fiery aura around her.

"My name is Susie Howard. I'm eleven; I'll be twelve in about three weeks. Our parents died in a car wreck when Simon was just a baby. Our great grand-mother, Nana, was our only living relative, so we lived with her. She passed away in August, and we went to live with Mrs. Crenshaw. She's the Director of Child Services in Willington. I love to draw, and I love music. I play the flute and the piano. I love science, math and history. I love to read all types of books. Simon and I read together every day, and have since he was a baby."

She smiled encouragingly at Simon; he grinned at her. Susie was sur-prised at how calm her voice had sounded. She was glad because Simon seemed less nervous now than what he had been.

"Thank you, Susie." Miss Pritchett kindly said. "Simon, would you like to share anything about yourself?"

Susie chuckled. That was like asking the fox if he'd like to babysit the chickens.

Simon perked up, knowing that it was now his turn to be in the spot-light. His baby blue eyes sparkled and danced, so much so that they seemed to glow.

"I'm Simon," he announced; "I'm four, but I'm almost five."

Pausing, he rolled his eyes as he tried to think of what next to say. He began to giggle. "I guess I love climbing trees the most. It's more fun than anything. The next best thing is reading with Susie because she does all the neat voices like Nana did. And I love coloring, and playing with trucks and all kinds of toys."

He looked at Susie with a quizzical look. He shrugged and said, "I guess that's all." Then he asked her, "Did I do good?"

She gave him a quick hug and whispered "yes" in his ear.

Laughing, Miss Hilda responded, "You did well, Simon."

"Absolutely," a grinning Miss Pritchett agreed.

———

Dinner ended late, which was apparently unheard of at Glen Hollow. Miss Pritchett rose from her chair, and everyone else followed suit. Susie was quick to assess what was happening; and she, too, rose from her seat, pulling Simon up as she stood. Everyone engaged in small talk with those around them while waiting to clear the dishes.

Miss Taryn and Miss Fiona quickly retrieved the tri-bin dish carts. Miss Taryn chose the side opposite of Susie and Simon while Miss Fiona proceeded along their side of the table. Miss Elsa followed behind Miss Taryn, collecting the pitchers, serving platters and bowls. As they passed, each person would carefully place into the bins their place settings; one for dishes, one for flatware and another for glassware. The serving pieces were handed to Miss Elsa by whichever adult was nearest to the serving piece.

After all items were cleared from the table, Miss Elsa, Miss Taryn and Miss Fiona headed toward the kitchen, rolling the carts as quickly as they could. Mrs. Coppersmith had already left several minutes earlier.

Miss Pritchett picked up the silver hand bell, ringing it three times. Soon the room was hushed; all eyes were on Miss Pritchett. Thanking everyone for making the evening meal so pleasant, she officially ended the meal. Noting that due to the lateness of the hour (it was seven forty-five), she excused the children immediately. All, that is, except for Susie and Simon. Miss Pritchett flatly stated that they were to remain in the Dining Hall.

As they all began to depart, a few of the children glanced covertly at the newcomers but most just simply ignored them. Within a couple of minutes, the only ones that remained in the room (besides Susie and Simon) were Miss Hilda, Miss Pritchett, Miss Thelma and Mr. Warbly.

Susie didn't think the other children could have moved any faster even if there had been a fire. She was very disappointed that none of the other children had been friendly; not so much for her sake, she reasoned, but for Simon's. She thought Timmy would have approached Simon after dinner, but Aaron whisked him away. It didn't appear to Susie that Timmy was interested in befriending Simon - he made no objection when Aaron ushered him out the door.

Before she and Simon had a chance to ask what they were to do, Miss Hilda enlisted them to assist her in the removal of the table linens. Simon's job was to make certain that all of the napkins were on the tablecloth. With great fervor and quite energetically, he began to race-walk ('no running allowed' as Miss Hilda had so kindly reminded him) around the table, verifying that all of the napkins were present. A few had fallen onto the chairs, or the floor, so he had to stop, pick them up and place them on the tablecloth. It took all of nearly five minutes for him to complete his task.

Next he began enthusiastically helping Miss Hilda and Susie with the task of folding the tablecloth over onto itself until it was small enough to be easily carried to the laundry room. She praised and lauded both of them for their excellent assistance. Simon beamed with pride and joy; Susie chuckled knowing full well that Simon's "helping" was more of a hindrance. She was appreciative that Miss Hilda didn't seem to mind that fact.

While the new arrivals and Miss Hilda were otherwise engaged, Miss Pritchett motioned to Miss Thelma to join her. They both walked over to Mr. Warbly who was looking, at this point, a little lost.

"Mr. Warbly," Miss Pritchett spoke as they approached, smiling graciously at him. "Mrs. Canton will show you to your room. There is a small parlor near your room that has a television as well as various reading materials. Please feel free to use it if you wish. We also have a Library that you're welcome to use. It's just down the corridor from here; Mrs. Canton will also show you its location. Breakfast is at six in the morning. Will you be staying for Chapel at nine?"

"No, Ma'am. I have t' get back. It'll take the better part of nine hours t' get home, so I'll need an early start. I thank you for askin'," he said with a smile and a respectful nod.

"You are most welcome," she replied cordially.

"If it's all the same t' you, I'd just as soon turn in. It's been a long day, 'n I'm real tired so there isn't anything I care t' read or watch."

"It's quite all right, Mr. Warbly," Miss Pritchett assured him.

Turning to Miss Thelma, she instructed, "Please show Mr. Warbly to his room."

She turned once again to her guest. "Good Night, Mr. Warbly."

He gave her a respectful nod and replied, "G'night, Miss Pritchett." He turned and escorted Miss Thelma out of the Dining Hall.

Miss Pritchett's attention was now focused on the trio at the dinner table, watching the theatrics playing out in the removal of the table linens.

Softly, she chuckled to herself as she observed Simon in particular and began walking toward them.

"Hilda," she spoke congenially; "when you're finished with your task, I would like to speak with Susie and Simon in my office in about fifteen minutes."

"We'll be done well before then," she assured Miss Pritchett.

"Won't we?" she asked Susie and Simon, seeking their concurrence. And she got it.

They both nodded and gave wholehearted replies of "Absolutely," from Susie and "Uh-huh," from Simon.

"Good; I'll see you in fifteen minutes," Miss Pritchett responded before exiting the Dining Hall.

It wasn't but a few minutes later when Simon announced he had to use the restroom (real bad, as he put it). Miss Hilda had just finished the last fold over, and she snatched up the tablecloth.

"Then let's go," she told him with a wink and a smile.

They headed at great speed out the door, into the southwest corridor, with Simon advising her "to hurry" every couple of steps.

Chapter 4

RULES, RULES; ALWAYS RULES

After Simon's emergency had been dealt with, Susie and Simon accompanied Miss Hilda to the Laundry Room in the Southwest wing. Miss Hilda had explained that there were several laundry rooms in the manor. The one they were going to, she had said, is used for table linens and kitchen aprons and cloths. The one in the South wing second floor is where all of the children's clothes, bedding and towels are laundered.

Simon slipped his hand out of Miss Hilda's, and he stopped walking. Miss Hilda and Susie turned to see why he had stopped and saw him staring dumbfounded at Miss Hilda. "*I* have to wash my clothes?" Simon asked incredulously, his voice squeaking an octave higher than normal.

"No dear," Miss Hilda laughed. "Miss Ginger and Miss Cora do your laundry. You are, however, required to put away your own clothes. They leave them neatly folded on your bed." She tousled his hair and added, "If you don't put them away properly, you will then be required to assist in the folding of towels until such time they think you will store your clothes properly."

Simon grinned. "No problem," he assured her, grasping her hand and, once again, renewing their trek to this wing's laundry room. Susie had her doubts, and with good reason. Simon *never* put away his clothes; if she didn't do it for him, Nana did.

When they arrived at the laundry room, Simon pleaded with Miss Hilda to allow him to place the linens in the hamper. He was most insistent, and she finally agreed that he could probably handle it on his own. He ran to the large hamper (more like a bin) and, with a great deal of struggling and a little help from Susie, lifted the lid.

He turned, did his little bouncy dance, and then held out his arms. Miss Hilda placed the large pile of linens onto his outstretched arms. It was hilarious; they couldn't even see Simon for the huge mound of linens. Like a little robot, he slowly turned to face the hamper and positioned his arms directly above it. He opened wide his arms, allowing the linens to tumble down into the hamper.

He turned and grinned. "All done," he proudly announced.

"Very good," Miss Hilda replied, smiling at him. "Now, we need to scurry on to Miss Pritchett's office. We don't want to be late."

Simon was a chatterbox all the way back down the southwest wing and on into the west wing corridor. Part of Susie wished there was an 'off' button on him; however, Miss Hilda is a new audience for him, and Simon *loves* an audience. Susie smiled watching the two of them. Miss Hilda didn't seem to mind his chattering; in fact, Susie was beginning to think Miss Hilda was actually enjoying it.

Again, Susie stole quick glances at the portraits they passed as they hurried along the west wing corridor. Miss Hilda had already informed her that there was no time to dawdle. They'd have the grand tour tomorrow. Afterwards, Susie could look to her hearts' content, but not now.

Halfway down the long corridor, they turned left into a narrow hallway and immediately saw a spiral stairway near its end.

"Where does that go?" Simon asked Miss Hilda as he tugged her toward it, trying to get a better view.

She smiled at him and responded, "It goes to the second floor living quarters and guest rooms."

"Can I see?" he queried.

"Not at the moment," she answered.

"Why do you have one there?" he pressed.

"Because the house is so large," she explained, her eyes twinkling at his insatiable curiosity. "If it wasn't there, we'd have to go to the foyer, or all the way back to the kitchen in order to get to the second floor. That's quite a lot of extra steps."

Simon nodded. "Okay," he replied, mulling over the logic of her answer.

They quickly resumed their pace until they came to another intersecting corridor and turned right. A short distance more and Miss Hilda guided them to the second door on their left. She smiled as she held the door open for them.

They entered a rather large sitting room, and did so a few minutes ahead of schedule. Miss Hilda, before leaving the room, told them she'd be back in a jiffy, telling them to have a look around. They proceeded to do just that…. and would have done so regardless. Susie surveyed the room from where she stood just inside the door. Simon plopped himself down in one of the chairs near the fireplace.

A nice fire was brightly burning, keeping the room comfortably warm. The fireplace was of average size; its surround and mantle were made from red oak. Carved into the round end columns were entwining vines bearing clusters of grapes, spiraling their way up to the mantelpiece. Upon reaching the mantelpiece, the vines wove their way along it, forming three long swags across the mantelpiece. Initially Susie thought carved bows were at the top of the vines and at the joining of each one of the swag uplifts. She moved closer and discovered that it wasn't bows at all. It was fairies.

"That's different," Susie softly commented aloud.

"What is?" Simon asked. He had left his chair and crept up behind her.

She smiled at him and pointed to the fairies. "They're fairies," she answered. "I don't think I've ever seen a fireplace that had fairies carved in it."

"Wow," Simon said as he leaned in for a better look, standing on tiptoe. He dropped back down flat and, due to his closer proximity, saw the vines more closely. "Look, Susie there's more! See…. here in the vines, and some are peeking out from behind the grapes."

Susie looked; he was right.

Simon reached out and touched one. "They look real, don't they?"

She had to admit; whoever carved it was really, really good. "Yes, they do." She turned away from the fireplace with its lovely fairies, continuing her survey of the room.

There were four wing chairs by the fireplace, each upholstered in dark, burgundy leather. Two chairs were placed on each side of the fireplace, facing each other and slightly turned toward the fireplace. Between the chairs were small cherry wood tables with dark gray marble tops. According to Simon, the chairs were "snugy-comfy", which was the highest form of praise that Simon could bestow.

To her left was a conversation area that boasted two long couches upholstered in an ice-blue velvet fabric. As she walked by, Susie ran her hand along
the top of the couch. It was so soft, just like a tiny kitten. She walked around
to the front and sat down, sinking into its soft, plush cushion. She leaned her
head back, closed her eyes and decided that she could just sleep right here.

"Susie, come look," Simon called to her.

With a sigh, Susie opened her eyes. Simon was on the floor, pulling at
the coffee table in front of her.

"What, Simon?" she asked.

"I think this is a drawer, but I can't figure out how to open it." His
face was contorted into his usual expression of frustration. "Help me!"
he demanded.

"It could be just a false front made to look like a drawer," she explained.
Susie walked around the table and sat down next to him on the floor.

"No," he said. "Look. See it's different here and here," he told her as
he pointed to four places where the carved ruts were deeper.

She felt along its edges and then underneath the table. There was no
apparent door or drawer; the table appeared solid.

"Maybe it is," she told him, "but we don't have time for this right now.
Why don't you see if there's a book you might want to read in one of those
bookcases?" She pointed to the cherry bookcase with the glass doors. It
was next to the overstuffed chairs, near the door to Miss Pritchett's office.

"Okay," he agreed cheerfully, jumping up and running over to the
bookcases.

With Simon now safely occupied, Susie turned her attention to the
south wall. There had to be at least a hundred photographs pinned to a
gigantic corkboard. She walked closer to examine the exhibit and was surprised to discover that they were pictures, past and present, of the children
since the start of Glen Hollow Orphanage in 1974. Under each photo was
a label, giving the person's name and their arrival date. The photos were
organized into sections by decades. Each decade column held a row of
photos, one for each year of that decade.

Susie looked closely at the photos as she scanned the first three rows,
wondering what had become of all these people. She stopped dead in her
tracks. "It's him!" she uttered, astonished.

"Who?" Simon had quietly walked up behind her, startling her when he spoke.

"Ed," she answered, pointing to a picture of a young boy in 1975. "That's Ed from the Diner."

"Whoa-a-a; that little guy is Big Ed?" Simon commented in disbelief.

Susie nodded. "Yes, it is." She removed the business card he had given her from her pocket. "See; his name on the card is Ed R. Jenkins, and the name plate shows the boy's name is Edward Randall Jenkins."

"Are you sure?" Simon challenged.

"I think so," Susie replied.

"It's a lot of faces, isn't it?" Miss Hilda's voice rang out with a chuckle. "We have formal portrait pictures in the Parlor. We take a group photo every Christmas, more often if there's a change in staff or children."

Susie and Simon turned and saw that she had entered the room and was nearly to the couches.

"Is this Big Ed?" Simon asked her, pointing at the picture.

She laughed loud and hearty, thoroughly amused by Simon's description. "I don't know that I've ever heard him called Big Ed. He certainly is big, though. But in answer to your question; yes, that is the Ed who owns the Diner and Service Station in Foxboro Station."

Simon stared at the picture, admiring Ed's transformation. "I hope I get as big as Big Ed when I'm grown."

"You never know," Miss Hilda replied, smiling at him.

"Nana was tall," Susie remarked; "and so were Mommy and Daddy." She turned and looked at Simon, seeing the hope springing forth in his eyes. "Maybe you will be, too." She smiled at him as she ruffled his curls.

With a sunny smile and cheery voice, Miss Hilda announced, "Come, children. It's time for you to meet with Miss Pritchett."

"Why does she want to meet with us?" Susie asked as they began walking toward the office door.

Miss Hilda smiled affectionately at Susie, and her tone conveyed her desire to assure them both that they had nothing to fear. "It's just to go over some general rules, dear; most you probably already know. But even so, it's still a good idea to review them. It'll be a short meeting since it's so late. Tomorrow afternoon, you'll both be given the grand tour of the manor and the farm. Anything not addressed tonight will be discussed then. And you can ask questions about the manor. If I don't know the answer, I'm certain Miss Pritchett does."

"Here we are," she said as they approached the door near the bookcase.

Simon pointed to a door directly opposite of Miss Pritchett's. "Where does that go?" he asked.

"It goes to my office. You'll see it tomorrow," she responded. Opening the heavy oak door, Miss Hilda ushered in Susie and Simon. "We're here," she cheerfully announced.

Miss Pritchett stopped writing, looked up and greeted them with a hearty smile. "Hello children; please come in." Motioning to the sitting area, she said, "Susie, Simon, if you'll please be seated, I'll be with you momentarily." She returned to writing in her ledger.

Miss Hilda deftly guided them to the cozy area next to the fireplace. Faintly glowing embers were all that remained of a fire that had been burning brightly. Though it had been quite some time since a log had been placed on its grate, the room temperature was still comfortable.

The sitting area was well furnished. It had a beautiful tapestry couch and, with its ornately carved mahogany arms and legs, Susie thought it was artwork more so than furniture. Across the back of the couch was an exquisitely woven scene. The detail was incredible. Three animals were prominently displayed across the center: a white tiger, a unicorn and a white wolf. The right side contained a Pegasus and a Dragon, while flying above them were an eagle, a phoenix and a falcon. The upper left side was a mountain valley scene displaying a variety of animals, including birds such as doves, owls and peacocks. The lower left side contained dolphins and mermaids playing in the sea, teeming with a vast array of aquatic life.

Placed opposite of the couch and facing Miss Pritchett's mahogany desk were two chairs upholstered in a dark hunter-green fabric. Placed between the two chairs was a narrow table with a matching coffee table between the couch and the chairs. The tables were made of mahogany and had the same detailed carvings as did the couch. Both tables were topped with dark green marble. An antique Persian carpet, in vivid colors and hues of purple, gold, green, red and black, covered the hardwood floor in the sitting area.

Susie would have preferred the couch because she was also intrigued by its front design. It appeared to be a forest scene with a myriad of plants and creatures. She wanted a closer look, but Simon had already jumped into the first of the chairs. He sank into its soft, deep padded upholstery and the sight was comical; he being so small versus the giant-size chair (giant-size in comparison to Simon).

Smiling at him as she walked past, Susie glided into the other chair, nearest the fireplace. She glanced at the fireplace casings and mantle; this one she really liked. Its design was simplistic; flat slabs of dark green marble with veins of muted white swirling through it.

Simon began bouncing in his chair almost immediately, eliciting from Miss Hilda the rapid shaking of her head. He stopped. She gave them both a big smile, turned and headed for the door. As Miss Hilda opened the door, Miss Pritchett looked up, smiled and softly said, "Thank you, Hilda."

Miss Hilda smiled, nodded and quietly left the room, closing the door behind her.

Miss Pritchett finished her task, put down her pen, closed the ledger book and rose from her chair. "Are you warm enough," she asked amicably as she walked toward them; "or should I place another log on the fire?"

Susie shrugged her left shoulder. "I'm fine," she said.

"And you, Simon; are you warm enough?"

He smiled shyly and his voice was bashful. "No," he spoke softly; "another log, please."

"Very well then," she smiled; "we'll make it a small one so everyone will be comfortable."

From the wood bin she selected a short, fat log and effortlessly placed it on the embers. She stoked the fire with the poker and, once the flames began darting up the sides of the log, she returned the poker to its stand.

Moving quickly to the couch, she seated herself and glanced at her watch. "It's eight o'clock," she said; "and is Simon's bedtime. For the older children, such as you, Susie, the rule is lights out at nine; therefore, we'll make this meeting as short as possible."

"Nine?" Susie asked surprised. "Nana always let us stay up until ten."

"I understand, Susie; however, we can't have separate bedtimes for each individual. Therefore, the younger children's time is set at eight, and the older children's time is set at nine," she answered courteously. "Wake up time for everyone is six a.m. Breakfast is served at seven, lunch is served at noon and dinner is served at six. All meals are served in the Dining Hall except for the lunch meal on school days. School lunch time is only thirty minutes; therefore, it is served in the classroom."

Simon tilted his head and looked up at her, his eyes twinkling mischievously. "What if I get sleepy before eight?" he asked.

Miss Pritchett smiled at him, thinking to herself he is definitely a live wire and would obviously make life interesting. "Then you may certainly go to bed before eight," she responded cheerfully.

"To continue," she said; "we have a simple rule regarding meals; if you are late, you don't eat. We have found that without this rule, everyone tends to wander in at various times. In addition to being rude to those persons already seated, it is an undue burden on Mrs. Coppersmith. She can't possibly serve a proper meal if we are not punctual."

Susie and Simon exchanged looks of surprise and apprehension at this revelation. Miss Pritchett smiled reassuringly at them and added, "There isn't any need to worry. Until you both are acclimated to your new surroundings, one of the adults will always see to it that you are punctual."

Susie raised her eyebrows at Simon, locking her gaze with his. He grinned back at her, signaling that he understood. (She would see to it that he didn't miss any meals.)

After a slight pause, Miss Pritchett began her welcoming speech. "Susie, Simon, this is your home, and I encourage you to think of it as your home." She smiled affectionately and continued. "Perhaps a family will adopt you soon, and that would be most wonderful for you. In the interim, we are your family; maybe a little different than most, but still a family."

Simon, clearly puzzled, interrupted. "But there's no Mommy and Daddy."

She laughed lightly, and her eyes twinkled. "Not in the traditional sense, Simon. You know there are some families that have stepmoms and stepdads, stepsisters and stepbrothers, and they are a family. We are similar. We are not related by blood, but we are still a family. As with other families, we live together, work together, share what we have and look after each other. As the head of the home, I function as the parent; Miss Hilda and the staff you can compare as to having aunts and uncles. The other children would be like having brothers and sisters or cousins."

Simon mulled this over, nodding his head and swinging his feet as his thought process whirled.

"How can '*we*' be a family; once we leave, we'll never see anyone again," Susie commented skeptically, a hint of disillusionment in her tone.

Her mind was in a whirlwind, wondering how long it would be before a foster home was found that would take them both. And what if they changed their mind; would she and Simon be returned here, or separated and sent to the State Homes; or would they be sent to another foster home, or even sent to separate foster homes? What if the cycle kept repeating, and they never found a permanent home or family? What if they had to grow up without each other, separated permanently because no one would take both of them?

Susie's head began to ache, and her stomach began to knot as variation upon variation began swirling, demanding to be heard. To break the seemingly endless rounds of possible scenarios, Susie forced herself to focus on a delicate porcelain box on the table in front of her. Her mind began to quiet, but the nausea remained.

Miss Pritchett's countenance looked a little sad, and she spoke in a very gentle voice. "While many families have members that part and never see each other, we also have had a few that followed that path. However, Susie, the majority of our children that have lived here, whether it was for one day or until they reached adulthood, always return for our annual reunion each June. And there are some who live nearby that we see even more frequently. Many that have gone away to college, or are in college now, return during schools breaks. This is their home."

Susie continued to stare at the trinket box on the table as if to shut out her words. Miss Pritchett's compassion for Susie's inner turmoil tugged at her heart. She understood well the grief and sense of loss that Susie felt.

Softly clearing her throat, Miss Pritchett continued. "As with all families, there are rules of conduct; and the same rules apply here."

She chuckled, looked at Simon, and said, "There'll be no sliding down the banisters, Simon." (Simon, his blue eyes mischievously dancing, flashed her one of his Cheshire cat grins.)

"Additionally, the third floor is strictly off-limits. That floor is the staff residences. The east wings are unused; therefore, the doors remain locked. You are welcome to use any of the other rooms once your schoolwork and chores are done."

"Chores?" both children echoed.

"Yes, you will have at least one assigned chore just as I'm certain you did with Mrs. Crenshaw and with your Nana."

"No-o-o, we didn't," Simon drawled while slowly shaking his head back and forth.

"Yes, we did, Simon," Susie corrected him. "Making our beds, putting away our clothes, cleaning our rooms and setting the table were our chores."

"Oh," he responded with his brow knitted and lips pursed. "I thought that was helping."

Susie sighed.

Miss Pritchett smiled at Simon and continued. "Actually, Simon, you are correct; it is helping, and you will have similar chores here. You will make your beds, keep your room tidy and put away your laundry. Additionally, you will be assigned one, age–appropriate chore. Also, please remember that if you use something, return it to where you found it when you're finished. Everyone assists in the clearing of the table as you did tonight."

"Who feeds the animals?" Simon asked as the thought popped into his mind.

"Staff members," she responded tentatively, uncertain as to why he was asking.

"Can I help?" he asked.

"It's 'may I'," Miss Pritchett corrected.

"May I help?" he repeated with hopeful anticipation.

His eagerness made her grin. "You may help on Saturdays, but first I'll need to clear it with Mr. Sean. If he agrees, you will need to let him know every Friday morning whether or not you'll be assisting him the following day. It's very important, Simon, that you remember to tell him every Friday morning."

Simon's face brightened. Vigorously nodding his head, he exclaimed, "I will; I promise."

"Good. Now the rules concerning chores are simple; there are only two. First, any chore worth doing is worth doing well; and second, slackers don't eat."

Susie eyes widened in surprise, then narrowed as she glared at Miss Pritchett.

Simon inquisitively asked, "What's a slacker?"

Her tone was casual as she explained. "A slacker, Simon, is someone who doesn't do their chore, doesn't finish their chore or does it in a sloppy manner. The word 'chore' is simply another word for work. At this stage in life, your work is your assigned task and school work. We must always do our best, whatever our best may be. If we fail to do our work, or not do it properly, then that places a burden on others. Understand?"

"Uh–huh,' Simon nodded; "that's what Nana called 'lazy bums'." Dramatically, he began slowly shaking his head. "Nana said lazy bums don't go to Heaven."

Slightly irritated with Simon, Susie interjected, "Actually, Nana said what we do is a reflection of who we are; people who are lazy tend not to do what's right because of who they are. .... She never said anything about them not going to Heaven. Nana would *never* judge anyone like that, and you know it, Simon." Her tone clearly revealed her anger toward Simon's misquoting of Nana. Susie gave Simon a stern look. He shrugged.

Smiling conciliatorily in an attempt to mediate between Simon and Susie, Miss Pritchett spoke calmly. "Your Nana was right in that how we comport ourselves is a reflection of who we are. However, I believe that even lazy bums, as your Nana called them, can change. It's a matter of finding the right incentive."

"Like not eating," Susie retorted.

"Yes, it generally is an effective incentive," Miss Pritchett said gently; "one that has been used for millennia, including by Captain John Smith of Jamestown. Perhaps you remember him from your history lessons?"

Susie gave her a hard glare before turning her focus onto the crackling fire dancing in the fireplace.

"What if I'm sick and can't do my chores?" Simon asked, his voice trembling and his eyes fearful.

97

"Then you are excused from chores until you are well," Miss Pritchett responded with a smile, leaning forward and lightly tousling his hair. "No one is ever assigned a chore that they aren't able to perform, so you needn't worry."

She straightened, sat back, and said, "Moving on. I'll take you on a tour of the manor tomorrow afternoon. Though it's large, the floor plan is quite simple. Just so you know, every floor has a lavatory in addition to the private bathrooms that are in both Dorms, the staff residences and in the guest suites. We are in my office on the first floor in the west wing. As you are already aware, the Dining Hall is also in this wing, at the very end. When you enter from the foyer, this floor has a parlor, a music hall, a media room, the operations office, Miss Bettye's clinic, this suite's sitting room, Miss Hilda's office, my office, a lavatory, a library and a dining hall."

"The southwest wing is just past the Dining Hall, and its first floor contains the butler's pantry, the kitchen, the food storage pantry, the staff lounge, a lavatory and a laundry room."

"We helped Miss Hilda take the linens to the laundry room, and I put them in the hamper," Simon told her, his face expressing his pride in his accomplishment.

"That's wonderful, Simon. I'm so glad you're such a good helper," she responded appreciatively.

"And I know where the bathroom is, because I had to use the bathroom *before* we went to the laundry room," he confided. "I almost had an accident," he said in a hushed tone as if including her in on a secret.

He shook his head vigorously a couple of times as he added gleefully, "But I didn't."

Miss Pritchett had to bite her tongue to keep from laughing. She grinned. "I'm glad for you, Simon. No one likes having an accident."

"To help you with your bearings," she continued; "the front door, where you entered when you arrived, is the north side of the manor. The south wing is through the doors that are directly across from the front door. The south wing's first floor contains a lavatory, the Cloak Room…."

"We went there before we had dinner," Simon informed her. "Miss Hilda helped me wash my hands."

"That's good, Simon; you should always wash your hands before eating. As I was saying, the first floor of the south wing also has the classroom, an arts and craft room and a garden conservatory."

"What's a con… conservatory?" Simons asked, wrinkling his nose as he endeavored to pronounce it correctly.

She smiled at him; he was so inquisitive and that delighted her. "That, Simon, is a large glass room with many types of plants. You could call it an indoor garden. It has areas that resemble a botanical garden with walking paths and has other areas that are open and spacious. There are different types of seating arrangements throughout the conservatory. We also have a really nice waterfall that's connected to a goldfish pond."

"Really?" Simon asked as he leaned forward, his eyes opened wide in awe. Susie was equally impressed, but she endeavored to hide it.

"Yes, we do," Miss Pritchett affirmed, nodding her head. "The conservatory doesn't have a ceiling; it has a glass roof that's higher than the roof of the second floor. From the conservatory, you may exit outdoors into the pergola. From the pergola, you may enter either the east or west gardens, or go straight to the Chapel."

"Whoa-o-o-o," Simon blurted, his face scrunched into a confused look. "What's a pergola?"

Miss Pritchett chuckled at his expressions. She glanced at Susie who was striving to ignore them. "Susie," she asked in an attempt to draw her into the conversation; "do you know what a pergola is?"

Susie shook her head. "Not really," she answered, striving to appear indifferent.

"A pergola is a covered walkway," Miss Pritchett cheerfully explained. "Ours has twenty-four columns on each side. Each column is carved into a lady representing a month of the seasons. The roof of the pergola is actually a lattice and is covered in ivy and flowering vines. Right now, the flowering vines are brown and don't have any flowers; but come spring, they will. And it will be bursting with color. So for now, we have the green of the ivy to give it color and make it pretty."

Leaning toward Simon, she smiled at his perplexed look and said, "You'll see it tomorrow, Simon, and then you'll understand."

Simon shrugged and said, "Okay."

"We have the most amazing statues and fountains in the outside gardens," she continued. "The west garden has two fountains; one is mermaids and the other is dolphins. They're not as large as the one in the east garden, but they're still pretty. (She now had their interest.) The fountain in the east garden has seven, life-sized dolphins sculpted out of marble. The artist was truly gifted. When you see it, you'll know why I say he was truly gifted."

"Can't you just tell me?" Simon whined.

She laughed. "Very well, Simon; the dolphins appear to be actually swimming in the ocean. You have to see it to believe it. We also have some very realistic looking statues," she said.

"Like what?" Simon asked.

Her eyes lit up, sparkling with a mischievous gleam as she answered. "Let see," she began playfully. "I think there are several types of woodland creatures, a fairy or two, some gnomes, a dragon and even a tiger."

"Wo-o-o-ow," Simon responded in awe. He looked at Susie. His eyes were flashing with excitement and wonder. "Isn't that neat? Susie," he asked. "Just like in Nana's stories," he uttered elatedly.

Susie gave him a demonstrative shrug of her shoulder as if to say she wasn't interested; but she was. Simon inquisitively looked at her, and then he smiled. He knew; he could see it in her eyes – she was very much interested.

"Oh, I almost forgot," Miss Pritchett said teasingly. "There is a statue of a unicorn, and it's as big as a very, tall horse."

Without question, that captured Susie's attention. Her mind flashed to the memory of the satin pillow with its embroidered white unicorn that Nana had presented to her on her tenth birthday.

"A unicorn?" The question had popped out of her mouth without time for her to filter it. As soon as the thought had entered her mind, it was already spoken.

Miss Pritchett smiled and chuckled. "Yes, a unicorn. The same artist that created the large dolphin fountain also created the unicorn statue. It truly is amazing."

Susie could feel her heart racing, her pulse quicken as a surge of energy sparked through her. She'd always had an affinity for unicorns, and so did

Nana. Obviously (she reasoned) the mention of the statue caused her to feel a connection to Nana and nothing more.

"I guess we'll have to go see them," Susie responded, trying her best to sound calm and casual. Simon parroted his agreement, nodding his head rapidly.

Grinning, Miss Pritchett sat back against the couch and continued describing the floor plan. "The second floor of the south wing has the Dorm Rooms, a recreation room that we call the Rec Room, and a laundry room. The two front suites are for Miss Cora and Miss Ginger and their families. Should you need anything during the night, you may go to them. You may also come to me, or to Miss Hilda, or even to Miss Thelma and Mr. Henry. Our suites are also on the second floor, but are here in the west wing. The second floor of the southwest wing has a large parlor, a laundry room and the guest suites. There are a few guest rooms here in the west wing on the second floor, above where we are now. That is where you will stay tonight. Tomorrow afternoon you will move into the Dorm rooms."

"What?" Susie looked up at her in surprise. Simon's hands tightly gripped the arms of his chair as he pushed hard against the back of his chair. He gave Susie a look of utter panic.

"Mrs. Crenshaw said that we'd stay together in the same room," Susie protested.

Miss Pritchett held up her hand, signaling them to be quiet. "She did request that you remain in the same room. However, that isn't the way things are done here," she explained gently.

Simon's eyes were shut tight as he shook his head repeatedly. "NO!" he exclaimed again and again.

"Mrs. Crenshaw *promised* that we would stay together until Simon was ready," Susie hotly challenged. Her piercing blue eyes flashed with the anger and the frustration that was swelling inside her.

Gently Miss Pritchett responded, "I understand that Susie; but when will Simon be ready? .. Will it be in a week, a month, or perhaps in a year? And what of the other siblings that are here? Is it fair to them for you to share a guest room while they remain in the Dorms?" Her eyes revealed the compassion and understanding with which she felt; but her tone was firm.

Susie fiercely glared at her while Simon's tears silently rolled down his cheeks.

Miss Pritchett spoke, her voice soft and kind. "I'm truly sorry that Mrs. Crenshaw made you a promise that wasn't hers to make. Your suitcases have already been taken to a guest room for tonight. Tomorrow afternoon, during free time, you will assist in moving your things to your Dorm rooms. Afterward, you may play, read or take a nap; whatever you decide to do, the rest of the day is yours. The remainder of your possessions will arrive next Saturday afternoon. We have plenty of storage space here, so there isn't any reason for your things to sit at a warehouse. Should a family adopt you, your things will be sent with you. Until then, they will be here, available to you, and not incur any more storage fees."

She rose, walked to her desk and picked up the phone receiver. Seeing the expressions on their faces, she wished she could relent. She paused before dialing and softly stated, "It is for the best; it may not seem like it now, but it truly is." She pressed a button on her phone and asked Miss Hilda to join them.

With tear stained cheeks and eyes like that of a wounded puppy, Simon looked to Susie, pleading for help. The sadness in her eyes told him that she could not help him, and his tears began flowing anew.

Miss Pritchett returned to the sitting area and knelt in front of Simon. His eyes were shut tight.

"Simon," she said very softly; "please open your eyes and look at me." They remained squeezed shut.

"Simon, open your eyes and look at me," she insisted.

He opened his eyes. His fear, his dread, shone through his tears. Their eyes met.

"You will be just fine. I promise," she assured him. Hugging him, she gently patted his back. "Simon, you will be just fine," she repeated as Miss Hilda entered the room.

Miss Pritchett released him and looked into his eyes. Smiling tenderly, she kissed his forehead. He gave her a half-hearted smile.

Rising to her feet, she instructed Miss Hilda, "Please take Susie and Simon to their room for tonight."

"Certainly," she replied. "Come now, children," she said as she held out her hands to them. Reluctantly they compiled, walking over to her. Reaching down, she clasped their hands in her own.

"Good night, children. I'll see you in the morning," Miss Pritchett said, her tone soft and gentle.

Miss Hilda looked first at Susie and then at Simon. She lightly squeezed their hands and prompted, "How do you respond to Miss Pritchett?"

With white-hot anger flashing in her eyes, Susie responded icily, "Good night, Miss Pritchett."

Choking back his tears, Simon mumbled, "'night, Miss Pritchett."

With that task accomplished, Miss Hilda escorted them out the door and on to their room.

———

During the entire trek to their room, Miss Hilda cheerfully told them about the manor. Some of its history she knew firsthand since she'd been here from the age of three. Simon perked up a little when she reminded them she would be giving them a personal tour of the barns tomorrow afternoon. And he became especially cheerful when she said he would be allowed to pet some of the animals. Soon he was laughing and talking with Miss Hilda as if he'd always known her. Susie was not as easy to cajole.

"This will be your room for tonight," (Miss Hilda smiled as she switched on the light); "and I'm right across the corridor should you need anything." She pointed to a door directly across from their room. "You know where Miss Pritchett's door is, and where Mr. Henry's and Miss Thelma's door is."

They nodded.

As they entered the room, Susie was surprised to see that someone had turned down the bed. The lamp on the nightstand gave off a soft, comforting light. Simon would be pleased since he hated sleeping in the dark. Someone also had unpacked their suitcases and laid out their pj's, robes and slippers. Everything else was either neatly hung in the closet, or properly folded in the dresser drawers.

Opening the bathroom door, Miss Hilda switched on the light for them. "Come brush your teeth and use the facilities, children. It's already after nine, so you need to get a move on." After which she walked over to the fireplace and chose one of comfortable looking chairs in which to wait.

Susie and Simon snatched up their pj's and headed into the bathroom, passing by the fireplace. Its small fire and glowing embers made the room feel a little more like home with Nana. And the thought of Nana rekindled anew their great loss, causing tears to begin forming in her eyes. Susie quickly darted into the bathroom before they could fall, and before Simon or Miss Hilda could see.

Simon made fast work of brushing his teeth in his hit-and-miss style; as usual, it was more miss than hit. He bounded out of the bathroom and jumped onto the bed. It was soft and springy, and he already decided that it could be fun.

Miss Hilda laughed. "That'll be enough, young man. The bed isn't a trampoline."

He stopped bouncing with a final, grand collapse onto the bed. His eyes sparkled, and his smile was impish as he watched her.

Susie exited the bathroom in a rush. "I guess we're ready for bed now," she stated a little haughtily as she walked over to the bed.

"Have you said your prayers?" Miss Hilda asked quietly.

Susie and Simon looked at each other. In unison, Simon responded with "I forgot" while Susie said "not yet".

"Well then, I guess you're not ready for bed yet." Her eyes twinkled as she smiled.

"I guess not," Susie admitted.

Simon jumped down beside the bed. With a great dramatic flair, he sank to his knees, clasping his hands together. Resting his hands against the side of the bed, he turned his face up to Heaven. "God bless Susie, God bless Mommy, God bless Daddy and God bless Nana. God bless Mrs. C. Amen."

"God bless--," Susie began.

"Wait, I forgot something," Simon interrupted, a sense of urgency in his voice.

"Go ahead, Simon," she replied with a patient sigh.

"God bless all the trees so that I won't fall out when I climb them, and God help me remember to feed the animals every Saturday. ... Oh, and help me remember to tell Mr. Sean every Friday that I will be helping on Saturday."

Simon halted briefly, sneaking a peek at Miss Hilda. Grinning impishly, his eyes flashed with glee as he added, "And God bless Miss Hilda, and everyone here. Amen." His final 'amen' was said with great emphasis and flourish, confirming to Susie that he was truly finished this time.

Susie began again, considerably reducing her usual litany. "God bless Simon, Mommy and Daddy, Nana, Molly and her family, and Mrs. Crenshaw and her family. God bless everyone here at Glen Hollow; help us all to be better people. Amen."

As soon as Susie said her 'amen', Simon sprang up and jumped onto the bed while she meticulously arranged the covers on her side prior to getting into bed.

Miss Hilda arose from her chair and headed in Simon's direction. Upon reaching his side of the bed, she pulled the covers down and held them up for him to slide under. He did so quickly. She tucked him in and kissed his forehead.

"Good night, cherub," she said fondly.

"Good night, Miss Hilda," he responded in sing-song fashion, giving her a big grin.

Miss Hilda proceeded to Susie's side.

"I don't need to be tucked in," she snipped. "I'm too old for that."

"If you say so," Miss Hilda said softly. "Good night, dear."

Susie smiled humbly at Miss Hilda and, in a more gracious tone, responded, "Good night, Miss Hilda."

Miss Hilda quickly retrieved a thin book from the chair where she had been sitting. She smiled and handed it to Susie. "I thought you might like to read a story to Simon. It's a little book; you can easily read it in fifteen minutes."

"Thank you," Susie said gratefully; "but what about the lights-out-at-nine rule?"

With a light-hearted chuckle she said, "It's already a quarter past; I see no harm in another fifteen minutes." She switched the table lamp setting from nightlight to reading light. "When you're finished reading, please re-set the lamp to nightlight. Okay?"

Susie nodded; both she and Simon said "Thank you".

Miss Hilda waved goodnight as she switched off the main light and closed the door behind her.

"I like her," Simon declared.

Susie smiled and agreed, "I do, too."

"Do you like Miss Pritchett?" he asked while crawling out from under the covers.

Susie slowly inhaled and exhaled. "I don't know. She seems nice," she answered noncommittally, attempting to deflect her own mixed feelings.

Simon nodded in agreement. "I like her a little, but I also don't like her a lot."

"Simon, you either like her or you don't," Susie responded with just a hint of irritation in her voice.

"Then I don't." To accentuate his opinion, he crossed his arms and gave a forceful nod.

"Why?" Susie asked calmly.

"Because she said we can't stay together like Mrs. C promised," he answered, his tone becoming part whine and part sulk.

Susie didn't respond, and Simon, too, became silent; but only for a moment.

His face became sad, and his voice carried a tremor as he asked, "Do you really think she won't let us stay together?"

Susie struggled to keep her own anger and frustration in check. She knew she needed to be as positive as possible for him; otherwise, he wouldn't be able to accept the changes that were coming. She shrugged slightly. "I think her decision is final, Simon."

"Then I don't like her!" he spouted angrily, slamming his fists into the soft bedding.

"Simon, please try to be nice. Maybe it won't be so bad," she said as conciliatory as she could muster. "Settle down, and I'll read to you."

"I don't want to settle down," he whined. "I want to stay with you like Mrs. C said." He was heading into full pout mode.

"I know, Simon; but we don't have a choice," Susie told him.

"Yes we do. We could call Mrs. C, and she'd fix it," he countered.

"No, Simon, Mrs. Crenshaw can't fix it. There's nothing she can do." Susie's tone held a strong sense of finality.

"We could go live with her again," Simon whined.

"She doesn't have enough room for us; remember how crowded it was," Susie reminded him.

"But she said we could." His whine was reaching the crying phase.

Susie decided to change tactics. "She did. But we promised Mrs. Crenshaw we would give this place an honest try. Remember?"

Simon was now in full pout mode. He hung his head, arms crossed over his chest, his eyes downcast and his bottom lip was sticking out. "Yes," he sniffed; "but that was when she said we were sharing a room."

"Are you going to break your promise?" she asked. "What would Nana think of you breaking a promise?"

He shrugged. "She wouldn't like it," he snuffled.

"That's right; she wouldn't like it. She would tell you to honor your word, to keep your promise."

He looked up at her, his brow furled. "But it's not *fair!*" he yelled.

Susie hugged him and sighed deeply. "I know, Simon," she said softly. She rocked him gently back and forth for a few minutes then released him. Smiling at him, she asked, "Feel better?"

"No!" he fussed. "When can I call Mrs. C?"

"You have to wait at least a week. She'll be here next Sunday, so you can talk to her then. Okay?"

"I will," he insistently promised.

"Now are you ready to settle down so I can read this book to you?" she asked patiently.

"What book is it?" he asked, pawing at the cover to get a better view.

Susie shook her head. "I've never seen this one before. It's called 'The Lost Prince and Princess'."

"That's us," Simon giggled.

Susie laughed. "Yeah, right; that's what we are. Now settle down, silly, so I can read."

Simon slid back down under the covers and snuggled up to Susie. With her arm around him, she began reading the story while gently rubbing his back. In five minutes he was fast asleep. She smiled at him and kissed the top of his head. She closed the book and laid it on the night stand. Carefully she raised him up and gently placed his head onto his pillow. Placing Binky beside him, she draped his arm over his favorite stuffed dinosaur and pulled the covers around him, securely tucking the blankets in all along both sides of Simon.

'Snug as a bug in a rug' – the thought entered Susie's mind in a flash. Nana had said that to them every night after she tucked them in, just before she turned off the light.

Susie reset the lamp to night-light and quickly slid down under the covers. She laid there listening to the soft crackling sounds of the fire and began to relax. Silently she prayed that everything would be okay. And slowly, ever so slowly, she gently drifted off to sleep.

Chapter 5

NEW BEGINNINGS

Susie awakened to the sight of Simon sitting cross-legged on the bed with his elbows on his knees and his chin resting on his hands, just staring at her.

"Good, you're awake," he quipped.

"What time is it?" she asked while yawning and stretching.

"Al...most...six," he intoned in staccato style, bobbing his head from side to side.

"Why are you up so early?" she mumbled through a sleepy yawn.

He shrugged, tilted his head and held his hands up, palms open as if to say 'I don't know'. He answered in a giggly, sing-song fashion, "Just woke up, I guess."

Susie sat up, rubbed her face and yawned once again. "How long have you been awake?"

"Since four." His tone accurately depicted the boredom his face expressed.

She shook her head. "You should have gone back to sleep, silly. You'll be ready for a nap before lunch."

Yawning, she stretched her arms high over her head, then swiftly swooped down and gave him a good-morning hug. He giggled, wiggled and squirmed his way to freedom.

"And you heard Miss Pritchett last night; you can't take a nap until this afternoon when we have free time," she reminded him, smiling at his pretense of not liking hugs.

"I don't think I like Miss Pritchett," Simon solemnly declared.

Susie shook her head and sighed with exasperation. "Simon, please don't start this again," she pleaded.

Simon frowned at her then crossed his arms across his chest in a huff, registering the depth of his frustration. "We didn't have a schedule on Sundays with Nana or Mrs. C."

"Yes we did, Simon," Susie disagreed. "You just didn't realize it."

Simon's eyes narrowed, giving her one of his best sulks. "How could it be a schedule if I didn't know it?" he snipped.

Susie inhaled slowly and then exhaled just as slowly. Sometimes Simon could really test her patience; she had to remind herself from time to time that he was only four and could not be expected to act any older.

"We got up at the same time every day, Simon. We had breakfast the same time every day. We went to school and came home the same time every day. We went to church every Sunday at the same time. We had lunch every day at the same time. We had the afternoons to play; and in the evenings we had dinner, bath time, story time and bedtime. *That's* a schedule, Simon."

Her tone was a little more acerbic than she had intended; she felt a twinge of remorse at the crestfallen look on Simon's face. She sighed, stacked her pillows against the headboard and sank back into them.

Simon pursed his lips as he mulled over Susie's words. A few seconds later he started making fish faces at Susie in order to make her laugh. It worked. She picked up his pillow and popped him on his head with it. He fell sideways next to her, laughing very loud and very much exaggerated. His laughter was infectious, and Susie soon found herself laughing with him. She dropped back against her pillows, chuckling at his antics.

After a few minutes, he stopped. He lay very still for several minutes, quite unlike Simon. Susie watched him, wondering what was coming next. Suddenly he sat up. He looked at her, and his expression was very somber. It matched the tone of his voice.

"Susie," he asked; "do you really, really think Miss Pritchett will make me stay in the Boy's Room tonight?"

Susie slowly nodded her head, maintaining eye contact with him. "Yes, I do, Simon; and I'll have to stay in the Girl's Dorm."

"It's not fair!" he cried out in anger, pounding his fists repeatedly on the bed. "Mrs. C said we get to stay together until *I* decide I'm ready to stay in the Boys Room."

Susie pulled him to her, hugged him and held him tight. She kissed the top of his head while gently rubbing his back. "I'm sorry Simon, but maybe Miss Pritchett is right."

"No she isn't!" his muffled voice insisted.

"Let me finish. Would you be ready in a week, or a month or a year? I don't think so, Simon. You wouldn't want to make the change, ever. And it isn't fair to the others. What about Jared and Juls? They're brother and sister, and they have to stay in the Dorms."

He pushed back away from her, scowled and shouted angrily, "I don't care! Mrs. C said that Miss Pritchett--"

"Stop it, Simon," she admonished him harshly, interrupting his tantrum. Seeing his expression of fear and dismay, she felt sorry for him and softened her tone. "It'll be okay. I promise. Just give it a try. I'll tell you bedtime stories and tuck you in every night."

"What if Miss Pritchett won't let you?" he mumbled, his shoulders drooping and his head hanging down to where his chin nearly touched his chest.

His quivering voice caused Susie's eyes to fill with tears. She swallowed hard and held her breath in an attempt to control her emotions. Softly she exhaled while quickly brushing away the water from her eyes. She had to be strong for Simon.

Susie cupped his little face in her hands and gently raised his head. She looked directly into his eyes. Very earnestly she said, "I'll do it anyway. *I* promise. I *will* tell you bedtime stories *and* tuck you in *every* night, even if we have to do it in secret."

Simon knew she meant it; Susie always kept her promise. He smiled at her. Then he launched himself at her, wrapped himself around her and gave her his best bear hug. They both started laughing as they fell, rolling sideways on the bed. After several minutes of playing Tickle Monster, Susie stopped, allowing Simon to catch his breath.

"We have to get up now, Simon. In twenty minutes Miss Hilda will be here to take us to breakfast, and we have to be ready." Susie got out of bed and headed for the closet.

"I like Miss Hilda," Simon declared with an affirmative nod of his head.

"Me, too. Come on, we have to get ready. After all," she now spoke mimicking Miss Pritchett; "breakfast is served promptly at seven. If you are late--"

"You don't eat," Simon chimed in as he began using the bed for a trampoline.

"Stop jumping," Susie ordered him. "Come choose what you want to wear, or I'll choose for you."

Immediately he stopped his trapeze act, jumped off the bed and ran to the closet. "I'll do it … I'll do it," he insisted.

"Okay, then do it."

Simon finally settled on a light blue shirt, navy sweater and his dark blue slacks, but only after Susie rejected several of his other choices. Some of them Susie was certain he chose just for the sake of clowning around, knowing all the while it would annoy her. Next up was the selection of a t-shirt, underwear and socks. The first two were easy enough; but the socks - they were a whole different ballgame. He was absolutely determined to wear his bright purple socks with the lime green dinosaurs.

Extremely frustrated after several wasted minutes of heated debate, Susie finally relented. She told him to wear whatever he wanted no matter how silly it may look, just hurry up and get dressed. From past experience she knew the chance was slim that he would. Susie pulled open her dresser drawer and retrieved her undergarments, then stomped over to the closet and selected her outfit. Ignoring Simon, she turned and stormed into the bathroom, slamming the door behind her.

She set a new speed dressing record (three minutes – her best time yet). Hastily combing her hair and then securing it in back with a glittery, pink butterfly barrette, she sighed at her reflection. "Not the greatest Sunday hair style, but it'll have to do," she said to her reflection.

Closing her eyes, Susie took in a slow, deep breath. Releasing it quickly, she said with resolve, "Now to get Simon dressed."

Upon re-entering the bedroom, she was pleasantly surprised to find Simon fully dressed, and he had just finished tying his shoes. He had actually done a decent job this time, Susie noticed. She combed his hair but, within seconds, it had already begun reverting back to its normal curl pattern.

"You look great Simon," she said with a winsome smile.

He swaggered over to the cheval mirror to check out her assessment. He nodded approvingly as he turned every which way in front of the mirror. With all the gyrations he was performing, Susie saw that he was indeed wearing his favorite dinosaur socks. She giggled.

Simon finished his critique and crawled into the chair next to her as Susie moved over to give him room. He leaned against her, placing his cheek against her arm and quietly asked, "After chapel, will you take me to see the statues?"

"I guess; but it might be too cold outside, Simon," Susie responded agreeably.

Simon looked up at her, giving her his best pleading look. "We won't stay outside long; I promise. I just want to see the dolphin fountain," he begged with just a hint of a whine.

Susie smiled as she looked into those big, seemingly innocent eyes. He definitely knew how to work her. She laughed softly. "Okay; we'll make a fast trip around the gardens. When it's warmer, we'll explore them to your heart's content."

Simon coyly smiled. "Thanks, Susie; you're the best."

"You're welcome, Simon," Susie responded. Then for good measure, she added in a firm tone, "But you have to mind me and come back inside when I tell you. Promise?"

Simon's smile expanded quickly into a full, toothy grin. "Promise," he vowed.

Susie grinned. "Okay; right after chapel we'll change into our play clothes, and then we'll go outside. We'll have plenty of time to take a quick look around before lunch."

Simon shook his head. "If we change our clothes first, we won't have time to see the dolphin fountain. I promise I won't get dirty."

Susie didn't answer; she studied Simon, contemplating whether or not it was a good idea to allow him to remain in his dress clothes longer than necessary.

Simon gave her his best begging face. "Please?" he pleaded.

Susie laughed. "You silly goose," she said, responding to his facial expression. "Okay, we'll go straight after chapel. But you better be good and mind me," she cautioned.

Simon's pearly-white baby teeth gleamed as he grinned at her. "I already promised," he reminded her.

They were interrupted by a knocking on the door. It opened, and Miss Hilda was standing in the doorway. She gave them a cheery smile and asked, "Are we ready?"

"We're ready," they said in unison as they exited into the corridor.

———

Breakfast this Sunday morning consisted of a small bowl of oatmeal, a fruit cup, toast and milk. Simon wrinkled his nose when his bowl was placed in front of him; he was not fond of oatmeal. He pushed it away and flopped back against his chair, quite clearly registering his disapproval.

Upon seeing his reaction, Mrs. Coppersmith made sort of a clicking sound with her tongue. She eyed him with that *'we'll have no more nonsense'* stare of hers.

"It may not be to your liking, young man," she quipped; "but it'll sustain you through the morning. Last thing you want is to be puppy dog full and fall asleep during chapel."

Undaunted, Simon grinned up at her. "What happens if I fall asleep?"

Mrs. Coppersmith chuckled slightly. 'He will surely liven this place up', she thought.

Her voice and facial expression were the epitome of concern as she leaned slightly toward Simon and answered, "Well, dear, I pity the poor soul that Miss Pritchett catches napping during chapel. Extra chores, hard ones at that, are assigned to the transgressor. And it's no easy task to get them unassigned." She gave him a curt nod of her head, moved on to Miss Hilda and began serving her.

The smile quickly faded from Simon's face, and his eyes widened in fear at the prospect of hard labor. Slowly he reached for his bowl, easing it back to its proper place in front of him. Susie leaned over and whispered to Simon that she would keep him awake. He smiled at her and nodded as he reluctantly took his first bite.

After breakfast, everyone made their way to the Chapel. Service began promptly at nine, and no one dared be late. Miss Ginger and Miss Cora made haste in herding the children down the corridors. Behind them the adults followed in groups, making small talk as they hurried on their way.

Susie and Simon walked with Miss Hilda at the rear of the column. Simon slid his hand into Miss Hilda's, giving her one of his best smiles as he squeezed her hand.

"You needn't be afraid of getting lost, Simon," she said affectionately. "There's plenty of people and noise ahead to guide you."

"But if I'm with you," he said coyly; "then I won't get lost."

She laughed. "True enough. That's excellent reasoning, Simon."

As they continued walking, Miss Hilda began telling them a little more of Glen Hollow's history. Simon was already bored and began wildly swinging his arm back and forth while attempting to take giant steps.

"No, Simon," Miss Hilda said, pulling him back to her side. "Walk properly. After all, you're dressed as a young man, and you need to conduct yourself as such. Susie chose well for you this morning."

"*I* chose for me," Simon informed her as he pointed to his chest; "not Susie."

"You did quite well then. It makes you look very handsome," Miss Hilda responded. He beamed and preened like a little peacock, his head held high as he strutted alongside of her.

Miss Hilda placed her arm around Susie and gave her a hug. "I'm quite certain you assisted him," she said softly. "You did well." Releasing Susie, she said in a normal pitch, "You look very pretty, Susie. Is pink your favorite color?"

Susie smiled and nodded. "Yes; it's always been my favorite. Purple is a close second."

Nodding, Miss Hilda said, "Purple's my favorite, and pink is a very close second."

During the remainder of their short walk, Miss Hilda reminded Simon that chapel is the same as church; the rules of behavior remain the same. She went on to enumerate what behaviors were not allowed, ending with what is expected of him. Simon gave Miss Hilda his solemn promise to 'mind his manners', after which she praised him for his spirit of cooperation.

Miss Hilda began telling them about the Reverend Josiah Tillman, their minister. He had retired from his congregation many years ago, but continued to serve as minister for Glen Hollow. He was very active in various

115

communities in the county, performing volunteer work in several youth organizations and in several shelters. Miss Hilda came to know him when her family moved to Glen Hollow; but he has known Miss Pritchett all her life, and was a friend of Miss Murielle, Miss Pritchett's mother. According to Miss Hilda, he lives in Micah's Landing, a small village about twenty-one miles northeast of Glen Hollow. It is a sleepy, little town with a population just slightly less than two hundred; that is, until summer when it comes very much alive with the tourist season.

They finally exited the south wing, entering the pergola with its tangled mass of vines that blocked most of the sun's light. The ivy's dark green foliage stood in sharp contrast to the brown stems of the vines that would have flowers come spring.

The pergola was made of white granite, including its floor, and each side had twenty-four columns, approximately six feet apart. The columns were of sculpted ladies clad in long flowing gowns, holding various types of plants or produce. Between each lady was a granite bench except for the spaces between columns seven and eight, and again between columns seventeen and eighteen. Those four spaces (two per side) were open, allowing entry to the flagstone paths of the east garden and to the west garden.

As they rushed along the pergola, Susie only had time to give just the briefest of glances to the small portion of the gardens that was visible. From what she could see, both gardens had a large oak tree, though neither was as large as the one in the field that loomed in front of the manor. Formal flagstone paths wound their way throughout the gardens like a path through a maze. Interspersed throughout were benches, fountains, statues, evergreen bushes, small trees and flower gardens (though none blooming this late in the year). It was beautiful even at the onset of winter. The air was a bit nippy, and so they made a short walk of it (more like a sprint) down the pergola to the portico in front of the arched door of the Chapel.

Providing a welcome relief from the bitter cold, they entered the vestibule, a small room and well heated. According to Miss Hilda, the staircase on the right led to the bell tower. The staircase to the left led down into the basement where a small furnace was located. Directly in front of them, leading into the sanctuary, was a set of thick, double doors made of white oak. The brass handles were highly polished and gleamed brightly, reflecting the light from the small chandelier above them.

Miss Hilda hastily ushered Simon into the Chapel and down the main aisle. Susie paused in the doorway, absorbing its atmosphere. She delighted in its beauty and in the serenity. The high, vaulted ceiling not only lent the impression of being a much larger room than it truly was, but also gave it the ambiance of a cathedral. There was a reverence here, an embodiment of worship in this place that she could sense, instilling her with peace. For a moment she remained motionless, closing her eyes and allowing the sensation to fill her spirit. She felt a connection in here, as if she had come home.

Upon opening her eyes, she was met with the beauty of the stained glass windows. She delighted seeing the morning light filtering gently inside, cascading a rainbow of colors onto the marble floor. There were twelve windows in all; six in the east wall and six in the west wall. The tall, narrow windows formed an arch at the top, and in the center of the arch was an octagon of a clear crystal. Though all of the windows were exceptionally beautiful, six weren't scenes normally depicted in a chapel or a church. Susie wasn't certain (since she'd never been inside a cathedral), but somehow she didn't think these would be found in a cathedral either.

The first odd window scene was of a strange configuration of planets and galaxies in addition to our solar system and the Milky Way. There were twelve in all, forming a circle around what appeared to be a starburst in the center. Each of the outer systems linked to each other, some more than others, but all linked with the starburst by the exact same amount.

The second was of an array of stars and constellations; some Susie recognized and some she didn't. It was stunning, like miniature diamonds cast in a sea of black ink.

The next window displayed a collage of mermaids and sea nymphs, Sirens, seahorses and underwater cities. It contained a host of images revealing all types of aquatic life, both the friendly (like dolphins) and the fearsome (like sharks).

The fourth window was of a scene containing pictures of a variety of earth creatures, both real and legend. Prominently displayed in its center were a tiger, a wolf and a unicorn.

The following window presented images of creatures of flight, real and fantasy. Among those shown were an owl, a dove, an eagle, a condor, a Pegasus, a dragon and a phoenix.

The sixth and last of the odd scenes presented scenes of people. Sort of. It had the typical Adam and Eve scene as well as other people; but it also had images of angels, demons, fairies, pixies, nymphs, elves, imps, hobgoblins, trolls and several other odd looking creatures.

Susie found herself smiling; whoever built this chapel had a sense of humor. She liked that. She hurried to catch up with Simon and Miss Hilda, now nearly to the front of the center aisle. With a quick look around she surveyed the interior.

At the front was a rosewood altar, simple in design. It had no ornamental carvings, no padded top. Positioned directly behind the altar in the center of the dais was the lectern, also made from rosewood. It, too, was of simple design, having no ornamentations. To the left of the lectern was a concert harp and to the right was a grand piano. Susie wondered who would be the musicians. Obviously, she thought, Miss Cora would be one of them since she's the music teacher.

The rich, dark red of the rosewood pews contrasted beautifully with their thick, dark-green velvet cushions, so soft and comfortable. (Simon had been quick to voice his approval once they had been seated.) The pews were obviously very old for they had the high, bench-style sides, and on the outside of each bench was a built–in niche for a lantern. She counted the pews as she followed Miss Hilda down the center aisle. It was no major chore; there were only twelve pews per side.

Apparently the children were required to sit in the front row. The other children were already seated in the right front pew along with Miss Cora, who was sitting at the far end of the pew next to the west aisle. Miss Hilda motioned for them to sit with the other children and then seated herself on the aisle end of the pew directly across from them. Susie pulled Simon around her and guided him into the pew, slipping in behind him. She removed his hat and scarf, stuffing them in his right coat pocket and then removed his mittens, placing them in his left coat pocket. Next she assisted him in removing his coat and motioned for him to sit.

Quickly Susie removed her own winter clothing, placing it on the back of the pew with Simon's. She sat down and leaned against the high end of the pew, relaxing for just a second. Simon, of course, decided he wanted to sit on the end. He pestered her until she finally surrendered, sliding over and giving him that spot. As she settled in, she recalled what Mrs. Crenshaw had said about Glen Hollow. She wondered if Miss Pritchett could remember the Sundays when the chapel was filled with her family and with all the staff members and their families. Sadness began to fill her heart as she empathized with Miss Pritchett - the realization that Sundays with Nana would no longer be, struck a common chord within her for the loss Miss Pritchett had also suffered.

Moments later, both doors abruptly opened. Miss Pritchett entered, escorted by an elderly man whom Susie rightly surmised as being the Reverend. He was tall and willowy, and looked very somber dressed in a dark, charcoal-gray suit and white shirt. His silvery hair was thick and bushy, just like his eyebrows. His weathered face was heavily wrinkled, and he looked to be "*at least two hundred*" per Simon's emphatic whisper in her ear.

Reverend Josiah Tillman's amber eyes sparkled and danced with the light of a soul that's forever young. He wore round, wire-rimmed silver glasses that elicited a giggle (more like a squeal) out of Simon as he whispered to Susie, "He looks like a hoot owl." Susie shushed him, but not before Miss Hilda gave him a stern look from across the aisle. Simon quickly sank back down onto the pew, hiding from Miss Hilda as he pressed up against the end of the bench.

The Reverend cheerfully greeted each of the adults in turn as he and Miss Pritchett made their way to the front row. Miss Pritchett introduced Susie and Simon to him; and, after he greeted them and the other children, he escorted Miss Pritchett to her seat. As he made his way up to the lectern, Miss Cora quickly seated herself at the piano, and Miss Fiona took the bench next to the harp.

They began playing an introductory call to worship, and the small congregation began to cease their conversations, heeding the music's plea for reverence. Susie closed her eyes and allowed the tranquil strains to uplift her soul, renewing her inner spirit. She loved the harp with its peaceful sound; this was the first time she had ever heard one live, and she was even more enthralled with the instrument than ever. No wonder it was the angels' choice of instruments; it resonated with the soul, imputing a keen sense of worship, of inspiration and of peace.

'I want to learn to play it', she told herself; 'I hope Miss Fiona will teach me.' Susie played the flute well; her mother had started teaching her when she was three. Nana had insisted that she take private lessons, so Susie had done so the past four years. Then three years ago, Nana began teaching her the piano. Although Nana taught her a great deal, she knew she was still a novice where the piano was concerned.

Service lasted about ninety minutes and, when it was over, Susie decided that she liked Reverend Tillman. He wasn't preachy; he spoke as if they were sitting at a kitchen table, just talking like friends do. He had a good sense of humor and everyone enjoyed it, laughing at the analogies and quips he used. The timbre of his voice was soothing, and his words she found both encouraging and comforting. Simon, too, seemed to like him; Susie noticed that he remained alert the entire time.

After the conclusion of the service, Miss Ginger and Miss Cora played a processional while the Reverend slowly walked toward the vestibule doors. As he passed by the benches, everyone began putting on their coats, scarves and hats. The children's row was second to file out, right behind the first row on the other side of the aisle. Simon insisted he could put on his own coat, and pleaded until she gave it to him.

Susie was ready to leave long before it was their turn; however, Simon was not. His knit hat and scarf were not a problem; unfortunately he seemed to be having a little trouble getting the coat buttoned. Finally he asked (more akin to a whine) for her help when he noticed that the other row was just about gone. Fast and easy, Susie buttoned his coat and put on his mittens just as the last adult left the first row. She turned Simon around and gently nudged him, signaling him to start walking toward the vestibule.

Simon was not at all happy with Susie keeping her hand on his shoulder. He kept squirming, trying to dislodge her grip. After several attempts on his part, Susie tightened her grip and pulled him close to her. She whispered in his ear, "If you don't start behaving, the trip to the dolphin fountain is cancelled."

Simon stopped in his tracks, gave her an angry look thinking she would relent. Her expression immediately caused him to change his demeanor and tactics. "Sorry," he said sweetly; "I'll be good."

Susie sighed as Simon resumed his walk toward the Reverend. One by one they filed past the Reverend, shaking his hand and chatting a minute with him before leaving the warmth of the vestibule.

Reaching down, she firmly clasped Simon's hand into hers - which was no easy task. His mitten was so puffy it was hard to determine whether or not she actually was holding his hand. They walked down the Chapel's portico steps and headed quickly to the entrance of the pergola. Even though they were well ahead of most of the adults, the other children had already entered the manor along with Mrs. Coppersmith, Miss Taryn, and Miss Ginger.

When they reached the first breakout section that led to the east garden, Susie quickly steered Simon onto the flagstone path.

"Hey, stop. Susie.... Simon. Come back here," a voice rang out from the pergola.

Susie and Simon turned around. It was Miss Hilda.

"Where do you think you're going?" she asked.

"Simon wanted to see the dolphin fountain that Miss Pritchett spoke of last night," Susie explained. "I promised him this morning we'd take a quick look after chapel," she added, hoping that Miss Hilda would allow them to continue.

"Don't you think it's just a little cold out here for that? Perhaps you should wait for a warmer day," Miss Hilda suggested.

Susie shrugged. "Maybe, but I promised Simon. We won't be long. We'll just take a quick look, and then we'll come inside."

Miss Hilda smiled and approached. "Fine, but I'll show you the way. You could end up wandering around for hours, not knowing the gardens." She clasped Simon's mitten hand in hers, briskly walking them toward the center of the garden.

Susie was very much glad that Miss Hilda had come along – there were far too many paths and turns that had to be taken in order to reach the dolphin fountain. Along the way, they rapidly strode past several statues, garden ornamentals, benches and reading alcoves. When they reached what Miss Hilda said was the center of the east garden, they made a final turn just past a grove of American Chestnut trees.

There it was! Simon phrased it best when he exclaimed, "Wow-whee!"

Susie stood silently in awe of such a wondrous work. The round fountain rose to a soaring height of at least ninety feet, not counting the stepped base that was approximately three feet high. The pool portion of the fountain appeared to be at least thirty feet across while its depth was probably about slightly less than two feet.

Simon broke free from Miss Hilda and ran to the pool, climbing up onto the ledge. Susie slowly walked toward it, admiring the exquisite creativity and craftsmanship of the person who designed it, and whoever carved such a marvel. The intricate and precise detail was so realistic, she felt as if she was standing at the ocean and watching the dolphins play.

The water portion of the sculpture was a blue-hued marble, blending into white tips at the crest of the waves. The life-size sculpted dolphins were interspersed among the waves and were made of a blue-gray sparkling marble, casting eerily an appearance of life. They encircled the fountain, spiraling ever upward toward the pinnacle where one lone dolphin emerged from the waves as if it were truly leaping out of the water.

Water jets at the base of the marble waves sent the water into a fan like burst, crashing against the sculpted waves and gently trickling down into the pool. It helped to create the illusion of motion, making it seem like the marble waves were actually causing the water sprays.

Each magnificent dolphin had a water jet hidden inside the blowhole, producing the appearance that the creature was alive and frolicking just as they do in the ocean. These water jets intermittently spurted a solid stream of water similar to that of a living dolphin. After her inspection of the fountain, Susie sat down next to Simon on the pool's ledge.

"Simon was just asking me why we don't have any fish in the fountain," Miss Hilda said. "I explained it's because of the additive that's required to prevent the pipes from freezing in the winter."

"Makes sense," Susie responded. "I wondered why it wasn't frozen."

Simon beamed at Susie. "I love it. Can we come here every day?"

Susie looked at Miss Hilda before answering. "I don't know. We probably should wait until the weather is a little nicer."

Simon frowned.

Miss Hilda smiled at him and cheerfully said, "Simon, when the weather is warm, you are allowed to play in the pool but only with adult supervision. I'm certain we can find a time schedule that will meet with your approval."

Simon grinned at her, then jumped up and gave her a hug. "Thanks, Miss Hilda," he said, pleased at what he thought was a victory on his part.

Miss Hilda gave him a hug and then asked, "Shall we go inside?" To his frowned response, she explained, "You need to change your clothes and be in the Dining Hall by noon. We're running out of time."

Simon grinned and nodded. "Okay," he agreed cheerfully, grasping her hand.

"Okay, then; let's go," Miss Hilda agreed, grinning at Simon. Hurriedly she led them back to the warmth of the manor.

———

Reverend Tillman joined them for Sunday dinner, served promptly at noon, and apparently he did so most every Sunday. Mrs. Coppersmith was a flurry of motion in preparing the meal and in overseeing the proper table placements. Everything had to be perfect. One would think this was Reverend Tillman's first dinner at Glen Hollow by her constant obsessing over every detail. Her effort was not wasted; the dinner was marvelous and very delicious. Reverend Tillman was as appreciative of her talents as were the residents of Glen Hollow.

Conversation ebbed and flowed on a wide variety of subjects. The Reverend would inquire as to the well-being of staff and their family members; others would freely update him on the trials and tribulations of family or friends. The children, too, were engaged in lively chats with the Reverend, relishing his attention. He loved their stories and their jokes, and there wasn't a short supply of either.

"We got a letter from Grammy yesterday," Timmy excitedly announced to the Reverend. "Aaron read it to me."

"That's wonderful, Timmy. How is she?"

"She's better 'cause she said she's going to come visit for Christmas. Didn't she Aaron?" His voice was demanding a confirmation from his brother, one that wasn't given.

With a wary look at the Reverend, Aaron's response was anything but hopeful. "She didn't say she was better, Timmy; and she didn't say she would visit at Christmas. She *said* she *hoped* she could visit this Christmas."

"Well, isn't that the same thing?" Timmy asked, his voice quivering, revealing his fading hope.

"No, it isn't." Aaron's brusque answer reflected his own anguish that he would not see her this Christmas.

Timmy's head dropped down in despair as his fork fell to his plate with a clatter. "But I want to see Grammy," he whimpered softly.

"Timmy, I'm certain your Grammy will come if it's at all possible," Miss Pritchett said, attempting to reassure him. "I'll phone her, and see if she needs any assistance in traveling. I'm certain we can work something out," she smiled affectionately at him. "Come to my office at three this afternoon, and we'll call her together."

His face brightened as he sat up straight. "See Aaron; Miss Pritchett knows Grammy will come."

"Aaron, does your Grammy have anyone staying with her yet?" Reverend Tillman asked.

Aaron nodded. "Yes sir, but only during the day." His brow furrowed with worry as he thought of his Grammy. "She really needs someone all the time but..." his voice trailed off, uncertain as to how much he should reveal.

"Would you mind if I try to find someone for night duty?" he asked.

Aaron was surprised. "Grammy can't afford it," he flatly stated. "No one will do it for what she can afford." Sadness and anger competed for dominance in his tone.

Reverend Tillman smiled encouragingly. "Let me worry about that, Aaron. Is it okay with you for me to contact your Grammy, and see what I can do?" he asked gently.

Aaron slowly nodded his head, keenly watching the Reverend. Timmy, unsure of exactly what was happening, popped out with, "Does this mean Grammy is coming for Christmas?"

Nearly everyone laughed; Miss Pritchett and Reverend Tillman both responded with, "We'll do our best to get her here."

Susie was silent; it hadn't occurred to her that some of the others had family that they could go visit, or that could come here to visit them. Tears began to well up in her eyes as she felt the sting of loss; loss of her parents and especially of Nana.

Simon looked at her, saw her tears, and became frightened. "What's wrong, Susie?" he whispered urgently.

She stoically forced back the tears, smiled at him and said as cheerfully as possible, "Nothing, Simon; I was just thinking how nice it is that their Grammy can come visit."

Her faint smile didn't convince him at all. He leaned toward her with arms outstretched, waiting for a reassuring hug. His expression and action was not lost on the attentive nature of most of the adults. A quick glance around the table told her all that she needed to know with regards to their powers of observation.

Susie quickly gave him a hug and then gently pushed him upright into his booster seat. "Thank you Simon," she whispered in his ear and smiled.

Satisfied now that all was right, his attention immediately shifted to the Reverend. His curiosity was bursting, and Simon just had to know the answer to a question that had been bugging him all morning.

"Mr. Reverend, why is your town called a landing?" he blurted.

The Reverend's eyes sparkled with delight. "The township, Simon, is called Micah's Landing. It was named after Micah McBride. He was the leader of a group of settlers who built a little village called New Hope about a mile west of the Falls. Micah built his business on the river bank a little further west from the village. He built a general store on one side of the building and a small inn for travelers on the other side. He also built a small wharf and dock on the River in front of his building. He called it Micah's Landing. As time passed, new settlers came to the area, built their homes and business around his place. Eventually, the boom around Micah's Landing grew and overtook the little village. They, in essence, became one village so the people voted that they become one village, and to keep the name of Micah's Landing."

"Is it big?" he asked.

"No, Simon," he chuckled. "It's still a little town; we have maybe two hundred people. From June through August we have a large number of tourists that come to view the waterfall and our quaint, old buildings. Some come for the peaceful, park atmosphere of our village. We have several artisan shops, art galleries, tea rooms and coffee houses. We even have a candy factory." (This last statement garnered a round of "oohs" and "yums" from the children.)

He leaned forward and winked at Simon (who sat across from the Reverend). "But I think people come for the fishing. The Anicaw has a lot of *really, big* trout." He gestured with his hands, extending his arms out as if measuring a six-foot fish. That elicited a variety of responses; from the children, amazed utterances of "wow", "golly", awesome", and "really"; whereas from the adults, most responses were "now, Reverend" and "don't tease them".

He laughed good-naturedly and corrected himself. "Well, perhaps, they're only this big," he said, gesturing about fifteen inches in length.

"Before I forget, Eloise," Reverend Tillman turned to look at her as he spoke; "the town will be celebrating its tri-centennial come July. The mayor asked me if I thought you would be interested in helping to plan the extravaganza. He would like a month-long celebration. Some council members want to take advantage of the tourist aspect and have the celebration activities last the whole summer, but that might be too much."

Miss Pritchett raised her eyebrows slightly, surprised at his request. "I'm not certain I'm the right person for such an endeavor."

"Nonsense; you are. And you needn't worry; you won't be planning it alone. You will have a committee... of sorts." He chuckled slightly, revealing in that laugh that there are very few committee members.

"Well, at least think about it. The mayor will probably phone tomorrow. It would be nice to have you on the committee with me," he concluded his inducement with a grin.

"What does Micah's Landing look like?" Jose asked.

Reverend Tillman launched into a vivid description of his town, captivating all the children. His eyes would twinkle as he relayed its colorful history, and his animated style reminded Susie a little painfully of Nana. Her thoughts drifted to Nana, and soon she had tuned out the Reverend and his stories. But when he asked if any of the children had heard the tale of the 'Witch of the Mist', Susie's reverie abruptly ended.

"Now, Reverend," Mrs. Copperfield chided; "please don't tell them that old ghost story. It's a silly superstition. Surely we can find a more suitable subject than that, especially on the Lord's Day."

The children immediately began clamoring to hear the story. Mrs. Coppersmith abruptly pushed back her chair and stood. "Would anyone care for more coffee?" she asked in a slightly irked tone. Several of the adults answered "yes", so she retrieved the silver coffee pot from the sideboard and began filling their cups.

"Well, Eloise, do you think it's a subject that should be left for another time?" he queried Miss Pritchett, his lilting tone revealing his amusement at Mrs. Coppersmith's reaction.

"No, I think it's just a story, no better or worse than most," she responded with a slight shrug of her shoulders. Grinning mischievously, she added; "Besides, everyone loves a scary story."

"Well then," he said rubbing his hands together gleefully; "let's sit by the fire. It'll be cozier and much more appropriate for storytelling."

He rose, walked to the fireplace behind the table and sat down on the hearth. The children quickly scrambled from their chairs and sat on the floor in front of him, forming a half circle.

"Come on," he motioned heartily to the adults. "Bring your chairs and join us."

Miss Pritchett laughed and said, "Why not."

She rose from her chair and carried it over to the fireplace, setting it down behind the children. Some of the other adults complied quickly, and some were reluctant. Most who were seated on the hearth side of the table just simply turned their chairs around and remained by the table. Reverend Pritchett teased and joked with the children, entertaining and being entertained while they waited for the adults to join them. When all of the adults were finally seated and quiet, he held his index finger to his lips, signaling to the children the time had arrived.

He leaned slightly toward the children and dropped his voice to a hushed level, denoting something mysterious was afoot. "This is a *very* old tale," he began; "about the fight between an evil, evil witch and good people."

The Reverend widened his eyes, hunched down and slowly looked around the room as if he was searching for someone or something. The children shivered and giggled as they, too, searched the room, expecting to find something or someone skulking in the shadows.

"Shh-h-h," he whispered with his index finger pressed against his lips. "Be very quiet for we do not want to wake her. Some say just the telling of the tale can begin to arouse her from her slumber, and give her the strength she needs. If we are too loud, she may awaken, and break free from where she's imprisoned."

As he spoke, he slowly nodded his head. And, ever so intently, he held eye contact with each child, one by one, captivating their attention and tantalizing their imaginations for the story that was to come.

Chapter 6

THE WITCH OF THE MIST

"Long, long ago," Reverend Tillman began in a soft, sing-song voice; "nearly four hundred years ago, a young man and his bride came to the Falls of the Anicaw River. It was just after the spring thaw. The waters rushed along the banks and gently cascaded down into a large pool of water; from there, the River continued on its journey, hundreds of miles on to the sea."

"The pool at the base of the Falls was the size of a small lake, and it brightly sparkled as the sunlight danced across its surface. The water was very, very deep and icy cold; and it was so clear, you could see all the way to the rock bottom. A mist would rhythmically rise and fall from the water's surface as if the pool was alive and breathing," he said, slowly moving his arms out and in, simulating the movements of deep breathing.

"The young couple was amazed by the size and strength of the Anicaw with its clear, cold waters flowing swiftly, rushing along as if running a race."

Reverend Tillman paused, slowly observing the spellbound expressions on each young face. He smiled, leaned forward and whispered, "And perhaps the River is; perhaps it's racing to keep the evil one from breaking free of the chains that bind it in the mist."

"In case you don't know, the word 'Anicaw' means 'spirit water' in the native language of the Icori people. It is their belief that the mighty River is the home of water spirits, what we call sprites. Do you know what a sprite is?" he asked.

One by one the children shook their heads and said "no."

"A sprite is a supernatural being whose physical essence," (he patted his arm), "is much like that of a fairy or even an angel. Their abilities are similar to fairies, but less than that of an angel. The Icori believe the water spirits live in the Anicaw River, controlling and preserving it. They keep it from flooding, and keep it clean and pure so that the fish, and the animals, and the birds and the people all have what they need to live."

The Reverend straightened and continued his tale, his rich baritone voice capturing their imaginations as he wove his tale with great animation. "As the couple gazed out at this land, its beauty completely captured their hearts. The River was full of fish, and the forest surrounding it was thick and lush with giant trees, providing shelter and food with its variety of nuts. Patches of wild strawberries, grape vines and berry bushes were plentiful. All types of animals, from the smallest chipmunk to the biggest bear, flourished in the deep, dark forests and in the small clearings alongside the River's banks. There were birds of every kind: pheasants living in the tall grasses, geese, ducks, turkeys, doves and songbirds as well as owls, hawks, ravens and eagles. They all shared this amazing land."

"The young couple decided to stay, that here they would build their home. They traveled downstream in search of a clearing large enough to build their farm. About a mile southwest of the Falls they found the most marvelous clearing. The land was flat, ready for building and for tilling. It was perfect, as if it were made just for them. "

"The meadow grasses were tall and thick, providing a ready-made pasture for their animals. The River would provide plenty of fresh water and fish. The dense forest, with its abundance of trees, would provide all the logs they would need with which to build a cabin, a barn and a corral. And the clearing, well, it was large enough to provide plenty of land to raise their crops and pasture their animals."

"They thought they had entered a paradise," he said with the tone of an awe-struck dreamer.

Suddenly dropping his voice to that of a hushed whisper, he added; "but soon they would discover *evil* also lived in this wondrous paradise."

Anticipation of what was to come filled their young faces with a mixture of fear and excitement. Some squirmed and giggled; others huddled together for the feeling of safety. Simon pressed against Susie, and she hugged him close to her.

Reverend Tillman smiled. Continuing his tale, his tone was now cheerful. "They began the hard work of making the clearing into their farm, living in their traveler's box wagon until they could build a proper cabin."

"They first staked out an area for the horses and cows to graze. Next he built a lean-to; and then, under it, he built a fire pit. It would provide the means to cook their food and serve as a heat source, helping to banish a little of the chill in the air that the spring mornings and evenings still held. They also placed two chairs and a small table under the lean-to, giving them a place to eat or to just sit and rest. "

"As soon as those tasks were done, they plowed and tilled the land, planting their crops. Knowing that harvest time was several months away, it was very important that they have the garden planted quickly. The provisions they had brought with them would only last another eight months."

"After planting the garden, they began felling trees. They had established an area to process the trees near the south edge of the clearing. Every day he would work in the forest, felling the trees and hauling them to the work area. She would help him strip the branches and the bark from each log. It was no easy task. They worked from sun-up to sun down; and six weeks later, they had finished the small barn for the animals. It was another two months before they had finished their tiny cabin."

"Life was good in that little clearing. The crops had grown well, and they were harvesting more than enough for them and their animals. Carefully the young bride stored in the root cellar the seeds for the next year's garden. She preserved enough food to carry them for two years. Whatever they didn't eat or preserve, they placed in the forest to feed the forest animals."

"It was early autumn now, just after daybreak. The young couple was sitting on their front porch and enjoying a steaming cup of tea. They made it a point every day to watch the sun rise and set together, giving thanks for all the blessings they had received."

His tone now changed to one of apprehension. "A man appeared at the far edge of the clearing to the east of their cabin. He just stood there, staring at them."

"The young man rose from his chair, walked to the edge of the porch, waved and called out 'Hello.'"

"Slowly the man advanced toward the cabin. He began to weave and stumble, and then fell to his knees. The young couple quickly put their cups down and ran to assist him."

"When they were near to him, they saw he was an Indian, quite elderly and badly injured. His clothes had huge slashes that were singed as if he were repeatedly struck by lightning. But these were no lightning strikes; they were deep, curved wounds with six slashes in each grouping."

"'The breastplate he wore was made of animal bones and rawhide strips. It was broken, hanging in pieces and dangling from the cord around his neck. He was covered in blood. Around his waist was a beaded belt fastened with a bone latch. Around each ankle was a band of feathers. His face, neck and hands had symbols drawn in what appeared to be a light gray mud. In his hair were seven eagle feathers.'"

"The young man pointed to the cabin, then to the Indian and made a walking motion with his index and middle fingers. The old man nodded, allowing them to help him stand. And with their support, he leaned heavily on them as they slowly walked to the cabin. Several times the old man groaned in such pain that the young couple feared he would not make it. When the elderly man's knees buckled, the young man quickly caught him and swiftly lifted the old man into his arms, carrying him the rest of the way to the cabin."

"The young bride gathered up quilts and blankets, making a pallet for him on the floor by the hearth. They helped him down onto the soft, makeshift bed, and he wearily closed his eyes. She covered him with additional blankets and quilts; after several minutes he stopped shivering."

"'What could have caused such wounds?' she asked her husband, fearful of whatever beast could inflict such grievous injury."

"The young man shook his head. He, too, was greatly worried. 'I don't know…I've never seen anything like it.'"

"'Should I dress his wounds now? If I don't, I fear infection may set in,' she said."

"'Let him sleep,' he instructed her; 'when he wakes, do it then.' He left the cabin to tend to his chores, and she began her own chores."

"Mid-morning, the old man awakened. He immediately tried to stand, but he was too weak. He fell back down onto the quilts. The young bride ladled into a cup the chicken broth she had made and quickly brought it to him."

"He refused it, pushing it back to her. She tried again to give it to him, but he again refused it. He kept talking to her, rattling on and frantic. He pointed to her, to the door; his tone was filled with fear. His eyes misted as he kept pointing to the door."

"She didn't understand. She didn't speak his language, and he didn't speak hers. She thought perhaps he was afraid of what was in the cup. She took a sip to show him that it was nourishment; with an encouraging smile, she extended the cup to him."

"The old man sighed. He looked at her so sadly; slowly he reached out and took the proffered cup. He drank it, smiled weakly at her before returning the empty cup to her."

"She returned his smile. Pointing at herself, she told him her given name. Next she pointed at him and asked his name. She couldn't understand what he said, but she thought it surely couldn't have been a name. There were far too many syllables."

"He began once again frantically pointing to her and to the door, his utterances sounding as frightened as the look in his eyes. She knew that whatever it was, it had to be important for him to be so agitated."

"It was then he gave up in frustration. He shook his head, closed his eyes and moaned 'Mon Dieu'."

"'French,' she exclaimed; 'you speak French!'"

"She asked him, 'Parlez vous François?'"

"He nodded emphatically and said, 'Oui!'"

"She asked how he knew the French language. He smiled at her, telling her that his people had traded with the French trappers for many, many years."

"They began to talk in earnest as she dressed his wounds. He was of the Icori people; his full name was Swift White Eagle Who Soars with the Ancestors and The People. He said to call him Swift White Eagle."

"He told her he had just come from the Falls, and that she and her man were in *grave* danger."

"'This land belongs to one who is very powerful and very evil, a spirit-witch,' he said somberly; 'and she exacts a great price from any who dare to invade her land. She had been bound for many years, but has escaped her chains. I have done battle with her, and she is bound once again.'"

"'But not for long,' he said with great remorse. 'I am not as strong a guardian as the father of my father's father was. It was he that summoned the water spirits. His strength and the strength of our ancestors filled them. They were able to bind her and keep her imprisoned in the Anicaw.'"

"The young bride dismissed his story. She told him the beast that attacked him had caused him to suffer such great trauma that he imaged this story. If he rested, he would remember what kind of beast it was, and her husband would hunt it down and kill it."

"The old man's anguish turned to anger. He pushed himself up, leaning heavily against the hearth, and then sat up straight. He stared intently into the young bride's eyes."

"His voice was harsh. 'The words I speak are true.' he declared. 'I am not long for this world. The wounds she inflicted on me I cannot survive. The Spirit Horse will soon come for me. You must listen to me. You and your man are in great danger; she will soon break free from the Anicaw and will come for you. You must leave this place.'"

"Weakened and tired, the old man closed his eyes. For a long while he was silent. Just when she thought he must have fallen asleep, he looked at her and spoke. His voice was eerily calm."

"'My son and his hunting party were seeking food for our people. They knew not to come here, but they also knew our people are hungry. They followed the deer onto her land. They killed five deer and began to return home. Just as they neared the edge of her land, she appeared in a vision.'"

"'She told them to leave the deer and get off her land, or they would die. My son was defiant and told her they would not leave the deer because our people would die without the food. She laughed and mocked them. That angered our hunters; they shouted at her, argued with her. The more she mocked them, the angrier they became. They did not understand their anger fed her more quickly than had they just left. She began the drawing of their life force.'"

"Swift White Eagle sighed heavily. 'My son, Gray Owl, did a foolish thing – he took his bow, drew an arrow and shot at her. He thought he could kill her with an earthly weapon. His pride and arrogance only made her stronger. With her attention focused on Gray Owl, the others tried to run. Only one of the ten made it back to our people.'"

"'He had deep wounds, like mine, and was struggling to remain awake. He told us everything that happened. He fell into a sleep that is near death, hovering between worlds, waiting for the Spirit Horse to come for him.'"

134

"The old man paused and closed his eyes. His strength was fading. He had to rest several minutes before continuing his story."

"When he opened his eyes, there was a hint of pride and of sadness in them. 'We all know of this evil one. The father of my father's father did battle with her and won; but at great cost. He grew old rapidly and died that night in great pain, but he saved our people for many winters.'"

"'We have heeded the warning of our ancestors and stayed away from this place. From time to time, other people find their way here. From them she draws the strength to break her bonds. When she breaks free, a guardian must bind her if he has the strength. If not, he will die. She will continue to harm the living until a guardian that does have the strength comes and binds her.' Swift White Eagle's eyes misted with tears, and he fell silent."

"'You think our presence here freed her?' the young bride asked, the thought too incredulous to her to be true."

"He shrugged. 'I know that the hunting party gave her strength. Whether or not she drew strength first from you and your man is a small matter.'"

"The old man smiled sadly. 'My son and his hunting party chose to ignore the warning of our ancestors. Their hearts were good; they wanted to save our people from hunger. Winter will soon be here, and there has not been enough meat dried to last through the snows. More and more the animals come to her land because they know we will not follow them here.'"

"They both lapsed into silence. She listened to the clock on the mantle above them ticking away the minutes."

"Softly the young bride asked Swift White Eagle, 'If she draws strength from others, why didn't she draw strength from you or your great-grandfather?'"

"Swift White Eagle smiled at her, a patient smile, one such as a parent would give to a child in the midst of learning. 'I am a guardian as was my father and his father before him, and all the fathers of our line. She has great power, but her power has a limit. She can kill a guardian if he is not strong enough; but she cannot use his life force.'"

"'What happened to you?' the young bride asked him gently."

"'I had to face her, to do battle and bind her. Our medicine man prepared the sweat lodge for me. I entered and began my vision quest. I saw my ancestors who had done battle with her. The line of guardians went far into the distance, too many to count. She is an ancient evil, from the time before man was placed upon this earth. They told me to be strong in my faith in the Great Spirit, and she would be bound yet again. In my vision, they began to give to me their wisdom.'"

"Swift White Eagle sighed and moaned slightly in pain. 'She broke into my vision before I could receive their wisdom. She drew me away from the place of my ancestors to the realm where she is. I saw her there, between worlds. It is a dark place, filled with fire and smoke; the smell of death is strong there. Lightning flashed, and the thunder roared in this realm. There was a great chasm between us. She rose upwards as if to fly away. But she didn't; she floated in the air, suspended high above me. She laughed as one who is victorious. Her eyes glowed red like fire as she showed me my son and the others. She told me to come for them if I dared.... I told her I would come.'"

"'I broke the vision. My son and the others were alive, but not for long. I knew I must prepare and do so quickly. The medicine man took me to the Sacred Rock on Spirit Mountain. There we built the ceremonial Fire and asked the Great Spirit for help in the binding of the evil one, and for the freeing of our hunters.'"

"'The medicine man took ash from the ceremonial Fire and mixed it with the sacred water from the Anicaw. He took the sacred mixture and painted me with the protective signs.' He pointed to the symbols on his face, neck, and hands."

"Swift White Eagle tugged at the leather string around his neck, pulling it out from under his shirt. He held it out to her. It was an eagle carving, about four inches high, and was carved out of white oak."

"The young bride marveled at the precision and detail of the carving. She held it, and her fingers lightly traced over its surface. It was so smooth, gleaming from the hours spent honing it to perfection."

"The eagle's wings were outstretched as if it were in mid-flight. In its talons was a large staff that touched the top of a deeply carved semi-circle. The wavy lines that surrounded and flowed across the semi-circle symbolized water. The totem seemed to suggest that the eagle was holding something or someone down in the water."

"'The medicine man blessed my totem,' the old man told her; 'it is a gift from the servants of the Great Spirit. In ancient days, it was given to the first guardian to protect his soul from the evil one during battle. It has been handed down from guardian to guardian since that time.'"

"After tucking the carving back under his shirt, he continued with his story. 'Next the medicine man wove eagle feathers into my hair to protect my mind from her powers. He held the Belt of Wisdom before the ceremonial Fire, then raised it up to the Great Spirit. He asked the Great Spirit to grant me the wisdom of all my ancestors in order to defeat this evil one. He placed the belt around my waist.'"

"'The medicine man placed the sacred breastplate upon me, sprinkling it with the sacred water and with ash from the ceremonial fire. It would shield my heart, my soul, from the evil one. Then he fastened around my ankles the feathers of a young eagle that I may be swift in my pursuit of her, enabling me to be faster than she. He handed me the sacred spirit catcher to absorb her power, to render her harmless. Last he handed me the staff, the sacred staff handed down from father to son since the beginning.'"

"Swift White Eagle was tired; he leaned back and closed his eyes. The young bride anxiously watched him; not certain of what to do or what to say. After several minutes, he opened his eyes and smiled at her. He could see that she had a good soul."

"'I was ready for battle', he spoke softly. 'I began my journey to the Falls, confident in my coming victory. The presence of our hunters and their actions gave her enough power to break free. From them she will draw enough strength to return her power to that of the ancient days. Not until I saw your lodge,' he paused slightly as sadness filled his face; 'did I know why her powers had grown enough to capture our hunting party.'"

"The young bride started to object but he held up his hand, motioning for her to be silent."

"'My time is short. I must tell you the rest before the Spirit Horse comes for me. You must believe my words. If you do not, you and your man will die.' He spoke sharply, as if he were correcting an errant child."

"'I did battle with her, and I have won for a short time. Her power is great; far greater than my strength. I could not give the water spirits what they needed to keep her bound. Soon she will break that binding, and then she will strive to break free from the Anicaw. I was able to free our hunters. I have sent them to our people, to warn them to leave this valley before she breaks free from the Anicaw. She will seek revenge.'"

"Swift White Eagle looked at her with such compassion that it moved her to tears. He spoke gently. 'Before the Spirit Horse comes for me, I had to warn you of the danger. I told our hunters to return without me. We have said our goodbyes, and my son will convey my last thoughts to our people.'"

"He smiled reassuringly at her, patting her hand as her tears began to stream down her face."

"'You must leave here,' he repeated urgently. 'She will continue to draw from the life force of you and your man. Soon she will be free, and she will kill you both. She will offer you as a sacrifice to her master, and her powers will be greater than ever. I do not know who would ever be able to stand against her.'"

"He shook his head in bewilderment. 'I do not understand why her power did not return in full before the hunting party arrived. You have been here some time, yes?'"

"She nodded. 'Yes,' she said quietly. 'We've been here six months.'"

"He sighed. 'I do not understand. She should have been free long ago.'"

"'What about your son?' she asked him. 'Why can't he bind her?'"

"The old man smiled wistfully. 'Gray Owl, though he is my son, he has never believed in the power of the Great Spirit. He is truly a great warrior among men. He is the best hunter in our tribe, and no other can match his skills in battle. Although the blood of the guardians flows through him, he cannot fight the evil one. He has never chosen to learn the wisdom of our ancestors, and weapons of this world cannot defeat evil.'"

"The aged warrior sighed heavily. 'It has grieved my heart greatly that my son has chosen not to follow the path of my fathers. He has chosen the path of this world. He has done what is right for him, and what he thinks is right for our people.'"

"The old man felt both sorrow and a sense of pride as he continued; 'He is the greatest of warriors in this world, and has earned a place of honor among our people. It saddens me to know that I am the last of the guardians. I do not know what will happen to my people when I go to be with my ancestors.'"

"Swift White Eagle began coughing. He sank back against the hearth. The young bride studiously watched him. His strength was fading quickly. His breaths were short and laborious."

"Sadness filled his eyes as he contemplated her fate and that of her man. 'I know you do not believe. I grieve the loss this world will bear when you die. You are a good soul and have a kind heart.' He sighed, one of surrender to fate, and closed his eyes."

"'If I were to believe you, what would I need to do to stop her?'"

"Surprised, the old man opened one eye. He closed it again, made a snorting sound and shook his head as if to tell her she was foolish. 'Nothing,' he stated, 'you are not a guardian.'"

"'How do you know that I wasn't led here for this very purpose?' she countered."

"Swift White Eagle struggled to sit upright and, with her help, he did so. He shook his head and laughed softly. 'You are brave, Little One,' he responded affectionately; 'like a white dove. Perhaps that is your spirit name.'"

"She smiled at him. 'Perhaps,' she said. 'Now tell me what I must do.'"

"The old man vehemently shook his head. 'Even if you are a guardian, there is no medicine man here to provide you the tools you need for protection and for battle. You cannot do it,' he stated emphatically. He folded his arms across his chest to signal the matter was closed."

"'Yes, I can,' she said softly but firmly. 'In my people's faith, such evil can be bound through faith in the Almighty One.'"

"From the set of her jaw, Swift White Eagle knew she meant it. He feared for her. She was not trained in such matters. 'It would be better for you and your man to leave,' he said flatly. 'You must leave. You are no match for this evil one.'"

"Swift White Eagle fell quiet and released a heavy sigh, one that was racked with pain. Turning his head, he gazed out the window. He sat motionless for a few minutes before turning to look at her. Sadly he said, 'My time is over. I hear the whinny of the Spirit Horse. He comes for me.'"

"'Not yet,' she retorted hotly. She stood, pulling him up with her. 'Honestly, I don't understand this attitude of surrender. Where's your faith? You're coming with me; and we're going to put an end to her, great evil or not.'"

"The old man started to protest, but knew that it would be useless. She had a strong spirit, and he could sense that she would not be deterred. He leaned heavily on her and out the door they went."

"They stepped off the porch just as her husband came out from the barn. He saw them, and his face was filled with concern. Anxiously he asked, 'Where are you going?' as he ran to them."

"'I don't have time to explain,' she answered hastily in French. 'He speaks French, and his name is Swift White Eagle. We must hurry. We have to stop an evil water spirit that resides in the Falls.'"

"The young husband looked at her and at the old man as if they had lost their minds."

"With a nod of his head, the old man told him, 'She speaks the truth.'"

"'Please, hurry,' she pleaded with her husband while attempting to pull him toward the path. 'I'll explain as we go.'"

"And so she did. By the time they reached the pool below the Falls, she had relayed everything to her husband ... with Swift White Eagle's help of course," the Reverend added with a wink.

Reverend Tillman paused briefly. Lifting his eyes up toward the ceiling, he raised one hand high up over his head, as if he were reaching for the sky.

"It was now mid-day," he continued in a quickened tone. "The sun was high in the heavens."

In a swift, fluid motion, the Reverend suddenly leaned down toward the children, startling them. Stretching out his arms and wiggling his fingers, he simulated the water's movements.

"Its bright light was dancing off of the water, glittering as if tiny diamonds were floating across its surface. The mist was rising, swirling and pulsating like a living thing."

"With the help of the young man, Swift White Eagle raised his hands to the heavens and began to chant, praying for the help of the Great Spirit. The young bride fell to her knees, praying to The Almighty One for His protection and for deliverance from the evil spirit-witch."

140

"Suddenly, there she was! She was visible in the mist. The drops of water were glistening and sparkling all around her. Her raven black hair floated gently out and around her as if it was being carried by invisible streams of water."

"She laughed with merriment at the three who came to challenge her. Her vivid blue eyes glowed, and sparks flashed within them."

"'Hello, Swift White Eagle,' she spoke with feigned affection. 'I see you have brought me gifts. How sweet! Perhaps I will spare you after all.'"

"Her laughter rang out, echoing in their minds. 'I have not seen such as these in many millennia. I am most pleased, Swift White Eagle,' she cooed to him."

"The evil creature turned her attention to the young man. Her voice became melodiously sweet and deceptively alluring."

"'Come to me,' she called to him as she held out her arms to him."

"'Do not listen with your physical ears,' the old man instructed. 'Use your spirit ears, or she will own you.'"

"The evil creature laughed again, greatly amused at his advice. She began slowly spinning around, arms outstretched. Her smile became sinister as she glared at them through the veil of miniscule drops of water. The mist began to swirl around her, becoming thicker and thicker as she drew more water up from the pool below. Streams of water now rose upwards, flowing constantly around her in a figure eight pattern."

"She raised her arms above her head, spinning faster and faster until the water took on a different form. Magically she transformed the water, cohering it into a translucent blue gown. It looked incredibly beautiful as it billowed and swirled around her in the air."

"Gone was the mist that held her; she was free. Her laughter cackled and cracked like the sound of a whip snapping in the air. She hovered high above them, and they beheld a creature whose beauty had no equal."

"Her skin was milky white and had the appearance of the smoothest, softest silk. Her large, cat-like eyes were a bright blue and exquisitely framed with sweeping black eyelashes. Long and thick, her luxurious black hair shimmered and gleamed in the light, flowing delicately on the air currents. The elegance and grace of her movements were as beguiling as was the sound of her voice. She looked like a goddess."

"'Come, my sweet,' she said softly, enticing the young man. 'I will give you power and wealth. I will make your life full and exciting. Come to me, and I will give you whatever you desire.'" Her smile was deceivingly sweet, but her eyes were deathly cold, devoid of all truth."

"She beckoned him with her arms, stretching them out to him and then pulling them back to her heart. Her spell was cast; her web woven. The young man, enraptured, began to slowly walk to her. He could not hear the words of the old man, nor those of his bride. The closer he came to the evil spirit-witch, the greater her power over him grew."

"Swift White Eagle began his chant once again. Louder and louder he chanted his prayer to the Great Spirit. He began the binding spell though he no longer had the ritual powders, the staff or the spirit catcher to aid him in his quest. He knew the Great Spirit honors those that have faith in Him, those that believe He hears and answers. So Swift White Eagle placed all of his hope and faith in the Great Spirit, praying his faith alone would be enough to capture the attention of the Great Spirit. And if his faith was strong enough, the Great Spirit would then honor his faith and answer him."

"As Swift White Eagle prayed, the young bride ran to her husband and pushed him back from the water's edge. He fell and struck his head on a rock. It was just a glancing blow; enough to break the skin, but not enough to cause serious harm. He sat there by the water's edge, dazed and with a vacant stare in his eyes."

"The evil one laughed and sneered at the young bride. 'He belongs to me,' she declared."

"'No, he doesn't!' the young bride challenged."

"'We shall see,' the evil one retorted arrogantly. Again she called out her sweet siren song to the young man. He stood up and, once more, began to walk toward her.

"Her laughter was shrill and loud; its malevolent sound echoed throughout the land. The forest became deathly silent and still. No longer were the birds singing, or the squirrels playing. The rabbits hid in their burrows, and nothing moved."

"The young bride turned around and cried out to Swift White Eagle. 'Get him out of here. Do it now!' she commanded."

142

"The evil one lowered herself behind the young bride, not more than ten feet from her. She started laughing, a low guttural noise that sounded much more like a growl than a laugh. It sent shivers through the young bride."

"Slowly the young bride turned around. Bravely she stared into those cruel, wicked eyes. Her heart was racing, pounding in her chest, but she summoned the courage from deep within and did not flinch."

"Swift White Eagle had now reached the young man and was attempting to get him to leave. The evil spirit-witch smiled; its insidiousness caused the young bride to shudder. But she stood her ground."

"'Do you really think you are a match for me?' the evil one contemptuously asked the young bride."

"Before the young bride could answer, the evil one thrust her hand forward, hard and fast, toward the men. They flew backwards through the air as if they had been struck by a powerful blow. They tumbled, rolling several hundred feet before they came to a halt."

"The young bride never took her eyes away from the evil one, watching through the reflection in those cold, glassy eyes. The young bride called out in a loud voice to the men, 'Are you both all right?'"

"Swift White Eagle slowly rose to his feet. 'Yes,' he responded, pulling the young man up and propping him against a rock. The young man seemed confused and disoriented."

"The old man reached down into the water's edge and wet his fingers. He quickly mixed it with the ash symbols on the back of his hand. He began a chant, low and soft, as he moved toward the young man. With the ash mixture on his finger, he began painting four interlocking circles on the young man's forehead. Inside each circle he painted a symbol. His chant changed and became louder until the young man collapsed on the ground, dropping into a deep sleep."

"Swift White Eagle began quickly walking back toward the young bride. His strength was continuing to fade, but he knew she needed him. He had to help her before it was too late."

"'Do you think you can defeat me?' the evil one snarled at Swift White Eagle. 'Your paltry, little spells are no match for my power.'"

"To the young bride, she scowled and pointed to the ground. 'Bow to me now,' she demanded; 'and I will spare you. If you do not, I will sacrifice you and offer your blood to my master. He will reward me handsomely for such an offering. Your man will be my slave forever, and I will torture this foolish old man for a very long time before I sacrifice him as well.'"

"Swift White Eagle stared hard at the evil one, perplexed at her words. He shouted, 'You have no power to sacrifice a guardian. You know this. If I expend all my strength in battle against you and die, I cross over to my ancestors. You have no power to draw my life force into yourself. You gain nothing from the shedding of my blood. Why would you lie to her?'"

"The old man looked at the evil spirit-witch and then at the young bride. ... He smiled. 'Unless,' he said; 'she, too, is a guardian. If she submits to you, you have a slave forever; one who's strengths can be used for evil. But you still cannot draw her life force, ever, so why do you lie?'"

"'Be silent!' she growled at him."

"In a flash the understanding unfolded in his mind. 'You fear her!' he proclaimed to the evil one, pointing at the malevolent creature. 'You want her to submit to you because you fear her.'"

"Turning to the young bride, Swift White Eagle told her, 'For her to fear you so, you must be a powerful guardian even if you do not know that you are.'"

"The evil spirit-witch was enraged. Throwing her head back, she released a shriek that chilled their very souls. Her eyes turned a glowing red as if a raging fire blazed inside them. She began to contort into her true form."

"Her skin changed from a silky appearance to one of thick scales, ashen green in color with erratically spaced blotches of black spots. Small tufts of short black hair, more like bristles, grew out of the spots."

"Flowing, beautiful hair turned into long, spear-like stalks with deadly barbs on the ends. They moved like snakes, seeking the best opportunity in which to strike its victim."

"Her head began to elongate and widen, becoming grotesquely dis-torted. Those flaming red eyes grew to triple their previous size and bulged outward, giving the appearance that they would pop right out of their sockets. Her ears stretched upwards and then narrowed into sharp points. What once was an elegantly, sleek nose twisted and shortened into a form similar to the snout of a wild boar. Her cheekbones jutted out almost as prominently as her massive jaw with its saber-like fangs and teeth that resembled daggers."

"Arms that were slim and graceful became gangly and misshapen. The upper arms shortened while the forearm extended to where her hands were now even with her feet. Talon-like six inch claws, razor sharp and black as coal, protruded from her gnarled fingers and toes. Thin tendrils of smoke emanated from the tips of those deadly claws."

"Instead of the pleasant floral fragrance that had permeated the air, the creature now emitted an odor of sulfur and the stench of rotting flesh. Gone was the incomparable beauty; in its wake was the hideous, true appearance of the evil creature."

"Thrusting herself high into the air, she pointed at them, screeching, 'You fools; you have no idea of the extent of my power. But you will soon learn.'"

"Swift White Eagle began his prayer chant, calling upon the Great Spirit to grant them protection and to bind the evil one."

"She laughed derisively at him, calling upon the forces of darkness to come to her and to do her bidding. Then she called upon the ancient evils, each by name, eliciting their help."

"The sun was blotted out; darkness descended upon the land like a thick, black shroud as the demons entered our world en masse. The air turned freezing cold and dank, such as one would encounter in a tomb. Howling like a wolf pack, the wind blew in great gusts around them. As the winds increased, the howling became terrifying shrieks as if the sounds coursed up from the bowels of hell itself. The young bride shivered, not so much from the icy coldness of the air, but more so from the terrifying images that the sounds conveyed."

"Lightning flashed as the evil witch hurled the demon fire at them. Smoke and sulfur filled the air each time one struck the ground… And each one missed its intended target."

"Her rage grew with each failure. She clapped her monstrous hands together; and each time thunder rolled in a shock wave through the valley, destroying everything in its path…. But it did not harm them. She commanded trees and boulders be uprooted, sending the projectiles careening toward them… It was also in vain, for each deadly object bounced above them and was deflected away. It was as if they were encompassed by invisible cages."

"The young bride stared in stunned silence. Though she could hear and see what was happening, it just did not seem real. She could feel the icy coldness of the air, feel the wind tearing at her and hear its howling as it swirled around her. And even though she could smell the sulfur and the stench of this creature, it just seemed surreal.... like something out of a nightmare."

"She stared and stared, trying to grasp hold of the strange reality displayed in front of her. And then, slowly, the sound of his voice broke through the walls of her mind."

"Swift White Eagle continued his prayers, thanking the Great Spirit for granting them protection. He asked again for the Great Spirit to bind the evil one."

"'You think you can defeat me,' she roared at him. 'I am just getting started!'"

"The evil creature disappeared, immediately reappearing directly in front of Swift White Eagle. "'Foolish old man,' she jeered; 'this time I will kill you; you will suffer much before you die.'"

"Swift White Eagle was unshaken. He looked right into those evil eyes and that hideous face, undeterred by the sight of her and the stench of her. With absolute confidence he said, 'The only power you have over me is that which the Great Spirit allows. He wrote the days of my life before I was born. I will join my ancestors at the appointed time.'"

"Ignoring her, he closed his eyes and returned to his prayer chants."

"She howled in anger. Her nostrils flared, and her eyes glowed brighter with the intense hatred that swelled within her. 'I will destroy you, old man,' she hissed at him. As she spoke, streams of spittle discharged from between her fangs and teeth, like a cobra spewing its venom. As the poisonous spray fell onto the plants, they abruptly withered, turned black and then died. But none of it touched Swift White Eagle."

"Swift White Eagle's chant began to change; he began to ask the Great Spirit to grant the young bride understanding and wisdom. He asked the Great Spirit to give her the strength to help him defeat the ancient evil."

"The evil creature's anger grew; she called upon her master, the overlord of evil for this land. While chanting prayers to her master, her countenance became eerily dark as the evil grew stronger within her being. She clenched her hulking paws and bared her ghastly teeth at Swift White Eagle. A low, menacing rumble began to emanate from her as she thrust herself at him. With one swipe she sent him lurching backwards. The second blow sent him flying through the air, crashing against a tree several hundred yards away."

"Instantly the evil one was face to face with the young bride, startling the young bride. The evil spirit-witch cackled."

"'Why aren't you begging for help like the old man? Or have you finally realized you can't defeat me?' she sneered. 'Bow to me now!' she snarled at the young bride."

"Even though the putrid stench of the creature was sickening, the young bride stood her ground. She stared face to face with the evil one and did not recoil. Calmly she responded, 'It isn't my place to defeat you. That is the place of my God, the Almighty One; the Creator of all things. And He has already done so. You have no power over me or over Swift White Eagle. By the authority of the Almighty One, and through the power of His Holy Name, I bind you. Return to the Abyss from which you came.'"

The Reverend's voice changed again, carrying the essence of surprise. "Suddenly the evil spirit-witch began shrieking and clawing desperately at the air all around her."

"'No!' she screamed repeatedly. For several minutes she struggled hard against unseen forces. She screeched a piercing, blood-curdling sound, and then ... poof ... she was gone."

"The sun was back again, bright in the sky. The air returned to its normal, afternoon temperature. The howling winds ceased, and everything returned to the way it had been."

Reverend Tillman stopped and smiled at his audience; they were completely engrossed in the story. He waited a few seconds before leaning forward and whispering, "It's said that when the mist rises and falls in a rhythmic pattern, it's her, trying to get free once more. When you see the pool breathing in that manner ... beware. Stay away, or she will use your life force to break free from the mist."

Reverend Tillman sat back, signaling the story was finished. His grin was one of satisfaction.

"What happened to Swift White Eagle?" some children asked, and some wanted to know what happened to the young couple. Others wanted to know the names of the young couple, and still others wanted to know the name of the evil spirit-witch.

He chuckled. "Well, Swift White Eagle didn't die; at least, not right away. He lived a good many years after that day. The legend is that he heard the Spirit Horse coming for him just after the evil spirit-witch was defeated. He asked the young bride to pray for him, for his healing. She did, and the Spirit Horse passed him by."

"The young couple insisted that Swift White Eagle return with them to the cabin; he needed to eat and to rest before attempting to find his people. When they reached the cabin, it was destroyed. The barn, too, was gone. Their animals had fled to the safety of the forest and began returning upon seeing the young couple approach. They salvaged what they could, and she prepared a meal for them while the young man made preparations for Swift White Eagle to travel."

"The old man asked them to join his people because the snows would come before the young couple would be able to build another cabin. The young man gave heed to Swift White Eagle's words, accepting his kind offer. He agreed that they would stay with the Icori through the winter, but would move on come spring."

"After they ate, they packed as much provisions from the root cellar as two of the horses could safely carry. They built small crates and placed as many chickens as they could in them and tied the crates to the travois they had made. Then they hitched the travois to the plow horses. The young bride had been steadily working on rope harnesses and collars as the men accomplished the building projects. Swift White Eagle was impressed with her skill; he smiled and nodded his approval. He and the young man placed the harnesses on the cows, securely tying their leads together. They placed the rope collars on the pigs and tied those leads together also. Finally they were ready to leave."

"The young man gave to Swift White Eagle the white stallion, a strong and spirited horse. He handed the old man the leads for the horses that were harnessed with the travois. The elder Icori tribesman began slowly guiding his horses on their journey. Riding a pale gray horse, the young bride held the leads for the pack horses and followed Swift White Eagle. Last to leave was the young man; he paused briefly, looking back at what once was their world. He sighed heavily; and with a fierce look of determination on his face, he guided his black mare onward, pulling the lead for the cattle and for the pigs, leading them away from their devastated farm."

"They arrived at the camp of the Icori people late that night. They were very fortunate to have found the tribe when they did. At daybreak the camp would be moving, heading further west. Everyone celebrated the return of Swift White Eagle and for the food brought to them. But, most especially, they celebrated the wonderful news that the evil spirit-witch was defeated. Swift White Eagle told his wife and son that he wanted to adopt the couple, make them a part of their family and a part of the tribe. They agreed, and Swift White Eagle presented their request to the tribal council. The council agreed and called for a tribal meeting, presenting the request to the people. The people agreed, celebrating and accepting the young couple as children of Swift White Eagle and his squaw, brother and sister to Gray Owl."

"Three days after he had returned to his people, Swift White Eagle had a visit from a holy one. As was his daily custom, he had gone to the River at daybreak to offer his prayers to the Great Spirit. When he finished, he started back toward his village."

"Suddenly, from nowhere, she appeared. There was a radiant, white hue around her; her face glowed like the sun, and her fawn-colored skin sparkled in the early morning light. Her long, black hair softly rose and fell with the gentle breeze that wafted through the meadow. She moved so gracefully it was as if she was walking on air."

"She approached him slowly, singing an ancient song. The words he did not understand, but the singing of them imparted in him a joy and a peace such as he had never known. Her voice was so beautiful, so perfect that tears filled his eyes. She spoke, and her speaking voice was as melodious as chimes floating on the wind. She told him she was sent to bring him a message from the Great Spirit."

"At first he thought he was seeing a vision. He closed his eyes and rubbed them several times. When he opened them, he saw her smiling at him. She held out her hand to him, instructing him to touch her so that he could see that she was no vision.

"He did. She was real. He marveled at this iridescent being. He bowed to her, overwhelmed by the presence of this holy one. She instructed him to stand, telling him that she was merely a servant of the Great Spirit. He obeyed and stood."

"She told him his prayers have been answered. Smiling, she told him that his son would learn the path of the Guardians, that he and his descendants would be great spiritual warriors. Swift White Eagle rejoiced at the news, thanking the Great Spirit that the line of the Guardians would continue. Her smile broadened as she waited patiently. When he ended his prayer of thanksgiving, she announced that the Great Spirit had also sent the young woman to him. He was to teach her their ways, passing his knowledge on to her. Through her and her descendants, a different line of guardians would emerge and continue. The holy one told Swift White Eagle that he and his people must learn from the young woman; she also had much wisdom to give."

"'Show me,' she commanded him; 'the symbol of the guardians.'"

"Swift White Eagle pulled the totem out from under his shirt and held it out to her."

"'As a sign to your people, so that they may know your words are true, this totem will shine from within. When her child is born, it will cease. On that day, she will become a guardian as will all her descendants.'"

"She stretched her hand toward the totem. It began to emit a soft glow as if somehow it had captured the sun."

"Then, as suddenly as the holy one had appeared, she was gone. She vanished before his eyes."

"Quickly he returned to the village and relayed to his people what he saw and heard. He showed them the totem, shining bright, lit by a holy fire. The Icori celebrated the visit of the holy one, and the news that the young bride would have a child."

"They taught the young bride the ways of the Icori and of the guardians. She was eager to learn, and she absorbed quickly all the wisdom that he and the medicine man knew. And they were just as eager to learn from her, so she taught them the customs and beliefs of her people."

"The following spring the young bride gave birth to her first child, a daughter. As soon as the baby took her first breath, two amazing things

150

happened. A faint smudge instantly appeared on the child's right cheek, and then the totem stopped glowing, just as the holy one had said."

"From his medicine bag, Swift White Eagle removed a totem he had carved for the child. The beautifully carved totem was suspended from a braided rawhide strap. Swift White Eagle showed the totem to the young mother, telling her of its meaning. She smiled and nodded. He kissed the totem and gently placed it around the child's neck."

"They remained with the Icori for two more winters. The spring that followed the second winter, the holy one returned. This time Swift White Eagle was not alone; he was with the child and the young mother, walking along the River bank. It was early morning, and the dew was still on the grass."

"The holy one appeared in a burst of light. They were startled, but the child wasn't; she ran to the holy one, arms outstretched, and hugged her. The holy one laughed, lifted her up and returned the embrace. She gently handed the child to the astonished young mother."

"The holy one told the young mother it was time for her to leave the Icori, that she would be guided by the Great Spirit to a place where they were to settle."

"The young mother was distressed and told the holy one that she feared for the safety of the Icori."

"The holy one's smile was patient, and her voice was as sweet as honey. 'You are to be a guardian of this world, not of the Icori. If you choose not to be a guardian, the Great Spirit will anoint another; the land will be in darkness until then. Either way, it is time for you to leave the Icori. They have their path, just as you have yours.'"

"Swift White Eagle placed his hand on the young mother's shoulder. He spoke softly. 'We will do as the Great Spirit asks.'"

"The young mother smiled through her tears, telling the holy one, 'Yes, I will follow the path set for me. It is my honor and privilege to be His servant.'"

"Stretching out her hand toward the child, the holy one commanded, 'Give to me the child's totem.'"

"Perplexed, the young mother started to ask 'why?', but Swift White Eagle quickly complied, removing the totem and gave it to her."

"In her hands the totem began to softly glow. She closed her hands around it, completely covering the totem. Raising her face heavenward, she began to sing a song, one that infused the soul with joy and peace, with strength and hope. In a steady, deliberate motion, she lifted her hands upwards, holding them just above her head. As the holy one opened her hands, she continued her song. In an instant the totem burst into a radiant light, streaming its brilliance outward like a miniature sun. Gradually the light dissipated until the totem was glowing again with just a soft hue."

"Smiling at the child, the holy one returned the totem to the child. One minute it was in her hand, the next it was around the child's neck. The little child laughed and laughed, clapping her hands and wanting the holy one to do it again. The holy one laughed with the child, telling her that once was enough. It was then that the holy one instructed the young mother that she was to never remove the totem. She told the young mother that when they reached the place they were to settle, another messenger would come. That one would teach her many things."

"The holy one disappeared; once again she left as miraculously as she had arrived."

"Ten years later, in mid-spring, a group of settlers arrived near where the young couple had their farm and began building a settlement. The Icori came to greet them, bringing them food and livestock as welcoming gifts. They asked the settlers if anyone had seen the young couple or knew of them. No one did. Swift White Eagle relayed to them the story of the evil spirit-witch of the Mist, and how together they were able to defeat that ancient evil."

"Why didn't the evil spirit-witch break free when those other people came?" asked Aaron.

The Reverend grinned. "Because, according to Swift White Eagle, the young bride's spirit was very strong, very powerful. Her faith was so strong that she enabled the water sprite's powers to bind together, making them much stronger than they were individually. The combining of their powers prevents the evil spirit-witch from breaking free from the Abyss."

"Forever?" several children asked nervously.

Reverend Tillman chuckled. "I believe so. However," his tone now became ominous as he leaned toward them; "some people believe that calling out her name when the mist rises will release her. But the legend says," he whispered now, speaking very softly; "there are only three ways that she can be released. If you go to the Falls during a full moon and call her name three times while spinning counter-clockwise, she will be freed. Or, if you go there during a Blue Moon and call her name four times, that will also free her."

He paused for effect, hunching down and looking around the room as if hiding from someone. "According to the Legend, the most powerful time to free her is during a Blood Moon. Performing a very specific rite will free her and restore all of her power. ... But don't tell anyone," he added with a twinkle in his eyes as he pressed his index finger to his lips; "or she might come and get us all."

"O-o-oh," Simon shivered fearfully and pressed hard against Susie, burying his face. Susie whispered in his ear, "It's just a story, Simon; you're safe."

"What's a Blood Moon?" asked Jared as Megan blurted "How can the moon bleed?"

The adults laughed, and various ones responded "it doesn't."

"Does anyone know what a Blood Moon is?" the Reverend queried, first looking at the adults and then at the children.

Jose raised his hand. "I know... I know!" he excitedly proclaimed.

"Okay, Jose," the Reverend responded with a chuckle. "Tell us what a Blood Moon is."

Jose sat up very straight and pushed his glasses back up to their proper place. "It's a total lunar eclipse. The color depends on how much dust, and dirt or ash is in the atmosphere, refracting the light. The dirtier the air is, the more the moon appears red. Clouds can also affect the color."

"You are correct, Jose," Reverend Tillman praised him, nodding his head approvingly. (Jose beamed.) "However, the full moon in October has also been called a Blood Moon, though most of the time it's referred to as a Hunter's Moon. Does anyone know why?"

The children all slowly shook their heads; all that is except for Jose. He again raised his hand, waving it.

"Does anyone besides Jose know?" he asked.

None of the children volunteered.

"Jose, stand and tell us why," the Reverend said as he smiled at him. Jose was his chess partner, and he never ceased to be amazed at this young man's mental acuity and agility.

Jose ceremoniously stood as if he were giving a presentation in class. "Because of the earth's relative position to the orbit of the moon, the moon rises sooner in the sky thus leaving no period of darkness between sunset and moonrise. Hunters were able to hunt for a longer time because of the extended period of light. Because they killed animals, some called it a Blood Moon instead of Hunter's Moon." He gave a quick nod of his head and a slight bow, signaling he was finished and then sat down. Everyone clapped.

Dani asked, "What's a Blue Moon?"

"Mrs. Coppersmith cleared her throat and softly said, "I've always heard it's a full moon on Halloween."

"True," Reverend Tillman said with a nod. "A full moon on Halloween is always a Blue Moon because that means it's the second full moon of the month which would also makes it the second full moon of the season. Generally, a Blue Moon is the second full moon in a season."

"What's her name?" Kat asked mischievously.

"Don't say it … don't say it," the other children implored Reverend Tillman.

He laughed. "I don't think we have anything to worry about even if I knew it … which I don't," he told them.

"Where did they go after they left the Icori?" Juls asked.

The Reverend shrugged. "Not sure. Some people think they started Rosemont or Turtle Pond. They're both slightly older than Micah's Landing. But it could have just as easily been Willow Creek, Eagle's Ridge, Deer Hollow or Flat Rock Creek."

"How long has Glen Hollow been here?" Susie asked Miss Pritchett.

Surprised, Miss Pritchett responded, "A little more than three hundred years, in some form or fashion. Originally my ancestors settled closer to the Anicaw Falls because the sound reminded them of the ocean sounds along the East coast. According to family history, their first home was a log house built in 1690, and it was added to several times. Additional log houses were built as needed as the family grew. The manor and the other buildings were started in 1840 and completed in 1852."

"How come they built such a big house?" Simon asked.

Miss Pritchett smiled. "Well, Simon; my mother's great-great-great grandmother had intended for all of the family to live together in one house. There were a lot of family members back then, so they needed a large house. It wasn't until about 1900 that they began moving away to cities, mostly to the larger cities. Some became architects, teachers, ministers, doctors and dentists – just a variety of different vocations other than farming."

She paused briefly and winked at Simon. "Not everyone likes living on a farm."

Grinning, Simon continued his inquiry. "How many brothers and sisters do you have?"

"Sadly, none, Simon. I'm an only child, as was my mother and my grandmother," she responded softly.

"It's because of Glen Hollow that Foxboro Station came to be," Reverend Tillman added. "There were no towns, so the Evermores built a staging depot where all the supplies, and materials and people could be brought before being taken out to the construction site. A freight depot and warehouse were built along with rooming houses, diners, a livery stable, a blacksmith shop and some other businesses sprung up too. After a few years, the railroad decided they were missing out on revenue so they built a station. Good thing, too, because they were able to move materials and supplies in much faster than with the freight wagons. It helped to reduce the time it took to build all of this."

He had once again captured the children's attention. All of them began asking if it was true, and how he knew it was true.

"Miss Pritchett's family kept a detailed record of all of their business transactions, including the construction of the manor and the other buildings," he answered.

"He's right," Miss Pritchett confirmed. "In my office I have all of those old records. They're very interesting because it isn't just a record of the cost of the construction; but they also recorded what happened each day."

"Why did the railroad name it Foxboro Station?" asked Jared.

"They didn't," Miss Pritchett answered, grinning. "The men that were building the freight depot found an empty fox den not far from the site, so they named it in honor of the foxes."

"Did the foxes come back?" Simon asked.

"No, Simon; once people came, the foxes found another place to live. Since the foxes gave up their home for the people to live and work, the station was named in their honor. The railroad kept the name because it was already well known by people, freight and stage lines and postal carriers. Eventually it grew large enough to become a town, and the people decided to keep the name. "

Although Susie had heard this portion of the conversation, it wasn't as interesting as the questions that kept her mind preoccupied. Her thoughts had been racing, whirling around a bizarre notion; could Glen Hollow be the ancestral home of that young couple? "What were the names of the young couple?" she asked the Reverend.

He smiled at her. "I don't recall their surnames; I'm not certain I ever knew it. The Journal states his given name was Brian, and hers was Brigit. But who knows?" he shrugged and grinned.

"Did it really happen?" Timmy asked, trying hard not to be afraid.

"Yes, it did," Simon said somberly, his voice soft and low. He was staring nearly trance-like into the fire.

"Well now, it's just a story," chirped Mrs. Coppersmith. "You children needn't worry about it. Nothing at all true of it; there are no witches, and certainly nothing evil is going to happen to you while you're here with us."

She wagged her index finger at Miss Pritchett and Reverend Tillman. Her clipped tone and curt manner registered her disapproval of such stories. "This is why I objected to the telling of it. It serves no useful purpose – it only frightens the little ones."

"Mrs. Coppersmith--," Miss Pritchett began and was interrupted by the Reverend.

"Allow me, please, Eloise?" he asked.

"By all means," she said, deferring to him.

"Mrs. Coppersmith," he began to explain in a gentle voice; "first of all, it serves the purpose of entertainment. As to the veracity of the tale, there are many recorded happenings throughout history that seem just as fantastic. However, there is the matter of Micah McBride's journal in which he recorded the tale, including the initial meeting that he and the others had with the Icori and their friendship afterwards."

"*The Journal*," Mrs. Coppersmith snorted. "Everyone acts as if it's the Gospel Book. For all anyone knows, it was just a story he made up to entertain his children."

"Actually, Mrs. Coppersmith," Miss Emma interjected; "his journal isn't the only record of the story. His has far more detail, but that's probably due to his friendship with Swift White Eagle. There are other sources that mention the couple, the Icori and the great battle."

"None with any more credibility than that journal, or any other tall tale," Mrs. Coppersmith retorted.

"My grandmother, White Dove Song, is Icori," Mr. Henry spoke softly; "full-blooded, too. She tells us the story every spring and every fall. It's a tribal tradition among the Icori to commemorate the defeat of the enemy, and the blessing of a new guardian." He looked up and smiled at the Reverend. "She didn't have a way of storytelling like the Reverend, but she has essentially told the same story."

"She believes it?" asked Miss Cora.

Mr. Henry nodded slowly. "Yes, she does. I recall her telling that her maternal ancestor was present at the birth of the child, and assisted in the birthing. And, if I remember correctly, it was about ten generations back from my grandmother, making me generation number thirteen."

He laughed as he said, "If I were superstitious, I'd be worried that my generation will see the return of the evil witch." With a playful wink to the children, he added reassuringly, "But I'm not superstitious, and I am not worried."

"My mother's line has always incorporated a part of the child's tribal name into the naming of their daughters," he added.

"Really?" Susie asked. "What was the child's name?"

He shook his head and gave a brief shrug of his shoulders. "I don't know, Susie. My grandmother might, but I doubt it." Mr. Henry glanced over at Samuel and Kevin, who had both remained quiet during the exchange. "Didn't your parents or grandparents ever speak of the Legend?" he asked quizzically. "I'm certain Kenatae has."

"Well, now that you ask," Kevin began as he stretched out his long legs, crossed them at his ankles, folded his arms across his chest and leaned comfortably back into his chair. "I can't remember a time when they didn't speak of it. The Tribal Council is considering a petition that requests Tribal sacred day status for March 9th and September 13th."

Grinning at his cousin, Kevin moved his left leg and gently prodded Samuel's foot with the toe of his boot. He quipped, "Father said that Dancing Sky Dove is planning the schedule of festivities."

This news surprised Samuel and Elsa, but neither of them responded.

"Who's Dancing Sky Dove?" Susie asked.

"My Mother," Samuel answered concurrently with Kevin's reply, "My Aunt."

"Will the festivals be only for the Icori, or will they be open to the public?" Miss Pritchett inquired.

"That's one of the issues being debated," Kevin answered as he sat up straight in his chair when addressing her. "Some are of a mind that the days belong only to the Icori since The People have kept the tradition alive. The majority believe all should know of the Legend, and that it should be honored and celebrated by everyone."

"I think it's a wonderful idea," Miss Hilda agreed. "Keeping good traditions alive and vibrant are an excellent way to build friendship and community spirit."

"Greater still than all of this," the Reverend interjected, attempting to get back on point; "the story teaches our young that though evil does exist, we need not fear it; nor should we run away from it. Our God is greater than all of evil combined. He will equip us to stand against it, and be victorious against it. Just like Swift White Eagle and the young bride, we must believe Him, and trust Him to do as He has promised."

Miss Pritchett, agreeing with the Reverend, expanded on his thought. "Don't you agree, Mrs. Coppersmith, evil cannot be allowed to thrive in any form or fashion, and that unless good people stand against it, evil will thrive?"

"Of course," she replied tartly.

"Children need to be taught this, Mrs. Coppersmith," the Reverend stated unequivocally.

"That's what Sunday Service is for," Mrs. Coppersmith countered dryly, her tone edging upon sarcasm.

The Reverend laughed cheerfully, delighting in the banter. "True, but our God has also instructed us to take every opportunity to teach our children about Him and His ways. Did He not?"

"Maybe so," she grudgingly admitted. She gave a quick shrug and stood. "All I know for certain is there are dishes to wash and a kitchen to clean." Giving Miss Taryn a perturbed look, she ordered, "Taryn, come along."

Turning to Miss Pritchett, Mrs. Coppersmith politely said, "If you'll excuse us, we'll tend to our duties."

Smiling with an amused smile, Miss Pritchett just nodded her head. Mrs. Coppersmith turned and headed for the kitchen. With a shrug of acquiescence, Miss Taryn followed Mrs. Coppersmith out of the Dining Hall.

Reverend Tillman rose from his chair. "I, too, need to take my leave. It's after two, and I have a bit of a drive ahead of me. As always, it has been a delightful visit, Eloise. I thank all of you; and, especially, I thank all of you children. You've been wonderful." He bowed graciously to them.

The children giggled and laughed, responding with competing, echoing choruses of "thank you" and "you're welcome".

Miss Pritchett glanced at her watch as she stood. "Thank you, Reverend. As always, you have made the day delightful for us as well. I'll see you out," she said as she walked toward the Reverend.

When she reached the door, she stopped and turned to Miss Cora. "Cora, please escort Aaron and Timmy to my office. We have a phone call to make when I return."

The Reverend offered his arm to Miss Pritchett, escorting her out of the Dining Hall.

As soon as they had left, everyone rose to also take their leave. Before the children had effected their escape, Miss Hilda quickly commandeered them (except Aaron and Timmy) to return the chairs to their proper places around the dining table. Once that task was completed, they all had the afternoon as free time. No one wasted any time in leaving the Dining Hall. They scattered like rats deserting a sinking ship.

Miss Fiona, Miss Ginger and Miss Thelma began the process of clearing the table and removing the linens.

Calling out to Susie and Simon, Miss Hilda asked them to wait. After she finished speaking with Miss Thelma, she asked them if they were ready for their tour of the barns and to meet the animals. Susie merely nodded; Simon jumped up and down, clapping his hands and very gleefully shouted, "Yes, yes, yes!"

Miss Hilda chuckled. "We'll have to hurry. Miss Pritchett wants to give you a tour of the manor at four, so we can't dawdle." She looked squarely at Simon as she said the part about dawdling.

He grinned up at her, his eyes sparkling with joy. Very adamantly he stated, "No problem."

Susie giggled. 'Fat chance,' she thought as they left the Dining Hall.

Chapter 7

FARM TOUR, ALL CREATURES
GREAT AND SMALL

After retrieving from the Cloak Room their coats, scarves, hats and gloves (mittens for Simon which were securely fastened to his coat sleeves), they hurried down the corridor of the south wing. Simon was exuberant and, in what seemed like an endless stream of chatter, asked Miss Hilda one question after another, barely giving her time to answer before he launched the next question. That abruptly changed when they exited the manor. The icy December wind whipped through the pergola, cutting through their clothes like a hot knife through butter. Susie pulled her woolen scarf over her nose and mouth in an attempt to keep the cold at bay. As her teeth began to chatter, she wondered if this might not have been such a good idea.

Miss Hilda ushered them quickly along the pergola, and they exited it midway onto a flagstone path in the east garden. They followed the path to the rear of the garden, race-walking all the way. From there they entered the portico of the southeast wing, crossed it and then picked up another flagstone path. Susie noted that at least she now knew the answer to her question upon first seeing the manor – the east side also has a south wing attached.

They hurried along this path as it wound its way toward the garage, which turned out to be a very large, two-story stone building located about half the length of a football field away from the manor. Miss Hilda explained that many years ago, long before she even came to Glen Hollow, it had been a carriage house where the carriages, buggies and sleighs were kept. She went on to explain that the footmen (they were the ones who drove the vehicles and assisted the passengers) lived in the rooms above the carriage house. Of course now the upstairs is used only for storage, and the first floor is where the modern vehicles are kept.

According to Miss Hilda, in those days, they had all kinds of wagons (big and small), and were kept in another building. Susie asked if it was one of the three old buildings (the ones without night lights) she had seen as they drove up the lane yesterday. Miss Hilda shook her head, telling her that the wagon barn was much farther away, down past the livestock barns.

"Then what are those buildings for?" Susie queried.

Miss Hilda smiled, amused at her curiosity. "We call them bunkhouses. The first week of June they're used by those who attend our Reunion. After that, they're used by the seasonal laborers who start arriving right after the reunion. Most stay through the end of harvest."

"What do they do?" asked Simon.

"A variety of things," she responded; "most work the fields and orchards, some help with the fencing and building repairs."

"Do we get to see the bunk houses?" he asked.

"Not today," she told him.

"How about the wagon barn?" he pressed.

Miss Hilda chuckled heartily. "Not today, Simon. We don't have enough time."

"What do they use the wagons for?" he asked while skipping along backwards in front of them.

She explained that the wagons were used a long time ago to bring the harvest in from the fields, for deliveries to market and, sometimes, for hay rides. Of course, Simon just had to know what a hay ride is, and so Miss Hilda explained the custom of hay rides. Both Susie and Simon thought it sounded like fun. Miss Hilda smiled and told them that they still had the hayrides every fall. Susie did her best to contain her enthusiasm, but it still showed. Simon, however, made no such attempt; he jumped up and down, clapping his hands in an ecstatic display of joy.

As they neared the end of the old stone carriage house, Simon wanted to know why they had sleighs when they had carriages, buggies and wagons. With the patience of a saint, Miss Hilda told him that, in the dead of winter, the deep snows and ice prevented the use of any vehicle other than a sleigh. Back then, they didn't have snow plows to clear the roads. The only way to travel was by sleigh. Simon looked sad. Wistfully he commented that he would have loved to live back then so he could ride in a sleigh like Santa.

Miss Hilda grinned. "It just so happens there are two sleighs inside."

Both children were excited, clamoring their desires to see, get in and to ride in one.

"Can we ride in one?" Susie asked as Simon begged, "I want to see!"

"Not now," she responded. "You may see them later; and when we have a heavy snow, we can take a ride."

Simon's response was to jump up and down as he spun around, making whooping noises and pumping his arms in the air as if to signal some major victory.

"Why did they keep them?" Susie asked Miss Hilda while watching Simon, amused at his clowning around.

"I suppose mainly for historical reasons," Miss Hilda responded. "Miss Pritchett does loan the sleighs to several small communities for their annual winter carnivals. And there are several communities and groups that borrow the carriages, buggies and wagons for parades and different celebrations throughout the year."

Miss Hilda's eyes began to twinkle; her smile broadened into a full grin. Her face glowed with joy as her memories surfaced. Softly she added, "It really is quite fun to ride in a sleigh, smelling the fresh, crisp air, hearing the sleigh bells and the soft whishing sound as the sleigh glides over the snow."

"How do you keep warm?" Simon asked. He just realized it was open, and there would be no heater.

Smiling tenderly at him, Miss Hilda answered as she pulled his knit cap back down over his ears. "First, you bundle up in warm clothes, a heavy winter coat, a woolen scarf, a warm knit hat and mittens or gloves. Then you cover your legs with a lap rug. And if it's super cold, you can always wrap a blanket or an afghan around you."

"How can you put a big ol' rug in a sleigh?" His puzzlement clearly showed on his face, matching his voice. He was trying to envision one of the gigantic rugs from the manor (or even the smaller ones of Nana's) fitting into a sleigh.

"Oh, Simon," Susie bemoaned.

From what seemed to be an endless source of patience, Miss Hilda devotedly explained. "A lap rug, Simon, is really just a heavily woven blanket. It's very thick; and it's small, just large enough to cover your lap and your legs while seated."

"O-o-oh," muttered Simon, mentally storing this new tidbit of information. He ran to the window closest to the garage door and tried to inch his way up the stone blocks, his fingers clinging to the window sill high above his head.

"Come along, Simon," Miss Hilda called out to him.

"I just want to see!" Simon yelled back.

"Now is not the time, Simon," she responded firmly. "If you want to see the animals, we must go now. I'll have Mr. Dale give you a tour of the garage and storage barns next week."

"Okay," he relented with a sigh, dropping to the ground and running back to where she and Susie were standing. "How many sleighs are there?" Simon asked Miss Hilda as she firmly grasped his hand.

"Not as many as you're hoping," she replied with a wink. "As I said, they only kept two sleighs. But they also kept two carriages, two buggies and three of the wagons. They're stored in the old wagon barn."

"Then what's in the garage?" Simon asked.

"Besides the two sleighs, we have four vans, a mini-bus, a pick-up truck and a cargo van. We also have three farm trucks, but those trucks are kept in the equipment barn with the other farm equipment."

"Let's go there," Simon suggested.

"Not today, Simon. We don't have enough time to see the animals and drive down to the equipment barns," she said as she pulled him along.

Sighing with disappointment, he sadly mumbled, "Okay."

Lightly squeezing his hand, she leaned down and said, "But next Saturday, I'm certain Mr. Sean can arrange for you to visit the equipment barn. Is that all right with you?"

With his famous Cheshire cat grin lighting his face, he bubbled an enthusiastic, "Yah!"

Firmly maneuvering Simon away from the stone garage, the three of them quickly made their way onto the side path. From there the smaller path led them toward the quaint cottages Susie had seen from the car. Simon, of course, broke free from Miss Hilda's grasp and ran ahead of them. He went from lamppost to lamppost, swinging around them as if it were a warm summer day.

When they reached the walkway that veered toward the cottages, Simon began a fast sprint down it. Miss Hilda promptly called him back.

"No, Simon," she said. "Stay with us."

Simon, grinning, ran back toward Miss Hilda and Susie. "Why? Who lives there?" he asked, brimming with curiosity.

"The farming crew lives in four of them; the others are vacant," she answered, gently pulling Simon along with them.

"Why so many houses if they stay empty?" he asked, puzzled.

Miss Hilda gave a brief chuckle and replied, "Because, Simon, a long time ago, Glen Hollow was a much larger farming operation; and all the cottages were filled. Now, the vacant ones are only used as guest cottages during the June reunion."

"Why don't they live in the main house?" Susie asked as Simon broke free from Miss Hilda and resumed his lamppost swinging.

"I suppose because of the hours they keep. The farmers are usually up at four in the morning and go to bed by eight at night," she responded while keeping a close eye on Simon.

"Why do they get up so early?" Susie asked, completely astonished.

Simon had stopped his lamppost twirling upon hearing their hours. His expression was one of disbelief.

Miss Hilda laughed. "Because, my dear, they start the day feeding and caring for the animals, and milking the cows by five. Then they have the fields to see after, fencing to check, equipment to tend to, as well as a host of other things. Living in the cottages allows them the ability to start their day without disturbing the sleep of everyone else."

"Except Mrs. Coppersmith; she has to get up and cook," Susie remarked, feeling a twinge of sympathy for her.

"No, dear," Miss Hilda informed her. "The kitchens are fully stocked in each cottage. They make their own breakfast, but they also join us for meals at the manor. And since they usually go to bed earlier than the rest of us, being here allows them to not be disturbed when they're trying to sleep."

Miss Hilda once again snatched Simon's hand. Hurriedly she began shepherding them along the path just as the sound of barking could be heard emanating from some of the cottages.

"Whoa," Simon yelled excitedly, attempting to pull Miss Hilda to a halt. "Do you have dogs?" he asked.

She grinned. "Yes, Simon; there are four dogs. They stay with the farmers, but the dogs work. They shepherd the cattle to and from the fields whenever the weather permits the cows to be outdoors," she replied.

"May we pet them?" both Susie and Simon begged.

"Not now; maybe later," she responded firmly.

Susie sighed and shrugged; Simon wheedled, "Why not?"

"We don't have time to visit all of the barns and animals if we make any more stops, Simon," she patiently explained. "This is your home now, so you'll have plenty of opportunities to visit each and every animal. That includes the dogs as well as the cats that live in the barns."

"Cats?" they parroted, they're faces lighting up with delight.

"That means kittens," Simon squealed for joy.

Miss Hilda made a brief sigh and stated firmly, "Come along, children."

As they hastily continued down the path, Susie asked the names of the dogs, to which Miss Hilda had replied, Archie, Gus, Roxie and Jill.

With the cottages a considerable distance behind them, Susie noticed that the forest was closer to them the further away from the residences they went. Up ahead, still some three hundred or so yards away, was a white shed that appeared to be the size of a three-car garage. The sloped, red tile roof had three vent pipes protruding from it. Windows, short in height but long in width, were evenly spaced all across the top of the building allowing for plenty of light to filter into the building. The windows had shutters as did the two large fans that were in the east and west walls, just under the eaves.

Susie stopped dead in her tracks, turning quickly to face the forest to her right. Motionless, she stared at the wall of trees, just slightly further away than the length of a football field.

"Susie," Miss Hilda called. "What are you doing?"

Susie continued her intense focus on one spot, the white tree in the middle of the clump of brown ones. "I saw something," she responded.

"It's just the branches swaying in the wind. Come along," she instructed.

Susie's gaze remained unbroken. She had that uneasy feeling again, the same one as when they arrived yesterday. "I don't think so," Susie yelled back. "I think I saw a person."

"Nonsense," Miss Hilda countered. "Come here now."

Susie drew in a deep breath then forcibly exhaled it. As she turned to comply with Miss Hilda's order, she saw it again. It was just a brief, fleeting glimpse; but she saw it. Someone, or something, was definitely there and was watching them. She ran as fast as she could to Miss Hilda and the not-so-patient Simon.

"I saw it again, just now," she puffed between breaths. Simon rolled his eyes, not impressed by Susie's adamant declaration.

"Susie, dear," Miss Hilda said with a lilt in her tone. "The shadows play tricks; no one is there. The wind moves the branches, and it just *appears* that someone is there." Her smile was meant to comfort Susie, and convince her that it was all her imagination.

Susie remained unmoved. She knew, just knew, she saw someone or something watching them. She kept close to Miss Hilda the rest of the way to the shed. When they were within a few yards of it, Susie could see that it was quite well protected. The shed had a very large pen (Susie guessed about fifty yards each direction) and was completely enclosed – including the top – in a sturdy wire mesh. To Susie, it was more like a giant, steel cage than a fence. The winter fescue in the yard was thick and green, and looked to be as soft as a carpet. Situated around the yard were automatic feeders and water bins. Miss Hilda held the gate door open and then closed it behind them, making certain that it was securely fastened.

As they approached the shed, Simon noticed that there were two small pet-door openings on either side of the door. "Why are there pet doors?" he asked Miss Hilda.

"So when the weather permits, the chickens can come and go whenever the door is shut."

"What if a dog or cat gets in?" Susie asked.

Miss Hilda chuckled. "More like a fox or wolf, but not even they can get through, under or over the fence."

She pointed to the secure fencing, both the peripheral and the top. "The posts and the wire are sunk three feet below ground. The wire mesh then folds and runs three feet back toward the lane, down another eighteen inches and back again toward the lane. It's very strong and secure." She smiled at Susie, reassuring her that they, and the chickens, were safe inside the fence.

"There are foxes and wolves here?" Simon asked wide-eyed, more so out of wonder than fear.

"Oh yes," she told him. "They live in the woods all around here. They've tried to get in, not so much anymore; but years ago they were constantly trying to get the chickens. Now we seldom ever see one."

"I bet Susie saw a wolf," Simon popped off gleefully. "I hope I get to see one and even pet one."

"I'm certain all Susie saw was the wind moving the branches," Miss Hilda replied firmly.

Bending down so as to look Simon in the eye, she added sternly, "Under no circumstance are you ever to try to touch a wild animal, Simon. They aren't pets; and they might harm you because they don't know you. Do you understand?"

Simon gave her a slight scowl, then answered with a reluctant, "Yes, Miss Hilda."

"Good," she responded with a smile. "Now, let's go see the chickens."

She opened the heavy door, and Simon bounded through it, eager to meet the chickens. He was thrilled to see the large flock of hens and chicks.

"There must be a million chickens!" he exclaimed.

Miss Hilda laughed. "No, not quite" she said. "I'd say we have about two hundred hens and pullets, a few roosters and a lot of chicks."

Susie was surprised to see how clean it was inside. The floor had a slight grade to it, sloping gently down to drains along the center of the floor. There were water pipes and faucets extending up from the floor, spaced evenly apart. Mounted to the wall, next to each faucet, was a hook that held a neatly coiled water hose.

Automatic, double-sided feeding stations and watering bins were positioned strategically around the shed. A few chickens were eating and drinking, and some were strutting around the henhouse. Most of the hens were snuggled down onto the straw filled nests or sitting on the perches.

Simon was laughing, trying his best to catch a hen. They eluded him at every turn. Finally he gave up and plopped down on the floor. Within seconds several hens cautiously approached him, checking out the newcomer.

"Be very still, Simon," Miss Hilda instructed. "Let them have a chance to get to know you."

She reached down and petted a couple of hens that had raced over to greet her. Susie followed her lead and lightly stroked the hens. Soon she had several more pressing around her, wanting attention.

Simon, too, was now able to pet them. His bright, blue eyes sparkled, and his face glowed as he squealed with delight. Grinning like a clown, he laughed. "They like me," he giggled.

"Of course, they do," she said, amused at his ecstatic hilarity. "Dorkings are a friendly breed."

Susie rolled her eyes. "Simon is so-o-o silly sometimes. He *knows* animals like him. Nana said we have a way with animals." She paused and quietly added, "All our family has."

With an intuitive twinkle in her eyes, Miss Hilda smiled at Susie and nodded in agreement. Turning her attention back to Simon she announced, "It's time to go. We need to hurry if we're going to have time to visit the other animals." Miss Hilda moved quickly to the door.

With a dramatic sigh, Simon reluctantly got up and brushed off his clothes.

"What's in those rooms?" Susie asked as she pointed to the doors on the south wall.

"In the room on the left, we store their food and medicines in there. We also have a dark area where we candle the eggs."

"What does 'candle the eggs' mean?" Susie asked.

Simon quickly blurted out, "What do you feed them?"

Miss Hilda smiled pleasantly and stated, "Susie asked her question first, Simon. In answer to your question, Susie, we gather the eggs twice a day, and then take them in the dark room. We hold them up to a bright light to see if the egg has been fertilized. If it has, we put it back in the nest. If not, we take it to the kitchen. Taryn washes them, places them in egg cartons and then stores them in the pantry's refrigerator."

"What's fertilized?" Simon asked.

"It means it'll become a baby chick when it hatches," Miss Hilda told him.

"Oh." Simon said. With a hopeful grin he asked, "May I help?"

She grinned. "Maybe; we'll see."

"And what's the other room for?" Susie asked.

"Wait," Simon protested. "You didn't answer my question. What do you feed them?"

"I'm sorry, Simon," she replied. "We did skip it. The chickens forage in the yard for all kinds of bugs and worms, and we supplement that with crushed oyster shell and grain. When the ice and snow begins, we keep them inside, feeding them earthworms and other bugs along with the crushed oyster shells and grain. We raise the bugs and worms in terrariums in the back room."

"Cool", he said! "Can I see?" Simon's enthusiasm for all things slimy or grimy was never on hold.

"It's 'may I', and the answer to that is, not now." She chuckled at his exuberance.

"So that's where you keep the bugs for the chickens?" Susie asked, slightly grimacing and wrinkling her nose.

Miss Hilda laughed, amused by Susie's aversion to the creatures. "Yes, the room on the left has the terrariums. As to the center room, it has the breaker box, some supplies and the control box for the sprinklers."

Pointing overhead to the pipe grid above them she continued, "If a fire breaks out, then the sprinklers turn on and put out the fire. The room on the right houses the furnace and a generator; they're used if our electricity isn't working," she said, finishing the discourse.

Miss Hilda opened the door, and Susie stepped through it to the fenced yard; Miss Hilda stopped in the doorway. "Simon," she called out to him; "let's go see the pigs. Afterward, we'll make a very fast stop to see the cows and horses. We need to return to the manor in an hour."

Simon quickly patted the hen one last time. He grinned at Miss Hilda and did his imitation of a chicken strut all the way to the door. She couldn't help but laugh; he was so comical.

Susie was waiting by the door of the enclosure, and Miss Hilda wasted no time getting it opened and then securely closed again behind them. The frigid air provided plenty of incentive to move quickly. Nearly at a running pace, they headed past the two large barns that were several hundred yards away, opting instead for a much smaller barn not too far from the second of the large barns.

On each side of the structure there was a large, fenced area that ran the entire length of the building. It was self-contained; no entrance to the pastures, but had plenty of trees and grass in the enclosed areas. The fencing and gates were heavy, galvanized steel and looked strong enough to withstand just about anything, including Simon. He was currently standing on the middle slat of the gate on the west side.

"What's that?" Simon asked as he pointed to the area in the center of the large yard.

"That's a mud pit," Miss Hilda answered, grinning at Simon's reaction.

"A mud pit?" he squeaked, partly from surprise but mostly with delight.

"Yes," she affirmed. "In the summer, the pigs like to bathe in the mud. It helps to keep them cool. Some will bathe in the mud, and some stay in the shade. There's one just like it on the other side of the barn."

Before he could ask his next question, Miss Hilda answered it for him. "And, no; you may not get in there, with or without the pigs."

Simon tilted his head coyly as his smile developed into a toothy grin. His eyes danced with a mischievous sparkle as he giggled. "How'd you know what I was going to ask?"

"Because you're not the first little boy that has lived here," she answered with a laugh, her eyes twinkling. "Come on, let's go inside."

She attempted to assist him, but he had already jumped to the ground and ran to the door. He turned around, facing them as he waited for them, bobbing and bouncing to music only he could hear.

As Miss Hilda opened the side door, Susie asked, "Miss Hilda, what are those cables for that run to all the buildings?"

Miss Hilda turned and looked to where Susie was pointing. "Those are our guide cables. When the snow is too deep or there's a blizzard, we can get from the manor to the various buildings by attaching this clip to a belt harness we wear." She jiggled the attached large metal clip that was hanging down from the cable.

"Why go outside in a blizzard?" Simon asked.

"We still have to feed and water the animals, Simon; and we have to make certain they're warm. If the power goes out, we have to start the generators. If the power is out for several days, then we have to build fires in the fire pits so they won't freeze to death," she explained.

"Oh," he responded thoughtfully.

"Does it go out often?" Susie asked, mentally noting to herself to make an emergency kit for Simon and one for herself.

Miss Hilda smiled said, "No, dear; not anymore." She held the barn's side door open and ushered them inside.

This barn was about a quarter of the size of the other two barns, and had two small enclosed fire pits, one on each end of the barn. The floor was concrete and slightly slanted downward; and, just like the chicken house, it too had drains in the floor. There was one large stall and one smaller stall lining each side of the center corridor. Just outside each stall was a water pipe, rising up through the concrete floor. Attached to the stall's frame were heavy iron hooks just above each faucet. Water hoses were neatly coiled and hung on the hooks. Susie glanced up and saw this barn, too, had a water sprinkler system just like the chicken house.

There were several corn cribs filled to capacity along with barrels that were labeled with a variety of different nuts and grains. Her observations were cut short by loud laughter and squeals.

Simon had already found a stall with young pigs. His arms were slid between the slats of the stall's gate, and was merrily petting them. He was squealing with delight as much as the piglets were.

"Look, Miss Hilda," he beamed. "They like to be petted."

"Indeed they do," she agreed. "They really love to have their bellies rubbed."

Susie knelt down beside Simon, reached between the slats, and began scratching one of the little piglets behind the ear. She smiled as it began sniffing the palm of her hand with its snout. She giggled. "That tickles," she told the piglet. Turning her face toward Miss Hilda she asked, "How many are there?"

Miss Hilda's brow furrowed slightly as she pondered that question. "In this stall, I believe there are two boars, twelve sows and thirty piglets that are four months old. We sold twenty of the piglets two months ago."

"Why did you sell them?" Simon asked.

Miss Hilda smiled as she cautiously answered, "We don't need that many, and we wouldn't be able to feed that many during the winter months."

Simon nodded his head, affirming that made sense to him as he continued tickling and petting the squirming heap of piglets, pressing up against the gate. It wasn't long until they also had to contend with the sows and boars who wanted Simon's attention as well.

Simon popped off with, "What are *sows*?" Scrunching up his face and wrinkling his nose at the sound of the word 'sows', he looked like he had just taken a bite out of a lemon.

Miss Hilda laughed. "It means a mother pig."

"Why not just *say* mother pig?" he asked, exaggeratedly shaking his head as if adults were just silly.

"I don't know, Simon," she said, smiling at him. "It's just a farming term that has been used for hundreds of years."

Simon returned his attention to petting the piglets and the pigs. All of them were pushing and shoving each other, struggling to get close enough to him to be petted.

"Are they mean?" Susie asked.

"No, Tamworths are a very gentle breed. So are the Choctaw hogs on the other side."

"Hogs?" Susie and Simon chorused in unison.

"Yes," she responded as Simon jumped up and ran across the barn to the other stalls.

"Hey!" he exclaimed. "They're not pink! They're black! Why are they black and the other ones are pink?"

"It's genetics," she answered and then realized from his expression he didn't understand. "Their size and color are determined by their parents."

"Their feet are different too. Look Simon, see the difference?" Susie pointed to the hoof of the nearest little piglet among the crowd that was now pressing hard against the wooden slats of the stall.

Simon looked close at the piglet and then turned his face to Susie. "Yeah," he said with a grin. "It has one big toe, and the pink pigs have two."

"The Tamworths have a split hoof, and the Choctaw hogs have what's called a mulefoot," Miss Hilda informed them.

"That's weird," Simon declared.

"No, not really, Simon," she explained. "No more so than you having blond hair and Susie having dark auburn hair. You each inherited certain traits of your parents. The hog parents have the same features so their babies look just like them. The same is true for the Tams."

She checked her watch and frowned. "We need to get going. We have forty minutes before we must go back to the manor."

Susie headed for the barn door while Simon reluctantly, and slowly, stood to his feet. "Not even a few more minutes?" he asked.

"It's okay with me, Simon," Miss Hilda cordially answered; "but we'll have to skip seeing the cows and horses today."

"No way!" he shouted as he ran to the door.

They left the pig barn and quickly strode to the nearest of the two large barns. Simon, having run ahead, was already waiting for them at the door.

Upon entering the barn from the south side, Susie saw that a quarter of the way inside was a large circular firepit, strategically placed atop a stone platform. Directly across on the far side of the barn was another firepit, also positioned a quarter of the way into the barn.

Black, wrought-iron mesh guards surrounded the open pits so that sparks could not fly out and start a fire. Brass chimneys sat atop the mesh guards and rose up through the roof, venting any smoke. Cords of wood were neatly stacked along the south wall and rose to at least five feet in height. Mirroring them was another stack along the north wall.

Susie glanced up at the roof; sure enough, there was a sprinkler system in here also. She smiled. She noticed the floors were identical to those in the pig barn, including the water pipe floor system running the length of the barn. Although there were far more faucets in here, they also had the neatly coiled hoses above each faucet.

There were two rooms on their right, one of which was a supply room and the other was a bunk room (each door was clearly labeled). To their left was a wall full of various tools and implements. Bundles of alfalfa were neatly stacked in the loft above them. It was packed full and so were the storage cribs on the ground floor. There were barrels of oats and barley strategically placed around the barn.

Susie froze. Her head tilted back, and her eyes focused intently on the loft.

"Susie, is something wrong?" Miss Hilda asked.

"Did you hear that?" she responded. (She didn't actually hear anything so much as she sensed that someone was there, watching. But she couldn't tell Miss Hilda that.)

"It's probably just one of the cats or maybe a mouse," Miss Hilda cheerfully explained, attempting to ease Susie's wariness.

Susie didn't respond; she waited to see if it was indeed a cat or a mouse. Finally the sensation left just as quickly as it had arrived. There had been no movement in the loft at all, nor was there a sound to reveal that any creature had been hiding there. Susie sighed and turned to join the others. She didn't understand why she was jumpy all of a sudden, ever since they arrived yesterday. It wasn't like her, and she didn't like jumping at shadows.

Simon ran to the first stall and was attempting to pet the cow inside it. Slowly the creature moved its head, dropping its muzzle into Simon's hand and blowing its warm breath into the palm of his little hand. Simon giggled with glee.

"It's soft!" he exclaimed.

"Yes, they are." Miss Hilda agreed, chuckling softly.

Susie joined them at the stall and gently began stroking the cow on her neck. "What's her name?" she asked.

"Daisy," Miss Hilda answered. "See," she added, pointing to the name plate next to the stall door.

"Hey, Susie, look!" Simon demanded. "Daisy looks like an Oreo cookie!"

Susie looked to where Simon was pointing, the side of the cow. Sure enough, Daisy was black with a wide band of white around her middle.

Miss Hilda's eyes twinkled, and she replied. "They do indeed. They're called Dutch Belted cows. The white band resembles a big, wide belt. Don't you think?"

Susie nodded in agreement, but Simon wrinkled his nose at the idea. "I think they should be called "Oreo" cows," he decreed; "'cause that's what they look like, and 'cause that's my most favorite cookie." Grinning up at Miss Hilda, he asked, "How many are there?"

"Besides Daisy, Bessie and Lily, we have sixty cows, three bulls and twenty-four calves. Most of the calves were sold in September when they were six months old."

Simon's eyes bulged as he raised his eyebrows and did his little head jutting motion. "Wow, that's a lot of cows! ...... I want to pet them all! .... *May* I?" he asked, giving Miss Hilda one of his super grins.

"Not today, Simon. We still have one more barn to visit. You'll be able to pet them all later, I promise."

Simon gave her a perky smile, nodded his head several times and said, "Okay."

"Do the cows give a lot of milk?" Susie asked.

"Oh, yes, most of them do." Miss Hilda confirmed. "Daisy, here…."

"How long do they live?" Simon interrupted.

"Simon, it isn't polite to interrupt. You need to wait your turn," Miss Hilda corrected him.

With a dejected look, Simon pouted and said, "Okay," and moved down to the next stall, petting Bessie.

Miss Hilda smiled at him, continuing her explanation to Susie. "As I was saying, Daisy and a couple more are too old to give milk. Daisy is our oldest; she'll be twenty-six come March," Miss Hilda said fondly as she petted Daisy. "The others give between five to seven gallons each day, and they're milked twice every day."

"That's a lot of milk," Susie commented.

Moving to Bessie's stall, Miss Hilda began scratching her gently behind her ear. Bessie really enjoyed it; she closed her eyes, tilted her head and leaned on Miss Hilda.

"It takes it, Susie." Miss Hilda said. "Besides milk for drinking, cooking and baking, we also make our own butter, buttermilk, sour cream, ice cream, yogurt, cottage cheese, and several other types of cheese." She smiled and then gave Bessie an affectionate kiss on her forehead.

"Who does all that work?" Susie asked astounded.

Miss Hilda smiled. "Mrs. Coppersmith spearheads the effort, but we all help."

Simon's attention was captured when he heard the words 'ice cream'; the expression on his face was one of sheer bliss. "I'll help make the ice cream," he volunteered eagerly.

Miss Hilda reached down and tousled Simon's hair. "Thank you, Simon. I'm certain Mrs. Coppersmith will be glad to have your help. Now, in answer to your question; most of the cows live about twenty years, but their milk production slows down by age fourteen."

"Why do you keep them if they don't have any milk?" he asked. He moved down one more stall and began petting Lily.

Miss Hilda paused reflectively for a moment before answering. "Well, I suppose it's because they've earned their retirement. They worked all their years providing for us, so they've earned their keep. And they still do. Daisy, Bessie, and Lily are the old matriarchs … mothers," she quickly added when she saw Simon's puzzled look. "They help keep the pregnant cows calm; they tend to mother all of the cows and especially look after the calves out in the fields. So, even though they aren't producing milk, they still help out in their own way."

Miss Hilda gave Lily an affectionate pat, and turned to leave. "Let's go."

Simon, still petting Lily, asked, "What happens when they die?"

Smiling softly, Miss Hilda answered, "We bury them. There's a field a long way from here where we bury them." She sighed slightly and stated firmly, "Let's go, children."

Simon nodded and ran ahead of them to the door.

When he was out of ear shot, Susie asked, "They're not raised for beef?"

Miss Hilda nodded briefly. "Some are; those that are, we send to the butcher at a year old."

Susie looked at her with a steady glance. "So the calves will be slaughtered in the spring?"

"Some," she acknowledged.

"Don't tell Simon," Susie tersely stated.

"This is a working farm, Susie. He has to learn someday," Miss Hilda responded gently.

"But not now," Susie insisted and quickened her pace to catch up with Simon, who was now impatiently waiting by the barn door.

They left the dairy barn and quickly darted the hundred or so yards to the horse stable, a very large, wooden building with a gray stone foundation. It had four chimneys and four ventilation turrets on the roof. The stable was painted cherry red with dark gray trim and was, in Susie's opinion, the prettiest of the farm buildings.

The east side of the stable had a training corral, and the west side had a large paddock. Entrance to the fenced areas from the barn was from one of the four sets of double barns doors. Both enclosures had gates on their north sides, leading into the pasture. The double barn doors on the south end were huge, big enough that Susie thought a tractor could easily be driven inside the barn if both doors were open. They were, however, closed, so they entered the stable through the people door (as Miss Hilda had called it).

Susie marveled at the interior; it wasn't what she expected. It was an open area and full of light. The ceiling was very tall (maybe as much as thirty feet) and had natural lighting fixtures throughout. The ceiling was solid; if Miss Hilda hadn't told her that there was a hay loft above it where bales of alfalfa were stored, she would never have realized it. That is, until she saw the freight elevators; then she would have asked why they had elevators in a stable.

Immediately to her left and to her right were the bunk room, tack and supply room, grain and feed storage room, a veterinarian medicine room and a small office. Susie noticed that the stable also had a sprinkler system as well as the water pipes and hoses for cleaning the stalls. The stable flooring, however, wasn't concrete like the pig barn. It was, however, like the dairy barn - the stall flooring was made of rubber tiles that gave a cushioned feel to each and every step.

The building had four fire pits (two on the south end and two on the north end); the fire pits were approximately twenty feet into the stable from the exterior walls. On the south end, one firepit was positioned ten feet from the first and second stall rows and the other was positioned ten feet from the third and fourth stall rows. The north side positioning of its fire pits mirrored exactly those on the south side.

The two outer stall rows had a six foot corridor that was between them and the outside walls of the stable. Separating the outer row of stalls and the inner rows were nine foot corridors. However, the widest corridor was the one in the center of the barn; it had to be at least fifteen feet across.

Susie noticed that the stalls in this barn are quite different from that of the dairy barn. Although in size they are about the same (maybe twelve feet by ten feet), the horse barn is quite different in construction. Black wrought iron rails in a lacy, open pattern comprise the top half of each stall whereas the bottom portion is solid oak boards. The wood on the outside has been so highly polished it gleams in the light. Inside the stalls, the wood is covered in a dark maroon padding, thick enough to protect the horse. Each stall has an ornate brass plate displaying the name of its resident.

She liked the stable; it seemed more like a bedroom for horses than that of being a barn. Several of the horses had already ventured to their doors, heads bobbing and weaving through the open space above the doors, waiting for attention and for the occasional treat.

Miss Hilda did not disappoint them. She moved to each one in turn, giving the desired affection and the expected apple slices. Susie and Simon followed along behind her, mimicking her movements. To their great delight, each one of the beautiful creatures bestowed upon them a muzzle kiss and an affectionate lip nibble, just like they did with Miss Hilda.

As they passed down the center corridor, Susie realized that the outer two rows were empty as were the majority of the inner two rows. Of the barns thirty-six stalls, only twelve had horses. She remembered Mrs. Crenshaw had said that there was a time when the Evermores were famous for their horses. If those horses were as beautiful as these, Susie could easily understand why people came to see and to buy them. She wondered what it must have been like to see the barn full of the horses, to watch the training and the shows.

With a hint of sadness, Susie began walking toward Miss Hilda, who was shouting "No, Simon!" as she ran to catch up to him. He was attempting to climb over one of the gates. Apparently he found a horse he liked. Susie bit her lip in an effort to stop the laugh that wanted to escape. Simon would only be encouraged if he heard her laugh.

Her attention, however, was diverted as soon as she reached the next stall. The name on the brass plate read: 'Moon Shadow Lacy Heart Treasure'. "What an odd name," Susie thought.

Without warning, the creature's head appeared, nose to nose with Susie. Startled, Susie jumped back and then began laughing. The horse moved her head up and down as if joining in with Susie's laughter.

"You scared me," Susie whispered as she reached out and petted the horse's neck. "You shouldn't do that."

The dappled, silvery-white horse gave a soft whinny, nodding her head again before dropping her nose into Susie's open hand. Her muzzle was velvety soft - Susie's heart melted. She was hooked. Susie looked into her blue eyes and asked, "Just what do I call you? You have too many names."

"Lacy," she heard a voice say. Susie looked around and saw no one. Puzzled, she turned once again to the horse.

She started to ask the horse if the creature herself had said it, but thought better of it. After all, horses don't talk. She continued gently stroking the horse on her forehead, mane and neck. Affectionately the horse rubbed her head against Susie's, even giving her a few kisses. She nibbled lightly at Susie's hair and snorted a soft whinny or two. Susie felt a bond with this creature and silently wished that someone would teach her to ride.

The horse moved her head again near to Susie's, enabling eye contact. For the briefest of moments, Susie thought she could see the memories of the horse. Someone, a woman, was riding through a meadow. Then it was gone. "What was that?" Susie whispered.

The only response she had was a soft nuzzle from her new-found friend.

"I see you've met Lacy," Miss Hilda said cheerfully. She had managed to corral Simon and had a vise-like grip on his forearm. "She a sweetheart," Miss Hilda said softly as she gently caressed Lacy's forehead.

"Her name is Lacy?" Susie croaked. Just for a second, she thought she saw a twinkle in Lacy's eyes. Lacy nodded in response to her question.

"Well, that's what we've always called her. As you can see, her formal name is a bit longer." Miss Hilda patted Lacy then gave her a kiss on her forehead. "She'll be thirty come Christmas Day," she said softly, speaking more to Lacy than to Susie.

She turned and pulled Simon along with her, heading toward the barn door.

"Let's go, Susie. We have less than twenty minutes to get back to the manor."

Susie gave Lacy one final pat and whispered in her ear, "I'll be back; I promise." She turned and ran, catching up with Simon and Miss Hilda just as Miss Hilda opened the door.

"Miss Hilda, why does Lacy have so many names?" Susie asked.

Miss Hilda smiled. "It's the custom. The horse is given its own name, and a name from each parent. Then you add a name from the dam's mother and from the sire's father."

Seeing Susie's blank look, Miss Hilda laughed. "In other words," she explained; "Lacy is her given name. Miss Pritchett named her Lacy because her dapple pattern gives the appearance of lace. Moon comes from part of her father's name, and Shadow comes from part of her mother's name. The name Heart comes from part of the name of her father's father. And the name Treasure comes from part of the name of her mother's mother."

Susie grinned. "I understand. My first name is really Arielle. I'm named after Mommy's mother. Simon is named after Daddy's father."

"So you do understand," Miss Hilda said with a chuckle.

Susie nodded.

They hurried past the chicken house, heading toward the cottages when Susie came to an abrupt stop and whirled around, facing a road that branched off toward the north. Straining to see, Susie stared down the farm road as it continued on well past the barns, and out of her line of sight. She could have sworn she saw a flash of white on the road, just at the edge of the trees.

"Susie, dear, don't dawdle. We must hurry. We don't want to be late for your manor tour with Miss Pritchett," Miss Hilda called out to her.

"I'm coming," Susie responded as she ran, catching up to Miss Hilda and Simon. "Where does the road go?" she asked, breathing hard as she attempted to keep pace with Miss Hilda.

Miss Hilda smiled and chuckled. "To other buildings and fields, and it also connects to several of our other farm roads. Years ago you could travel all the way on the farm roads to several towns bordering Glen Hollow. Miss Pritchett's father gated and locked those entry points, oh, I guess nearly fifty years ago now. ... Why do you ask?"

"Just wondering," Susie answered. "Have you ever been down any of those roads?" she asked.

Miss Hilda nodded. "Certainly, when I was little; both Miss Pritchett and I would go with my Dad when he'd check fences, buildings and road conditions. Sometimes when he was walking the fences, we'd get out of the truck and play."

She winked at Susie and continued, "We weren't supposed to, but we did. ... And on many occasions, we rode the horses, just the two of us. We went everywhere, all over Glen Hollow. There was this one meadow that was her favorite place for a picnic. We went there at least once a week until I left for college."

Chuckling softly, Miss Hilda admitted, "We had a lot of fun." Her smile was wistful, and her eyes held a joyful glint as she remembered.

"Do you still ride?" Susie quietly asked.

"We do from time to time. We just don't ride as far as we did when we were young," she said with a hearty laugh.

Quickly they scurried past the cottages; and at a frenzied pace, sailed past the old stone garage, as they hurried to the manor. They rounded the corner of the east wing and saw Simon ahead of them, running down the pergola, racing his way to the door.

"Wait for us, Simon," Miss Hilda instructed him.

He stopped just a few feet shy of the door, turned and held out his arms, letting them drop in an exasperated fashion. "Hurry up, slowpokes," he ordered.

Miss Hilda quickened her pace – which Susie could not believe was possible – and within a very few minutes, they caught up to Simon. Miss Hilda assisted Simon in opening the heavy oak door. Quickly they entered into the soothing warmth of the manor, leaving behind the frigid December air.

Chapter 8

THE MANOR GRAND TOUR

Rapidly shedding their outside attire, Miss Hilda deftly hung Simon's things, then her own while Susie made short work of hanging her own coat and accessories. They made a quick stop at the restroom (Simon insisted) only it turned out not to be so quick. After his business was concluded, Simon became distracted by the enormity of the linen closet, discovering that it made a great hiding place because it was actually the size of a room.

After causing Miss Hilda and Susie to search for him for nearly ten minutes, Simon also discovered that there is such a thing as an appropriate time for play ... and this was not it. Miss Hilda proceeded to sternly lecture him. Susie attempted to intervene on his behalf, but Miss Hilda would have none of it. Quite harshly she instructed Susie to remain silent. Susie bit her lip momentarily, then launched into defending Simon. Miss Hilda again told her to be silent, warning Susie that if she had to tell Susie once more she would be punished. As it stood, Simon would receive a ten minute time-out after dinner.

Miss Hilda grasped Simon's hand and hurriedly strode through the door with Susie trotting close behind. With great haste, Miss Hilda propelled them toward Miss Pritchett's office. Several times Simon strenuously attempted to break free from her iron grip, but without success. Consequently, they had to listen to him whine the entire way that Miss Hilda was walking too fast and squeezing his hand too tight.

They arrived at Miss Pritchett's door just as the grandfather clock began chiming the four o'clock hour.

"There you are," Miss Pritchett cheerfully said as they entered her office. "Right on time," she added as she rose from her chair and quickly joined them.

"Certainly; we wouldn't dream of being late," Miss Hilda responded while giving Simon a stern look.

Undaunted, Simon challenged, "What happens if we were late?" The gleam in his eyes was most definitely mischievous, and his tone was that of a playful imp. Susie instinctively held her breath, silently praying Simon would cease his shenanigans.

Smiling, Miss Pritchett leaned back against her desk, her hands loosely clasped in front of her as she studied him for a moment. She chuckled lightly, and her eyes were twinkling with amusement. Bending slightly toward him, she answered, "Well Simon, that all depends on the age of the offender, and whether or not it's a first offense."

"What if it's me?" he asked, emphatically pointing to himself.

"You could have an extra chore assigned or even a time out," she responded.

Pausing briefly, Simon stared back at her as he processed this information. "What if I couldn't *help* it?" he pressed his case, crossing his arms over his chest, signaling his triumph of logic.

Enjoying his banter, Miss Pritchett's smile increased. "Normally there isn't an excuse for being tardy. However, occasionally, a circumstance arises that is beyond one's control. In that instance, tardiness is excused. .... Just what sort of circumstance do you think would be an acceptable excuse? "

His smile quickly spread to a full, perky grin. His eyes sparkled as he assumed his Peter Pan stance. "What if I was in the Library all by myself, and I was busy reading?"

Miss Pritchett laughed heartily. "Oh, I would love for you to love reading that much, Simon. However, do you know how to tell time?"

"Yes," he responded proudly.

"Well, Simon, you would have no excuse because there are clocks in the Library," she informed him.

Not to be dissuaded from his mission, he contorted his little face into a faux scowl and challenged, "But what if some chairs aren't where you can *see* a clock."

Nodding in agreement, she readily responded, "True, some are ... Do you know how to count?"

Puzzled, he answered slowly, "Yes, I can count to a hundred. Susie taught me."

"Excellent," she declared vibrantly. "Then you would be able to count the chimes of the mantle clocks and know the time. Again, my dear, no excuse for being tardy," she said, smiling fondly at him.

"I'll think of something," Simon promised.

"I'm certain you will, Simon; and I look forward to hearing your ideas. However, now we need to take a quick tour of the manor," she responded as she gently turned Simon around, guiding him out the door.

———

Their first stop was across the sitting room to Miss Hilda's office. It was furnished much like that of Miss Pritchett's office. After a quick look, Miss Pritchett signaled it was time to go. Miss Hilda took her leave, remaining in her office, while Miss Pritchett escorted Susie and Simon on the manor tour.

As they entered the corridor, Miss Pritchett explained that the portraits hanging in the corridors throughout the manor are of her ancestors. The various other artworks were painted by previous residents. As they passed by, Susie noticed that the portraits all had a silver name plate denoting the person's name and the year the portrait was commissioned.

The first place they visited after leaving Miss Hilda was to Miss Bettye's office, directly across the corridor. They entered and found themselves in the waiting area. The dropped ceiling held rows of lights underneath opaque panels, chasing away any and all shadows yet softly lighting the room. Three tapestry loveseats, with six upholstered chairs, were the sole source of patient seating. Magazines were neatly stacked on the tables. A large carpet covered most of the oak floor in the waiting area.

Miss Pritchett led them to Miss Bettye's office, situated to the far right as they entered the office suite. Separating her office from the waiting area was a wall of frosted glass blocks. Her desk and chair, credenza and filing cabinets all matched the waiting area furnishings. There were two chairs placed in front of her desk, their backs to the waiting area.

Curious, Susie asked how Miss Bettye would know when someone entered. Miss Pritchett smiled, answering that there is a light that flashes in

Miss Bettye's office and in all of the other rooms whenever the door opens. Miss Pritchett pointed to the light above Miss Bettye's door.

Miss Pritchett ushered them out of the office, guiding them to the door directly across from the entrance. She opened it, and they entered into a small hallway. Three doors opened into other rooms. The first two were exam rooms, and the third was a dispensary and supply room. Susie checked the hallway and the three rooms; they each had the light over the door just as Miss Pritchett had said.

Guiding them back into the reception area, Miss Pritchett explained that if they are not feeling well or are injured, this is where they come or are brought. If it's something minor, Miss Bettye treats them; and they remain at Glen Hollow. If it's a serious illness or injury or requires surgery, then Miss Bettye treats what she can and assists in taking the person to the hospital in Foxboro Station.

Seeing Simon's uneasy expression, she assured him that they hadn't ever had any serious injuries or illnesses. He grinned at her, shyly asking how she knew what he was thinking. Smiling and chuckling, she told him he was not the first person to wonder, or ask, about hospital trips.

After they had seen everything, or nearly everything, Miss Pritchett ushered them out of Miss Bettye's office suite and back into the corridor.

Simon had to try each and every chair, and peer into every cabinet and chest along the way. It surprised Susie that Miss Pritchett didn't seem to mind; she just smiled and occasionally chuckled, making small talk with Susie as they walked along.

Next they visited the Operations office. It was an enormously large room, but the dropped ceiling, ambient recessed lighting and the various potted plants helped to create a pleasant, homey atmosphere.

The immediate center of the spacious room (where they entered) showcased a large area carpet; upon the carpet, four long sofas were arranged in a square formation. Small oak tables were positioned at the ends of each sofa, and in the center of the carpet was a large, square coffee table.

At the far left of the room were four distinct office areas, each complete with an executive desk, chair, credenza, computer, printer and phone.

In the very back of the office complex was an oak conference table with twelve chairs, a wet bar with microwave oven and a coffee maker.

To the far right, was a bathroom and also a utility room which housed the supplies, file storage, facsimile and copier. The entire wall between the conference area and the utility room was lined with built-in bookcases, filled with books.

Simon had a blast trying all the different seats. He especially liked the conference chairs; they swiveled and rocked.

Miss Pritchett guided them back into the corridor and proceeded to the next stop.

"This is the Media Room," Miss Pritchett informed them, opening the door. "But it is actually a suite of rooms."

Entering into a cozy living area, its focal point was the large-screened television, fastened to the wall. Miss Pritchett explained that the children may watch Saturday morning cartoons in here without adult supervision as long as the older children are with the younger three. She smiled, adding that the television has parental locks that prevent it from being used except for pre-approved shows.

The room boasted a u-shaped couch, upholstered in a plaid, corduroy fabric. It was big enough, Susie thought, that it could easily seat two dozen people, maybe more. The coffee table had to have been made especially for this couch, Susie determined, because it conformed perfectly to it. A dozen or so plush floor pillows were stacked in bins along the back wall. Simon ran to them immediately, examining them and approving of their comfy soft texture.

Miss Pritchett laughed, telling Simon that sometimes even the adults prefer to lay on the floor using the pillows. Simon then wanted to know what was in the cabinets. Smiling, she told him the cabinets held blankets, lap quilts and some afghans, explaining that sometimes, in the winter, you need a little extra layer to keep the chill at bay.

Quickly she led them to a room behind the television area. It was a theater room. The screen was enormous, almost as large as the movie theaters. Miss Pritchett laughed when she saw their reaction, assuring them that it wasn't a movie screen but was a television. She told them it receives satellite television, and operates other devices as well. The chairs looked just like the comfortable stadium seating at the theater, complete with the drink holder and a small folding tray.

Moving them along, she led them out of the theater and to the right. The next door opened into a large room with walls that were mirrored from floor to ceiling. It had hardwood floors and no furnishings. A stationary barre was fastened to the mirrored wall at the far end of the room and a portable one stood several feet away. Positioned in the corner of the room and bolted to the ceiling was a large media screen. Miss Pritchett explained that this was where Juls practiced and also received her dance instruction.

Guiding them out of the room, Miss Pritchett moved them on to the last door. This room also had hardwood floors, but the floor was mostly covered by a thick mat. In here, only two walls were mirrored. There was a recessed storage unit that held various types of martial arts equipment. In one corner, there was a large bag that was suspended from the ceiling. It looked like a duffle bag, but Miss Pritchett explained it was a practice bag. This room, too, had a media screen suspended from its ceiling. As Miss Pritchett explained, Jared practices in here as well as receives his instruction.

"Doesn't practicing martial arts require you to practice with another person?" Susie asked.

"Yes, I believe some things do require a partner," Miss Pritchett agreed. "In those instances, Kevin practices with Jared. He has a black belt in several disciplines."

"Why doesn't he teach Jared?"

"Kevin has responsibilities that come first. In his spare time he practices with Jared."

Miss Pritchett stated it was time to move along, so they quickly left the Media Room. From there, they made their way to the Music Hall, a room that even impressed Simon. Miss Pritchett slid open its doors (they were pocket doors,) turning on the lights just as Susie and Simon stepped into the room.

Susie felt as if she had just been transported into one of Nana's stories. As if she were in a daze, Susie entered the room slowly, gazing at her surroundings. Perfectly spaced, in neat rows, were hundreds of white chairs, exquisitely carved and gilded, covered in a beautiful tapestry fabric. Above them in the vaulted, arched ceilings were twelve chandeliers, each having seven tiers of sparkling crystals that dazzled the eyes even lit at the low level Miss Pritchett had set. Floor to ceiling mirrors lined the walls, left and right, reflecting the light of the crystal chandeliers as if it were the noonday sun when fully lit.

At the farthest end of the conservatory was a raised platform. To the right was a concert grand piano and to the left was an elegant concert harp, contrasting and complementing each other. The piano was a glossy, black walnut whereas the harp was painted a glossy ivory with inlays of gold.

"Why are they so far apart?" Simon asked. "You could fit a whole army in there."

Miss Pritchett laughed at his analogy. "Sometimes, we have musicians that play other instruments. When we do, they're seated in between the piano and the harp," she explained.

"How many people can fit in here?" Susie asked.

"It depends," she answered reflectively. "If we're having a concert or music recital, we can seat three hundred people comfortably. If we're having a dance recital or a play, then it's somewhere between two hundred and two hundred and fifty. It varies depending upon the size and number of props that are needed."

"Who's in the performances?" Susie asked a little warily.

Miss Pritchett smiled. "Only those who choose to be," she assured Susie. "The only time we have performances anymore are at Christmas, Easter and our Reunion every June."

Simon had been plucking the strings on the harp, but now was quickly moving to the piano.

"Are you interested in taking lessons, Simon?" Miss Pritchett asked as they joined him at the piano.

"Maybe," he said, slowly bobbing his head. "I just wish there were drums."

Miss Pritchett's eyes twinkled. "Well, then; come with me. I have something to show you," she said, extending her hand to Simon.

Eagerly Simon clasped her hand, and she guided him toward the mirrored wall, stopping a few feet shy of the entrance wall. Lightly she pressed the edge of the mirror; it immediately popped open, revealing a hidden cabinet. Inside were kettledrums, snare drums, bass drums and tenor drums. On shelves above the drums were tambourines, xylophones, triangles, chimes and cymbals.

"Wow!" Simon exclaimed! "That's neat!" (Susie nodded her head in agreement with Simon.)

Miss Pritchett laughed and moved to the next mirror, pressing its edge. It, too, popped open, revealing four cellos and shelves holding violins, violas, guitars and banjos. The next cabinet revealed various clarinets, flutes, oboes, piccolos and saxophones. The last cabinet contained trombones, trumpets, tubas, French horns and two bagpipes.

"Who plays all of these?" Susie asked.

"We have several talented adults and children who play at least one instrument," she answered. "If you're interest in learning, I'll see to it that you have lessons." She smiled at Simon, adding, "The older children are required to practice for an hour every day, but your requirement would be only thirty minutes. That means, Simon, you must practice before playtime or reading with Susie."

Simon scrunched his nose. "That's okay," he said. I'll learn when I'm bigger."

"It's up to you, Simon. What about you, Susie?" she asked.

"I play the flute and the piano," she responded, remembering her last piano recital. She had played Nana's favorite first (Fur Elise) and then her own favorite (Pathetique). "I'd like to continue with lessons after Simon's settled in here, and I'd like to learn to play the harp."

"I'm certain we can arrange that," Miss Pritchett said with a smile. "Well, let's go to our next room," she stated, moving toward the door.

Miss Pritchett ushered them across the corridor and into a room that was larger than the Music Hall and Media Room combined. The double doors opened wide to reveal an elegant parlor, used in days gone by as a social hall. Susie held her breath – she felt as if she had stepped back in time. Slowly looking around the room, she drank in its contents.

Its two fireplaces were large, nearly as large as those in the Dining Hall, and were accented with carved marble casings. The wallpaper had an oriental look with its brightly plumed birds, plum trees, lotus flowers and pale blue background. The oak floors were highly polished, softly reflecting the light that filtered through the large windows in the north wall.

There were several conversation areas containing small couches and chairs upholstered in a velvet fabric. Though the main color was a pastel yellow, the fabric's pattern had trees with cherry blossoms and pale blue feathered birds. Some birds were in flight while others were sitting on the branches. The chairs were covered in an ice blue color of crushed velvet, creating a shimmering effect like sunlight on water.

The paintings that decorated the walls were beautifully displayed in ornately carved frames. There was only one seascape; it was positioned on the east wall, midway between the fireplace and the beginning of the north wall. It was much larger than all of the other paintings. Susie felt drawn to it and wanted a closer look.

Unfortunately, Miss Pritchett called her back, reminding her that she and Simon would have plenty of time to explore later; this was just a cursory tour. Susie turned around and headed back to Miss Pritchett, and it was then she saw the annual group photographs Miss Hilda had mentioned – they lined the south wall. She made a mental note to herself to find the time to examine them alone – Simon would be too much of a distraction considering he would never willingly agree to spend time doing so. His attention span was far too short; he would whine and pester her to leave, or his boredom would cause him to get into something that he shouldn't – again causing her to leave. No, she would definitely have to do it alone.

Exiting the Parlor, Miss Pritchett ushered them to the left and headed toward the foyer's double doors. However, when they reached the small intersecting hallway in front of the double doors, Simon darted to the left.

"Where does that go?" he asked, pointing to a wide door at the end.

"That is our elevator," she answered with a smile. "It requires a key to open it, and to operate it."

"Why?" Simon queried.

"To make certain little ones don't get into it and possibly get hurt," Miss Pritchett responded, repressing the urge to laugh. Although successful, her wide grin and twinkling eyes gave her away - she enjoyed his banter and his curiosity.

Simon nodded as if agreeing with her. Susie knew him well enough to know that was unlikely. Truth be told, he was only processing the information until he could figure a way to open it without a key.

Quickly Miss Pritchett guided them to the right. And a short distance later, Susie realized they were now at the main corridor of the west wing, the one they use every day going to and from the Dining Hall.

Turning left, they began moving toward the south wing. As they traversed along the corridor, Miss Pritchett told them that the entire south wing was once the garden conservatory. The memories caused her expression to glow with happiness, and her voice became soft like a gentle summer rain. She spoke with fondness of the times she and her mother had afternoon tea in the area that is now the classroom. And, sometimes, just the two of them would have breakfast in the area that is currently being used as the arts and craft room. Many times, her mother would read to her in a little grotto, now serving as the Lavatory and Linen Room.

Her eyes sparkled with gladness as she told them how sunny and bright it had been in the conservatory in those days. Although the current conservatory still receives considerable sunlight, she added; it isn't near the amount of light as it once had. She laughed softly at Simon's puzzled look, then explained that the walls and the entire roof are made of glass.

Simon was impressed, amazed that it didn't break and said so. Miss Pritchett's laugh had such a happy ring that Susie was almost certain she truly enjoyed Simon's constant questions. Smiling sweetly at Simon, Miss Pritchett tousled his hair and told him that the glass is "specially made to be super strong". Simon, naturally, took this to mean that a superhero had to have made it. She laughed and agreed, telling him in a way, one did.

As they entered the south wing, Miss Pritchett had said that it was remodeled after her mother died. Her voice sounded a little sad, but she managed a smile. Until the remodeling of the south wing was completed, she told them; her father had all of their things moved into the west wing from the east wing and closed the east wing. And it had been closed ever since.

When Simon asked why he did that, Susie nearly choked. She gave him a very stern 'it's-none-of-your-business' look. As usual, it had no effect on him. For a fleeting second there was an intense sorrow in Miss Pritchett's expression; then it was gone. Her face now showed no emotion, and her voice was equally bland. Very calmly she stated she didn't know; he never told her. Her smile was forced as she added that she was certain he had a good reason.

Simon wouldn't let it drop. He pressed her further by asking if Miss Pritchett asked him. She gave him a look that Susie was certain had been seen on her own face many times – a look of exasperation and irritation.

Completely surprising Susie, Miss Pritchett began to chuckle softly, and her face softened. Smiling warmly at Simon, she told him she was only seven years old when her mother died. It never occurred to her to ask. Then, she further revealed, her father died when she was eleven. Once again the sadness returned to her face as tears misted her eyes. In a quiet voice, not much more than a whisper, she told Simon that she never had the chance to ask.

Simon eyes grew wide as he began to understand that Miss Pritchett lost her Mommy and Daddy just like he and Susie. His eyes filled with tears of compassion. He threw his arms around Miss Pritchett, giving her one of his best bear hugs.

In silence and in a shared consolation, Miss Pritchett returned his hug. To Susie, anyone watching might think that they were mother and child. Susie wasn't certain how she felt about that. She wanted Simon to be happy, but she didn't want him to forget their real parents or Nana.

As she watched them, understanding filled her. Now she fully realized that remembering Mommy and Daddy would be impossible for Simon since he was just a baby when they died. His memories of Nana would be sparse in comparison to hers. Susie smiled – she knew what to do. She would do as Nana did; she would tell him about all the things they did and show him the pictures in the albums. Susie fought her own tears, resolving to remain strong. Simon needed her strength, and she wasn't going to let him down; not ever.

Miss Pritchett released Simon, kissing his forehead and thanking him for his hug. Her countenance glowed as she told him that she felt much better. Simon nodded his head and chirped, "Me too!" He grinned so big, Susie was certain his sweet face would lock in that position. Sauntering on down the corridor, Simon began strutting like a little peacock.

Miss Pritchett resumed her oratory, telling them that the garden conservatory had been decreased in size to allow for the addition of the rooms, both upstairs and downstairs. The second floor was added but not as high as in the main section of the manor, enabling the garden to receive some sunlight through the remaining portion of the glass wall and roof.

She went on to tell them that the upstairs was made into her bedroom, bathroom, linen room, laundry room and playroom, in addition to suites for her nanny and for her governess. The downstairs is the same as it was when she was a child, she told them. After she left for college, the south wing was unused except for the garden conservatory. When she decided to start the orphanage, she changed a portion of the upstairs into the Dorm Rooms.

Since they had seen the Cloak Room and the lavatory last night, they proceeded to the classroom. Miss Pritchett opened the door, allowing them to enter first.

"Why did you start the orphanage?" Simon asked as Miss Pritchett entered the room.

Susie inhaled sharply. "Simon," she admonished; "it's none of your business."

"It's all right, Susie;" Miss Pritchett softly answered. "A bad thing happened to me, Simon; and it made me very sad. I felt so lonely in this big house. It was really much too big for just me and the staff. One day it occurred to me that I could use this house to help children who need a place to live. I discussed it with my best friend, Miss Hilda, and with my attorney. He handled all the legal work to make Glen Hollow Orphanage a reality. We have been able to help a lot of children, just like you and Susie."

Simon's face had an odd expression, a cross between curiosity and misgiving. "Our Miss Hilda?" he asked.

"Yes," Miss Pritchett acknowledged, grinning.

Seeing that Simon was about to continue, with no telling what, Susie quickly spoke and effectively stopped him. "That was really nice," she told Miss Pritchett.

Miss Pritchett smiled warmly as she tenderly looked at them. "I do hope you and Simon will like it here. If you don't, I will find a place that both of you will like."

She stepped further into the room. "This, as you can see, is the class-room. The rows are in order of youngest in the front, and the oldest children in the last row."

Susie glanced briefly around the room. It seemed so odd to her for such a large room to have so few desks. She wondered why they didn't move the classroom to a smaller room. Then it hit her - - there weren't any smaller rooms!

Like her previous schools, the classroom was arranged with the teacher's desk at the head of the class and the blackboards behind her desk. Large windows lined the entire back wall of the room, allowing for plenty of light and a good view of the east garden.

Eight retractable wall maps hung along the side walls of the room, depicting the world at various stages in history. A wallpaper border ran all around the room, just below the ceiling. It was a timeline of the history of the planet. Susie stepped a little closer to get a better look. It was all hand drawn! Susie wondered who had done such meticulous work. The paper seemed to be fairly old (it was beginning to have a yellow cast to it), so it couldn't have been Miss Emma.

Turning her attention to the rest of the room, she noticed that between the desks and the windows was a long table. It was unique in that the table would be uncomfortable for adults; it was obviously made for children. Matching benches were placed on each side of the diminutive table. Against the wall and not far from the table was a cabinet. The doors were closed, so Susie couldn't tell what was inside, but she figured it had to be related to the table. Probably, she thought, it has the tablecloth and napkins.

Along the length of the side walls of the room were open-box shelving. Stored in them were several types of toys, puzzles, construction papers, poster boards, crayons, glitters and, glue. It seemed that every type of school and art supply that could ever be needed was in abundant supply. Simon was already pawing through the bins, looking at everything.

Miss Pritchett called both of them to come back to her. Simon quickly complied, but Susie had noticed something in the garden that caught her attention. Actually it was two somethings, and she was trying to ascertain just what she saw.

"Class begins at eight o'clock," Miss Pritchett was saying. She was currently standing by the door with Simon, waiting for Susie.

"Susie," Miss Pritchett called out to her a little sharply. "We're ready to continue our tour. Please join us."

Susie turned away from the window. "I'm sorry, Miss Pritchett," she apologized; "I saw a white flash over there (Susie pointed to where she had seen it).

Miss Pritchett smiled. "Yes, I'm certain you did. The flash was prob-ably the unicorn statue. The white granite tends to reflect the sunlight."

"Awesome," Simon remarked. "Can ... I mean, may we go see it?"

"Not today; I promise you'll have plenty of time in which to explore the manor and the grounds," she said smiling. "We need to continue our tour if we want to finish before dinner."

As she guided them to the door, she added, "Since school lunchtime is only thirty minutes, it is served in here at the table. After lunch, class resumes for the older children. Simon, Megan and Timmy will have their naptime."

Simon rapidly shook his head. "I don't take naps," he informed her.

"You may choose not to sleep, but you will rest. Miss Cora and Miss Ginger will escort the three of you to the Rec Room. You each have a mat that you will lay on and sleep or daydream. But you will be quiet and rest. After naptime, you are free to play in the Rec Room."

Scowling, Simon crossed his arms. "I ... don't ... take ... naps," he told her again forcibly.

"Simon, you…" Susie began but stopped when Miss Pritchett held up her hand.

"This isn't a debate, Simon; nor is it open for discussion," she firmly stated. "We shall proceed to the Craft Room, and from there we will visit the Garden Conservatory."

They left, following her to the Craft Room. Miss Pritchett only allowed them to peek in from the doorway. There were a dozen work tables in various heights so that all children would have a table that suited them, whether standing or sitting. There were storage shelves and storage cabinets where all the supplies are kept. Currently, on one of the taller of the tables, a model jet was in the process of being assembled. There were easels that held paintings in various stages of completion, and several clay modeling projects in process.

Next it was on to the Garden Conservatory. As they entered, they were amazed and spellbound by such a marvelous room. If it wasn't for the metal beams of the glass roof, you would forget that you were actu-ally inside. There were birds chirping and singing, flying from one tree to another. There were butterflies flitting from flower to flower just as they did outside.

Miss Pritchett firmly grasped Simon's hand as she led them from the entry area and down one of the pathways. Susie could hear the waterfall long before she could see it. It was fantastic. The rock waterfall was at least twenty feet high and looked as if it was springing forth from the side of a mountain. The water gently cascaded down the rocks and splashed into the pool below. There were goldfish swimming in the pool, some little, some big. Sunlight streamed in through the glass roof causing the water to sparkle like glitter.

"Awesome!" Simon exclaimed. "What do they eat?" he asked.

"A special food that gives them all the vitamins and minerals they need," she replied.

"Who feeds them?" he quickly lobbed.

"Myself and Miss Hilda usually," she answered.

"May I?" he asked, eyes wide in hopeful anticipation.

"Only if I, or Miss Hilda or Susie is with you," she stated. "I'm serious, Simon. If you feed them too much, they will die."

Worry showed on his little face. "They'll die?"

Very somberly she nodded her head. "Yes, Simon; they will. It's very important that you not feed the fish unless you tell me first. Do we have a deal?"

Sending his curls into a bouncing frenzy, Simon rapidly nodded his head. "I promise," he sincerely vowed.

"Very well," she said, opening a small canister. She retrieved a small scoop, filled it with the fish food and leveled the food to the rim of the scoop. Showing it to Simon, she told him, "This is how much you feed them. We only feed them once each day, and it's usually at night. This is my week to feed them, so we'll go ahead and do it now."

She handed the scoop to Simon. He beamed as he took it from her.

"Gently shake it back and forth over the water," she instructed. Simon complied, and the food gently fell on top of the water and floated. Within seconds the fish had detected the food; moving like torpedoes, they quickly swam to it. They darted to the surface, gobbling it up as fast as they could.

Simon squealed with delight, clapping his hands and jumping up and down.

Susie smiled; it was good to see Simon enjoying himself.

Miss Pritchett retrieved the empty scoop from Simon, returning it to the canister. "Don't forget our deal," she reminded him.

"I won't," he assured her.

"Let's go; we're running out time," she told them, grasping Simon's hand.

They hurried back to the entrance and out into the corridor. Instead of returning to the main foyer, Miss Pritchett quickly guided them to the left, rapidly striding toward the rear door that led outside to the pergola. She explained they would use the spiral staircase near the end of the corridor, saving time.

Reaching the second floor minutes later, Miss Pritchett ushered them hurriedly to the next stop – the Rec Room. She opened the door, allowing them to step just inside the door. She greeted the few children inside the room; they responded like automatons before returning to their activities.

As they continued down the corridor, Miss Pritchett reminded Susie and Simon that the Rec Room was one of two places the younger children could be without supervision of either an adult or one of the older children. Smiling at Simon, she firmly stated that he, Timmy and Megan were only allowed in the Dorm Room and in the Rec Room without any supervision.

He frowned and began what Susie could only guess would be a complaint. However, Miss Pritchett stopped him cold with just a look. Susie silently wished she had that talent.

Across the corridor was the Laundry Room. Miss Pritchett allowed them to peek inside, stating they only needed to know where it is located. She laughed at Simon's expression, qualifying her statement with the addition that only those assigned with laundry duty use this room.

Quickly she took them to their next stop – the Girls Dorm. Opening the door, she stepped into the Common Area. Simon barged in right behind her with Susie closely following him.

The Common Area was comprised of two dark-green couches that faced each other, and four comfortable looking, overstuffed chairs that were a mushroom color. Between the couches was a small coffee table bearing several different magazines. A large braided rug covered the hardwood floor of the seating area. There were several small bookcases, and a rather large grandfather clock. Three, large Palladium windows encompassed most of the east wall, allowing for plenty of bright sunlight to fill the room every morning. Overlooking a portion of the east garden, the view was incredible. The windows also afforded a partial view of the east wing and the southeast wing, both of which were dark and dismal.

To the right was another door; and, in answer to Simon's question, Miss Pritchett stated that it led to the bathroom. Amused by his curiosity, she added that the girls' rooms were down the hallway to their left. With a lively grin, Simon ran down the hallway, eager to see what they looked like.

The first room was Susie's, Miss Pritchett said. Peering in, Susie was surprised and delighted to see that it was larger than her old room at Nana's. And she was astonished for someone had beautifully decorated it in a creamy white with accents in a multitude of shades of pink. She loved it!

"When your things arrive, you may replace any of the bedding or the curtains with what you had at Nana's, if you prefer," Miss Pritchett said softly.

Susie shook her head no. "I love it," she admitted.

Simon darted down the hallway to the next room. Miss Pritchett quickly followed, closing the gap between them. Susie was surprised to see that all of the rooms were the same size, and were furnished with the same delicate-looking furnishings, antique white with gold accents. Each room had a four-poster bed, nightstand, desk and chair, a small dresser with mirror, an armoire, a cheval mirror and a four-drawer chest. What made each room unique were the different choices of décor - colors of bedding, throw pillows, posters, toys and stuffed animals. Each room also had shelves and a large chest that could be used to store treasures, toys or extra quilts and blankets.

There was only one difference that Susie could see; all of the other girls had interior rooms. She was the only one that had a window. She smiled.

Miss Pritchett hurriedly ushered them out of the Girls Dorm and across the corridor to the Boy's Dorm. It was laid out exactly like the Girl's Dorm, right down to the same furnishings in the Common Area. Their Dorm also had three, large Palladium windows, only these offered a view of the west garden, and partial views of the west wing and the southwest wing.

As soon as she had told him which room was his, Simon ran as fast as he could to see his room. Miss Pritchett managed to catch up with him halfway down the hallway. She led them to his room which was the last one on the inside wall. Although he pouted a little that he didn't have a window, he was very pleased with the room. Simon's room was decorated in a bold plaid with shades of red, blue, purple and green. Someone had even made for him a lap quilt with what she guessed to be a Binky (his favorite dinosaur) appliquéd in the center. Simon was ecstatic when he saw it. Squealing with joy, he snatched it up and hugged it.

All the boys had sturdy oak furnishings; beds, nightstand, desk and chair, a small dresser with mirror, an armoire, a cheval mirror and a four-drawer chest. They also had shelves and a storage chest just as the girls did.

Citing they had to hurry because it was nearly time for dinner, Miss Pritchett guided them out of the Dorm and toward the main staircase. She pointed to Miss Cora's and then to Miss Ginger's suites as they rushed past on their way to the landing.

Quickly she ushered them down the main staircase. She repeated the rule of 'no bannister sliding' as they descended, and Susie was positive it was directed at Simon. She was also positive that he was ignoring her directive. Upon reaching the ground floor, Miss Pritchett hurried them along the west wing corridor, the same corridor they always use in order to get to the Dining Hall. As they went, Miss Pritchett answered Simon's questions.

He wanted to know why the entire left wall of the corridor looked like the porch of the Chapel, and why this one had windows. Miss Pritchett corrected him, telling him that it was a portico, not a porch.

She explained that while a porch may run around a building, a portico is a long, covered walkway that connects the buildings. Giving him an encouraging smile, she told him that he had a good eye because he had noticed the similarities. (That made him grin, and strut his little bouncy walk.) The reason they look the same, she explained, is due to the fact that this corridor was once a portico. After her mother died, the changes to the west wing were part of the renovations her father had done.

Years ago, she told them, the ground floor of the west wing held only the Dining Hall, the Library, a Grand Parlor and a Ballroom. All of the rooms had windows and French doors that opened out onto the portico. The renovation removed the windows and doors, replacing them with walls. The arches of the portico were enclosed with glass, thus creating the main corridor of the west wing. This afforded everyone a view of the west garden as they walked the corridor, and gave them protection from the weather. The Grand Parlor and the Ballroom were reduced to a third of their original size, allowing for the new rooms. It also gave space for the corridor between the rooms, and the smaller hallway between the Library and the new rooms.

Simon's curiosity prompted him to ask if the bedroom he was in last night was new, too. She laughed and told him that the second floor has had some changes, but not to that room. Smiling, she told him that before her mother died, the second and the third floors of the west wing were for guests. The east wing's second and third floors were where her family resided. That caused him to give her a "Huh?" With a soft chuckle she told him that resided means lived. Simon shrugged and told her she should have said so in the first place. Grinning, she nodded in agreement, telling him that at least he now knows a new word. That made Simon grin.

When they passed by the small hallway to their right connecting to the corridor that led to the where they had begun the tour, the image of the manor's layout was now firmly entrenched in Susie's mind. Miss Pritchett was right when she said it was a simple plan – it was.

Miss Pritchett stopped at a pair of large double doors. Framed in white oak, the heavy glass doors were decorated with a frosted etching. Susie had wondered what this room was when they passed it yesterday, and again this morning. Miss Pritchett pushed open one of the doors and motioned for them to enter. They did. It was the Library.

Susie was in heaven – here she could lose herself and find contentment. The Library would be her sanctuary. Its vaulted ceiling gave it the appearance, the ambiance, of an ancient cathedral. Adding to that effect was the white marble pillars and the highly polished marble floor. Plush carpeting, dark hunter green in color, covered the aisles. They quite effectively muted sound so that whoever was using the Library wouldn't be disturbed by echoing footsteps.

Very appreciatively, Susie looked all around. There were rows and rows of tall, double-sided bookcases as far as the eye could see. "Awesome," she whispered.

Three main aisles led away from the reception area, north (straight ahead), west and east. Miss Pritchett guided them to the west section. As they walked quickly, Miss Pritchett explained that, in addition to the stacks, the Library has four reading areas and four study areas. Simon asked what a stack is. She chuckled lightheartedly and explained that it is a library term that meant the bookcases. He gave her one of his *'that's absurd'* looks which only made her laugh even more.

When they reached the west section, Miss Pritchett pointed to the four double-sided bookcases (each about three feet tall), stating that they only contained children's books. Each section of the Library had these same bookcases, but with different books of course. (She added that last part, smiling at Simon.)

"Neat-o!" Simon exclaimed approvingly.

At first Susie thought he was referring to the many bookcases just for children. No so. He was halfway to the built-in bookcases lining the west wall and flanking both sides of the fireplace. Rising to the thirty–foot ceiling, the shelves were filled with books of all sizes and colors; some were old while others were fairly new.

To reach the highest shelves, a sturdy oak ladder was inserted into a groove in the floor. The ladder was attached at its top end to a thick rail and the rail was anchored to the wall just above the bookcases. Additionally, there were thinner rails that were attached to every third shelf of the bookcase and anchored to the end walls. The ladders were attached to the thin rails by metal brackets. Simon was headed for the ladder and running as fast as he could.

"Simon," Miss Pritchett called out sternly. "Come here immediately."

Simon dropped to a dead stop and whirled around. His little face was scrunched into a very unhappy expression. "What?"

"You must stay with us," she firmly stated.

Simon's shoulders slouched as he shuffled his way back to them, looking very dejected. Susie was certain it was a ploy to get Miss Pritchett to allow him to check out the ladder. If it was, it didn't work.

Miss Pritchett looked him squarely in the eyes and repeated, "You are to remain with us. The Library isn't a playground, and the ladders are not for children. Understand?"

Simon huffed a little sigh, crossed his arms and pouted slightly. "Yes, Miss Pritchett."

"Good, now come with me," she said cheerfully, leading them toward the fireplace.

"This is one of the reading areas," she explained; "the other three are similarly furnished, although only the east and west sections have a fireplace."

Arranged on a large Persian carpet were three wingback chairs, upholstered in a tapestry fabric, and one cushiony, overstuffed chair which was upholstered in a buttery-soft leather. A coffee table was positioned in the center of the grouping, and each chair had its own accent table and reading lamp. Simon had to try all of the chairs. Watching him as he flitted from chair to chair, Susie thought of the story of Goldilocks and giggled. Although Simon admitted they were all good, his favorite was the burgundy leather chair. As far as he was concerned, it was "his" chair, and he loudly proclaimed title to it.

Susie wondered why the reading area was so far from the fireplace since most people enjoy the warmth of a fire while they read. She began to ask and stopped. She suddenly realized that the fireplace was as large as the ones in the Dining Hall, and that meant a very hot fire if the big logs were used. And, she further realized, that if a small fire was built, the raised hearth would still afford a nice place to sit and read.

Miss Pritchett smiled and checked her watch. "Time to go," she stated.

As they quickly began their trek back to the Library doors, Miss Pritchett told Susie where she could find the other reading areas as well as the four study areas. Smiling, she mentioned that Susie should avail herself of the Library whenever the Dorm Room is too noisy in which to study. Susie nodded - she already had thought of it.

As they reached the doors, Miss Pritchett said, "Susie, I have decided what chores will be assigned to you, and there will be two." (Susie's expression was a guarded one.) "First, you will be responsible for waking the girls every morning at six. Miss Cora arrives at six-forty to escort you all to breakfast. Normally, I don't assign this until age twelve. However, in three weeks you will be twelve, so I think you can handle it now. Second, you are assigned the task of taking the girls' dirty clothes from the hamper each afternoon and place them in the laundry room's hamper. But not the towels and linens; that chore belongs to Juls."

Miss Pritchett paused briefly then asked, "Any questions?"

Susie coolly replied, "No, Miss Pritchett." Silently she thought how unfair it is to make her pick up after the other girls. After all, they were just as capable of putting their dirty clothes in the laundry room as she. And, she further reflected, why should she be responsible for getting everyone up; wasn't that Miss Cora's job?

"What about me?" Simon asked eagerly. "What are my chores?"

Miss Pritchett softly laughed. "You already have chores," she answered. "Remember? You are to make your bed every morning. You are to put your dirty clothes in the bathroom clothes hamper every day. You are to put your dirty towels and wash cloths in the linen hamper every day. You must put away your toys when you've finished playing with them. You must neatly put away your clean clothes. You must remember to put things back after you've used them, like games or toys, in the Rec Room. And, most important, you are to do your school work every day to the very best that you can."

Simon frowned. "Everybody has to do those things," he said.

"Yes; and when you get older, you'll have more chores assigned." She smiled. "I think you have enough right now, don't you?"

He sighed. "I guess."

"Good," she cheerfully responded; "I think we should proceed to the Dining Hall. We have only a few minutes before it's time for dinner."

Miss Pritchett held the door open for them, allowing them to exit into the corridor. "We'll forego visiting the southwest wing," she stated as they passed through the doorway. "I believe you saw the majority of the rooms there last night on your trek to the laundry room."

Simon bounced his head rapidly in agreement. "But we didn't get to go in," he countered; "just the bathroom and laundry room."

"Miss Hilda told us what the rooms were as we passed by," Susie reminded him.

"But we didn't get to *see* them," Simon objected.

"You will, Simon," Miss Pritchett assured him.

"Miss Pritchett," Susie began her quest; "Will it be all right for me to read to Simon at bedtime? We've always done that with Nana, and I continued it at Mrs. Crenshaw's."

"I would prefer that you didn't," Miss Pritchett responded. "Bedtime needs to be bedtime, Susie. Perhaps you could read to him in the Library in the afternoon," she suggested. "Four o'clock would be a good time," she quickly added.

Flabbergasted, Susie just stared at her, and then slowly her gaze focused on Simon. He was very upset.

"I don't see why we can't have a Story Time at bedtime. We always have," Susie vigorously protested.

"Yeah," Simon joined in the debate. "I want my bedtime story," he wheedled.

"Is there any reason why you can't have a Story Time every day in the Library at four in the afternoon?" Miss Pritchett countered pleasantly.

"I want my bedtime story," Simon fussed, becoming more insistent. "Mrs. C let us!"

"Simon needs it," Susie hotly argued. "He needs things not to change so much. I think it's important, and I don't think he should do without it," Susie obstinately insisted, her voice becoming loud enough to be heard by anyone even remotely nearby.

Miss Hilda entered the corridor and approached. Her expression clearly showed she was quite concerned with what she heard, not so much the words but the hostile tone with which they were said.

"It's time for dinner," she calmly reported, giving Susie a brief glance.

Miss Pritchett checked her watch. "So it is." She smiled at Susie and Simon. "We'd better hurry. We have four minutes." She motioned for them to walk on ahead. Miss Hilda lingered behind, softly conversing with Miss Pritchett as Susie and Simon headed toward the Dining Hall.

Susie quickly steered Simon into the Hall and to his chair. As she assisted Simon into his booster seat, she leaned down and whispered, "Don't worry; when everyone is asleep, I'll sneak in and read you a story."

He looked up into his big sister's eyes and smiled at her. His eyes danced with joy for he knew she would.

Chapter 9

A LONG DAY ENDS

Susie lay still, listening to the chiming of the grandfather clock, counting each chime. Ten o'clock. Silently she crept out of bed, pulling on her robe and her slippers. She picked up her flashlight and the book Miss Hilda had given them the night before, tiptoed to the edge of her room and paused, listening. All was quiet.

Cautiously Susie made her way down the hallway, through the Common Area and to the door. Carefully she eased open the door, just a smidge, and peeked into the corridor. She could see Miss Hilda and Miss Ginger talking, standing near the second floor landing.

Although glad they had not seen her, Susie was slightly irritated that they were delaying her rendezvous with Simon. Simon was not patient, nor did he have the ability to be still for any length of time. This could be a problem Susie well knew; left to his own devices, Simon could easily start playing and awaken all of the boys. The more time that passed, the more anxious Susie became. She peered again into the corridor.

"Rats," she whispered softly. Miss Hilda and Miss Ginger were still talking.

Slowly she closed the door, deciding to give them a few minutes before making another attempt to leave the Dorm. The grandfather clock noisily ticked away the minutes, and Susie decided to try again after another five minutes had passed. This time it was a go – the corridor was empty.

She slinked out of her Dorm, ears keenly listening for the faintest sound that someone was near. It was eerily silent. Quick as she could, Susie dashed across the large corridor to the Boys Dorm and carefully opened the door. She peeked in. She smiled. No one was stirring. Susie entered, closed the door softly and, hastily moved through their Common Area and down the hallway to Simon's room.

He was sitting up, waiting for her and passing the time playing with his dinosaurs. Upon seeing her, Simon grinned. "I thought you'd never get here," he fussed.

"Shh," she whispered; "we have to be very quiet." Susie slid in next to him, picking up his dinosaurs and placing them on his nightstand.

"Okay," he loudly whispered.

Susie balanced her flashlight on her left shoulder, using the headboard to help stabilize it. Opening the book, she began reading as Simon cuddled up to her. Gently she rubbed his back as she read to him from the book 'The Lost Prince and Princess'. Fifteen minutes later, as she read the last paragraph, Susie saw that he had fallen fast asleep.

"Good timing," she whispered to him, gently kissing the top of his head.

She switched off her flashlight, closed the book and laid them on the nightstand. Carefully she shifted Simon down into his bed and covered him, tucking the covers around him. Retrieving his favorite stuffed dinosaur, Binky (a lime green stegosaurus with large, purple spots), from the foot of his bed, Susie placed it against him and draped his arm over it.

She watched him for a few minutes, sleeping peacefully, and kissed his forehead. Susie whispered a short missive to Heaven, praying that Simon would be happy here. She picked up the book and flashlight, and left him sleeping, dreaming his little boy dreams.

Quiet as a cat, Susie retraced her steps, moving quickly back down their little hallway, through their Common Area and back to the door. Opening it just a sliver, she peered into the corridor and saw no one. Easing the door open a little further, she slipped through and closed the door quietly behind her before making a mad dash back to her Dorm Room and to her own bed.

Flopping down onto her bed, Susie gave a big sigh of relief. She had been successful. Feeling an irresistible urge to laugh, she grabbed her pillow and held it against her face. Susie laughed and giggled with abandonment, knowing her roommates couldn't hear her. She didn't know why she had this irrepressible urge – she just knew she felt better, more like her old self, in relinquishing to it.

A few minutes later, when all the giggles had been released, Susie fluffed her pillow and lay back down. Quickly she said her prayers and, when finished, smiled a happy, little smile as she slowly drifted off to sleep.

Unknown to Susie, when she exited the Boys Dorm, Miss Hilda and Miss Cora were standing slightly to the side of the entryway landing. Susie did not see them as she darted across the corridor to her own Dorm. But they saw her.

"What in the world was she doing in there?" Miss Cora said, surprised.

"Probably reading Simon a bedtime story," Miss Hilda answered dryly. "She had a book and flashlight with her." She frowned and added, "Eloise had told her earlier today that she could read to him in the afternoons, but not at bedtime. The children did not take it well and were very upset. It appears they have decided to ignore Eloise."

"Well, I'll just go have a chat with her right now," Miss Cora declared.

"No," Miss Hilda said softly; "let it go. I'll speak to Eloise and see how she wants to handle this; then I'll let you know."

"All right, then. Goodnight, Hilda," she said.

She gave Miss Cora a reassuring smile. "Good-night, Cora."

Miss Cora quickly entered her suite as Miss Hilda descended the foyer staircase, taking the steps quickly as she hastened to Miss Pritchett's office for their meeting.

———

"Surely, Eloise, you know Susie is going to continue to read to Simon at bedtime every night, don't you?" Hilda asked her, perplexed at her friend's laissez-faire attitude to what she and Cora had witnessed.

Eloise chuckled lightly. "Of course I do, Hilda. I never said she couldn't."

"I thought you did?" Hilda was perplexed.

Eloise chuckled lightly and poured them both another cup of tea. "No; what I said was that I would prefer that she didn't, knowing that she will. I told her bedtime needs to be bedtime. I suggested that she read to Simon in the Library during the afternoon."

"And you're not going to stop her from reading to him at bedtime?" Hilda pressed.

"Heavens, no," Eloise said with a hearty laugh.

Hilda shook her head. "Then I don't understand. You intimated to her that she was not to have a bedtime Story Time with Simon. We both know that's how she interpreted what you said. She'll secretly defy you, and you know this; but you don't intend to stop her."

"She isn't defying me, Hilda, because I didn't actually say she couldn't."

Eloise gently began massaging her forehead and her temples as she explained her rationale. "To do it in secret will require that she elicit the help of the other children. They will work together as a team and, as a result, form familiar bonds. To form those bonds they must trust each other, to let down their walls and to stop being so withdrawn. And the result will be happier children."

"Why not just tell them that and have their Story Time openly? They would be able to take turns choosing and reading to each other. Wouldn't that also create bonds?" Hilda countered.

"No, because they wouldn't do it. They need to be united in a common cause," she responded softly as she picked up her teacup and slowly sipped her tea.

"It just seems to be the hard way around." Hilda sighed, stirred her tea and took a sip.

"I know," Eloise replied with a soft sigh. She stared at her teacup, momentarily lost in thought.

Still focused on her teacup, she quietly said, "When they learn to trust each other, they will be able to begin the process of trusting us. Then I will let them know that I think the Story Time at bedtime is a good idea. Everyone wins." She looked at Hilda and smiled.

"Maybe so," Hilda agreed reluctantly.

The two sat quietly, sipping their tea, listening to the soft, crackling sounds as the fire danced its way toward becoming nothing more than faintly glowing embers. The gentle chiming of the mantle clock announced that the hour was late; a quarter to midnight.

"This group of children seems particularly difficult to reach," Eloise spoke in a soft, contemplative tone. After a slight pause she added, "I don't think we've ever had such a difficult group."

"Oh, yes we have," Hilda responded quickly. "You've forgotten. Perhaps conveniently?"

Eloise smiled. "Perhaps," she acquiesced.

Hilda raised her right eyebrow and grinned. "Remember Peter Cook; now that was a little devil if ever there was one. And look at him now - he's a minister in Shadow Grove. He has such a great love and compassion for people. His ministry has touched the lives of so many. It's humbling to know we had a part in raising him, mentoring him and helping him to find the right path for his life."

Eloise just chuckled, sipping her tea as Hilda continued their journey down memory lane.

"Oh, and what about the Andersen twins, Devon and Darin? ... I swear, Eloise; I thought you'd have to send them to the State Home. But you didn't give up; and because you didn't, we reached them. They've grown into fine men, owning their own construction business that they built up from *nothing* into one of the state's largest firms. Look how many people they've employed over the past twenty years, not to mention the kids that they've taken in and taught a vocation. When I think of all the youth centers and the homes for charity they've built for just the cost of materials, I am absolutely amazed and humbled that we had a part in their raising. We've had many successes over the years, Eloise. We've lost a few, but we've had far more successes than losses."

"Yes, we have," Eloise concurred, smiling.

They sat quietly for a few minutes. Suddenly Eloise began to laugh, a hearty, rolling laugh. Within a few minutes, she had contained it to a quieter giggle. Grinning at Hilda, she said, "I'll never forget the look on your face the first time Sheriff Atkins brought Kyra home at two a.m."

"You were just as shocked as I was," Hilda chuckled, her eyes flashing in delight at the memory. "That child had the makings of a great escape artist."

Hilda paused momentarily as the memories replayed in her mind; a little sigh escaped from her, revealing she missed those days and Kyra as well.

"She was a defiant soul, that one," Hilda continued, slowly nodding her head, remembering the many times they had been awakened in the middle of the night.

Each time Sheriff Atkins would apologize for the lateness of the hour; but he knew Eloise didn't want Kyra taken to juvenile detention. Kyra would glare at them, storm upstairs and be insolent for days, angry that her fun was impeded. They had even gone to the trouble to have special locks installed on all the doors in an effort to prevent her midnight escapades. How she was able to sneak out was still a mystery – Kyra never would tell them just how she managed it. To this day, she'd only smile when asked.

"She was indeed," Eloise agreed. "Whoever would have thought she'd be a juvenile court judge now?"

"You did," Hilda said softly. "You've always had a gift to know the children, to help them on their journey." She smiled, adding, "Not all have responded as we would have liked; but then the same can be said for one's natural child. There are no guarantees."

"So true. Maybe I'm just too old to do this anymore." There was a hint of sadness in her voice.

"Well, I don't think that's true," Hilda shrugged; "but you can always close the Orphanage, and return Glen Hollow to just being your home. If you sell some of the timber acreage, you won't have so much work trying to manage this place."

"I can't do that," she responded, slowly shaking her head.

"Why not? It belongs to you; it's yours to sell," she stated, a hint of puzzlement underlying her tone.

Eloise released a heavy, troubled sigh. She looked up at her dear friend. She struggled with her thoughts, uncertain whether or not she should confide something she had never told anyone.

Hilda could clearly see the inner conflict with which Eloise was besieged. She sat quietly, sipping her tea, allowing Eloise the time to sort through her thoughts. She knew Eloise well enough to know that whatever it was, she wouldn't discuss it until she was ready. And knowing Eloise, it might be never.

After several long minutes of silence, Eloise spoke. Her voice was quiet, almost a whisper. "Mother, the night she died, made me promise never to sell any portion of Glen Hollow. Even then I knew how important it had to be. As weak as she was, she pushed herself up onto one arm and leaned close to me in order to look directly into my eyes. She held my hand so tight, insisting that I promise. …. and I did."

"You were only seven years old!" Hilda responded, her tone one of utter incredulity. "How could you possibly be expected to keep such a promise, especially in light of what your father did?"

Eloise hesitated, staring at the teacup in her hand. She continued, her voice strained with the anguish she had for so long kept buried. "I know, Hilda; but you know he was never the same after Mother died. He was so different after her death … totally different."

Her face clouded with the pain of sorrow and sadness. "He blamed himself for her illness. He never said as much, but I knew he did. I don't know why he blamed himself. …. I wish I did."

She looked up at Hilda. "He never got over her death and that destroyed him. You know that; you watched him, just as I did, sink into despair until he finally died."

Concern for her friend flooded her heart, reflecting in Hilda's face and in her voice. "Eloise, you turned eight years old two days after your mother died. You were a child. There was nothing you could have said or done to change that event, or change your father's reaction to it, nor his behavior following her death."

Eloise smiled appreciatively at Hilda. "I know, Hilda."

They drifted into silence, quietly sipping their tea, each lost in their own thoughts. The chiming of the clock, announcing the time was now twelve-thirty, broke the reverie. Eloise continued her tale.

"The night she died, after I gave her my promise, Mother collapsed back down onto her bed. Mother smiled at me as she told me that she had placed all of Glen Hollow in a trust; and on my twenty-first birthday, I would receive it. Until then, Reverend Tillman would be the trustee. She said he would protect and preserve Glen Hollow. She kept repeating that I was never to sell any portion of it, that I was to protect and preserve it, and to remember my promise."

Eloise pressed her lips together. She raised her head and looked at Hilda. She laughed slightly as if that laughter would drive away all the sorrow and sadness. "I know; it sounds silly to hold onto that promise now since I was so young when I gave it … It was important to Mother ….and I promised. I have kept that promise and will continue to do so."

She paused for a minute, sipping her tea. Her expression was one of being slightly perplexed when she looked up at Hilda. "Mother was rambling something about a secret. … Her fever was so high … she probably didn't know what she was saying."

Eloise shook her head slightly, trying to sort through the distant memories.

"Is that all she said; that she had a secret?" Hilda asked, also puzzled by such a declaration.

"No; she kept repeating that Glen Hollow *held* a secret. She said it was important for me to know it, and that she had to tell me. Mother started crying and kept saying that it wasn't time yet. Then she started mumbling something about 'no more time', and that I was too young to bear the responsibility...... I don't know; it was probably just her fever."

Hilda said nothing, just watched and waited, allowing Eloise the freedom to release the imprisoned memories, or to keep them locked away.

After several minutes had ticked away, she looked up at Hilda with a stone cold gaze. "Do you remember when we went to New Orleans with Lydia, Ellie and Beatrix? You remember; it was right after I graduated from college, just before you got married?" she asked.

Uncertain as to where this was leading, Hilda slowly nodded her head as her facial expression registered her bewilderment. "I do."

"Do you remember the little shop in the French Quarter?" Eloise asked softly.

"Which one?" she responded.

"The one called 'The Healing Garden'." She smiled as she watched Hilda struggling to remember. "You remember; the one with the psychics?" she prompted.

The memory now restored, Hilda replied, "Oh yes ... I do remember; only they called themselves spiritual advisors, not psychics. Besides being an apothecary, they had such a cute, little store. If I recall correctly, they had every type of cross, charm, candle and a host of other trinkets for sale. The jewelry was really beautiful. ..." She paused, reflecting for a moment, and added, "That's where I bought my amethyst set and this watch."

Hilda grinned as she fingered the pendant watch pinned to her blouse. It was in an elegant, sterling silver case that had exceptionally detailed scrollwork. The greatest surprise came when she had opened the cover to reveal that the face of the watch was ringed in alternating miniature stones of blue diamonds and deep purple amethysts. The younger of the ladies had told her it was a very special, very powerful amulet; it would protect her from harm. She chuckled at the memory. What the lady didn't know was that she intended to buy it even without the sales pitch.

Eloise grinned and softly laughed at the memory. "Yes, we got caught up in their stories. I think we all bought several of their wares that day." She fell silent again, lost in thought as she sipped her tea.

Hilda nodded slowly as the memories of that day so long ago resurfaced. "Was it that shop where you purchased the antique necklace, or was it at the little boutique where we purchased the hats?"

That broke her reverie. Her eyes moved from her teacup to Hilda. She smiled as she replied, "No, it was The Healing Garden." She chuckled softly, reminiscing. "I haven't seen it in ages. I wonder where I put it. The elder lady said it was a talisman of great power, to protect me and anyone within its vicinity from evil." She laughed lightheartedly and then dropped into silence, mulling over the memories from that day so long ago.

"Eloise," Hilda asked, breaking the silence after a long wait; "why the reminiscing about the shop?"

Her friend, startled from her contemplation, looked up and then began chuckling, more out of embarrassment than amusement. Closing her eyes, Eloise sighed and then rested her head back against the sofa. In a faint whisper she asked, "Do you remember the reading you received?"

Bewildered, Hilda responded, "No; why do you ask?"

Eloise smiled and opened her eyes. "I remember my reading, and I also remember what you said the young woman told you."

Confused by this turn in the conversation, Hilda replied tartly, "I'm certain if I dwelt on it long enough I'd remember. It was thirty-eight years ago, Eloise; forgive me if I'm a little rusty."

Eloise laughed heartily and sat upright. "All I meant was that that memory surfaced earlier this morning, and I haven't been able to stop thinking about it. I just wondered if it ever crossed your mind."

"No, I can't say that it ever has," she responded slowly, wondering where this was leading.

Eloise took several sips of her tea before continuing. She set the teacup back down in its saucer, folded her hands in her lap and leaned toward Hilda. Very quietly she stated, "The elder woman told me that my life would soon be at a crossroad. I would meet a charming man,

214

and I would have to decide which path to choose. She said he would bring great heartache and sorrow in my life; but that, out of the ashes, eventually happiness would come. She said if I chose the other path, I would fulfill my destiny, and would walk with the ones of light and keep the darkness at bay."

She paused briefly and then added, "Don't you think it has come to pass, and doesn't it make you wonder what might have been had I not married Everitt?"

Hilda placed her cup and saucer gently onto the coffee table, contemplating her response. Leaning forward, she looked intently into her friend's eyes. "Eloise, I know you realize that reading was so vague it could apply to anyone and to any situation."

Hilda sat back and laughed, amused at the memory that had resurfaced. "Remember, I was told that I would have a house full of children, and I only have one."

Eloise grinned, picked up her cup and saucer and slowly raised her teacup to her lips. She paused before taking a sip and playfully responded, "In a way, you have had a house full of children. We've kept a house full of children since 1974."

Grinning saucily, Eloise lifted her cup to Hilda in a salute before calmly sipping her tea.

Caught off-guard, Hilda just sat staring at Eloise. Then she laughed. "Okay, I guess one could say I have a house full of children; but, again, the prediction was so vague it can easily be applied to anyone or any circumstance. ….. You know this, right?"

Eloise toyed with her teacup for a moment before continuing. "I know; it's just that….I don't know how to explain it, Hilda. There are times it seems as if this place speaks to me; it's like someone who's whispering just far enough away you hear the faint sounds, but not the words. I've always felt that there's something missing about my heritage and that someday, if I hold onto the land," she sighed heavily; "then somehow I'll find what it is. Ever since this morning, I can't help but wonder that if I hadn't married Everitt, I would have known it years ago."

Seeing Hilda's expression, Eloise laughed heartily. "I know; I sound crazy. I guess I am getting old and senile."

Hilda gently smiled. "Neither one, if you ask me. You're just feeling a bit blue because we've not made as much headway with these children as we had hoped. But surely you know the ice began to crack last night at dinner. Except for Dani and Aaron, all of the children shared. And Kat, well, I never expected anything from her. I was certain she would refuse again, but she didn't. I never thought she would ever share any of the pain she has suffered, but she did."

Nodding, Eloise agreed. "Yes, I, too, was a little surprised. I was positive she would leave the table again after I called her bluff. It seems she appears to feel a connection with Susie. I noticed during her sharing that she kept her focus on Susie almost the entire time."

"I think," Hilda responded quietly; "that the walls are crumbling. It takes time and the right catalyst. For whatever the reason, I think that catalyst is Susie ... and Simon, too. I truly believe we'll start seeing improvement in all of their sociability in the next few weeks, Story Time notwithstanding."

She leaned slightly forward and stated emphatically, "We will break through the walls and help them, Eloise. We always have."

"You're right." Eloise admitted and smiled. "We will find a way."

Hilda drained the last of her tea, set her cup down onto its saucer and slowly stood. "I'm going to bed. It's late, and these old bones need their sleep. Are you staying up much longer?"

She was concerned that the melancholy mood Eloise was sinking into would cause her to stay late, further casting her into a mire of sadness. The anniversary of Murielle's death was less than two weeks away, and Hilda was certain that that impending date had a considerable influence on Eloise's mood this evening. It usually did.

Eloise glanced up at Hilda, saw the concern etched in Hilda's eyes and in her expression. "No, I'm calling it a night in just a few minutes," Eloise said with a smile; "otherwise I'll never be able to get up when the alarm sounds."

"Good-night, Eloise," Hilda said as she headed for the door.

"Good-night, Hilda," she responded. Hilda softly closed the door behind her as she exited.

Sitting quietly for a moment, Eloise watched the embers faintly glowing, now barely a pinkish color among the gray ash. She rose and extinguished them completely. Picking up the teacups and saucers, Eloise began walking to the door. Changing her mind, she walked over to her desk, setting the cups and saucers down on her desk.

Eloise reached over and picked up the sterling silver frame containing a miniature portrait. Lovingly she touched the glass above the lady's face. Her smile was bittersweet as she gazed at the painted face smiling back at her.

"I miss you, Mother," Eloise whispered.

She kissed the portrait and returned it to its proper place. Turning away, she walked to the door, switched off the lights and then slowly made her way upstairs to her suite.

Chapter 10

AND SO IT BEGINS

When her alarm clock began its announcement that the night was officially over, Susie was already awake and had been for more than an hour. Sleep had been, for the most part, elusive and fleeting.

Strange sounds had awakened her several times during the night, and had kept her awake for seemingly endless stretches of time. Sometimes it was the sound of wind rushing against her window, rattling it as if someone was outside desperately trying to come inside her room. After the third time of trekking to her window and seeing that there wasn't any wind blowing whatsoever, she stopped getting out of bed and did her best to ignore the sound. Soon afterwards the various creaking and groaning sounds began, like that of floorboards or doors. Each and every time she rose and checked to make certain that the girls were all still in their beds – they were.

The most unnerving of all of the sounds, however, were those that resembled voices whispering. The first occurrence had been at three o'clock. Initially, the sound was faint, barely audible. Slowly it grew louder and louder, enough to where she thought she could distinguish at least three voices. Certain it was Juls, Kat and Dani, Susie bolted out of bed determined to catch them in the act.

Darting into the hallway and exuberant at the thought of victory, she loudly proclaimed "Ah-Ha!", only to find it empty. The feeling of triumph quickly dissipated, leaving in its wake a feeling of hollowness and confusion. She tried to determine to where they could possibly have scurried so swiftly without being seen. Neither direction gave them any cover, so *how* did they do it; it was a puzzle.

On a hunch, Susie ran to the Common Area and then to the bathroom – both were also empty. Quietly she tiptoed down the hallway, pausing at each one of their rooms. All were fast asleep. Bewildered, Susie turned and headed back to her own bed. As she placed her slippers next to her bed, it was then that she realized the whispering sounds had ceased. Odder still, was the realization that the sounds had done so when she had left her room; none of the sounds were heard anywhere but in here. A little unnerved, Susie slowly crawled back into her bed.

Repeatedly Susie told herself it was just the sounds of an old house settling and nothing more. She had tried sleeping both under her covers and under her pillow hoping for silence, but to no avail. The disturbing sounds came and went like the ocean tide. As the sounds gradually diminished, Susie would just begin to drop off to sleep as they finally abated only to be awakened as they rolled in once again.

Though tired and sleepy, she willed herself to rise and shut off the alarm. She stepped into her slippers, put on her robe and shuffled out of her room, beginning the process of awakening each of the girls. It went smoothly enough with Kat and Dani; however, Megan and Juls were another story.

Susie lightly shook Megan, softly calling her name. No response. Susie shook her again, this time telling her to get up a little more loudly. Though Megan didn't appear to hear her, Susie knew she did. The corners of Megan's mouth curled ever so slightly into the faintest hint of a smile, revealing her act.

Susie sat down on the bed next to Megan, trying not to laugh. "Wow, that Megan sure can sleep through anything," she said in mock amazement.

Megan's smile increased just a little more.

"I don't know how I'm going to get her to wake up," Susie said, feigning bafflement. "Oh, I know," she added with a triumphant lilt. She reached her arms under Megan, pulling the small waif up against her, giving her a big hug. "This should do it," Susie said, laughing along with Megan's squeals of delight.

Megan returned Susie's hug. "I guess I just sleep hard," Megan offered as an explanation for her apparent deep sleep.

"Really?" Susie responded affably. "Are you sure?"

Megan nodded, still clutching Susie. "Uh-huh; I think it takes a hug to wake me up," she answered as innocently as possible.

"Well," Susie said, suppressing a laugh; "I guess I'll just have to give you a hug every morning."

Megan giggled and pushed back so she could see Susie's face. "Really?" she asked.

"Really," Susie promised. "Now, go use the bathroom and come right back. I'll wake up Juls, and then I'll help you get dressed."

"O-KAY!" Megan heartily agreed as she jumped out of bed, scurrying away.

"Don't run," Susie called out after her.

"I'm not! I'm just walking fast!" Megan yelled back, continuing her frenzied pace.

Susie laughed lightly, sighed and rubbed her face. 'Life is definitely going to be different', she thought.

She rose and went to wake up Juls, who by now Susie was certain had to be awake considering the noise level that Kat, Dani and Megan projected. However, such was apparently not the case. Juls was snuggled down under her covers, not even a strand of her hair to be seen.

Susie gently shook the bed, calling out softly, "Juls, it's time to get up."

"Go away!" a muffled voice demanded.

"Sorry, but it's time to get up," Susie repeated cheerfully.

"Leave me alone!" Juls shot back angrily.

Susie closed her eyes, silently counting to ten. Calmly, she stated, "You have to get up now."

The covers flew down, and a very hostile Juls glared at Susie. "No ... I ...don't. Go away and leave me alone." She promptly shut her eyes, as if to mentally will Susie to leave.

"Juls," Susie began, her tone not quite concealing her annoyance; "if you don't get up, I'll come back with a wet, ice-cold washcloth and put it on your face."

Her eyes snapped opened. "You wouldn't dare."

"If that's what it takes to get you out of bed, I'll do it. Now, get up. Miss Cora will be here in thirty minutes." Susie turned and left, leaving a sulking Juls to stare after her.

Susie helped Megan get dressed and then made a mad dash to get herself ready. As she hurried through the Common Area on her way to the bathroom, Kat and Dani were arguing over who had first dibs on the current issue of some magazine. Ever since they woke, they had been bickering nearly non-stop about everything and anything.

A few minutes later Susie exited the bathroom just as Juls paraded through the Common Area on her way to the bathroom. Her exaggerated stride lent the impression she thought she was a debutante on a promenade. With a dramatic flair she sauntered past, deliberately not greeting anyone.

Ignoring Juls' little act, Susie rushed to her room to get dressed. She had finished in record speed and returned to the Common Area, barely having time to get comfortable in one of the chairs when Miss Cora arrived right on schedule. Of course, Juls wasn't ready.

Miss Cora smiled as Dani and Kat quickly volunteered that Juls had just left the bathroom. She proceeded down the corridor to Juls' room, to see if she could assist her, as Miss Cora had phrased it.

Five minutes later, a smiling Miss Cora returned with a scowling Juls in tow. "Come girls; we'll have to double time it, or we'll be late," she said cheerfully as she held the door open for them.

And double time it they did, arriving just in the nick of time.

Simon and the rest of the household were already seated at the table when Susie, the girls and Miss Cora arrived. As soon as she entered the Dining Hall, Simon perked up, eyes twinkling as his smile broadened into a full grin.

"Susie!" he yelled and waved. "I didn't think you were coming!"

"Use your inside voice, Simon," Miss Hilda gently reminded him.

Simon gave her a shy smile and coyly whispered, "I'm sorry, Miss Hilda. I forgot because I was so happy to see Susie."

Miss Hilda smiled affectionately at him. "I know. Just try to remember we don't yell indoors."

He nodded and stretched his arms up to Susie. She hugged him, kissed the top of his head and then slid into her seat next to him. "Sorry, I didn't mean to worry you. Some people have a hard time waking up."

Miss Hilda laughed, amused at Susie's diplomatic stance. "Yes, Juls isn't a morning person."

Susie giggled. "That's for sure."

Miss Pritchett rang the hand bell promptly at seven, signaling it was time for the Blessing. This time the privilege fell to Miss Ginger who obviously believed in being as concise as possible.

They made short work of the scrambled eggs, bacon and the pancakes that were topped with creamy butter and hot maple syrup. While conversations were sparse and short among the adults, it was non-existent among the children.

Thirty minutes later, Miss Pritchett dismissed the children and Miss Emma. Susie sighed internally – school was about to begin, another major portion of her life that was about to change irrevocably.

Susie looked at Simon and smiled, watching him as he took one last, fast swipe at his mouth with his napkin, eager to get started with school. His face was lit up as if today was Christmas or his birthday. He was so excited that he was attending school with the big kids instead of preschool like he did in Willington. It didn't matter that he, Timmy and Megan would only attend the morning session. Simon noticed her smile and grinned back at her, his eyes twinkling with joy.

Miss Emma stood and waited at the door as the children all began moving toward her. After they were all assembled, she turned and led them out the door. Walking in front of the procession, Miss Emma firmly held Megan in her left hand and Timmy in her right hand. Directly behind them was Juls, scowling, arms crossed and shuffling her feet as they traversed the corridor. Several paces behind Juls, in single file, were Aaron, Jared, Dani and Jose. Kat allowed a considerable distance between herself and the others. Simon held Susie's hand tightly as they walked at the rear of the column. Susie noted glumly to herself that it looked as if they were in some sort of weird parade.

Susie caught a glimpse of movement to her left just as they entered the south wing corridor. It was in the shadows of the doorway that led to the east wing. She stopped and focused, straining to see if anyone was truly there.

"What's wrong?" Simon asked.

Susie turned her attention to him. Just as she began to answer him, Kat turned and looked back at her. Tilting her head slightly, Kat raised an eyebrow and smiled that eerie half smile of hers. Susie felt a wave of goose bumps rising on her skin as a tingle cascaded down her spine. Susie swallowed hard, forced a smile on her face and told Simon everything was fine.

"Then why did you stop?" he pressed her, a little annoyed at her.

Susie shrugged. "I thought I saw something over there by the doors."

Simon tried to head to the doors, but Susie held him back. "No, Simon. Let's go; we don't want to be late for class."

Simon scrunched up his face, trying to understand his big sister. "I thought you wanted to see what's there."

"I'm sure it's nothing. We can look later," she said with a smile.

He shrugged. "Okay, but I thought we were going to the Library later."

"We are; now, come on," she agreed, pulling him along as they hurried to catch up with the others.

As they entered the classroom, each child took a wet wipe from the dispenser, wiped their face and hands and then tossed it into the waste basket by the door. Susie pulled out two, handing one to Simon. She watched as he wiped his hands and face, and was surprised that he actually did a decent job for a change. She pointed to the wastebasket as she threw hers into it.

"I know," he said, giving her a spry grin as he tossed it into the basket and headed to the first row of desks. (Megan and Timmy were already seated, leaving only one desk vacant.)

Susie made her way toward the last row which she shared with Aaron, Juls and Jared. The row in front of her held Dani, Jose and Kat.

Miss Emma wasted no time getting down to business. She drew their attention to the chalkboard upon which she had written the assignments for the older children. "Please begin your assignments," she instructed.

She walked over and sat down in the chair placed in front of the first row, where Megan, Timmy and Simon eagerly awaited. Miss Emma smiled at them, instructing them to open their workbooks so they could begin their lesson. The rest of the class started on the assignments listed on the board under their name; Susie did likewise.

After Miss Emma finished with the first row, she assigned them a page in their workbooks before moving to the second row, beginning their lessons. When finished with Jose, Dani and Kat, she instructed them to continue with their board assignments. Now she turned her attention to Susie's row, repeating the process with each level as she had with the previous two rows.

Watching Miss Emma as she worked with each group reminded Susie of Mrs. Fairfield, Susie's former teacher in Stonebridge. Susie missed her. Mrs. Fairfield made the subjects not only interesting but also fascinating. She had a way of making what she taught come alive, never dull or boring. To Susie, Miss Emma had that same knack, and was very much like Mrs. Fairfield – just a much younger version.

The morning flew by quickly, and soon the morning assignments were completed. They had covered a lot of material in each of the subjects, far more than Susie's previous school in Willington. Susie was surprised it was already lunchtime when Miss Hilda arrived with the lunch cart.

They moved to the rear table near the windows as Miss Hilda began distributing the meals. She enlisted Susie and Miss Emma to assist her, and the process went fast.

Timmy, Megan and Simon were chatterboxes, each one trying to top the other as they vied for Miss Hilda's attention, regaling her with their versions of the day's lessons. It was actually Miss Hilda's fault; she had asked how class had been. Neither Timmy nor Megan spoke. So Simon, being Simon, enthusiastically and quite animatedly began his rendition of the morning's events. Not wanting to be left out, Timmy and Megan quickly chimed in with their own versions of the morning's lessons. Their spirited discourses were every bit as boisterous and as colorful as was Simon's. Thus the result was three, very lively voices in competition to be heard, and to outdo each other's version. The other children remained silent, continuing to eat their lunch, and ignoring the rowdy "babies" as much as possible.

Miss Hilda seemed to thoroughly enjoy their responses, asking more questions and praising them for paying attention in class. This led to more excited responses from all three of them, keeping the cycle in perpetual motion.

When lunch was finished, the dishes were cleared and were all tucked neatly back onto the cart. As if by a mental call, Miss Cora and Miss Ginger entered the room, ready to take their youngest charges for their naptime. They, of course, didn't want to go and began to loudly protest; however,

Miss Hilda gave them "The Look", rapidly silencing their protests. They left the room, shuffling along beside the women with their heads drooped, giving the appearance they were being led away to face some horrible fate.

The remainder of the day passed quickly enough, and the subjects were handled a little differently than the morning session. It was more of an open forum, with each of the levels being taught together. Susie watched the group, picking up on little nuances. Within a few minutes, she realized the children actually liked Miss Emma. In spite of all their protests, sulks and fussing, they respected and liked Miss Emma - so did Susie. The thought popped into her mind that perhaps Glen Hollow wasn't such a bad place after all. She smiled and focused her attention on Miss Emma, currently discussing ancient civilizations.

Miss Emma apparently loved the interaction of discussion and debate. With relative ease she drew her students into open discussion. She enabled and encouraged them to express their ideas or to launch their questions, thereby allowing for their growth of understanding, comprehension and articulation of the subjects. Well, some of them anyway.

Juls was not particularly interested in discussing anything other than ballet. Her attitude was unmistakable – she had no intention of participating, and was most hostile to any effort on Miss Emma's part to encourage her to do so.

Her brother, Jared, in addition to his love of physics, chemistry and the martial arts, was also a history buff. He not only knew dates and events, but had a keen insight as to the many interwoven nuances of the circumstances that led to the major dates and events. He also had an ability to correlate those past events and circumstance with those more current. He was impressive, Susie thought.

Kat, of course, was true to her nature and refused to co-operate period. Whenever Miss Emma would call on her, Kat would shrug her shoulders or just stare at Miss Emma. There was no acrimony or rebellion, just a stare of indifference as if none of this mattered.

With Aaron, math and science were his forte. When those subjects were discussed, he seemed to lose the shroud of sullenness in which he kept himself cloaked. His whole demeanor changed, becoming vibrant and full of life and energy.

For Jose, the languages were his main love; however, he also was most eager when they began reading and discussing poetry. Miss Emma called on him first to read. Listening to him read the poem, Susie could feel the emotions of it, to see, and hear and feel what the author intended. It was incredible to witness the transformation on Jose's face; it was as if he had been transported into the poem and was living it. When he finished reading, Susie found herself smiling. Like Nana's friend, Amelia, Jose had the soul of a poet. She wondered if Jose realized he had such a gift.

Dani was very bored during that particular portion of class and laid her head down on her desk. Naturally that prompted Miss Emma to call on her, requiring her to read aloud the next poem. Dani was not happy, but she complied. Her rendition left much to be desired. Her sour mood elevated a little, though, when they began the portion of class devoted to music and art.

The afternoon seemed to be gone in a flash; all too soon for Susie class was over. Miss Emma dismissed them, reminding them to do their homework as they hurriedly rose from their chairs and exited the classroom. Susie was amazed at how fast the others exited the room, leaving to go their separate ways for the rest of the afternoon. However, Susie also had plans – Simon would be waiting for her by the Library. Pausing at the classroom door, Susie turned and looked back at Miss Emma, currently in the process of erasing the blackboard.

"Thank you, Miss Emma," she said. "I like the class. You remind me of my teacher in Stonebridge, and she was great."

Miss Emma stopped erasing, turned toward Susie and smiled, genuinely surprised by Susie's words. "Thank you, Susie. I appreciate you telling me."

Susie smiled a little remorsefully and shrugged. "I just wanted you to know I think you're a good teacher. I didn't have the chance to tell Mrs. Fairfield, so I thought I should tell you while I can."

"Perhaps you could write her a letter; I'm certain she would love hearing from you," Miss Emma suggested. "I know I would if I were her," she added.

Susie's face brightened. "Thanks, Miss Emma. That's a good idea."

"You're welcome, Susie," Miss Emma responded cheerfully.

Susie left in search of Simon, a little more light-hearted than she had been. It was short lived – a few minutes later she reached the end of the south wing corridor. Recalling the shadow from that morning, she cast a wary eye toward the east wing doors as she hurried past. Nothing appeared to be out of the ordinary for the moment (no shadows or weird feelings); she quickly left the south wing, making her way toward the west wing.

She sighed, wondering why she felt so uneasy and why her imagination was in overdrive. "It's an old building; and, like all old buildings, they have drafts which cause noises," she reminded herself.

"Old buildings also settle as the ground shifts, again causing noises," she tried further to alleviate her own apprehension "Miss Hilda's right; light and shadow create illusions – it just seems as if something is there when it's really nothing," she told herself, giving herself a mental pep talk.

"So why am I so uneasy?" she asked.

Glancing at the portraits lining the walls of the corridor as she strolled past, the thought popped in to her mind – 'Did any of them have the same feelings I have?'

Something deep inside her screamed a resounding "yes", startling her and causing her mind to shift back to her first glimpse of Glen Hollow. She remembered the feeling of foreboding that had crept its way through her, causing her to shiver; she remembered the tingling sensation that coursed down her spine and the resulting goose bumps.

She found herself staring at the portrait of a happy, young girl, about her own age. The silver nameplate revealed her name to be Evangeline Elizabeth Evermore. The portrait was painted in 1819. Her smile and glowing face seemed to say that Susie was being ridiculous.

Susie began laughing at herself and her childish fears – all due to some silly thought she had when she first saw Glen Hollow. "How stupid is that?" she chided herself. "Grow up," she further admonished herself; "there is nothing wrong with Glen Hollow, and there isn't any reason to be afraid."

Rounding the corner at a fast pace, Susie entered the portion of the corridor that led to the Library and saw Simon, further elevating her mood. He was sitting crossed-legged by the Library door, intently watching the corridor for Susie's appearance. Simon beamed joyously as soon as he saw

227

her, jumping up to greet her. He came running to her, throwing his arms around her and fiercely hugged her.

Walking back toward the Library, arm-in-arm, she asked him how his afternoon went. He shrugged and said it was fine. He frowned as he reiterated that he shouldn't have to take naps because Nana never made him take naps, and neither did Mrs. C. She agreed with him, attempting to appease him, then changed the subject by asking what he did after his nap.

He grinned gleefully, telling her all about the inspection tour of the solar heating system. Allan Roy had been waiting for them after naptime and took them straight to see it. Then, JT came and took them to the basement to see the furnace.

"It's really neat and super big!" he excitedly informed her. "You should see it. It's awesome," he declared.

"Maybe I will," she replied, smiling at his zeal for it.

His expression became a little more somber as he continued. "It's spooky down there. There's a lot of weird noises, but JT said all buildings make noises."

Susie nodded. "He's right, Simon."

He shrugged, slowly moving his head back and forth. "Not these noises – it sounded like whispering."

Susie inhaled sharply. She looked at Simon, studying his face. She knew he was telling the truth. 'So he's heard it, too,' she thought to herself. Aloud, she said jovially, "Silly goose; JT is right. It's just the building settling when the ground shifts."

Changing the subject, she asked, "What else did you do today?"

His eyes sparkled, and he grinned from ear to ear. His giggle was lighthearted. Simon was his old self again, and that made her smile. He told her that Miss Hilda took them to the kitchen for ice cream. He frowned (more like a pout) when he relayed that Megan was already there. After that, Miss Hilda took them all to the Rec Room where they played Candy Land with Miss P (he was now referring to Miss Pritchett as Miss P). But, he informed her, Miss P had to leave after only *one* game, so Miss Ginger came and stayed with them. Then (to his utter amazement) Miss Cora came a few minutes later and took Megan away with her.

Having now arrived at the Library, Simon stopped Susie as she reached to open the heavy oak and glass door. "Why did Miss Cora take Megan away?" he asked, perplexed.

"I don't know, Simon. Did you ask Megan or Miss Cora?"

Simon nodded his head rapidly, sending his curls into a bouncing fury. "Uh-huh; Miss Cora said Megan had somewhere to be."

His face scrunched up revealing his confusion as he lifted his hands, palms facing upward. "What does *that* mean?"

Susie shrugged. "I don't know, Simon. When you see Megan, ask her."

"But what if she won't tell me?" he persisted, a little on the whiny side.

"Then it's none of your business," she answered tersely.

Simon's eyes narrowed as his face began the process toward a pout. "Why not?" he demanded petulantly.

"Simon, you know you like to have your time when no one bothers you. Maybe Megan likes to draw, or color, or play with her toys *alone*, just like you…. Okay?" she responded, this time her tone was gentle.

Simon drew in a deep breath, releasing it hard and fast. "Okay," he reluctantly agreed.

As soon as they entered the reception area of the Library, Simon took off like a bullet. Running as fast as he could to the end of the reception area, he darted down the aisle and was quickly out of sight. Susie heard him calling out for her to follow him because he had a feeling that this was the way to the best books. Susie, who was accustomed to Simon's 'feelings', followed close behind, repeatedly telling him to stop running - which he totally ignored.

When he reached the west side of the Library, Simon announced that 'this is it'. He ran to the large, overstuffed chair and promptly jumped into it.

"This is my chair," he proclaimed to Susie, as she entered the area. "Remember?!"

"I think it belongs to anyone who chooses to use it," Susie replied.

"Na-uh," Simon disagreed; "It's mine."

"Okay, Simon; have it your way," she replied. "Let's go look for a couple of books."

They walked over to the children's bookcases and began looking through the titles. Simon kept nixing everything Susie suggested.

"You know what I want," Simon told her. "'Maury Mouse and Carrie Cat: The Circus Comes to Town'," he added in sing-song fashion.

"Why? You know it by heart, and so do I," Susie objected.

Simon crossed his arms and tilted his head back. "I don't care. It's my forever favorite!" he adamantly stated.

Susie sighed heavily. "Simon, *please* choose something else."

Simon leveled his gaze at her, narrowing his eyes in determination and forcefully putting his fists on his hips. "No! One has to be 'Maury Mouse and Carrie Cat: The Circus Comes to Town'. You," he pointed at her dramatically; "can choose the other."

He gave a single, swift nod of his head denoting that the matter wasn't open for debate.

"Fine," she muttered.

She searched through the children's stacks until she found his *'forever favorite'*. She handed it to him; he spun around and scrambled to his chair, making himself comfortable. He began perusing its pictures while waiting for Susie.

Several minutes later, she joined him, bringing with her a large, thin book. Smiling enticingly, she held it up for him to see the exquisite cover.

"It's called 'The Magical World of Mr. Horatio Wedgilwog'," she told him, leafing through its beautifully illustrated pages to pique his interest. It worked; he decided to have her read it now and save his *'forever favorite'* for bedtime.

Susie slid into Simon's chair; he snuggled up to her, ready for the new adventure. She opened the book to its first page, a beautifully detailed illustration that filled the entire page. The scene was of a large, old growth forest surrounding a small clearing.

A strange looking creature (part penguin and part hedgehog) was featured in the center of the drawing. He had the body shape and coloring of a penguin but had the head, fur, limbs and feet of a hedgehog. He wore a bright purple bow-tie, had a dark red cane and little square glasses perched on the end of his stubby, little nose.

The odd looking creature stood in front of his home. It was a bizarre looking plant that appeared to be a cross between a tree and a mushroom.

It had a trunk, just like a tree, and some lower tree-like branches; then it ballooned upward into a giant, mushroom-like stalk with a mushroom cap that was shaped like a clover. The tree portion was a lime green color with bright orange leaves; the mushroom portion was a brick red color and had big purple spots randomly displayed on its cap.

The door was in the tree trunk portion, rounded at the top, and had an oval-shaped, little window centered in it at eye level for Mr. Horatio Wedgilwog. To the right of the door was a dark blue plaque. The name 'Mr. Horatio Wedgilwog' was painted in a lemon yellow color and outlined in black. Directly below his name plaque, there was even a cute, little mailbox that resembled a black top hat.

The story began on the opposite page. It was about Mr. Horatio Wedgilwog, his friends and many of the other creatures who all lived in the old growth forest. After giving Simon ample time to examine the picture of Mr. Horatio Wedgilwog, his home and the surrounding forest, Susie told him to hush his questions so she could begin the story. After all, she reminded him, the story was also new to her; the only way to answer his questions was for her to read the story. Simon nodded his agreement, snuggling up close to her as Susie began to read.

The story captivated Simon; Susie even had to admit she enjoyed it. As she began reading the last page, the mantle clock chimed. Susie looked up – it was a quarter to six; they were nearly out of time!

She told Simon she would have to read fast, so he'd better pay close attention. He did. She flew through the last page, finishing just five minutes later.

As she returned the book to its place on the shelf, she told Simon to bring her the other one.

"Why?' he asked

"So I can put it away," she answered.

Simon hugged the book tightly and glowered at her. "No! I want this one tonight," he demanded.

"We'll come back after dinner and get it," she assured him. "You can't take it to dinner."

"What if someone else gets it?" he asked, not certain he wanted to trust leaving his 'forever favorite' behind.

"They won't. We'll come straight here after dinner and get it. I promise," she pledged, holding her hand out for the book.

Reluctantly Simon released the book to her, watching closely where she placed it.

With that task finished, Susie grabbed Simon's hand as she rushed down the aisle toward the entrance. "Hurry, Simon; we don't want to be late."

"No problem," he assured her, slipping from her grasp and running as fast as he could.

Laughing, she decided to join him, catching up with him just as they reached the Reception Area. They stopped and caught their breath before Susie opened the door. After all, she reminded him, it wouldn't be smart for anyone to realize they had been running.

With his eyes sparkling, Simon gave her his famous Cheshire cat grin and held a finger to his lips. He'd keep the secret.

Susie opened the door and they quickly walked to the Dining Hall, arriving with only a minute to spare.

True to her word, as soon as dinner was over, Susie took Simon back to the Library to get his *'forever favorite'* book. As they entered the Library, Susie thought she heard someone talking.

"Did you hear that?" she asked Simon.

He nodded. "Someone's over there," he answered, pointing to the first aisle on their right.

"Let's go see who it is," Susie suggested.

"No!" Simon objected. "I want my book."

"It'll just take a minute, Simon. Come on." She answered as she headed down the aisle. Simon huffed as he shuffled along behind her.

They walked the entire length of the main aisle, checking the smaller side aisles as they went – no one was in sight.

"Where'd they go?" Simon asked Susie, slightly baffled.

"I don't know, Simon. Maybe they passed us when we were looking the other way."

"No way!" he argued. "I was looking both ways, and I didn't see anybody," he staunchly declared.

Susie had that uneasy feeling again; but she choked it back, forcing herself to sound unconcerned. "Well, obviously, Simon, we missed whoever it was. Never mind, let's go get your book so you can put it in your nightstand."

That was all the distraction that was required. Simon chirped "Okay", spinning around and running toward the resting place of his *forever favorite*.

Fortunately, the book was exactly where Susie had left it – otherwise, she'd never hear the end of it from Simon. Susie stopped at the reception area, quickly signed out the book to Simon (and entered her name also), and then they headed upstairs.

Simon decided that the nightstand wasn't a safe place; he adamantly insisted that Susie put it under the mattress. After several minutes of lively debate, Susie acquiesced, placing his treasured favorite under the mattress, at the head of the bed.

They left the Boys Dorm and headed for the stairs when they came upon Miss Ginger, Miss Cora, Timmy and Megan, the latter two looking a little morose.

"There you are, Simon," Miss Ginger greeted him with a smile. "I was looking for you."

"Why?" he asked.

"It's bath time," she replied pleasantly.

Simon shook his head. "Nu-huh," he disagreed.

"I believe so, young man. After bath time, you'll have a few minutes in the Rec Room before bedtime."

Simon began what Susie knew would be a challenge to Miss Ginger's schedule. She cut him off by quickly intervening. "Yes it is, Simon. Remember what we talked about yesterday?"

His brow furled, revealing his confusion. Suddenly, he grinned and nodded rapidly. "I'm ready for my bath," he exuberantly told Miss Ginger, grasping her free hand.

Miss Ginger gave him a quizzical look, uncertain as to what brought about this sudden change. Timmy and Megan looked at him, and then at each other, as if Simon had suddenly gone loco. Simon just grinned, waving good-by to Susie as they proceeded on down the corridor.

"See you later, Susie," he called back to her.

"See you later, Simon," she responded, hoping that neither Miss Ginger nor Miss Cora would suspect anything by Simon's sudden change in demeanor. She headed to the Rec Room.

———

Susie entered the Rec Room, discovering that all the others were already there. Juls was busy reading a book as was her brother, Jared. Dani was coloring; Aaron was engrossed in building a model jet; Jose was playing a computer game of chess, and Kat was drawing in her sketch pad. Dani was the only one that looked up as she entered. She gave no acknowledgment that Susie was there; no smiles or hello, just the briefest second or two of a glance before returning to her coloring.

Susie walked to the window seat that overlooked the west garden and sat down. As casually as possible, she observed the others through their reflections in the window. They were all withdrawn into their own worlds, wary of everyone. Susie understood; she also felt like an alien now that everything she knew, and everyone she loved, was gone. Well, everyone except for Simon. She smiled at the thought of Simon. He was like a ball of fire; yet he also had the distinct ability to endear himself to everyone without even trying.

She sighed, turning her attention to the garden below. Her eyes wandered to her right; in the reflection she noticed that Kat was watching her. She turned and smiled at Kat. Kat did not reciprocate; her eyes continued to dart up and down, and Susie realized that Kat was sketching her! Kat raised her hand, motioning for Susie to turn and face the window again. Susie smiled and complied.

Several minutes later, Kat had finished her sketch. Sauntering over to Susie, Kat handed Susie the sketch pad before slinking down onto the window seat beside her. Susie was amazed at the realistic quality of Kat's drawing. What concerned her, though, were the odd emanations that seemed to surround her image, in addition to the strange, ethereal shapes that seemed to hover around her, inside the room and just outside the window.

"Your talent is amazing," Susie told her admiringly.

Kat's smile was genuine, not that eerie one, or the smirking one that she usually displayed. "Thanks," she replied, pleased by the recognition.

"You're welcome. I'm serious, Kat; you have a gift," Susie reiterated. "I wish I was this talented."

Kat grinned, enjoying the praise.

"I'm curious though; what are these things supposed to be?" Susie asked a little apprehensively. She pointed to the translucent shapes hovering near her seated image, and to the ones outside the window and finally to the odd markings around her image.

Kat's pleasant grin deteriorated into that eerie half smile of hers that could freeze the blood in your veins. Kat locked her gaze onto Susie. There was a cunning light in those pale gray eyes that made Susie shiver.

Kat leaned in toward Susie and whispered, "You know."

Startled, Susie quickly moved back from Kat. "No, I don't," she stated firmly.

Kat's expression was like that of a cat toying with a mouse. "Yes, you do," she said without inflection as if it were a matter of fact and not of conjecture. "Think about it," she added; "and you'll remember."

Kat rose, abruptly retrieved her sketch pad from Susie's hand and left the room. Susie stared after her, astonished and unsure of what to make of Kat's little performance.

She didn't have much time to contemplate it. Seconds later, Simon, Timmy and Megan burst through the door, immediately dissipating the quiet calm from the room. Simon ran to Susie as fast as he could, with Timmy and Megan just a step or two behind him.

"Miss Ginger said we have fifteen minutes before bed time," Simon announced. "Can we play Candy Land?"

"Sure, but we won't have time to finish it," Susie agreed.

"That's okay," they all chimed together.

"Then go get it, we'll play at one of the little tables," she instructed.

"I'll get it," Megan yelled, running to the game shelves.

"No way," Simon countered as Timmy shouted, "No, I'll get it." They both took off like jack rabbits, trying desperately to catch up to Megan.

"Boys, come back," Susie ordered. "Megan will get it. Timmy, you choose the table, and Simon will get to return the game to the shelf when we're finished. From now on, you'll take turns. Okay?"

They both replied with a disgruntled "okay", and Timmy chose the table (with a lot of input from Simon).

Susie made short work of setting up the game, and they got started. It was fun; they all laughed and had a good time. Too soon for their liking (but right on schedule), Miss Cora and Miss Ginger arrived to take Simon, Timmy and Megan away for bedtime.

"I have to put the game back first," Simon dutifully informed Miss Ginger.

"That's okay, Simon," Susie hastily interjected. "Since I forgot to allow time for it, I'll do it this time." She smiled affectionately at him.

Simon gave Susie a hug and whispered in her ear, "Don't forget you know what."

She whispered back, "I won't forget."

Smiling, Simon strutted to Miss Ginger and said, "I'm ready."

Both she and Miss Cora chuckled at his antics as they shepherded the children out of the Rec Room.

Susie rose, returned the game to its place on the shelf and followed them out. She had an hour to do her homework before the official lights out time. However, she planned to work a little past that at her desk. After the girls were all asleep, she'd sneak out and go to Simon, read him his *'forever favorite'* and get him tucked back into bed; no one the wiser. Hopefully Simon would keep the secret.

———

The grandfather clock in the Common Area began chiming the ten o'clock hour. Susie switched her desk lamp off and gently eased back her chair. Softly she tiptoed down the hallway, checking to be certain that each girl was fast asleep. They were.

Quickly and quietly she made her way to the door. She held her breath as she slowly turned the knob, wincing as it made its distinctive click. Pausing momentarily, she then slowly opened the door slightly to see if anyone was in the corridor. It appeared to be empty. Opening the heavy door just wide enough to slip through, Susie quickly pulled it shut behind her.

The entire corridor was empty, and she heard nothing to indicate that anyone was approaching. She made a mad dash to the Boys Dorm, repeating the process of cautiously opening the door, verifying that no one was in the Common Area and then proceeding to Simon's room.

Simon was awake, all right; he was under his covers, the light from his flashlight clearly shining through his bedding.

"Simon," Susie whispered sternly as she removed his covers. "What did I tell you?"

"No one saw me," he whispered back. "I waited until *after* Jared, and Aaron and Jose went to bed," he proudly informed her.

"What if they had to go to the bathroom?" she countered.

He shrugged. "Doesn't matter," he quipped. "Their beds are up front," he said with a grin.

Susie shook her head and had to chuckle. Simon was amazing. She nudged him over so she could slide in next to him.

He handed her his book. "I was looking at the pictures," he explained.

She took the book, opened it and waited for Simon to settle in next to her. After he had stopped his wiggling and squirming, she took her flashlight and positioned it upon her shoulder, balancing it against the headboard. Once its light properly shone upon the book, she began reading his '*forever favorite*', 'Maury Mouse and Carrie Cat: The Circus Comes to Town'.

Several pages and ten minutes later, Simon was fast asleep. Switching off her flashlight, she laid it and the book upon his nightstand. As she slid out and off the bed, Susie gently moved Simon into a sleeping position. She tucked the covers around him and kissed him on his forehead.

Quietly Susie eased open the drawer in his nightstand, placed the book in it and then gently eased it closed. She looked around for Binky, his stuffed dinosaur. Binky had fallen between the bed and the nightstand. She retrieved Binky, placing it under Simon's arm for safe keeping. She moved the nightlight lamp a little closer to the bed, bathing Simon in a soft, warm glow.

Susie watched him a few minutes; then she quietly slipped back to her own Dorm and to her own bed.

Chapter 11

STRANGE THINGS ARE A HAPPENIN'

Susie awakened, bolting upright in a state of panic, her breathing was labored and shallow. Her heart was racing, beating hard like a drum, and as fast as if she had just run a marathon. Perspiration dampened her hair and her pajamas; her skin was moistened with its tiny droplets. At first her eyes were opened wide in fear; then, as she began to realize where she was, Susie slowly relaxed.

"A dream," she muttered; "it was only a dream."

She sighed heavily, a sigh of relief more than anything else. Drawing her knees up to her chest, she wrapped her arms around them and rested her head on her knees. After a few minutes she decided to sit up in bed for a while, mostly due to being slightly apprehensive that the dream would return. Susie grabbed her pillows and propped them against the headboard. After she had them arranged just so, she leaned back, sinking into them. Her eyes drifted to her alarm clock – it was three in the morning.

Wearily she closed her eyes. She hadn't had such a bad nightmare in years. Nana always made her feel better after she had had one until she finally stopped having them altogether. Tears began rolling down her face. "Nana," she whispered; "I miss you."

Nana had held her after each bad dream, rocking her and gently stroking her hair. Nana would softly hum the same song every time.

"What was it?" Susie asked, straining to recall.

Her forehead scrunched tightly as she tried to remember. Gradually, like a fog that dissipates with the heat of the morning sun, the melody came drifting back into her mind. She remembered! And Susie knew where she had first heard that tune – her mother!

Stunned, Susie sat still, staring at the clock while listening to the tune as it played itself over and over again in her mind. The memories came flooding back – her mother had done the same for her as Nana did. Just like Nana, her mother had dispelled the terrors. Now she remembered how her mother, like Nana, would coax Susie into telling her about the dream.

And like Nana, Mommy would say, "It can't hurt you, Susie; it's only a dream. If you recall it and tell it, then its power to frighten you is broken."

Susie breathed in slowly, a deep, cleansing breath, and released it just as slowly. Closing her eyes, she began to center her thoughts on the dream. At first she couldn't remember anything other than the intense fear and terror she had experienced during the dream. She focused her breathing, forcing it to remain steady, channeling her thoughts to push past the emotions and on to the dream itself. After several minutes, the dream burst through the opaque memory veil like water breaking free from a dam. Susie remembered it completely, and in all of its terrifying detail.

In the dream she was standing at the edge of a great precipice, rising thousands of feet into the air and jutting outward over a huge chasm. There wasn't much light; everything was cast in shadows. The air had a thick, suffocating quality to it, smelling rancid and putrid as if all that had ever decayed in the world was in this one place. Vapors in the air began to collide and thicken, becoming a wispy, shroud-like fog.

She wasn't dressed anything at all like herself and appeared to be a little older in the dream, maybe late teens or early twenties. Her hair was very short, much shorter than she thought she'd ever cut it. Even more bizarre, (now that she remembered), was a white, jagged streak on the left side, giving the appearance that she was prematurely graying in that one spot.

Susie opened her eyes in surprise. "That's weird," she said aloud. "Why would I be older in my dream? That doesn't make sense."

Susie closed her eyes again and pressed lightly on her temples. Slowly she moved her fingertips toward her hair, repeating the process several times, enabling her to return her focus on the dream. Once again overwhelming terror began creeping its way through her, filling her with the desire to run and hide.

"It's just a dream; it can't hurt me," she reminded herself repeatedly until her body began to relax. Concentrating on her breathing, she focused her thoughts, allowing the visions of the dream to resurface. In a flash the scene unfolded in her mind as fully as the petals of the evening primrose unfurl when the silvery light of the moon touches them.

She realized she wasn't alone in the dream. Several yards from where she stood, Susie could faintly see the outline of someone on the ground, quite still as if sound asleep. The haze was too thick for her to see who it was, or even if it was someone she knew. She saw herself walk over and kneel beside the person, crying as she laid her hand on the person's head. Out of nowhere came an arid blast of scorching wind, eerily howling like it came from the depths of hell. She watched herself rise to her feet, slowly turning to face the source of the wind.

Now she could see why the dream had frightened her so. On the precipice directly across the chasm was a great blackness. It was swirling, heaving and surging, twisting and stretching. In one great burst, sending the blackness into oblivion, it had taken form – a monstrously, gigantic snake; one so huge it could easily cross the vast chasm as if it were merely crossing the smallest of mud puddles.

Chills ran through Susie, deep to the bone, causing her to inhale sharply and open her eyes. As much as she hated spiders, she hated snakes even more so. Her immediate thought was to forget trying to remember the dream. But memories of Nana and her mother won out; she knew she had to break the dream's power.

In spite of the rising trepidation within, Susie forced herself to continue. She returned her mind to the image of the snake. Half coiled as it was, it was at least two hundred yards in length, and quite possibly more than twice that when uncoiled. Its scales were the darkest black and had a spiraling stripe that encircled its body. The stripe was a deep, dark red color, much like the color of blood. Its body was twice as thick as the largest of redwood trees, its head the size of building. As lethal as any weapon was the barb on the end of its body; its size alone made it deadly. Its fangs, those enormous fangs, gleamed in the dim light, deadly and strong. Of all its frightening attributes, none were more terrifying than its eyes. Evil resided within; a terrifyingly malevolent presence emanated from behind those eyes.

The creature laughed at her; it was a petrifying sound, penetrating to the very core of her soul. She watched herself as she stood her ground, facing the snake, unafraid and unconcerned.

"Do you think you can defeat me, little girl?" it hissed sardonically. "I have destroyed many far older and having much greater experience than you."

"Perhaps," she replied calmly; "but today is your judgment day. Today you return to the Abyss from which you came."

It rose upward and then stretched outward toward her, closing the distance nearly halfway across the chasm within seconds. Its eyes gleamed with the anticipation of her defeat.

"You are a fool," it taunted her. "Join me, and I will spare you. I will give you great power," it promised, sneering at her.

Pausing briefly, it smiled wickedly at her. "You can even rule the earth," it added in a deceptively seductive tone, slowly moving its upper body to her side of the chasm.

"You have no power to give," she responded. "Your master has limited power that he can give; but even he is no match for the Almighty One, the Creator of all."

Its hiss was more evil than ever as it raised its head high into the sky, maneuvering itself into a striking position. "Then you will die!" it declared vehemently.

"Possibly," she acknowledged; "You may kill my body, but you cannot kill my soul. If you destroy this body, another will come; and that one will defeat you. Know this, demon: I, through the power of the Almighty One, will defeat you today. You will return to the Abyss."

"You insolent, little fool," it jeered. "You will suffer much before I take your life!" it seethed in anger.

Instantaneously its eyes changed from yellow to black, and then to red, glowing as if lit by the very fires of hell itself. Its head arched backward, mouth wide open, fangs fully exposed and dripping with venom. It hurled itself toward her.

She watched herself move her arm from behind her back, exposing an odd-looking sword. It began to shimmer softly, twinkling like starlight when the clouds move across the night sky. Finally it began a bright, steady glow as she held it high.

The snake hissed and snarled, diving fast toward her to deliver its death blow. It was close enough now that Susie could see her own reflection in its eyes, smell the rancid, foul stench of its breath, and see the bucket-sized drops of venom oozing from its fangs.

Susie saw herself leaping up and forward, swinging her sword upward into an arc, bringing it down hard toward the base of the head of the snake. Their eyes were locked onto one another; neither one flinching, both fiercely determined to be the victor. In that moment, life and death hung in the balance. It was precisely at that moment Susie had awakened.

Susie sighed heavily, still a little unnerved by the dream. Her fingers began gently toying with her pendant as she muttered, "What a crazy dream; me as some kind of warrior-chick."

As she thought about it, she began to chuckle an amused, little chuckle – one of incredulity at the very idea of her battling a snake, let alone a giant, demon one. Gradually increasing, her giggling finally erupted into a full scale, side-splitting, rolling laugh. She buried her face into her pillow to muffle the sound – the last thing she wanted to do was to wake the other girls and explain why she was laughing like a hysterical hyena in the middle of the night.

After several long minutes, Susie's laughter abated. She laid there, sides aching and breathing hard. Rolling over, she looked up at the ceiling and silently thanked her mother and Nana; they were right – the dream's power to frighten her was now broken. The tune popped into her mind again, and she began to softly hum it.

The steady ticking of her clock caught her attention; it was now four o'clock. She had two hours in which to finish her literature homework before it was time to awaken her roommates. Susie sighed, put her head in her hands and slowly moved her head back and forth.

"I just have to make it through this week," she moaned. "Surely Simon will have made friends with Timmy by then. I'll have to help it along; otherwise, next semester I'm never going to have time to do homework."

Wearily Susie pulled herself out of bed and shuffled to her desk. She switched on the desk lamp as she slid into the chair. She opened her literature book and began reading.

———

Susie nearly jumped out of her chair when her alarm clock began its ringing. Though it seemed as if only minutes had passed, indeed it had been two hours; and she had only read three pages. She had fallen asleep, her head anchored between her palms, her elbows firmly planted in front of the book.

She slumped back against her chair. "Rats," she fumed, her frustration being to show.

Susie got up, grabbed her robe, putting it on as she headed into the hallway to awaken the girls. Another day had begun, and Susie hoped this one would be less troubling than yesterday.

———

For the most part, Susie got her wish. The most frustrating and irritating thing that happened thus far was in trying to awaken Juls. It had required three wake-up calls. Not until Susie had actually threatened to physically pull Juls out of bed that her head finally popped out from under her covers. Glaring at Susie with daggers shooting from her eyes, she snarled a spiteful "*get out!*" to which Susie had sarcastically responded with "*my pleasure*".

The day progressed pleasantly enough without any major rattling of nerves. No spine tingling sensations, no voices, no uneasy, edgy feelings and no mysterious movements in the shadows.

Class time was fun and interesting. Several times even Kat and Juls were somewhat cooperative. Everyone seemed to be in better spirits, and Susie decided that that must be the reason she felt more at ease in spite of being so tired. She even got lucky in that the only time Miss Emma didn't call on her was for the literature assignment. Silently she vowed that she would catch up tonight – no matter what.

However, just before class ended, Miss Emma wrote the homework assignments on the chalkboard, and Susie's heart sank a little - how in the world would she be able to do all that *and* see after Simon, she wondered. Determinedly, she reminded herself that she just had to make it through this week. After that, she had the Christmas break to help Simon make friends with Timmy. She smiled and sighed; she knew once they became friends, Simon would be preoccupied with Timmy, allowing her the freedom to do homework after dinner.

She scooted out the classroom door and headed toward the Library where she knew Simon would be waiting. Sure enough, he was there – impatiently pacing the corridor. His scowl turned into a sunny smile when he saw her.

"Susie!" he yelled and ran to her.

Laughing, Susie opened her arms and caught him, returning his hug. "Simon, I'm glad to see you, too; but you know you're not allowed to run in the house. And you know you're not allowed to yell," she reminded him.

His eyes twinkled and danced mischievously as he grinned at her. "It's okay," he said earnestly; "nobody saw me or heard me."

"It doesn't matter if no one else was here, Simon," Susie rebuffed him. "You know better. What would Nana say if you did that at Nana's?"

Simon's face scrunched into a pout as he crossed his arms. "I'm not home, so it doesn't count," he pertly informed her.

Susie dropped to her knees and held Simon by his shoulders, preventing him from escaping. She put her forehead against his, their noses touching and looked directly into his eyes.

"It counts, Simon," she answered him softly; "because we are home. This is where we live now, so it is home. You have to accept that this is our home now."

"But I want to go live at Nana's," he whined, protesting her opinion, tears filling his eyes. "That's our *real* home."

Susie choked back her own tears, resolving to remain strong for him. "I know, Simon; but we can't until we're older. In a few years we can go live at Nana's."

"Promise?" he pleaded.

"I promise," she vowed.

Simon broke her grasp, hugged her and then began one of his little jigs all the way back down the corridor, stopping only when he reached the Library doors.

She made no attempt to catch up with him, continuing her normal gait. She'd had a difficult time the night before in convincing Simon that they still had to have a Story Time every afternoon. Miss Pritchett and Miss Hilda would know something was wrong if they didn't. After all the fuss on Sunday that she and Simon had made about not being allowed to have Story Time at bedtime, they would know; they would figure it out that no afternoon Story Time meant they were having Story Time at bedtime.

Susie wasn't sure what punishment would be meted out to her or to Simon; however, she was certain neither of them would like it, and she told him so. Finally, she persuaded him when she told him that, if they got caught, not only would there be no more bedtime stories, but they probably wouldn't be allowed to have one in the afternoon either.

Simon quickly disappeared into the Library, bolting through the door as she held it open for him. He darted past the reception area and down the aisle that led to the west side and to his favorite chair. As he burst out of the stacks and into the west area, he stopped dead in his tracks. Miss Claire was sitting at a table, playing cards. She glanced up at him when she heard his thunderous approach.

She smiled at him. "Bonjour, Simon. What is your hurry?"

Smiling shyly, he answered softly, "Susie's going to read to me, but I get to pick the story."

"Très bien," she responded, praising him, "How wonderful that you are interested in books. It's important to know how to read; and you can never start too early, ma petit chèr. Have you learned your ABC's?"

"Yes," he nodded emphatically. "I can read *easy* books, but I like the ones that Susie can read." He crawled into the chair next to her, peering intently at the strange looking cards in front of her.

His face scrunched. "What kind of cards are those?" he asked, perplexed and intrigued by them. "I've never seen those before." He reached out, picked one up and examined it. "Hey!" he exclaimed, looking up at her in surprise. "It's made of wood!"

Chuckling delightedly at his expressions, she gently retrieved the card from his hand, replacing it on the table. "They are called The Mystery," she answered. "They are very ancient, and have been in my family for countless generations. They reveal the answers to many of life's mysteries."

"Like what?" he asked, his curiosity budding.

"The past, the present, the future, choices with which you need help to make," she replied casually.

Simon didn't respond; he just bobbed his head a few times as he continued his study of the ornate circles. Each thin, circular card was made from a single block of wood and had intricately carved designs. Even after so many years, the cards still displayed an amazing array of colors. So much so, that even one as young as Simon could appreciate the amount of work required to craft them.

Simon heard Susie approach and turned to greet her.

"Look, Susie; look at these cards. They're made of wood," he announced. "And guess what?" he added excitedly; "they tell the future."

Susie glanced at the cards briefly. "Really?" she responded skeptically, raising her eyebrow as she skeptically glanced at Miss Claire.

"Oui, to an entent, ma chérie. In life, there are many choices with which we are confronted. Some seem small, but can have a great effect in our lives. It is much like a small pebble tossed into a pond. The splash is tiny, and the ripples start small. But they grow larger, each one increasing in size until the ripple stretches across the whole pond. So it is with life. We have many choices, some better than others. The Mystery Cards act as a guide to choose the right path," Miss Claire explained, maintaining Susie's eye contact.

With a smile and wink at Simon, she added, "Occasionally, the angels that guide The Cards are not as talkative as at other times. Sometimes they are difficult to understand; but to one who has the gift, the Mystery will reveal its knowledge."

Susie chuckled, rolling her eyes. "It's Tarot, Simon; and it's just a game."

"No!" Miss Claire retorted sharply; "not Tarot! The Mystery is for those who seek answers from our Heavenly Father for many of life's difficult choices. The seeker must be of a pure heart and mind for the angels to direct The Cards and reveal the message."

"How do you know if you have a pure heart and mind?" Simon asked apprehensively.

"Do you have malice … wish bad things to happen to anyone?" she asked him.

Simon slowly shook his head. "No, but sometimes I say mean things when I'm mad."

He paused and looked up at her sadly, his eyes brimming with tears. "Like to Megan, and Susie and … Nana," he continued as tears began to spill down his cheeks.

"Mon ami," Miss Claire began sympathetically as she gave him her handkerchief. "Are you sorry you have said such things?"

Simon nodded.

Smiling tenderly at him she asked, "When you say your prayers, do you ask God to forgive you, and to help you do better?"

Again Simon nodded, wiping his eyes and blowing his nose.

"Then ma chèr, you are forgiven," Miss Claire told him. "God has said He will forgive if we are truly sorry, and ask Him to forgive. You have done this, and you try to do better, yes?"

Simon nodded; his eyes still downcast. Miss Claire leaned down as she gently raised his head up so that they were eye to eye.

"You are forgiven, Simon. According to God, it is as if it never happened. That's what forgiveness is," she said softly. "So now you must forgive yourself."

Susie watched as the truth of her words resonated within him. Slowly the sad, regretful expression changed to one of joy as he began to understand.

"Your heart and mind are pure," she answered, smiling as she gently caressed his cheek. Simon beamed at her a full, toothy grin and straightened in his chair, perky and as vibrant as ever.

"Feel better?" she asked, smiling happily.

Simon nodded. "Yes, thank you."

"Bon; as I was saying, the Mystery is not Tarot. Tarot began as a parlor game, centuries ago, in Northern Italy. After it became very popular, some people who practiced fortune-telling began using the Tarot cards instead of the bones, or dice or the stones that they had been using. Hundreds of years later, those that practice the dark arts began using Tarot cards as well."

"What's the difference?" Susie asked.

""Yeah, what's the difference?" Simon parroted.

Miss Claire smiled graciously at Susie, gently tousling Simon's hair as she gave him a wink. "The difference, précieux chèrs, is that The Mystery is far older than Tarot, and only the direct descendants of the priestesses can use them. They do not predict the future because the future is unwritten. There are many choices that come in our Life Path, some good and some not. The one who has the Gift can reveal what paths are ahead, and which would be the better choice."

"So these are those Cards?" Susie asked with a hint of cynicism.

Miss Claire's laugh was light hearted. "No, ma chère. These were made ages ago by one of my ancestors. It is said that the first Cards were given to a young girl by a very powerful Angel. Some have speculated that it was the Archangel Michael," she shrugged; "but no one knows for certain."

Tilting her head slightly, Miss Claire asked in an enticing tone, "Would you like me to tell you the story of The Cards?"

Simon's eyes widened, thrilled at the prospect of a new story. "Yes, please," he responded excitedly, clapping his hands. He looked up at Susie, noticing her expression was a dubious one. A little anxious, he asked, "It's okay; isn't it, Susie?"

Susie gave a brief glace at Miss Claire before smiling at Simon. "Sure," she answered; "but we'll only have time for one small book afterwards."

Simon rapidly bobbed his head, affirming his agreement. "That's okay," he hastily responded, then turned to face Miss Claire. "Tell the card story, puh-le-e-ease," he directed, grinning like the Cheshire cat.

Chuckling softly, Miss Claire replied, "Très bien." With an elegant wave of her hand, she motioned for Susie to be seated as she said, "Susie, s'il vous plaît."

Her tone changed, becoming soft as a whisper. Her demeanor revealed she was quite adept as a storyteller, and the children fell under her spell as she spun her tale.

"The Mystery is very, very old. It goes back further than recorded history, back to ancient times when the Angels frequently visited with us. It was in those Days a mighty Angel gave the Mystery Cards to a young girl because her love for the Almighty God, and her faith in Him, were unequalled."

"She taught many of Him and would speak of Him to everyone she saw. People came to her for prayers, for guidance and for her to interpret their visions and dreams. To aid her, the mighty Angel gave her The Cards and taught her how to use them. They were not like these; the first Cards were made of a strange metal. When the message was given, the metal would become clear as glass, and the etchings would glow. She would read each one in the order that they glowed, and the one who received the message would have their answer."

"Where are they now?" Simon interrupted.

Miss Claire shrugged slightly. "No one knows for certain, ma chèr; but it is said they are hidden in a very old book."

"What book? Is it here in the Library?" he pressed, his hope rising as his head began swiftly turning, scanning the books in the stacks around them.

She laughed. "No, Simon. They are not hidden here. No one knows where they are. Now, please, allow me to finish the story."

With an eager smile, Simon rapidly nodded his head several times.

Miss Claire smiled, and her voice once again took on the spell weaving quality of a skilled storyteller. "Many thousands of years ago, long before our oldest recorded histories, there was a very large city in an enormous mountain valley. It was a beautiful place, with crystal clear rivers and streams, and with forests of giant trees that seemed to nearly touch the clouds in the sky. They were famous for their beautiful gardens and buildings. But the most famous building was a temple built high on the top of the mountain. The only way to it was through the city gates in the valley below. The temple was very large and very beautiful. It was made of the finest white marble and was decorated with gold, silver and precious jewels. It gleamed like a big, white pearl topped with a gold cap. People came from great distances. Some came just to see the marvelous temple, but most came to worship and to receive instruction. They would bring their offerings, and some would even leave gifts for the poor."

Simon perked up at the mention of gifts. "What kind of gifts?" he asked.

Miss Claire grinned, chuckling to herself at his reaction. "Same as they do now, I would think. Perhaps some food, or shoes, or clothing, or blankets would be left in large bins, but mostly money would have been placed into the collection boxes."

"How would they get it?" he asked, completely puzzled by this idea.

She laughed softly and then responded. "I'm certain they had helpers who were given the task to deliver the gifts to the people who needed it, just as we have today."

Simon bobbed his head up and down as he mulled it over. He abruptly stopped, looked dead-straight into Miss Claire's eyes, and solemnly asked, "Can anybody give to the poor?"

Surprised by his question, Miss Claire slowly stammered, "Oui; I mean, yes, Simon; anyone can give to the poor."

"How?" he pressed further.

"A variety of ways, ma petit chèr," she responded. "You can give through your church, or through many different organizations." She reflected briefly and, with her curiosity piqued, she asked, "Why do you ask, Simon?"

He dropped his gaze and tightly pressed his lips together. A few seconds later he released a sigh. "Promise you won't laugh?" he asked as he lifted his eyes to meet hers.

"I promise," she solemnly affirmed, laying her hand over her heart.

Simon looked down at the table. "Well, I've been thinking about what the Reverend said, and I thought that maybe I could share some of my toys with the poor."

Simon looked up at her, his sincerity quite obvious. "I have lots and lots of toys. As soon as my stuff gets here, I thought I could put some of them in a box like you said, and then I would be doing what the Reverend said and helping others."

Her eyes brimmed with tears as she humbly whispered to herself, 'Mon Dieu, such is the kingdom of heaven'. Softly she replied, "That would be a wonderful thing to do, Simon."

"Can you help me get a box? I'll need a *really, big* one," he informed her. His head bobbed up and down, accentuating that it would truly need to be a large box.

"I would be honored to help you," she answered. Leaning toward him, she gave him a kiss on his cheek.

Simon giggled, flashing his dimples and his little, pearly-white teeth. He looked at Susie and saw that she was sporting as goofy a look on her face as what Miss Claire had. Susie got out of her chair and promptly gave him a big hug, kissing him on the top of his head.

"I am so proud of you, Simon," she told him as she knelt down beside him.

Simon rolled his eyes, pretending not to enjoy the attention. "Puh-le-e-ease," he fussed; "I want to hear the rest of the story."

"As you wish," Miss Claire responded, barely able to contain her laughter.

Susie quickly returned to her chair, still grinning at Simon.

Miss Claire continued her tale. "Well, many hundreds of years had come and gone; and the city grew to be very great in size. It was known far and wide that it was a place of safety, and fairness, and justice and of great prosperity. They had many powerful kings over the course of time, and they were good kings. Until one day a king ascended to the throne who was a bad man. He did not hold to the laws of the land. He began to impose new laws on the people, restricting their freedom and increasing the money they had to pay him to live and work in the city."

"His greed grew more every day. When he realized how many visitors came to the city, he decided that they would have to pay a fee just to enter the city. Many of the people who came to the city were just visiting their families or friends, not the gardens or the temple. But the evil king didn't care – he wanted more money. The people who lived in the city began to complain amongst themselves. When the king heard of their grumbling, he became angry. He made a new law that charged a fee for every person in the city. Most families could not afford the new fee because it was not just for adults, but for every child as well. The people asked the priests to intervene with the king on their behalf."

Miss Claire paused for dramatic effect as she slowly shook her head. "That only made the king even angrier. He yelled at the priests and told them they would pay for meddling into things that wasn't their business. Several days later a new decree was sent out to all the people. In it the king ordered that anyone who came to the temple would owe a fee for each visit. The amount was very high – more than the people could pay. The king's guards were placed at each of the twelve temple gates to collect the money."

"The king laughed for he was certain that the temple was doomed. Not so. Every day the priests and priestesses held meetings in the market square so people could come and receive instruction and guidance. The people brought offerings for the temple and gifts for the poor. At the end of the day, the priests and priestesses would distribute the gifts to the poor before returning to the temple."

"On the second day of this new arrangement, the king heard what had happened. He was furious! He ordered his guards to bring the high priest and the high priestess to him. And they did."

Miss Claire shook her head slightly, making a slight clicking noise with her tongue. She sighed, and her face became sad. "It was then the king did a very bad thing."

"What did he do?" Simon asked, fearful of what the imagined bad act could have been.

"Well, Simon, he told them that they were to stop what they had been doing, or he would have all of them arrested and killed. The high priest agreed, but only if the king would reduce the temple fee to an amount the people could afford. The high priestess would not agree. She told the king that what he was doing was wrong, and that it was an evil act. Oh, the king was so very angry with her. How dare she defy him! The king glared at her, but said nothing. She met his hostile glare without fear. He stared at her for the longest time, his rage fueled by hate. But the high priestess … she did not wavier. She knew she had spoken the truth. Then the king ordered her to return to the temple."

"After she left, the king told the high priest that the House of Priestess would be closed that very day forever. At sundown, the king's guards would arrest all of the priestesses; they would be executed on the third day of the festival, exactly seven days from that day. He said this would show the people that to defy him meant death."

Simon's eyes filled with fear, and he swallowed hard. "Did any of them die?" he asked timidly.

"A few did, Simon," she answered solemnly; "a few did."

She paused slightly and continued the story, her voice now resonating thankfulness. "But most were saved because of a very brave act by a slave girl in the king's household. She overheard the high priest and the king. The slave girl ran as fast as she could to the high priestess, telling her everything she had heard. The high priestess thanked the young slave for her courage and gave her a blessing. After the young slave had left, the high priestess went to her prayer chamber, lay before the altar, cried out to the Creator and then waited in humble silence. Her faith was rewarded. A gentle, rustling wind swirled around her, calming her. It was then she heard Him – it was the Creator's voice."

Simon leaned forward, captivated and asked, "What did He say?"

Affectionately, Miss Claire touched his cheek. "Just wait, ma chèr; allow me to finish the story as it has been told to me."

She smiled and continued, "The high priestess now knew what to do. She sent her servant to all of the other priestesses, commanding them to come immediately to the Chamber of the Sacred Flame. Of course they all came quickly, curious as to what could possibly have caused such a summons. As they took their places around the circle, the High Priestess walked to the center and stood before the holy flame, staring into the celestial fire. She raised her hands high and began to recite a prayer of thanksgiving to the Creator. When she finished, she turned and faced the women."

"She told them what had happened that morning. Then she told them what the slave girl had reported. The women were very upset and frightened, but the high priestess ordered them all to be calm. When they had quieted, she told them what the Creator had said – they were all to leave, and do so immediately. They were to gather their families quickly and return to the House for a Blessing Ceremony before going their separate ways. They were each to take a censer and light its wick in the holy flame. They would bring the knowledge of the Creator to all corners of the earth."

"Did they escape?" Susie asked.

"Oui; most did," Miss Claire answered. "There were some that refused to leave. Their families were of important rank, and they thought that would protect them. …. They were mistaken. Those who remained were arrested and killed on the third day of the festival. Those who left never returned."

"After the Blessing Ceremony, those who chose to stay remained in the Chamber of the Sacred Flame, praying for those who had decided to leave. Those who left did so secretly through a hidden staircase that led down to an underground passageway. It extended many miles, deep into the forest. The high priestess stood at the exit, handing a sealed scroll to each priestess as she and her family headed into the woods. The high priestess whispered to each priestess where they were to travel. She told every one of them that they were to not to stop any longer than necessary for the next three days. On the fourth morning, they were to open the scroll and to burn it after it was read. The scroll revealed the place where they were to meet thirty years from that night of exodus."

She smiled at them, giving a slight nod of her head to signal that the story was finished.

253

"Did they meet again?" Susie asked, curious in spite of herself.

"Oui, they did. Down through the centuries, they have done so many times, meeting in secret every thirty years. They each kept records of their own group; and at the meetings, they shared with each other their news."

"Have you ever seen this Record?" Susie asked, still a little unconvinced.

"No, I have not. However, my mother, my grandmother and my great grandmother have all seen it," she answered with conviction.

"Who has it?" Susie pressed, her interest definitely now rising.

Claire hesitated, uncertain as to how she should answer, and realizing that, perhaps, she has said too much. "That I cannot say," she finally said, forcing a smile.

"What happened to the bad king?" Simon asked, concerned that he escaped punishment.

"The same that happens to all bad people, Simon," she responded with a quiet tone. "As the king's greed grew, he took more and more from the people. They, also, had to leave or die. In large numbers the people began leaving the great city, searching for a better place to live. Eventually the great city became weak from the loss of so many of its people. The king's enemies attacked and destroyed the city, taking everything of value back to their own city. Those that had remained in the city died in battle, or became the slaves of their enemy. Nothing now remains of the great and mighty city, or of the beautiful temple. The king's enemies destroyed everything."

"That's a neat story," Simon said appreciatively. "Is it true?"

"But of course, ma chèr," Miss Claire answered sincerely.

"What happened to the first Cards?" Susie asked, trying to maintain the aura of just a faint interest in spite of her genuine curiosity; "you know, the metal ones?"

Smiling satisfactorily, Miss Claire responded in a hushed tone. "It has been told that the high priestess was a direct descendant of the young girl who received the first Cards. She kept them in her prayer chamber. They were hidden in a special box that looked like a book, so it was easy for her to hide them amongst her things when they fled from the bad king. She gave it to her first born daughter, and each generation since has passed it on to the next. Unfortunately, no one seems to know who that is."

Miss Claire had deftly picked up The Cards as she spoke, returning them to the velvet pouch. She handed the pouch to Susie. "Here, chère," she said cheerfully. "Take the pouch. Close your eyes and allow an image to enter your mind. Then place The Cards on the table in front of you in that very shape."

Susie shook her head, "No, thank you."

Simon begged, "Do it, Susie." Then to Miss Claire, he asked, "May I if she doesn't?"

Simultaneously, Susie said, "No" as Miss Claire responded, "Yes."

Simon looked from one to the other.

Miss Claire gave a little shrug; she gestured with her hands as if to say it was of no consequence. She smiled at Susie. "There is no harm in playing with them; however," she sighed dramatically; "if you do not wish to have a little fun, then that is your choice."

Simon gave Susie his best pleading look. She returned it with one of her exasperated looks. He didn't waver; she did.

"All right," she acquiesced; "for fun."

Susie accepted the pouch. "Do I pour them out onto the table?" she asked.

"No, chère," Miss Claire answered. "Remember, you must first close your eyes and allow an image to enter your mind. Then you remove one Card at a time, placing it on the table to form the image revealed to you. So, close your eyes, chère, and clear your mind. Allow the image to appear."

"Okay," Susie responded, closing her eyes.

A brief moment later, she opened her eyes. "I saw...."

"No, no, no, chère," Miss Claire quickly interrupted. "You must not tell me; just place The Cards as I instructed you."

"O-o-okay," Susie responded, reaching into the bag and removing The Cards, one at a time. She placed one Card directly in front of her. Then she began placing the other Cards, one by one, on the table until a pattern had formed.

"Mon Dieu," Miss Claire whispered, crossing herself. With a slight edge in her voice, she asked Susie, "Where have you seen this pattern?"

"Just now," Susie answered, slightly confused by Miss Claire's reaction. "Why? Did I do it wrong?"

Seeing the worried look on Simon's face and the confused look on Susie's, Miss Claire quickly regained her composure and attempted to assuage any fear on their part.

"No chère," she said with a forced smile. "You have done nothing wrong."

She exhaled heavily and then clasped her palms tightly together as she held her hands to her chest. "It's just that … it is … such an unusual pattern," she said with her eyebrows slightly pinched together.

With a dramatic shrug, she raised her hands, gesturing that the matter was unimportant. "I am certain that I shall be able to give you a proper reading," she declared.

Susie and Simon exchanged looks of surprise and of skepticism.

Miss Claire focused intently on Susie and leaned in toward her. "Are you certain that you have not seen this somewhere else, and not just now?"

Susie, slightly annoyed with all the drama, answered flatly, "Positive."

Miss Claire straightened in her chair and gave a brief nod to Susie. "Très bien; we shall begin," she stated resolutely, rising from her chair and moving to stand next to Susie.

As her eyes fell upon The Cards displayed, they widened; her face registered alternating emotions of surprise and awe. Slowly, as if in a daze, she looked at Susie, then at Simon and then back again at The Cards.

"What's the matter?" Simon asked impatiently.

Miss Claire didn't respond; she kept staring at The Cards.

With her curiosity now elevating, Susie looked up at Miss Claire. "Is something wrong?" she asked.

Softly clearing her throat, Miss Claire answered, "No, chère; nothing is wrong."

She forced herself to make eye contact briefly with Susie, managing to give Susie a weak smile just before her eyes were drawn back to the array of The Cards. Finally, with great effort, she forced herself to give each of them a big smile.

"I have never seen this array of The Cards. It is such a complex pattern; one that shall require much study. It would be best if you both run along and read your books. I shall tell you later what I have learned."

Susie shrugged and said "Okay" while Simon moaned his disappointment. "Can't we just stay here?"

"No, ma chèr; I must not have any distractions," she answered, smiling as she patted his head.

"Come on Simon," Susie said as she pulled him toward the aisle. "I'll read two short books if you can pick them out in the next five minutes."

Simon broke free of her grasp and ran toward their reading area, Susie not far behind him.

———

Immediately after Susie and Simon had left, Claire returned her full attention to The Cards displayed in front of her. A tingling sensation ran down her spine causing her to shiver. She drew in a long, deep breath and then slowly released it.

Closing her eyes, Claire began to recite the prayer her mother had taught her long ago. It invoked memories of when she was so little, watching her mother, grandmother and great-grandmother as they worked together on difficult readings. She opened her eyes, staring intently, waiting for the revelation. Again, she felt that tingling sensation; only this time, it was much stronger and far more intense. Her body began shaking and shuddering involuntarily as the strong pulsing sensation slowly coursed its way from the top of her head all the way down to her toes.

Claire shoved her chair back with a forceful thrust and leapt out of it. She anxiously paced back and forth in front of the table, wringing her hands and shaking her head. "I cannot do this," she muttered softly to herself.

She stood staring at the table, uncertain of what to do. She sighed; it was a heavy sigh, one of frustration. "If only Nini (her great-grandmother) or Mimi (her grandmother) were here. I know they could read it; perhaps even Mama could."

In defeat, Claire silently stared at The Cards. Releasing a small sigh of resignation, she picked up the velvet pouch and reached to retrieve The Cards. Her hand froze in midair as the thought flashed into her mind. *'Take a picture of it, and email it to their shop.'*

Smiling as one who just won a victory, she pulled her digital camera from her pocket and snapped several pictures. Quickly she collected The

Cards, returning them to their pouch and hurriedly left the library to return to her suite.

Once inside her sitting room, Claire nearly ran to her desk, quickly settling herself onto her antique, French provincial chair. Trembling with apprehension, Claire retrieved the memory stick from her camera, inserting it into her computer. With haste she retrieved the images, saving them to her hard drive. Immediately she accessed her email account, uploaded the images and typed in one short sentence in the subject box: "urgent: pictures attached – please advise". Pressing the send icon, she sent the pictures on their way. She closed the email account and opened the images again, staring at them.

After waiting five minutes, she picked up the phone receiver and quickly called the shop. As always, it was answered on the third ring. Claire smiled; it was nice to know that some things never change.

Her mother, Michele, answered the phone; it was good to hear her mother's voice, and a wave of relief washed through her.

"Hello, this is the Healing Garden. How may I help you?"

"Mama, it's me, Claire."

"Hello, my baby girl," she joyfully responded. "I hope all is well with you and Taryn. Unfortunately, I have some stressful news. Nini is refusing to come and spend Christmas there," she informed Claire. "Perhaps you can speak to her and change her mind, yes?"

"I will speak to her, Mama," Claire assured her. "Is Mimi coming without her?" she asked, a little concerned that Nini, who is ninety-four, might be left alone. Nini was opinionated and strong-willed; it wouldn't be the first time she sent Mama and Mimi packing. Claire chuckled to herself, remembering several incidents just last year.

"No; she told Nini that she will leave her, but that is only to try to convince her to come. If Nini does not come, neither will Mimi." She gave a heavy sigh. "I do not want us to be separated during the holidays," she began, sadness filling her tone as she worked her charm on Claire. "Nini may not be with us much longer. I could not bear it if on her last holiday we are not together."

"I will speak to her, Mama, and I will convince her to come," Claire promised.

"Très bien," Michele ecstatically proclaimed; "you are such a good daughter."

"Thank you, Mama," Claire replied with a small laugh. Her mother was the quintessential manipulator of all time; however, Mama always had the best of motives and intentions.

"Is there a particular reason you called, my sweet dove?" she asked with just a hint of misgiving in her voice. "Please do not tell me that Taryn has again changed her wedding date. First it was June, then September and then moved all the way up to February. So, what is it now?" Her tone had shifted, displaying irritation and a little exasperation.

"No, Mama; the wedding is still February." Claire hesitated, not certain as to how to broach the subject with her mother. It had always been a battle between her and her mother, with Mimi and Nini always siding with her mother. Claire decided to launch into it quickly, hoping there would be no forthcoming lecture.

"Mama, I have sent an email to you that I need you to see immediately. Please print the pictures and tell me what it means."

"What is this about?" her Mama queried suspiciously.

"Please, Mama; just do it," Claire pleaded.

The urgency in Claire's voice halted the barrage of questions Michele was ready to ask. Instead, she responded gently, "Very well, Claire; I will do it. Shall I call you back, or do you want to wait?"

"I'll wait, Mama; it won't take but a minute," Claire responded, relieved and grateful that her mother had chosen to comply so easily.

"Très bien," Michele replied, and laid the phone receiver down on the counter.

A few minutes later she returned.

"Claire," she spoke in a clipped tone; "What is this? I have never seen such a pattern as this one. It causes me to feel a little uneasy. When did you do this?"

"I did not do this, Mama. Someone here did it a little while ago. I could not read it. I tried but …. I couldn't." Claire paused, the frustration and apprehension building within her made it difficult to talk.

She took a deep breath and slowly released it. "Mama, I tried to read it, but there was a power I don't understand. …. I've never felt it before, and it frightened me. I thought maybe you, or Mimi, or Nini might be able to read it for me. ... I have a feeling it's important. .. I don't know why."

"It's okay, Claire," her mother assured her in a soothing voice. "Do not fret so. Wait a minute; I'll show it to them, and see what they think. I'll be right back." She laid the receiver down, taking the pictures into the back room where her mother and grandmother were having afternoon tea.

"What's wrong?" both women asked upon seeing Michele's face when she entered the sitting room.

"This," she said, placing the pictures on the table in front of them.

Mimi's brow furrowed, perplexed and apprehensive by what she beheld.

Nini gasped and slowly raised her eyes to meet those of her grand-daughter's. Pointing a slender finger, gnarled from arthritis, at the image before her on the table, she narrowed her deep, green eyes as she stared at Michele. In a husky whisper she demanded, "Child, where did you get this?"

Unsettled by Nini's reaction, Michele nervously answered, "Claire sent it, Nini. She needs help reading it. I don't think I can, so I thought I'd see if either of you recognized this pattern and the sequence. Claire's on the phone waiting to talk to you."

Nini immediately pushed herself up from her chair, grabbed her cane and the photo, and proceeded to stride rapidly toward the door.

"What is it, Mother?" Lisette asked, greatly disturbed by her mother's reaction.

"Come," Nini instructed brusquely. "You will hear what I have to say when I talk to Claire. I do not wish to repeat myself."

She turned, exited the sitting room and quickly ambled to the counter. Michele and Lisette were seconds behind her. Michele sprinted to the writing desk, removed the ornate tapestry chair from its position and quickly brought it to the counter for Nini. When Nini and Lisette reached the counter, Lisette pushed the speaker button on the box next to the phone. She smiled at her mother and said, "So we can all hear." Nini nodded assent.

Nini sat down and then addressed Claire. "Claire, we are all here. Now tell me, where did you get this?"

"Why, Nini? What is it?" Claire countered.

"Answer me, Child," Nini responded, her tone edged with agitation.

"A young girl here did it," she answered meekly. "Have you seen it before?" Claire asked hesitantly.

Nini was silent a moment; then she spoke softly. "Only in The Book."

"The Book," Lisette and Michele echoed reverently in unison while Claire asked, "What Book?" as innocently as possible.

Nini closed her eyes, exasperation swelling with her. "*The Book*, Claire," she spoke tersely; "The ancient journal of our ancestors."

"Oh," Claire responded, trying to sound unconcerned; "*that* Book. I remember you, and Mimi, and Mama speaking of it."

"I never showed it to you because you never took your gift seriously, little one. It was a toy to you; something to play with, like a parlor game, whenever it suited you. Worse, you dabbled into areas you had no business toying with ---", Nini's sharp discourse was interrupted.

"But Nini --,"Claire began her protest and was promptly cut short.

"Do not interrupt me, Child," Nini's tone was harsh; "Do not make excuses. Do not try to deny it."

Nini paused for a moment, calming herself.

When she continued, her tone changed, the sharp edge was gone and a softer, a more gentle, inflection was now prevalent. "Do you think I do not read for you, for my daughter and for my grand-daughter? I read for all of you every day. I pray daily to the Blessed Virgin that she will watch over, and protect, and guide all of you in the right path. I have seen in the Mystery the things you have done, and I have wept. I know how you secured jobs for Peter, for yourself and now for Taryn. Did Peter know? Does Taryn?"

Claire was stunned. She knew Nini had a very powerful gift, but had never known the extent of her ability. She felt ashamed that Nini knew, and now Mimi knew, and so did Mama. Tears began spilling down her cheeks.

"No Nini; I never told them. ... I didn't know you knew. ... It was harmless, Nini," Claire haltingly stammered, attempting to justify her actions. "No one was hurt. Peter needed the work. When he died, I needed work. And Taryn needed the job so she could stay here."

261

Nini made a clicking noise, tapping her tongue against her teeth; a sound Claire was all too familiar with – a sound of serious disapproval. She stopped and then released a heavy, dramatic sigh. "Ma petite Cœur, how can you say no one was hurt? Those you caused to leave, they were hurt by no longer working there. And Peter, he lost his life working in a job that was not his. You dabbled in the dark path as if it were merely a child's game. There are always consequences, Claire; you know this. Peter paid for your misdeed; and now I fear for you, or for whoever will pay for the other misdeeds you have done. This must be rectified," she commanded; "and soon."

Nini fell silent briefly, choosing her words carefully. "I love you, ma petite Cœur; you know this. I tell you this not to hurt you, but to help you. You must go to confession so that your soul and your spirit will be cleansed."

"Yes, Nini, I will," Claire promised.

"Bon," Nini responded. "That is settled; we will mention it no more. Now tell me what happened. Did you try to read the Mystery?"

"Yes, Nini; I tried, but couldn't. I tried twice. The first time, I felt a tingling sensation run through me. The second time the feeling was much stronger ... like an electric current discharging from the top of my head all the way down to my toes. I was frightened, and I stopped. That's when the idea came to me to take pictures and send them to Mama. I hoped she could read it; but if she couldn't, then maybe either you or Mimi could."

Nini chuckled softly. It was one of amusement. "Do you know why you couldn't read it?"

Claire, irritated by Nini's question, answered tartly, "Obviously because I don't have your ability."

"Watch your tone, young lady," Nini snapped.

Claire sighed. "I'm sorry Nini. It just seems obvious to me why I can't; and it should be obvious to you."

"What is obvious is that you still take the easy way out, making excuses instead of taking responsibility," Nini corrected her. "You have the gift. I've told you this all your life; but you have chosen to ignore your calling, and have used it to amuse yourself and others. What you felt was the connection you have through your gift, your ability, with the unseen world.

You could not focus your ability and receive the reading because you never learned to do so. ..... But it is there, still waiting to be honed and perfected in order to be of service. I will come for the Holidays if you want to start learning what your ability truly is," Nini offered, her tone now gentle.

"Okay, Nini," Claire responded; "I will learn from you. But, will you read this, and tell me what it is?"

Nini's voice became very somber and held a slight tremor. "Yes; but before I attempt this, I will need to go to confession and pray to the Blessed Virgin. I will need her guidance and protection. This is a very old, very old pattern. It has not been seen in more than three millennia. It is one that channels great power; so much so that our ancestors decided long ago it should not be used. The Book displays this pattern and others that were forbidden. Twice in my life I have seen a pattern that was in that section of The Book; once during Mardi gras in 1947, and again in June of 1970."

Nini paused and sighed heavily. Her voice carried sadness when she continued. "Both women were about to face a crossroad that, if they chose the wrong path, could have devastating consequences. Both times it was the same pattern and the same Cards; the only difference was in the sequence. This pattern is different; this one is the most powerful of all, and is the first of the ones to be forbidden by the Council."

"No one has taught this pattern since it was forbidden," Nini continued, her tone one of bewilderment; "nor do we ever show the banned patterns. Only the Holder of The Book has access to them. What I do not understand is how a child knew this pattern."

Nini stopped her narrative, closed her eyes, bowed her head and began quickly to recite a prayer. Lisette laid her hand on her mother's right shoulder and Michele laid her hand on Nini's left shoulder. They closed their eyes and bowed their heads as she recited the prayer.

When she finished, Nini spoke in a voice, soft and low. "I have prayed for these women many times over the years, and have never seen another pattern from the forbidden section until now. There must be a reason for this – there must be a connection."

Nini's face took on a look of fierce determination. "Claire, answer me; who laid out this pattern?"

"It was one of the children; a young girl named Susie. She and her little brother just arrived here," Claire answered. "There is something very different about her, Nini. I don't know what it is exactly."

"Bon," Nini responded. "Now, how did it come about that she had your Mystery Cards?"

Claire inhaled sharply and tried to simulate a nonchalant tone to her voice. "She and her little brother, Simon, saw me with them and wanted to know what I was doing. I told them the story of The Cards. Then I …. I told the girl what to do and gave her The Cards. I never expected anything to really happen, Nini. But, Voila! The result is as you see in the pictures. … I asked if she had seen this anywhere before, and she said no. I believe her."

Nini rubbed her temples; her head was beginning to ache. "Claire, why would you do such a foolish thing? Never mind …. What's done is done. … There is something very special about this girl; that is a certainty. Something is brewing in the spiritual realm. I will know more when I perform the reading. … Be careful, my little heart," Nini added softly.

"Careful of what, Nini?" Claire asked, perplexed and beginning to feel frightened.

"As I said, something is brewing in the spiritual realm. This child is very special, and possibly her little brother. I will know more after the reading. Perhaps, Claire, you have been afforded the opportunity to atone for your past misdeeds. Perhaps our Blessed Virgin has placed you there for this very purpose. It will be a very sacred honor for you if what I think is in The Mystery is truly what is there. For now, you must watch over them, make certain they are safe."

Bewildered, Claire responded; "Okay, Nini; and how do I do that?"

Nini sighed; it was one partially due to fatigue, but mostly due to the annoyance at having to state the obvious to one that should already know these things. "First, you must immediately go to confession; now, today. Afterward, you must light candles for yourself, for your Mama, for Mimi and also for me. Most importantly, you must light a candle for Glen Hollow – it will represent all those that live there. You must pray to the Blessed Virgin for her help to guide you in what you must do. You must ask her for her protection for you and all those that live at Glen Hollow. Then return home, ma petite Cœur, and pray these prayers every day, morning and night. She will answer you, Claire; you will see."

"I will, Nini; I promise."

"Bon; I, too, must go now to church. Girls, say good-bye," Nini ordered.

Michele and Lisette quickly piped up, telling Claire good-bye as Claire returned theirs with one of her own. Claire said good-by to Nini. Nini smiled, told her good-bye, and that she'd call her soon with the answer. They each hung up their receivers.

Claire sat still for a moment, staring at the phone. Her eyes slowly directed their focus to the grandfather clock in the corner of the room which proclaimed the time to be five-twelve.

"Mon Dieu," she whispered. "It is so late. But I promised."

She turned to her computer, accessed her email and quickly typed a note to Miss Pritchett explaining that she had an errand to run in Foxboro Station and not to expect her for dinner. She pressed the send button, exited out of the program and then shut down her computer.

Claire rushed to the coat rack and removed her dark green, hooded wool cape and a matching cashmere scarf. Hastily she put them on, snatching up her purse as she strode to the door of her suite.

She stopped, thought of Taryn and quickly returned to her desk. With lightning speed, she wrote her daughter a note and took it to Taryn's bedroom. She knew Taryn would be here to freshen up before dinner and would read the note and not worry about her absence. Sliding the note into the frame of Taryn's dresser, she froze as she noticed her own reflection – a face that looked haunted and frightened appeared in place of the usual vivacious beauty she was accustomed to seeing.

Quickly she turned away and left, making her way out of her suite and out of the manor. With great haste she headed to Foxboro Station, intently focused on her mission.

———

Susie had just finished reading the second book when they heard the chiming of the mantel clock. Simon had chosen two thin books, nothing that he couldn't have read himself. When she pressed him as to why he chose these, he coyly grinned and told her he liked the way she reads (meaning the various versions of character voices, and the mood inflections she performed). He also admitted that two small books *seemed* like more reading time than just one book.

"It's five-thirty, Simon. We finished in plenty of time. Let's put these away, and then we'll go to dinner," she told him, handing him the books.

Simon took the books and laid them on top of the first bookcase as he scurried passed it on his way to the door.

"Simon," Susie called after him; "is that where you found them?"

He stopped, whirled around, and grinned mischievously at her. "Close enough," he answered saucily.

"No, Simon," she countered. "If you want to use the Library, then you have to return the books to their proper place."

"You used them," he argued. "You put them back."

"I don't know where they belong, so you need to return them. Next time, wait for me to get the books if you want me to do it," she stated firmly.

Simon gave a shrug and then bobbed his head from side to side, marching back to her in his '*giant–walk*' stride. He grabbed the books, returning them to their proper places on the shelves with a grand thrust. When finished, he sighed heavily as if he had completed some monumental task that had required great effort.

"Can we *go* now?" he asked, more of a demand than a question.

Susie grinned. "It's '*may we*', and the answer is yes."

When they passed by the table where Miss Claire had been, Simon ran in front of Susie and began running backward. "Where did Miss Claire go?" he asked.

"Probably to get ready for dinner," she answered matter-of-factly.

"Why didn't she wait for us? And why didn't she come tell us what the cards mean?" he pressed.

"I don't know, Simon."

"Why was she acting so funny?" he asked, continuing his inquiry.

"I don't know, Simon," she again responded.

"Do you think she saw something bad?" he asked, frightened at the idea.

"No, Simon," Susie answered. "She didn't see anything. It's just a game; okay?"

"You sure?" he asked, squinting skeptically at her.

"I'm positive," she told him. "Now turn around before you end up getting hurt. We're almost to the door."

He gave her a goofy grin and quickened his pace just enough to allow him to back into the door. Feigning injury, he dropped to the ground, holding his head.

"O-o-oh," he moaned; "I think I've knocked my head off." Simon parted his fingers just enough to peek up at his sister, allowing Susie to catch a glimpse of his eyes twinkling with merriment.

"Come on, silly," she said with a laugh, reaching down to help him up.

Giggling like a loon, he launched upward and nearly knocked their heads together.

"Simon!" Susie fussed at him; "be careful."

Wrapping his arms around her waist and shrieking with laughter, he gave her a bear hug.

Returning his hug, she chuckled and said, "Let's go, silly; we don't want to be late."

Simon quickly released her and together they left the Library.

———

Dinner went rather quietly; most of the conversations were held by the adults. Occasionally someone would ask a question of one of the children. Answers were generally short and vague. Susie noticed that Miss Claire was absent and wondered why. No one had offered an explanation; since she wasn't comfortable asking, she decided to not ask.

Timmy was still pouting, even though not as much as when they first sat down to dinner. When he and Aaron had entered the Dining Hall, Timmy had asked Miss Hilda if he could sit next to Simon. She told him not presently, but perhaps at a future time. He began to whine and wheedle, prompting Miss Hilda to quickly inform him that his behavior suggested that he was not yet mature enough to sit next to Simon. Unfortunately, that observation only fueled his pout.

Throughout most of the dinner, he picked at his food and barely ate. He sat with his lips pursed in a pout, taking turns glaring at his plate and Miss Hilda. Periodically Timmy would cross his arms over his chest and release a big sigh. Aaron ignored him; he was accustomed to Timmy's frequent bouts of pouting. Several of the adults had made attempts to cajole Timmy into eating, but none were successful. Quite the contrary, their attempts only served to increase his theatrics.

Finally Miss Pritchett stated that only Timmy knew whether or not he was hungry. She smiled at Timmy, telling him that if he wasn't hungry he may skip dinner and perhaps his appetite would return in time for breakfast. After a brief pause, she added that she hoped his appetite didn't return during the night - he would be hungry for hours before breakfast time arrived.

Everyone proceeded to ignore him, finishing their meal and continuing their conversations. After several minutes of contemplation, Timmy apparently had a change of heart. He began slipping little pieces of his biscuit into his mouth, darting glances around the table to see if anyone was watching him. A few minutes later he began to devour his food.

As soon as dinner was over, Timmy ran up to Simon, wanting him to play.

"Bath time first," Miss Ginger reminded them. "Come along; let's get it done, and then you'll have until bedtime to play."

She smiled affectionately at them, placing her arms around them as she scurried them out of the Dining Hall. Meanwhile Miss Cora had corralled Megan for her bath time, and they left amongst the straggling group of children and adults. Susie watched them leave, allowing them plenty of time to get out of sight.

"Susie, are you all right?" asked Miss Fiona. She had returned to the Dining Hall to remove the table linens and noticed Susie sitting alone on the hearth.

Susie smiled as convincingly as she could muster. "Yes, I'm fine."

She was, however, completely exhausted. After two nights in a row with little sleep, she felt as if she would fall over in a dead faint at any second. However, the last thing she wanted to do was to admit to anyone that her imagination had run wild Sunday night keeping her awake, or that she had a bad dream last night that prevented much needed sleep.

"Would you care to help? You don't have to, but you may if you wish," she offered congenially.

Susie nodded as she slowly rose to her feet. "Sure, I'd like to help."

Trudging to the opposite side of the table, Susie began assisting Miss Fiona in folding the tablecloth back upon itself as they walked down the length of the table. Every now and then either she or Miss Fiona would stop, bend down, pick up a napkin, toss it onto the table and then resume folding.

"So, Susie; what do you think of Glen Hollow?" Miss Fiona asked with an amused lilt in her voice. It matched her perky grin, and her twinkling eyes.

Cautiously, Susie answered, "Okay, I guess. It's big … and interesting. It's different. I like it so far. … Everyone seems nice."

Miss Fiona chuckled merrily. "Even the children are nice?" she asked teasingly. "Mercy me; you are a diplomat, I think."

Susie blushed slightly and laughed. "No; I guess they're not all nice. But maybe it's because they're fairly new here, too, and just trying to deal with the circumstances that brought them here."

Miss Fiona smiled approvingly. "You have a kind heart, Susie. You'll do fine," she added with a wink.

They returned to the process of gathering up the table linens, and were nearly finished when movement near the fireplace on the far wall caught Susie's attention. She froze, quizzically staring at the fireplace and its immediate surroundings. It was too dark to see much of anything now that the fire had died down to a scattering of embers.

"Is something wrong?" Miss Fiona asked with a little mischievous undercurrent in her tone.

Susie didn't respond at first, continuing to search the area, trying to detect if one of the older children was perhaps hiding in the shadowy gloom. She saw no further evidence of anything – not a person, a mouse or any other creature. She shook her head.

"No," she answered; "I just thought someone was there by the fireplace. I guess I was wrong."

As she began to turn around, Susie caught the strangest glimpse out of the corner of her eye – Miss Fiona was softly glowing and had large,

gossamer wings like a butterfly! Susie whirled around to face Miss Fiona
…. It was just Miss Fiona … no glow and no wings. Susie's expression
went from incredulous to disappointment, and finally to confused and disturbed in just a matter of seconds.

Miss Fiona was smiling; not a cheery smile, but one that seemed to suggest she understood and knew exactly what Susie was experiencing. Susie's
inner radar was loudly ringing, sending waves of tingles all over her skin.

"I wouldn't worry about things like that," Miss Fiona said, gathering
up the folded table linens and proceeded to the door. "Old buildings have
a way of playing on our imaginations."

Stopping in the doorway, she turned, and her eyes were sparkling.
"Besides, like I said before; you have a kind heart, Susie dear. You'll do just
fine here. You'll see." She gave a little nod of dismissal and disappeared
into the corridor.

Susie sank down onto the hearth, allowing the faint heat from the
dying flames to gently warm her back. She chuckled softly, remembering
the character from the book that she had read to Simon yesterday – 'The
Magical World of Mr. Horatio Wedgilwog'. The character named Lashir
was a fairy, glowed, and had exactly the same gossamer wings that she
imagined Miss Fiona had.

"She's right," Susie muttered. "Old buildings do make us imagine
things. So does the lack of sleep."

Susie lingered a moment, enjoying the warmth from the fire; then the
realization struck. "Oh no!" she groaned. "I have a ton of homework to do."

Disheartened, Susie closed her eyes, dropped her face into her hands
and quietly prayed, "Please help me to get it finished quickly. I really need
some sleep."

Susie dragged herself up and slowly headed for the Rec Room, knowing that Simon would be there waiting for her, and more likely than not,
waiting a little impatiently.

———

Susie arrived in the Rec Room to find that Simon was indeed already there;
however, he wasn't waiting for her. He and Timmy were busy playing with

a box of Lincoln Logs, creating their own version of a farm. Apparently it was their rather unique representation of Glen Hollow. They seemed to be having a great time, laughing and snickering, obsessing over every detail and giving each other high five's periodically. At their insistence, Susie inspected their progress, giving both of them the praise and recognition that they deserved for a job well done; and, as she told them, for playing so well together.

Simon rolled his eyes, grinning and bouncing like a jack-in-the-box. He loved the attention even though he pretended he didn't. The same held true for Timmy; he loved the attention, but made a comical expression and jokingly said, "Aw, shucks". She laughed and gave both of them a hug.

Giggling and snickering profusely, the boys returned their attention to their farm, ignoring her. Susie realized that Fate had intervened; her prayer had been answered. She asked Simon if it would be okay with him if she went to her room to do her homework since he and Timmy were playing. He nodded, focusing his attention on the proper placement of the miniature tractor he held in his hand. He couldn't decide whether to place it in the barn, outside the barn or in the area they had designated as the field. He was leaning toward placement in the barn, and Timmy was voting for the field. They compromised, and it was placed outside the barn.

Now that the major decision was done, Simon looked up at her, very serious, and told her he didn't care just as long as she didn't forget about the *"you know what"*. Susie assured him she wouldn't forget. He grinned and waved goodbye. Susie quickly left before Simon had a change of heart.

Susie dove into her homework, first catching up on the literature assignment from yesterday. She noticed during class that, both yesterday and today, Miss Emma would often refer back to a previous lesson. No way would she be caught off guard if Miss Emma calls on her tomorrow, Susie determined.

Time flew and before she knew it, Miss Cora was escorting little Megan to bed. Megan ran into Susie's room with Miss Cora two steps behind.

"Megan, don't bother Susie; she's studying," Miss Cora instructed.

Megan put her hands on her hips, furrowed her brow and pursed her lips into a pretty, little pout. "I'm not bothering Susie," she unequivocally informed Miss Cora. "I'm here for my goodnight hug." She punctuated her declaration with a sharp nod of her head, sending her spiral curls into a bouncing frenzy.

Miss Cora's attempt to not laugh was successful; however, her grin gave her away (at least to Susie) – she was very amused at Megan's little performance. "If it's okay with Susie, then it's okay with me," she cordially consented.

Megan sauntered over to Susie, her expression very serious. "I forgot to tell you I also need a hug at bedtime. I can't sleep good without one," she said sincerely, slowly moving her head back and forth.

"Megan, the proper word is 'well' instead of 'good'," Miss Cora corrected. "Please state the sentence correctly."

Susie had to choke back a laugh when she saw Megan's comical expression as Megan repeated in a sing-song manner, "I can't sleep *well* without one."

Susie bit her tongue to keep from laughing. Smiling, she said to Megan, "Oh, well, we can't have that. You need to sleep well."

Susie held her arms open, and Megan rushed into them. As they hugged each other, Megan whispered, "I didn't used to sleep well; but I do now because you're here. My angel told me that you're here to help."

"Really?" Susie asked, trying to disguise her astonishment.

Megan pushed back and stared solemnly into Susie's eyes, her own revealing the earnestness with which she spoke. "Yes," she whispered. Megan smiled and then added with a giggle, "I really don't have to have a hug; I just like them."

"Guess what," Susie responded with a chuckle as she playfully tickled Megan; "I like them, too."

Megan gave her a fast hug, and then skipped to the doorway where Miss Cora was patiently waiting. "I'm ready for bed now," she sweetly chirped, smiling up at Miss Cora as she passed by, skipping all the way to her room.

Miss Cora's face expressed appreciation and affection as she smiled at Susie. "That was very nice, Susie. Thank you."

Susie shrugged. "I like Megan; she and Simon are a lot alike. If you don't mind, I'm going to go give him his bedtime hug now."

Nodding, Miss Cora told Susie to go ahead before Miss Ginger turned off the lights. Moving quickly, Miss Cora proceeded to Megan's room to tuck her in for the night. Susie switched off her desk lamp and hurriedly left the Dorm.

———

Susie returned from the bedtime hug fest with Simon feeling energized and ready to finish her remaining homework. She felt certain she could finish by the nine o'clock curfew, or possibly eleven at the latest. Never had she ever looked forward to bedtime with such eagerness; however, she desperately needed some sleep and that had changed her outlook. She selected her world history textbook, 'Ancient Civilizations', opening it to the reading assignment and began. Next she tackled her US history assignment, leaving math and biology yet to be done.

Susie was nearly finished with her US History assignment when she heard a loud commotion coming from the Common Area. It was Kat and Dani yelling at each other as they entered the Dorm, blaming each other for some perceived affront.

After several minutes of the ruckus, Miss Cora's voice rang out above the fray, terse and a bit exasperated. "That's quite enough, both of you. This bickering must stop. Tomorrow, you both will report to Mrs. Coppersmith after class. You will sweep floors, mop them or do whatever else she assigns you to do. And you will do it without grumbling, mumbling or fighting with each other. If you misbehave, you will have kitchen duty after class every day until you start behaving properly, no matter how long that might be. Do you understand?"

A very contrite voice responded with "Yes, Miss Cora" (Susie was certain it was Dani), whereas a more sullen, icy voice answered, "Fine!" (That voice had to be Kat).

Miss Cora, now more composed and less shrill, responded, "Good. Get ready for bed; lights out in ten minutes."

Within a couple of minutes, Dani shuffled past Susie's room, walking as fast as she could without it being deemed a run. Kat, however, sauntered past a few minutes after that, taking her own sweet time, attempting to further annoy Miss Cora. As she strode by, Kat peeked in and gave a sassy, little smirk at Susie. Kat quickly turned away, continuing her journey to her room.

Susie chuckled – Kat seemed to enjoy pushing people to their limit, and, most especially, poor Dani.

Several minutes later Juls passed by Susie's doorway on her way to bed. She made no attempt to acknowledge Susie's presence. Susie couldn't help but wonder what her problem was; she couldn't think of anything she had said or done to antagonize Juls that would account for her obvious dislike of Susie from the beginning. But then, as Susie contemplated the enigma that was Juls, Susie realized that Juls was aloof with everyone, preferring to be alone. Even in the midst of so many others that live here, Juls somehow managed to truly be alone. Susie wondered why – her brother, Jared, wasn't like that. Well, at least not to the same extent as Juls, Susie corrected her premise.

"Lights out, girls," Miss Cora said as she walked up and down the hallway, verifying that they all were in bed.

Night lights were permitted, of course, but only Megan chose to have one. Susie switched off her desk lamp and quickly slid into bed. It felt heavenly to allow her body to sink into its softness.

"Good night, girls," Miss Cora called out from the edge of the Common Area. The girls all responded with "Good night, Miss Cora". A few seconds later, Miss Cora switched off the lights as she left.

As soon as Miss Cora was gone, Susie got up and switched on her desk lamp, continuing with her studies. She finished her US history assignment and started her math assignment, finishing it just as the grandfather clock began striking the ten o'clock hour. She sighed; she still had her biology reading yet to do, not to mention finishing the essay assignments.

Susie removed her flashlight from her desk drawer, switched off her desk lamp and quickly made her way out the Dorm, across the corridor and to the waiting Simon.

He was sitting up and waiting for her, his arms wrapped around Binky. He grinned and whispered loudly, "I was afraid you forgot." He handed her his *'forever favorite'* book as she approached.

"Silly goose, I wouldn't forget," she whispered, sliding in next to him and giving him a hug. He cuddled up to her as she opened the book, and began reading from where they left off the previous night.

At first Simon was restless, constantly fidgeting and resettling himself. Susie kept reading, knowing that soon he would calm down enough to drift off to sleep. Halfway through the second chapter, he did just that. Susie tucked him in, stored the book in his nightstand and kissed him on his forehead.

Quietly she made her way back to the door, pausing briefly to be certain that no one else was awake. Slowly she opened the door and peeked into the corridor. It was empty so she slid out the door, pulling it carefully shut behind her to make certain no sound was made when it closed.

Darting across the corridor, Susie abruptly stopped halfway. There was a scent of lilac in the air. She looked around, but saw no one, and certainly nothing, that could account for the scent. With a sense of unease slowly creeping its way into her mind, Susie began again to walk toward her Dorm. Three steps taken, and she froze – now she heard the faint sound of a wind chime, soft and melodious. Its peaceful tone was barely audible, sounding as if it were miles away and being carried to her by a gentle breeze.

Susie stood in the middle of the corridor, uncertain as to what she should do. Nothing could explain the sound or the scent - and she wasn't certain just where she should look, or if she should look for the source at all.

A few seconds passed as she debated her course of action when a flash of white captured her attention. Turning just in time, Susie caught a fleeting glimpse of a woman, dressed in a long, flowing white gown, walking across the landing from the west side toward the east side. Susie couldn't see her face, but something seemed familiar about her. She ran toward the landing; when she got there, the woman was gone.

"How is that possible?" Susie asked herself, puzzled by the seemingly impossible feat. "There's nowhere to go."

Susie stood motionless, bewildered for a few moments. Slowly a smile formed upon her lips as Susie realized what the answered was. "Of course, she must have a key to the east wing," she deduced.

Excited at the prospect of entering the forbidden zone, Susie ran along the balcony walk toward the doors of the east wing. Forcefully she pulled and pushed – the doors didn't budge.

"How did she get them unlocked, get in and re-lock them before I got to the landing?" Susie wondered.

Contemplatively, Susie walked back to the landing of the south wing. She turned and looked back at the doors – they were still closed, and the woman was still sight unseen.

"Who has a key?" Susie pondered, quickly walking back to her Dorm. "Miss Pritchett would, of course, and Miss Hilda," she reasoned; "and probably Mr. Henry and perhaps even Mrs. Coppersmith. But none of them could have been her. …. So who else has a key?"

Susie opened the door and crept quietly through her Dorm and back to her room. She sat down at her desk, switched on the desk lamp and opened her biology book. Several minutes later, she realized she had been staring at the same paragraph without a clue as to what it said. Her mind was constantly wandering to the mystery woman. Susie promised herself that she would investigate this mystery woman, discover who she is and why she has a key.

"But now," she muttered; "back to biology."

—

Susie finally finished her homework and switched off the lamp. Wearily she stumbled toward her bed. She was so exhausted she could barely stand, yet it felt good that she was able to actually finish all of her homework.

Dropping onto her bed, she pulled the covers up and allowed her body to sink into its soft, billowy comfort. Susie began saying her prayers but never finished, drifting peacefully into a deep sleep. The last thing she heard was the sound of the grandfather clock chiming the three o'clock hour.

Chapter 12

CONCESSIONS

The day began as did the previous two with Susie's alarm shrilling its pronouncement that night was over and, therefore, so was the luxury of sleep. Surprisingly, she awoke refreshed and eagerly anticipating what the day would bring. Bounding out of bed, she turned off the alarm and strode into the hallway to begin her morning ritual.

First she made a brief stop to give Juls the first of what would probably be three wakeup calls. As expected, Juls ignored her. It was obvious she was awake because Susie saw her quickly pull her covers over her head upon hearing Susie's approach. Though slightly miffed at Juls and her game playing, Susie chose to let it go and moved down the hallway – her next stop was Dani and then Kat.

Neither of them were what Susie would deem a morning person; however, they awakened fairly easy. Dani was pleasantly civil, and Kat was Kat – aloof and a little surly. It was refreshing that both girls required little effort to awaken them, and they wasted no time in getting up and starting their day.

After Dani and Kat, Susie returned to Juls and to, yet again, give her a wakeup call. This time, Susie quietly approached her room. Peeking around the doorway, she watched as Juls was leafing through a magazine. Stealthily Susie took several giant steps backward, and loudly called out to Megan she would be there in just a minute. She darted into Juls' room; true to form, Juls was back under her covers, pretending to be asleep. Again she ordered Juls to get up and get moving; and, in classic Juls style, Juls ignored her.

Susie shook her head – this was ridiculous. She spun around and marched down the hallway to Megan. Megan, of course, was always awake when Susie approached her bedside – she pretended to be asleep in order to receive her morning hug. Susie would gladly give her morning hugs without the pretense; however, Megan enjoyed the attention, so Susie played along with her. After their current hug session, Megan jumped out of bed and tore down the hallway, racing to the bathroom.

"No running," Susie called out to her.

"It's an emergency!" Megan yelled back, increasing her speed.

Susie laughed; then she turned her attention to the task at hand. The one she dreaded was Juls – never had Susie seen such a sour puss. Since twins are supposed to be alike, she wondered if Miss Ginger had the same problem with Jared. Granted, they aren't identical twins; but even fraternal twins are purported to have some sort of psychic connection. Perhaps that trait would lend itself to similar behavior patterns. But then, she recalled, Jared doesn't seem to be quite as moody as Juls.

"Correction," she chuckled to herself; "no one is as moody as Juls!"

Susie began walking toward Jul's room, dreading this morning's session with each step. Although Monday was no picnic in getting Juls vertical, yesterday was even worse. Juls had required three (count them, three) wake ups calls. Even after the third time, Susie wasn't certain that Juls was going to get out of bed. However, at six-thirty, she came dragging through the Common Area on her way to the bathroom.

Completely unconcerned that Miss Cora would be there promptly at six-forty, Juls then slowly shuffled back to her room to get dressed. Every day Miss Cora would arrive and give Juls a minute or two before seeking her out to hurry her along. Juls would whine and complain, seething at the audacity of anyone who expected her to be ready at such an early hour.

Every morning it was the same whine - when her parents were alive, she attended a prestigious private school; classes started at nine, and she never had to get up before eight. Each time this elicited from Miss Cora the simple response of, "That was then; this is now." And every morning, Juls would be infuriated, once again, that her wish was not being granted.

Each morning during the entire trek to breakfast, Juls would fume, making snarky comments about Glen Hollow, denigrating it in comparison to her old school. Miss Cora ignored Juls, and actually seemed to be amused by, what was now, The Juls Morning Ritual. How Miss Cora managed not to shake the living daylights out of Juls, Susie didn't understand. Her own patience with the resident prima donna was fast nearing an end; and this was only day three.

One thing Susie had noticed, however, was that Juls never slighted any of the people, not the children nor the adults. She figured that either Juls had done so once and was severely reprimanded for it, or that Juls was smart enough to know that that would be crossing the line of acceptability and tolerance.

Today was no exception in The Juls Morning Ritual. She had totally ignored Susie's first two attempts to get her up and mobile. This time Susie grabbed her covers and gave them a hard pull, slinging them completely off the end of the bed.

"It's now six-thirty, Juls," Susie impatiently scolded her. "Get up!"

Juls bolted upright, glaring daggers at Susie. "Look what you've done!" she screamed at Susie. "Since you destroyed my bed, you will make it," she demanded.

Laughing, Susie looked at her in utter disbelief. "I don't think so. You chose to stay in bed, so it's your problem."

Susie turned to leave. When she reached the doorway, a pillow came crashing into the back of her head. Susie whirled around, anger rising within, and saw the smug look on Juls' face. She decided not to give Juls the satisfaction.

"Looks like you have one more thing to pick up before Miss Cora gets here," she calmly stated, then turned and strolled into the hallway.

As she walked back to her room to get ready, Susie heard an extremely angry Juls scream, "O-o-o-oh, I hate you!"

Susie smiled.

———

Class time, like breakfast, flew by, and it was already time for lunch. Simon and Timmy were bonding well; they were now best friends, or 'best buds' as they called it. Unfortunately, they had decided 'no girls allowed', leaving poor, little Megan out in the cold, so to speak. Susie decided that this afternoon she'd have a little chat with Simon about Megan before she read to him.

Lunch was over all too soon, and Simon, Timmy and Megan were escorted away for naptime. Susie was amused at how slow they could move when it suited them. After they were finally out the door, Miss Emma resumed class, and Susie was so glad that she had finished her homework. Every question Miss Emma had asked of her, she was able to answer thoroughly.

The day came to an end with Miss Emma reminding them that their essay assignments are due on Friday. She had assigned the essays at the beginning of the semester, three in total. For literature they were to read a book from the Reading List and write an essay; the ancient civilization essay assignment was to choose and write about one of the civilizations they had studied; the third essay was to be written on a pivotal person or event in early US history. Each of Susie's essay assignments had a minimum requirement of five hundred words. Juls, Jared and Aaron had four hundred; Kat and Jose had three hundred and Dani's were assigned at two hundred words each.

Miss Emma had offered to change the essay requirements for Susie to subject matters discussed just since Susie had arrived; however, Susie declined the offer. Susie felt confident that she could perform at the same level as the others, regardless of having previously attended school elsewhere. Miss Emma had smiled approvingly when Susie declined the offer, agreeing with Susie's assessment of her own abilities.

However, with so little time left in which to finish, Susie wondered now if that had been a hasty decision on her part. Simon required far more of her time and energy than she had anticipated. She sighed as she walked out the door, muttering to herself.

She had chosen for her literature essay the book, 'The Scarlet Letter'. Her literature essay was finished, and for all intents and purposes so was her ancient civilization essay. Since she had previously read "The Scarlet Letter" twice, Susie felt comfortable writing the essay without the benefit of reading the book again this week. She chose ancient Greece, specifically the time of Plato, for her ancient civilization essay. It was complete except for the need to proofread it, and perhaps add a finishing touch or two. Susie hadn't decided yet what the subject would be for her US History essay; and the pressure of time constraints was causing her anxiety level to rapidly increase.

Susie hastened to the Library where Simon was waiting for her just outside the doors. As was his usual habit, he beamed when he spotted her, ran to her and hugged her. Susie returned his hug, lifting him up and swinging him around, holding him tightly against her so that he wouldn't fall. He giggled and squealed, loving the attention and the airplane ride. Finally she stopped spinning him around and set him down, holding onto him until his equilibrium returned.

"Have you had a good afternoon?" she asked.

He nodded, "Yeah; Timmy and me got to play a little." He frowned, furrowing his brow, and continued; "But then Megan kept bothering us. So we ran and hid." He giggled. "She couldn't find us. We hid real good and watched her. It was so funny. Timmy almost giggled too loud, but she didn't hear him. Then Miss Hilda came, and she went with Miss Hilda."

Holding the door open for him, Susie followed him into the Library. "I'm glad you told me, Simon, because I want to talk to you about Megan."

Turning around to face her, Simon began walking backward, grinning at her. "Are you going to tell her to stop bothering Timmy and me?" he asked, his expression hopeful.

"Not exactly," she answered, smiling at him. "Turn around before you fall and get hurt," she instructed.

Tilting his head slightly to one side, he slyly grinned at her. "Okay," he chirped; he turned and ran the rest of the way to his chair.

When she arrived at the reading area several minutes later, Simon was sitting in his chair, wildly swinging his legs up and down

"Slow poke," he teased her as she approached.

"No, I'm not a slow poke. You know you're not supposed to run. You keep doing it, Simon, and one of the adults will catch you; and you'll get punished. Is that what you want?"

Simon hung his head. "No," he answered sullenly.

"Simon, please look at me," Susie said gently.

Slowly he raised his head, his eyes narrowing, suggesting the beginning stages of a pout.

"I want you to listen to me, okay? It's important," she told him. The serious tone in her voice reaped the result she wanted – she had his full attention.

"I'm very glad that you and Timmy have become buddies –", she began.

"Best buds," he corrected her.

She laughed softly. "Okay, best buds then. I'm glad, but I want you to think about what it's like not having any friends or buds. Do you remember how that feels?" she asked.

His look was a suspicious one. "Yes," he answered warily.

"Good; now think about Megan. Only you and Timmy are about her age; she has no one else as playmates, or friends or buds. Don't you think it would be the right thing to do to at least include her sometimes when you and Timmy are playing?" she asked, hoping she was persuasive.

Simon's brow furled deeply. "She's a girl," he objected. "She just wants to do girl things."

"I'm a girl, Simon; haven't I played board games, card games, tickle monster, tag, red light – green light, hide-n-seek and a lot of other games with you?" she reminded him.

Simon's mind began whirling around this reference – he didn't think of Susie as a *girl*. After all, she's his big sister. He just thought those were the kind of games that big sisters play.

"Don't girls play with dolls and have tea parties?" he asked, a slight hint of repugnance seeping into his voice.

"Some do, and I'm certain Megan does. But, Simon, Megan also likes other games. Give her a chance. I think you and Timmy will like her."

Simon nodded and grudgingly said, "Okay; but if we don't like her, we don't have to play with her anymore, right?" he bargained.

Susie laughed as she hugged him. "If you give her an honest chance, Simon; but only if you give her an honest chance."

She held him back so that their eyes met. "That means, you and Timmy need to include her at least five different days before you can decide that you don't like her."

He grinned. "No problem," he assured her. He snickered slightly; he had a plan.

"And," she added firmly; "you must both be nice to her."

"What?!" he exclaimed, sitting up straight at the shock of such a condition.

"I'm serious, Simon." Susie's determined expression reinforced her words. "If either of you are mean to her to keep her from wanting to play with you, then it won't count as one of the five days. If you keep being mean to her, then I think our bedtime stories will have to stop until you decide to be nice."

Surprised and in a quandary at such a dilemma, Simon couldn't believe his ears. 'How did Susie know my plan?' he wondered.

His eyes narrowed as he stared intently into her eyes, studying her expression. 'Did she read my mind? Can big sisters *do* that?'

His thoughts churned like a whirlwind, terrified at the very idea that she could know all his thoughts. 'Does she know me and Timmy are going to climb the big oak tree out front the very first nice day? And does she know me and Timmy sneaked into the kitchen after naptime and took cookies and hid them in our secret place?'

Simon quickly inhaled and held it for a moment, his eyes popping wide open. 'Does she know where our secret place is?' he wondered, panicked at the idea that their secret place was no longer a secret.

Simon swallowed hard and smiled feebly at Susie. He nodded and shrugged his shoulders, surrendering to her condition. With a heavy sigh he sadly agreed, "We'll be nice, I promise."

"Thank you, Simon. Now, let's go find a couple of books," she said as she stood to her feet.

Simon hopped down from his chair, shuffling his way to the bookcases. From his hunched shoulders, hands thrust into his pockets and eyes glued to the floor, Susie knew he was unhappy with the bargain he made.

'He did give in fairly easy,' Susie thought. 'I wonder why?'

Quickly she decided it didn't matter – the important thing was that he did agree to be nice to Megan. She knew he would because he had promised. In a matter of minutes, Simon's demeanor had returned to his normal vivacious state, Susie noticed, and she smiled.

Simon had begun looking through the various books in the middle bookcase, not seeing anything that caught his fancy. He wandered around to the other side and began walking along it, just glancing at the various size books and their colors. Soon he had disappeared altogether, Susie completely unaware of his vanishing act. She finally had selected two books; one was a secondary favorite of his ('Maury Mouse and Carrie Cat in Down on the Farm'); and the other was one neither of them had seen,

'Tidwell Turtle, Space Adventurer'. It was a thin, large book, and had plenty of brightly colored illustrations.

"Simon," she said as she stood; "look at this." And that's when she realized Simon was nowhere to be seen.

"Simon! Where are you?" she shouted.

Soon she heard squeals of laughter and followed the sound, dropping the books onto the coffee table as she ran passed. On the far side of the west wall, she found him on one of the library ladders; he had climbed nearly to the top.

"Simon, come down," Susie firmly ordered.

Ignoring her instructions, he responded, "Look, Susie; it has a brake. Watch this!"

He pressed the lever with his left hand, and gave a little pull along the rail with his right hand. Slowly the ladder began to move. Then he released the lever, and the ladder stopped. He turned, grinning from ear to ear, his eyes flashing with excitement and delight.

"Isn't that neat? It has a brake every third step."

"It's great, Simon. Now come down," she instructed.

Simon started giggling, his countenance alight with mischievous intent. He pressed the lever again and tugged hard on the railing, putting the ladder into motion.

"Simon, stop!" Susie ordered; he, of course, totally ignored her.

Simon continued pulling the ladder along, forcing it to move faster and faster. As he neared the fireplace, he slowed it down, bringing it to a complete stop. He then repeated the process for the return trip, Susie all the while ordering him to "stop and get down". As his speed increased, so did his laugher. His face, lit with joy, was as bright as a full moon in the midnight sky. His peals of laughter were becoming more and more ecstatic.

As he flew past the place where she was standing (where he had begun his ride), she shouted, "That's it, Simon! If you don't stop and come down right now, we won't have Story Time today or tomorrow!"

That did it; his little head whirled around to face her, dismay most apparent in his expression.

"I mean it, Simon!" she reiterated sharply.

He glared at her. "All right!" he yelled; slowing his ride to a stop. "Can I at least ride it back to you?" he asked, hoping she'd say yes even though he knew she wouldn't.

"No!" Susie responded flatly, extremely irritated with him.

Simon's face scrunched into a scowl as he descended, stomping hard each rung of the ladder. By the time he had reached the bottom, Susie was waiting there for him. Bristling with anger, he glared up at her.

"Party Pooper!" he hurled at her, storming away to his favorite chair.

Susie's frustration level was peaking; she wanted to snatch him up and shake the living daylights out of him. Fortunately, she was able to defuse her anger by the time she reached him – she very slowly counted to fifty, taking slow, deliberate steps. When Susie approached, Simon sharply turned his head, facing away from her.

She sat on the edge of the coffee table in front of the chair in order to be eye level with him. He still stared at the fireplace.

"Simon," she said, concern for him revealed in her tone; "you could have been hurt."

Slowly he turned his head. He stared at her, eyes narrowed in obstinacy. "Na-uh, I know how to do it," he snapped at her.

"I'm sure you think you do; but accidents happen, and I don't want you to get hurt," she said with a tone of finality.

Susie twisted around and retrieved the books from behind her where she had dropped them on the coffee table. Turning quickly, she handed them to Simon, smiling as cheerfully as she could muster.

Simon was unmoved. Refusing to accept the books, he crossed his arms and just glared at her.

"Come on, Simon," she pleaded. "Don't be mad."

He continued his glare.

Look," she said, holding up one of books for him to see. "It's one of your *favorites*," she told him, emphasizing the word 'favorites' in a sing-song fashion.

Coyly he titled his head, looking at the book she was offering. "Really?" he asked skeptically.

Susie nodded.

Simon knew full well that she was tired of the Maury Mouse and Carrie Cat series. It pleased him immensely that she caved in to his much loved favorites. "Okay," he said with a giggle; "which one?"

"It's 'Maury Mouse and Carrie Cat in Down on the Farm'," she replied; "and I have a new one (she held it up for him to see) called 'Tidwell Turtle: Space Adventurer'."

He looked at the two books, pursing his lips in and out like a guppy as he tried to decide which one he wanted to have her read. "That one," he said, pointing to the new book.

"Not Maury Mouse and Carrie Cat?" she asked in surprise.

He grinned. "It's a fatter book, so it takes longer to read," he explained; "I'll save that one for bedtime *after* we finish the Circus one."

Susie laughed. "I should have known. Scoot over," she instructed, and he happily complied. Simon snuggled against her, peering intensely at the colorful illustrations displayed as she held the book open for him to view.

In what seemed no time at all, the mantel clock began chiming five o'clock. Susie increased her pace, causing Simon to object several times to the speed in which she was reading. When she pointed to the clock, telling him that they wouldn't finish the story before five-thirty if she didn't hurry, he nodded his assent and she continued. All too soon the mantle clock chimed the half hour; Susie finished the sentence she had started, and then closed the book.

"Wait," Simon protested, pawing at the book in an attempt to re-open it.

"We have to go, Simon," Susie replied, trying to keep it out of his hands.

Rapidly shaking his head, he countered, "But there's only one page left. We have time. Please?" he begged.

Susie opened the book, adding her own stipulation, "I'll finish the book, but you have to promise no monkey business. We can't be late for dinner."

Giving her his most serious look, he vowed, "I promise."

Susie read the last page, then closed the book as Simon jumped out of the chair, snatching his Maury Mouse and Carrie Cat book. Susie returned

Tidwell Turtle to its place on the shelf as Simon danced around the book-cases, constantly urging her to hurry so they wouldn't be late.

Upon joining him, she noticed the book in his hand. "Simon, I thought you were going to put it away," she stated crossly.

Simon rapidly shook his head. "Na–uh; I want you to read this one after the Circus book," he staunchly reminded her.

"Give it here," she demanded, extending her hand.

Simon promptly moved away from her, holding the book behind him. With a frown and furrowed brow, he squinted his eyes as he jutted his jaw slightly forward. "No," he answered firmly.

"You can't take it to dinner, Simon," she said tersely. She paused and calmly added, "You know you can't. Remember how we came and got the circus one after dinner? Well, we'll come get this one after dinner tonight."

He showed no inclination to comply so Susie added, "I promise."

Simon grinned, handed her his treasured favorite and began his little jig. Susie quickly ran to the bookcase, placing the book on the shelf "Let's go, Simon," she said, as she returned to him. Simon grinned mischievously and ran down the aisle at break-neck speed.

"Simon, wait!" Susie yelled.

"You keep up!" he yelled back, laughing and increasing his speed.

Shaking her head, Susie closed her eyes and clenched her teeth. "Oh, that Simon," she fumed, then quickly ran after him. Slowing her speed as she entered the reception area, she found that he was waiting for her at the Library entrance, grinning like the Cheshire cat.

"Slow-poke," he giggled, pointing at her.

"You are not supposed to run," she sternly chided him.

"Neither are you," he retorted haughtily.

Abruptly he turned and began shoving the Library door as hard as he could, managing to get the heavy door open just a smidge. "Coming?" he asked without looking back at her.

Although part of her wanted to throttle him, she couldn't help but be amused. 'He sure is an odd little duck', she thought.

Leaning forward, she pressed hard against the door, pushing it open further. Simon slipped through, and she followed him into the corridor and on to the Dining Hall.

Dinner was delicious – Simon loves fried chicken, especially the drumsticks, as did his best bud, Timmy. They had an undeclared eating contest, Susie surmised, as to who could eat the most drumsticks in light of the fact that they were devouring them nearly whole, taking the most modicum of time to chew their food before swallowing. In their current rush to consume, Susie likened their appearance to be more like the dinosaurs they love than the little boys they are. After they each had eaten four drumsticks and begged for another, Miss Ginger informed the boys that they had had enough chicken and needed to concentrate on their veggies. That elicited a frown and a chorus of groans from both of them. Miss Hilda and Miss Pritchett quickly reinforced Miss Ginger's decision.

Exchanging snide glances, the boys began a round of snorting and snickering. Miss Pritchett cleared her throat before snapping her fingers once, immediately capturing their attention. They sat as still as church mice, wide-eyed, and were focused intently on her. Their faces were frozen in that "Uh-oh" look, clearly displaying their realization of their bad behavior.

Quite calmly Miss Pritchett asked if they thought this behavior was acceptable. They quickly shot a glance at each other before they each responded with a very demure 'no'. Her expression was nearly akin to that of the proverbial cat that caught the canary. She held up the hand bell, informing them that the next time they misbehaved at the table, she would ring the bell.

"When I do that," she continued gravely; "Miss Ginger will escort you both to bed where you will remain until the next meal time." Their eyes bugged out, dismayed at such a restriction placed upon their food and especially their playtime.

She gave them both a steely gaze, first focused on Timmy and then piercingly at Simon. In a tone that left no room for doubt as to her resolve, she asked the contrite duo, "Do you understand?"

Both boys, their faces frozen in trepidation and their eyes locked onto Miss Pritchett, swallowed hard before giving a meek verbal acknowledgement.

"Excellent, "she responded amicably. "Now that we have come to an understanding, we can continue with our pleasant meal that Mrs. Coppersmith has so wonderfully prepared."

Conversations began again; soon the boys were their usual selves, just a little less rowdy. Several long segments of talk were devoted to Miss Taryn's upcoming bridal shower and wedding. Apparently, the only remaining issue was the bridal gown – she wanted a new, store-bought gown, whereas her mother wanted her to wear the gown that had been passed down for several generations.

"Family tradition," Miss Claire stoically insisted; "is most important and should be honored."

Though many agreed with her, Susie thought it was interesting that Miss Elsa and, apparently, Miss Cora did not. Miss Elsa stated that it was Taryn's day; and that she should have what will make her day complete, even if that means foregoing an old tradition in favor of starting a new one. Miss Cora nodded her head in agreement, interjecting a simple 'absolutely'. A very pleased Miss Taryn promptly thanked both of them.

Miss Claire, sighing dramatically, held her hands up, palms to the ceiling as she looked upward, as if pleading to Heaven itself. Then she clasped her hands together, pressing them against her heart.

"Bon; if that is what my little girl wants, then so be it. All I ask, as your Mama, is for you to first see the gown before making a final decision."

Smiling adoringly at her daughter, Miss Claire added, "Your grandmother, and Mimi and Nini will be here next week. They are bringing the gown and veil with them. If you do not approve, then it will go back to New Orleans with them."

Affectionately, Miss Claire gently guided her daughter's hair away from her face. "Then we will shop until we find your perfect gown."

Miss Taryn's eyes welled with tears, and she hugged her mother. "Merci, Mama. I will look at it to please you; but I know what I want. We'll have fun shopping together like we used to do." Smiling happily, she released her mother. Miss Claire half-heartedly returned her smile.

Conversation shifted once again, this time concerning the impending winter weather. Discussions regarding preparations occupied most of the remaining time. When dinner was finally over, everyone dispersed, going their separate ways. It didn't escape Susie's notice that Kat and Dani had been exceptionally quiet all during dinner, and that they were the first ones to disappear. She chuckled to herself, wishing she could have been a fly on the wall during their kitchen duty earlier. She wondered how Mrs. Coppersmith had fared with those two hellcats.

A squeal from the door caused Susie to quickly look that direction. Miss Cora had captured Megan at the door. She had attempted to sneak out between the various adults, desperately hoping they would provide cover from the watchful eyes of Miss Cora. Such was not her fate, and Miss Cora whisked her away for bath time. Fortunately for the boys, Miss Ginger had been momentarily detained by Miss Pritchett. Timmy had disappeared all too quickly when he saw Miss Ginger was preoccupied - his whereabouts unknown. Having his new best bud vanish without him left Simon dismayed and forlorn.

"Come on, Simon," Susie attempted to cheer him. "Let's go to the Library or the Rec Room. You choose," she said, smiling.

He shrugged his shoulders, feeling disconsolate. "I don't care," he responded, staring down at his shoes.

'He needs something different', Susie thought; 'something that will spark his interest.' An idea struck. "What if we go exploring?" she offered.

His little face bobbed up, filled with anticipation. "Really?" he asked. "Can we go to the plant room and see the waterfall?" he asked excitedly.

Amused, she answered, "It's called the garden conservatory; and yes, we can."

"Oh, boy!" he shouted, jumping up and down and clapping.

"Shh-h-h," Susie shushed him. She noticed that he had captured the attention of Miss Ginger and Miss Pritchett. "Hurry, let's go," she urged him, pushing him out the door.

"Can I feed the fish?" he asked, trotting along beside her.

"Only a little; remember what Miss Pritchett said on Sunday."

He nodded rapidly, assuring her that he remembered.

"Hurry, we don't have much time," she said, grasping his hand, forcing him into a race walk.

Upon entering the south wing, Susie again thought she saw someone moving in the shadows that encompassed the area around the east wing door. She stopped walking, continuing to stare at the area, trying to determine if someone was truly there, or if it was just an illusion, a trick of light and shadow.

Simon tugged at her hand, pulling hard enough to jolt her. "Come on, Susie," he fussed; "I want to feed the fish."

Susie was certain this time she caught a fleeting glimpse of a shape as it moved in the shadows. "Who's there!" she called out to the undistinguishable shape.

Simon stopped tugging on her and followed her stare, focusing on the area near the doorway.

Again there was movement; someone had moved into the doorway and was now pressed against the east wing door. "Who is it?" she demanded, her temper starting to flare.

"No one's there, Susie," Simon told her. "Let's go feed the fish."

An uneasy feeling settled over her; someone was there – she knew it.

Simon tugged on her shirt three times to get her attention. "Want me to go look?" he offered.

Surprised by his brave offer, Susie glanced away from the shadows and into his cherubic face. She could see the concern in his eyes. 'How cute', she thought; 'he wants to protect me'.

"No, Simon;" she said aloud; "I guess I just have a case of the jitters. You know," she shrugged; "this being a new place for us; and it's so big."

Simon slowly nodded, and his expression became anxious. "Sometimes I think I hear people talking, but no one's there."

Susie scrutinized his face, hoping he was joking. He wasn't. To dispel the gloom and fear, Susie forced herself to laugh a carefree giggle. "Listen to us; we sound like a couple of willy-nillys."

Grinning with as lighthearted an attitude that she could summon, she clasped his hand firmly in hers. "Come on, Simon; we have fish to feed." Hand in hand they ran the rest of the way.

Initially Simon demanded giving the fish a scoop of food as Miss Pritchett had shown him. Susie quickly reminded him that they weren't supposed to feed the fish without prior approval. When she repeated Miss Pritchett's warning about feeding the fish too much, Simon readily agreed to a tiny amount, telling her he never wanted to ever hurt them. Susie had smiled and placed the tiniest amount of food into his open hand. Simon grinned and sprinkled the food on top of the water, giggling joyously as the fish gobbled each and every morsel.

After feeding the fish, Susie allowed Simon to sit on the rock wall that formed the pond so he could splash his hands in the water. He made several attempts to catch a goldfish. He didn't have any luck. They eluded his every try, yet he remained undeterred. Then he got the bright idea to put the fish food in his hand and hold it underwater, hoping the fish would eat out of his hand. Susie tried to tell him it wouldn't work – that the fish food would float away as soon as he opened his hand. He insisted, so Susie placed a small amount of fish food in his hand. Her reward was the joyous exuberance shining from his little face.

Several attempts later, the fish now came closer to his hand, gobbling the food as it floated in the water. He giggled with delight every time a fish came close enough that he might actually catch it, but they always darted away at the last second. After ten minutes of effort, one brave goldfish actually nibbled on his hand.

It looked up at Simon – directly at him for several seconds – with its little mouth moving as if talking to Simon. Then it returned to its nibbling fest. He kept his hand very still, and several more joined the first fish in the greeting ritual. Simon looked up at Susie, a heavenly joy illuminated his face.

"They like me, Susie," he whispered, his tone filled with awe.

Susie, amazed at the spectacle, smiled and nodded. "Yes, they do, Simon. They know you're their friend, and you won't hurt them," she acknowledged softly.

He nodded and returned to watching his new-found friends as more and more of the goldfish began arriving.

After allowing Simon several more minutes, Susie told him it was time to go. Simon, crestfallen, wanted to stay, but she convinced him that he could come back tomorrow and visit the fish. That sufficed; he got up, waved good-by to the fish, telling them he'd be back tomorrow. To her utter amazement, the fish all watched him as he waved and spoke.

Not until he had marched past her did they resume their normal swimming patterns. Susie watched Simon strutting down the path, and a new appreciation began developing in her for him. Her reverie broke quickly, however, when he darted down a side path, causing her to spring into motion to retrieve him.

Herding Simon to the door was no easy task. He continuously kept trying to dart down the various pathways, and Susie had to forcefully pull him back each and every time. They finally reached the sitting area near the door just as the clock began chiming, announcing it was now seven-thirty.

"Sorry, Simon; Miss Ginger will be looking for you. It's bath time," Susie reminded him, half dragging him out the door and down the corridor toward the spiral stairwell.

Wrinkling his nose and furrowing his brow, he grimaced. "Why do I have to go to bed at eight? It's not fair," he whined.

Silently, Susie had to agree – Nana always allowed him to be up until ten. Simon, like her own self, had high energy, and Nana had always said if the body isn't ready to sleep, sleep won't happen. To Simon, Susie just answered, "I know, Simon, and I'm sorry. The rules are different here; that's all I know. We just have to make the best of it, okay?"

He narrowed his eyes, giving her a look as surly as his tone. "I don't want to!"

"Simon, if you don't be good, then we can't have bedtime stories," she whispered. "They'll watch us more closely if you misbehave. You know I'm right."

"But it's not fair," he adamantly repeated, breaking free of her grasp and demonstratively putting his fists on his hips, a stance that made him appear very much like a little Peter Pan.

With her patience having worn a bit thin, Susie frowned at him. "Then fine," she snapped; "I guess bedtime stories are over since you want to be bad."

Panicked, Simon quickly surrendered. "I'll be good. I promise."

Susie feigned to be unconvinced at first. Simon repeated his promise to be good, only this time he was far more sincere. She smiled and hugged him. "That's better. Now, let's go find Miss Ginger, and you be nice."

"Okay," he agreed halfheartedly.

They climbed the spiral stairwell, Simon leading the way with Susie close behind him, making certain he didn't fall. When they reached the landing, Miss Ginger, with Timmy in tow, was just entering the corridor from the main staircase landing. Obviously she had found one of the rascals, and had diligently been searching for Simon.

"There you are," she called out to him. "I've been looking for you." Her voice carried the tone of one who was just a little perturbed and slightly aggravated.

Simon gave a dramatic shrug and responded cheerfully (a little too cheerfully, Susie thought), "Here I am."

"Where have you been?" she asked him, glancing briefly at Susie.

"Susie helped me feed the fish," he announced proudly.

Miss Ginger's expression softened a little. Grinning, she said, "Fun, isn't it?"

Simon beamed and nodded vigorously.

Timmy, feeling left out, piped up. "Hey, I want to feed them, too."

"Not now, Timmy; it's bath time," she reminded him. Seeing his downcast expression, she added, "Tomorrow, after naptime, I'll bring you both to feed the fish."

Timmy and Simon began their whooping shouts, dancing around her and performing their little victory jigs. Firmly grasping each one by their shoulder, she sharply told them to use their inside voices. Then she sternly reminded them that if they misbehave between now and time to feed the fish, they would not be allowed to feed the fish. That calmed both boys immediately.

Susie giggled inwardly; and, not wanting to add fuel to the fire, covered her mouth with her hands so the boys couldn't see her smile.

"Simon, give Susie a goodnight hug," Miss Ginger told him, catching Simon off-guard.

"What?" he asked. "It's not time. We get to play in the Rec Room before bedtime," he hastily reminded her.

"Yeah," Timmy echoed Simon's sentiments.

She smiled and slightly chuckled. "Not tonight, boys," she responded, to which they stared at her in disbelief. "It's now seven-forty. I've spent the better part of thirty minutes looking for you two, minutes which you could have had in the Rec Room after your bath if you hadn't been hiding."

Pausing slightly to allow the consequence of their actions to sink into their minds, she then added, "Tonight, you barely have time to have your bath before bedtime. So, as I said, give Susie her goodnight hug now, Simon."

Remorsefully, Simon slowly walked to Susie as she knelt down, arms opened wide. As they embraced, she whispered in his ear, "I'll be there shortly after ten, so be quiet and don't let anyone know you're still awake."

Simon hugged her tighter and whispered, "Okay."

They parted; Simon promptly marched to Miss Ginger, took her hand, looked up at her and grinned. "Let's go Miss Ginger; I'm ready for my bath now."

Warily Miss Ginger glanced at him, wondering what sparked such a change in his demeanor. She looked at Susie, quizzically raising her eyebrow.

Susie responded with a smile, calling out to Simon, "Good night, Simon."

He turned and waved, grinning from ear to ear. "'Night, Susie," he replied cheerfully.

Though her expression remained curiously suspicious, Miss Ginger didn't pursue the reason for the change in his attitude. She turned, and guided the boys down the corridor to their Dorm.

Susie watched the boys giggling and whispering to each other, conspiring only heaven knows what, as they disappeared into the Boys Dorm. She turned and began a fast stride to the main staircase. Since no one was about, she hastened down the staircase, taking the steps two at a time. She had to retrieve Simon's book from the Library (she promised, after all), and get her homework done.

After entering the Library, Susie sprinted across the Reception area and down the aisle to where she had left his book. It was still there, and she silently whispered a prayer of thanks. Simon would have been impossible to handle had it been gone. It didn't matter that she could recite the entire book from memory, not to mention so could he. And even though Simon had all the illustrations committed to memory, it also was irrelevant as far as he was concerned. He still wanted the book - he wanted it read, so he could read along with her and see the pictures. Susie removed it from its place, and began browsing among the others. She selected two small books, enough to finish out the week for their bedtime Story Time.

With the books tucked tightly in the crook of her arm, she hurried back down the aisle toward the entrance. Just as she reached the reception area, she heard a woman's voice. Susie stopped and listened. .... Silence. ....

She waited, wondering if perhaps she had been mistaken. Just as she decided to go ahead and check out the books and leave, she heard the voice again. It seemed to be coming from somewhere ahead, nearer the east side of the Library. Susie took three steps and paused. An uneasy feeling settled upon her. Inhaling slowly to steady her nerves, she exhaled softly and began moving cautiously down the aisle.

The deep carpet muffled her footsteps, and Susie heard no other sounds. When she reached the halfway point, she stopped. "No one is here. This is stupid," she silently chided herself.

Still, Susie wanted to know if she imagined the voice, or if someone was here and had moved deeper into the recesses of the Library. Deciding to continue, she sprinted down the aisle, glancing quickly between each of the stacks lining both sides of the main aisle as she hurried past.

Susie darted past the study area and continued on toward the east section of the Library. As she entered it, she came to a dead stop. It was Miss Fiona's voice – and she didn't appear to be alone. Quickly Susie took several steps back, returning well into the main aisle, just shy of the lighted area. Using the last stack to conceal herself and hoping that she had not been seen, Susie waited motionless for several minutes. No one approached, nor called out to her – she was relieved; she hadn't been seen.

Slowly, cautiously, Susie moved halfway down the side aisle between the stacks. Miss Fiona and the other lady were standing near the north wall of the east end, some forty or fifty feet away. Peering through the books, Susie could see the back of Miss Fiona but nothing of the other person. Though their voices were audible, no words were detectable from this distance; however, it was obvious to Susie that they knew each other well. They were laughing and talking as if they were long-time friends. Susie listened to the sound of the other voice, concentrating on its tone and timbre. She didn't recognize it. It didn't belong to anyone at Glen Hollow.

'Apparently Miss Fiona has a visitor,' Susie thought; 'she must be spending the night. It's getting a little late to drive anywhere now.'

Susie smiled wistfully – she recalled how she and her best friend, Molly, used to talk and giggle the night away during their sleepovers. They had a lot of fun planning what they would do after school, weekends and holidays. And the summers – oh, they always had great fun.

Earlier this fall, before Nana died, they had decided that they would be business partners when they were grown. They would go to New York, and take the fashion world by storm. She had the design talent, and Molly had the sewing talent. Over the summer, they had made several outfits, and they wore them when school started. The outfits were a big hit! All of their friends wanted them to design and sew an outfit for them. They even had girls they didn't know approaching them for outfits, especially party dresses. That sparked the idea of a fashion business they would run together. Together they would be unstoppable.

Tears misted Susie's eyes, spilling down her cheeks as the painful realization came crashing in on her that that future would never happen. Her tears coursed down faster and faster as her mind whirled, reminding her anew of the loss of Nana, of her home, of her parents and now of Molly. She turned away, ran back to the main aisle and sprinted back to the reception area.

Stopping briefly at the desk, Susie quickly signed out the books amid the droplets of tears splashing onto the form. After scooping up the books, she quickly changed her mind and laid them back down on the desk, wiping away her tears as she leaned against the front of the desk. She couldn't let anyone see her like this, she thought. Susie began to control her breathing, in slowly and out slowly, attempting to calm herself and stop the flood of tears.

A few minutes later, she accomplished her goal – the tears had stopped, and she felt calmer. She gathered up the books once more. As she began to leave, her eyes drifted toward the main aisle that led to the east section. She smiled wistfully, silently wishing Miss Fiona and her friend all the happiness in the world.

Closing her eyes momentarily, Susie gave a brief sigh before she opened them. She left the Library with a renewed determination to make the best of whatever time she would be here at Glen Hollow.

Susie put the finishing touches on her ancient civilization essay just as Megan came bounding into her room. (Miss Cora was seconds behind her.)

"Good night, Susie," she chortled, throwing herself into Susie's arms. She gave Susie a very strong hug for one who appeared to be as fragile as a porcelain doll.

Susie returned her hug, giving her a kiss on her cheek. "Good night, Munchkin," she softly whispered.

"Munchkin?" Megan asked, her puzzled expression matching that of her voice. "What's that?"

"A Munchkin is an adorable, cute, little person," Susie explained; "and you are adorable, and cute, and –"

"And little," Megan interjected gleefully, clapping her hands. Her eyes twinkled, and her face beamed, delighted with the attention.

"That's right," Susie agreed, tapping the tip of Megan's nose with her index finger.

Megan turned and skipped to Miss Cora. "I'm a Munchkin," she proudly informed her as she skipped out into the hallway and all the way to her room. Miss Cora grinned at Susie before following Megan.

Fervently, Susie returned to work, completing her current homework. She was thankful that Miss Emma had only given them one page of questions in each of their language courses.

Too soon for her liking, Dani and Kat came strolling past her doorway. Although they arrived several minutes apart, both were quiet and sullen. Neither spoke to her as they hustled past and on to their beds. Even though she tried to hold it in, an amused chuckle escaped from her as the thought danced through her mind that apparently kitchen duty had had the desired effect.

Miss Cora popped her head into Susie's doorway and smiled. "Lights out, Susie, in five minutes," she announced.

"Okay, Miss Cora," she responded, switching off her desk lamp.

Miss Cora returned to the Common Area and, five minutes later, she switched off the overhead lights and left the Dorm.

Treading softly, Susie returned to her desk, and turned her lamp on again as she sank into her chair. Opening her US History textbook and scanning the chapters, she spent the next fifty minutes trying to decide who or what should be the focus of her essay. Betsy Ross and the women of the American Revolution would be her focus, she finally decided, closing her book. Tomorrow, she would have Simon choose his own books while she checked the Library inventory for anything on her topic.

Turning off the lamp, she rose from her chair as she picked up Simon's books from the Library. Quietly she opened her desk drawer and removed her flashlight. She walked softly to her doorway. All was quiet; she breathed a sigh of relief, cautiously making her way down the hallway, through the Common Area and out the Dorm.

The corridor was quiet as well, so she ran to the Boys Dorm and peeked into their Common Area. No one was up, and all was quiet. She slipped in, quietly pulled the door closed and crept silently to Simon's room.

He was playing with his dinosaurs, quiet as can be, and with no lights other than his nightlight. Susie was impressed. She whispered to him how proud she was that he could be so quiet. He flashed a big, happy grin at her as he scooted over so she could crawl in next to him. She removed the book from his nightstand, placing the new books inside the drawer and settled in beside him.

Opening his forever favorite, 'Maury Mouse and Carrie Cat: The Circus Comes to Town', Susie held it so Simon could see the illustrations and began reading. He snuggled up close and every so often would ask her to repeat what she had just read. Each time she smiled – that meant he was getting sleepy, and nodding off for a second or two.

Fifteen minutes later, Simon was fast asleep. She closed the book, placing it in the drawer of his nightstand. Carefully she slid out of bed so as not to awaken him; gently she maneuvered him down into the bed, pulling the covers snuggly around him. Picking up his favorite dinosaur, Binky, from the floor where it had fallen, she tucked him under Simon's arm. Lastly, she gave Simon a kiss on his forehead before leaving.

The corridor was empty, and no sound of anyone approaching could be heard. Fast and quiet, Susie closed the door behind her and began crossing the corridor to her Dorm. Halfway there, she again caught the faintest essence of lilac. She paused, slowly turned around, expecting to see one of the adults catching her breaking curfew.

The corridor remained empty. She was alone, yet the fragrance persisted. Slowly, hesitantly, she walked toward the main landing, carefully watching the doors to the suites of Miss Cora and Miss Ginger as she passed them. Susie wasn't certain where, exactly, she could possibly hide should either of the doors open; but, all the same, she didn't want to be caught off-guard.

As she neared the landing, Susie first positioned herself to be able to see down the west wing walkway. Leaning forward slightly, she peeked out – the balcony walkway was empty. Pulling back, she sprinted across the corridor and repeated her actions, this time to view the east wing. Again, the balcony walkway was empty.

Susie leaned against the corner of the wall, sliding to the floor where she sat, obscured in the shadows. "This is crazy," she muttered pensively; "can it be just the lack of sleep?"

No sooner had that thought ended than the soft, tinkling sound of a wind chime began its light serenade, just as it had the previous night. With it came the wafting scent of lilac, stronger than minutes earlier. Susie looked down the corridor toward the Dorms, and again down the balcony walkways. Nothing could account for either the sound or the scent.

Susie stood to her feet, crossed to the east side of the corridor and began walking to her Dorm. A cold draft blew around her, chilling her to the bone. From somewhere behind her a voice called out her name. Susie spun around – no one was there. She was alone. She ran to the landing – both walkways were empty as was the foyer below.

"No one could possibly have had the time to run down the main staircase and hide under it, or in one of the corridors off of the foyer." Susie was certain of that. "And they certainly couldn't have made it from the landing along the balcony walkways to the west wing without being seen," she silently reasoned.

'Or *the east wing*', the thought leapt into her mind, screaming as if demanding to be heard.

"But who would want to play a cruel joke on me?" Susie asked softly, perplexed at the idea that this was some elaborate hoax targeting her. "How are they doing it?" she further pondered, struggling to find the answers.

The hairs on her arms began to stand on end, as if static electricity had suddenly surrounded her body. She began to return to her Dorm, taking three steps. She paused. ...... Music, she heard music. Faint strains of music!

Susie spun around and ran back down the corridor, stopping briefly at Miss Cora's door. Next she darted across the corridor to Miss Ginger's door. It wasn't coming from their suites. Her heart began to beat faster as her mind began to whirl, flitting from possibility to possibility.

Tentatively she made her way toward the landing – the music seemed to be growing stronger the closer she came to it. She stepped out from the threshold of the south wing corridor and onto the landing. Other than directly beneath the landing of the main staircase, Susie could see the majority of the foyer below. The front door and the main entrances to the east and west wings were clearly visible. In plain view were the balcony walkways, as well as the entrances of both the west wing and the east wing.

No one was in sight, yet the music persisted. She stood, frozen in place, staring at the east wing doors. A chill ran through her as she realized the music was coming from somewhere inside the east wing, and she began trembling. Before she could spring into action, it took her several minutes and a few deep breaths to regain her composure. After steadying herself, Susie felt an intense surge of energy. Like lightning across the sky, she sprinted to the east wing doors, rapidly covering the distance. Grasping firmly the handles, Susie gave them a solid tug; the doors refused to budge. They were still locked.

Dropping to her knees, Susie leaned against the right door, placing her ear against the keyhole and listened...... It was louder now, but not by much. The composition was beautifully inspiring yet immensely poignant. It was as if its melody could reach into your innermost being and capture your soul. As Susie listened, tears welled in her eyes. She found herself grieving a profound loss that she did not understand, and conversely a joy sprang up within her so deep and so intense that it also moved her to tears.

Pushing herself back away from the doors, Susie began sobbing uncontrollably. She leaned against the railing, tucking her knees tightly against her chest and rested her forehead upon her knees. She sat still, trying to comprehend what was happening to her as her chest heaved with the short, staccato breaths the intense emotions produced. Her tears flowed like rivers, coursing down her face and saturating her pajamas. Slowly the music faded away, and Susie no longer heard its incredible sound. Several more minutes passed before she realized the hauntingly beautiful strains were completely gone, and so were her tears.

Susie felt exhausted, completely spent. And yet, strangely enough, she felt renewed as if a catharsis had taken place. Knees still drawn to her chest, Susie began rocking slowly, desperately trying to make sense out of it. Several minutes later, she ceased rocking and sat very still, staring at the massive oak doors that were barring her way to the truth.

The manor was quiet; too quiet, she realized. Susie looked around, uneasy in the complete absence of sound. Nana had taught her that there is an explanation for everything – just sometimes we don't know what the explanation is, or we don't want to accept the explanation. Nana always said we either have to figure it out, or wait for the answer to be revealed.

Susie kept repeating to herself it could all be explained, reminding herself that she'll figure it out in due time. Slowly she felt herself relax, and the tension began to fade from her body. Sighing, Susie rose to her feet, knowing full well that the longer she was out here, the higher the risk of being caught breaking curfew. She began slowly trotting back down the walkway, heading for the landing of the south wing. As Susie entered the south wing, she caught a glimpse of something white out of the corner of her eye. She turned quickly, but it was gone.

Susie stared at the east wing doors – no way did someone enter and close them before she was able to turn around. 'Something's amiss,' she thought; 'Glen Hollow has secrets, and the east wing holds the brunt of them.'

"I will discover your secrets," she whispered to the doors. "Whatever they are, I'll find them. I promise you that," she adamantly vowed.

Instantly a cold draft fluttered around her, billowing her pajama top and fluffing her hair. The scent of lilac was back, and so was the sound of the lovely wind chimes.

Susie laughed. "If I didn't know better, I'd think that was an approval."

Realizing the sheer absurdity of talking to thin air, Susie turned and quickly made her way back to her Dorm. Carefully shutting the door so that no one was awakened, she moved stealthily through the Common Area, down the hallway and to her bed. Collapsing onto it, she started laughing at herself.

"I'm nuts," she whispered; "certifiably nuts. Do I really think a ghost wants my help? ... What else can it be? ... No one living here could possibly do what's been done?" ... Or could they?" she pondered.

Susie began trying to think of ways that someone could create the sounds, the smells, the visual effects and the physical, such as the cold breezes. "I guess it's all possible to create," she reasoned; "just a matter of knowing how."

Silently she mulled over another option – that it was all her imagination due to sleep deprivation and nerves. "If that's it, then why lilacs?" she asked herself. "Mommy wore 'White Shoulders', and Nana wore 'Lily of the Valley'."

After several minutes of reflection, she giggled. "Lilacs, of course," she popped her forehead with the heel of her right hand, not believing how silly she had been. In addition to all of the other trees and flowers, Nana also had several lilac trees and lilac bushes. Nana's cottage was filled with cut flowers, especially lilacs since they were Nana's favorite. Nana even made potpourri with the dried blossoms.

Susie smiled and began to relax now that she had begun to make sense of it. As she further contemplated, she realized that Nana also had many wind chimes, all sizes and sounds. Some were on the porches, some were scattered in various places around the outside of the house, and some were even in a few of the trees. The woman in white could represent Nana in her nightgown or her robe, Susie reasoned. She laughed at herself and her silly imaginations. So all of this was because she missed Nana, she chided herself.

'Well, not all', she posited mentally. The music she heard emanating from the east wing was still problematic. She was fairly certain she had never heard it before. At least not at Nana's ......

"Mommy could have played it on the piano or flute," Susie's mind flashed, grasping for a reasonable explanation.

"That's it," she whispered aloud, triumph ringing in her tone. "It's been hiding in my subconscious all this time. I'm in a strange place, I'm tired; and because I miss Nana so much, my mind has triggered it."

Stretching her arms over her head, Susie interlocked her fingers and cradled her head in her hands as she sank down into her pillow. She released a contented sigh. Grinning and quite pleased with her powers of deduction, Susie gazed up at the ceiling, content that she was on the right track. As she continued to revel in her supposition and in her powers of deduction, the air around her became chillingly cold. Susie shivered and drew her covers up tightly around her body.

Her windows flew open with a loud bang, allowing the frigid night air to flood inside. Susie leapt out of bed, quickly closing the windows and securely fastening the locks. Troubled by how easily they had flown open, she checked the locks twice this time to be certain they was fastened properly. Susie hadn't checked them today, but she was positive they had been secured.

She shrugged. "Obviously not," she muttered as she moved away from the windows.

Vigorously rubbing her arms in an attempt to dispel the chill, Susie ran back to her bed. Crawling under her covers, the haunting refrain that she had heard earlier began again. Susie closed her eyes and pulled the covers over her head. The melody persisted, growing louder as the scent of lilac permeated the air. Softly the wind chime began its soothing jingle, sounding as if it were right next to her ear.

Flinging her covers off, Susie bolted upright, her eyes darting around her room. She was alone, but she didn't feel alone. An eerie, tingling sensation seemed to bolt through and over her, coursing its way continuously along her skin and through her blood. Pressing back against her headboard, Susie pulled the covers up as far as she could, leaving just her fingers and face exposed.

"Okay," she whispered into the stillness of the room. "Maybe I was right the first time. Maybe you're a ghost, and you're trying to tell me something."

Susie swallowed hard, tightly grasping her covers in an attempt to steel her nerves. "Whatever it is, I'll listen. I'll find out whatever the secret is in the east wing as long as you show me the way. I'll help you if I can."

As quickly as it all had descended upon her, it now retreated. Silence ensued, the fragrance disappeared, and the temperature returned to normal. Susie released her death grip on her covers, exhaling a hard, fast breath.

Contemplating what had just happened, Susie reaffirmed to herself that she would indeed discover whatever secrets the east wing held – no matter what. "And I can't tell anyone," she whispered aloud; "they'll think I'm crazy."

She giggled. "Maybe I am," she added wistfully.

Shaking her head, Susie decided, "No; I'm not crazy. What happened is real. I don't know if it's a ghost, or an angel, or just what; but whatever it is, it's real, and it wants my help."

As soon as the words were spoken, Susie remembered Megan had told her the same thing last night; only Megan had said *her angel* had told her that Susie was here to help.

"Megan's talking to angels?!" Susie marveled at the thought.

Feeling a little overwhelmed, Susie began saying her prayers; this time she included one for Glen Hollow – it had a secret that was meant for her to find. She prayed she would be able to deduce its deepest mystery, whatever it is, and help in whatever way she was meant to help.

Susie smiled, took in a deep, cleansing breath and slowly released it. She felt better. She relaxed into the soft comfort of her bed, snuggling under the covers and began drifting off to sleep. The last thing she remembered was hearing the grandfather clock strike the three o'clock hour.

Chapter 13

NOT BAD, JUST ALL BOY

Susie rounded the corner in a fast trot, not slowing down in the slightest as she entered the west wing. She was expecting to see Simon waiting for her outside the Library; but the corridor was empty. Surprised that he wasn't already here, Susie slowed her pace to a brisk walk, wondering where he could be.

The thought popped into her mind that perhaps Simon got lost after leaving his playtime with Timmy. She promptly rejected that thought; Simon already knew his way around the old manor quite well. It amazed her how quickly he had adapted to Glen Hollow, and seemed to like it here even though it was spooky and unnerving at times. His acclimation was probably due in large part to his friendship with Timmy, she surmised. Apparently, the two were having great fun playing Hide and Seek in addition to their own version of Cops and Robbers.

Susie couldn't help but smile remembering the animated tale they told this morning in class. No one knew why Miss Emma was late, but they had entertained themselves while waiting for her - Simon and Timmy shared one of their latest exploits. It seems the dynamic duo, Simon and Timmy, have vivid imaginations that translates into their play.

Recounting their latest escapade from yesterday afternoon with all the flamboyance that would rival a seasoned thespian, their faces shone with exuberance as they divulged the afternoon's events. With great delight, they had regaled the class with their accidental traumatizing of poor Miss Thelma. Though they fully intended to surprise her, they had no idea as to how intensely surprised she would truly be. In this particular instance of their creative games, they were the cops and were fast closing in on the armed and dangerous robbers. Stealthily they approached their quarry (Miss Thelma) who, it seems, was completely oblivious to their presence, which, they proudly declared, was as it should be because they are great detectives.

Miss Thelma was busy, working steadily, polishing the furniture in the front corridor of the west wing, not too far from the Parlor. However, to the trained eyes of the master detectives, she was stealing priceless objects from a museum.

Out of nowhere they pounced, yelling *"freeze, maggot"* as they poked her in her back with their imaginary pistols, which as it happens was actually their fingers. Needless to say, poor Miss Thelma let out a blood-curdling scream and nearly jumped out of her skin. She clutched her chest as she stumbled back, crashing against the wall, her face contorted into an expression of shock. The boys fell to the floor, rolling around with laughter, holding their sides as their bodies ached from the spasms the intense laughter produced.

Hearing the thunderous commotion, Miss Pritchett came running from her office, expecting to see some sort of disaster and fearing the worst. By the time she arrived on the scene, Miss Thelma had regained her composure, somewhat, and was fiercely chastising the boys for their wretched behavior. Her face had become flushed with anger, according to the boys, but Susie felt certain it was also due to embarrassment. She was yelling at them and shaking her finger in their faces, droning on about what horrible, vile children they were for nearly causing her to have a heart attack.

Miss Pritchett quickly intervened, calmly stating she felt certain that the boys did not intend her any harm. Smiling at the boys, she asked, "Am I correct?"

With their heads bobbing like fishing floats, Simon and Timmy answered with a quick "Yes, ma'am".

Miss Pritchett heartily concurred adding, "Of course; you were just playing as children often do."

As she looked at Miss Thelma, her eyes were twinkling with amusement. Laughingly, she added, "I seem to recall several instances where Jason had done the same to all of us at one time or another; not to mention the many practical jokes he perpetrated well into his teens."

Pausing for a moment to allow Miss Thelma time to reflect, Miss Pritchett then gently asked, "We survived all of those antics, didn't we?"

Miss Thelma's face softened, and she half-heartedly smiled. "Yes, we did," she acknowledged; "but we were a lot younger then."

"True," Miss Pritchett readily agreed; "however, it's only been a few years since the last group of children were this age. We seem to have survived those playful antics as well."

She turned her attention to the young culprits and stated, "I am certain that they will not ever sneak up behind you again. Am I correct, boys?"

Simon and Timmy nodded vigorously and chorused, "Never again", and "Yes, ma'am" with faces that were properly contrite. Rushing to Miss Thelma, they wrapped their arms around her, telling her they were sorry for scaring her so much.

For a brief moment, Miss Thelma seemed surprised by their affection, and to not know what to do. Within seconds, she apparently resolved her inner conflict for she slid down to her knees and gave them both a big hug.

"I guess I've just forgotten what it was like to have little ones around," she admitted softly.

She released them so as to look directly into their eyes. "You did nothing wrong," she told them; "but let's not make this an everyday thing, okay?"

The boys solemnly promised, and Miss Pritchett then told them to go play in the Rec Room. They scampered away, giggling and whispering to each other, hatching up their next great adventure.

Susie had now reached the Library doors and leaned against the wall beside them, hoping that Simon would be along soon. She really needed to look for some reference books for her essay. Simon wouldn't likely entertain himself for long, but she hoped it'd be long enough for her to at least find one reference book.

Bored, Susie began slowly walking back down the corridor, glancing at the various portraits that lined it. Based on the style of clothing worn, she guessed that the portraits were of Miss Pritchett's ancestors, and not any that were recent. Hastily she perused the paintings, though not particularly interested - she was just killing time until Simon arrived.

She moved from painting to painting, spending very little time at each one, until she saw the fourth painting from the end. It was a painting of a horse; Susie moved quickly to the next three – each one was of an individual horse. The first painting was of a white horse, the second was of a black horse and the last two were of dappling grays. Susie rapidly strode back to the first of the horse paintings, her curiosity rising.

'Why would there be portraits of horses?' she wondered. As she reached the first painting, she remembered Mrs. Crenshaw had mentioned that the Evermores had once been famous for their horses. "Perhaps these four were champions," Susie pondered, focusing on the image on the wall.

The first of the horse portraitures was of a breathtakingly beautiful creature that actually appeared to be gazing back at her. According to the brass plate that was centered on the lower frame, she was a grand champion dam whose name was Nime Chuit Angel Aurora Pax. Susie knew that Aurora was Latin for Dawn, which referred to the Roman goddess of the dawn or daybreak. She also knew that Pax was the Latin word for Peace. What she didn't know is what the words 'Nime' and 'Chuit' mean, or even what language they are.

"I'll ask Miss Emma," she noted to herself.

She turned her attention to the painting, feeling drawn to it as if it were a kindred spirit. The horse's coat was as white as freshly fallen snow. Its snowy mane was long and flowing, like silken threads gently blowing in a light summer breeze. Something about the eyes drew you in - large, ice blue eyes that on the surface would seem cold and aloof, yet somehow they gave the sense of just the opposite, of being warm and friendly. The artist had captured the spiritual essence of the noble creature so well that the painting exuded a sense of gentleness and kindness, a knowing of love and loyalty.

Instinctively Susie reached out and gently touched the horse's forehead, half expecting to feel the warmth of its body and the softness of its skin. Instead, all she felt was the rough, dry oil paint, and was surprised to find herself feeling disappointed. Slowly her gaze returned to the eyes that seemed to entreat her to stroke its mane, its forehead and to gently caress its muzzle and neck. Staring into her eyes, Susie felt the sensation of wind blowing into her own face, of seeing the trees, the pastures, the dirt lane and of hearing hooves beat the ground as the horse trotted along. Susie stepped back, her heart pounding, mesmerized by this strange encounter. It felt as if she had actually been riding this magnificent creature.

Forcing herself to look away, Susie's eyes drifted to the bottom right corner of the painting. The name of the artist was written in an elegant, cursive script. The artist was Elizabeth N. Evermore. The date underneath the name was June 1950.

"A relative," Susie whispered, a sense of awe rising in her for the talent that created such a treasure.

She ran to next one, checking the artist's signature. It, too, was painted by the same woman and had the same date. "Maybe she was Miss Pritchett's aunt, or her grandmother or maybe her cousin," she whispered aloud, remembering Mrs. Crenshaw had told her that Miss Pritchett's mother was Murielle Evermore.

Susie's eyes slowly wandered up the painting, scrutinizing the vibrant work. This horse was as dark as a cloudy, midnight sky without benefit of stars or of moon. His eyes and mane were just as black and glossy as his coat, the only color being that of a sliver of white in the corner of his eyes, and a slight hint of blue in the center of each pupil.

Susie leaned in close, staring at the wisp of blue. "Oh my stars," she exclaimed softly. The little wisp of color in each pupil was actually a perfectly formed flame.

Moving back, she looked at the horse, drinking in the essence of his image. This was a creature of strong spirit – the haughty poise of its head, the defiant gaze, its ears perked inward and angled slightly back resembling horns, the wildly, streaming mane and its flared nostrils all echoed the sentiment that this was not a creature to be trifled with, nor challenged.

However, Susie sensed something else as she stared into that face; here, too, was conveyed a sense of love and loyalty, of protection and power. Her gaze fell to the brass name plate on the frame – he was indeed a grand champion; his name was Chride Baile Gabriel Verum Ignis. Instantly she knew the Latin words Verum means Truth, and Ignis means fire. However as to what 'Chride' and 'Baile' meant, Susie didn't have a clue.

"If Miss Emma doesn't know, maybe Jose does," she whispered, staring into the hypnotic eyes that seemed to hold her spellbound.

A feeling of lightheadedness suddenly descended over her, causing her to reach out, steadying herself against the wall. Susie pushed herself upright and back, resuming once again her scrutiny of the painting.

The light feeling was still with her, creating the sensation that she was floating. Slowly her eyes wandered upward, meeting squarely the eyes of Chride Baile Gabriel Verum Ignis. The flames in his eyes seemed to be dancing; she could hear him snort, feel the heat of his breath. Her hand intuitively reached up, her fingers gently touching his muzzle. At that instant, Susie knew; somehow she knew that these were the grandparents of Lacy. She would ask Miss Hilda. If Miss Hilda didn't know, she'd check the records in the stable's office. Until then, she'd see if Miss Emma could translate the words.

"Wait a minute," Susie mumbled to herself. "I know!" she whispered excitedly. "Miss Hilda said the names Moon and Shadow came from Lacy's parents. The name Heart came from the grandfather, and Treasure came from the grandmother."

Susie's excitement soared. She'd narrowed it down. The name 'Heart' was either 'Chride' or 'Baile'; and the name 'Treasure' was either 'Nime' or 'Chuit'. She smiled; Lacy was definitely a heart's treasure.

A merry peal of laughter broke through, capturing her attention. Faint though it was, she knew instantly it was Simon; and it was coming from inside the Library. Susie quickly gave one last glance at Gabriel and then at Angel. She whispered to them, "I'm going to find what secrets are here, and I'm going to find out all about both of you."

Running as fast as she could back down the corridor, Susie entered the Library about as subtly as a bull moves in a china shop. Her anger was rising with each step - she already knew what Simon was doing. Instead of waiting for her by the Library doors, he had entered without her and was playing on the ladder. Susie ran all the way to the west section. As she ran, she wondered how he managed to get the door open. Someone must have let him in – but who?

Upon entering the west side, Susie saw him – midway up the ladder, hanging on as it was moving fast along the rails. She arrived just in time to see him slowing it down to a stop.

"Come down, Simon; right now!" she demanded.

He laughed (more like a squeal), shook his head and climbed higher, scampering up the ladder like a monkey

"Wait till you see what I can do!" he boasted as he scurried toward the top.

Reaching the top rung, he firmly grasped the shelf in front of him, pulling himself along. Faster and faster he flew, giggling and laughing with delight. Intermittent declarations of "This is fun!" and "You should try it, Susie!" would escape between his peals of laughter.

No matter how many times Susie ordered him to stop, he just laughed and kept going, his eyes shining with glee. Several "whees" were shouted, loud and clear, echoing throughout the Library much like the sounds you hear around carnival rides.

On his seventh pass, a voice harshly rang out from behind Susie.

"Simon Michael Howard! Stop immediately, and come down." It was Miss Hilda, and none too pleased by the look of her.

His little head whirled around at the sound of her voice; his expression was akin to that of a deer caught in headlights. Slowly he brought his amusement ride to a complete stop, descending the ladder to the waiting Miss Hilda. He looked up at her so innocently, as if riding the ladder had been the most normal thing to have done.

"Do not *ever* do that again," she said sternly. "You could have been hurt."

Simon shook his head, disagreeing with her. "I was safe," he proclaimed. "I held on real tight once I got my speed up," he explained patiently, thinking that Miss Hilda wasn't aware of his safety precautions.

Unyielding, Miss Hilda's response was terse. "The ladders are not toys, young man; nor are they playground equipment. You are not to use them. All of the children's books are in the small bookcases. If you do this again, you will be severely punished."

His eyes widened in horror at the idea of a severe punishment, even though he had no idea what Miss Hilda considered severe.

"As this is," she continued, her tone now a little less harsh; "your first and your *last* offense, I think only a light punishment is in order. Tomorrow after naptime you will assist me in folding towels."

Simon hung his head, revealing his despair at being punished.

Miss Hilda smiled tenderly at him, cupping his chin in her hand. She raised his head up to face her. "Now, go with Susie and allow her to read to you. I'm certain you can find something that interests you in one of the children's bookcases."

Smiling at Susie, she added, "Don't forget; dinner is at six, and to be on time."

"We won't forget," Susie promised her. Simon had already scurried to the bookcases and had begun hunting through the children's books for just the right one.

Miss Hilda gave Susie a cheery smile and a nod, leaving them to their reading.

Releasing a heavy sigh (part frustration and part irritation), Susie stood still a few minutes, gathering her thoughts. Then she turned and headed toward Simon, determined to corral his behavior. She found him sitting on the floor between the first and second bookcases, pulling books from the shelves.

"Simon," Susie began as she sat down next to him; "you can't pull all of these books. We only have time to read one, little book today; so choose just one, "she instructed him a little tersely.

Quizzically, Simon looked up at her and asked, "Are you mad at me?"

Susie pressed her lips tightly for a second, before responding as calmly as she could while returning the books to the shelves. "No, but I am disappointed with you."

"Why?" he asked innocently, placing his hand on her shoulder and giving her a little push in order for her to face him.

His motion achieved the desired goal – Susie stopped and focused her attention on him. Studying his face, she realized that he truly didn't understand. Patiently she explained, "Because, Simon, you know better than to get on the ladders, but you did it anyway. Getting in trouble is a sure fire way for us to be watched more closely. It could stop our afternoon story time, and that could lead to our getting caught at bedtime."

"And then there's this," she said agitatedly, pointing to the books still remaining on the floor. "You know better. Why are you doing this?"

Puzzled and a little crestfallen, Simon meekly responded, "How am I going to know if I want the book if I don't see the front or what's inside?"

Susie's heart melted as she watched his little face. Reaching over, she drew him to her and hugged him. "I'm sorry, Simon. I shouldn't have been so cross with you. I'm only trying to protect you. I don't ever want you to get hurt or in trouble."

"Okay," his muffled voice croaked; "but you're smothering me." She giggled and released him.

His face, slightly flushed, reflected his usual inner joy. "I promise I'll be good," he vowed. With a sad sigh he added, "And I'll stay off the ladders."

"Thank you, Simon," Susie responded with a grin. "Now, if you decide you don't want to read a book, please put it back before you take another one, okay?" she reminded him gently.

He nodded.

Susie's tone changed to one that was slightly apprehensive. "I have to find a book for one of my classes, Simon. Will you be good and stay right here? I'll only be gone a few minutes." Susie intently searched his face for any sign of mischievous intent. There wasn't any.

Dramatically, Simon pointed down to the floor as he quipped, "I'll stay right here."

"Good," Susie said, leaning forward and kissing his forehead. "I'll be back in ten minutes," she added as she hurried away.

———

In a rush, Susie scurried back to where she had left Simon. She hadn't been gone long, only about fifteen minutes; however, experience had taught her that that was more than enough time for Simon to find trouble. Susie felt good, though, about the outcome of her quest for a reference book. She had been fortunate to find three really, good books – now all she needed was the time and energy to actually read them and then write the essay.

Half expecting to find no trace of Simon upon her arrival, Susie was delighted (and relieved), Simon was exactly where she left him, still looking through the books. He grinned when he saw her.

"See," he said proudly; "I stayed right here." He flashed her one of his best, precocious grins.

His sparkling exuberance tickled her, and Susie chuckled. "I see; and I'm very proud of you," she said, leaning down to kiss the top of his head. She gave him a quick kiss and straightened. "Have you chosen one yet?"

Simon nodded and handed to her a small, thin book, not much larger than a travel brochure. It was entitled, 'The Great Banana Caper'. The book was banana yellow with dark green block lettering, outlined in a dark shade of mustard yellow. It had bananas raining down all over the front cover, and monkeys with baskets trying to catch them.

With a dubious look on her face, she raised her eyebrows and looked at him. "Are you sure?" she queried.

He nodded his head rapidly several times, grinning from ear to ear. "I like the pictures," he explained.

"Okay," she replied, reaching for his hand. "Come on. We should be able to finish it before dinner."

Simon beamed at her, clasped his hand in hers, and began chattering away about all the really neat books he had found. He was amazed at how many books they had that he liked. Hesitantly, Susie asked what he did with them. Simon gleefully laughed, quickly realizing what she meant. He assured her that he had returned each and every one to its proper place. He crowed with pride as he informed her that he had memorized where they were so that he could find them for future Story Times.

They settled into Simon's favorite chair, and she began reading to him.

———

Susie finished the book with plenty of time before dinner, closed it and handed it to Simon. "Please return it to where you found it," she told him.

He took the book and ran to the bookcases, performing his task quite happily. Susie picked up her reference books and waited for him by the main aisle. Within a couple minutes, he came skipping toward her.

"Ready!" he chirped as he skipped past her.

Susie chuckled and followed him on to the entrance. Stopping at the front desk, she removed a large rubber band from a box and bound the books together.

Simon watched and finally asked, "What are you doing?"

"I'm leaving them here with my name on them so no one else will take them," she patiently explained. "I'll pick them up after dinner just as I do for your books."

"While I'm taking a bath?" he asked.

"Yes, Simon," she answered inattentively, writing her name on a slip of paper and sliding it under the rubber band. Then she placed the books by the check-out sheet.

Simon shrugged and headed for the door with Susie right behind him. She pushed open the door; he darted out into the corridor and began race walking to the Dining Hall.

"Simon, would you mind if I skip the Rec Room tonight, and you just play with Timmy?" Susie asked as she caught up with him. "I have some homework I have to finish. I'll still come and give you a goodnight hug, and then come back for our secret time."

Simon's brow furrowed slightly. "But I told Timmy you'd play Candy Land with us," he pouted.

"I'm sorry, Simon; but if I don't get this homework finished, I'll have a bad grade. I'll make it up to you and Timmy, I promise. We'll play Candy Land tomorrow night after bath time. Okay?" she offered.

Simon frowned. "It's no fun without you," he wheedled.

"You and Timmy could ask Aaron to play tonight," she suggested.

"He won't," Simon fussed. "Timmy says he thinks he's too big to play with us."

"I think if you both ask him really nice, he'll do it," Susie countered. "Maybe tomorrow night both of us will play with you and Timmy. Megan might even want to play."

Simon didn't respond.

"In fact," Susie continued coaxingly; "if you include Megan tonight, that would count as one of the five times of our agreement."

Simon's head sharply turned to face her, a grin spreading across his cherub face. "Really?" he asked.

She nodded. "Really," she affirmed.

Simon began his peacock strut as he mulled it over. "Okay," he agreed. "You do your homework, and Timmy and me will play with Megan and Aaron," he consented as they approached the doors to the Dining Hall.

Pulling back hard on Susie's hand, he loudly whispered, "Wait, Susie."

She stopped and looked at him, wondering what now.

"You promise you won't forget about my hug and our secret?" he asked, his expression fully revealing his anxiousness.

Leaning down, she whispered in his ear, "I won't forget. I promise."

He grinned at her, happy as a lark, and they strolled in to dinner.

———

The other children were already seated, and nearly all the adults were already in the Dining Hall when Susie ushered in Simon. Only Mrs. Coppersmith and Miss Taryn were absent. Of course, that was as it should be since they were running back and forth between the butler's pantry and the Dining Hall bringing in the food. From the looks of the table, the only thing missing were the pitchers of milk, and soon that would be rectified.

As she hurried Simon to his chair, Susie noticed Miss Claire watching her. She appeared to be listening to Miss Fiona and Miss Elsa, but her eyes were on Susie. Embarrassed by Susie catching her, Miss Claire's face flushed slightly; she gave Susie a quick smile and a brief nod of acknowledgement before returning her attention to the other ladies.

Tentatively, Susie returned her smile, and then assisted Simon into his chair. She was puzzled by Miss Claire. Nearly every time Susie saw her (which was mostly at mealtime), Miss Claire seemed to be watching her. At first Susie just thought she was mistaken – but now, Susie was certain that Miss Claire was actually watching her. It was a little weird, to be certain; but, even more so, it was a little disconcerting. It was as if Miss Claire was worried about her.

'But why,' Susie wondered silently. 'Come to think of it', Susie calculated mentally, 'it's only been since yesterday morning that she's been watching me.'

With Simon now safely in his booster seat, Susie slid his chair closer to the table. As she pulled her chair back from the table, the realization struck: 'Wait a minute; that was the day after she told Simon and me that story, and we played with those cards of hers. She wasn't at dinner that night, so the first time I saw her after the Library was at breakfast yesterday morning!' Susie decided that she'd have to find a way to talk to Miss Claire and find out what was the problem.

As Susie seated herself, Timmy appeared, grinning like a loon, and standing between her chair and Simon's. Immediately she was bombarded with requests for a favor by the best buds. She listened as they pleaded their case - they wanted her to ask Miss Hilda to allow Timmy to sit next to Simon. When she told them she didn't think that was a good idea, they began to pout.

Shaking her head slightly, she sighed in exasperation. "That's one of the reasons why Miss Hilda will say no," she informed them. "You misbehave when you don't immediately get your way."

Both boys protested with a vigorous "Na-uh!", and Susie noticed that Aaron quickly turned his head to face the opposite direction. But not before she saw the amused grin spread across his face.

"If Miss Emma doesn't mind, maybe Miss Hilda will allow Timmy to sit next to Miss Emma," Susie suggested. "That way, you're across the table from each other; and, if you both behave, then maybe she'll allow Timmy to sit in my chair."

Miss Emma grinned. "I don't mind at all," she stated pleasantly.

Simon and Timmy exchanged grins, happily agreeing with Susie's counter plan. Next they exchanged covert whispers and began giggling.

"All right, Timmy. It's time for you to get in your chair," Aaron ordered.

Timmy shook his head rapidly, giving his brother an exaggerated frown. "Na-uh; Miss Pritchett hasn't rang the bell yet." That elicited an energetic round of snickering from both Timmy and Simon.

"If you want Miss Hilda to let you switch chairs, you'd better be on your best behavior. And that means being in your seat before the bell rings," Aaron responded sharply.

Timmy looked at Simon – they broke out giggling, each one trying to outdo the other. Simon glanced at Susie. Upon seeing her expression, he immediately ceased his antics. He looked at Timmy, began shaking his head and placed his finger over his lips.

Timmy got the message; he stopped, turned and grinned at Susie. He turned back to Simon and said, "Gotta go."

Mrs. Coppersmith and Miss Taryn came through the swinging doors, carrying trays that each held four large pitchers of milk. Just as they approached the table, Timmy whirled around and darted away. Poor Miss Taryn nearly collided with Timmy. She let out a high pitched squeal. By the grace of God, he ducked down just as she began raising her tray higher, barely missing him.

Mrs. Coppersmith began chiding Timmy, telling him that he ought to already be in his seat. As they began distributing the pitchers, she fussed at Aaron for not seeing after Timmy, and then began admonishing Miss Ginger for not properly attending to the little one.

Before Miss Ginger could respond to such unwarranted criticism, Miss Pritchett hastily intervened. "Mrs. Coppersmith, I'm certain that Timmy meant no harm. I have not as yet rang the bell (she smiled at Timmy who was now securely fastened in his booster seat) so Timmy was not actually out of place. Fortunately, Taryn was able to avert the accident. Thank you, Taryn, for your quick action."

Miss Taryn smiled but said nothing. She was still fluctuating between panic and anger. Part of her really wanted to throttle Timmy.

While Mrs. Coppersmith and Miss Taryn finished placing the pitchers on the table, the rest of the adults quickly took their places. Miss Emma waited until Miss Hilda had seated herself, and then launched Susie's plan before Susie had the opportunity to do so. "Miss Hilda, if you don't have any objections, would it be permissible for Timmy to sit next to me?"

"Why?" Miss Hilda queried, giving her a guarded look.

"The boys would like to be seated together. Across the table from each other seems to be the best solution as opposed to actually sitting next to each other," Miss Emma explained casually. "Susie and I have discussed it with them, and we believe that Susie's alternative is the better choice." She smiled and winked at Susie.

Miss Hilda darted a quick glance at Susie before asking Miss Emma, "Do you think they can properly behave?"

Miss Emma shrugged slightly and honestly answered. "I believe so. They sit next to each other during class and at lunch time, and they behave well. I see no reason why they wouldn't behave here at the main table."

Miss Hilda's gaze fell squarely on Timmy and then on Simon. "Well, boys; will you properly behave yourselves if allowed to sit across from each other?"

With expressions that were nearly angelic, both boys sincerely promised to be on their best behavior. Miss Hilda nodded ever so slightly and then smiled. "Okay; Miss Emma if you will please assist Timmy's move to this chair, I would appreciate it."

Miss Emma rose and quickly assisted Timmy out of his current chair, into the chair besides hers and, therefore, he was also next to Miss Hilda. As Miss Emma reseated herself, both boys flashed grinning faces as they each gave her an exuberant thank you.

Accepting their expressions of thanks, Miss Emma asked if they forgot someone. Immediately they turned to Miss Hilda, coyly smiled and properly thanked her as well. Softly Miss Hilda chuckled, thanked the boys and then suggested that perhaps they should also thank Susie, considering it was her idea. Quite animatedly, both boys expressed their appreciation to Susie between rounds of giggles. Susie smiled, reminding them that good behavior from them would be thanks enough. The boys then delved into plans for later, after bath time.

Susie caught the look that was exchanged between Miss Hilda and Miss Pritchett. There was a message in those glances, one that to Susie appeared to be triumph. Both Miss Hilda's and Miss Pritchett's eyes were twinkling and dancing like never before. There was no mistaking the grin that spread across Miss Hilda's face; however, with Miss Pritchett, there was only the faintest hint of a smile that graced her lips. In spite of her efforts, that little smile escaped and spoke volumes to Susie.

A loud, clattering noise behind Susie distracted her. She, like most of the others, jumped at the sound and quickly turned to see what had happened. Apparently, as Miss Taryn attempted to place an empty tray on top of the other empty trays, it slipped from her hand, crashing down onto the stack. Fast and nimble, Miss Taryn collected the trays that had scattered, carefully returning them to the stack.

Miss Taryn, embarrassed and blushing, muttered a quick apology as she slinked to her chair. Though Mrs. Coppersmith spoke not a word, the look she gave Miss Taryn said it all. Susie felt sorry for Miss Taryn; it wasn't her fault – that could have happened to anyone.

Susie couldn't understand why Mrs. Coppersmith didn't like Miss Taryn. True, Susie didn't know for a fact that that was the case, but it sure seemed as though Mrs. Coppersmith didn't like her. Miss Taryn never seemed to be able to do anything that pleased her. She was always frowning at Miss Taryn, or chiding her about something. Susie wondered why Miss Taryn wanted to work for Mrs. Coppersmith; she could easily change jobs with Miss Elsa or Miss Fiona. Both of them assisted Mrs. Coppersmith a great deal, and always at Mrs. Coppersmith's request. Obviously Mrs. Coppersmith liked them.

Susie's pondering was brought to an abrupt halt by the sound of the dinner bell. As soon as Mrs. Coppersmith and Miss Taryn had taken their seats, Miss Pritchett picked up the silver hand bell and rang it, signaling that it was time for the Blessing. Conversations ceased immediately, and Miss Pritchett asked Miss Claire to lead them in prayer.

———

After dinner, Susie quickly made her way to the Library, retrieved the books she had left at the desk and disappeared into her room. She wasted no time, diving into the first of the three reference books. It was the smallest volume, and thus she was certain that she could finish it by eight o'clock. And she did. Shortly before eight, she had finished it, and had started the first paragraph of the second book when Megan came running into the Dorm, calling out her name. Megan burst into Susie's room, racing as fast as she could, launching herself into Susie's arms. She gave Megan her goodnight hug, receiving Megan's best hug in return.

Megan, as was now her custom, chitchatted about her entire day, telling Susie all the events that she could remember, especially those of her favorite pets, Hazey and Mazey. Hazey is her purple and white stuffed unicorn, and Mazey is her green and white stuffed dragon. Apparently they lead very full and interesting lives. Megan, being deemed a special human by a royal proclamation of their King, was privy to all of the tales of their adventures; and occasionally they allowed her to participate.

Megan, lively as ever, had begun spinning her fascinating story of their most recent exploit. She was in the midst of how they were to rescue the baby dragon prince, Rayta, from the evil overlord, Shaknor. Miss Cora finally interrupted, telling Megan it was bedtime. Megan gave Susie one more hug, whispering to her that she'd finish telling Susie later. She turned and skipped all the way to her bed, Miss Cora following close behind.

Susie hastened to see Simon, giving him his goodnight hug. He informed her that Timmy and he played with Megan and Aaron. He grinned from ear to ear, apparently surprised that he actually had fun playing with Megan. Susie pretended not to know. Megan had already recounted this bit of information just minutes earlier. Megan, too, was pleasantly surprised that the boys asked her to play with them. And, bless her little heart, Megan was so happy. She had gushed on and on to Susie about how much fun they had had, and that she looked forward to more play times with them.

Simon shyly smiled and told Susie that Megan wasn't so bad, even Timmy thought so. He nodded, bouncing his little head up and down like a yo-yo. Suddenly he stopped and grinned at her, a big toothy grin. "You knew that," he said matter-of-factly. "That's why you wanted me to play with her."

Susie nodded and smiled.

"We'll play with her sometimes," he announced as if he were a judge pronouncing a sentence; "but not every time. Some things are just for boys."

Susie laughed, amused at his logic. "Okay, just as long as you include her some of the time."

Miss Ginger popped her head in his doorway. "Let's go, Susie. It's after eight, and past his bedtime."

They quickly gave each other one final hug. Susie tucked him in, and kissed him on his forehead, whispering, "I'll see you later."

He whispered back, "Okay."

They waved to each other as Susie left his room with Miss Ginger escorting her out of the Boys Dorm.

———

Susie was so engrossed in her second book that she had not heard Dani, Kat or Juls parading past her room. It wasn't until Miss Cora started flashing the overhead lights that she realized what time it was. A minute later, Miss Cora was standing in her doorway. "Lights out, Susie; it's already ten after nine," she cordially reminded her.

Susie sighed. "I know, Miss Cora. I was just finishing some homework. I only have one more chapter in this book to finish," she replied, hoping to gain a few more minutes.

Miss Cora smiled understandingly. "Well, I suggest you read it quickly before breakfast tomorrow morning. I'll give you five minutes to get into your pajamas," she said softly; "then I turn out the lights."

"Thanks, Miss Cora," she responded, switching off her desk lamp. She smiled at Miss Cora as she retrieved her pajamas out from under her pillow. "Goodnight, Miss Cora."

Miss Cora returned her smile, nodded and responded warmly, "Goodnight, Susie."

She left Susie, and returned to the Common Area by the door. Punctual as always, five minutes later exactly, Miss Cora turned out the overhead lights and left the Dorm.

As soon as Miss Cora had left, Susie got up and switched on her desk lamp, continuing with her studies. She finished the second book and quickly moved on to the third and last book. This one, she'd have to skim for she didn't have time to thoroughly read it. She finished it, and began writing the outline for her essay. Next she began writing a summary under each point of the outline. Susie was nearly finished with her summary points when the grandfather clock began striking the ten o'clock hour. She sighed; she still had so much to do.

Switching off her desk lamp, Susie quietly slid out of her chair. She made her way, quiet as a cat, to the waiting Simon.

Tonight he seemed a little petulant, not his usual effervescent self. When pressed as to what was bothering him, he finally admitted that he wanted Timmy to share in their bedtime Story Time. Susie shook her head no, offering instead to include Timmy in the afternoon Story Time. Simon was not to be dissuaded. Adamantly he insisted that Timmy be included in both Story Times because they were now best buds, and best buds do everything together. Susie leaned in close to Simon, harshly reminding him about the need for secrecy at bedtime.

Unfortunately, Simon was unmoved. He whined and pleaded, assuring her that Timmy would never tell. After all, he reminded her, best buds always keep secrets because you can't be a best bud if you don't.

Susie sat silent, contemplating what her next argument would be, hoping to persuade him. She couldn't think of anything. Finally, Susie surrendered, telling Simon that Timmy would be included in both Story Times;

however, with one caveat. Simon pressed his lips tightly together, certain he would not like whatever condition she was about to propose.

"Timmy can join both Story Times if Megan can join the afternoon one," she stoically told him.

Simon rapidly shook his head back and forth, glaring at her. "No way," he hissed. "Only best buds," he insisted.

Susie shrugged. "Then I guess Timmy won't be joining us at all," she countered.

Simon crossed his arms and narrowed his eyes in defiance. "Yes he will because I'll tell him!"

Susie inched her face close to his, nose to nose. "If you do, then we won't have any Story Time, ever; not in the afternoon, and not at bedtime."

Simon's brow furrowed; he stared into her eyes, hoping to see if she was bluffing. He could tell she wasn't. He gave an exasperated sigh, and then acquiesced. "Okay; Megan can come to the afternoon Story Time, but Timmy gets to do both. Right?"

Susie grinned and kissed his forehead. "Right," she confirmed. "Now I want you to invite both Timmy and Megan tomorrow at naptime for the afternoon Story Time. Okay?"

"Okay," he responded glumly.

"We'll meet at the Library door. And remember," she firmly instructed; "don't go in until I get there."

With all sincerity, Simon casually replied, "Then don't be late."

Susie looked at him – there was no hint of malice, no judgment in his demeanor. She smiled, realizing he meant no offense. "I won't," she responded. "Now there's one more thing; we only have one small problem with the bedtime Story Time."

"What problem?" Simon asked, his tone a little cross for he saw no problem at all.

"We'll have to change the time, Simon," Susie informed him. "I can't go wake Timmy up, nor can the two of you hide out in here because you'll get caught."

"No we won't," Simon disagreed.

Susie warily looked at Simon. "Yes you will. You'll start wrestling, or giggling, or something, and you'll get caught." She sighed – how in the

world would this work, she wondered. After a few minutes of contemplation, an idea struck. "Tomorrow night," she whispered, "I'll come in just
after Miss Ginger leaves. That way, the two of you will be in here alone.
I'll read one, little book, or only one chapter from a bigger book. Okay?"

Flashing his famous Cheshire cat grin, Simon hugged Susie and whispered, "You're the best. I love you, Susie."

"I love you, too, Simon. Now, get settled. I hope we can finish this
chapter."

Simon snuggled down into his bed, sidling up close to Susie as she
opened his 'forever favorite' book and began reading the last chapter. By
the time she finished it, he was fast asleep.

Susie tucked him in, stored the book in his nightstand and kissed him
on his forehead. Watching him sleep, she had to agree with Miss Hilda's
assessment on the day they arrived – he did look like a cherub. His behavior, however, was not always so angelic, but Susie loved him as fiercely as a
mother bear loves its cub. Chuckling softly to herself, she had to admit he
really wasn't so bad when he was awake. Not that she'd ever admit that to
him – he has a big enough head as it is, she told herself.

Quietly she made her way back to the door, pausing briefly to be certain that she hadn't awakened any of the other boys. All was quiet. She
cautiously opened the door, peered into the corridor and exited, softly closing the door behind her and ran across the corridor to her Dorm.

———

Wearily, Susie rose from her chair, turning off the desk lamp. Her back
and neck were so stiff, they ached - she stretched several times, hoping to
relieve the tension and the soreness. Her U.S. History essay was finally
finished, and she hoped it was in good order. She was out of time – she'd
have to turn it in without proofreading it.

She trudged to her bed, allowing her body to drop onto it. Yawning,
she kicked off her slippers and crawled under the covers. She ran through
her prayers quickly, giving a very condensed version of her usual litany.

Glancing at her alarm clock, she groaned when she saw the time; four–
fifty. She yawned, closed her eyes and within seconds she was fast asleep.

Chapter 14

AN UNEXPECTED CONNECTION

"Good grief," Susie groaned as she wearily raised her head from her pillow. Barely opened, her eyes were still heavy with sleep. Her room was blurred, much like a picture taken using the wrong focus setting. After slowly squeezing her eyes opened and closed a couple of times, she was able to restore her perfect vision. She turned her attention to her clock.

Glaring at the unwelcomed noisemaker that was so annoyingly proclaiming that morning had arrived, she flung her arm up and over, bringing her hand down hard and fast, smacking the alarm button and ridding her head of the noisy intruder. For the moment, she didn't care that she had nearly knocked the clock off of her nightstand. It slid across the nightstand, coming to rest, not just near the edge but partially hanging over it. She dropped back down onto her pillow, enjoying the silence. She just wanted five more minutes.

"That's all," she mumbled. "Then I'll be ready to get up."

Her eyes closed quickly as she relaxed back down into the soft, warm comfort of her bed, her blankets and her pillow. She yawned three times, each one longer than its predecessor. Her body felt heavy as if it were descending, sinking into an endlessly deep cloud.

Just as she began to drift into slumber, she jolted awake. It felt like a bolt of electricity had just charged its way through her. She sat upright, torn between feeling exhausted and startled. The clock boldly displayed the time – 6:20.

"Rats, I'm late; and now everyone will be late," she muttered, dragging herself out of bed.

No time for slippers or robe, she quickly ran to Kat and then Dani, telling them to get up and hurry – they were late, and had no time for dilly-dallying. She ran to Megan's room and was pleasantly surprised to find Megan sitting up and waiting for her. As she entered, Megan stood on her bed, arms outstretched, ready for her hug. Susie quickly and readily complied.

"I heard what you told Kat and Dani," Megan confided; "so we'll skip our regular time today, and start again tomorrow," she offered.

Susie smiled. "Thanks, Megan. You're so sweet. Thank you for being so grown-up and helping me."

Megan flashed Susie a precocious grin. "You're welcome. We girls have to stick together, don't you know." She emphasized her statement with a short nod of her head, sending her blonde ringlets bouncing.

Susie couldn't help but laugh, wondering where Megan had heard that particular sentiment. "That's right," she agreed. "Now, go to the bathroom; when you get back, I'll help you choose your clothes and get dressed."

Megan shook her head slowly, making a full swing from side to side. "No, I can do it myself," she informed Susie.

Susie looked at her quizzically. "Are you sure?"

Emphatically Megan answered, "Yes!" She grinned, giving Susie a radiant smile. "But only for today 'cause we're late."

"Okay," Susie replied.

Megan tore down the hallway, heading to the bathroom as quick as she could while Susie headed to Juls' room, dread and anger mounting with each step. To be truthful, she was beginning to resent having the chore of getting Juls up every morning. The others girls, she didn't mind; but Juls was another story.

'It isn't fair that it's my responsibility to make Juls get up when everyone knows what a colossal pain she is,' Susie groused silently. 'And really, why should it be my responsibility?' she asked herself. 'After all, I'm not an adult; I can't *make* her do anything. It's not fair for me to get punished for what she does.'

Susie entered Juls' doorway, anger just bubbling below the surface. She forced herself to pause and calm herself before attempting to get Juls out of bed.

"Juls, it's 6:30," Susie stated as benignly as she could. "There's no time for your nonsense this morning. You need to get up right now."

Juls peered out from under her covers, glaring daggers at Susie. "Why didn't you wake me at six?" she demanded haughtily.

Irritated at her inference that she would have gotten up sooner, Susie glared at Juls, seething. "Since when do you get up at six? You never get up much before 6:30 no matter how many times I wake you; and you know it!" Susie's tone left no doubt as to her current state of mind.

With all the grace and fluidity of a prima ballerina, Juls rose up as she arched her back, slowly raising her arms above her head as she sat upright. She made several stretching movements that appeared more like an elegant dance than a call to her muscles to awaken. All the while her focus remained on Susie, her eyes sparkling with satisfaction.

Grinning saucily at Susie, she stated dismissively, "I require a gentle wakeup over the course of at least thirty minutes. I need to ease into my day."

Susie realized that she had fallen prey to Juls' purpose, which was to antagonize Susie – and she had allowed Juls to do so. Susie's eyes narrowed slightly as she thought, *'never again'*. From now on, one way or another, she would get Juls out of bed and on time.

Susie shrugged. "Well, today I overslept. Deal with it." She spun around and strode down the hallway to her room.

———

The remainder of the morning had gone smoothly enough. Juls wasn't speaking to her; but then, what else was new. There was always someone she wasn't on speaking terms with, and usually it was most of the residents at Glen Hollow simultaneously.

Upon arriving in the classroom that morning, they were surprised and delighted to see on each desk was a present, wrapped in bright, pretty Christmas papers and tied with ribbons and bows. Miss Emma explained that she was going home for Christmas and would not return until just before class was to restart.

Everyone was a little sad to hear that news; Miss Emma was truly a favorite, even to Juls. However, they were glad (and a little envious) for her to be able to be with her family. She showed them pictures of her family and promised to bring pictures from her Christmas. Promising to share all the details of her time away, Miss Emma elicited promises from each of them to also tell her everything they did while she was gone.

"Our first day of class will be a reunion," she said cheerfully. "Please remember to write down anything you want to share."

That was greeted with a rousing chorus of various promises to do so.

She laughed and the warmth of her laugher instilled a sense of happiness in each of them. "Who would like to be responsible for bringing pictures of your Christmas?" she asked.

There was an immediate avalanche of volunteers shouting their intent to be the one to bring pictures.

Though delighted at their overwhelmingly, enthusiastic response, she quickly restored order. Smiling affectionately, she said, "I have an idea. Let's make a scrapbook of the Christmas break."

Miss Emma paused, removing from her desk a large, padded leather scrapbook and held it up for them to see. It was a dark, hunter green with embossed gold lettering that stated, 'Our Treasured Memories'. The binding had a braided cord entwined with gold, burgundy and hunter green threads. Each end of the cord held tassels made of the same thread as the cord.

As they 'oohed' and 'ahhed', she continued explaining her idea. "There will be a lot of preparations and events between now and New Year's Day. You can capture everything in pictures, and then place them in our scrapbook."

"Who will be taking the pictures?" Jared asked.

"Yeah; and where are we going to get a camera?" Aaron chimed.

Miss Emma chuckled, and her eyes danced with glee. "It just so happens that I have a disposable camera for each of you. Each camera has forty-eight color exposures so you'll each have plenty of pictures to place in the scrapbook, and also keep some for yourself."

Lifting the lid from the box on her desk, Miss Emma began distributing the cameras, instructing that they were not waterproof, so they should all be careful. Susie figured that remark was mainly directed at Simon, Timmy and Megan.

"Now, to organize our project; Susie, Jared and Megan will choose the order of the pictures. Dani, Juls and Simon will secure the pictures in our scrapbook. Kat and Aaron will write the captions. Jose and Timmy will place the letters you write in the scrapbook and choose the sequence."

"What letters?" everyone shouted.

She grinned. "Oh, I guess I forgot to mention it. Your only homework assignment over the break is to write a letter to Santa. You may write whatever you wish; however, you must include at least one paragraph telling him what, or who, you are thankful for in your life."

Dismay and disapproval had begun finding its voice as several of the children made comments or other noises that were obviously meant to convey their great displeasure at such an odious assignment. Miss Emma took it in stride, smiling as if they were all eagerly willing to compose said letters.

After several minutes, the room fell silent. They all realized Miss Emma was still leaning against the front of her desk, unmoved, and was still smiling as she observed their discussion. After everyone had quieted, she spoke. Her voice was soft and gentle.

"Everyone, and I do mean everyone, has at least one thing or one person in their life, past or present, that has been good, and for which you are thankful. All I want you to do is to include whatever you are thankful for in your letter. You may certainly write what you don't like, or what you hope for in the future. But you must include one thing or person for which you are thankful."

She studied their faces, watching the varied expressions. "Any questions?" she asked.

No one responded.

Miss Emma chuckled. "Just so you know, I will also write a letter to Santa, and it will be placed in the scrapbook with yours. Fair is fair."

That statement seemed to relieve the group somewhat; but not nearly as much as she had hoped.

"What about pictures?" Simon asked. "Are you going to include pictures from your Christmas?"

Surprised, Miss Emma just laughed, shaking her head no. The other children began pressing her to provide pictures, parroting back to her, 'Fair is fair'. Finally she conceded. Nodding her head in agreement, she smiled and said she would be happy to provide pictures for the scrapbook.

Time to leave came all too soon. Miss Emma dismissed them, giving them ample time to be in the Dining Hall for lunch.

———

Mr. Henry and Miss Thelma were absent from lunch due to the fact they volunteered to take Miss Emma to the train station in Foxboro Station. It seemed strange for Miss Emma not to be seated across the table from her, and Susie felt a little sad that she would be gone the next two weeks.

Her pensive thoughts were soon disrupted by a chorus of loud laughter, mingling with quips and teasing. Megan, Timmy and Simon had relayed to the adults the scrapbook project. They had also warned everyone that they were going to be secret Ninja picture takers, taking pictures when everyone least expected it. For some reason, the adults thought it was funny and didn't seem to mind. That surprised Susie. It was one thing to have photos taken when you are aware they are being taken, in which case most people willingly participate. It's another thing entirely to have someone skulking around, snapping candid photos that perhaps you wouldn't want anyone to see.

Everyone was bantering good-naturedly back and forth about who would have the zaniest photos, and who would be the most caught off-guard and thus the most embarrassed. Conversation eventually wound its way to the coming festivities. From the discussions, it appeared that there was a great deal of preparations ahead, not just for the holidays but also for the guests that would begin arriving next Saturday.

Susie's mind wandered as the adults hashed back and forth all the details. She was remembering the simple holidays with Nana, and the Christmas she was six. That was the last one with her parents; now this would be the first one without Nana. That renewed realization caused her eyes to sting with tears. Blinking rapidly, she quelled their flow, returning her mind to the conversation at hand. She darted little glances at Miss Hilda and Miss Pritchett; relieved that they had not noticed her tears.

Mrs. Coppersmith was stating that she would have all the popcorn ready for stringing by Wednesday evening. Apparently they had been discussing the tree and manor decorations when Susie was mentally absent.

"So after dinner, we'll all start stringing the popcorn after we've cleared the dishes from the table," Mrs. Coppersmith informed everyone.

"I don't know how to do that," Dani said. Her sentiments were echoed by Juls, Jared and Megan.

"It's easy," Jose laughed. "Anyone can do it."

"That's true," Mrs. Coppersmith agreed. "For those that don't know how, you'll be learning a new skill come Wednesday night," she added with just a hint of a smile.

"Why are we stringing popcorn?" Jared asked.

"Popcorn strings are used to decorate the tree and other evergreens," Miss Elsa patiently explained. "It's a very old tradition, and it's also fun. We tell stories while we do it, and the time goes by so fast, you're done before you know it."

It was decided that the search for the perfect Christmas tree would be on Thursday. Once found, the men would cut it down and bring it back to the manor where everyone assists in trimming the tree.

"Me, too?" Simon asked, his face glowing with excitement.

"Yes, Simon," Miss Pritchett answered with a chuckle. "Decorating for the holidays is a family tradition, and we're a family."

The chorus of agreements from the other adults echoed as they began reminiscing about past holidays. There was talk of sleigh rides, bonfires, and the fun of decorating the manor, both inside and outside. Apparently practical jokes were a common occurrence, and everyone seemed to delight in the memories of who did what and to whom.

Jared asked if he could help in the search for the Christmas tree.

Mr. Sean laughed heartily. "It wouldn't be much of a family tradition if the children didn't help find it," he answered.

The children were ecstatic to learn that they were included in the search for the Christmas tree. They began laughing and bragging about who would be the one to find the perfect tree. Well, not all; Juls and Kat adamantly were opposed to such pursuits and loudly protested their inclusion. It was then that Miss Pritchett assured them that no one is required to participate; they could remain in the manor if that was their preference.

Miss Fiona piped in that she would need helpers in the morning to gather the pinecones and evergreen boughs, holly branches and mistletoe. "It takes time to prepare and decorate the boughs for hanging, and also for draping the staircase," she explained. "It all must be done before next Saturday."

Both Juls and Kat remained silent, but Miss Fiona had plenty of other volunteers.

Mrs. Coppersmith teasingly suggested that perhaps Juls and Kat would like to assist her in the kitchen this next week preparing all of the extra foods for the holiday season. The stunned look on their faces caused everyone, even Miss Pritchett, to burst out laughing. Susie couldn't resist laughing either. The mere thought of Juls getting her hands dirty making bread, or pies, or peeling potatoes and onions or washing a dish was hysterical. The girls were teased until finally Miss Pritchett rang the bell – she had tried to be heard over the commotion but to no avail. The bell, however, caught everyone's attention.

With an amused smile, Miss Pritchett graciously said, "Perhaps their talents can be put to better use. Juls, we know that your first love is ballet. Perhaps you would like to perform for us on Christmas Eve."

"Perform what?" Juls drily responded.

"A dance from the Nutcracker, or from Babes in Toyland," she suggested.

"By myself? I can't do that. I need props and other dancers," Juls flatly stated.

"Use your imagination, dear," Miss Hilda encouraged.

"Juls, it's a great idea," Miss Ginger told her. "Both The Nutcracker and Babes in Toyland have scenes with little children and toys. I'm certain we can help put together anything you would need. You have Megan, Simon and Timmy available to be the little children in whichever scene you choose. I'm certain some of the other children will be happy to help as well." (The Munchkin's eyes grew wide in surprise at this idea, and they began looking at each other and at Miss Ginger.)

Juls' eyes lit up with glee, and she began to genuinely smile. "Okay," she agreed. "I'll do it if they'll help."

Miss Ginger looked at them and asked, "Well, will you help Juls?"

Megan was the first to say yes, bubbling over with excitement. Simon grudgingly agreed, but only because Susie insistently nudged him under the table. Timmy finally agreed when Simon told him it could be fun.

"Excellent," Miss Pritchett commended them. "We look forward to seeing your performance. Shall we set the time for three in the afternoon, Christmas Eve?"

"Yes," Juls responded elatedly.

"Good; now Kat," Miss Pritchett turned attention to her; "with your artistic talent, would you like to assist Miss Taryn in designing the wreaths and the table decorations?"

Kat shrugged. "I don't think I'd be any good at it," she replied.

"Nonsense," Miss Taryn rebuffed her. "I've seen your artwork; we all have. I need the help. Mama is willing to help, but there's more work than just the two of us can do. If you're not interested, just say so. I'll get someone else to help us."

Kat's sideways glance at Miss Taryn was one of suspicion. Miss Taryn never shared her design duties and jealously guarded her position. Kat sighed. She knew she should participate in something for the holidays, but she really wasn't looking forward to spending time with Miss Taryn. Only thing worse would be to spend time with Juls. Kat forced a smile, then gruffly agreed to assist Miss Taryn.

That settled, Miss Hilda announced that there would be additional assignments to help during the holidays due to the impending visit of additional family members. Beginning Monday, Dani would have morning laundry duty assisting Miss Fiona; Susie would have morning kitchen duty; Jared would have afternoon laundry duty assisting Miss Elsa, and Juls would have afternoon kitchen duty. Jose would be in charge of hanging the greeting cards along the foyer staircase. The following week, those that weren't given an assignment today would be given one then. "After all," Miss Hilda said cheerfully; "we must all help each other with the extra work."

When lunch was finished, Miss Ginger quickly snared Timmy and Simon and made a grab for Megan. It was naptime for them; they weren't happy about it and were determined to convince her that they did not need naps. When their logic failed, they began pleading and whining, and finally begging to be released from naptime. Miss Ginger wasn't assuaged, informing them that their present behavior was proof that they did need naptime. With a tone reminiscent of a drill sergeant and a firm grasp on all three, she maneuvered them out the door. Their whining could be heard for a considerable time after they had left the Dining Hall, gradually diminishing the further from the Hall they went.

Susie decided that now would be a good time to slip away and find the unicorn statue that Miss Pritchett had spoken of last Sunday. From her bedroom window, she could see its horn and the very tip of its head. By day, it glistened in the sun's light; by night, it seemed to glow in the moonlight. The thought of it enticed her, beckoned her, and she was determined to find it.

Simon would be down for his nap for an hour. Afterward, he would be serving his sentence with Miss Hilda and be occupied with folding towels for two hours. That would give her ample time to find the statue, and then spend some quality time alone in the Library.

Unusual for daytime, the corridors were clear; Susie didn't have to hide from anyone and that gave her a sense of relief. Hastily she put on her coat, scarf, hat and gloves. Dashing out of the Cloak Room and into the corridor, she hurried to the door, praying her mission would not be interrupted.

Pulling the door open, the blast of icy air took her breath away, causing her to shiver. Susie lost no time in covering her nose and mouth with her woolen scarf as she ran along the pergola. At the first opening, she darted out of the pergola and down the flagstone path. Susie continued running, hoping it would help to keep her warm. It didn't; her teeth began chattering within seconds of leaving the pergola.

Susie ran along, taking path after path, winding her way ever closer to the area where she thought the statue was located. Ten minutes later, she finally found it. She rounded a bend and discovered it neatly tucked in an alcove of hedges. It stood on a large granite platform, bearing a plaque that said:

TRUTH
Seek: earnestly search, you will find it.
Believe: once found, you must choose it.
Live: choose it, you will live.

"What does that mean? ... Weird," she muttered.

Turning her attention to the statue itself, Susie was awestruck by the impressive, realistic horse in front of her. Granted the horn wasn't typical of a horse, but surely the artist must have used one of the Evermore's horses as the model for this statue, Susie mused.

The white granite statue sparkled in the sunlight, causing little bursts of light to dazzle her eyes. It was like watching the brilliant stars twinkling in the velvety blackness of a clear night sky.

'Miss Pritchett is right,' Susie thought; 'it is amazing.' Instinctively her hand reached up and touched the nose, half expecting the statue to come alive. ... It didn't.

"How did the artist do it?" Susie whispered. "How could he make you look so real? ... How did he make the dolphins, and the ocean waves look real?" she softy asked the statue.

Realizing that her toes and fingers were beginning to become numb, Susie turned to leave. It was then she saw the carved inscription in the side of the platform.

It read:

A refrain of hope, a song of mirth,
With joy, dance at the noble one's birth;
Since creation's dawn, through days of yore,
They reveal the Way to Truth's One Door.

A heart that's pure is required to see,
This glor'ous one, so noble and free;
For he will come, revealing himself,
To one whose heart is of purest wealth.

Not silver, gold or such trifling things,
Could e'er obtain its priceless off'ring;
To Truth's Purveyor sing loud and strong,
Your reward will be your heart's new song.

When sought by a heart so pure and true,
The Truth's Purveyor shall come to you;
In a lightning flash so white and bright,
You'll wing away on heavenly flight.

"That's the song Nana taught us," Susie whispered in astonishment.

Time seemed to stand still as she stared at the poem. She no longer heard the music of the birds, or the wind rustling the trees nor felt the frigid December air. The sunlight seemed to become brighter, causing everything around her to fade from view. Except for the unicorn, all was lost in a sea of the bright haze. The unicorn appeared to glow as if he was somehow causing the changes. For the briefest of moments, Susie thought she saw the unicorn move. She was almost certain she saw the head nod. Within an instant everything returned to normal, and she was once again freezing.

Gazing at the magnificent face of the unicorn one more time, Susie smiled - the sunlight had reflected just then off of the eyes, making it appear as if the unicorn had blinked. She patted the neck of the statue. "I'll be back when it's warmer," she promised.

Susie turned and ran all the way back to the manor. Once inside, she began shedding her outer garments as she trotted down the corridor to the Cloak Room.

———

Upon entering the Library, Susie immediately felt uplifted. She loved the atmosphere in here. It was quiet and peaceful. Susie began down the aisle toward their usual reading place when she heard laughter. It was coming from the east side of the Library.

Curiosity getting the better of her, Susie changed course; she began walking toward the source of the laughter. As she neared the east side, she thought she recognized one of the voices – Miss Fiona. The other one she wasn't certain who it could be; it didn't really sound much like anyone at Glen Hollow.

She stepped out of the aisle, entering the wide reading area of the east side. No one was there. Susie looked around; she was alone. She sighed. "Maybe they went down one of the side aisles as I was coming down the main one," she reasoned.

Suddenly there was a hint of lilac in the air, and the soft knell of a wind chime. Susie froze mid-step, remembering the events from Tuesday and from

Wednesday nights. Nothing happened. No lady in white, no voices and no music. The scent of lilac and the sound of the wind chime suddenly stopped.

Slowly and feeling a little uneasy, Susie walked to the fireplace, nervously glancing around with each step. Standing in front of the fireplace, she stretched her hands toward the flames, warming herself in the heat of its embers. She turned around, allowing the heat to warm her back, giving her the opportunity to casually inspect the area. Looking all around the vicinity, she saw no one. Whoever had been here had left along the far aisle, and must have done so at the same time she entered from the main aisle.

"That's the only reasonable explanation," she told herself.

A flash of light suddenly appeared in her peripheral vision, and she turned to see what it was. It came from a small alcove near where the east wall met the north wall. Gleaming faintly in the soft light of the wall sconces was a beautiful bookcase made of oak and beveled glass. Susie began walking toward it, drawn to it as if she were a moth and it a flame. Each step caused a slight tingling sensation along her spine. She shivered as the goose bumps rose on her skin.

The legs of the bookcase bowed gracefully outward as they descended to the floor, resting atop carved feet that resembled the paws of a cat. The front of the top piece had the vague appearance of a crown; its center rose into a peak higher than its sides. A carving, unique and intricate in its detail, was in the center of the crown. The carving clearly displayed an oak tree, and standing in front of the tree were three creatures: a tiger, a unicorn and a wolf.

The center section of the bookcase had three glass shelves, each shelf holding four large books. Their leather bindings were a rich, midnight blue color. Embossed along the spine in gold lettering was the title, 'Histories', and directly under it was the word 'Volume'. The only apparent difference in the books was in the Roman Numerals that followed the word 'Volume'.

Susie pulled gently on the silver handle. It was locked. She felt extremely disappointed. Her search for the key was cut short by the sound of the mantle clock chiming the four o'clock hour.

"Later," she promised the bookcase as she left it to go meet her reading group for their afternoon reading session.

Susie ran all the way to the entrance, not wanting them to wander away because she's late. They were definitely waiting for her; she heard them well before she reached the door. Apparently they were in the middle of a very heated dispute, arguing who would get to choose the book that was to be read. Susie opened the door, telling them to come in, and to stop arguing.

Noticing that Megan had brought a book with her, Susie decided that they would read it. The boys were none too happy with that decision, and began to strenuously object. Susie held up her hand, and they quickly became quiet. She told them that they would take turns choosing; today it would be Megan since she already had a book. The boys glared at Megan, still unhappy with the decision. Megan responded by slipping her hand into Susie's, giving Susie a sweet, little smile.

Susie returned Megan's smile. As cheerfully as possible, she said she was glad they were all going to be friends. The sullen look the boys gave her cast serious doubt as to the veracity of the word 'friends'. Susie sighed internally; it was definitely going to be an uphill battle to get the boys to be friends with Megan; but Susie was determined.

As she guided them toward their reading area, Susie asked Simon how his towel folding duty went. Simon rolled his eyes, made an exaggerated horror face, and bemoaned how awful it was. He had to fold towels for "two whole hours, and some were really big". Then he started giggling. His eyes sparkled as he bounced along, walking backwards so he could face Susie. He admitted that it wasn't so bad; Miss Hilda was really nice, and she told the funniest stories.

When they entered the reading area, Simon immediately ran and jumped into 'his' chair, motioning for Timmy to join him. Susie walked past, choosing instead to sit on the hearth of the fireplace. Motioning to them, she told them to come sit on the carpet in front of her. Megan quickly joined her. Timmy and Simon slowly complied, heads bent toward each other as they whispered and giggled.

"May I pick the book tomorrow?" Timmy asked.

"Yes," Susie replied; "and Simon can choose on Monday."

"Who chooses on Sunday?" Megan asked.

"No one," Susie answered. "We probably won't have time for our Story Time," she explained. "I think Reverend Tillman tells a story after lunch, so I guess in a way that is our Story Time."

"Okay," Megan shrugged, her face still saddened at the thought of not having Story Time with Susie. Then she noticed the whispering and giggling between Simon and Timmy as they looked at her and then each other.

Megan's eyes narrowed as she demanded, "Are you talking about me?"

Both boys shook their heads and declared, 'Nope!", then burst into another round of giggles.

"You are so!" she challenged.

Again they denied that she was the subject of their laughter. The fact that they were giggling throughout their denials did little to assuage Megan's belief. Unconvinced, Megan began to pout.

"I would never be mean to you," she told them, her voice as equally sad as her face.

Timmy and Simon giggled, and then gave her the "oh, please" look. Simon was trying his best not to giggle, and was completely unsuccessful

"We're not being mean to you," he declared between chuckles.

"And we're not talking about you," Timmy added, snickering.

"Oh, really," Megan snapped back at them.

"You are such a girl," Timmy responded, making a goofy face at her. "We were laughing because we still have a Story Time that you don't."

Simon began bobbing his head in agreement, giggling gleefully. Like a dam filled to overflowing, he burst out the secret. "We're best buds so we have a secret Story Time."

Realizing that the boys were on the verge of disclosing the secret, Susie hastily intervened. Attempting to derail the subject, she reminded them that they only have an hour left for Story Time. Susie opened the book and held it up in front of her, telling them to be quiet so she can start reading.

It was to no avail.

"No you don't," Megan countered Simon's declaration.

"Yes we do. We're best buds so we have a secret hiding place, and a secret code, and now we have a secret Story Time every night," Simon informed her.

In an effort to show disdain, Megan folded her arms across her chest, giving her head a little toss. "I don't care," she protested. "I have secrets, too. I have secret friends, and I have secret tea parties every day."

"Secret Story Time beats a tea party any ol' day," Simon guffawed. He and Timmy giggled incessantly at this last taunt.

Susie sat quietly, giving the boys enough rope with which to hang themselves. They had no idea just how smart Megan truly is; but she was certain they were about to find out first hand.

Megan pressed her lips tightly together, peering at them as if they were road kill. Abruptly she changed tactics, smiling at them, a saucy, little smile. She laughed, rolled her eyes and told them she didn't believe them. After all, they are just boys, and everybody knows boys will say anything.

Timmy eyes grew wide with indignation. Hotly, he defended his best bud. "We didn't make it up. Susie is going to read to us every night right after Miss Ginger leaves."

"That's right," Simon chimed haughtily; "you ask Susie."

Suddenly, Simon's eyes grew wide with dread, and his face registered the realization of what he and Timmy had just done. Megan's face, however, registered satisfaction; the same kind of satisfaction you would see on the face of a cat that had just finished a bowl of warm cream. Panicked, Simon's eyes darted to Susie. She was laughing! She had that I-told-you-so look on her face. Puzzled and confused, Simon just stared at her. He thought she'd be mad.

"Sorry boys," Susie said, amused. "You broke the rule. Now Megan knows, and it isn't a secret any longer."

"You better not tell," Timmy growled, glaring at her.

Megan's brow began to furrow; her eyes began to mist, and her lips began to quiver. "Friends don't squeal," she said softly; "and you're my friends."

Tears began to roll down her cheeks, obvious to all that her feelings were genuinely hurt. Megan wasn't a tattletale; Susie knew this to be true from her time spent with Megan. In spite of being so young, Megan had a deeply-rooted, intuitive sense of honor. Even the other girls could attest to that fact; they'd all been the recipients of her discretion at one time or another, some more than once.

Susie stared harshly at Simon, and then at Timmy; both boys quickly averted their eyes, focusing their attention onto their shoes.

She turned to Megan and smiled soothingly. "Megan," Susie asked; "would you like to join our secret Story Time?"

The boys were horribly dismayed. After all, how could Susie do such a thing? First they looked at each other, then at Megan and finally at Susie. Simon began shaking his head, hoping to get Susie to retract the invitation.

Sniffing dramatically, Megan gave Susie her best sad face as she timidly answered. "Yes, but I can't because they don't want me."

Susie leveled her gaze at the duo and replied firmly, "Sure they do; otherwise they wouldn't have told you about it. Right, boys?"

Neither said anything; they just stared at their shoes, feeling miserable.

"I said, right boys?" she repeated curtly.

They mumbled something that was completely unintelligible causing Susie to chuckle. "Thank you, boys, for your sweet invitation to Megan." She smiled at Megan. "Well, Megan, are you going to join us?"

Megan grinned, her face beaming with elation. She began bobbing her head up and down. "Yes!" she declared emphatically.

"Great. Every night, after Miss Cora and Miss Ginger leave, you and I will meet Simon and Timmy in Simon's room," Susie explained.

Then she pointed slowly to each of them, one by one. "It's very important that none of you tell anyone else. This has to be kept a secret, our secret only. Do you understand?"

They all readily agreed to keep the secret, crossing their hearts and pledging to stick needles in their eyes if they lie. Susie quickly informed them that that punishment would not be necessary.

Holding the book up in front of her once again, she told them to settle down and pay attention. They only had thirty minutes left so she would have to read fast. As they inched closer for a better view of the pictures, it occurred to Susie that this would not work for the secret Story Time. Simon's bed was not big enough for them to sit in a semi-circle.

Susie quickly told them of the dilemma. Smiling, she admitted she had the solution – she would tell them one of Nana's stories every night. At first, Megan and Timmy weren't thrilled with the change of plan. But once they saw how excited Simon was, they changed their minds, especially when Simon assured them that Nana's stories were better than most books.

That resolved, Susie told them all to quiet down so she could read to them. Quickly they complied, hands clasped and resting in their laps as they leaned forward in anticipation of the story to come.

———

Susie, with Megan's hand firmly clasped in her own, peered out into the corridor. It was empty. She thrust the door open, pulling Megan into the corridor. Scooping Megan up into her arms, she made a mad dash across the corridor to the Boys Dorm.

Motioning for Megan to be quiet, she gently eased opened the door and peeked inside. Susie smiled at Megan, pushing the door wide open. They slipped inside, and Susie gently closed the door. She set Megan down, and they ran down the hall to Simon's room. Timmy and Simon were there, quietly waiting on Simon's bed as instructed. Megan climbed onto his bed, setting herself next to Timmy as Susie sat at the end of the bed.

"Everyone ready?" she whispered.

"Yes," came three loudly whispered responses in perfect unison.

Susie giggled softly. "You're like the three musketeers," she told them. "You're in agreement, and of one accord."

All three gave her puzzled looks which only made her laugh again.

"I thought you said I was a Munchkin?" Megan asked.

"Well, you are; and so are Timmy and Simon," she responded. To resolve the baffled look on the boy's faces, she explained, "Munchkins are adorable, and cute, and …"

"Little!" Megan whispered loudly, finishing the sentence for Susie.

At first, the boys wrinkled their noses in disgust at such a description for them until Susie told them that being a Munchkin made them very special. They decided, in that case, it was okay for Susie to call them a Munchkin, especially once they learned that Megan had already received the title.

"Okay, let's get started," she told them; "this story is one of Simon's favorites."

Simon's eyes sparkled, and his face lit up with anticipation. "Is it the one about Ketar?" he asked.

"Yes," she confirmed.

Simon began giggling, gleefully clapping his hands and bouncing on the bed. Susie promptly shushed him, and he settled down.

"This is the story about a little boy named Ketar. He is no ordinary boy. He is a magical creature known to us as fairies. He lives in the beautiful fairy kingdom of Shashur," she began, using her best storytelling voice just like Nana had done.

Chapter 15

DISCOVERIES ABOUND

It was Saturday at last! Before going to bed last night, Susie had set her alarm for three, placing the alarm clock under her pillow. That way, no one else would be awakened when it began its high-pitched trill. She woke feeling energized, eager to continue her exploration of the manor. Finding time and privacy in which to roam was not an easy accomplishment. Class time, homework, chores and Story Time narrowed considerably the amount of time available for such pursuits. And it seemed as if there was always someone around; if not the staff, it was Simon or one of the other children. It had been a week now since she and Simon had arrived at Glen Hollow; and, to date, she had explored very little of the manor. Very little, that is, in comparison to the whole.

Returning her alarm clock to its proper place on her nightstand, Susie quietly slipped out of bed. Cautiously making her way to her dresser, she was very careful not to step on the floorboards that creaked. Ever so slowly she eased the bottom dresser drawer open to prevent the squeak it makes when opened at a normal pace. Susie selected a pair of her dark pink jeans and then, just as cautiously, slid the drawer shut. Proceeding to the next drawer, Susie repeated her efforts and removed a light pink sweatshirt and then eased that drawer shut. Last, she opened the top drawer, accomplishing her final tasks of retrieving her undergarments, socks and a pair of white cotton gloves.

After assembling her clothes, Susie shed her pj's and dressed quickly, stuffing the cotton gloves into her back pocket. She pulled her hair into a ponytail, securing it with a neon pink fluffy band and added a pink, lacey headband to secure her bangs. After all, exploring was serious business, and she didn't want to be distracted by her bangs falling into her eyes at the wrong moment. Hastily Susie scooped up her tennis shoes (pink, of course), making short work of putting them on before she crept down the hallway to the Common Area. Stealthily, she crossed the Common

Area and silently slipped into the corridor, after she first had verified it was empty. Gently Susie closed the door behind her.

———

Susie felt an elation she hadn't felt in months – not since before Nana's passing. Like a gazelle at play, she sprinted along the corridor to the foyer landing and down the stairs to the first level, taking the stairs two at a time. She was excited, exuberant even, at the thought of having the manor to herself. She could explore anywhere; well, anywhere that is except the east wing. The doors on all three levels were locked and stayed that way, which was a mystery yet to be solved since no one apparently knew why, not even Miss Pritchett.

Last night, while she had been waiting for sleep to come, she had decided her first exploration would be the Library. During the guided tour last Sunday, Susie fell in love with this room. She loved to read. She especially loved old books for they gave her a sense of history, of continuity; and this Library had thousands of books. She had immediately felt at home in the Library, a kindred spirit, despite its immense size. It invoked a reverence for knowledge, for learning; and Susie decided from that first day she would spend as much time here as she possibly could. The Library afforded her a sense of sanctuary since the other children didn't come here. At least, they hadn't this past week. Other than having afternoon Story Time, the Library seemed to be vacant most of the time; she hoped that trend would continue.

Susie darted through the south wing entrance on the first floor, dashing around the corner and entered the west wing corridor. Slowing her pace to a fast walk, she glanced briefly at the portraits of Gabriel and Angel as she sailed past them. Mentally she wished them a good morning and was almost certain she heard two distinct sounds (like a soft whinny) as if they were also telling her good morning. She giggled silently and ran on to the Library, determined not to be deterred from her mission.

She thought of Simon as she neared the Library and laughed, remembering Thursday's little mishap. The memory of Miss Hilda's face upon seeing Simon on his amusement ride, and Simon's face when his punishment had been pronounced, was so comical Susie couldn't help but laugh. Simon's interest in reading was increasing with each passing day; and fortunately, being reprimanded and punished didn't derail Simon's love of books.

Instinctively, Susie reached for the heavy door on the right and pulled it opened. She stepped inside and realized she was still smiling, grinning actually. Simon had that effect on her -- and most everyone, she acknowledged with amusement.

Having just entered the darkened library, Susie paused inside the doorway to allow her eyes time to adjust to the dim light. She knew she couldn't use the main lighting; whoever passed this way would see the light - not that she wasn't allowed to be in here; she was. If anyone was actually up and about this time of morning, they might, however, question why she was here so early and what was so important. Susie just didn't want to be interrupted, so no main lights; and hence the early wake–up time. Small Tiffany lamps, used as night lights, were placed strategically around the Library. Their faint, soft light provided very little illumination initially; but now her eyes had adjusted sufficiently.

Confident she could now make her way through the Library without stumbling or bumping into anything, Susie sprinted toward the far corner of the east wall where yesterday she had seen the bookcase. Now, at last, she had the Library and the bookcase to herself.

As she approached the bookcase, she had that tingling sensation again. An illusion of a halo seemed to surround it.

"An effect created," Susie told herself in an effort to steady her nerves; "by the soft light of the wall sconces on each side of the bookcase."

Susie searched the small writing desk near the bookcase. No key. She searched the other desks in the area but without success. Next she searched the various ornamental boxes on the tables and on the fireplace mantle. Still no key. Hastening to the other study areas, Susie searched those desks, and anything that she thought might hold the key. She didn't find it. Slightly frustrated, she returned to the Library's east side and dropped into a chair by the fireplace. The mantle clock began softly chiming five o'clock.

The sound of the glowing embers popping and crackling in the fireplace gained Susie's attention in its cry for another log. Arising from her chair,

Susie retrieved another log and placed it on the fire. After several minutes of waiting for the log to start burning, Susie realized that more kindling was need so she added some kindling to the fire. Immediately the kindling took hold, and the fire began dancing upward onto the log. She warmed her hands for a moment before turning her attention back to the bookcase.

From the corner of her eye, Susie caught a glimpse of an odd shape against the wall. The fire cast just enough light for Susie to see it pressed up against the wall behind the library ladder. Curious, she stared at it, trying to determine just what would be placed there. As she concentrated on the object, it dawned on her that it was a small step stool. At first she thought it strange that a two-step stepstool would be in use when there was the ladder. She dismissed it with a shrug. Until she realized, it wasn't *for* the wall bookcase!

Excitedly, Susie hurried over to the step stool, picked it up and placed it in front of the oak bookcase. Stepping onto its top step, she still had to really stretch to reach the small ledge in front of the crown. Pressing her right hand firmly against the wood frame of the cabinet door, Susie braced herself. Cautiously she reached up, and the fingers of her left hand searched diligently for the elusive key. She was rewarded; she found the key. It was pushed back from the edge, directly under the carved unicorn.

"Yes!" she exclaimed as she jumped down.

The key weighed heavily in her hand, and appeared to be made of silver. Quickly Susie inserted the key and turned it. The distinctive click of the lock sent another round of cascading tingles down her spine. Cautiously she pulled the silver handle; and, this time, the door opened. Immediately the scent of the leather wafted outward, mingling with the scent of antiquated vellum parchment and antique ink.

Removing her gloves from her back pocket, Susie put them on, interlocking her fingers and pressing the gloves firmly down onto her hands. Ever so carefully, she removed the first book labeled 'Histories Volume I' and reverently carried it to the desk.

Gently Susie laid the book on the desk and switched on the desk lamp. For a moment she sat very still just gazing at the book, absorbing the beauty of its simple elegance. Then her hand, in its white cotton glove, gently caressed the cover. Its deep blue color was now apparent, sharply contrasting against her white glove as the light from the desk lamp shone upon it.

'Much like the ocean appears black at night,' she thought; 'and blue again in the light of day.'

Susie could hardly contain her excitement; this was an incredible find. She had learned from Nana that antique books were fragile, and must be handled with the utmost care. Nana had several such books; most were written in Latin, and a few in another, very ancient language that Nana had promised to teach her someday. Susie winced slightly as the sting of Nana's loss renewed in her mind. She sighed and then scolded herself, reminding herself 'to focus and not be distracted'. Slowly and deeply she inhaled and then, just as slowly, gently released her breath.

Her gloved, left fingers lightly touched the gold lettering of the book's spine as she admired its brilliance. Peeking at the edges of the book, she saw that the thick, vellum pages were also gilded. She opened the book. Her eyes widened; she inhaled rapidly, and she held her breath, spellbound at the beauty of the page displayed.

She exhaled softly as she whispered, "Awesome."

The title page had an ornate border, an intertwining, lacey pattern. It was outlined in midnight blue while the lacey pattern was decorated in gold, silver and copper. Gleaming softly, the metal inlays appeared to dance as the light from the desk lamp flickered across the page. Each corner of the page comprised a diamond shape inside of a circle, and were connected to each other by intertwining tendrils of the lacey border. A beautifully illustrated painting filled each of the diamonds, and the detail – well, it was mesmerizing. Susie just stared in wonder at the magnificent paintings. So realistic were they that it was almost like looking through a window at the real place or object instead of viewing an image.

The top right diamond contained a painting of a body of water with a shoreline partially along its right side, suggesting a lake, or the ocean, or even perhaps a wide river. The hues of blue varied, creating the effect of waves in perpetual motion.

In the top left diamond was a meadow with trees of various sizes and shapes, slightly bowed as if enduring a strong breeze. Leaves were blowing along the ground while others were captured in a small whirlwind, swirling ever upward. A large, grayish-white cloud, having a semblance of a face, dominated the brilliant blue sky. Like the paintings of Old Man Winter, the face in the cloud was blowing down toward the trees, evident by the translucent ghostly puffs that were swirling and streaming downward.

The diamond on the bottom right contained an illustration of a mountain. Its peak was snow-capped, and the meadow below was green and lush with grass. All along the mountain sides were clusters of trees, diminishing in size as they advanced upwards toward the peak.

The bottom left diamond contained the figure of a solitary, dazzling blue flame. The vibrant hues of blue were arranged in such a way as to give the optical illusion of a living flame.

Slightly below the top border, in the center, was a crest; the same crest as was carved into the crown of the bookcase. There was an addition to this crest that the carving did not have - a tri-ring border encircling the crest and edged in a thin band of gold. The first ring after the gold band was a thin band of midnight blue followed by a wide circle of ebony, which was followed by another thin ring of midnight blue. Ending the crest's border was yet another thin band of gold. In each border ring were symbols, no two alike.

The background of the crest's inner circle was a pastoral illustration of a lush, green meadow, and a sky strewn with cottony clouds floating on a sea of cerulean blue. Prominently featured in the center of the scene were three creatures; on the left sat a white tiger, in the center stood a white unicorn and on the right sat a white wolf. Behind the creatures was a mighty oak tree, its branches thick with foliage and acorns.

Susie looked closely at the symbols printed in the border rings. Some looked vaguely familiar. She kept staring at them until she realized why they looked familiar. Not only were some of them in the foyer floor of the manor, but some she had seen in Nana's books. Books, Nana said, that had belonged to their family for many years, and would one day belong to both she and Simon. Those books, along with their other possessions, were to be delivered later today.

Susie could hardly wait for their belongings to be delivered! She felt the adrenaline rush; her heart racing, her breathing quickening at the thoughts, the ideas and the possibilities swirling and popping in her mind. She closed her eyes, steadied her breathing and willed herself to be calm, to focus. She opened her eyes and continued examining the book.

Just below the crest was the book's title. The hand lettering, done in exceptionally precise calligraphy, was in midnight blue ink and outlined in gold leaf. It was surrounded by an outline of a box in the same midnight blue ink as the lettering.

The title simply stated:

History of the Evermore Family
Volume I

Cautiously, Susie turned the page and began reading its short declaration:

The Evermore Family began in Ancient Days, in the Time before Time.

Their traditions have been meticulously passed down from generation to generation, in secret, from one Keeper to the next. They have been recorded in the Journals of the Keepers.

These volumes record only their lineage, not their secrets. The most ancient of Journals have not been translated. I do not know their native tongue, and thus those Journals are not recorded here in these Volumes. The journals that have been translated into these Volumes reflect a lineage of nearly seven thousand years.

I am not a Keeper; my beloved wife, Josephine, was. I do this to honor her memory and that of her lineage.

Published This Date: In the Year of Our Lord, May 05, 1852

Vols. I through XII

The chiming of the clock broke Susie's concentration. In panic she saw the time: 5:45.

Where had the time gone! Quickly she closed the book and hastened to the bookcase, returning the volume with great care. Susie gently shut the door, locked the cabinet and returned the key to its hidden location under the unicorn. Carefully she returned the stepstool back against the wall, under the ladder, exactly how she found it.

Stealing one last look at the clock as she ran past it, Susie increased her speed. She had nine minutes to get back to the Dorm and awaken the girls on time, or explain why she was late. Hurriedly she ran toward the Library entrance and out the door.

———

Immediately after breakfast, Miss Pritchett took Susie aside. "Please come with me, Susie. I have a chore that I am assigning to you for today," she said as she gently guided Susie toward the spiral staircase located just outside the kitchen.

"It's an important task," she stated; "one that requires someone who doesn't need constant supervision. You are that someone, Susie. You're nearly twelve, and are certainly old enough to perform chores without constant supervision."

Susie nodded her head in agreement; Nana hadn't supervised her chores since she was eight.

Miss Pritchett smiled. "We have several attic rooms that are empty, and one in particular is perfect to use as a workroom. However, before it can be used, it must be cleaned. Mr. Henry has already cleaned the chimney, the firebox and its grate, and he has stocked the wood bin. Miss Thelma will finish her tasks as soon as you have finished yours."

"My tasks?" Susie repeated.

"Yes. I want you to clean and polish the andirons, clean the fireplace tools, vacuum the floor, dust the storage shelving and clean the windows. Mr. Henry has replaced the light bulbs in the light fixtures as needed; however, you will need to clean the glass globes. Miss Thelma has already taken the supplies you will need to the attic room so that you may get started immediately."

"But what about my regular chores?" Susie asked.

"I've reassigned them for today only," Miss Pritchett responded. "Come along; we're wasting time." And with that said, she headed up the stairs. Susie sighed, following her up the stairwell.

When they reached the third floor landing, Miss Pritchett stopped and turned to face Susie. "Remember, today is an exception to the rule," Miss Pritchett reminded her. "And what is the rule regarding the third floor?"

"Children are not allowed on the third floor because it is the staff's residence," she responded.

Miss Pritchett smiled. "Very good, Susie. Now, come; the attic door is down the front corridor." She quickly headed toward it with Susie just a step behind her.

Upon their arrival at the attic door, Miss Pritchett removed from her pocket a long, thin black key. Its end was square, having four prongs that protruded downward, curving slightly inward like the fangs of a snake. The handle was a large, open circle with three interlocking circles within it. She unlocked the door and returned the key to her pocket.

"Susie, please bring that doorstop over here," she requested, gesturing toward it.

Susie walked across the corridor to an ornate accent table to retrieve the doorstop placed next to it. The doorstop was small (about six inches tall), brownish in color and looked like an acorn.

'It's too small,' Susie thought; 'it'll never hold that big door.'

In a fluid motion, she leaned down, stretched her arm out, grasped the acorn and …was totally surprised! It didn't budge. Her graceful motion came to an abrupt, and comical, halt.

"What is this made of?" she asked between huffs. Using both hands to lift and carry it, she still struggled with its weight.

Miss Pritchett smiled and chuckled. "It's made of cast iron, and makes for a very effective doorstop."

"Totally," Susie grunted in agreement as she placed the doorstop in front of the door.

She stepped back and looked into the gloomy entrance. Only the first few steps were visible; the rest of its steep stairway was swallowed up in the darkness. She had that tingling feeling again.

Miss Pritchett stepped up onto the first step, reached up and flipped a switch; a soft light flooded the stairwell, dispelling the gloom and darkness.

"Be careful, Susie, not to trip," Miss Pritchett warned her. "The stairway is wide; but it is steep, and the steps are somewhat close together," she said, continuing her ascent up into the attic.

Susie tentatively followed her, holding tightly to the handrail. Upon reaching the top of the steps, Miss Pritchett flipped another light switch, and the room was bathed in a bright light.

Her supplies were indeed waiting for her. Miss Thelma had set up a utility table; on it were rolls of paper towels, bottles of window cleaner, wood cleaner, brass cleaner, multipurpose cleaner, dry cloths, a box of trash bags, a dust pan and a pair of rubber gloves. Leaning against the table was a broom and a dust mop. A large ShopVac was placed beside the table. Rounding out the supplies was a tall waste basket sitting next to the table.

Miss Pritchett picked up a clipboard from the table and showed it to Susie. "This is your checklist. As you complete each task, mark it off. There is much to do, as you can see, so I'll leave you to it."

Tilting her head downward ever so slightly, Miss Pritchett peered over her reading glasses at Susie. "I expect you to do a proper job, Susie, and in a timely fashion," she stated, handing Susie the clipboard.

After several awkward moments of silence, Susie averted her gaze to the floor. She muttered, "Yes, ma'am."

"Do you have any questions, Susie?"

Susie nodded, still focused on the floor in front of her. "How will I know when it's lunch time?" she asked softly.

"I will send someone for you early enough to allow you plenty of time to clean up, and change your clothes before lunch. Any other questions?"

"Umm, yes. There's no bathroom here, is there?"

"No, Susie, there isn't. When you need a bathroom break, you may use the bathroom in your Dorm Room. Any other questions?"

Susie hesitated, pressing her lips tightly together. A fierce determination filled her. She stood up straight and looked directly at Miss Pritchett. "I read to Simon in the Library every day at four. Will I still be able to do that?"

"That depends entirely on you, Susie. When you've finished your task, then the rest of the day is yours. Are there any other questions?"

Susie shook her head. "No, ma'am."

"Very well, then; I'll leave you to it," Miss Pritchett said and headed for the stairwell.

Pausing at the landing, she turned around and asked, "Susie, what's the rule regarding chores?"

Susie parroted, "Any chore worth doing is worth doing well."

Miss Pritchett nodded her head once and asked, "And what is the rule regarding the quality of chores performed?"

Susie sighed as she said, "Slackers don't eat."

Miss Pritchett smiled and responded, "Very good, Susie. You should be able to be finished by three this afternoon. I will inspect your work at that time. If you have not finished, or should your work be improper, I will inspect it again at five. If, at that time, you still are not finished, or the quality is unacceptable, you will not have dinner. You will, however, have breakfast tomorrow morning. After that, only when the work is properly finished will you join us for meals."

Miss Pritchett gave Susie a nod of dismissal, turned and descended the steps, leaving Susie to her task.

Susie surveyed the attic room. It wasn't overly large; she guessed it to be about thirty feet in length and maybe forty feet wide. Granted the stairwell took a chunk out of the width, but not too much.

On the north wall were three, large Palladian windows that encompassed nearly the entire wall, having barely a foot of wall space between the windows. Beneath each window were wooden benches, solidly anchored to the wall and to the floor.

'On a sunny day', thought Susie contentedly; 'this room will be bright with sunlight. …. But, not today,' she sighed.

Turning, Susie faced the table that was loaded with supplies. For a moment, she felt a little daunted at the task that lay before her. Shaking her head, she forced herself to remain positive, dislodging the negative feelings – "No problem," she told herself. "Just like Nana always said; I can do anything I set my mind to do. I just have to want to do it."

With determination of spirit, Susie strode to the table. Taking one of the paper towels, she saturated it with cleaner, walked over to the center window and rubbed a small circle free of its grime.

It was cloudy and gray outside; the forecast had been for snow and lots of it over the next few days. She peered outside through the little opening and saw that the flakes had already begun to sporadically fall. They were big and fluffy, floating and swirling down to the ground. Most were melting as soon as they touched the ground, but she knew within a few hours that would change.

Turning away from the window, Susie began mentally developing her cleaning strategy. It dawned on her that the room actually *was* bright. She looked up at the ceiling light fixture above her. It was clean. She looked at the next one; it also was clean. She inspected the other seven. They were all clean. Someone had cleaned the ceiling light fixtures in addition to installing new bulbs.

"Thank you Mr. Henry," Susie said in a sing-song fashion.

Swiftly Susie headed to the fireplace, warming herself for a moment before starting her monumental task. The flagstone fireplace, in the center of the east wall, was six feet wide and rose all the way to the ceiling. Its hearth, made of the same stone, rose about three inches off the floor and extended out about eighteen inches in front of the fireplace. The interior firebox looked to be three feet in width, plenty big to heat the room.

Mr. Henry had built a nice warm fire in it for her. (She decided she would thank him at lunchtime.) She opened the iron door to the wood box; he had filled it with neatly stacked logs. Checking the tinder box revealed that he had also filled it with kindling. It was then Susie noticed that the fireplace tools were clean, and the brass andirons had been cleaned and polished.

She grinned. "Bless you, Mr. Henry Canton."

Flanking each side of the fireplace were recessed cabinets. Though not very deep (maybe a foot, she estimated), they stretched from the end walls to the fireplace and up nearly to the ceiling. 'Nine feet high, maybe,' Susie thought as she eyed it.

Fortuitously, a sturdy six-foot work ladder had been placed in front of the recessed cabinets, allowing her to easily reach the top shelves. She then saw that someone (Mr. Henry perhaps?) had placed a small clock on a bottom shelf next to the fireplace. Susie smiled; it would enable her to keep track of her progress.

Susie decided to start with the floor since it would take the least amount of time. She grabbed the ShopVac and started on the north wall by the windows. Susie worked hard and fast all morning - she was determined to be finished before three.

At eleven fifteen, Miss Hilda came up the stairs. "Goodness me," she exclaimed. "You've done a marvelous job, Susie."

Susie turned around and beamed at Miss Hilda. "Thank you," she responded, pleased with her own progress.

In three hours she had finished the floor, both of the recessed cabinets, the stairwell banister and one of the windows. She had just started cleaning her second window when Miss Hilda arrived. She tossed the grimy paper towel in the waste basket (which was nearly overflowing) and sauntered over to Miss Hilda.

"I think I need to take a quick bath before lunch," Susie commented.

Miss Hilda laughed, and her green eyes sparkled. "I think you're probably right." She gave Susie a big hug. "Come on, we'll get you presentable in time for lunch."

"Okay," Susie agreed, following Miss Hilda down the attic stairs.

———

True to her word, Miss Hilda selected clean clothes for Susie while Susie quickly took a bath. As soon as she was dressed, Susie dried her hair and pulled it up into a ponytail with her pink butterfly holder.

"You're definitely the belle of the ball," Miss Hilda cheerfully told Susie. "Now, we'd better scoot. We have a whole ten minutes to get there."

Susie laughed. "No problem," she assured Miss Hilda.

At lunch, Mr. Henry and Miss Thelma were noticeably absent. As they were clearing the lunch dishes, Susie had asked Mrs. Coppersmith where they were. With a curious look, Mrs. Coppersmith had told Susie they had gone to Foxboro Station, and wouldn't be back until late this afternoon. Susie was a little disappointed that she had to wait to properly thank him for all that he did, but she would catch him as soon as he returned.

After lunch, Susie returned to her Dorm Room, changed back into her grimy clothes, pinned her bangs away from her face, and headed to the attic room. She was energized and couldn't wait to finish. She was still floating from the praise Miss Hilda had lavished on her all during lunch.

Miss Pritchett had smiled at her, saying she was looking forward to seeing Susie's accomplishment.

Pausing at the attic landing and surveying her work, Susie was pleased. "I did great," she boasted to herself. She looked at the clock; one fifteen. Susie headed straight for the windows and with great fervor, tackled the remaining two windows.

Finally finished with cleaning the windows, Susie tossed the last grimy paper towel into the waste basket. Her eyes were drawn to the clock on the shelf as it continued ticking away the minutes. It was now two-twenty. Standing in the center of the room, she smiled, admiring her handiwork. At long last, the room was sparkling clean. She was tired, very tired; but she knew that Miss Pritchett would have to approve of her performance when she came to inspect it at three. That thought made her grin.

Hearing laughter coming from the front of the building, Susie wandered over to the center window. She sat down on the window seat and watched the Munchkins, Dani and Jose playing on the front lawn. Susie was glad to see Simon having fun. He had been so sad and quiet after Nana died. Her eyes began to mist. She leaned against the window, resting her weary head against its frosty panes and closed her eyes.

The first week after Nana's death, Simon had nightmares every night. No one could convince him they were just dreams, and that he was safe. He finally sneaked into Susie's bed one night; he said the bad people wouldn't come to her room (which she shared with Mrs. Crenshaw's daughter.) He begged her to let him stay. He told her the good ones always came and chased away the bad ones, but the bad ones frightened him. He told her that at Nana's, the bad ones never came into the house, only the good ones. And the bad ones always left him alone if Susie or Nana was with him. He cried, telling her that Nana made them go away; and for a long time, they were gone. But now the bad ones were back, and he was afraid.

At first Susie told him he couldn't stay, but she conceded when she saw the fear in his eyes, and the silent tears cascading down his face. She had Simon add in his bedtime prayers for Nana to help make them go away again. After several nights secretly sleeping in her bed, he became calm and eventually stopped talking about the bad people. When Mrs. Crenshaw discovered he was sneaking into Susie's room, she told him he had to stay in his bed. Simon cried, and Susie interceded on his behalf – insisting that he be allowed to stay with her because it calmed him, and he slept better. Recognizing the truth in Susie's plea, Mrs. Crenshaw had relented, allowing him to stay with Susie.

Susie had feared those dreams would start again since Simon had to sleep in his own bed here at Glen Hollow. And it didn't help any for him to hear Kat's fantasy tales the day they arrived; but the bad dreams hadn't returned, and she was so thankful. She didn't understand how Kat or Simon could convince themselves it was real. Obviously they had, but she still didn't understand it. She felt sorry for them – the fear they lived with was horrific, and even worse was the fact it was of their own making. It was real to them, and Susie could only hope in time they would see it wasn't real at all.

Another round of squeals, shouts and laughter caught Susie's attention, breaking her reverie. She looked down from her lofty perch and laughed at the pandemonium below. The snow was just beginning to stick to the ground, forming a thin, white blanket over everything. It was falling much heavier now, causing the air itself to appear a grayish white. They were squealing with delight, running and chasing the flakes, trying to catch them in their mouths or on their tongues. Occasionally they would run into each other, and it seemed to her that perhaps it was more intentional than accidental. Their playtime was cut short by the voice of Miss Cora, calling them to come inside before they caught pneumonia.

Susie turned away from the window, yawned and stretched, and then leaned back against the window. She considered lying down on the window seat, but decided against. If she fell asleep - and she was so tired she probably would - Miss Pritchett would most likely disapprove.

Rising to her feet, Susie yawned and stretched again. She shook her head, attempting to drive away the sleepiness she felt. One of her hairpins fell out and flew across the room. She heard the distinctive ping it made as it dropped onto the floor. It was somewhere near the recessed cabinet that was closest to the window and the east wall.

Exasperated, her head slunk down, and she released a big sigh. "Great, just great," Susie muttered. Straightening herself, she went in search of the missing hairpin.

After crawling on her hands and knees for ten minutes, Susie found the elusive hairpin. But, to her delight, she found something even better. The hairpin had landed in front of the center section of the recessed cabinet. When she picked it up, Susie felt a cold stream of air lightly blowing on her hand. She laid her head down on the floor and saw that the center shelving did not touch the floor. Little puffs of air blew on her face, and she smiled. There was a slight space (just a sliver, really) between the bottom of the cabinet and the floor; not more than a sixteenth of an inch. The other two sections rested squarely on the floor.

Susie pushed herself up and ran to the cabinet on the other side of the fireplace, dropped to the floor and looked at its sections. All three rested squarely on the floor.

"It's a door!" Susie jumped up, thrilled by her discovery. "It's a secret door!"

Quickly she checked the clock; two forty. She had at best fifteen minutes to find a way to open the door before Miss Pritchett arrived.

Susie ran to the ladder and dragged it over to the center shelving. She climbed to the top and began searching for a latch. Slowly she felt along all the edges of the top two shelves. Nothing. She retreated down a few steps on the ladder and began feeling along the edges of the middle shelf. Again, nothing.

Tenaciously, Susie jumped down to the floor and moved the ladder out of her way. She carefully searched the lower two shelves. Once again, she found nothing. She stood back staring at it, puzzled.

"There has to be one," she muttered.

Feeling slightly frustrated, she shook her head and folded her arms across her chest. Susie pressed her lips tightly together, staring at the cabinet.

"There has to be one," she repeated to herself; "think."

Carefully she scrutinized the cabinets. Both had five shelves and three sections. Where each of the vertical panels met a horizontal shelf, there was an ornate square carving for a total of twenty-four carvings per cabinet. No two carvings were the same, and they were all carved with great care and skill. There were animals, plants and flowers; some Susie recognized, and some she didn't. Some were of real subjects, and some were of mythical ones.

And then she saw it. There were four carvings that did not match the other categories. They were the carvings on the center shelf of the hidden door. One carving had three mountain peaks, one had three lighted candles, one had three curly lines slanting in and downward from its top right corner, and the final carving had three wavy lines rising up from its bottom edge.

Susie looked at the other cabinet, focusing on the center shelf; its four center carvings were of two animals and two plants. "Yes!" she declared in victory; "this has to be the key."

Glancing quickly at the clock, Susie's heart sank; it was 2:55. Scarcely a second had passed after checking the clock when she heard Miss Pritchett entering the stairwell. She turned and faced the stairwell just as Miss Pritchett's head came into view.

"All finished and ready for inspection, Miss Pritchett," Susie announced proudly.

Miss Pritchett's smile encompassed her whole face as she observed the room from the landing. "I'm very impressed, Susie. You have done an outstanding job."

She walked around the room, glancing first at the floor, then the light fixtures and then appreciatively at the windows and window seats. Occasionally Susie would hear Miss Pritchett say softly "wonderful" or "amazing" as she made her way around the room. When she reached the recessed cabinets and the fireplace, she nodded her head several times, signifying approval of Susie's efforts.

Miss Pritchett gave Susie a hug and said, "Absolutely a marvelous job, Susie. I'm very pleased and delighted. I am so proud of you."

"Thank you," Susie responded, beaming with pride.

Tears misted Miss Pritchett's eyes, and her face glowed with a strange mix of joy and sorrow. She looked past Susie, actually more like through her, as if Susie wasn't there.

"Miss Pritchett, are you all right?" Susie asked.

Her question broke the spell, and Miss Pritchett smiled fondly at Susie. "Yes, dear; this room holds a great deal of memories for me. I haven't been here since I was seven. ... It was my mother's studio," she answered softly.

Susie nodded slowly, understanding. "When I saw those windows on the north wall, I thought it would be a great place to draw or paint." Susie sighed softly, her own eyes beginning to water. "Nana painted. Her workroom had a large window on the north wall. Nana said the northern light was the best light to use."

Miss Pritchett handed Susie a handkerchief. "I know you like to draw, so I thought this room would be the perfect place to store your Nana's things, and for you to have as a studio." Her smile became a grin as Susie's face registered complete surprise.

"Thank you, but what about the third floor rule?"

"Today you have proven yourself to be responsible, and mature enough to be granted an exemption." Miss Pritchett reached into her pocket, removed the key and handed it to Susie. "This is your key. You are responsible for it," she said.

"Thank you. I'll take good care of it," Susie told Miss Pritchett, clutching tightly the antique key in her hand.

"I know you will, Susie." She smiled and added, "I did, however, have the foresight to have a duplicate made as a precaution." She showed Susie the second key, obvious a current duplicate and not as intriguing as the original. "I'm hoping it won't be needed," she stated.

"Miss Pritchett…," Susie began and then faltered.

"Yes, Susie?"

Susie hesitated and then launched into her question. "Why didn't you use this room?"

Miss Pritchett's eyes closed for the briefest of moments; her smile was bittersweet. She sighed. "A few weeks after my mother died, my father removed all of her things from this studio and closed it. I had just turned eight. … I found the key three months ago, quite by accident."

With a light shrug and a gentle shaking of her head, Miss Pritchett opened her eyes, returning her focus to the here and now. "My mother was a wonderfully gifted artist, Susie; but I did not inherit her gift," she confided. "I have a talent for painting that has served me well as a relaxation exercise, but nothing in comparison with my mother. This studio needs to be used by someone who is gifted, and I have heard that you are."

Her smile was genuinely happy as she added, "This studio will serve a dual purpose; it'll provide you a place to store your things, and also to have that quiet, special place in which to create."

"Thank you so very much, Miss Pritchett," Susie stammered, quickly giving Miss Pritchett a hug.

Miss Pritchett affectionately returned Susie's hug, responding, "You're most welcome."

"Do you have any of her paintings? I'd love to see them," Susie asked.

"My father never said what he did with them. I assume they're stored somewhere in one of the many attic rooms. The rooms are all locked, and most of the keys have been lost over the years." She grinned mischievously. "I do, however, just happen to have one miniature that he didn't know about."

"Really?" Susie asked, her eyes sparkling with anticipation.

Miss Pritchett laughed softly and smiled. "Yes. She painted a miniature portrait from a picture she had of the two of us. I kept it hidden so my father never knew of it. I would take it out at night and look at it; … remembering her…. remembering us."

"May I see it?"

"Certainly," she said; "come to my office anytime, and I'll be glad to show it to you."

"Thanks," Susie beamed with appreciation.

With a light-hearted laugh, Miss Pritchett said, "Come on; let's go. You need to clean up, and then the remainder of the day is yours."

Placing her arm around Susie, she guided her to the stairs and followed Susie down the staircase.

When they exited the attic, Miss Pritchett closed the door but didn't lock it. As if reading her thoughts, Miss Pritchett smiled at her and said, "The delivery truck will be here between four-thirty and five. I think it's safe to leave it unlocked for now. If you wish, you may be present when they deliver your things. I thought you might have a preference as to where things are placed."

Susie nodded animatedly. "Yes, thank you."

She was surprised and excited. First because Nana's things would soon be here, and the studio would now feel like home; and second, because the studio held a secret. She decided that tonight, when everyone was asleep, she would slip upstairs to the attic and find the way to open the secret door.

They parted company on the second floor; Miss Pritchett continued down to the first floor, and Susie headed to the Dorm Room. It was empty, and Susie felt a wave of relief. She was tired and in desperate need of two things, a bath and a nap. She quickly completed the former and then collapsed onto her bed.

Susie awoke, with a start, and bolted upright. Looking around the room, she saw nothing that should have caused her to awaken in such a fright. But she did; and that tingling feeling had returned, only for a split second, but it had been there. Susie sank back against the headboard and released a sigh, trying to dispel the silly notions that were attempting to invade her thoughts.

She turned her head and looked at her clock; three thirty-nine. She had been asleep for all of ten minutes.

"Well, so much for a nap," Susie muttered.

Susie arose and left the room.

Heading to the Library to meet the Munchkins, Susie saw Mr. Henry entering the corridor that led to the kitchen. Quickly she changed her direction and followed after him. She rounded the corner in haste, bolting through the swinging doors of the kitchen.

Much to her disappointment, the kitchen was empty except for Mrs. Coppersmith. She was sitting at the large, mission style table, having a mug of tea. She looked up when Susie barged through the doors. "Here, child, what's wrong?"

"Nothing; I thought Mr. Henry came in here," she explained, her confusion readily apparent.

"He did," she nodded, eyeing Susie; "but he went on through to the staff lounge. Why did you want to see him?"

"I just wanted to thank him. He did some of my chores this morning."

Mrs. Coppersmith let out a derisive snort. "That doesn't sound like Henry. He'd lend a hand if you needed it, but he wouldn't just do it for you."

"Well, he did," Susie adamantly defended him.

With a chuckle, Mrs. Coppersmith rose from her chair by pushing herself up from the table. "If you say so, child. Have a seat; I'll let him know you're here."

She ambled over to her desk, stationed in a generously proportioned niche. She picked up the phone receiver, punched a button on the phone and waited. After a few minutes, she said, "Tell Henry someone wants to see him in the kitchen." After placing the receiver in its cradle, she returned to her chair and sipped her tea.

A few minutes later, Mr. Henry entered the kitchen. "You wanted to see me, Bernice?"

"Not me," she said. She nodded her head toward Susie. "Susie does."

Susie, feeling a little embarrassed, jumped out of her chair and approached him. "Yes I do, Mr. Henry. I just wanted to thank you for your help this morning."

"What help?"

"You know; ... the attic."

"I just did what Miss Pritchett instructed me to do."

"I don't understand... She told you to?"

"Yes, ma'am. Yesterday, she told me to replace the light bulbs, sweep out the chimney, clean the firebox, the grate and the wood box. She wanted the wood box filled with wood, kindling in the tinder box and wanted a fire built before breakfast this morning. So I did."

He looked at Mrs. Coppersmith and shrugged. He grinned at Susie and asked, "You didn't expect to do that yourself, did you?"

Perplexed, Susie shook her head. "No sir, but that isn't what I meant. I just wanted to thank you for cleaning the light fixtures, the fireplace tools and for polishing the andirons."

Now it was his turn to look confused. "Don't know what you mean, Susie," he said. "It wasn't me."

Susie smiled as an idea flashed into her mind. "Oh," she said; "then it must have been Miss Thelma. I guess I need to thank her."

Mr. Henry and Mrs. Coppersmith looked at each other, then burst out laughing.

"Oh, I hardly think that she would be the one," Mr. Henry sputtered in between his howls of laughter.

Mrs. Coppersmith wiped the tears from her eyes, nodding in agreement. "Dear me, no," she agreed. "Thelma Canton would never do such a thing."

"Then, who?" Susie asked, slightly annoyed by their laughter.

Mr. Henry's chuckles continued as he shrugged his shoulders. "I don't know, but I can tell you for certain it wasn't my wife."

Mrs. Coppersmith finally stopped laughing, but her grin and the twinkle in her eyes revealed her amusement had not yet waned. "Child, if you want to know anything in regards to the manor, ask Miss Hilda," she instructed, her voice light with merriment. "She and Miss Pritchett are the only ones that know everything about this place."

"Thank you," Susie replied stiffly, slightly perturbed by their laughter.

She left the kitchen in search of Miss Hilda, but her search was postponed when the chiming of the grandfather clock in the butler's pantry reminded her that Simon, Timmy and Megan were waiting for her in the Library. Racing down the corridor, Susie darted into the Library, and dashed down the aisle that led to Simon's favorite chair.

He looked up at her, smiled coyly and said, "You're not supposed to run in the house, Susie."

"You're right, Simon," she answered apologetically. "I was wrong, but you are supposed to wait for me. How did you get in?"

Impishly he grinned. "Miss Fiona let me in," he stated.

"Where is she?"

He shrugged. "I don't know. She was leaving when I got here."

"She shouldn't have left you alone in here," Susie told him.

Simon grinned, flashing his little pearly white baby teeth. His look was absolutely mischievous. "I told her you were coming any minute. But you were late."

"You're right; I am late, and I'm sorry. From now on, Simon, you wait for me outside the door. I don't want you to get into trouble for being in here without supervision, okay?"

Simon gave her a frown, shrugging his shoulders.

"Where are Megan and Timmy?"

With a slight pout, Simon answered. "Megan is doing something with Miss Fiona, and Timmy is talking to his Grammy on the phone."

Susie smiled. "That's good because today we only have time for a really, small book." She indicated how small by inching her index finger slightly above her right thumb.

"Why?" he shot back, his brow furling.

"Because our things and Nana's things are being delivered in about thirty minutes," she answered as she reached over and began tickling him. He giggled and squirmed with delight.

She slid in next to him, picked up the first book and began to read. When she was finished, Susie returned the books to their places on the shelf and escorted Simon to the door. Giving him a hug, she told him to go play with Timmy while she checked on the delivery status.

"I want to come," he insisted.

"No, Simon. After everything is in place, I'll take you there."

"You promise?" he asked petulantly.

"I promise," she answered solemnly, holding the door open for him.

"Okay," he chirped and darted down the corridor in search of Timmy.

Susie had checked the clock as they had left the Library; it was exactly four-thirty. There was plenty of time before arrival, so she decided to seek out Miss Hilda and ask her who had performed some of her tasks in the attic.

———

"Miss Hilda," Susie knocked on the doorframe as she poked her head into Miss Hilda's office. "May I talk to you for a minute?"

"Of course, dear," her cheerful voice encouraged. "Come in and have a seat."

Susie entered and slipped into one of the burgundy leather chairs positioned in front of Miss Hilda's desk. She hesitated; she wasn't certain just how to pose her question.

"Is something wrong, dear?" Miss Hilda asked concerned.

"No, nothing like that. It's just that, well... some of the cleaning chores in the attic room had been done already."

"Is that right? What do you mean?" Miss Hilda asked.

"Someone cleaned all of the glass globes, the fireplace tools and polished the andirons. I wanted to thank whoever did it; and ... I guess ....
I need to tell Miss Pritchett that I didn't do all of the cleaning. I thought
Mr. Henry had done it, but he said he didn't. Then I thought it was Miss
Thelma, and both he and Mrs. Coppersmith said that she wouldn't have
done it. ... I don't know who to thank. ... I thought maybe you would
know."

Slowly nodding her head, Miss Hilda responded. "Well, that does seem
to be a mystery." She smiled and leaned forward, folding her arms in front
of her as she rested them on her desk. "I think you need to ask Miss
Pritchett. She assigned the chores to that room. She would be the one to
ask; don't you think?"

Susie shrugged. "I guess."

The phone rang, and Miss Hilda picked up the receiver. After a brief
pause she answered, "On my way," and returned the receiver to its cradle.
Rising from her chair, she smiled at Susie and said, "The delivery truck is
here. Shall we go?"

Susie nodded and answered with an enthusiastic "Yes" as she jumped
from her chair.

———

Miss Hilda and Susie met the delivery men at the door. Per her instructions, each of the four men each brought a small box with them as they
followed her through the doors to the west wing. Turning right, she
strode quickly the short distance to the elevator, unlocking and opening
the elevator door. Miss Hilda inserted a key into the interior panel lock,
pressed the button for the third floor while giving them instructions on
its use. The door opened, and they followed Miss Hilda to the attic
studio.

Giving the supervisor her elevator key, Miss Hilda explained that they
now know where the delivery destination is without her having to make
repeated trips with them. She ardently informed the supervisor that she
would collect her key upon completion of the delivery.

When Susie entered the attic studio, she was pleasantly surprised. Someone (Mrs. Canton, perhaps) had cleaned the walls, mopped and waxed the hardwood floors and placed a large oval braided rug in front of the fireplace. It felt more like home already.

The men made short work of delivering the items. Miss Pritchett and Miss Hilda assisted Susie in determining where the boxes and the other furnishings should be placed while awaiting unpacking, but they allowed Susie to decide the placement of Nana's parlor furniture.

The massive attic fireplace was very different from the small fireplace in Nana's parlor; but, somehow, her things just seemed to belong here. Susie suddenly felt a barrage of overwhelming emotions; sadness, joy, gratefulness, loss and of belonging. Her eyes misted as she struggled hard to keep the tears from falling, and her fierce determination was rewarded.

Miss Hilda gave Susie a quick hug. "It looks lovely, dear," she whispered as she nodded her approval.

Turning to the delivery men, she said, "Thank you for your fine work. I'll see you out." She headed for the attic stairwell, descending rapidly with the four men scrambling behind her.

"You're welcome to use the studio any time during your leisure time. School work and chores must always come first," Miss Pritchett gently reminded her.

Susie nodded. "I promise."

"Very well, I'll leave you to it." Pausing briefly at the stairwell, Miss Pritchett smiled and said, "Remember, dinner is at six. Don't be late."

"I won't," she promised.

As Miss Pritchett began to leave, Susie blurted out, "Miss Pritchett, may I ask you something?"

Miss Pritchett turned and nodded slightly. "Certainly."

"It's about the studio," she began haltingly. "I didn't clean everything. ... Someone else cleaned the glass globes, the fireplace tools and polished the andirons. I wanted you to know because I didn't want you to think I did it all when I didn't. I also want to thank whoever did it for me, but no one seems to know who did it. .... Miss Hilda said to ask you because you assigned the chores for the studio, and would know who it was. ... I really would like to know, so I can properly thank the person."

Miss Pritchett grinned and laughed lightly. "You just did."

"Excuse me?" Susie responded, quite perplexed.

"You could have easily finished everything on your own by three; however, I decided to give you a helping hand. I'm glad you appreciate it, Susie. I'm also delighted that you are honest enough not to take credit for someone else's work. It's another sign of your maturity, your responsibility and your integrity."

Her eyes sparkled with the pride she felt for Susie. "Now I have other things to attend to as I'm certain you do also." She smiled at Susie, gave a nod of dismissal and began her descent down the stairs.

Susie took in a deep breath and slowly exhaled. She had forty minutes before she had to be in the Dining Hall. She sank down into one of Nana's soft chairs, allowing its familiarity to comfort her.

Chapter 16

SECRETS, SECRETS

Susie was awakened by the soft trilling sound of her muffled alarm clock. It was one o'clock in the morning. After her roommates had settled in for the night, she had wrapped it in a shirt and slid it, along with her flashlight and a change of clothes, under her pillow. She lay there quietly, listening for a few minutes. Susie had to be certain that her alarm had not awakened anyone else. … It hadn't. She sat upright and retrieved her clothes from under her pillow, making short work of changing into her clothes and putting on her sneakers

Fast and quiet, she crept out of her room and to the door of the Dorm. Gently she opened the door, wincing as it made a soft creaking sound. Peering into the corridor, she saw the coast was clear and slipped into it.

After carefully closing the door to prevent any audible sound, she leaned against the wall and yawned several times. She was so tired yet her mind felt alive, excited even. She'd had a difficult time falling to sleep; she couldn't stop thinking about the secret door in the attic studio. Well, she would take a nap this afternoon and make up for the loss of sleep, she promised herself.

Sprinting along the corridors, Susie headed for her attic room. Though she was fairly confident everyone was asleep, she remained alert for any sign to the contrary.

The soft click as she turned the key in the lock of the attic door made her smile; this really was her special place. Susie opened the door and stepped up into the stairwell. A slight tuft of air encircled her, causing her to experience anew cascades of tingles down her spine.

Gently she pulled the door closed. Susie turned on her flashlight; its soft light created a tunnel through the darkness, dispelling her jitters. Tucking the flashlight under her arm, she turned, inserted the key into the lock and turned it. Its soft click told her it was locked. Shining the light up the stairwell, she ascended the stairs, making certain the light remained fixed on the steps ahead of her. At the top of the stairwell she switched on the ceiling lights, illuminating the room with a cheery brightness.

Strolling to the recessed cabinet on the left, Susie's focus was solely on the center shelf and its four distinctive carvings. Her fingers lightly felt the carved squares. They were so smooth, so delicately carved.

"They are the key," she said softly; "I know it."

She attempted to turn the squares, but they didn't budge. Next she tried pulling out on them; again they remained fixed. Susie pressed in on the square with the three wavy lines; it moved, simultaneously emitting a whisper of a click. Exuberant, she quickly pressed the other three, receiving the same soft click as each one moved.

Nothing happened; no movement of the door, not a hint that it had unlocked. Susie pushed and pulled on the shelf as hard as she could, but the door remained closed.

Susie sighed heavily. "Rats; it probably requires a certain sequence," she muttered; "and it'll take forever to try every possible sequence."

She shook her head, a little in disgust and a little in frustration, staring at the elusive door. The carvings triggered a sense of something familiar, yet she couldn't quite place why. The longer she stared at the carvings, the more determined she was to find the answer.

Sitting cross-legged on the floor, she braced her elbows on her knees and rested her chin in the palms of her hands. After several minutes, she emitted a long, loud yawn. She was so tired; her eyelids felt as if they were made of lead. Slowly they would droop until they closed; and Susie would force them open, shake her head and rub her eyes in an attempt to revive herself.

"Think!" she commanded herself aloud. "It's just a puzzle."

Silently her inner voice added, 'If I weren't so tired, I'd have solved it by now.'

That made Susie giggle, and then burst out laughing. Slowly she quieted and sat there, just staring at the bookcase, allowing the familiarity of the carvings to absorb into her mind. Knowing she had never seen them before, there wasn't any reason they should be familiar. And yet they are.

A big grin slowly crept on her face; she started laughing triumphantly. "That's it," she declared; "the carvings represent the pictures in the Book."

Upon further reflection, she realized they were not in the same order as in the Book. Moments later, she chuckled again. "I've got it!"

She pressed the square with the three slanting lines, then she pressed the one with the three wavy lines. Next she pressed the one with the three peaks, and lastly she pressed the one with the three lighted candles.

With a soft, whooshing sound the door slowly gave way. It slid quietly back and then to the left, behind the recessed cabinet abutting against the north wall.

Susie could hardly contain her excitement. She jumped up and down in celebration, arms raised in triumph, pumping the air as she emphatically cried "Yes, Yes, Yes!!"

Grabbing her flashlight, Susie switched it on and shone the light into the blackness. Puffs of wafting air circled around and over her, brushing lightly against her. The air was a little stale and smelled heavily of dust. Straight ahead in her beam of light was the rock wall of the circular section of the manor. It was about three feet away from the back wall of the cabinet.

She leaned in, shining the flashlight to her left. Between the back of the secret door and the rock wall was a circular staircase leading down. Susie smiled, realizing that meant there were more secret doors on each level. 'It'll be fun to see where they all lead,' she thought.

Pulling back into the studio, she began searching the studio for something with which to wedge the door. 'Just in case,' she told herself.

Her eyes alighted onto the fireplace tools; quickly she ran over and snatched the poker from its position on the stand. Returning to the doorway, she wedged the poker into the shallow groove, leaning the handle against the doorframe. "That should do it," she proclaimed.

As an afterthought, she ran back to the fireplace - this time snatching the shovel from its position. She smiled as she thought, 'It'll come in handy whether battling spiders, mice or just about anything else.'

Now she was ready. She approached the gaping hole of darkness, armed with flashlight and shovel. Susie shone the light to her right; the secret passageway appeared to follow the rock wall. How far, she didn't know but was determined to find out, wherever it might lead.

Cautiously entering the passageway, she slowly began her mission. Moving the flashlight back and forth between straight ahead and along the wall to her right, Susie noticed the various cobwebs along the way. Shuddering involuntarily, she consoled herself with the fact that she had not yet seen a spider.

"Perhaps the cold winter air has killed them," she said aloud in an attempt to bolster her courage.

It was cold; so cold, in fact, that Susie found herself wishing she had thought to bring a jacket or at least a sweater. It hadn't occurred to her that with no direct heat, the secret passageway would be little different than being outside. Her sweatshirt just wasn't enough to keep her warm. She picked up her pace, hoping that would help offset the lack of clothing layers.

About thirty feet into the passageway, she saw a lever attached to a vertical beam. She pulled it down. Immediately, a panel slid sideways, revealing a narrow opening into another attic room. Susie shone her flashlight into the darkness and peered inside. Everything was covered in what appeared to be white sheets, and veiled in a light layer of dust. There were cobwebs everywhere. The tall, thin sheets that were sporadically placed around the room were most likely covering torchieres, coat racks or even reading lamps.

Susie quickly backed out of the doorway, pushed the lever upright, and the door slid shut. She continued her journey and came upon two more such levers. They also opened doors into rooms where everything was covered with dust sheets.

Continuing her course, she came to the end of the straight portion of the rock wall, curving its way to the left just as it does on the lower levels. The passageway now split; Susie had a choice to turn to her right or follow the passageway on around the wall to her left. She chose the left passageway, hoping it would lead to the east wing.

Walking faster now in direct correlation to the surging exhilaration she was feeling, she followed the rock wall as it continued its course onward toward the east wing. Several minutes later, there it was just like the manor below; the passageway continued to the left and to the east wing. Without hesitation, Susie increased her speed as she followed the curve of the rock wall, anticipation growing with each passing moment. Her heart was racing, pounding its response to her excitement. Abruptly it came to an end barely two-thirds of the way down the passageway.

Susie stared in disbelief. "How could it stop here?" she asked aloud. "Why would it stop here?"

Frustrated, she walked back and forth along the wall, shining the light from top to bottom. Ever so slowly, Susie methodically inspected every inch of the wall. She saw no visible trigger, latch or lever that would reveal a hidden door.

She was freezing, and getting colder with each passing minute. Her fingers and toes were numb from the cold, and she had been shivering the past hour, virtually nonstop. Susie checked her watch; 3:49. She really wanted to remain here, to find the door that would grant her access to the east wing. But in an hour or so, people would start milling around. And Mrs. Coppersmith, well, she was always in the kitchen by four every morning to start preparing breakfast. ... So was Miss Taryn. She knew she didn't need to run into either of them and explain her dirty clothes, or why she was up so early.

"Tomorrow after church, I will find your secret door," she promised the wall. Laughing, she amended her promise, "I guess it is tomorrow already. Make that later today," she said, giving the wall a friendly pat.

She spun around and trotted back. As she passed by the place where the passageway curved toward the east wing, the light shone on an alcove previously unnoticed. Curiosity getting the better of her, she decided to investigate. It was another hidden stairwell.

"They must be everywhere," Susie mused. A smile slowly spread across her face. "This is great," she giggled. "There must be hidden doors all through this place; maybe every room has one," she added gleefully.

Shining the light down the stairwell, Susie closed her eyes and shuddered. "Ugh! Spiders!" she cried. She looked again and saw that there weren't any actual spiders; but there was, however, a very thick covering of cobwebs, extending down as far as the light could shine.

"No way," she told herself. "Not until I find a way to get rid of them."

She stood up and sighed. "Now what," she thought. Then she knew. "I'll bet the ShopVac can remove all of the cobwebs in a jiff. I just have to find out where it's stored."

She headed back along the passageway, trotting quickly in an effort to make up for lost time. She reached the fork, returning her to the west wing.

From there, it was a short jaunt to where she had entered this secret passageway. Back inside the attic studio, she returned the shovel to its proper place. Removing the poker from the groove, Susie also returned it to its rightful place next to the shovel.

Pressing the carved squares, Susie was expecting the door to close. Nothing happened. The door remained open. "This isn't good," she thought. She tried several more times, but the door refused to close.

Slightly aggravated, she began pacing in front of the door. She was tired, more so than she had realized; after just a few passes, she had to sit down. She felt weak and a little dizzy. Rubbing her face, Susie sighed and then yawned as her hands dropped wearily into her lap.

"Please let me get it closed," Susie whispered, frustrated at herself and her inability to maneuver through her mind fog.

She yawned several more times. Her eyes were heavy with sleep, and it was difficult to keep them open. She began to drift into a light sleep when suddenly she felt a hand on her shoulder. Startled, she turned to look. No one was there. She was, however, now fully awake, adrenaline pumping and coursing through her veins. She jumped to her feet.

Susie didn't actually hear a voice; but, yet … she did. It told her to reverse the order that opened the door. So she did … and the door slid shut. Susie shivered again as the tingles crawled up and down her spine.

Darting toward the stairwell, Susie turned on her flashlight as she sprinted across the room. She switched off the ceiling light, scampered down the stairwell and unlocked the door. Slowly she opened the door and peered into the corridor. It was empty. Slipping past the threshold, she quickly closed the door and locked it before running all the way to the foyer staircase. Taking the stairs three at a time, she landed on the second floor with a soft thud, and began swiftly running to her Dorm Room.

Quietly she made her way to her bed, undressed and got back into her pj's. Susie heard the grandfather clock chiming five o'clock as she dropped off to sleep.

Chapter 17

REALTY OR ILLUSION

Susie found it extremely difficult to concentrate on Reverend Tillman's sermon, partly because she was exhausted. Mostly it was due to her discoveries from yesterday afternoon, and during the wee hours of this morning. She tried and tried to focus on his words, but her thoughts kept drifting back to her discoveries.

To be fair, she also was a little preoccupied with Mrs. Crenshaw's impending visit scheduled for later this afternoon. Part of her wanted to confide in Mrs. Crenshaw; however Susie just knew that if she did, Mrs. Crenshaw would insist she stop exploring, citing the possible danger of such activity. Susie was certain she had already considered any such problems, not to mention those already encountered. However, Susie's main concern was that Mrs. Crenshaw might tell Miss Pritchett, or require Susie to tell Miss Pritchett what she found. And Susie wasn't ready to do that just yet.

'Something is very different about this place; something - - not sinister exactly, but definitely peculiar,' Susie thought; 'and I'm going to find out what it is.'

Susie drifted back to the sermon once again in time to see Miss Hilda watching her, quite concerned by the expression on her face. At breakfast, Susie had had to endure inquiries from nearly everyone as to whether or not she was ailing.

There was no hiding the ill effect from the lack of sleep; she had tried very much to disguise it, but was unsuccessful. Before getting dressed, she had splashed her face several times with icy cold water, hoping color would return. It didn't. Repeatedly she pinched her cheeks, hoping for a good, healthy blush. All that accomplished, besides the pain, was a few seconds of a pinkish color. Surrendering her pallor to the inevitable, Susie then concentrated on the dark circles under her eyes. Attempting to diminish the zombie look, she lightly dusted a little baby powder on the dark circles.

It made it much, much worse, so she washed her face, resigning herself to looking as if she was one step away from death.

"Might as well," she had muttered as she had exited the bathroom; "I feel like death warmed over." That thought immediately caused to her chuckle and grin - it was one of Nana's favorite sayings whenever either she or Simon looked a little under the weather.

Susie gave Miss Hilda a broad, perky smile, hoping to assure her all is well before turning her attention once again onto Reverend Tillman. Determinedly, Susie forced herself to focus on the Reverend's words, and to appear to be as alert as ever. The service ended right on schedule, though not soon enough for Susie. Her curiosity was growing with each passing minute as the possibilities regarding her recent discoveries tantalized her. Her mind raced with questions and with plans.

Reverend Tillman began his processional walk down the center aisle, slowly moving toward the vestibule doors. As he passed each pew, the congregants would rise and begin putting on their coats, scarves, hats and gloves. They would patiently wait their turn to file out of the pews, greet the Reverend and then exit.

Simon wasn't in the mood to wait, and he coaxed Timmy into joining him. Like a couple of overgrown hamsters, they hurriedly wove their way through the line, pushing and squirming their way to the doors. As soon as they reached the doors, they darted outside the Chapel as if escaping, leaping and waving their arms, reminiscent of birds set free from a cage.

Susie stepped outside; the blast of glacial air stung her face and was a shock to her lungs. Knowing how cold it was outside prior to exiting was still no match for its reality, especially after having been in the toasty warmth of the Chapel for the past ninety minutes. It felt as if long fingers of ice had wrapped around her lungs, squeezing them and chilling them to within a fraction of being frozen solid.

The frigid December air bit right through her thick winter coat; '*straight to the bone as Nana would say*', Susie thought. She pulled her pink woolen scarf up over her nose and mouth, quickly descended the three steps and headed toward the manor as fast as she could.

Far ahead of her, Simon and Timmy were running in and out of the pergola, jumping over and onto the granite benches as they darted, much like the erratic movement patterns of hummingbirds. They were playing their version of tag while everyone else hastily made their way toward the door of the south wing, trying not to collide with the boisterous duo during their frequent passes through the pergola. On the next pass through, Miss Ginger quickly snared both boys, compellingly them into the comforting warmth of the manor.

"Susie, wait please," she heard a voice call out from somewhere behind her just as she reached the manor steps. It was Miss Hilda.

Susie stepped inside and waited by the window beside the door. The warm air from the manor entwined with the frosty outside air, creating a swirl of hot and cold spots. Susie shivered, and drew her coat tighter against her body in a futile attempt at keeping out the freezing air. Her nose began to run, forcing her to hastily retrieve her handkerchief from her pocket. She waited in silence as the others filed past her, chatting about the sermon or their plans for the day while she nervously tried to anticipate the questions Miss Hilda would ask. Finally she was alone in the corridor. All the others except Miss Pritchett, Miss Hilda and Reverend Tillman had already entered the manor.

"Thank God," Susie whispered, breathing a sigh of relief as she watched Miss Pritchett and the Reverend interrupt Miss Hilda's route toward Susie.

Their conversation was spirited, and the three of them began laughing as they resumed their course toward the door. They stopped about twelve feet away from the steps, their conversation appearing now to be a little more serious. She could hear them rather well through the glass. However, as tempted as she was to remain, she was only truly interested in retreat now that the opportunity had presented itself. She knew this was only a temporary reprieve; Miss Hilda would find her later. But still it was a reprieve, and she was glad for it.

Cautiously so as not to draw attention to herself, Susie slowly backed away from the window. Abruptly she turned, quickly darting down the corridor to the Cloak Room, removing her coat as she ran. She entered and wasted no time in placing her coat on a hanger. Quickly stuffing the pockets with her gloves and hat, she wrapped her pink woolen scarf around the neck of the hanger.

Pausing at the Cloak Room door, she peeked down the corridor, looking back toward the door to the pergola. Apparently, they were still talking outside despite the cold because the corridor was empty. Susie scurried into the corridor, making a mad dash to the foyer. Quickly she crossed the foyer, darting into the West wing and on toward the Library. In there, she could lose herself among the stacks until the last possible minute, and could easily race walk to the Dining Hall in five minutes, a feat she has already performed several times.

Entering the Library, Susie waited for a moment and made a brief sweep of the corridor behind her. No one was there; no one had seen her. She smiled as she slowly closed the Library door. With all the stealth and speed of a cat, she began to make her way to the east side of the Library. As she came upon each aisle, Susie would stop and cautiously check both sides to see whether or not anyone happened to be in those particular aisles. No one was in any of them.

She was alone. She had the entire Library to herself. Susie smiled and almost giggled. She felt relieved and exuberant at the same time, and found herself skipping down the aisle the remainder of the way to the east side. Upon arriving, the fireplace had a roaring fire blazing away. Someone had built a lovely fire, and had tossed in cinnamon sticks; their fragrance was lightly scenting the air as they burned. Susie stepped closer, absorbing the warmth of the fire.

Inescapably her eyes were drawn to the oak cabinet in the alcove. Briefly she considered getting down the key to the cabinet, and continuing her examination of the Histories of the Evermores. Susie shook her head. 'Not enough time,' she told herself.

Instead, she turned away from the cabinet with its enticing volumes and began slowly walking down the first row of stacks. Susie began to relax as she wandered through the Research stacks, her eyes skimming the book spines as she went. She wasn't looking for anything in particular, just looking; killing time until she had to be in the Dining Hall… which was in exactly forty-five minutes. She checked the mantle clock when she heard the single, melodic chime.

She found several books that piqued her interest, making a mental note to come back and get them. Susie had noticed earlier in the week that there wasn't a sign that stated a limit on the number of books you could check out. Now that she thought about it, Miss Pritchett didn't mention one either when she gave them the tour last Sunday. Surely it can't be less than three at a time, Susie guessed. *'Maybe I'd better ask'*, she thought.

Susie continued her perusing until halfway through the third stack. The book seemed to leap out at her; not literally, but it captured her attention without any reason for doing so. There was nothing overtly noticeable about the book.

It was a thin book, taller and wider than most of the others on the shelf, and was not much more than a quarter of an inch thick. Its cover was a muted olive green cloth (a little drab) with intermittent, nearly imperceptible, tiny threads of gold. The spine displayed only the surname of the author, Von Richter; the lettering was a nondescript tan color, outlined in dark brown.

Susie slowly reached for the book. As her index finger touched it, she felt a gentle sensation, a little like warm, bubbly water flowing over her skin. She pulled her hand back, and for a moment she just stared at this plain book. An urge, an overwhelming urge, began to fill her, compelling her to pick up the book. Without thinking and without resistance, she reached for the book. Her slender hand moved with the speed and precision of a lightning strike, removing the book from its place. Instantly, upon touching it, she again felt that soothing warmth in her fingers, and now in her hand. The book began to faintly glow, much like the soft light of a child's night light.

"This is really weird," Susie whispered. "I feel like I've stepped into some sort of alternate dimension. It's probably just the lack of sleep," she said, attempting to dismiss the apparitions.

She turned the book and looked at its front cover. Her mind flashed back to Friday afternoon, to the east garden with its magnificent unicorn statue, its unusual inscription on the plaque and to the poem she already knew. A strange, bubbly sensation began in her brain, tingling, making her feel lightheaded and yet incredibly alive. Susie inhaled deeply, slowly releasing her breath, calming herself.

"More secrets," she whispered to the book; "this place seems to have a lot of them. Why?"

No answer was offered. Not that she actually expected one; however, just the act of acknowledging it aloud became a balm, steadying her. Susie shrugged and smiled. "I will find out what they are," she vowed.

Turning her attention once again to the book, she began to closely examine it. Across the top of its cover, printed in gold lettering with a thick black outline, was the name of this little volume: 'Unicorns: Purveyors of Truth'.

At the bottom of the front cover was the author's full name: Helga Gretchen von Richter. It was printed in the same tan lettering and dark brown outline as the lettering on the spine of the book.

Displayed in the center of the book's cover was a golden oval; standing in that oval was a handsome, white unicorn. The artist's rendition was incredible, creating the illusion that the animal was alive; that its strong, muscular body would leap right off the cover. Susie stared into the blue eyes of this creature, half expecting it to blink. .. It didn't.

Suddenly she was aware that she had been holding her breath. She chuckled at herself, and her over active imagination. As Susie opened the book, she could have sworn she heard a voice whispering. Startled, she looked up and all around. There was no one

"Get a grip," she mumbled, chastising herself.

Susie took the book and curled up in one of the comfy arm chairs near the fireplace. According to the inside front cover, the book had originally been printed in Germany in 1846. This edition, however, had been re-printed in England in 1882. It was not the only book published by this author.

According to the first page, the author had published seven other books, each with a slightly bizarre title: 'White Tigers: Guardians of the Realms' in 1847; 'Wolves: Protectors of Seekers' in 1848; 'Doves, Eagles, Falcons and the Phoenix: Heralds of Hope and Peace' in 1849; 'Elephants: God's Gentle Giants, Embodiment of Love & Patience' in 1850; 'Dolphins: Knights of the Seas' in 1851; 'Dragons & Pegasus, Angels & Demons: Warriors All' in 1852, and the last title, 'This Wondrous Universe: World Without End' in 1853.

There was no mention as to whether or not they were also reprinted in England; Susie hoped they had been. If not, she was fairly certain Miss Emma could probably translate them for her. It'd be a while yet before she would be fluent enough to do so herself. She decided that later she'd check the card catalogue just in case the books were here.

Turning the page, she now came to the title page. It was rather plain, displaying only the book's title and the author's name; there weren't any decorative designs or artwork. There wasn't an elaborate border, or any border for that matter; and the lettering was in the same dull colors as was the author's name on the book's spine and cover. Susie felt a little disappointed ... until she turned the title page.

"It's beautiful," she gasped, gazing at the scene displayed before her.

Across the next two pages there was a breathtaking scene showcasing a pastoral meadow. In the left background were seven tall waterfalls pouring down from a majestic mountain range. Growing between the waterfalls on the rocky cliffs, and sprouting out of the clefts, was an abundance of plants and flowering vines, splashing a vibrancy of colors along the rock face.

Like an enormous curtain of water, the largest waterfall plunged directly down into the waters of the crystal blue river. The force of its energy as it collided into the river caused the water to rise up into billowy clouds of mist, ascending nearly halfway up the curtain of water. The six smaller waterfalls (three on each side of the main waterfall) flowed with considerably less force, cascading gently down the cliffs, level to level, until the water eventually merged seamlessly into the river.

As beautiful as any bright, summer day, the sky was a brilliant blue with clouds that were white and as fluffy as cotton balls. There were large trees, dazzling wild flowers and meadows, lush with green grass as thick and plush as a deep carpet.

Butterflies and bees were flitting from flower to flower. A vast array of brilliantly plumed birds was present. Some birds were flying; others were sitting on branches, singing their songs, while some were foraging for worms or seeds. Squirrels and chipmunks were scavenging the various nuts that had fallen on the ground while others were scampering about, chasing each other.

Featured in the foreground was a herd of white unicorns. Some were lying down, some were standing at the river's edge and others were drinking its crystal clear waters. Many were in small clusters, giving the appearance that they were conversing with one another. Scattered around the meadows were unicorns that were eating, and those that seemed to be asleep.

There was, however, a portion of the painting that enthralled her so much so that it seemed as if her heart skipped a beat. Standing next to a prominent oak tree was a unicorn and a maiden. He was taller and more muscular than the other unicorns and, as such, it was obvious the artist meant to portray him as the leader. But what was so astonishing to Susie was that the scene was exactly like her brooch, the one Nana gave her nearly two years ago.

"How weird is this," Susie mumbled, her fingers lightly touching the unicorn and the lady. For the briefest, most fleeting of moments, she heard the Lady's voice. Then she heard a male voice – it seemed to emanate from the Unicorn. The voices were pleasant and soothing. Though Susie couldn't understand the words, they seemed familiar, much like a distant memory struggling to find its way from the unconscious to the conscious mind.

Quickly Susie moved her hand away from the picture. The voices stopped. Sitting very still for a few moments, Susie tried to formulate an explanation for what happened. Her hand remained poised over the scene. She closed her eyes and shook her head, attempting to clear away the fog in her mind.

"It must be the lack of sleep," she told herself, then opened her eyes.

She laid the book in her lap, staring at the scene. Several times she started to touch it, and each time she pulled her hand back.

"This is ridiculous," Susie scolded herself and then firmly placed one hand on each page of the scene as she closed her eyes.

Immediately she was flooded with sensations as if she had just stepped into the picture. Susie felt happy, a profound joy that welled up from deep within her soul. It settled around her, wrapping her in a cocoon of peace and tranquility.

A cool breeze lightly caressed her face and body, while the warmth from the sun kissed her skin. She could hear the rustling of the leaves in the trees as the wind swirled and floated through them. Susie could smell the fragrances of the flowers, the meadow grass and the crisp, clean air. She could hear the buzzing of the bees as they flew around her, and felt the gentle vibrations from the beating of the wings of the butterflies. She could hear the birds singing and chirping, letting the world know their joy. Susie could hear the sounds of the squirrels and chipmunks at play and at work, gathering their food. She could hear the water as it fell, rumbling and thundering, dropping into the river.

Susie listened to the gentle lapping of the waves against the shore as the river's current drew the water downstream. She could hear the munching sounds of the grass being eaten, and the snoring of those currently asleep. Susie could hear the whinny and snorting sounds, and the hoof beats of the young at play. She could even hear various voices, male and female, ebbing and flowing with the natural rhythm of conversation. But these weren't human voices, nor did they speak in a language she understood. The language sounded as it did when the Lady and the Unicorn had spoken just minutes before.

Susie opened her eyes, staring at the portions of the pages visible between her fingers. Slowly her hands melted away from her sight; the pages of the book began enlarging until they surrounded her, engulfing her. It seemed so real; she could see, and feel, and hear and smell *everything* - and it was all in motion, not just pages in a book.

She saw the water cascading down, flowing into the river, feeling its misty spray as the breeze gently carried it to her. Susie watched as the river's gentle current pulled the water along the river bank, listening to the roar of the water colliding with the river and then the gentle sounds as the water lapped against the riverbank. She saw the wind ruffling the flowers and vines along the rocky cliffs, and rustling through the leaves on the trees; she felt it moving through her hair. She marveled at the beauty of the flowers, and trees and grasses, delighting in their varied aromas and in their vivid colors.

Happily Susie watched the squirrels and chipmunks at play, the birds singing and flying, the bees and the butterflies flitting all around the meadows. She could see unicorns: some sleeping, some eating, some drinking and some huddling together and talking. She laughed while watching the young unicorns romping and playing, seeing them laughing and yelling.

She found herself giggling with a carefree abandon, joy springing from within her and creating the desire to run and play with them. Slowly she spun around in circles, and then did a few cartwheels in the meadow, enjoying the elation she felt. Dropping down onto the cushiony thick grass, she sat quietly as she surveyed this miraculous place.

The dream seemed so real, but she could not understand how. All Susie knew was that she loved it here; and, at this very moment, she was content with that. Part of her hoped the dream would never end. As if drawn by an unseen force, Susie slowly turned her head toward the oak tree. She watched the Lady and the Unicorn as they spoke to one another, wondering what it was they were discussing.

And then, they saw her. The Lady and the Unicorn turned and looked directly at her, telling her not to be afraid. Susie began to panic. She had been certain this was all a dream; a wonderful dream, but a dream nonetheless. That was why she could enjoy it and not be seen by the inhabitants. But they saw her! They knew she was here. So how could this be a dream?

"Where is here?" she wondered aloud, feeling the panic steadily rising within her.

The Lady and the Unicorn began to slowly walk toward Susie, again telling her not to be afraid, that all would be explained. They smiled at her, and welcomed her. Stunned, Susie realized that she could now understand what they were saying. The other unicorns began moving toward her, joining the Lady and The Unicorn in greeting Susie with pleasant welcomes.

Susie could feel herself shaking her head. "No," she heard herself say; "this isn't real. It can't be real. I'm dreaming."

The Lady and the Unicorn were calling out to her, but now their voices sounded faint, as if their voices were traveling a long distance to reach her. "Wait, we have much to tell you, much you need to know …" Their voices dissipated as Susie willed herself back to the Library.

She removed her hands from the book as if its pages were scalding hot. Breathing rapidly, confused and frightened, Susie sat silently, staring at the book in her lap. The pastoral scene was just an illustration; beautiful, but nothing more. Slowly inching her hand toward the open book, Susie cautiously allowed her fingers to touch the illustration. Nothing happened.

Exhaling forcibly, Susie breathed a sigh of relief. 'It's just a book', she scolded herself silently.

Susie began laughing, a nervous laugh that came from the tension that had wound its way throughout her body. Her laughter shifted into one of amusement as the tension slowly ebbed. After the tension had dissipated, Susie realized the fear was also gone. In its place was a profound and overwhelming sense of curiosity.

"Was it real, or was it hallucinations from sleep deprivation, or from an over active imagination?" she whispered softly.

Susie remembered how Nana had told her many times that her imagination was always in over drive, and that she had no shortage of it. Rubbing her face vigorously several times, Susie hoped that would at least provide some alertness, if only temporarily. As soon as lunch was over, she'd take a long nap, and then be as good as new, she promised herself.

The mantle clock kept ticking away the minutes as she sat very still, intently staring at the book that lay open in her lap. She was hesitant to touch and turn the page, not wanting another sleep deprived hallucination to further rattle her nerves.

Finally her curiosity won; she turned the page and was thankful to see it was nothing more than a note from the author. Relaxing, Susie emitted a little sigh of relief and began reading the Preface note from the author.

Preface
Dear Fellow Seeker:
Unicorns are the Purveyors of Truth. They have been entrusted since
before Time began with the Ancient Secrets, The Mysteries of the Ages.
Of all of God's creations, they alone hold within their being the infinite
Knowledge of the Universe and the immense Wisdom of the Ages.
They impart this vast repertoire only to those whose heart is pure.
If you are of a pure heart, seek them. They will come. They will test
your heart to prove its worthiness. Should your heart be found, indeed,
to be pure, they will honor you; they will bestow upon you their gift.
I pray that your Spirit is as strong as your heart is pure, and pray that the
Almighty Creator grants to you the strength that you will need. For a
strong and vigilant Spirit is required for one to remain on the
Path of Light and not succumb to the subtle, insidious enticements of
those who walk the Path of Darkness.
An amazing journey, a marvelous path lies ahead for you. Make no
mistake – it is in no way easy. Count the cost before you embark.
Know this; it is worth whatever the cost.

May the eyes of your heart be fully enlightened, enabling you to truly see and understand this wondrous Universe we inhabit.

> *With much affection,*
> *Helga Gretchen von Richter*
> *January 08, 1846*

A warm sensation, bubbly like sparkling cider, flowed from the top of her head all the way down to her toes. It was a pleasant sensation, making her feel happy and as light as air.

Sensing the presence of someone nearby, Susie bolted upright in her chair and looked around. She saw no one .... Yet still she had this feeling, a profound sense that she was not alone.

The mantle clock began chiming the quarter hour, jolting her from her daze and causing her to nearly jump out of her chair. She began laughing, chuckling at the gullibility that the lack of sleep had obviously caused. Closing the book, she rested her head against the chair. She had fifteen minutes until lunch time, plenty of time and no need to rush. She yawned several times, her body's way of reminding her that sleep was sorely needed.

Rising slowly to her feet, Susie returned the book to its place, patted it and softly said, "Until later. I'll come back for you tonight."

She strolled lightheartedly down the aisle, out the Library doors and casually headed to the Dining Hall. Halfway there, she realized that she was humming the little song Nana had taught Simon and her on her tenth birthday, the same song as the poem on the Unicorn statue in the east garden.

Smiling, she entered the Dining Hall, her spirit as light and as happy as her smile.

Chapter 18

KAT FIGHT & A TEA PARTY

Susie was so glad lunch was over. As soon as she had entered the Dining Hall, Miss Hilda and Miss Bettye had cornered her. Miss Pritchett was watching even though she was pretending not to notice. Both Miss Hilda and Miss Bettye pressed her about her state of health. At breakfast, they were all concerned because she was so pale. Now, they were concerned because she had a little color; flushed, they called it.

Miss Hilda felt Susie's forehead, admitting Susie had no fever though not yet convinced that Susie wasn't ailing. Miss Bettye, also, checked Susie's forehead for fever, and Susie's throat for any sign of infection. She, too, shook her head, declaring that Susie had no apparent fever or sign of illness. However, she firmly stated that she would check Susie again later, just to be certain. Susie sighed and smiled, acquiescing to their concern.

As they were proceeding to their places around the table, Miss Hilda asked Susie why Susie didn't wait for her after service, and where had she been since then. Before Susie could answer, Miss Pritchett rang the dinner bell. Susie silently said a prayer of thanks.

"After lunch, I want to speak with you," Miss Hilda whispered. Susie nodded while secretly praying for another miracle.

In another stroke of good fortune for Susie, Miss Hilda was diverted as soon as lunch had ended. Miss Pritchett asked Miss Hilda to join her and the Reverend in her office. Miss Hilda quickly complied, but not before telling Susie that she would talk with her later. Susie nodded, affirming Miss Hilda's plans and did her best to refrain from smiling.

'*Another reprieve*,' she thought. Susie turned and began jauntily strolling to the Dining Hall doors. She smiled. She couldn't help it. Apparently, the Powers That Be were helping her today.

Darting down the west wing corridor to the foyer and up the main stairs, Susie quickly made her way to the Dorm Room. With Simon headed for naptime after changing his clothes, she had things to do before Mrs. Crenshaw's visit; and time was short. Though she considered taking a nap, she no longer seemed to need one. She was alert and felt full of energy. "Nana called it 'getting your second wind'. That must be it," Susie decided.

Her roommates had already changed out of their Sunday dresses and into their everyday clothes. As she made her way to her room, Susie heard an argument brewing between Dani and Kat. It wasn't their first one this week and not even their first one today. This one, however, sounded as if it were escalating fast into a full blown brouhaha. There would be the usual name calling and end with Dani stomping away and yelling a variety of threats. Susie sighed and did her best to ignore them – they could be, oh, so-o-o childish sometimes.

From her dresser, Susie chose a pastel lilac top, deep purple jeans and a pair of dark purple socks. She changed her clothes and, as she sat down on her bed to put on her shoes, she heard a blood-curdling scream. It was followed in a split second by the sound of a couple of "Uh-Ohs" and loud wailing (actually, more like high pitched squeals).

Susie quickly finished tying her shoes, jumped off her bed, ran down the hallway and into the Common Area. Dani and Kat were standing over little Megan who lay crumpled on the floor in a fetal position, hands covering her face and screeching at the top of her lungs. Juls was sitting on the couch, pretending to be totally disinterested in their shenanigans. The smirk on her face fully revealed that she was enjoying their little drama.

"What happened?" Susie asked, parting the girls and kneeling down beside Megan.

"Dani tried to hit me in the gut, and I sidestepped," Kat said smugly. (She truly was as nimble as her nickname implied.)

"That's because you *stole* my bracelet, and won't give it back!" Dani glowered at Kat, seething with anger. "It's *your* fault Megan got hurt."

"No it isn't," Kat protested. "*You* hit her," she retorted, pointing at Dani.

"Enough!" Susie demanded. "Both of you be quiet."

Susie sat next to Megan. Sliding her arms under Megan, she lifted her off the floor and placed Megan into her lap, cradling Megan up against her body. She gently rocked Megan back and forth, stroking her hair and telling her that she'd be all right. After a few minutes, Megan's cries became whimpers, quickly diminishing into an occasional gulping sob.

Gently easing Megan back so she could inspect the damage, Susie winced at the sight of it. Already a fairly large bruise had formed, and a bump the size of a goose egg was in the center of her forehead.

"Well," Susie commented optimistically in an attempt to defuse the potential of a full scale fit; "if you didn't have any war stories before, you do now."

Megan started to wail again so Susie kissed her boo-boo and said, "Megan, you're okay. You really are."

Megan refused this diagnosis, burying her face up against Susie. "I don't *feel* okay," she moaned. "**It hurts!**" she yelled.

Susie patted her back, and began slowly rubbing Megan's back as she had done numerous times for Simon. "I know," she said softly, comforting Megan. "It'll hurt for a little while, and then it will stop. We'll put some ice on it; that will make it all better faster."

Megan continued her sobbing.

"Oh, come on Megan; how bad can it be?" Kat asked, her tone a little trivializing.

Susie gave the two culprits a stern look. "Bad enough," she chastised. "Both of you need to apologize to Megan. ... Now! It might help lessen your punishment from Miss Hilda and Miss Pritchett if you at least show some remorse for what you did."

"I didn't DO anything!" Kat repeated emphatically, insulted that she was being blamed.

"Yes you ---", Dani shouted, but was interrupted by Susie.

"Quiet, Dani," Susie ordered. Turning her focus to Kat, she continued, "Yes you did, Kat. You started this fight by taunting Dani. Give her back her bracelet, apologize to her and then apologize to Megan."

Kat glared harshly at Susie for a moment while thinking it through. Exhaling a short, forceful burst of air, she shrugged, conceding at least somewhat that she is partially responsible. "Okay," she said.

Kneeling down beside Megan, Kat gently rubbed her back. "I'm sorry, Megan. I didn't mean for you to get hurt. I would never want that." Her tone was sincere; and by her expression, Susie knew Kat meant what she said. Susie smiled at her appreciatively, nodding her approval. Kat shrugged and grinned.

Inhaling a slow, deep breath, Kat released it forcefully as she stood and reluctantly turned to face Dani. "I'm sorry, Dani. I shouldn't have taken your bracelet. I was mad at you because yesterday I saw you trying to open my diary…. I just wanted to get even. I knew it'd make you mad if I took it," Kat shrugged dramatically; "so I did."

Reaching into her pocket, Kat withdrew the stolen item. She handed it to Dani. "I'm sorry."

"Thanks," Dani said sheepishly.

"Dani," Susie said sharply; "your turn."

Dani sighed. She looked at Megan, still pressed up against Susie and hiding her face. "I'm sorry, Megan. I didn't mean to hurt you."

Dani reached down and lightly tapped Megan on her shoulder. Megan turned her face toward Dani just enough for one eye to see her. "I would *never* hurt you on purpose, little sis," Dani said with an affectionate smile.

Megan buried her face up against Susie, not yet willing to forgive the transgressors.

Dani looked at Susie, held her hands up and gave an exaggerated shrug as if to say 'Hey, I did my best; what else can I do?'

"Dani, you're not off the hook yet," Susie began. "Did you try to open Kat's diary?"

Dani's eyes darted from Susie to Kat and then to the floor. "Yes," she replied softly. "I thought she might be writing something about me."

"You owe Kat an apology," Susie stated firmly. "How would you feel if someone did that to you?"

Dani looked truly remorseful. "I wouldn't like it."

"Neither does Kat." Susie responded gently.

Dani turned to face Kat, tears of remorse misting her eyes. "I'm sorry, Kat…. I just want you to like me. … I don't know why you don't. … I've tried *everything* I can think of to get you to like me. I thought that if you wrote something about me in your diary and I read it, then I'd know what to do different so you'd like me."

"You goof," Kat chuckled; "I do like you." Shaking her head, she let out a sigh of exasperation. "It's just that sometimes…. sometimes you get under my skin. You irritate me. … You're always following me, copying everything I do or say. … It *really* bugs me." Kat paused, smiled and then added, "But I do like you … even though you're goofy."

Surprising everyone, Kat reached out and gave Dani a hug. It was returned by Dani with great enthusiasm. "I guess you're my little sis," Kat said with a smile. Dani nodded, grinning from ear to ear.

"Great," Susie said, pleased that her diplomatic efforts thus far were successful, at least temporarily. "Now that that's settled, perhaps we can think of a way for the two of you to make it up to Megan." She raised her eyebrows, nodding her head toward the little ball curled in her lap, clinging tightly to her.

The room was suddenly uncomfortably silent. The other girls – Juls, Kat and Dani - mostly viewed Megan as a nuisance. Megan was always under foot, trying to keep up with them and constantly whining. They liked Megan – well, as much as you could like a five year old. After all, they were so much older, and much more mature than she. Since the arrival of Susie and Simon last week, Timmy had stopped hanging around his older brother, Aaron, and played with Simon. They were quite relieved that the boys had started inviting Megan to play with them; so, for the most part, Megan now left the girls alone. And for that reason, Juls, Kat and Dani were glad that Susie and Simon had arrived.

That is until today; Simon and Timmy had already told Megan that they were doing *"boys stuff"* today, and she wasn't invited. Megan was back to following the girls, trying to keep pace with them. Unfortunately, she was only inches behind Kat when Dani took a swing at Kat, receiving the blow meant for Kat.

"What about a tea party; I'm certain Megan would *love* to play tea party with Dani and Kat," prompted Juls mischievously. She had been sitting on the couch in the Common Area, reading her magazine and watching the whole show. She seemed genuinely amused and delighted in their reaction to her suggestion.

Kat and Dani rolled their eyes. The last thing they wanted to do was to play pretend tea party with prissy Juls and fussy Megan.

Megan's face turned toward the girls. "A tea party?" she asked between sniffles.

Dani sighed. Then she asked Megan, "Would you feel better if we all play tea party with you today?"

Megan's eyes brightened; she sat up straight and nodded her head several times.

"Okay," Susie agreed, "a tea party it is. What time?"

"Three o'clock," Kat offered.

"I can't," Susie responded glumly. "That's when Mrs. Crenshaw is coming to visit. She's bringing Simon a bunch of pictures of Glen Hollow that were taken fifty years ago."

"Really?" Kat asked as Dani asked, "Can we see them?"

Juls had left the couch and joined them. "May we, Susie?"

Susie nodded and said, "Sure, I don't see why not."

Megan's face clouded; crossing her arms, she puckered her lips into a giant pout. "What about my tea party?" she whined, irritated that she and her boo-boo were no longer the center of attention.

The trio – Dani, Kat and Juls – looked crestfallen. They looked to Susie, eyes pleading for help in dealing with Megan.

"Wouldn't you rather have a *real* tea party?" Susie asked Megan, turning Megan to face her.

Megan's scowl turned to a look of confusion until she suddenly realized what Susie meant. "Yes!" she shouted gleefully, clapping her hands.

"Okay," Susie said, giving Megan a hug. "Let's go ask Mrs. Coppersmith if she'll help us set up a tea party for you and Mrs. Crenshaw."

Susie lifted Megan up to her feet and quickly followed suit. "We have less than two hours to pull it together, so no more fighting. Okay?"

The girls unanimously echoed their 'Okays' and headed for the door.

"Wait!" Megan yelled.

They stopped in their tracks and turned around. "What?" they asked in unison.

Megan ran to them. She hugged Dani and then Kat. She stepped back, proudly stood tall and said, "It's my turn. I forgive you, Dani; and I forgive you, Kat." She gave both of them the royal nod as she bestowed her forgiveness on them. The girls all laughed; Dani and Kat both thanked her for her benevolence.

"Let's go get an ice pack for your bump," Susie told Megan as she ushered the group to the door.

"We'd better hurry," Juls said with an impish, little smile. "Miss Cora will be here any minute to take Megan for naptime."

Panic registered on Megan's face, and both Dani and Kat appeared a little unnerved at the thought. Having Miss Cora, or any of the other adults, see the huge goose-egg on little Megan's forehead was certainly not what they wanted. At least, not until it had time to dissipate at least a little.

Susie laughed. "No problem," she assured them. "Megan's bump comes first. We'll use the back stairs."

"Then let's go," Kat insisted, opening the door.

Peeking into the corridor, the girls looked like a comedy routine; five heads, vertically in a line, peering around the doorpost – Megan at the bottom, then Dani, then Kat, then Juls and ending with Susie at the top.

"Coast is clear. Let's go," Susie whispered.

Dashing out the door, they scurried down the corridor to the circular stairwell. From there, they quickly and cautiously hurried to the kitchen.

———

When they entered the kitchen, Mrs. Coppersmith was aghast at the bump protruding from Megan's forehead. She demanded to know what happened. They all began talking at once. She held up her hand, signaling them to be silent. Focusing her piercing gaze intently on Susie and, in a rather sharp tone, she insisted that Susie do the explaining while she tended to Megan.

Susie complied. She began explaining the fiasco while Mrs. Coppersmith clucked and fretted over the lump on Megan's forehead. Mrs. Coppersmith led Megan over to the deacon's bench situated against the wall by the fireplace. She insisted that Megan lay down, propping one of the decorative pillows under the little cherub's head. Quickly Mrs. Coppersmith removed a compress from the freezer. Gently she placed it on Megan's forehead, instructing Megan not to move until she was told to do so.

Turning around, Mrs. Coppersmith focused her attention on the girls and lit into Dani and Kat. Wagging her finger at both of them, she chided them for their deplorable behavior. Next she lit into Juls and Susie for not intervening before Kat and Dani came to blows. She launched into a mini-lecture about how the four of them were older and should be protective of poor, little Megan, and how they should be setting a good example for her instead of such a pitiful one. She continued with how they were fortunate to be here, to be a part of this wonderful family.

Mrs. Coppersmith paused briefly, her expression softened, and her voice became tender as she told them, "That's what we are, don't you know? We are a family. And family means looking out for one another, not trying to harm each other."

Dabbing the tears from her eyes with the hem of her apron, she cleared her throat and continued by stating how much each and every one of them were loved and wanted by all the members of Glen Hollow. Her eyes still glistened with her tears as she smiled so tenderly. "You are our children; maybe not by blood, but certainly by our choice."

She paused and nodded her head a few times. "Enough said."

Surprising all of them, she gave each girl a big hug. Kindly she told them to each take a chair from around the table and go sit by Megan. She gave them strict instructions to watch Megan and not allow her to fall asleep. She returned to her desk located in an alcove across the kitchen. The girls happily complied, telling Megan jokes to keep her amused.

After a few minutes Susie left and hesitantly approached Mrs. Coppersmith. She quickly launched into the tea party idea, adding that she thought maybe everyone would like to come.

Mrs. Coppersmith smiled at Susie, and her eyes twinkled. "That's a wonderful idea, a nice gesture, too," she said as she gave Susie a quick hug.

"Megan loves tea parties. We'll do it up right," she announced enthusiastically. "A real tea party, not like what she and I have. We'll get the word passed; the tea will be served at four. You might want to mention it to Miss Pritchett and Miss Hilda yourself."

"You play tea party with Megan?" Susie asked, the surprise quite evident in her voice and her expression.

Mrs. Coppersmith chuckled and said," Of course; at least once a week Megan and I have our own little tea party. Nothing fancy; just a cup of tea, a cookie and some girl talk."

Susie didn't know what to say; she just stood there, staring. It had never occurred to her that any of the adults would play tea party with Megan, the exception being Miss Cora, and Miss Pritchett and perhaps Miss Hilda. Finally she stammered, "That's really nice."

Mrs. Coppersmith shooed Susie away, back to the chairs with the girls for, as she put it, "she had lots to do and little time in which to do it".

Spinning into action, she picked up the phone and called Mr. Henry. Enthusiastically she informed him they had a guest coming at three for a tea party at four. She told him to spread the word that everyone is invited. (She had stressed the word "everyone" in such a way that Susie felt certain Mr. Henry received her inference that it was actually a command invitation.). Then she told him she needed tables set up immediately in the Grand Parlor: three large, round tables for the adults and one of the smaller ones for the children. Lastly, she reminded him to bring enough chairs for everyone.

Next she phoned Miss Fiona and Miss Elsa, instructing them to report to the kitchen straight away to assist her. Turning to Miss Taryn, Mrs. Coppersmith instructed her to get the tables set, to '*do it up fancy*', and then return to the kitchen and assist in the final preparations. Miss Taryn nodded and hurriedly left the kitchen. Her face lit up as her smile turned into a full grin – she was thrilled to be able to use her design talents for such a festive and formal occasion.

Mrs. Coppersmith was a whirlwind of activity. The girls were very surprised to see how fast, how efficient, she was. There was no wasted motion; there was no duplication of effort in obtaining kettles, or pans, or bowls or supplies. When Miss Elsa and Miss Fiona arrived, she put them to work preparing the tiny cucumber sandwiches and the chicken salad sandwiches while she prepared the petit fours and the dainty chocolate confections. She barked out instructions to them while continuing with whatever project she happened to be performing.

After twenty minutes had passed (Mrs. Coppersmith had been watching the clock Susie noticed), Mrs. Coppersmith removed the cold compress from Megan's head, checking her lump. It had reduced in size by half. After repeated assurances from Megan that her head didn't hurt any more, Mrs. Coppersmith accepted Megan's declaration. Smiling, she told the girls to return the chairs and then have a seat at the table. Not knowing what to expect, the girls nervously complied, hoping her next call wasn't to Miss Pritchett, or Miss Hilda, or Miss Bettye or even Miss Cora.

In a flurry of motion, Mrs. Coppersmith removed from a cupboard five ice cream bowls and five spoons from a drawer, setting them on the table, one in front of each girl. From the freezer she removed a container of ice cream and placed a small scoop of strawberry ice cream (Megan's favorite) into each bowl. She received a resounding chorus of 'thank-you' from the surprised and grateful girls.

After returning the container to the freezer, Mrs. Coppersmith came back to the table. She told them there was something she forgot to say earlier, should have said and was remiss in not having done so. She smiled. She told the girls how proud she was of them for the way they resolved the conflict. Her eyes twinkled, glistening from her tears that began forming again. Beaming with pride, Mrs. Coppersmith told them that she was most especially proud of them all for uniting together to care for little Megan the way they did.

Her smile widened into a full grin as she added, "Perhaps you've already come to see yourselves as sisters after all. At any rate, I'm mighty proud of the lot of you." She left them to enjoy their snack as she continued making the preparations for the tea party.

They quickly ate their ice cream, setting a record, Susie was certain. After placing their bowls and spoons in the sink, they each gave Mrs. Coppersmith a hug, thanking her yet again for helping Megan and for the ice cream. They rushed to Miss Hilda's office, hoping that they'd be finished in time to help Miss Taryn. They didn't get far from the kitchen door when they ran into Miss Hilda.

"There you are, Susie," she said. "I've been looking for you."

"We've been looking for you," the girls said in unison.

Miss Hilda was now close enough to see Megan's face. She saw the dark bruise and the lump on her forehead.

"What on earth happen to you, Megan?" With a swift motion, she reached and gently held Megan's chin in her hand for a closer inspection, turning her face to the right and then to the left.

"Mrs. Coppersmith put an ice pack on it," Megan announced proudly. "I now have a war story."

Susie grimaced slightly as Dani and Kat fidgeted. Juls just grinned.

"Indeed you do," Miss Hilda responded with concern; "how did you get hurt?"

Dani and Kat quickly looked at each other and then at Susie, pleading silently for her help.

"Well, which one of you is going to tell me what happened?" Miss Hilda prompted, her tone becoming just a little terse. "Susie, you tell me."

Very calmly, and with a touch of sophistication, Susie explained. "Dani and Kat had an argument which became physical. In short, Dani tried to hit Kat; Kat moved, and Megan was hit instead. Mrs. Coppersmith put an ice pack on her bump. Dani and Kat have apologized to Megan and to each other. Megan has forgiven them both. They've resolved it."

"Is this true?" Miss Hilda asked the three involved in the scuffle, giving them all an intense scrutiny.

"Yes," Dani and Kat chorused in unison, wanting the questions to end.

Megan smiled gleefully, rapidly nodding her head several times for emphasis as she quickly informed Miss Hilda, "We're going to have a *real* tea party, not a play tea party."

"Is that so?" Miss Hilda asked, arching her eyebrow.

Susie took in a deep breath and began talking fast. "Yes. We were going to have a pretend tea party with Megan today to make up for her being hurt; but I couldn't because Mrs. Crenshaw is coming to visit at three o'clock. The other girls wanted to see the old pictures of Glen Hollow that Mrs. Crenshaw is bringing. Simon asked Mrs. Crenshaw last week if he could see the pictures, and she said she would bring them today. So everyone wants to see the pictures, and that upset Megan since her play tea party would have to be postponed."

Susie took a fast breath and continued rapidly, "We offered to give her a real tea party with Mrs. Crenshaw so she could still have her tea party today. We asked Mrs. Coppersmith, and she is happy to prepare it for us; but she said that we would need to tell you and Miss Pritchett about it. And that's why we are looking for you; we wanted to tell you about the tea party, and also see if you or Miss Pritchett would like to come. Everyone is invited. Mrs. Coppersmith said that tea will be served at four."

Miss Hilda smiled warmly. "It sounds wonderful, dear. I'd love to attend, and I'm certain Miss Pritchett will also."

She looked at her watch. "We'll discuss this incident later. Mrs. Crenshaw will be here in forty minutes. Susie, Miss Pritchett would like to see you in her office. The rest of you may go on to the Parlor and help Miss Taryn."

Smiling fondly at Megan, Miss Hilda patted Megan's head. "Off with you now," she instructed; "and mind what Miss Taryn tells you."

The girls looked at Susie with concern, but not enough to question Miss Hilda as to why Susie was wanted in Miss Pritchett's office. They gave Susie a chagrined look, shrugged their shoulders and rapidly ran toward the Parlor.

"No running," Miss Hilda sharply called out to them whereupon they immediately dropped into a frenzied walk.

"Come along," Miss Hilda said to Susie, walking briskly toward the front corridor of the west wing. "Are you certain you feel okay? You're not as pale as you were at breakfast, and not flushed as at lunch; but you still look a little peaked." Miss Hilda looked very concerned.

Susie smiled. "I'm fine. I just didn't sleep much last night. That's all."

"And why do suppose you didn't sleep well?" she pressed.

"Too excited, I guess. There's so much to see and do; I guess I just couldn't stop thinking," Susie responded as casually as she could.

Before Miss Hilda could ask another question Susie decided to ask one of her own. "Why does Miss Pritchett want to see me? Am I in trouble?"

Miss Hilda chuckled. "Not at all, dear. There are just a few things you need to know. Simon is already there."

When they reached the sitting room door, Miss Hilda opened it and held it open for Susie. Upon entering the room, Susie saw that Simon was indeed already there. He was sitting on the couch facing the door, laughing and talking with Miss Pritchett and the two men that sat on the couch opposite of him. As she and Miss Hilda approached, Miss Pritchett smiled and stood. The two men followed suit.

"Hilda, Susie; please come join us," Miss Pritchett said cheerfully.

Susie walked over and stood next to where Simon was still seated; Miss Hilda stood next to the elder of the two gentlemen. Susie noticed that both men had a leather briefcase.

"Gentlemen, I believe you already know Hilda. Susie, allow me to present Mr. Ethan Hawks and Mr. Milton Aimes." She indicted the elder gentlemen first (Susie guessed he was at least eighty), and then the younger man, whom she thought was in his late twenties or early thirties.

"Ethan, Milton, please allow me to present Miss Susie Howard."

They each said "hello" to one another; then Miss Pritchett sat down, and everyone else did the same.

Miss Pritchett spoke softly, "Susie, I've asked you and Simon here because I wanted to introduce you to these gentlemen and allow them to explain what it is they do." She turned and nodded at Mr. Hawks.

He smiled affectionately at Miss Pritchett. "I've known Miss Pritchett all her life. Her mother was a good friend of mine, so Glen Hollow has a special place in my heart. I do what I can to help."

Mr. Hawks, in fluidity of motion, reached into his pocket, retrieved a small, silver case and opened it. He removed a business card and handed it to Susie. Simon promptly stuck out his hand. Mr. Hawks grinned and repeated the process, giving Simon his own card to keep.

"I'm an attorney, and I handle the legal matters for Miss Pritchett and for Glen Hollow. Mr. Aimes is an associate in my firm."

Mr. Aimes now handed one of his business cards to Simon and then to Susie. Delighting in being handed the card first, Simon sat up straight, proud as a peacock.

"With that said," Mr. Hawks continued, "there are two matters of business that we need to discuss. First, I have set up trust accounts for both of you. Miss Pritchett's custom is to have such an account for each child that lives here, and I am the trustee of those trusts. You may not receive the funds until you are eighteen. It is intended that the funds help to provide for your college education together with scholarships or other student aid."

Susie was shocked. She looked at Miss Pritchett. "How can you afford that?" she asked.

Miss Pritchett's eyes twinkled, and her smile was kind. "We have been very blessed that Glen Hollow has always provided what we need. When I first started Glen Hollow, I refused to accept the money from the state for the children's care and tried to return it; the state would not allow me to do so. Nor would they allow me to set it aside for your future use. Therefore, I decided that I would place funds equal to what is received into trust until the child reaches the age of eighteen. At that time, the money is transferred into your personal bank account, and the trust is closed. It is my hope that you will further your education with it, or use the funds to start your own business."

"Thank you," Susie mumbled, humbled at this generous gesture.

Mr. Hawks said, "Our second business that we need to address is the property that you and Simon inherited from your great-grandmother, Sophie Tremont."

"Her name is Nana," Simon politely corrected him.

He smiled at Simon. "Yes, of course. Nana left to both of you her home and her bank account, in addition to her personal belongings. I believe the personal items were delivered here yesterday, is that correct?"

Susie, Simon, Miss Hilda and Miss Pritchett all chorused "Yes" in answer to his question.

"Excellent," Mr. Hawks responded. "Miss Pritchett arranged to have those items brought here in order to stop the storage fees that were depleting Nana's account. In other words, to enable you to keep more of the money Nana left to you. As your legal guardian, Miss Pritchett instructed me to set up another trust, in both your names, that will hold the bank account and your Nana's home. I have done so; and again, I am the trustee on that trust."

Leaning slightly toward Susie, his expression became quite serious. "If you attend college, monies will be dispersed from the joint trust to help defray the cost. When you turn twenty-one, whatever funds remain from your half of the trust account will be disbursed to you. The same holds true for Simon. Additionally, on his twenty-first birthday, the home will be deeded in both your names, if you've not already sold it."

He returned to sitting upright and continued, his tone taking on a functional, instructional quality. "As your legal guardian, Miss Pritchett has decided not to sell the home at this time in order to allow you the option of living there in the future. For now, we'll rent it, and those funds will be deposited into the trust account. I, or Mr. Aimes, will keep a close watch on the home to ensure that it is well cared for by the tenants. Any maintenance or repair costs will be deducted from the trust account, as are insurance and tax payments. Just so you know, normally I charge a fee for such service. However, for Glen Hollow the work is done pro bono."

Perplexed, Simon asked, "You work for a bone?" Everyone laughed. Simon was not amused.

"No, Simon; 'pro-bono' is a legal term," Mr. Hawks patiently explained; "it means 'without charge'. Free, in other words."

Simon scowled. "Why didn't you say that?"

Mr. Hawks smiled, leaned toward Simon and winked. "Next time I will, Simon."

He turned his attention to Susie. "I give an accounting to Miss Pritchett every month; and we have a formal meeting annually, which you and Simon will attend. You are welcome to ask questions of Miss Pritchett, or myself or Mr. Aimes at any time. Do you have any questions?"

She shook her head and answered softly, "No, sir."

He smiled fondly and said, "Should either of you ever have any questions, please ask."

Simon asked of Mr. Aimes, "Where do you live?"

He grinned. "I live in Foxboro Station."

"Have you always lived there?" he pressed.

Chuckling at Simon's curiosity, he answered, "No, not always. I've lived there for four years now."

"Where did you live before that?" Simon asked, continuing his interrogation.

"In Willington; I went to law school there. Why do you ask?" he questioned Simon.

Simon shrugged. "Just wondered," he responded. He grinned slyly and asked, "Do you have any children?"

Mr. Aimes laughed robustly. "Not yet, Simon; I've only been married a year."

"All right," Mr. Hawks intervened; "I believe we're finished."

Miss Pritchett rose, extended her hand first to Mr. Hawks and then to Mr. Aimes, shaking hands with them. "I believe so. Thank you both for coming. I'll see you out."

Gracefully she moved around the end of the couch and walked to the door. Both gentlemen quickly said their goodbyes to Miss Hilda, Susie and then to Simon, following Miss Pritchett out of the door.

Miss Hilda smiled at Susie and Simon as she moved toward the door to her office. "Mrs. Crenshaw will be here in fifteen minutes," she told them; "run along and join the others."

"Aren't you coming?" Susie asked as she followed Miss Hilda.

"Yes, dear; but first I have a couple of things to attend to in my office. You go on ahead; I'll be there directly."

Miss Hilda crossed the room and entered her office just as Susie and Simon reached the door to exit the sitting room. Simon darted out the door, then noticed that Susie wasn't following him. He re-entered the sitting room to find Susie at the Wall of Fame.

"What are you doing?" he asked, slightly annoyed.

"Checking out a hunch," she answered, not bothering to turn around.

"What are you talking about?" he asked, lightly pushing her in an attempt to get her undivided attention.

"Stop it, Simon," she ordered. "I'm looking for something."

"What?" he demanded. "Mrs. C is going to be here any minute. Let's go," he insisted.

"Just a minute," she responded in a sing-song fashion, attempting to quell his impatience.

She continued searching the photos. "Aha!" she exclaimed. "I knew it."

"Knew what?" Simon asked.

She pointed to a picture. It was a young boy, age twelve, from 1990. "Milton Jared Aimes," she pronounced with an air of satisfaction.

Simon shrugged and said irritably, "So."

"So," Susie explained; "it means that Mr. Aimes once lived here."

"Cool," Simon stated. "*Now* can we go see Mrs. C?" he asked peevishly.

"Sure, let's go," she agreed. Simon ran out the door as if the house was on fire, Susie right behind him.

"Do you think we'll be punished?" Dani asked Susie as soon as she entered the Parlor.

Apparently Dani had been nervously waiting by the door for Susie. She was anxious and rightly so, Susie thought. Megan could have been seriously injured. For that matter, so could have Kat if Dani had landed that blow in her abdomen as Dani had intended. Kat, however, did not appear to care that there could be consequences for herself or for Dani.

Susie shrugged. "I don't know. Maybe they'll take into consideration that it's already resolved, and that we're really having this tea party for Megan." She smiled encouragingly, hoping Dani would relax and enjoy the tea party.

Miss Taryn had done a marvelous job in such a short amount of time; they were awed by her talents. She had re-arranged the furniture so that the large, round tables would easily fit without the room appearing over-crowded. The adult tables were placed facing a fireplace and formed a semi-circle. The children's table was placed in the center of the semi-circle, almost forming the letter 'e'.

Fastidiously, Miss Taryn directed the men as to the precise place-ment of each table, exasperating them a time or two with her penchant for perfection. Miss Claire, together with Miss Ginger, Miss Bettye, Miss Cora and Miss Emma made light work of re-arranging the smaller pieces while Mr. Henry, Dale, JT and Allan Roy attended to the moving of the heavy furniture. Miss Thelma's assistance mainly consisted of voicing her approval or disapproval of the choices made by Miss Taryn; however, she did help when it was time to set the tables.

As soon as Miss Taryn pronounced that their chores were complete, the men hurriedly left – they needed to clean up and change clothes in time for the tea party. Mr. Sean, Joe, Kevin and Samuel, currently still at work in the barns, would go directly to their cottages for clean-up prior to attend-ing the tea party. Although tea parties were not one of the men's preferred activities, they were quite interested in seeing the pictures Mrs. Crenshaw was bringing.

Susie thought that the decorated tables were amazing. 'Miss Taryn is definitely talented', she thought as she admired the finished work.

First, Miss Taryn had placed on the tables a white, satin brocade cloth that nearly touched the floor. On top of it, she placed a smaller silk cloth, creamy white in color, and draped nearly three-quarters of the way down the brocade cloth. The corners of the silk cloth each displayed a vibrant bouquet of red and gold roses; pretty green leaves surrounded the bouquets, very much reminiscent of fresh, floral arrangements. Running along the edge of the cloth, creating a unique border, was a ribbon of leaves connecting each beautiful bouquet. Lastly, she draped a white, sheer cloth over the silk one; it gracefully extended to just above the floral bouquets of the silk cloth.

Miss Taryn had just finished laying out the last of the place settings as she and Simon entered the room. The elegant gold-trimmed crystal, the gold flatware and the red and gold roses of the Old Country Roses china perfectly complemented Miss Taryn's selection of table linens.

Her choice of items for the table centerpieces was also incredible. A scalloped gold plate held a trio of white taper candles in china candle holders that matched the china service. Encircling the decorative plate was a ring of diminutive silk roses, alternating gold and scarlet colors; truly a perfect apex for the table décor.

Miss Pritchett and Miss Hilda entered the Parlor accompanied by Mrs. Coppersmith, Miss Fiona and Miss Elsa, just moments prior to the arrival of Mrs. Crenshaw. The atmosphere filling the room was festive, bursting with excitement and anticipation. Everyone was talking and laughing, teasing and joking, eagerly waiting for their guest of honor. Mrs. Crenshaw arrived promptly at three, and was immediately ushered into the Parlor by Miss Cora, who had faithfully been waiting by the front door for her arrival.

Simon rushed over to Mrs. Crenshaw, giving her one of his best bear hugs. "Mrs. C!" he gushed excitedly; "you came!"

"Well of course I did," she responded cheerfully, returning his eager embrace.

Susie gave Mrs. Crenshaw a quick hug and began the introductions, first the adults, beginning with Miss Pritchett who insisted that Mrs. Crenshaw address her by her given name, Eloise. Mrs. Crenshaw readily agreed, providing that Miss Pritchett would reciprocate and call her by her given name of Ruth. Miss Pritchett also readily agreed, prompting the other adults, (except Mrs. Coppersmith), to also insist on the use of their given names. Mrs. Crenshaw laughed and said that she doubted that she could remember so many names, and to please assist her whenever she faltered. Naturally everyone volunteered to assist, especially Simon.

As soon as Susie had finished the adult introductions, Mrs. Crenshaw smiled and thanked them for their gracious efforts. She noted that the tables looked divine, humbly stating how pleased she was that they would go to so much trouble for her.

Mrs. Coppersmith gave "credit to where credit is due", as she had said, proudly telling Mrs. Crenshaw that the design arrangements were all Miss Taryn's talent. Miss Pritchett, also complimented Miss Taryn, agreeing that she was a treasure. Most of the other adults also gave a wide range of accolades, citing many examples of her talent.

Flushing slightly from such high praise (especially from Mrs. Coppersmith), Miss Taryn smiled and thanked everyone, adding that it was her pleasure. Susie noticed that Miss Claire was radiant as she gazed lovingly at her daughter.

With a twinkle in her eye, Mrs. Coppersmith excused herself and her helpers, Miss Taryn, Miss Elsa and Miss Fiona, citing they had to finish the preparations. Swiftly the ladies left, closely following Mrs. Coppersmith.

Susie began her introductions of the other children. When it was Megan's turn to be introduced, she marched right up to Mrs. Crenshaw, pointed to the goose egg on her forehead and proudly announced that she had a war story.

"Indeed?" Mrs. Crenshaw responded, slightly concerned. "And what might that be?"

Megan pointed to Dani. "She tried to hit Kat (now pointing to Kat) and missed 'cause Kat moved, and then Dani hit me 'cause I was behind Kat."

Megan slowly moved her head back and forth. With all the seriousness she could muster, and in an attempt to exonerate Dani, she added, "Dani didn't know I was there. She didn't mean to hit me."

Megan flashed Mrs. Crenshaw a dimpled smile, nodded her head rapidly as she confided, "It was an accident."

Susie watched Miss Pritchett as Megan relayed the story. Since there was no hint of surprise, Susie concluded Miss Hilda must have told her about the incident prior to their arrival for the tea party. She wondered what would be the repercussions for Dani and Kat. Suddenly Susie realized that having helped Megan elude naptime, she could also be facing some repercussions of her own. She swallowed hard and turned her attention back to Mrs. Crenshaw.

"My goodness," Mrs. Crenshaw said, serious concern filling her expression. "Are you all right, Megan?"

Megan nodded, affirming that she was. "Mrs. Coppersmith put ice on it, and then gave us strawberry ice cream." She giggled a little, confessing, "It's my favorite."

"That was very nice of Mrs. Coppersmith," Mrs. Crenshaw responded, casting a wary glance at Miss Pritchett.

Megan nodded, agreeing. "Yes, and we're having the tea party for you, and for me," she proudly informed Mrs. Crenshaw.

"That's wonderful, but a tea party for me isn't necessary," she said smiling as she gently removed a few stay strands of Megan's hair from her eyes.

"Yes it is," Megan adamantly countered. "We were going to have a play tea party because I got hurt. But Susie couldn't play because you were coming. They all wanted to see your pictures, so Susie said let's have a *real* tea party for *me* and for *you*. That way we get to have a tea party *and* look at the pictures." She ended her little speech with a sharp nod of her head, signaling the end to her performance.

Mrs. Crenshaw laughed lightheartedly. "I think that was very wonderful of them, and certainly a fine gesture for the girls to do all of this in order to apologize to you. They must like you an awful lot," she said smiling at Megan.

Megan flashed Mrs. Crenshaw a coy smile and shrugged her shoulders. "I don't know," she said, feigning shyness.

"Can we see the pictures now?" Simon interrupted, slightly annoyed by Megan's monopoly of Mrs. Crenshaw.

"What is the proper way to ask?" Mrs. Crenshaw responded, smiling at him.

Simon thought for a moment and grinned. "*May* we see the pictures now, ple-e-ease?" he asked sweetly.

"Yes, you may," she chuckled. She opened one of the four tote bags she had brought with her and began laying the first of the photo albums onto the coffee table.

"Now before we start, we must observe three rules. First, you must sit around the coffee table to view the albums. Second, you may not remove the pictures from the albums. Third, you must not touch the pictures. Does everyone understand?"

A chorus of "yes", and "uh-huh", and "you bet" competed for audible triumph as all of the children scrambled for a position around the large, oval coffee table.

She smiled at them and continued. "There are twelve albums; four are from 1954, four are from 1955 and four are from 1956. Please be careful with them."

As she laid an album in front of each child, she gave a final instruction. Placing her hands on Simon's shoulders, she stated, "Simon will be the starting point." (He grinned and bounced a little jig at this honor.) "As you each finish your album, you will carefully pass it to the person sitting on your left." She leaned down and asked the child on Simon's left, "What is your name, dear?"

The girl grinned at Mrs. Crenshaw and said, "Juls."

"Juls," she repeated as she straightened. "Simon will pass his album to Juls, who will pass her album to Susie and so on. Does everyone understand?"

Again, a variety of chorused responses acknowledging that they understood were loudly articulated.

"Then you may begin," she responded, leaving the children to their albums. She joined the other ladies, seating herself next to Miss Bettye.

It was obvious that the flaw in this system was that the younger children lost interest after viewing a few pages. They passed their albums on much faster than anyone else was ready to receive. As a result, a bottleneck of albums ensued. Simon, Timmy and Megan decided to go play one of the many board games that Miss Ginger had so thoughtfully brought for them from the Rec Room. Not long after they had left the table, Dani, Aaron, Jose and Jared also left, leaving only Kat, Juls and Susie pouring through the albums.

Mrs. Crenshaw quietly rose from her position on the couch and walked over to the girls remaining at the coffee table. After verifying with them which albums they had not yet seen, she left those with the girls. Taking the albums that had been viewed, she distributed them among the adults.

Everyone was amazed by the pictures, chatting away about the grandeur of the festivals and what fun they must have been. Susie looked up and noticed that Miss Pritchett and Miss Hilda were very quiet. Both appeared to be sad, Miss Pritchett more so than Miss Hilda. She began to regret that Simon had asked Mrs. Crenshaw to bring the pictures. As the adults began asking questions about the festivals and about Glen Hollow, Miss Pritchett and Miss Hilda were jolted out of whatever memories that had caused the sadness. They began to regale everyone with their memories and stories; soon they were laughing along with everyone else.

'Perhaps it was a good idea after all', Susie thought.

The grandfather clock chimed the four o'clock hour; with her usual precision, Mrs. Coppersmith entered the Parlor and announced that "tea would now be served".

Stepping aside, she allowed Miss Taryn, Miss Elsa and Miss Fiona to enter, each pushing a tea cart laden with teapots full of tea, and serving dishes filled full of goodies.

———

The tea party was actually a great deal of fun. Everyone seemed to be enjoying themselves. Mrs. Coppersmith, in her infinite wisdom, had the foresight to also include milk on the tea carts for whoever decided they didn't like, or want, hot tea.

Though very delicious, the cucumber sandwiches did not gain much popularity among the men or the children, the exceptions being Juls and Susie. Again, Mrs. Coppersmith had anticipated that possibility and had provided miniature peanut butter and jelly sandwiches in addition to sandwiches made of her tasty chicken salad. However, the greatest hit of all was the sweet desserts. Everyone greatly enjoyed the petit fours, and the variety of candies that Mrs. Coppersmith had so expertly prepared.

It was strange, but the good kind of strange, to see how so many people that were so different could relax and enjoy each other's company. The conversations never ceased, flowing seamlessly from one subject to another whether started by an adult or a child. Susie found it fun to watch and to participate in the ebb and flow of the camaraderie.

The afternoon passed far too quickly, and soon the grandfather clock was chiming five-thirty. "Oh dear," Mrs. Crenshaw said as she realized the lateness of the hour. "I really must be going. It's been such a wonderful afternoon. Thank you ever so much," she added as she rose from her chair.

"It was our pleasure," Miss. Pritchett responded, rising from her own chair. "I'll see you to the door. Susie, Simon would you like to accompany us?"

They both nodded 'yes', and they vocalized it as well. Simon volunteered to carry one of her tote bags, but quickly discovered it was too heavy for him to carry. As they prepared to leave, everyone came over to say 'good-by', wishing her a safe trip and hoping that she'd come back soon for another visit. Mrs. Crenshaw assured them that she'd visit again.

Simon started to run ahead, but quickly dropped into a fast race-walk. He looked back to see if Miss Pritchett had noticed his change of pace. If she had, she didn't show it, so he quickly continued his course toward the front door.

"Are you driving back to Willington tonight?" Susie asked Mrs. Crenshaw.

"No, Susie," she responded. "It's too far for that. I arranged to have tomorrow off as a personal day, so we'll drive back in the morning."

"We?" asked Miss Pritchett.

Mrs. Crenshaw smiled. "Yes, my children and I visited with my mother this weekend. They're with her now."

"How many children do you have?" Miss Pritchett politely inquired.

"Four," she responded with a grin.

"That's a houseful," Miss Pritchett responded.

"Yes, it is." Mrs. Crenshaw smiled sadly at Susie. "I would have loved to have kept Susie and Simon, but… I just couldn't."

"It's okay, Mrs. Crenshaw. We didn't want to leave; but with only two bedrooms, we knew you didn't have enough room for anyone else. And we really like it here," Susie assured her.

Miss Pritchett smiled fondly and said, "Thank you, Susie. I'm glad you and Simon are here, and I am very delighted that you like Glen Hollow."

411

"I'm glad you like it, too, Susie. I felt certain you and Simon would do well once you both adjusted to the change," Mrs. Crenshaw said with a big smile.

They had reached the foyer, and Simon was impatiently waiting by the door. "What took you guys so long?" he asked impertinently. Seeing the reaction on their faces, he quickly amended his question with, "I was getting worried someone fell and got hurt."

They laughed, and he gave a chagrined little smile as he pranced over to Mrs. Crenshaw.

Miss Emma came scurrying into the foyer, carrying Mrs. Crenshaw's coat and rubber boots. "I'm sorry it took so long, but I had to break up a slight disagreement between Jared and Aaron. Nothing serious," she assured Miss Pritchett.

"Thank you," Mrs. Crenshaw said to Miss Emma as she accepted her coat and boots. She sat down on the bench and quickly put on her boots. She stood and slid into her coat. From one pocket she removed her hat and scarf, placing the former on her head and the latter around her neck. Removing her gloves from the other pocket, she quickly slid her hands into them.

Susie gave Mrs. Crenshaw a hug, telling her to please come back soon and visit longer. Simon followed Susie's lead and did the same. Mrs. Crenshaw promised she would, but sighed as she told them it would be after the holidays. She patted Simon on the head and asked, "Does your bedroom have two beds, or do you and Susie share the same bed?"

Simon proudly stated, "We don't share a room; I sleep in the Boys Dorm."

"Excuse me?" Mrs. Crenshaw responded, quite taken aback. Susie and Simon started talking at once; Susie trying to explain and prevent any further damage, whereas Simon just wanted to brag about his 'big boy' status.

"Susie, Simon, please be silent," Mrs. Crenshaw firmly requested. She set her sights on Miss Pritchett. Her voice had a slight edge to it. "I distinctly remember informing you that Susie and Simon were to share a room until he was ready to do otherwise. Would you kindly explain to me why they are not sharing a room?"

Miss Pritchett's relaxed demeanor and hearty smile were genuine. "Certainly, Ruth. Simon, if left to his own device, would never choose to be separated from Susie. To force him to do so after adjusting to his new life here would be far more traumatic for him than to require him to begin his new life here sleeping in the Dorm Room. Their first night they did share a room, but only for that night because they had arrived here so late. They barely arrived in time for dinner. Both have adjusted well as you have witnessed this afternoon."

"Honest, Mrs. C; I like it here. I like sharing a room with the other boys. And I have Timmy and Megan to play with," Simon assured her.

"It's true, Mrs. Crenshaw," Susie affirmed. "Simon is doing great. At first, we were both very angry with Miss Pritchett. Simon wanted to call you immediately (to this statement Simon begin rapidly nodding his head); but I told him when you visited today, he could tell you himself if he was unhappy here."

"I'm not unhappy, Mrs. C. I *really*, **really** like it here; and I don't want to leave," he insisted. Giving her a soulful, pleading look, he added; "Please let me stay here."

"And you, Susie?" she asked, studying Susie's expression closely.

Susie nodded slowly, keeping eye contact with her. "I really like it here, Mrs. Crenshaw. I want to stay."

Mrs. Crenshaw was still a little apprehensive about leaving them in a place where her instructions were not followed. After a few moments of reflection, she affably stated, "Very well; if you're happy, then I'm happy."

Giving them each a quick hug, she smiled affectionately at both of them and said, "I'm very proud of you both. You kept your promise to give Glen Hollow an honest try." Susie smiled and nodded, and Simon beamed his very best Cheshire cat grin.

Extending her hand, Mrs. Crenshaw shook hands with Miss Pritchett, thanking her for taking good care of Susie and Simon, and for such a pleasant afternoon. She smiled and added that she looked forward to getting to know all of them, staff and children alike.

Miss Pritchett smiled fondly at both Susie and Simon, assuring Mrs. Crenshaw that Susie and Simon were a delightful addition to the Glen Hollow family. They said their good-byes, wishing Mrs. Crenshaw a safe journey.

Chapter 19

THE TROUBLE WITH JULS

Dinner now finished, everyone fell into their routines. Mrs. Coppersmith, Miss Taryn and Miss Fiona had already left the Dining Hall, pushing the heavily laden carts to the kitchen. The farmers (Mr. Sean, Joe, Sam and Kevin), Miss Elsa and Miss Bettye all said their goodnights and quickly left for their cottages. Mr. Henry, Allan Roy and JT were standing by the fireplace, laughing and talking. Dale skulked away, citing he had to get up early when invited to join them.

The children all scampered away, pursuing their interests. Except for the Munchkins; as usual, Miss Ginger and Miss Cora were waiting at the doors for them, thwarting any chance of escape. Thus snared, they were led away for their nightly baths.

Susie slipped out of the Hall before anyone could detain her. For the most part, she was trying to avoid the other girls. She didn't have a chance after lunch to retrieve her Unicorn book. The brawl between Dani and Kat and its aftermath, the meeting in Miss Pritchett's office suite, Mrs. Crenshaw's subsequent arrival and the tea party, all worked in concert to derail Susie's plans.

Fortunately, she had the Library to herself again; hurriedly she ran to the east side and to the precious volume. She slid it out of its resting place, holding it tightly against her body as she ran back to the Library entrance.

Peeking into the corridor, Susie breathed a sigh of relief – it was empty. Debating whether she should use the main staircase in the foyer (as was allowed) or the spiral staircase (that no one had actually said she couldn't), Susie opted for the spiral staircase. After all, Miss Hilda did say its purpose was to save time and steps, Susie rationalized.

Stepping into the corridor, Susie quickly made her way to the connecting hallway, and did so in as close a pace to running as possible without actually running. Pausing, she cautiously peeked around the corner before entering the hallway. It was empty so she rushed to the spiral staircase. Taking the stairs two at a time, Susie arrived at the second floor landing within a couple of minutes. Her luck held; no one was there. She continued on up the staircase to the third floor, again pausing when she reached the landing. Slowly rising up to where her eyes were just above the floor, she peered around the area. She grinned; the corridor was empty. With great haste, Susie exited the stairwell and ran to the attic room door.

Pulling the key from her pocket, she unlocked the door and stepped onto the stairs, pulling the door closed behind her. Placing her hand firmly on the banister, Susie carefully climbed until she reached the switch, flipping it and flooding the stairwell with its soft light. Running up the steps, she flicked the switch for the room's light as she strode past it. Everything was as she had left it. But then, she really didn't expect anything to be amiss. Crossing the room, Susie placed the treasured volume in the bookcase. It looked lonely, having no company other than the little clock.

"Don't worry," Susie told it; "I'll bring the other volumes here, too; if they're in the Library."

As she turned to leave, she thought of something else. Susie spun around and giggled. "And I'll start unpacking some of Nana's books. That'll keep you company."

She laughed and skipped to the stairwell. In less than ten minutes, the Munchkins would be in the Rec Room and ready to be entertained. Susie turned off the overhead light and made her way down to the stairwell light, switching it off as she sailed passed it. With the stairwell now completely veiled in darkness, Susie carefully continued down each step, reaching the door within a few minutes. Opening it, she darted into the corridor, quickly closing the door and locking it.

"Unpacking?" a voice behind her asked.

Startled, Susie jumped. "Yes," she stammered.

"I'm sorry; I didn't mean to frighten you," Miss Fiona said, smiling impishly.

"No problem," Susie replied; "I didn't see you when I came out, and I didn't hear you behind me."

"Obviously," Miss Fiona agreed, her tone amused. "So, you're settling in then?"

Susie nodded. "Yes; I thought I'd unpack some books and knick-knacks."

Miss Fiona laughed merrily. "Are you telling me the Library doesn't have enough books for you, or none that's to your liking?"

Susie blushed. "No," she quickly explained. "I just thought I'd unpack some things that reminded me of Nana."

Leaning slightly toward Susie, Miss Fiona grinned playfully. Her eyes flashed and sparkled with glee. "I'm just teasing you, child. I understand about needing things to help keep the memories fresh. We all do. But I am glad to see that you're making yourself at home."

Susie sighed. "It doesn't really feel like home. Up there it does a little, but … I don't know."

Miss Fiona smiled encouragingly. "It will. No transition is ever fast enough to suit us. The place will grow on you, and you'll come to love it here."

Her eyes held a light that Susie had never before seen, similar to a strobe light alternating between faintly glowing and then dimming. It was strangely calming. Somehow Susie now had a sense that Miss Fiona was right, that, in time, Glen Hollow would be home to her.

Upon reaching the second floor landing, Miss Fiona said goodnight to Susie, continuing on down to the foyer. Susie turned and trotted quickly to the Rec Room. As she entered, the Munchkins were waiting for her with the game already set up, loudly debating who would be what color. Susie interrupted their heated exchange by telling them to take turns. She assigned each of them a color and told them if they could not get along, she would not play with them. That quieted their contentious quarreling as fast as an ice cube melts when left in the summer sun.

The rest of the evening went smoothly. They laughed and had a good time; it ended all too soon, even for Susie. It seemed as if just a minute or so had passed since they began playing when suddenly Miss Ginger and Miss Cora were standing in the doorway, announcing that it was bedtime. Each Munchkin gave Susie a hug, one by one, before running to the ladies. From the doorway they gave Susie a last wave and a wink, chorusing a hearty "good-night, Susie" before they exited.

Susie began picking up the game pieces. After collecting all of them, she closed the lid and returned the game to its proper shelf. On her way to the door, she smiled at Jared as she passed by the couch. He smiled back, and Susie was delighted that his smile was genuine.

The pleasant mood was destroyed upon Juls' entrance. Having come straight from her practice session, she was still dressed in her ballet exercise attire. She sashayed into the room as if she owned the place. Having seen the pleasant exchange between Susie and Jared, she was slightly miffed. Glaring at Susie, she snidely informed Susie that Susie was to wake her promptly at six tomorrow morning - to do otherwise would ruin her entire day. Juls then sauntered over to Jared and sat next to him, smugly staring at Susie.

Though difficult, Susie managed to contain her anger and not respond. Turning abruptly, she left. Once out of sight, she stormed across the corridor and entered her Dorm room, still seething.

"Susie; is something wrong?" Miss Cora asked. She had just finished getting Megan to bed.

Susie shook her head. "No," she answered tersely.

Miss Cora's expression was one of disbelief; however she smiled and responded, "Very well."

As Miss Cora opened the door to leave, Susie uttered, "Miss Cora, may I talk to you for a minute?"

"Of course, dear," she replied as she turned and walked to Susie. "What's bothering you?"

Susie took a deep breath and forcefully exhaled. "It's Juls. It's her attitude. I can't get her to get out of bed in the mornings. It takes at least three wakeup calls every morning. And then, every time, she is so rude and hateful. Everyone knows what a pain she is. She's impossible. I can't make her do anything, and I don't think it's fair that Miss Pritchett made it my responsibility to make her get up every day. Do you think it's fair that Miss Pritchett gave me this chore?"

Miss Cora smiled gently. "Is it possible that you have misunderstood Miss Pritchett's instructions? What did she tell you?"

"Miss Pritchett said that because I am the oldest and almost twelve, it is my responsibility to get them all up at six o'clock so they can be ready for breakfast on time," Susie answered, her tone a little clipped.

Miss Cora grinned. "Really; are you certain that is what she actually said? I think, perhaps, your paraphrase is incorrect. Think about it, Susie; and when you do, you'll realize just what you have misconstrued."

Miss Cora stopped in the doorway, turning to face Susie. "When you figure it out, your mornings will be a lot less stressful." With an amused smile, Miss Cora nodded and left.

Susie didn't have a chance to think about it – Megan came running to her.

"I thought she'd never leave. Now we're late," she petulantly told Susie.

Susie opened the door slightly and peeked into the corridor. The coast was clear. Grabbing Megan's hand, they made a mad dash across the corridor to the Boys Dorm. Timmy and Simon were impatiently waiting for them when they arrived.

Bombarding her with questions regarding their tardiness, Susie alleviated their anxieties by assuring the boys that she hadn't forgotten, and that she was sure Miss Cora didn't know about their secret. That said, she launched into the next segment of their story about Ketar, the fairy kingdom of Shashur and the rescue of the baby dragon.

———

Staring at the ceiling above her bed, Susie contemplated what Miss Cora had said earlier. She thought over and over again what Miss Pritchett had told her regarding the wake-up chore she had been assigned. Susie was certain that her memory was correct.

Yawning profusely, she decided that she needed to say her prayers and get some sleep. She quickly ran through her litany, making certain not to forget anyone. Just as she began drifting into sleep, Miss Pritchett's words came back to her, as clearly and as precisely as if Miss Pritchett was in the room with her now and speaking to her.

Susie laughed. "I know what my mistake is," she giggled; "and I won't make it again."

With a sigh of satisfaction, Susie closed her eyes and promptly fell fast asleep.

Chapter 20

WINTER BREAK BEGINS

The sun was bright, riding high in the cloudless, blue sky. It was pleasantly warm, and a light breeze was softly blowing, tugging gently at her hair. She heard peals of laughter, and then realized it was her own voice; she was laughing and running through the meadow. The fragrant perfume of the wildflowers easily caught her attention; she stopped running, dropped to her knees and drank in their wondrous scent. She lay on her back, looking up at the richness of the various hues of blue in the sky. The warmth of the sun gently caressing her skin made her drowsy, lulling her to sleep. She closed her eyes and considered taking a nap.

The serenity of the meadow was suddenly broken; a voice called out to her. Reluctantly she sat up to see who it was. At first she saw no one. Ever so slowly a figure appeared, far in the distance, coming up over the hill. Watching and waiting, she sat very still. The figure, clad in a long, hooded robe, stood alone on the hilltop, beckoning her to come. From somewhere behind her a familiar voice, soft and sweet, quietly spoke. "It's time; you must go. You have much to learn, much to do; and the time is short."

Slowly she rose to her feet, turned and saw her mother, smiling, with arms held open toward her. She ran and lost herself in her mother's arms, allowing the safety, the security, and the love to cover her like a warm, fluffy blanket.

Eloise awakened. She often dreamed of her mother; but this time it was different. The feelings of loss, of sadness, were gone. This time she awakened with joy and peace, with happiness and with love abounding deep within her being. She smiled and suddenly realized she was humming a song she had learned as a child. It was a silly, little ditty that her mother had taught her; and, until just now, she had forgotten it. She chuckled softly, remembering how exuberant and flamboyant her mother at times could be.

'A free spirit if ever there was one,' she thought, releasing an amused sigh.

Arising, Eloise yawned and stretched as her eyes wandered to the alarm clock on her nightstand; three-thirty it proclaimed. Rubbing her face in an attempt to wipe away the sleepiness that clung to her, she considered momentarily going back to sleep. The alarm would ring at four, awakening her at the proper time; however, she knew from past experience that she would feel much worse for that thirty minute nap than if she remained awake. Decision made, she leaned over and shut off the alarm, tossing back the bedcovers.

As she shuffled her way toward her bathroom, Eloise began contemplating the dream. It was so different from any other she'd previously had regarding her mother. For one thing, she remembered all of it and in the greatest of detail.

'It seemed so real,' she thought; 'as if I really was there with her.'

The dream's sensations were so intense that her sensory memory retained all of it, and not just the mental images of the dream. Instinctively she slowly rubbed her arms as the sensory memories flooded her. She could still feel the warmth of the sun on her skin, the gentle breeze swirling around her and through her hair. Eloise grinned; the delicate scent of the wildflowers was still with her, as was the beauty of the sky and of the meadow.

But the greatest of the sensory memories now washed over her, filling her again with an innate sense of joy, of love and of peace. It was the sound of her mother's voice, and the absolute certainty she had of her mother's arms holding her. Eloise struggled, trying to determine just what was so different. It wasn't just the ability to recall the dream, nor was it just the change in emotions she felt afterward; it was more than that.

'Who was that lone figure on the hill?' she wondered; 'What was the meaning of my mother's words?' she puzzled.

Eloise entered her bathroom, removed a towel from the linen closet and placed it on the towel rack beside the shower door. Her mind was still mulling over the dream, happily revisiting the meadow. She began to remove her robe when suddenly she stopped and began laughing heartily; she realized she knew the meadow. It was the one she had played in with her mother when she was a small child. They went every week and had a picnic there – just the two of them.

At first, she rode with her mother on her mother's horse. When she was six, she was allowed to ride her own horse. Well, Buttons was actually an old pony; however, to a small child of six, Buttons was big and excitingly dangerous. Eloise smiled fondly at the memory of Buttons – she hadn't thought of him in years. He was so gentle and had the kindest eyes. Even when she outgrew him, she still walked him every day, brushing him and bringing him treats. Throughout the years, Eloise had confided in him all her secrets, her dreams and her fears. Somehow he knew just when to nuzzle her, and blow her kisses to make her feel better. She was seventeen when he passed away - Buttons was twenty-nine.

When she was eight, the meadow was also the first place she took her friend, Hilda, that first warm day in March. Sadness began to creep into her heart - the memory reminded her that she took Hilda because her mother was no longer with her. As more memories resurfaced, the sadness was dispelled, replaced with happy memories of she and Hilda riding in the meadow, or playing tag, picnicking, cloud watching and picking wild flowers. Eloise couldn't help but laugh when she remembered their girl talks, and all the plans they had made. As she turned to the shower door, her eyes noticed her own image in the mirror, clearly reflecting the immense joy she was feeling.

Reaching to start the shower, she stopped. Momentarily she was frozen in place, her hand just resting on the faucet's handle. She knew. ... The difference this time was that she wasn't a child in the dream as in all her previous dreams; she was in the dream as she is now.

A chill swept through her at the realization, and inadvertently she held her breath. Suddenly, she felt a presence in the room. A subtle scent of lilac filled the air. Within seconds, Eloise heard the soft sounds of a wind chime. Instinctively she turned and walked toward the sound, stopping at the chair in front of the vanity.

"Mother?" she whispered hoarsely, the word catching in her throat as she struggled to make sense of what could not possibly be. "It... can't ... be," she stammered.

As if to reorient herself, she closed her eyes and took several deep breaths, slowly inhaling and exhaling each time. When she opened her eyes, she caught a glimpse of a faint silhouette near the window.

"What on earth?" Eloise began, but the words froze in her throat as chills cascaded down her spine. She began to tremble, grabbing hold of the vanity to keep from falling.

A light appeared and began glowing, softly at first and then brighter and brighter until she could not see. Slowly it dissipated, and then disappeared altogether. Standing near the window, but still cloaked in the shadows was what appeared to be a young woman. The apparition told her not to be afraid, and stretched out her hand toward Eloise, touching Eloise on her forehead. Immediately her body ceased trembling. A profound peace and strength flooded her. The visitor softly told her that soon all would be revealed, and then repeated the words her mother had said in her dream. Eloise stood transfixed, uncertain whether she was dreaming or hallucinating.

"Who are you?" Eloise whispered.

"I am a messenger," the apparition said; "watch and be ready." It was gone just as quickly as it had appeared.

Stunned, Eloise stood staring where the figure had been. 'Was that an angel?' she wondered, which prompted her to ask herself why would an angel not fully appear? 'And,' she asked herself; 'why would an angel visit me? Why would I have a vision, if that's what it was?'

Even as Eloise struggled with the questions, there was no denying the deep peace and strength she felt. Whatever the visitor was, it meant her no harm. She decided that she would visit Reverend Tillman and tell him. He would help her make sense of this. Then she thought of Kenatae, and decided to also seek his council.

Whether an angel, a hallucination or a vision, she knew at the right time she would understand what it meant, and what the dream meant. Until then, she would carry on with the business at hand.

Eloise quickly readied herself for the day; and, having done such, headed to the Chapel for her morning quiet time.

———

The annoyingly incessant trilling of her alarm clock awakened Susie from her dream. Wearily she raised her head, barely opening her eyes as she stared at the intrusive noisemaker. It was six-twelve, and her alarm clock had been loudly proclaiming the end of the night the past twelve minutes. She had slept soundly, which was a good thing for she needed it after having such little sleep for far too many consecutive nights. She sat up, yawned and stretched several times, trying to awaken her brain; it felt as it is was filled with pea soup, foggy and obtuse.

'What was I dreaming?' she wondered.

The images of the dream were lost; but the impression of peace and happiness lingered, as did the sense of importance and urgency. She wished she could remember it.

With a heavy sigh, Susie gave a look of longing at her pillow and the nice warm blankets; she really wanted to sleep a couple more hours. Maybe the dream will return, she thought wistfully. But with her stomach already growling, she didn't dare miss breakfast. Besides, if she did, she'd have to endure another round of inquiries as to why she was ill, and that would destroy any chance of exploring for today and possibly even tomorrow.

"Can't have that," Susie muttered as she forced herself to stand.

Today was the first day of the school winter break, and she intended to use this week to do some serious exploring. Even though they had a two-week break, with all the company that was due to start arriving on Saturday, she knew that the next five days would afford her the most opportunities for exploration.

"Time to wake up, girls!" she called out, walking up and down the hall-way. "Everybody up! We're late!! No time for dilly-dallying!" she shouted loudly, hurrying to Megan.

Grinning precociously, Megan reached out to Susie for her morning hug. Susie swept Megan up into her arms, hugging her tightly and swinging her around a couple of times before setting her back down on her bed. Megan's bright eyes flashed with glee. She laughed merrily, fully showing her pearly white baby teeth. Her dimples deepened as her smile widened into a full grin.

"Do it again, Susie; do it again," she pleaded.

"Okay," Susie agreed; "just one more time. Then we have to get ready."

Megan nodded her head vigorously in agreement. "Okay!"

Susie wrapped her arms around Megan, twirling her around several more times before returning her to her bed. Megan's delightful laugh was so ecstatic and carefree that Susie couldn't help but laugh along with her.

"Okay; time to get ready," Susie finally told her. "Let's choose your clothes, then you go to the bathroom. When you get back, I'll help you get dressed."

Megan shook her head. "We're late, remember? I'll chose my clothes. You go wake up Juls."

Susie just grinned at the impish look on Megan's face. "No problem," she replied.

Megan rolled her eyes and giggled. "If you say so," she responded in a sing-song fashion. "Gotta go," she added, dashing into the hallway, heading for the bathroom.

Susie laughed and shook her head. 'Megan is amazing,' she thought as she returned to her room.

Quickly she chose her outfit, raced into the bathroom and got ready to meet the day. As she hurriedly dressed, she mentally devised her list of 'must-do' things for today. At the top of the list was finding the location of the ShopVac. Next was how to get it to the attic studio without being seen. She mulled it over while brushing her teeth, and the solution flashed into her mind – just *ask* Miss Hilda if I can use it.

"After all," she reminded herself aloud, pointing her toothbrush at her image in the mirror. "Miss Pritchett did say I could unpack some things. That's sure to make a little mess that needs cleanup."

She re-entered the Common Area just as Dani and Kat were crossing it, heading for the bathroom.

"Good morning," Susie greeted them cheerfully.

Dani was quick to reciprocate. "Good morning, Susie," she merrily parroted and disappeared into the bathroom.

Kat was definitely not a morning person this morning. Surly and scowling, she glared at Susie. "I hate perky people this early," Kat snarled as she stomped past Susie.

Susie chuckled at how different her roommates are. Dani and Kat were notorious for sleeping in until the last possible second. Dani was usually pleasant or, at least, cordial. Kat, on the other hand, was usually silent and sometimes sullen. Megan was always awake, just feigning sleep while she waited for her hug from Susie. Susie didn't mind; Megan was truly a sweetheart, cheerful and was a lot of fun.

Juls, however, was not. Every morning it was the same. Juls would cover her head with her blankets and ignore Susie, hoping she would go away. Susie would give her until six-twenty and then pull down her covers.

That always elicited an icy, cold stare and a hostile attitude from the resident prima donna.

Today was no exception.

"Get up Juls," Susie urged. "You know as well as I do that in fifteen minutes Miss Cora will be here."

"Ask me if I care," Juls snapped back at her, pulling her covers back over her face. "It's my vacation. I don't have to be in class, so I don't have to get up. Now, go away!"

Smiling sweetly, Susie said, "Have it your way, Juls. I've done what I'm required to do, which is to *wake* you. That's it! If you want Miss Cora to find you still in bed when she gets here, fine with me."

Pausing in the doorway, Susie added, "From now on, you only get one wake-up call. If you choose to ignore it, it's your problem."

Juls tossed her covers down, staring in disbelief as she watched Susie walk away. Scrambling out of bed, Juls grabbed the clothes she had laid out the night before. Rapidly she stomped down the hallway, stopping when she reached the Common Area. She stood there for a moment, defiantly glaring at Susie, who was reading a magazine and pretending not to have noticed Juls' dramatic entrance.

Not getting the reaction from Susie that Juls had sought, she sauntered (in her best promenade form) through the Common Area, toward the bathroom. As she passed by Susie, Juls smugly commented, "Apparently someone woke up on the wrong side of the bed this morning."

Susie, unperturbed, chuckled and continued reading her magazine. Soon she was joined by Dani, Kat and Megan. Megan, of course, crawled into Susie's lap, handing her a brush and a ponytail holder.

"Make mine like yours, please?" she asked sweetly after giving and receiving another hug from Susie.

As Susie complied with Megan's request, Dani asked Susie, "When do you think Mrs. Crenshaw will visit again?"

"I don't know, Dani. She said yesterday it'd be after Christmas."

"Do you think Miss Pritchett or Miss Hilda have any pictures from that time?" Kat asked.

Susie stopped brushing Megan's hair and quickly wound her silky, blonde hair three times through the ponytail holder. With any luck, it'd

425

make it through breakfast before Megan pulled it out. She shrugged her shoulders and responded, "Probably."

"Do you think they'd let us look at them?" Kat pressed the subject.

"I don't know. Why?" Susie asked her, wondering what Kat was thinking.

"Just because….. I mean, I thought Mrs. Crenshaw's pictures were interesting, didn't you?"

Susie nodded slowly. "Yes, but that doesn't necessarily mean that they have any pictures, or want to show them if they do."

"You could ask." Kat softly suggested. The expression on her face revealed to Susie that it wasn't a suggestion; Kat wanted her to ask.

"Why?" Susie countered.

"Why not?" Kat charged back.

"What's the big deal?" Dani asked. "They're only pictures, and it was a long time ago. Who cares?"

Neither Kat nor Susie responded. Megan, however, filled the void. "I'll ask," she volunteered. "It could be funny to see Miss Pritchett and Miss Hilda when they were little. Mrs. Crenshaw didn't have any of those pictures."

"No, she didn't," Susie spoke softly as she realized Megan was right.

"Hey that's right," Dani agreed. "That seems a little weird."

"Why?" Kat asked a little flippantly. "Mrs. Crenshaw's family wasn't taking pictures of anything but the festivals and their *own* family."

"True," Susie acknowledged; "but I do know that one exists."

"Really?" asked Dani, while Kat asked "Where is it?", and Megan demanded, "I want to see it!"

"Yes, it really does exist, but I don't have it. When Simon and I were staying with Mrs. Crenshaw, she told us a little about Glen Hollow and about the festivals. She said her mother had a picture of her when she was five sitting on a large, white horse with Miss Pritchett's mother. That was 1956."

"Did you see it yesterday?" Kat asked.

"No, I didn't," she answered reflectively; "which is strange because Mrs. Crenshaw had promised Simon she would show it to him."

"Maybe she forgot to bring it," Dani offered. "What's the big deal? Call her and ask her to bring that one the next time she comes."

The door opened and Miss Cora swept into the room like a spring wind, pleasant and full of vitality. "Good morning, girls," she greeted them.

"Good morning, Miss Cora," they echoed in unison.

"Where is the lovely Juls?" she inquired; "still asleep?"

Three answered "No" and Megan answered loudly, "In the bathroom," pointing the way.

Before Miss Cora could respond, Juls thrust open the bathroom door. Standing in the doorway, she gave her best interpretation of one who has been seriously annoyed and, thus, perturbed by their mere presence. Miss Cora was not impressed. Impervious to Juls' performances (or tantrums), she just laughed lightheartedly.

Checking her watch, she smiled and said, "There you are Juls; only thirty seconds late this morning … Not bad; you are improving."

Opening the door for the girls, Miss Cora stood in front of it and held it open. "Shall we proceed to breakfast, ladies? I believe I heard Mrs. Coppersmith mention something last night about pancakes this morning."

The girls were out the door in seconds, even Juls.

———

Mrs. Coppersmith had most certainly prepared pancakes for breakfast, and they were the lightest, fluffiest buttermilk pancakes Susie had ever eaten. They just seemed to melt in her mouth. There was a variety of hot syrups from which to choose as well as several fruit compotes. Ample supplies of scrambled eggs, sausage links, bacon, slices of honey ham (Simon's favorite), breakfast potatoes with onions and peppers and an assortment of sliced fruits were available for their choosing. A small glass of juice and also one of cold milk were placed in front of each child. Susie wasn't certain, but she was almost sure the orange juice was fresh squeezed. It was great!

Chatter at the breakfast table this morning was filled with playful banter and a considerable amount of teasing. Occasionally the conversation steered toward business; but, for the most part, it remained in the realm of fun.

Simon was delighted that Mr. Sean had agreed to allow him to help feed the animals every day during the winter break. He could hardly contain his enthusiasm; one such outburst of arm waving caused his glass to tip, spilling a little milk. Luckily, Miss Hilda caught the glass before it spilt its entire contents. Timmy, apparently feeling left out, began badgering Mr. Sean for the same privilege as Simon.

"Are you certain Timmy?" Mr. Sean asked. "You've not shown any interest in feeding the animals."

Timmy rapidly nodded his head several times, hurriedly chewing and swallowing before answering. "I didn't know we could," he explained, his tone suggesting to think otherwise was just plain silly.

"It's hard work. You can't quit because you get tired or want to play," Mr. Sean cautioned.

"I know," he insisted very maturely. "Simon told me all about helping you on Saturday. I want to help too."

Mr. Sean glanced at Miss Pritchett. She smiled. He looked back at Timmy, smiled and nodded his approval. "Okay. After breakfast, we'll go feed some animals."

"All right!" Timmy and Simon both yelled at the same time, performing their little victory jigs in their booster chairs.

"Boys, I'm only going to say this once, so pay attention," Mr. Sean spoke sharply. Immediately Timmy and Simon ceased their victory dances. They looked at him, eyes wide, expecting to be told that their helper status was cancelled.

"Feeding the animals isn't play time. Yes, it's fun, but it's also important work. I want you to think about it the same way you get fed every day."

He paused for a moment, watching the puzzlement increase on their little faces. "What if no one prepared any meals for you? How would you eat? How would you live?"

As the understanding began to dawn on them, the light of it began to show in their expressions. "We wouldn't," Simon said somberly; Timmy responded sadly with, "We'd starve."

"That's correct; and the same is true for our animals. Now, how would you feel if your meals were late, or just tossed around haphazardly so that you had to hunt for it?" he asked them.

"I wouldn't like it," Simon answered earnestly.

Timmy slowly shook his head. "Me neither," he responded seriously.

"No one would, boys. Neither do the animals. We must show them respect just as we want respect. If you do, you'll see that the animals you care for will also care for you." Smiling at them, he added, "I am very pleased that you both want to help; after all, you may like the animals enough to be our future farmers."

"Yeah!" they proclaimed, bobbing their heads again and pumping their arms; "future farmers!"

"Settle down and finish your breakfast, boys," Miss Hilda instructed, interrupting their show.

They looked at her, then at each other, giggled, and quickly began stuffing their mouths with pancakes.

———

As soon as breakfast was over and the dishes cleared from the table, Susie accompanied Miss Elsa, Miss Taryn, Miss Fiona and Mrs. Coppersmith. This week she had been assigned morning kitchen duty, and that was a two hour block of time. She began by unloading the carts. First, she scraped into the compost bin any remaining food from the plates. After which she pushed the bulky, heavy carts to the large, stainless steel sinks. As she did so, Miss Taryn and Miss Fiona unloaded the pots and pans from the dishwashers, returning them to their proper places in the various cabinets and bins. Meanwhile, Miss Elsa and Mrs. Coppersmith were busy putting the leftovers in storage containers, labeling the containers and getting them properly stored into the refrigerators.

Susie's next task was to rinse the dishes and place them onto the counter; dishes, flatware and glasses to her right and the serving dishes to her left. As Susie placed the items onto the counters, Miss Taryn and Miss Fiona quickly loaded them into the dishwashers. After the dishes were done, Miss Taryn, Miss Elsa and Miss Fiona left the kitchen just as Mrs. Coppersmith brought in a large sack of potatoes and a smaller sack of onions. It was twenty pounds of potatoes and two pounds of onions.

"Have you ever peeled potatoes?" Mrs. Coppersmith quizzed Susie.

"'Yes," Susie responded warily.

"Good," she replied with a quick nod of her head, "then I don't need to show you how it's done."

Mrs. Coppersmith laid the sacks onto the large wooden table, turned and walked to the counter behind her. Reaching down into the cabinet to her right, she removed two large, stainless steel colanders. Next she opened the middle drawer and pulled out two potato peelers, placing them into the colanders. Sliding two large knives out of the wooden block, she placed one into each colander. Returning to the table, she saw Susie still standing by it. "Have a seat," she said, motioning toward the chair in front of Susie.

Susie slid into the chair, eyeing the huge sack. Mrs. Coppersmith placed one of the colanders in front of Susie, laid a potato peeler and knife to the side after which she sat in the chair directly across the table from Susie. The other colander, knife and peeler she placed on the table in front of herself.

Opening the large sack, she pulled out potatoes, lots of them, rolling them into the large space between them. Susie was pleasantly surprised that they had already been washed. She didn't mind peeling potatoes, but she hated washing them.

"Get peeling," Mrs. Coppersmith told Susie, grabbing a large, red potato.

"How many do we have to peel?" Susie asked while reaching for a potato.

"All of them," she responded nonchalantly.

"Wow, that's a lot of potatoes." Susie was slightly disheartened for she feared it would take all morning. That is until she saw how fast Mrs. Coppersmith was at peeling potatoes.

"Not really," she responded. "It'd take a bit more potatoes if we were preparing them as a side dish; you know, mashed, or boiled or fried. We're making potato soup for lunch today."

"Is that all we're having for lunch?" Susie was surprised, and the inflection in her voice clearly revealed that surprise.

Mrs. Coppersmith chuckled loudly, stopped peeling and grinned. "Do you not like potato soup?"

Susie's face flushed, slightly embarrassed. "It's okay. ... I... I was just thinking that it doesn't seem to be much of a lunch for the men," she answered.

Mrs. Coppersmith's eyes twinkled with merriment. She nodded her head a few times, still chuckling as she continued with her task in hand. "Don't you fret about that; we'll be having the soup and garlic bread as the first course. Main course will be baked ham, spinach soufflé, glazed carrots, lima beans and yeast rolls. Desserts will be pecan pie and chocolate cake."

Teasingly, she asked, "Do you think that might meet with their approval?"

Susie laughed and nodded assent. "Possibly," she answered jokingly.

They both fell quiet as they continued peeling potatoes. After several minutes, Susie spoke, "Mrs. Coppersmith?"

"Yes dear?"

"Did you know Miss Pritchett's father?" Susie asked tentatively.

Mrs. Coppersmith's laugh nearly made Susie laugh. It sounded like a cross between a snort and a cough. "Heavens, no. I started working here in July of 1974. Mr. Pritchett had passed on some thirteen years before that."

Peering at Susie with a wary look, she inquired, "Why do you ask?"

Susie shrugged and responded, "Oh, no reason in particular. I was just curious as to what he may have been like." She continued peeling the potato she held and tried a different tact. "Other than Miss Pritchett and Miss Hilda, have you been here the longest?"

"Yes I have," she answered, nodding her head and grabbing another potato from the pile.

"Was that when Glen Hollow first became an orphanage?" Susie asked, attempting her best to sound as if she was just making small talk.

Mrs. Coppersmith began laughing heartily. "What is it you want to know, child? Why don't you just ask instead of beating around the bush?"

Surprised, Susie blushed lightly. "Nothing…. I was just curious."

She swiped a few more peels from the potato, placed the potato in the colander and quickly picked another potato. An idea stuck. "Is there a reason I shouldn't ask questions? Is it a secret when Glen Hollow orphanage started?"

Mrs. Coppersmith ceased peeling her potato. Her expression was one of a guarded calculation as to whether or not Susie's motives were for good or for ill. Finally she determined that she would trust her first impression of the girl.

431

She responded casually, "No secret; Glen Hollow itself has been here a very long time. All of Glen Hollow belongs to Miss Pritchett. The Orphanage, as such, only exits on paper. It is a real corporation, but the corporation does not own anything. The Orphanage is actually Miss Pritchett opening her home, Glen Hollow, to children that have no home, and have little prospect of finding a good home. She began the Orphanage June of 1974."

"Then why have an orphanage? Why not just have foster children, or adopt?" Susie asked.

"Back then, child, they wouldn't allow a single woman to adopt or to foster a child, let alone a dozen. By having a legal orphanage, she could provide a home for up to two dozen as the manor is now, more if the east wings were in use."

Susie nodded her head slightly as she contemplated the new information. "Mrs. Crenshaw said that Glen Hollow only accepts twelve children. Why not twenty-four?" she asked.

Mrs. Coppersmith smiled and answered patiently, "Same reason folks shouldn't have more kids than they can afford to clothe and feed. Oh, we have the room to take in more little ones even now, but it wouldn't be right. She'd take in a hundred if she could. Miss Pritchett has a good heart; but she wants to be certain that we can amply provide for the ones that come here to live."

She looked at Susie intently. "Mind, I'm not just speaking to feeding; there's more to providing than just mere food. There's education, medical care, shelter and clothes. And there's the teaching, the training of virtues and values so that each and every one of you grow to be fine adults and good citizens. That takes time; the more children you have, the less time you have with them. So, to be fair, and to give each of you the best possible future that we can, Miss Pritchett decided the maximum number of children we could properly raise would be twelve."

Mrs. Coppersmith paused briefly then added, "Mind you, we grow most all of our own food, as well as the feed for the animals. Some years are not as good as others; and, in those years, we just barely can provide for twelve."

Slowly she shook her head and a worried look clouded her face. "It'd be heart breaking for everyone, children and adults, if we had to send any child elsewhere because of a poor harvest or several consecutive bad harvests. I pray every day that never happens."

Her eyes were glistening with tears which she quickly wiped away. She cleared her throat and gave an encouraging smile to Susie. "And as long as I've been here, somehow we've always managed, even in the leanest of years."

Susie was silent, focusing her gaze onto the task of peeling the potato she held. She hadn't realized how much thought, and preparation and work had gone into the choice of caregiving for so many extra people.

Breaking the silence, Mrs. Coppersmith casually said, "Come June, you'll get to meet a considerable number of those who have lived here... That is, providing you're still here."

"What do you mean?" Susie asked, startled.

"Why nothing, dear, other than if you're adopted before June, your adoptive parents may not be able to bring you here for our annual reunion. But, perhaps they will in the future. It's a grand time, a week-long celebration."

She looked quizzical at Susie's expression. It was not what she expected to see. "Child, is something wrong?"

Susie shook her head several times rather quickly as she gathered her thoughts. She stared at the potato in her hand. She didn't want to leave. She had assumed that she and Simon would remain here. Softly she asked, "Do most of the children get adopted?"

"No; usually not," she cautiously responded. Her eyes narrowed slightly as she studied Susie, trying to determine what Susie was thinking.

Reflecting for a minute, she continued softly, her voice kind and gentle. "Miss Pritchett usually accepts only those children that would be difficult to adopt. On occasion, the younger children are easier to place; but much depends on the child's circumstances. .. And Miss Pritchett will never allow siblings to be separated; so sometimes adoptive homes aren't readily available, and sometimes not at all. .. Is that what concerns you, dear; that Simon and you might be separated?" she queried, leaning in toward Susie and trying to determine just what was troubling Susie.

Susie looked up and met her gaze. "No.... Mrs. Crenshaw told us that she wouldn't let us be separated; but she may not have a final say, so ...

433

" Her voice trailed away as she tried to gather her thoughts. She sighed. "It's just that ... well, I like it here. Simon does, too; and I think he'd want to stay here. I know I do."

Mrs. Coppersmith grinned, nodded her head approvingly and straightened in her chair. "That doesn't surprise me, dear. You've a sharp mind and a keen eye. This is a great place to live, but it may surprise you to learn that not all children have thought so. Some have not liked the country life, and others do not care for the chores, or the large number of people that comprise our little family. For those, adoption is necessary, vital even; and Miss Pritchett works extra hard to find them just the right home."

Susie remained silent, diligently peeling the potato she held tightly in her hand. Several times she looked up at Mrs. Coppersmith, starting and stopping the next question that was impatiently waiting to be released from her mouth. Finally, she could hold it back no longer.

"Mrs. Coppersmith," she began with a slight tremor in her voice; "what if I don't want to be adopted? Are we forced to go with them?"

Mrs. Coppersmith stopped peeling immediately, laying the potato and the peeler on the table in front of her. Reaching across the table, she patted Susie's hand, attempting to reassure her. "No child, never; Miss Pritchett would never send you somewhere you didn't want to be."

Quickly she left her chair and came to Susie, giving her a hug. Mrs. Coppersmith kissed the top of Susie's head and then stepped back in order to face her, holding Susie's face in her hands. "You mustn't fret so, Susie dear. Share your concerns with Miss Pritchett, and you'll see; she'll always be your fiercest advocate."

Susie smiled weakly, not certain that she was ready to take that plunge just yet.

Mrs. Coppersmith reseated herself and picked up her potato and peeler. She made short work of that potato and the next several ones. They made small talk, mostly about Mrs. Coppersmith's late husband, Edward Marvin Coppersmith. Her eyes shone and sparkled whenever she spoke of her late husband.

Susie learned that they never had children; Mrs. Coppersmith said that she believed that The Good Lord had placed her here where so many children need love. To her, all the children that pass through these doors are hers to care for and to love. She winked and smiled at Susie, adding that that included both her and Simon. Susie couldn't help smiling in return.

Mrs. Coppersmith went on to say that Mr. Coppersmith had been a supervisor of a crew of lineman for the phone company. He was always traveling and was gone more than he was home, especially in winter. Mrs. Coppersmith said she didn't mind so much, for she had her work here to keep her busy; but she would have preferred it if he'd had a job that allowed him to be home more often. He'd had a heart attack in August of 1993; she still missed him every day, she proclaimed, and would until she saw him again. She smiled, wiped away the tears that had filled her eyes, and confided to Susie that she visited his grave daily, weather permitting. Noticing the perplexed look on Susie's face, Mrs. Coppersmith smiled warmly and explained that Mr. Coppersmith was buried in the cemetery behind the Chapel.

"There's a cemetery here?"

Mrs. Coppersmith nodded. "Of course," she stated. "The cemetery is behind the Chapel a might bit, and the Evermore Family Mausoleum is in the center of the cemetery. Anyone who has ever worked for the Evermores has the choice to be buried in the cemetery here if they prefer. Mr. Coppersmith loved this place, and so do I." She shrugged. "It didn't seem right to bury him anywhere else."

Gently tossing the potato she had just peeled into her colander, Mrs. Coppersmith grinned and said, "I believe we're done."

Without realizing it, thirty minutes had passed, and all the potatoes were now peeled. Susie was amazed.

Mrs. Coppersmith rose and carried both colanders to the sink, rinsing the potatoes and allowing them ample time to drain. Placing a towel under each colander, she brought them back to the table. Quickly she retrieved from the countertop two small cutting boards and two, very large, stainless steel bowls. She placed one bowl, a cutting board and a colander on the table in front of Susie, repeating the same ritual on her own side of the table.

After returning to her side of the table, Mrs. Coppersmith picked a potato out of the colander and placed in on the cutting board in front of her. "Watch me," she instructed, "and do exactly as I do. You first cut the potato lengthwise," she instructed as she slowly sliced the potato. "Hold the knife up, tip end onto the board like this. Then holding the two sides together, you simply slide the potato under the knife and carefully bring the blade down."

She demonstrated each step ever so slowly as she explained. She stopped, smiled at Susie and said, "Go slowly until you learn how. After you're more experienced, you'll be able to do it quickly without injury." To illustrate her point, Mrs. Coppersmith took a large potato and, within seconds had cut it into mid-sized chunks. "See," she said.

Susie grinned. "That's fast," she acknowledged, removing a medium-sized potato from her colander and, just as quickly, sliced it into mid-sized chucks, astonishing Mrs. Coppersmith. Susie laughed and said, "Nana taught me."

Mrs. Coppersmith chuckled. "Very well, then; let's get to it."

Within minutes all of the potatoes had been cut and were in the bowls. While Susie had been slicing the last dozen or two of the potatoes, Mrs. Coppersmith had peeled and chopped the two pounds of onions, placing them into her bowl. She picked up her bowl and headed to the huge, commercial stove, calling out to Susie to also bring her own bowl.

She lifted the lid from the large stock pot, and the wonderful aromas of green onions and celery wafted into the air. Carefully Mrs. Coppersmith slid the contents of her bowl into the boiling water. Placing her bowl on the counter, she took Susie's bowl and repeated the process. After stirring the contents of the pot, she placed the lid back on it.

"We'll let that simmer a bit before we add the cream and herbs to it," she informed Susie. "And while we're waiting, we'll clean up our work area," she added. "You bring the bowls and utensils to the sink while I clean the table."

"Sure," Susie agreed and quickly gathered up the bowls, colanders, cutting boards, peelers and knives. Cautiously she laid them into the sink, rinsing them and them placing them into a dishwasher. She had finished just as Mrs. Coppersmith returned from taking out the peels.

"You're all done with kitchen duty for today," she cheerily announced. "Would you like a cup of cocoa before you go?"

"Yes, thank you," Susie eagerly responded, hastily returning to her chair.

Mrs. Coppersmith set about preparing the cocoa. While it was heating, she withdrew several large jars of various herbs and headed back to the stove. "Susie, be a dear and bring me four quart bottles of cream. They're the ones with the purple tops," she said as she lifted the lid from off of the stockpot.

Susie jumped up and quickly retrieved the bottles from the refrigerator and carefully carried the glass bottles to the stove. She removed the lids and handed one of the bottles to Mrs. Coppersmith.

"You pour it in, dear," she said; "do it slowly, stirring as you pour."

"Okay," Susie said and did as she was instructed.

After she had emptied the last bottle, Mrs. Coppersmith handed Susie the herbs, one at a time, telling her to smell them and add them as she saw fit. Susie did so; when the last one had been added, Mrs. Coppersmith held the pepper grinder over the pot and began grinding the peppercorns into the soup.

"Tell me when you think it's enough," she said, smiling at Susie.

After a few seconds, Susie said, "I think that should do it."

Mrs. Coppersmith placed the pepper grinder onto the counter as Susie continued to stir. Removing two spoons from the top drawer, she handed one to Susie. "Take a taste, and see if it's to your liking."

Susie did; it was great, and she said so. Mrs. Coppersmith took her own sample.

Grinning, she pronounced Susie was correct. She turned the burner down to a low setting. "It just needs to simmer a little while longer. Now let's have that coca."

Susie returned to her chair and, in a few minutes the cocoa was ready and piping hot. Mrs. Coppersmith poured the cocoa into the two mugs she had set out on the counter, brought them to the table, placing one of the mugs with its delectable aroma in front of Susie.

Sitting back down into her chair, she cautioned Susie, "It's very hot. You may have to blow on it a bit before drinking."

Nodding, Susie began to gently blow on the top on her cocoa and then stopped, allowing it to cool on its own. "Mrs. Coppersmith, did you start here as Head Cook?" she asked.

"Heavens, no; I started as an assistant thirty-four years ago. Louise Smithfield was Head Cook then. She retired in 1987." She smiled at the memory. "I learned a good deal from her," she said with a soft quality in her voice.

"How long had she been here?" Susie asked.

"She started two months before I did. She'd been Head Cook at Willington University for twenty years, retired and came here. She was sixty-eight when she retired from Glen Hollow ... Great cook, truly a great cook."

Mrs. Coppersmith took a sip of her cocoa and then continued. "Louise moved to Florida to be near her children, and grandchildren and, now, her great-grandchildren." Mrs. Coppersmith began to chuckle. "She's still going strong, busy with volunteer work and her family. We talk every month."

They sat silently sipping their cocoa for the next few minutes.

"Has Miss Pritchett's family always lived here, or did they buy Glen Hollow from someone else?" Susie asked as she took another sip.

"Glen Hollow, as far as I know, has always been in her family. Obviously, it was originally land that belonged to the Icori people. The story is that her ancestors had performed a great favor for the Icori. As a reward, the tribal council had allowed them to purchase land." She took a sip of her cocoa before continuing. "When the territory became part of the new country, the Evermores purchased the land from the new government."

"Why? The land was already theirs," Susie asked.

Mrs. Coppersmith chuckled. "That was the way of it back then. The European countries staked claim to the Indian lands because they didn't recognized the Indian's right to it. And it didn't matter to them if there was an agreement between a settler and the Indians. So when the new government decided to buy territory from the European countries, the new government now owned the land and sold it as they saw fit."

"But that wasn't right!" Susie protested.

Mrs. Coppersmith shrugged. "Right or not, it's what they did. Anyway, dear, that's ancient history. Fortunately, the Evermores had strong enough ties with the new government which allowed them to purchase their land back. Since the Icori were bound to lose their land, including their sacred places, the Evermores agreed with the Icori to purchase all the surrounding land, preserving it for the Icori tribe. The tribe would still have their homes, hunting grounds and sacred places without fear of removal from the government."

"Wow; that was nice. Do the Icori still live on Glen Hollow?" Susie asked.

"Not on the Glen Hollow proper of today," she replied while blowing gently on her cocoa. "Some live on the outskirts of the property, up by Eagle Ridge, Ravenswood, Spirit Canyon, Flat Rock Creek and, I think, Turtle Pond. Those areas all once were part of Glen Hollow, but were deeded years ago to a land sanctuary established by Miss Pritchett's grandmother."

Susie nodded in admiration. "That was a lot of land."

"To be sure, but Glen Hollow still has over seventy thousand acres; most of it is forest." She paused and took a large swallow of her cocoa. "It's my understating," she continued; "from village gossip (she grinned, and winked at Susie) and not from first-hand knowledge, that shortly before Miss Pritchett's mother passed, she added the Icori Tribal Council to the Land Sanctuary Board and also Reverend Tillman. Gossip also has it that Miss Murielle made it a condition that they would add Miss Pritchett when she came of age."

Susie took another sip from her mug. She was impressed by Miss Pritchett's family. She wished she could have known Miss Murielle and her parents. An idea struck. "Mrs. Coppersmith," she began; "did Miss Murielle and her parents know the Icori well?"

Mrs. Coppersmith rapidly nodded, "Most certainly. The Icori attended all the festivals here, and Miss Murielle and her parents – that'd be Mr. Jerome and Miss Elizabeth, God rest their souls - attended many of theirs. The last one held here was September 1956. I attended that one with my family, of course, since I was just a child."

"What about Miss Pritchett? Did she attend the Icori festivals?" Susie pressed.

Mrs. Coppersmith raised her right eyebrow, contemplating where this inquiry was heading. "I'm certain she did."

"Does she still attend them?" Susie asked, pushing the subject.

Mrs. Coppersmith smiled slightly; then took another sip of her cocoa before answering. "Some; she also attends some of their Council meetings. From time to time, they meet with her here... Why?"

"Just wondering," Susie responded, deflecting the question as she organized her thoughts. She sat quietly sipping her coca, focusing on it and attempting to ignore the curious glances from Mrs. Coppersmith.

"Well, if it eases your mind any," Mrs. Coppersmith replied with an amused lilt in her voice; "it's no secret. Miss Pritchett is a generous soul. Whatever we produce above what we need, she donates to the Council; they distribute the food among their people who have need." Mrs. Coppersmith drained the last of her cocoa then set the mug down on the table. "Her family has always done so. It's been reciprocal, too," she added matter-of-factly.

"Really?" Susie asked.

The twinkle in her eyes matched the grin on her lips as she answered, "Absolutely; you need to ask Miss Pritchett. She'll be able to give you more details."

"I'll be sure to ask her," Susie mumbled as she quickly swallowed the last of her cocoa. "Thank you for the cocoa, Mrs. Coppersmith," she said as she stood.

"You're most welcome, Susie," she responded heartily.

As Susie turned to take her cup to the sink, Mrs. Coppersmith told her to leave it; she'd take care of it.

Susie smiled at Mrs. Coppersmith, thanked her and moved toward the door. She stopped, ran back to Mrs. Coppersmith and gave her a hug.

"Thank you, for everything," she whispered, kissed her cheek and then ran as fast as she could out the door, leaving an astonished, happy and misty-eyed Mrs. Coppersmith behind.

———

As Susie hurried along the corridor toward Miss Hilda's office, her mind raced over the information she had gleaned from Mrs. Coppersmith. The most important item being that what Mrs. Coppersmith had already told her Saturday was true; Miss Hilda and Miss Pritchett are the only ones left that know Glen Hollow's past. She feared that it might prove challenging to extract information from them, but she was determined to find out everything she could.

"Wait a minute!" she chided herself. "Last Sunday, Miss Hilda said that the *Reverend* had been a friend to Miss Pritchett's mother." She smiled. "I'll have to find a way to talk to him alone."

She entered the sitting room and walked quickly to Miss Hilda's open door. Knocking lightly on the door jam, she entered when Miss Hilda greeted her.

———

Ten minutes later, Susie was dashing to the Library just as the grandfather clock chimed eleven o'clock. Miss Hilda had been very accommodating. Without any great detail from Susie, she had graciously agreed to allow her the use of a ShopVac for as long as Susie needed it. Tomorrow, after breakfast, Mr. Henry would meet her at the attic door and carry it up for her.

Susie entered the Library and went directly to the card catalogue. She looked up the name Helga G. von Richter. There they were; all eight volumes and, according to the inventory listing, all were located on the same shelf. Susie could barely contain her excitement, running all the way to the bookcase, back to where she had found the Unicorn book. She searched and searched; not just the appropriate shelf, but all the shelves in that entire bookcase. The other books were missing. Her excitement quickly faded into disappointment.

"Rats!" she fumed; "every time I think I've found a clue, I get blocked."

Susie wandered to the chair by the fireplace, and unceremoniously dropped into it. Her eyes were drawn to the cabinet far across the room with its alluring Histories volumes. She sighed. She knew there wasn't enough time; lunch would be ready in fifteen minutes.

She stood and began slowly making her way toward the Library doors; and, from there, reluctantly on to the Dining Hall.

Chapter 21

AN ENEMY BORN

The lunch fare was delicious. Mrs. Coppersmith had told everyone that Susie had been a major contributor to the preparation of the soup. She grinned and winked at Susie as everyone began thanking her. Susie blushed, insisting that she hadn't really done all that much. But Mrs. Coppersmith wouldn't hear of it. She heartily proclaimed that Susie was welcome any time to help her cook.

That surprised everyone for Mrs. Coppersmith seldom allowed Miss Taryn to assist in the actual preparation of the meals, even though she is Mrs. Coppersmith's assistant. Most of Miss Taryn's duties consisted of gathering and washing the eggs from the chicken house, loading and unloading the dishwashers, stocking the pantry shelves, polishing the silver and ironing the table linens. It was a rare occasion that Miss Taryn actually was allowed to do anything that even remotely resembled cooking. Truth be told, Miss Fiona and Miss Elsa did more food preparation than Miss Taryn, and they weren't even assigned as kitchen staff. They helped as needed in the kitchen, but their main duties were in housekeeping.

Susie expressed her thanks to Mrs. Coppersmith and to the others for their gracious compliments. However when she glanced at Miss Taryn, Susie was startled to see the sheer hostility expressed. Miss Taryn quickly turned her head away, facing her mother instead.

She returned to sipping her soup, a little unnerved by Miss Taryn but determined to find a way to apologize to her. Not that she *owed* Miss Taryn an apology, but Susie felt bad that Mrs. Coppersmith had made such a fuss. Maybe she and Miss Taryn could make a surprise dessert, one of Nana's specialties; that would show everyone Miss Taryn's cooking ability, Susie decided.

'*Unless she truly doesn't have an ability to cook*,' the thought leapt into Susie's mind without effort or intention, as if it were a voice other than her own.

With a tiny sigh, Susie watched Miss Taryn, now chatting away with Miss Ginger about the upcoming fabric sales in Willington and Stonebridge.

Apparently both stores were having bargain basement sales; they were comparing notes as to which items should be purchased. Observing her lively and sunny demeanor currently being displayed, Susie would never have believed that such a strong animosity toward her was harbored by Miss Taryn if she hadn't seen it for herself. Apparently no one else saw it. Susie had checked with a quick glance around the table.

Much of the remaining conversations centered on Simon's and Timmy's adventure in the realm of farming. Both boys took great delight in relaying every detail of their helper status, trying to top each other's stories and voices. Several times Mr. Sean had to reprimand them, insisting that they lower their voices and stop flailing their arms. With each exaggerated gesture, they were sending food particles around the table like miniature cannon balls.

Once their exploits had been fully reported, they begged Mr. Sean to allow them to help after lunch as well, promising to be on their very best behavior. He chuckled, turned to Miss Pritchett and said, "I don't mind," he told her; "as long as you don't have them assigned to anything else."

She grinned. "No, that's quite all right," she responded affably. To the boys, she asked, "Are you certain you want to work this afternoon?"

They responded with a hearty "yes", and with vigorous nodding of their heads.

"Very well," she concurred heartily; "you may continue to assist Mr. Sean until two-thirty."

Their faces looked crestfallen, and they began to object. She held up her hand, motioning no discussion was allowed. "It'll be a very, long day for both of you. You'll both need a bath and a short nap before Story Time, or have you forgotten about it?"

It was obvious they had; both their faces registered surprise when she mentioned Story Time.

"She's correct, guys. You're not accustomed to such a long day," Mr. Sean told them as he lifted his folk to his mouth. Taking a brief pause, he winked at them and then added, "Besides, you'll need your strength if you want to help me again all day tomorrow."

"Okay," they chimed in unison, eyes wide with excitement as they looked at Mr. Sean with adoration.

"Then you better finish eating; I can't have weak, undernourished helpers," he said with a jovial lilt in his voice.

The boys turned their attention to each other, began bobbing their heads and giggling with glee before they dived into finishing their meal.

Miss Pritchett chuckled and nodded her head slightly toward Mr. Sean, signifying that he had indeed handled them perfectly. No one else seemed to notice the exchange; but Susie did.

———

Lunch ended, and everyone had begun leaving the Dining Hall. Miss Cora corralled Megan, dashing her hope that she might have a reprieve from naptime. She went without incident; well, for her it was without incident. She whined that it wasn't fair that the boys got to wait to take their naps. Persistently trying to convince Miss Cora to allow her also to wait, Megan could be heard long after they had left the Dining Hall, her whimpers gradually fading until the sound disappeared altogether.

Miss Taryn and her mother, Miss Claire, had already made their exit. This struck Susie as being unusual since Miss Taryn always remained behind to take the dishes into the kitchen. Since Miss Elsa was performing that task, Susie assumed that she must have coaxed Miss Elsa into taking her place. Juls had afternoon kitchen duty this week and was sighing loudly her dismay as she trudged along behind Miss Fiona. Clearing table linens and cleaning dishes was definitely not her idea of how a future prima ballerina should be treated.

Susie hurriedly left the Dining Hall, darting down the corridor to the Library doors and slipped inside. She heard the sound of voices coming from further inside the Library, and she froze dead in her tracks. The voices at times were raised, so it was either a spirited discussion, or a heated argument was ensuing. Susie immediately recognized the voices – it was Miss Claire and Miss Taryn.

Without a sound, Susie quickly moved down the main corridor and quietly made her way to the west section of the Library, allowing the sound of the voices to guide her. As she neared the end of the main corridor, Susie stepped into a side aisle, second aisle from the entrance into the west section. She listened, acquiring a bearing for their position. Slowly

Susie inched her way toward the voices, being careful to remain unseen. Definitely they were arguing. That fact had been easy to deduce just a few seconds down the main corridor. What had drawn Susie was the mention of her name several times by both Miss Claire and Miss Taryn. Now she was positioned close enough to see them, and to hear exactly what they were saying about her.

"You must not be so hostile to Susie," Claire cautioned her daughter. "You must change your behavior and your attitude."

Taryn glowered at her mother. "Did you *hear* what Mrs. Coppersmith said?" Taryn countered angrily, nearly shouting at her mother. "That little brat is worming her way into **my** place. I've worked hard for that woman, and all she does is criticize me," Taryn fumed.

"This is not true," Claire differed politely; "just yesterday she paid you a great compliment at the tea party."

"Big deal," Taryn responded scathingly. "One measly compliment does not make up for all of the humiliation and insults she's heaped on me."

Claire smiled tenderly at her child. Gently she removed Taryn's bangs from her eyes. "Ma Chère," she responded softly; "Susie is not trying to take your place. No one can do that. Mrs. Coppersmith is severe with you because you tend to dream, to forget what you are doing. Always with you it is the design, the creations. She is trying to make you practical, like herself; nést-ce pas?"

Taryn tossed her head, pulling sharply away from her mother. Her expression did not soften. "I don't want to be like her, and I don't need to be like her to cook," she spewed, seething with resentment. "I tried to show her my designs for new linens, new drapes and for redecorating this dismal place. She wouldn't even look at them, Mama. She told me to stop wasting my time, so I told her I'd show them to Miss Pritchett. She told me if I did, I'd never do anything but peel onions and garlic. Can you believe that witch?"

"First of all, Chère; this place is not dismal. It is filled with elegant tapestries, murals, carpets and furnishings," her mother responded sternly. "I realize you do not like her antiques; however it isn't your place, Taryn, to criticize or attempt to cast aside Miss Pritchett's family heirlooms."

Pausing reflectively, Claire closed her eyes, choosing her next words carefully. "Second, Chère, you must change your attitude toward Mrs. Coppersmith. It is unacceptable for you to call her a witch, or any other name."

Opening her eyes, she looked upon her daughter with great sadness. "I know you know this," she spoke softly.

"Oh Mama," Taryn responded apologetically. "I'm sorry. I didn't mean to upset you. I get so angry and so frustrated with Mrs. Coppersmith. I don't know why she doesn't like me," she whined.

"Nonsense, child;" Claire hugged her daughter. "Of course she likes you. How could she not."

Releasing Taryn, she affectionately patted her daughter's face. "Please, for me, be nice to Susie," she requested.

Crossing her arms, Taryn's posture reflected the insolence in her voice. "Why? "

Claire sighed a troubled sigh. "Ma petite Cœur; please listen to me. I told you last week that Nini, Mimi and your Mema will be here this week. What I did not tell you is the reason." She paused momentarily, hoping to garner Taryn's interest. It worked.

Taryn's tantrum attitude changed to one of curiosity in spite of herself. "I assumed it was to spend Christmas with us. Obviously there must be another reason. Well," she demanded; "tell me why."

Her mother's smile was one of victory. "There was a pattern of The Cards I could not read. The pattern has to do with Susie," Claire began tentatively.

Breathing in a quick, steadying breath, she continued. "I took pictures and emailed them to the shop. Nini told me that the pattern is very old and very powerful. Nini was able to read it." Quickly she added, "*After* confession and much prayer. But Nini has not told me the meaning. All she would say is the message is very important, that Susie is most important and must be protected. And she will only explain the meaning in person."

Taryn shrugged. "Who cares?" she commented with disdain.

"You should care," Claire reprimanded her daughter. "This is your heritage. The Gift and the Mystery are your heritage."

"So," Taryn repeated; "who cares? I don't. Since when have you ever taken the so-called Gift, and The Cards and The Mystery seriously? It's always been a game to you," Taryn challenged derisively.

Aghast, Claire drew in a sharp breath as her fingers covered her mouth. Her eyes widened in shock as she stared at her child, unable to believe what she just heard. Tears filled her eyes, spilling down her face like little streams. Slowly she shook her head and closed her eyes. The ensuing silence was crushing. After several minutes Claire clasped her hands together, holding them at her heart. "You are my heart," she whispered. "Everything I have done, I have done for you."

When she opened her eyes, she saw the scorn in Taryn's expression. "I realize now that perhaps I made wrong choices," Claire said with great sorrow; "however, you would be wise not to discard what you do not understand."

After a fleeting pause, her tone changed, becoming harsh and authoritative. "When Nini comes, she will explain the reading. You will not be disrespectful. You will be courteous, and you will show your elders the respect that is their due. You will be nice to Susie, and to all the others here. If you do not behave yourself properly, I will send you away."

Shocked and angered by her mother's tone (one that she had never heard before), Taryn challenged, "You can't send me away. I work for Miss Pritchett; not you, Mama."

Claire's expression was devoid of any emotion, almost as bland as her voice, and both had a hard edge. "You were not her choice, my child. I asked Miss Pritchett to hire you until you married Joe, or until you left for Design School. If I tell her you must go, she will send you packing. Her tolerance of your insolence is wearing thin. She has the patience of a saint, but I see that your attitude is taking its toll on her as well. If you wish to remain, and marry Joe here in the Chapel as planned, you will heed my words."

"You are wrong," Taryn smugly hissed. "Miss Pritchett would never cancel our wedding. I do not have to like Susie, nor do I have to be nice to her. I don't like the way she watches everything and everyone. She's too smart for her own good. Someone needs to bring her down a peg or two, and I may do just that," she retorted haughtily.

"Do not be a fool, Taryn," her mother responded icily. "If Miss Pritchett is forced to choose between her legal charge and her employee, whom do you think she will choose? You? Never! She will send you away whether or not you are engaged to Joe, or have married him. How do you think Joe will feel toward you if you show such hatred to a child? How do you think he will feel toward you should you be the cause of him having to leave his home and job because Miss Pritchett has had to send you away?"

Taryn stared at her mother in disbelief. Never had her mother spoken harshly to her. Never had her mother been so forceful. Meekly Taryn responded, "I'm sorry, Mama. Please forgive me. I do love Joe, and I want to marry him. It's just that … well, I want to design. Every day it consumes me. My mind is constantly in a whirl with concepts. I sketch every moment I can, but no one cares. I could do so much here if anyone would give me the chance. It makes me angry that no one will listen to me."

"Perhaps, Chère, we can find an outlet for your talent even if you insist in remaining here," her mother suggested. "You do not have to live in a big city to start your own design company."

Taryn looked at her mother with surprise. "You mean the internet?"

"Oui, Chère. You can sell from here; even place your designs in our shop. I am certain that we can find room there to display whatever you wish to design. Perhaps you will design an exclusive line of dresses, or robes, or hats for just our shop."

Taryn looked hopeful as she asked, "Do you mean that, Mama?"

"But of course, ma petite Cœur," she responded with a smile. "I will consult The Cards. Come to the suite after you have finished your duties this afternoon."

Taryn shook her head. "Mama, I really don't think…."

Claire held up her hand, stopping her daughter's protest. "You will come out of respect for me. There is much I need to teach you. We will start this afternoon."

Taryn sighed heavily. "All right Mama. I'll be there at three."

"Bon," Claire joyously declared, hugging Taryn and kissing her cheek. "Now, we will speak no more of disagreeable things. We will focus on your wedding, and your new business," she decreed, linking her arm in her daughter's as she escorted Taryn toward the main corridor of the Library.

Susie darted quickly to the end of the aisle, rounding the end of the stack just as Miss Claire and Miss Taryn sashayed into the corridor. Her heart was racing, pounding in her ears as she flattened herself against the end of the bookcase, praying that they had not seen or heard her. She waited a few minutes before following them to the exit.

After they exited the Library, Susie ran to the door and peeked into the corridor of the west wing. She watched as they turned and entered the southwest wing. It was then she slipped out of the door and headed for the south wing. She wanted to go to her attic room and think about what she heard. Miss Claire had certainly said some very strange things.

'Miss Taryn, too', she mused. Susie had an uneasy feeling about Miss Taryn. An inner bell was ringing, telling her that the contrite apology was false, and that Miss Taryn was not to be trusted.

As she neared the south wing, she heard the unmistakable voices of Dani and Kat.

She heard Dani say, "Let's get Susie to play it with us."

Kat answered, "Okay, but where did she go?"

"Let's check the Library. She's *always* in there," Dani responded flippantly.

Running as fast as she could, Susie made incredible time getting back to the Library. Susie pulled the Library door shut behind her and ran all the way back to the East section, back to the alcove that housed the cabinet with the Histories volumes.

"This was stupid," she chided herself. "Now I'm trapped! Why did I run here? There's no place to hide."

With great haste, Susie looked all around, frantically hoping for a place to hide. She heard their voices as they entered the Library. Willing herself to be calm, she focused on where she might hide. She desperately wanted to spend the afternoon exploring and not playing games with Dani and Kat.

Standing still, she began to slowly look around the area. She heard a voice. Very faint, still and small, but she heard it as clear as day telling her to go to the alcove and look at the wall next to the cabinet. Without hesitating, she did. The panels of wainscoting held a row of little squares along its top edge, and in each square was a carving. Instinctively she

449

pressed the tiger, then the unicorn and finally the wolf. A panel opened, revealing a passageway. Peering at the inside of the door, Susie saw a pull handle and the release latch. She stepped in and pulled the secret door closed, keeping one hand on the release latch and one on the handle.

Within seconds of closing the door, Susie began shivering. She knew it was as much probably from the pitch blackness of the passageway as it was from the bitter cold. She could hear the girls; they were calling out to her, yelling actually. She stifled a giggle when she imagined how Dani, or Megan or Juls would react to being in this place.

'Kat would probably feel at home', she mused with a silent laugh.

Her teeth began to chatter; and, to her, it sounded like a string of fire-crackers popping. She just knew they could also hear it. But they didn't, and soon Dani and Kat had left the Library.

Susie popped the release latch and re-entered the Library, practically running to the fireplace. There she remained for several minutes warming her body by the fire, trying to dispense the chill that seemed to have set deep into her bones. A smile began to slowly fill her face as the realization dawned.

There must be secret passages all throughout this place like a honeycomb. I bet every room has a secret door to them,' she thought.

She turned and faced the sitting area, allowing the fire to give its warmth to her back.

'Where would someone have put those books?' she wondered. 'Did they accidently return them to the wrong shelf, or was it intentional?'

Leaving the comforting warmth of the fireplace, Susie began walking up and down the aisles, looking at all the bookcases surrounding this area. Slowly she began expanding her search among the rest of the stacks in the east section of the Library. Discouragement set in as she realized trying to find the misplaced books among the thousands in the Library would be akin to searching for the proverbial needle in a haystack. As she continued to mull it over, an idea flashed into her mind, creating a ray hope. "Perhaps someone thought they belonged with the children's books," she uttered excitedly.

Alive with a new found energy, Susie raced to the children's bookcases in the East section. No luck. Undeterred, she next checked the South and the West sections; still not finding the books, she quickly ran to the North section. Eureka! She found all seven books in the third bookcase she searched. She nearly danced for joy, so absolutely elated was she that she had found them. It was as if she had found a pirate's treasure; something so precious that it had been hidden away, just waiting for the right person to discover it.

She removed the books from the shelf and quickly made her way to the door. Quickly she signed out the books, scrawling the information and her signature beside each entry. Cautiously she opened the door ever so slightly, listening to see if anyone was in the corridor. No one was. Slipping out of the Library, Susie ran all the way to the spiral staircase, praying that no one would enter either of the corridors.

When she reached the staircase, she climbed them two at a time, losing her balance only once along the way. She fell hard against the metal steps, scrapping her shins and nearly dropped the books. That would have been a disaster - she would have had to climb back down to the ground floor and risk being seen. Of course, no one would care unless it was one of the girls; then she would have had to explain where she was going, and subsequently spend the remainder of the afternoon with them instead of in grand pursuit of the Secret of Glen Hollow.

As she neared the second floor, she paused and listened before continuing on past the second floor landing. No one seemed to be in the corridor. As fast as she could, she scurried on up the staircase, past the landing and on toward the third floor. Again, she paused just before reaching the third floor landing. Her heart was beating so hard and so fast it sounded like a big bass drum in her ears. As luck would have it, this corridor was also as empty as the others. Stepping onto the landing, Susie quickly exited the staircase, running the short distance to the attic room door. She fished the key out of her pocket, unlocked the door, opened it and quickly entered.

Setting the books down on the first step, she ran up the next two, reached up and turned on the light switch. The familiar, soft light shone, cheerfully illuminating the stairwell. Susie turned, ran back down and quickly closed and locked the door. Scooping up the books, she hurried to the top of the stairs, flipping on the light switch as she went past. Susie delivered her newly found treasures to the bookcase, setting them along side of the first volume. Susie felt a sense of completion surge within her being.

"The books belong together," she told herself and smiled.

The clock on the mantle revealed the hour to be two-thirty; not enough time remaining to explore before Story Time, but certainly enough time to read, she decided. Susie retrieved the Unicorn book from the shelf and laid it onto the little table by Nana's chair.

Since she was going to stay in here and read, she decided the attic was a little too frosty and in need of a small fire. Susie placed two small logs and some kindling in the fireplace. Striking a match, she held it against the kindling in three places, smiling as each one took hold. She waited for a few seconds before tossing the match into the fire that had now ignited all of the kindling. Using the poker, Susie stoked the fire until its flames began licking at the bottom of the logs.

Dropping into Nana's chair, Susie covered herself with Nana's afghan while she waited for the fire to take hold. Soon the fire was burning nicely, warming the area around it quite well. Susie yawned a few times, lulled into drowsiness by the warmth of the fire. Slowly she drifted to sleep as she listened to the comforting sounds of the fire's popping and crackling.

———

Drifting gently between twilight sleep and consciousness, Susie began to awaken ever so slowly. Dressed in a flowing, pale blue gown, a beautiful lady was gently shaking her. Still in her dream-like state, Susie sleepily smiled at the woman. The lady returned Susie's smile with one of her own. It was a pleasant smile; one that was cheerful and kind, comforting and gracious. Susie hazily looked at the radiant lady. She had the most vivid, dark red hair that gleamed with a golden hue, giving her hair the appearance of having been sprinkled with gold dust. Her skin was smooth and soft, and as white as the finest alabaster, sparkling as if lit by the noonday sun.

Susie's sleepy eyes finally met those of the lady, staring vacantly into the lady's eyes. She couldn't help staring; the lady's eyes were so pretty. They reminded Susie of the ocean when the sun shines on it, all sparkly and filled with a myriad of blue tones from the faintest hint of blue to its deepest midnight color.

The lady's voice - it was so pleasant. It was like listening to your mother sing to you a lullaby or as soothing as the prettiest of wind chimes, ringing gently in a light breeze. "Wake up, Susie," the lady insisted. "You must wake up now."

Susie finally rejoined the land of the living; and for a fleeting moment, she thought she truly saw this lady. She bolted upright, pulling Nana's afghan tighter around her body as she shivered in the cold. Squeezing her eyes shut for a moment, she attempted to clear her mind of the sleep that tried to persist.

Suddenly she knew what was wrong, and her eyes sprung open with dismay. Glancing at the fireplace, Susie could see that fire had long since died. Panic set in as she looked at the little clock – a quarter to six. She flung the afghan onto the chair and jumped to her feet. She'd been asleep for three hours!

Racing to the stairwell, she scurried down it and nearly dropped the key in her haste to unlock the door. Finally she managed to steady her hand enough to unlock it. Opening the door, she dashed into the corridor, slammed the door shut behind her and then re-locked it.

Only when she entered the spiral stairwell did she realize that she had forgotten to turn off the attic room lights. "Can't be helped," Susie muttered as she took the spiral stairs three at a time, all the way down to the first floor. Running to the Dining Hall, Susie arrived just in the nick of time. Everyone was just taking their seats.

As she slid into her chair, Simon scowled at her and said a little crossly, "Where were you Susie? We tried to find you. You weren't in the Library, so we didn't get Story Time."

She smiled, rubbed his back with a few short stokes and said, "I was reading and fell asleep. I'm sorry." Leaning down, she whispered in his ear, "I'll make up for it at bedtime. I'll read two, small stories tonight, or continue with Nana's story. You get to choose. Okay?"

She straightened just enough to nearly be nose to nose with him. Simon grinned, and his eyes twinkled. He nodded his head in approval of her plan.

———

After dinner, Susie spent the evening with the others in the Rec Room. As soon as their baths were finished, Simon, Timmy and Megan burst through the door and came running to Susie. Simon and Timmy had to regale her and the others once again of their helper exploits from that afternoon. After playing several rounds of 'Go Fish' with the Munchkins, they decided they wanted to play Candy Land. Just as they were ready to start the game, Miss Ginger and Miss Cora entered the room.

"Eight o'clock bedtime," Miss Ginger announced.

All eyes were drawn to the antique grandfather clock. It declared that the time was 7:59. The Munchkins quickly jumped to their feet and joined the ladies at the door. Their little faces were beaming at the ladies as they eagerly hurried out the door.

Miss Ginger looked at Miss Cora, a little surprised, and said, "It's amazing that they don't seem to fight bedtime anymore. I wonder why that is."

Miss Cora chuckled (she knew why). "Does it matter?" she asked.

"I guess not," Miss Ginger concurred as she turned and headed out the door.

Miss Ginger quickly caught up with the boys as Miss Cora raced to catch up with Megan, who had already entered the Girls Dorm on her own.

———

"Hey, Susie, you want to play chess?" Jose asked hopefully, holding the chess board out for her to see.

"I can't right now, Jose. Ask Jared; I'm sure he will," Susie suggested, smiling politely.

"I'd rather play with you. … Why can't you?" he countered, dropping onto the couch next to her.

She looked at the clock; Megan would be expecting her in about five minutes.

She smiled at Jose and said, "I'm just not really up to it tonight. Would tomorrow afternoon in the Library, say about three, be all right?"

He shrugged. "I guess. I'll see if Jared wants to play." He rose and headed in Jared's direction.

Susie breathed a sigh of relief. She stood, leisurely walked to the door and left the room. Quickly she ran to the Girl's Dorm. Opening the door, she peered in; there was Megan, standing not two feet from the door.

Susie chuckled. "Come on," she whispered as she took Megan's hand.

They sprinted across the corridor and into the Boys Dorm. All was quiet as they hustled through the Common Area, then along the hallway the short distance to Simon's room. Timmy and Simon were perched on the bed with the silliest grins as they patiently awaited her arrival. Megan jumped onto the bed and settled herself down next to Simon.

"Okay," Susie whispered. "I told Simon that I'd read two, little stories tonight, or continue with the next part of Nana's story; so what do you want?"

"I want to hear the next part of the story," Megan said with just a hint of a pout.

Timmy furled his brow a moment as he thought it through. Then asked, "If you read two stories tonight, will you tell the next part of Nana's story tomorrow night?"

"Yes," Susie answered.

He shrugged. "Then I don't care."

"Simon, what do you want?" Susie asked.

He thought for a fraction of a second before his grin spread from ear to ear. Softly he whispered, "Nana's story, please."

Susie nodded, smiled and said, "Okay, let's begin."

Delving into the story, Susie began using the same traits and skills that Nana had performed so many times for her and for Simon. She delighted in watching their facial expressions change from excitement, to wonder, to apprehension and fright, and back again to relief, wonder and joy.

Just as she finished telling the final installment of 'Ketar and the Kingdom of Shashur', Aaron appeared, startling them all.

"What's going on? What are you and Megan doing in here?" he demanded tersely.

The three Munchkins began to panic. Remaining calm, Susie looked at him and said, "They want bedtime stories, so I give them one every night."

"Do the adults know?" he queried, his tone just slightly suspicious.

"No, they don't," she responded softly while Simon, Timmy and Megan each echoed their own versions of "no". "And we would appreciate it if you didn't tell them," she added with a pleading tone.

He grinned, resembling the proverbial cat that caught the canary. "No problem as long as I get to sit in."

"No way," Simon protested. "This is our secret club."

"That's right," Timmy agreed with his 'best bud'. "It's just for us Munchkins," he insisted, pointing to Megan, Simon and himself.

Aaron glanced at Susie, raised his eyebrows, and shrugged his shoulders. "If that's the way you want it," he said as he turned to leave.

"Wait Aaron, please," Susie implored. "Guys, I think it would be okay to have Aaron join us. Story Time isn't just for little Munchkins; it's for everyone."

"What about it being our secret?" Simon asked, a little perturbed that their secret club was expanding.

"Yeah," the other two chorused.

Susie sighed. "Unfortunately it isn't a secret now." Susie paused and then asked, "Simon, did Nana exclude you from Story Time?"

He shook his head slowly back and forth.

"No, she didn't," Susie concurred. "You were a lot younger than me, but she included you even before you could talk. Don't you think we should include Aaron? Isn't that what Nana would do?"

"Yes," Simon agreed reluctantly.

"Timmy, Megan, you agree?"

Megan nodded rapidly as she smiled at Aaron. She liked Aaron. Timmy giggled and said "Okay," grinning at his big brother.

"You're in," Susie told him cheerfully.

"Okay," he said. "So what's the skinny?"

Timmy was quickest to respond. "We meet here every night right after Miss Ginger leaves. Susie tells us a story; and then we get back in bed, and then Megan and Susie leave."

"So, is it over for tonight?" Aaron asked Susie.

"Yes," she answered. "They need to get back into their beds, and I've got to get Megan into hers before the nine o'clock bedtime call."

"I'll get them in bed; you take care of Megan," Aaron offered.

"Thanks," Susie said, surprised and appreciative. She gave Timmy and then Simon a quick hug and kiss goodnight. Grabbing Megan's hand, they made a mad dash toward the door. It would be close tonight – the grandfather clock showed it was already eight fifty-two as they hurried past it.

She peered out the door and saw that the coast was clear. They darted into the corridor and across to the Girls Dorm. Hurriedly they ran to Megan's room and promptly got her into bed. After a fast and strong goodnight hug from Megan, Susie tucked her in, giving her a kiss on her forehead.

Not a minute after picking up a magazine and stretching out on the couch, Miss Cora and the girls came bounding through the door.

"There you are Susie," Miss Cora commented. "We were wondering where you were."

"Just relaxing," Susie said and smiled at Miss Cora.

"It's time to get ready for bed," she told Susie.

"Yes, ma'am," Susie answered, smiling, as she stood and headed for the bathroom.

When the girls exited the bathroom, Miss Cora was in her usual spot, waiting by the door. They quickly filed past her, saying goodnight as they each headed toward their beds. Five minutes later, Miss Cora left the Dorm, turning off the lights on her way out the door.

Chapter 22

DISCERNMENT AND COMPASSION

Susie sat quietly, just staring at the crackling fire as it danced its way closer to becoming mere embers. Her thoughts were racing, unstructured, as they darted and flitted from one idea to the next. She had finished all eight books by Helga Gretchen Von Richter, and had the most amazing thoughts envelop her mind while doing so. Each book was like the first; not just in cover and lettering, but also in its attention to detail in all of its artistry. With each book Susie had the same sensations as she did with the first, only now it did not frighten her. Instead, she found herself intrigued by the experience as well as the thoughts expressed by the author. Much of her stories were similar, even identical at times, to Nana's.

"Makes you wonder," Susie mused aloud.

Her eyes wandered back to her journal, revisiting the conversation she had overhead yesterday in the Library. There were so many questions plaguing her mind, and no answers. She wondered if there was any chance that Miss Clare's Nini would talk to her.

"Probably not," she sighed despondently, answering her own question.

Relaxing against the window, Susie reflected on yet another strange, unexplained discovery. Before coming to her attic sanctuary, she had slipped into the Library to take a quick look at the newest of the "Histories" volumes. She was hoping to find that it contained the additions to the family since the volumes were printed in 1852. It did.

Oddly enough, Susie noticed that only the first-born daughter inherited Glen Hollow. Even more strange was that only the first-born daughter kept the surname "Evermore". All other children were given their father's surname.

The last volume began with Josephine Lee Evermore, the wife of the man who commissioned the 'Histories'. As with all of the other records, her page prominently displayed her name at the top. Under her name was recorded her date of birth (May 05, 1788) and also her date of death (November 02, 1849). The cause of death was listed as pneumonia.

The following section listed the names of Josephine's parents with a notation referring the reader to the previous Volume and the page number of her mother's record. After the parent's section came the listing of Josephine's husband, Horace Ansel Stanford.

Last was the section for children; names, dates of birth, dates of death, names of spouses and dates of marriage were all recorded. A total of ten children were born to Josephine and Horace. Their second child, Annabel Lee Stanford, had died of pneumonia in 1824 at the age of fifteen. All the other children lived long lives, several living into their nineties. However, Susie's interest peaked when she saw that Josephine's first-born daughter was Evangeline Elizabeth Evermore, the girl from the portrait. She was born January 04, 1808 and was eleven when that portrait was painted.

Somehow learning details about this young girl who lived so long ago created a sense of connection in Susie. She could envision young Evangeline running and playing with her brothers and sisters, whether in the house or outside. She smiled as the images surfaced, of the fun times, the holiday celebrations, family outings, and, most likely, times of arguments and hurt feelings. But she could also see images of a strong love and bond between them.

"Like Simon and me," she mused affectionately at the thought of her little brother.

Susie wondered what happened to them, where they went and if any of their descendants knew about Glen Hollow. Or had it been lost to them, forgotten over time and distance. June was homecoming at Glen Hollow – homecoming for the residents and staff, current and past, but no mention had been made of any relatives of Miss Pritchett attending.

'There must be some somewhere,' Susie thought.

She turned her attention to the change in penmanship. The calligraphy writing had ceased beginning with the record for Elizabeth Noreen Evermore, born in 1882 and was Miss Pritchett's grandmother. The script was now an elegant, formal script, but not calligraphy. The same person that recorded Elizabeth Noreen's page also recorded Miss Murielle's page, and the beginning of Miss Pritchett's page; however, the hand was not as steady and precise with Miss Pritchett's page as with the other two.

Susie found a Baptismal Record folded and stuffed into the book's crease at Miss Pritchett's page. The Baptismal Record revealed Miss

Pritchett's legal name was Evermore, just like all the other first-born daughters. That made Susie wonder why she used Pritchett instead of Evermore. Also stuffed into the binding was her Marriage Certificate. Lastly, Susie found a birth certificate – the child's name was Dara Evangeline Evermore. The parents were listed as Eloise Noreen Evermore and Everitt Wendell Sheridan. Susie held her breath, staring at the document in her hand. A sense of overwhelming grief flooded her; her breathing became rapid and shallow as the waves of emotion rolled through her. Slowly the sensation dissipated, ebbing away like ripples in a pond.

Turning the page, she expected to see a Record started for Dara. There was none, and she couldn't help but wonder why. Although Dara had been kidnapped, it seemed to Susie that there should be a page. As she pondered it, the answer came. Miss Pritchett didn't know about the Volumes. Being tucked away at the very back of the Library, they weren't all that noticeable.

Whoever had written Miss Pritchett's Record was elderly and had passed away long before Dara was born. Someone else put the documents in the book. But who? And why weren't they recorded?

"Another mystery," Susie mumbled to her reflection in the window. "And still another; why wasn't Miss Pritchett told about the Volumes?"

Her eyes strayed to the mantel above the fireplace. The little clock readily showed that the morning was fast disappearing, leaving her fifteen minutes to return to the Dorm room and awaken the girls. She'd had little more than two hours of sleep, having risen at midnight in order to slip away and read the books. Increasingly her body felt that lack of sleep, and even now cried out for just a nap. Although she'd had a three hour nap before dinner, it wasn't enough to balance the scales, currently still leaning heavily toward sleep deprivation.

Reluctantly she rose from Nana's chair, returning her journal to its hiding place. She grinned – she had found this unique, little spot quite by accident tonight when she set the clock on this shelf. Why she hadn't noticed it before now, she didn't know. Not that it mattered; she had found it, and it was a great hiding place.

Someone had carefully worked free from its mortar the second stone back from the front. When replaced properly, the stone appeared to be a solid part of the fireplace. It wasn't until she set the clock on the shelf that she noticed something was amiss – the stone was sitting slightly askew. She touched it; it moved. Gleefully, her fingers locked onto it and pulled; the stone came free, revealing a nice little hiding place, just perfect for her journal.

Gently she refolded Nana's afghan, draping it carefully across the back of the chair just as she had seen Nana do for so many years. A bittersweet smile formed on her lips as the realization struck her.

"I miss you, Nana," Susie whispered to the framed picture perched on the table next to the chair. It was her favorite. It had been taken on a family picnic the week before her parents died. They were all sitting on the blanket with Nana in the center between her parents. Mommy was holding Simon in her lap, and Daddy was holding her in his. Nana's outstretched arms wrapped around both she and Simon, like an eagle protecting its own.

Nana had told her many times about the nice, young couple who had taken the picture for them. Susie didn't remember them; but she did remember playing hide-n-seek with Daddy, and singing songs with Mommy and Nana. No memory of that couple, no memory of the food or of the trip itself.

"Funny," she contemplated; "what little I remember about that day." Susie sighed lightly as her fingers gently touched the picture, lightly tracing the images.

Attempting to dispel the sadness, Susie inhaled deeply before slowly releasing her breath. Knowing she had to start her day, she forced herself to walk to the fireplace and extinguish the smoldering embers before exiting her sanctuary. She made certain none would burst back into flame.

——

After breakfast, Susie hurriedly left the Dining Hall, heading to the kitchen to get started on her assigned kitchen duty. Simon and Timmy had just left with Mr. Sean to start their farming chores. Behind her, but still in the Dining Hall, she could hear Megan whining. Kat and Dani were attempting to get away from Megan, prompting her wails - she had no one to play with and was decidedly unhappy about it.

As she exited the Dining Hall, Susie heard Miss Ginger ask Megan if Megan would be her sewing partner. Megan was ecstatic, bouncing up and down, clapping her hands and squealing with delight. Susie chuckled, thinking to herself that that was a nice thing for Miss Ginger to have done, especially when you consider Megan would be more of a hindrance than a help. Susie couldn't imagine just what Megan would be able to do, but she knew that Miss Ginger would find something that would give Megan the satisfaction of accomplishment.

"And for that," Susie surmised with amusement; "Dani and Kat owe her a big favor."

The morning went fairly well. Miss Taryn was surly as usual, and shot Susie hostile glances every now and then. Susie noticed, however, that whenever Mrs. Coppersmith was within earshot, Miss Taryn would pay Susie a compliment. She even managed to feign a smile if Mrs. Coppersmith happened to be near enough to actually see Miss Taryn's face. Susie was not fooled – she already knew Miss Taryn was not to be trusted. Today's behavior only reinforced her intuition.

Finishing the last of her kitchen chores (peeling and chopping onions), Susie was thrilled she had done so ahead of schedule. Humming a little tune, Susie rinsed the knife and cutting board and laid them in the sink. Lastly, and according to Mrs. Coppersmith's instructions, she covered the bowl with plastic wrap and headed to the refrigerator.

"What are you doing?" Miss Taryn inquired. Her tone was anything but curious.

"Putting the onions in the refrigerator," Susie answered politely, opening the door of the refrigerator.

"Leave them on the table," she ordered. "We'll be using them when we prepare lunch."

"But Mrs. Copp -," Susie began and was interrupted.

"Don't argue with me. You will do as I tell you," she snapped. "Put the bowl on the table now. Get the broom and sweep the kitchen."

"But I finished the chores Mrs. Coppersmith gave me," Susie replied earnestly. "She said I could leave whenever I finished."

"Did she? I think not," Miss Taryn retorted caustically. "You are assigned kitchen duty for two hours every day, missy. You still have thirty minutes of duty time, so get sweeping!" she ordered.

"Here now; I told Susie to put them in the refrigerator, and that's where they'll go, Mrs. Coppersmith barked.

She had entered the kitchen from the employees lounge, unseen by both Taryn and Susie. Mrs. Coppersmith stormed over to Taryn like a mother bear protecting its cub.

"Who do you think you are telling her what to do? This is *my* kitchen, and I'll thank you to remember that. You do not give the orders here, young lady. I gave her the chores for today, and I told her she could leave when she finished. I don't care if she did get done early. Do you have a problem with that?" She huffed, jutting her chin slightly forward and placing her fists solidly on her hips.

Taryn looked frightened and took a couple of steps backwards. "No … I mean, I didn't know you had told her to put them in the refrigerator." Her composure quickly returned, enabling her to launch a counteroffensive. "She should have told me," she declared haughtily.

Mrs. Coppersmith crossed her arms, eyeing Taryn with a hard glare. "She would have if you hadn't cut her off," she responded drily. "Don't bother denying it; I heard every word," she added as Taryn started to speak. Mrs. Coppersmith pressed her lips firmly together, rapidly shaking her head several times as if she were trying to come to a decision.

Suddenly her motion ceased, and her expression held a look of finality. When she spoke, her voice was resolute. "I have had enough of your attitude, young lady. I had serious misgivings about you being my assistant; but, as a favor to Joe and to Miss Pritchett, I obliged. You need to think seriously about your attitude; I can't use you unless you change, and truly want to be my assistant. Now, you go somewhere and give heed to what I've said. I'll be expecting an answer before lunch."

Stunned at such a reprimand, Taryn's face flushed deep red. "I don't understand," she stammered as she sank into a chair. "Are you saying you don't want me as your assistant?"

Mrs. Coppersmith's expression softened. "No, child; I have doubts that you want to be my assistant. Your attitude and behavior has only served to show that you do not want to be here. What is it you truly want? Do you even know?" she asked kindly.

"Yes I do," Taryn declared hotly in her own defense. "I was born to design. I have talent; everyone who has ever seen my sketches has said so."

"Then why are you here? Why aren't you in New York?" Mrs. Coppersmith fired back.

Taryn took in a fast breath and released it quickly. "Because of Joe," she responded acerbically; "he won't leave here."

"It seems you have a decision to make, don't you child?" Mrs. Coppersmith gently laid her hand on Taryn's shoulder. "You can stay, marry Joe and choose to be bitter, working in a job you hate; or you can choose to go to New York, do what you love, and seek your future there without him."

Patting Taryn's shoulder, Mrs. Coppersmith added, a humorous hint in her voice peeking through the serious tone, "*Or* you can stay, marry Joe and find a way to do what you love even here in the country. You're not the first woman to have to choose between the desired career and the man she loves. You can have both; you just have to be a little more flexible in how you achieve both."

Taryn looked up, tears filling her eyes. "That's what Mama said."

Softly Mrs. Coppersmith replied, "Then listen to your mother." Smiling, she added, "Go on; take the morning off and gather your thoughts."

Miss Taryn rose and headed for the door. She paused on the threshold and turned to face Mrs. Coppersmith. "Mrs. Coppersmith, I already know I want to work for you as your assistant. That is, if you'll have me."

Nodding, she responded, "Of course, child. Now off with you. Everyone needs a break now and again. Be here promptly at eleven-thirty."

"I will," Miss Taryn answered and hurried toward the door, a wicked, little smile creasing her lips. Mrs. Coppersmith didn't see, but Susie did; Miss Taryn had intentionally turned her head slightly toward Susie as she left the room.

"Come have a sit down," Mrs. Coppersmith called out to Susie, patting the chair next to hers.

Susie promptly slid into the chair.

"Don't you worry about Taryn," Mrs. Coppersmith told Susie, noticing Susie's hard stare as Taryn left. "I doubt she'll change, but it doesn't matter. I know she planned to quit as soon as she marries Joe; which is fine if that is truly what she wants. Somehow I don't think she knows what she wants." Mrs. Coppersmith's tone was strained. For all her blustering, Susie sensed that Mrs. Coppersmith was worried about Miss Taryn.

"Well, child, you're done for the day. Would you like to accompany me to visit Mr. Coppersmith? Afterward you may explore the cemetery a little, if you like."

Susie was surprised and delighted at the offer. "Yes, thank you."

"Come then; we'll go out this way, and save time and some steps," Mrs. Coppersmith instructed. "You may use one of my capes."

Mrs. Coppersmith led Susie out of the kitchen, down the southwest corridor and into the vestibule. She selected a short, purple cape, complete with matching scarf, hat and gloves. Smiling as she handed them to Susie, she said, "It's meant to be waist-length; but, on you, it'll be full-length."

As Susie donned the garments, Mrs. Coppersmith chose her navy, full-length cape for her own use. Now ready to brave the elements, Mrs. Coppersmith opened the door and out they went.

As they hurried along the portico, Mrs. Coppersmith began telling Susie a little of the history of some of the "residents" of the cemetery and mausoleum. Staff members and their families were buried in the cemetery; the Evermore family members were buried in the mausoleum.

Apparently, Miss Pritchett's parents, grandparents and other ancestors had been quite well known, entertaining Presidents, Congressmen and even visiting dignitaries, some of whom were royalty. A memory surfaced, and Susie recalled what Mrs. Crenshaw had said - the Evermores were famous for their horses, and for the festivals.

A twinge of sympathy for Miss Pritchett flooded Susie; she truly began to realize just how much Miss Pritchett's world had changed when her parents died. How different Glen Hollow is now compared to what it once was; and yet, Susie marveled, Miss Pritchett seems okay with it. More than okay – she seems happy. Susie couldn't help but wonder, 'will I ever be happy?'

Mrs. Coppersmith had stopped talking, noticing the far-away gaze in Susie's eyes. Jolting from her reverie, Susie came crashing back to reality upon hearing Mrs. Coppersmith's laugh and subsequent question, "Earth to Susie; are you okay, child?"

Embarrassed, Susie laughed lightly. "I'm sorry, Mrs. Coppersmith. I was just thinking how different Glen Hollow is now, and how Miss Pritchett must miss what it used to be."

Giving Susie a knowing glance, she replied, "To be sure, it is different; better in fact than the time right after the passing of her mother. I should think it was very hard to be a child and not be allowed to speak your mother's name, nor have anything that had belonged to her."

Susie nodded. "Miss Pritchett told me that her father had removed all of her mother's things except for one miniature portrait that she had kept hidden."

Mrs. Coppersmith reached her arm around Susie and hugged her tight. "You see, child; everyone who has ever lived has had some heartache in their life at one time or another. We can choose to let the circumstances destroy us and make us bitter, or we can choose to let them make us stronger. And we can also help others to cope with their heartaches since we know what it is ourselves to suffer."

"Thanks, Mrs. Coppersmith." Susie hugged her.

"Enough blubbering," Mrs. Coppersmith responded. Although her tone tried to sound gruff, her twinkling eyes revealed how tender-hearted she truly is. "I want to introduce you to Mr. Coppersmith. He's going to just love you," she added cheerfully.

Having left the portico near the Chapel, they began the long walk to the cemetery, nestled behind a screen of tall cedars. The flagstone path led between two such behemoths, ushering them into an expansive garden of rose bushes, lilac trees, oak trees and (according to Mrs. Coppersmith) a kaleidoscope of colors from the array of flowers that would start blooming come spring. Currently, the only flowers in bloom were the deep red camellias, also known as the Christmas rose according to Mrs. Coppersmith.

Holly bushes, loaded with red berries, lined the walkways and were trimmed so that they were short hedges, not more than three feet in height. Park benches were strategically placed, some under trees and some in the open. There were several small fountains, each with its own theme, but none as grand as the dolphin fountain in the east garden.

Mrs. Coppersmith shared with Susie that, had they entered through its main entrance in the center of the cemetery, Susie would have seen the mausoleum. "A truly beautiful building," she said admiringly. However, this entrance is closer to the southwest wing; and it is far too cold, she said, to be out any longer than necessary.

As they passed by the graves, Susie remarked how beautiful the cemetery was, more like a park than what she had mentally pictured as a graveyard. Her face clouded with sadness as she told Mrs. Coppersmith that there was no one to care for Nana's grave or her parents' graves. Shaking her head, Mrs. Coppersmith told her not to worry because Miss Pritchett has already seen to it. She winked and smiled at Susie's astonished look, adding that, come spring, Miss Pritchett would allow her to have day trips to place flowers on the graves; Susie would see for herself that their graves were well maintained. Mrs. Coppersmith's smile and confidence made Susie feel better.

Five minutes later they arrived at his "resting place" (as Mrs. Coppersmith called it). Susie was beginning to get hot and removed the scarf, hat and gloves. Though the sun was shining brightly and warmed her skin, the air was still quite chilly. Mrs. Coppersmith quickly fussed at her to put them back on before she caught her death, so Susie complied. Susie smiled as she listened to Mrs. Coppersmith tell Mr. Coppersmith that she had to watch the children every minute, and that it was a wonder any of them ever survived to adulthood.

Then Mrs. Coppersmith introduced Susie and her late husband to each other. Upon doing so, she noticed that Susie was uncomfortable and asked why. Susie cautiously responded that Mr. Coppersmith isn't in the grave - that he's in Heaven.

Mrs. Coppersmith laughed heartily, her eyes crinkling with delight. Nodding affably, she said, "Oh, to be sure; he most definitely is. Never was there a man as kind and decent as he."

Her face shone with joy as she explained to Susie that facing the headstone was just a matter of courtesy. "After all," she stated matter-of-factly; "he can still hear and see us even if we can't hear or see him. By facing the headstone, he can sit on the headstone, or stand in front of it, when we're speaking to him."

Pausing ever so briefly, she asked playfully, "Where else would you know to look when addressing him if you didn't face the headstone?"

Susie grinned at Mrs. Coppersmith, admitting that made a little sense.

Mrs. Coppersmith smiled and told Susie she wanted some alone time with him, giving Susie permission to explore the grounds nearby. Although Susie wanted to see the mausoleum, Mrs. Coppersmith had told her absolutely not, citing that the mausoleum was too far, and it was too cold today to be outside in it for that length of time. After seeing Susie's disappointment, she tenderly added that come the first nice day, Susie could explore it to her heart's content.

"Now be a dear, and don't go far. We'll be heading back to the manor in about five minutes," Mrs. Coppersmith instructed.

Susie nodded and began walking back down the path, looking at the headstones. All were of the same granite as the manor. "Must be a quarry nearby," Susie concluded. Most all of these were more recent graves, so Susie scampered her way further into the cemetery, keeping within sight of Mrs. Coppersmith.

As she hurried along, the path now split into three directions. The left path led toward the center (to the mausoleum, she figured), the center path (the one she was currently on) proceeded straight and the one on the right led to a large tree. Susie hurried toward the tree, discovering that the path ended by circling around the tree. A solitary bench was placed under the white ash tree, granting the visitor shade from the heat of the summer sun.

Smaller trails led away from the main path and down the rows of gravesites. Susie chose the furthest trail and wandered slowly, reading the headstones as she passed. Several of the headstones were so old and so weather-worn that the names and dates were nearly illegible. She recalled how Miss Pritchett had said that the first portion of the manor was built nearly 270 years ago; before that, there had been a log house. Some of these must be from that time, Susie realized.

Susie stopped. The gravestone read:

Priscilla Grace Albright
Born Mar 20, 1744
Died Dec 20, 1744
Our beloved child

Susie noticed that the next three gravestones were also of Albright children, none older than two years of age. Following those graves was the headstone of a woman; her name was Ada Mae Albright, 57 years old when she died. Beside her grave was a man's, whose name was Elijah Aaron Albright; age 54 at death. The next two graves were also Albrights - Benjamin Aaron Albright (son of Ada and Elijah), age 55 in death, and Mary Alice Boothe Albright (Ben's wife), age 53 when she passed. Next to her, in succession, were their children, children's spouses, and grandchildren.

The rows varied, some only had one person and no apparent relatives, others had a few and still others seemed to fill many rows, with generation after generation living and working here at Glen Hollow, just as Mrs. Coppersmith had said.

"Susie! Where are you?" Mrs. Coppersmith called, her voice sharply cutting through the stillness.

"Here I am," Susie responded, running to the top of the hill. She waved at Mrs. Coppersmith and continued running until she met up with her.

"Child, I thought I told you not to go too far," she admonished. Her voice revealed that though she was worried, she wasn't upset. She linked arms with Susie, swiftly guiding her back to the entrance.

"I'm sorry, Mrs. Coppersmith," Susie apologized. "I was reading the headstones and just kept following the path. Some are really old and hard to read," she explained.

Mrs. Coppersmith nodded. "True enough; it's a good thing they're all listed in the Record Book, including where they're laid to rest," she informed Susie.

"Really; where is the Record Book?" Susie asked.

Mrs. Coppersmith chuckled lightly, amused by Susie's curiosity. "There's an office in the Mausoleum," she replied. "You can look through them some other time," she added, intuitively answering Susie's next question before she was able to ask.

The breeze had turned bitterly cold, blowing in forceful gusts as it whipped around them. They pulled their woolen scarves over their noses in an attempt to stave off the effects of the icy air. With arms linked tight, they bolted back to the inviting warmth of the manor.

Upon entering the kitchen after their near-Artic expedition, Mrs. Coppersmith quickly made them two steaming mugs of hot cocoa. Its warmth seemed to spread throughout her entire body, removing every last vestige of the icy chill.

Mrs. Coppersmith thanked Susie for accompanying her, and for being willing to meet Mr. Coppersmith. She had said that not many people, especially young ones, were willing to visit with their departed loved ones. Sighing wistfully, Mrs. Coppersmith began taking Susie down memory lane, revisiting the days when she was a young girl. Mrs. Coppersmith's countenance took on that starry-eyed gaze of one that was here physically, but had retreated mentally and spiritual into another time, a time long since passed.

She regaled Susie of the day trips to the beach, or the picnic grounds at the lake, or a park. Longingly she spoke of the winter carnivals at Half Moon Bay. She chuckled at Susie's expression – it was obvious that Susie had no idea where it was.

"Half Moon Bay," she said; "is a little village in Half Moon Cove on Moon Lake. The lake is halfway between Foxboro Station and Rosemont, but to the west, near about thirty miles."

She continued her recollection about Half Moon Bay, laughing heartily when she told Susie that the Winter Carnival December 1957 was when she received her first kiss at age twelve. It was at a kissing booth; her best friend, Maggs (given name, Margaret) had dared her to do it. She, of course, double dared Maggs, and they both paid the fifty cents. She howled with laughter as she admitted how nervous they both had been; both wanting to back out, but not wanting to be called 'chicken'. She shook her head, still laughing, as she said they were absolutely terrified that their parents might happen by and see them, either waiting in line or receiving the kiss.

"Mind, it was just a peck; not a romantic kiss at all; but to us, it was as if we were kissing Ricky Nelson himself." Sighing happily and with twinkling eyes, she fondly remembered "the good ol' days" as she called them.

With their coca now gone, Mrs. Coppersmith winked at Susie, telling her that she'll save the story of how she met Mr. Coppersmith for the next mug at a later time. Shooing Susie on her way, Mrs. Coppersmith gave her a hug, telling her she knows that Susie has better things to do than to listen to her yammering about yesteryear.

Smiling tenderly, she added, "But I thank you for listening."

Susie grinned at her, and returned her hug. "I love to hear the stories, Mrs. Coppersmith. Thank you for sharing them with me."

With a nod and a, "Scoot now", Mrs. Coppersmith just glowed.

———

Susie decided to spend the remainder of the morning in the Library, looking for books by her two favorite authors. One wrote a detective mystery series, whose protagonists were a teenage girl and her zany black cat, and always centered around the host of trouble that seemed to find them wherever they went. The other wrote historical mysteries, but the characters, places and subject matter were different with each book.

Searching through the Library inventory listing, she found that there were many books by her favorite authors. Unfortunately she had already read them, and some of them several times. However she did happen across one book that seemed interesting. She hadn't read any by this particular author, but its storyline synopsis appealed to her.

She decided to give it a try, so she found the book and began perusing other titles around it on the shelf. Several others had potential, Susie noted, after reading the first few pages of the first chapters of the books.

The chiming of the clock ended her excursion. She had ignored the other chimes, but this one she couldn't – it was now 11:45. Time to go.

Taking her book to the reception area, Susie left a note with her name clipped to the book so no one else would borrow it. She left it on the shelf behind the desk, vowing to come back for it right after lunch.

———

Lunch had come and gone; nothing out of the ordinary had transpired. Most of the conversations were centered on the holiday preparations and Miss Taryn's wedding (which all of the children were tired of hearing about and most of the adults too, more than likely). The food was wonderful, as always, and Susie had wondered if Mrs. Coppersmith had ever had a dud.

Somehow, she didn't think so. Mrs. Coppersmith's talents and gifts were definitely culinary, no doubt about it.

Jose had reminded Susie that they were playing chess at three in the Library. She laughed, telling him that she hadn't forgotten, and apologized again for missing yesterday's game. He grinned at her, a little shyly, telling her it was okay because sometimes he also fell asleep when reading or watching television.

Simon and Timmy, tired of the attention being everywhere but on them, began a series of dramatic reenactments of their helper status. Today it had been Kevin that they had been assigned to help; and the boys regaled them with all of the different things they helped Kevin do. Of course, they also had to share what things only Kevin could do, but they were allowed to watch Kevin perform those tasks.

Kevin had told the boys that when they were just a little bigger, then they could help him do those things, too. Susie, of course, congratulated them on doing such as great job. The other children joined in, offering their own "atta boys", thoroughly pleasing both Simon and Timmy. During their entire discourse, they were very excited, and their voices grew quite loud. Several times they caught the withering look from Miss Ginger, or Miss Hilda, or Miss Pritchett and even a couple from Mr. Sean. Though each time they quieted immediately, it didn't last for any length of time.

Megan had to try to top their exploits with news regarding her sewing feat with Miss Ginger. She began a long, detailed discourse on the sewing project Miss Ginger was teaching her. She also, quite proudly, informed everyone that Miss Ginger told her that she was Miss Ginger's best student. (Susie chuckled silently, realizing that Megan didn't realize that she was Miss Ginger's only student.) To Megan, Susie praised her for being such a good student and for working so hard. The others joined in, singing her praises, making her very happy.

Lunch ended; Megan had naptime to face, and the boys returned to the barn with Kevin, their naptime being postponed again until two-thirty.

Susie dashed to the Library, determined to get her book and get it upstairs long before her chess game with Jose. She hurried, hoping not to have her plans derailed.

Entering the Library, she was pleased that her book was still there, waiting for her. Quickly she signed her name on the check-out sheet, picked up her book; and with a jaunty spirit, she headed toward the doors.

Lilac; a very faint essence, scarcely there yet lingering in the air. Susie froze, her hand resting against the door. Chimes, the sound of wind chimes began to peal. Barely audible but there, nonetheless.

Slowly she turned around, her heart beginning to pound as the adrenaline began rising in her blood. Susie breathed in deeply and slowly exhaled, calming herself.

Cautiously she crept forward, pausing at the edge of the Reception area and the Library's main corridor. Susie waited, trying to determine which direction she should search. The scent was gone; so was the sound of the wind chimes. She hesitated – 'maybe I imagined it,' she thought. 'No,' she countered herself; 'it was real.'

Susie walked into the main corridor of the Library, standing still momentarily as she glanced down each direction. The corridor was empty. Chiding herself for being a hysterical ninny, she turned to leave.

A flash of white appeared in her peripheral vision. The lilac essence returned, stronger this time. She heard the soft knell of the wind chime, beckoning her to come find it. Whirling around, Susie caught a glimpse of the lady in white, darting into the east section.

'Not this time,' Susie thought firmly; 'you won't get away from me again.'

Running as fast she could, Susie quickly began closing the gap. With each step, the scent became stronger and stronger, as did the sounding of the chimes, taunting her to come find the source. She knew, whoever it was, had to pass this way, either using the main aisle or one of the perpendicular aisles. It didn't matter which one the mystery woman chose, Susie was going to catch her and put an end to the games.

Darting into the east section, Susie's sense of impending triumph came to a dismal halt, throwing her into a sense of shock, disbelief and bewilderment. It was empty. Except for her own presence, the entire east section was empty. Stunned, Susie surveyed the section; the reading areas, the study areas were empty. She quickly scanned all of the short stacks of the children's bookcases – they offered no protection, no ability to shield yourself from view.

Susie knew it wasn't possible; she had to be here. Susie had carefully watched each and every aisle as she ran past. The lady in white had to be here; there is no other way out of the Library.

Suddenly she knew – the lady in white was hiding in the secret alcove. There is no other explanation, Susie reasoned.

Quickly she ran to the north wall and opened the secret door to the alcove. Empty.

Shaking her head, Susie muttered, "It can't be. She has to be here. How did I miss her?"

Slowly the scent of lilac began perfuming the air. Within seconds, the light sound of the wind chime began. A chill crawled its way down Susie's spine; she shuddered. Swallowing hard a few times, Susie stepped back into the east section of the Library. No lilac scent; no wind chimes. She entered the secret alcove again, and both the scent and the sound returned.

Praying she wasn't making a mistake, Susie removed the key chain from her pocket, switching on the little pen light. Its illumination was not much better than that of a single match, but it was better than fumbling around in total darkness. She closed the alcove's secret door and began cautiously moving along the narrow passageway.

Shaking from the freezing cold, Susie's teeth began to chatter; but she pressed on, determined to find where this passageway led, and to find the lady in white. Carefully she moved along, seeing several levers and handles as she passed by them. Susie began to laugh, realizing that these must be secret entrances into Miss Hilda's office, their office sitting room, Miss Pritchett's office and now the Parlor.

Slowly she continued along the passageway until it ended at the stone wall of the foyer and a circular stairwell. Excited, Susie nearly shouted for joy; obviously, this would lead all the way up to the stairwell just outside her attic room. Her earlier premise that there must be secret passageways all over the manor is true. She was elated.

Susie shone her little pen light into the stairwell to begin her ascent. She stopped, frozen in disbelief. The stairwell also led down! It led to the basement. Susie was ecstatic. This meant that there had to be a secret entrance to the east wing from the basement.

Climbing rapidly, Susie reached the second floor in a matter of minutes. At the alcove's second floor landing, Susie noticed immediately a little leather strap attached to a knot in the wood. She gave it a gentle tug, opening a small peep hole. Laughing, she couldn't help but think how easy it would be to play practical jokes if you knew where all the secret doors are.

The second floor balcony walkway was empty, and Susie saw no reason to go all the way back to the Library. She easily located the lever, pulled and the secret door swung open, allowing her access to the second floor. Watching as it closed, Susie found the little button on the wall, just below the top of the wainscotting.

Strolling to her Dorm, Susie laughed. Glen Hollow is an amazing place; she definitely agreed with Miss Fiona's assessment. The more she discovers, the more there is to discover; and the more unanswered questions there are.

Susie entered the Dorm and was delighted to find it empty. Darting into her room, she leapt onto her bed, landing as if she had performed a seated drop on a trampoline. Quickly she stacked her pillows against her headboard and sank back into them. She decided that since she had a little more than two hours before she needed to meet Jose, she'd get started on this new book.

Opening the volume, Susie began reading.

———

Susie awoke with a start. "Oh, rats; not again," she moaned.

Her alarm clock showed the time to be three-fifty. She had missed her game date with Jose once again.

Jumping up, she ran all the way to the Library.

———

Story Time went rather well except for the hurt feelings that Jose was having, and the occasional frosty look he gave her. She had apologized profusely as she ran into their reading area. Although he had said it was okay, it was obvious to all that it wasn't. Susie had to agree. This wasn't like her, and she knew it couldn't continue. She had to find a way to get sleep and manage better her explorations.

Walking to dinner together, Jose barely said two words to her. She did her best to convince him how sorry she was, but it seemed as if he was not ever going to believe her, or forgive her.

Dinner proved to be awkward – Jose talked with everyone but Susie. The other children pretended not to notice, but they did. Susie realized they were giving Jose and her space to work it out, and move forward. She apologized again to Jose, promising him that, if he would give her one more chance, he'd see that she would be there. Simon vouched for Susie, animatedly telling Jose that Susie never breaks a promise. Finally Jose agreed; and it was decided that they'd meet in the Library at three tomorrow afternoon.

After that, Jose returned to his usual sunny disposition; they all began to share jokes and tall tales. Mentally, Susie breathed a sigh of relief. More than ever, she was determined not to disappoint Jose again.

Chapter 23

THE HIDDEN ROOM

For the longest time, Susie lay awake, tossing and turning in a wasted effort to fall sleep. Periodically she'd sit up, pound a few times on her pillow in a futile attempt to create a softer, more sleep-friendly pillow. She knew well that the real culprit for her inability to sleep was the nap she'd had after lunch. Unfortunately, she had missed her chess date with Jose for a second time because of it. However, she would not miss today's game; she was determined.

Her alarm clock incessantly kept ticking away the minutes as she struggled to ignore it. She peeked once again at the time – 12:45. "Rats, I'm never going to get to sleep."

Prior to going to bed, she'd set her alarm to awaken her at two, enabling her to have just over three hours to explore the passageway barrier. She knew, she just knew, there had to be a secret door.

'Probably leads to another storage room,' she thought dismally; 'but I want to know; I have to know. It just doesn't make sense to have that section blocked like that.'

After staring at the ceiling for a few more minutes, Susie made her decision. Thrusting her hand into the clothing bundle again, she removed her clock and re-set the alarm for six.

Swiftly, Susie changed into the clothes she had used as a muffler to drown out the noise of the alarm. This time she made certain she wore plenty of clothing in order to stay warm. She put on two thermal, long-sleeved cotton t-shirts, a dark pink turtleneck sweater, a neon pink sweatshirt, a pair of thermal pants, two pairs of dark pink knee socks, neon pink leg warmers and a pair of sweatpants that matched her sweatshirt. Grabbing an iridescent pink, elastic hair band, she quickly pulled her hair into a ponytail at the nape of her neck, stuffing her ponytail under her sweatshirt.

After tying her pink sneakers, she stealthily moved down the corridor, through the Common Area and reached the door without disturbing the other girls. Slowly she opened the door just enough to see whether or not the corridor was empty. All appeared quiet. Susie slipped out of the Dorm and headed toward the foyer landing. She paused at the landing, listening for any sound that would reveal if anyone else was also awake. There was none. Quickly she sprinted down the corridor, racing her way to the stairwell that would take her to the third floor.

With the manor so quiet this time of morning, Susie now decided that this is the best time to explore. And once she had figured out the mystery of the passageway barrier, she would start exploring the east wing, using the Library passageway she found earlier today. Her excitement at the prospect of exploring the forbidden zone caused her to giggle.

With her exuberance soaring, she darted into the third floor corridor without first checking to see if the coast was clear. A door opened; Susie froze in place then darted back into the alcove, her heart pounding as the adrenaline raced through her veins. Attempting to stave off the panic that was trying to engulf her, Susie forced her lungs to breathe slowly. With each deliberate breath, she felt the fear releasing from her body. Since whoever it was hadn't called out to her, Susie felt confident she hadn't been seen.

Cautiously Susie peeked into the corridor. It was Miss Taryn!

Slinking back into the darkness of the alcove, she watched as Miss Taryn strode rapidly past her and entered the main landing.

'What's she doing out this late?' Susie wondered; 'and where is she going?'

Without hesitation Susie followed her, an impulse from within urging her to hurry. With each step she took, Susie's curiosity rose. The attic intrigue would have to wait; discovering what Miss Taryn was up to was far more important. Susie paused at the entrance to the landing and cautiously peered into it. No sign of Miss Taryn. She crept quietly to the banister and looked down. Miss Taryn had just entered the main foyer and was heading to the west wing.

'Wow, she moves fast when she wants to; not at all like she does in the kitchen,' Susie observed.

Running toward the stairs, Susie tried to close the distance between them. The irony of her constantly admonishing Simon for running and leaping down the stairs was not lost on her. She smiled and laughed softly as an image vividly flashed into her mind of what his expression would be in catching her running, and subsequently chiding her for doing so.

Susie landed on the main foyer floor with a soft thud, having jumped from the seventh step. Rapidly she sped toward the west wing, arriving just in time to catch a fleeting glimpse of Miss Taryn entering the Dining Hall.

That really piqued Susie's curiosity. 'Why would she be going there this time of night?' Susie asked herself as she raced down the corridor. Susie slowed her pace as she neared the entrance.

'How odd,' Susie mused; 'she didn't turn on the lights.'

Stealthily Susie peeked into the Dining Hall, and into the gaping, black hole of its current state. Just as she wondered how Miss Taryn could possibly see, a small flicker of light emerged. Its size quickly increased – she had lit a candle.

"At least I know where she is," Susie muttered silently, watching the flame move slowly toward the west wall. Miss Taryn had obviously taken one of the candles from the sideboard because she certainly wasn't tall enough to reach the candles in the torchieres.

Susie crouched low, scurrying quietly along the floor. As she neared the fireplace, she whispered a prayer, thankful for the cover of darkness and hopeful that Miss Taryn wouldn't notice her. Sliding under the table by her usual chair, she eased her way to Miss Elsa's chair.

With a mixture of curiosity and fascination, Susie watched Miss Taryn slowly moving the candle all around the mantle. It was obvious that she was searching for something, but what Susie had no idea. During her search, Miss Taryn would periodically emit sounds of frustration and exasperation, emotions with which Susie herself was quite familiar, having recently experienced them a number of times. She smiled as she thought of what was awaiting her in the attic.

'Is she looking for a passageway?' The thought jolted Susie upright, causing her to nearly collide with the table.

Susie froze in place as Miss Taryn swiftly moved the candle, holding it toward the table. Susie held her breath, praying that Miss Taryn would not see her. It seemed as if an eternity had passed before Miss Taryn turned her attention back to the fireplace. Susie quietly breathed a sigh of relief.

After a long, intense search, Miss Taryn made her way back to the sideboard nearest to the doorway. Susie heard Miss Taryn mutter that she must have read it wrong, otherwise it would be there. Miss Taryn blew out the candle, returned it to the sideboard and left the Dining Hall. Susie waited a few minutes just to make certain she had really left.

As she crawled out from under the table, she couldn't help wonder what could possibly be so important that it would coax Miss Taryn to search so late at night. Obviously it had to be important, or she'd search during the day; and it would appear that she didn't intend for anyone else to know of it. It must be a treasure of some sort, Susie reasoned; and something she's read because Miss Taryn had said she must have misread its whereabouts.

Her mind flashed back to yesterday afternoon, when she had overhead Miss Taryn and Miss Claire in the Library. Perhaps she found a book in the Library that referenced a hidden treasure in the fireplace before Miss Claire caught up with her.

Susie's mind raced, excited at the idea of another mystery, but the excitement was short lived. It suddenly dawned on her that there are thousands of books in the Library, and she had no way of knowing which one Miss Taryn had read.

Smiling at the challenge, Susie confidently thought, 'I'll just have to keep a close watch on her. She'll lead me to it.' With a start, Susie realized that Miss Taryn could already *be* in the Library, and not in her room as she had initially supposed.

Susie dashed out of the Dining Hall into the corridor. Running as fast as she could, she headed to the Library, fearful that Miss Taryn could be anywhere in the Library and then gone before she could find her.

Her luck held; she entered the Library and crept cautiously to the edge of the reception area. Peeking to her left, she saw Miss Taryn moving quickly down the main corridor, heading to the west section. Quietly Susie moved down a side aisle and then entered an aisle running perpendicular to the main corridor. Stealthily she approached each cross section, making certain Miss Taryn was not in either aisle before continuing.

Finally she saw Miss Taryn turn to her left, into a side aisle. Softly Susie moved into the aisle next to where Miss Taryn had gone. Stealthily she crept, quickly closing the distance until she was within a few feet of Miss Taryn, her only cover the shelves loaded with books. Susie watched as Miss Taryn removed a book and began reading it. Smiling triumphantly, Susie memorized the place where the book belonged.

Several minutes later, Miss Taryn placed the book back on the shelf; she turned quickly and headed back to the main corridor. Susie had nowhere to go. There wasn't time to make it to the end of the aisle and around the end of the stack. She did the next best thing – she ran as far as she could toward the end of the stack and quickly dropped to the ground, flattening herself against the floor and praying that the shadows would help hide her as Miss Taryn passed by. It worked. Miss Taryn walked past about two seconds after she had hidden herself, obscured by the shadows.

Allowing Miss Taryn a few minutes head start, Susie rose and decided to choose the perpendicular aisle on this side of the main corridor. Following it as far as she could until it ended, she turned into the side aisle, quietly and rapidly making her way toward the main corridor. Now she was within visual range of the reception area, and watched as Miss Taryn exited the Library.

Just to make certain that Miss Taryn really was returning upstairs, Susie followed her as far as the foyer, watching as she ascended the foyer stairs all the way to the third level. Satisfied that Miss Taryn was done for the night, Susie made her way back to the Library and to the mystery book.

Its cover was a padded leather, bearing the title, "Hidden Niches and Nooks: A Guide to Hidden Treasure".

Summarily fanning the pages, Susie found the page Miss Taryn had earmarked. It was a picture of the fireplaces in the Dining Hall. The caption beneath the picture gave the name of the sculptor, stating that he had made this style for many prominent homes and was known for creating hidden niches and nooks to be used as secret hiding places. The book cited a few examples of where some of those hidden niches and nooks could be found. But it also revealed that the sculptor did not keep records of just where he had made the hiding places; it differed depending on the owner and placement of the fireplace within the home.

Susie laughed softly. "So that's it; she is looking for hidden treasure."

Susie returned the book a little remorsefully. "It'll have to wait," she sighed; "I have a more important mystery to solve."

Scurrying quickly to the Library door, Susie took the time to check first before entering the corridor. It was empty, so she ran to the circular stairway. From there she cautiously made her way to the third floor and then to the attic door. After closing the door and locking it, she leaned against it, relieved that she had not been caught.

'Although...,' she thought amusedly; 'even if Miss Taryn had caught me, she would be hard pressed to explain to Miss Pritchett just what she was doing, too.' Susie giggled as the image popped into her mind of Miss Taryn trying desperately to explain to Miss Pritchett just what she was doing in the Dining Hall.

Switching on her flashlight, she scrambled up the steps, entering her attic room. Her gait was lighter now, here in her sanctuary, as was her mood. She smiled at all of Nana's things as she passed by them, making her way to the secret door.

Quickly she opened it, securing it with the poker from the fireplace. Stepping into the blackness, Susie shivered a little from the cold. Her flashlight did little to dispel the darkness, but it did illuminate the path directly in front of her; and that was enough. Her nose wrinkled at the smell of the stale air, and she coughed slightly as her lungs offered a protest. Ignoring all of this, she pressed onward toward the oddity that cried out for resolution. Somehow she knew that there was a hidden door in that wall. And wherever it was, she would find it.

Without delay, she hurried along the passageways. Mentally she reviewed every inch of the wall and of her previous search for a hidden door as she trotted along the passageway. Arriving at her challenge, Susie dropped her gait to a walk, slowly approaching it. She was ready to try again. Susie closed her eyes, clearing her mind of all the distractions, centering her thoughts on the wall in front of her.

Instantly the realization struck – the wall was solid. There were no seams such as you would find in paneling or flooring, or in a stone or a brick wall. It was one, large block of wood. She smiled. She knew. The wall *is* the door. It must slide, and now all she had to do is find the lever that opens it.

Slowly and meticulously Susie shone the light up and down, covering every inch of the wall. First she checked the stone wall where it connected with the wood. Nothing. Repeating the same process, she scoured the opposite attic wall where it joined to the wood. After nearly an hour of intense scrutiny, she found it - a tiny, little button that was the same color as the wood around it. Susie pressed the button and held her breath. The wall began to groan and shudder; and then it slowly moved. Amazed at the sight of this massive wall disappearing, her skin began to tingle, causing her to shiver. A sigh of satisfaction escaped from her.

"Awesome," she whispered. The wall had now completely vanished.

Susie pointed her flashlight into the black hole in front of her. It was a room, but not a storage room.

"A parlor or sitting room maybe," Susie pondered; "but why up here?"

Small particles of dust were floating in the air, swirling around as they slowly cascaded downward. Everything was covered in a thick layer of dust. Cobwebs hung in the corners of the ceiling. She panned the light across the floor; solid dust. No one had walked in here for a very long time.

The room was only about a quarter of the size of her attic room, but it still was a comfortably sized room. A swift search with her flashlight revealed that the room contained an elegant writing desk with a lattice backed chair, a tall oak secretary and a furnished sitting area in front of a small fireplace. Two silver candelabras and a dozen or so framed photographs adorned the fireplace mantle. The sitting area comprised of a small sofa, two wing chairs and an oval accent table. Draped across one of the chairs was a lacy afghan, covered in dust

"Spiders, too, I bet;" she muttered, shuddering a little at the thought.

Along the north wall was a small bookcase, like the ones for the children's books in the Library, and with it what appeared to be a toy chest. Its lid was raised slightly, and several dolls could be seen peeking above the edge of the chest. A large, braided area rug was placed in front of the bookcase and toy chest, obviously meant for a child's play area.

Turning to her right, Susie panned the east wall again until she came to the oak secretary. Keeping the beam of light focused on the oak secretary, she crossed the room in a fast stride. The oak furnishing was tall and narrow, and its main cabinet had two doors. Pulling the handles ever so gently, the doors moved seamlessly as she eased them open. Inside were three rows of pigeonhole bins sitting atop, and slightly inset of, three rows of narrow drawers. The open bins held a variety of office supplies. The drawers beneath held mailing supplies and stationery of various sorts (paper, cards, postcards, envelopes).

The ledge in front of the bins and atop of the drawers displayed an ornate silver letter tray. A letter and an opened envelope, addressed to 'Mrs. Murielle Evermore', were lying in the tray. The envelope's postmark was dated December 03, 1956. Susie picked up the letter. It was from Foxboro Station Mayor, Wilbur Hartsen. He was confirming their scheduled meeting for December 10th regarding the upcoming Winter Festival.

Remembering what Mrs. Crenshaw had told her two weeks ago, a chill went through her, and Susie dropped the letter back into the tray.

'The Festival was cancelled because Miss Murielle died,' she remembered.

She closed the cabinet's doors. The bottom section of the cabinet had one large drawer. Susie pulled it open; it contained a blanket, a quilt and several afghan throws.

Susie moved to the desk. Other than completely covered in dust, it was well organized. The silver inkwell and pen set appeared to be very heavy. She lifted the inkwell lid, shining the light in the inkwell. The black ink had long since dried and had become solid. Its cracks were erratic, reminiscent of mud as it dries in the sun. The matching silver letter sorter was empty except for a spider that now called it home. In the center of the leather-bound desk blotter was a single sheet of scalloped linen stationery. It was held down by a silver letter opener that looked more like a small dagger than an office tool. Susie lifted the letter at its corner, shaking the dust from it. She shone the light on it and read:

December 18, 1956
To my darling daughter;

I regret that I will not be with you on your birthday in three days. It grieves me to know that it will be a day of sadness for you, but in time that will not be so. As time passes, it will heal your heart as you come to understand that our spirits live on, and that one day we will be reunited.

Know that I love you with a love that neither time nor death can diminish. I will love you always. I will miss our special times here in this place. I hope you will come here often in remembrance of me.

When the proper time has arrived, you will take your rightful place here and in the Inner Sanctum. May your memories in this place always give you great joy; of me, of Grandmother Noreen, of us and, in the distant future, of your daughter.

Over the past two days I have written a packet of letters for you and have placed them in our secret hiding place. These letters will serve as an introduction regarding your destiny. Follow them exactly and in the proper sequence. Then you will be ready to contact Ashara. She will teach you all that you need to know in order for you to take your rightful place as the Keeper.

Normally, instruction begins at age ten with the barest of knowledge. Unfortunately, circumstances have dictated an accelerated time table for you. You are so young to have to experience these things now; but I know the strength of your spirit. Your abilities will even surpass that of mine.

Until the day we are reunited, take care of your Daddy; he loves you so very much.

> *All my Love,*
> *Mommy*

Susie's eyes welled with tears. Miss Pritchett had never seen this letter from her mother. 'Why?' she wondered. 'She'd been here with her mother; did she forget how to open the door?'

Carefully Susie folded the letter and slipped it into her pocket. "What is the 'Inner Sanctum?" she whispered. "What is a Keeper?" ... "And who is Ashara?"

Susie exhaled softly as she wiped the tears from her eyes, continuing to scan the room with her flashlight. The walls held brass light sconces and several framed paintings. None of the details were discernable due to the heavy layers of dust and cobwebs. The painting hanging on the rock wall was the largest and looked to be at least seven feet tall and four feet wide.

One final pass with the flashlight along the east wall caused Susie to notice that the dust was moving inexplicably faster in the northeast corner of the room. Unable to resist this peculiarity, she walked over to it, keeping the light fixed on the area. As she approached, she realized it was a spiral staircase.

"That's weird," she mused, having expected to see cobwebs filling the stairwell; but there were none. It was as if someone had cleaned only the stairwell.

Decision made, she carefully descended the stairwell, following the light as she went. The stairwell ended on the second floor and brought her into a small alcove behind an enormous room, which apparently was a closet and dressing room. Peering into the room, Susie noticed that all of the mirrors, chairs and tables were covered in large cloths, completely obscuring them from sight. The light from her flashlight suddenly reflected, and Susie was amazed to see that all the built-in closets and chests had glass doors.

Susie stepped into the room; upon doing so, the lights automatically sprang to life in each of the closets and chests, clearly displaying all of their contents. Marveling at the vast array of clothing and accessories, from the most casual to the most elegant formal attire, Susie slowly inspected each one.

Two smaller rooms to her left also automatically lighted upon her entrance. Though they were smaller than the main room, they were by no means tiny. Nana's living room would have easily fit into either of the alcove rooms. One room was lined with glass cabinets filled with footwear of all types and for every occasion. The other room held glass cabinets and drawers filled with the exquisite jewelry, from the rarest gems to the most casual of costume jewelry. Realizing that these were all Miss Murielle's things, Susie now knew that Miss Pritchett's father had not removed everything as Miss Pritchett had been told. It didn't make sense to Susie, and she felt a little sad for Miss Pritchett that all this had been kept from her.

"Why would he do that?" Susie puzzled, moving to the door that led out of the dressing area.

Susie peaked into the next room and saw it was an antechamber. The furnishings were covered just as in the dressing room. Two doors led out of the room; one straight ahead and the other to her right. Susie chose the door on her right and discovered it led to another dressing room and closets that were filled with men's clothing and accessories.

Returning to the antechamber, she crossed the room, opened the other door and stepped inside. Her flashlight did little to dispel the darkness other than the narrow swatch of light directly in front of her. Although she wished it provided more than what it did, she was thankful and relieved to have some light. The gloomy blackness and the stale, icy air enabled her fertile imagination to run wild. Apprehensively she began her examination of the room, slowly panning the light from side to side.

This was obviously a bedroom, quite large and lavishly decorated with its crystal chandeliers and Tiffany lamps. The tall windows were covered in drapery, its color lost under the decades of dust that had accumulated. They had been left drawn, blocking out all light as if the room wanted to remain in the shadows. The elegant marble fireplace was a rose color with veins of a creamy color scattered through it. A beautiful, silk wall covering displayed roses in a lattice-work pattern. The colors created warmth, a sense of comfort in a room now freezing cold.

Framed photographs, in a multitude of sizes and shapes, adorned the fireplace mantle. Two chairs were placed near the fireplace, making a great conservation area, or a place to read and warm oneself on a cold winter night. Both were covered to prevent dust from collecting on them. For a fleeting moment Susie considered lifting one of the cloths to see what they looked like; but decided against it. Her curiosity wasn't stronger than her fear of the prospect that a nest of spiders might now call the chairs home. She turned her attention to the massive four-poster bed. Decades of dust covered the wood for the dust cloth only protected the bed portion.

Feeling a bit uneasy, Susie decided it was time to keep moving, and quickly sprinted across the bedroom. She opened the double doors to find that it led to an ornate sitting room.

As in the bedroom, these drapes were also covered in layers of dust, but were only partially closed. Between the thick walls of the brocade fabric, the faintest sliver of moonlight cascaded into the room. It cast an eerie aura upon the room, but none more so than its ghostly illumination of the portrait prominently displayed above the fireplace. It was a portrait of a young woman cradling an infant in her arms. The artist's rendition was exceptional.

Susie's gaze dropped to the corner of the painting. In a precise hand was written: Elizabeth Noreen Evermore, March 21, 1949. Susie suddenly released her breath, unaware that she had been holding it. It shouldn't have surprised her, Susie realized; she had seen the horse portraits and knew Miss Murielle's mother was gifted. Why wouldn't she paint her daughter and granddaughter?

The longer she lingered over the portrait, the more she found herself wishing that she had this type of gift. True, she had talent, but nothing compared to this.

'Practice and time is what it takes,' a voice in her head advised. Susie chuckled at the thought, gazing up at the woman.

Miss Murielle was stunningly beautiful, and the joy on her face as she looked upon her infant was unmistakable. Susie inched closer to the painting and noticed the markings. Miss Murielle had a faint, little birthmark in the form of a starburst on her right cheek. So did the infant. Susie realized immediately that the birthmark was in the same place as Miss Pritchett's jagged scar.

"What happened?" Susie whispered as she continued to absorb the amazing details of the portrait.

At any moment Susie expected to hear Miss Murielle's voice and the baby's cooing sounds. Miss Murielle's eyes exuded a kindness; her demeanor was of grace and gentleness. Susie sighed longingly, wishing she was still with Nana and her own parents.

Turning away from the portrait, Susie shined her flashlight around the room. There were framed pictures everywhere, but the bulk of the collection was on the grand piano. A delicate lace runner was draped across the piano, protecting it from the metals and woods of the eclectic assortment of frames. Miss Pritchett was in most of the pictures, but not all. In some of the pictures she was alone; but most of the pictures were of her and her mother, some included another couple that Susie guessed must be the grandparents. Several photographs were of adults that Susie could only surmise were grandparents and other relatives. A few were of Miss Murielle during various stages of her childhood and early adulthood.

Susie wondered if Miss Pritchett remembered these rooms. Suddenly she knew why Miss Pritchett hadn't been in the Hidden Room and found the letter. As a young child, she would have only entered with her mother, and that would have been through the closet stairwell. Miss Pritchett didn't know about the passageways or the secret doors. And because her father told her he got rid of everything and had locked the east wing, Miss

Pritchett never came back here. Because of that, Miss Pritchett never got to see the letter from her mother, nor find the hidden ones mentioned in her letter. Susie's eyes stung with new tears as compassion and sadness for Miss Pritchett began to fill her heart.

She turned and ran back to the stairwell and climbed up to the Hidden Room, quickly crossing to the secret door. Susie decided that she would restore this room; it would be difficult, but worth it. There were secrets here in Glen Hollow that she was determined to know and understand. And, perhaps in the process, help Miss Pritchett. As that thought blossomed in her mind, Susie was unaware that she was actually nodding her head in approval of the idea.

Pausing at the entrance of the Hidden Room, Susie took one last look before closing the door. Moving the flashlight slowly around the room, its beam of light flickered across the front of the desk. Susie hadn't noticed it before, but now she did.

A small drawer, the only drawer, in the desk was there in the center front portion of what appeared to be just part of the oak trim. A tiny, silver handle resembling a teardrop was in the center of the drawer, reflecting the light.

Feeling a sense of urgency to open the drawer, she ran to the desk. Pulling the chair back out of her way, she reached and slowly opened the drawer. A small tray held two items, an ink blotter and a small, burgundy leather book. Susie picked it up and opened it. Inside the cover, on the title page, was written:

Murielle Dara Evermore
Journal, December 1956

Susie's heart pounded. Her mind raced. This journal had definitely belonged to Miss Pritchett's mother. Like the letter to her daughter, these were her last words, words that no one had ever read.

A prickly, tingling sensation ran throughout her body again much akin to having a lightning bolt race through her veins. She swallowed hard several times. She closed her eyes and inhaled slowly, deeply. Then, just as slowly and deliberately, she exhaled.

Susie opened her eyes, turned the page and began reading.

Saturday, December 1st:

His moods have darkened considerably, and now he has taken to drink and gambling. He stays gone for days at a time. His behavior is erratic at best and at worst there are times I fear he may do me harm. His love for our child, Eloise, seems to be the only thread that holds him to a semblance of sanity that prevents him from total destruction.

I don't understand what is happening, but I fear the worst. I don't know why or how, but my spirit tells me that Gorza is responsible. I hope I am wrong, that it is only a medical issue. I have prayed and asked God for guidance. I don't know how to approach Dorian with it without him becoming enraged. God will provide the perfect timing. I will trust in Him.

Sunday, December 2nd:

I had hoped that Dorian would come home for the picnic. He didn't. Eloise misses him terribly, and it becomes increasingly more difficult with each passing day to explain his absences.

I pray he will be here for her birthday. She's only turning eight; but some days, she seems so much more mature than that. However, she is still very much a child, and she adores her Daddy. It will crush her if he isn't here.

I pray that whatever is distressing him, he will share it with me so we can resolve it together. As we have for so many years, I pray we will once again be able to trust and depend on each other.

Wednesday, December 5th:

He came home today, disheveled and angry. The coldness in his eyes frightened me, but the hate and the loathing in his voice terrified me. He accused me of being a witch.

I was stunned and asked how he could possibly say such a thing, let alone believe it. The contempt in his eyes, and the hostility he exuded was frightening. He told me that while he was in Willington a woman approached him. She appeared to know me and Eloise, asking as to our well-being. Then she asked him if he liked living with a witch, and if he feared for his safety and that of Eloise's. I asked him who she was.

He could not remember her name. I asked him to describe her; he could not remember. The harder he tried to remember, the more agitated he became.

All he could remember were her words and her voice; 'it was smooth as silk', he said.

The horror I felt as I realized what has happened, is happening, to him. Someone has cast a spell on him. But who? It must be Gorza. But how? She has not come through a portal. I have since verified this with the others.

I told Dorian that the idea was ludicrous, and I would not entertain such a notion. He seemed surprised by my composure and somewhat confused. Then he left. How could I explain to him the difference between a witch and the Keepers?

If I had tried he would never believe me, not in his current state. He will accuse me of being a witch, of casting the spell. For now, he is content to brood on his thoughts, locking himself in a guest suite. Some thread of the truth of my words still retains a hold on his mind. I could see it in his eyes before he left. But how long will that last?

I must contact Ashara and tell her what has happened. If I have Ashara's help, perhaps there is still time to undo what has been done. We will prevent whatever wicked plan Gorza is hatching, and Dorian will be made whole.

Monday, December 10ᵗʰ:

I am heartsick; I do not know what to do. I am so furious with Dorian, so angry. Yet I know it isn't he that has done these things. A dark, evil power has descended upon him.

I had an early morning meeting with Mayor Hartsen in Foxboro Station regarding our annual Winter Festival this year. Everything is ready for the three day festival beginning on Dec 21ˢᵗ. It will be lovely. I am so looking forward to it. The planning of it seems to keep me focused and from succumbing to despair.

Arriving home shortly before eleven I had come home much earlier than expected. When I entered the foyer, I was stunned to see carpet had been laid over the floor, and a large table sitting in its center.

Never, ever has the crest been hidden. I went in search for Dorian. I didn't find him. Instead, I found a group of artists. They were painting out the family birthmark on everyone in every portrait. They were just finishing the last six portraits as I entered the east Parlor. I was furious! I demanded to know where he was. They didn't know.

I went in search for Mr. Madsen, the new butler Dorian brought back from Willington nearly six weeks ago now. He reluctantly informed me that Master

Dorian was out on business and would return in time for dinner on Thursday. I left instructions that I was to be notified immediately upon his return.

My emotions, my thoughts, were in a whirl. I couldn't believe he had done such horrible things. But I knew why. The spell that had been cast on him was strong; it must be Gorza. She must have told him about my family's starburst birthmark. But she did not tell him of its true meaning for he obviously believes it to be a sign of a witch. That must be the reason he had the portraits changed. And I'm certain she also convinced him to cover the protective seal of the Evermores.

I went upstairs to our suite to lie down; my head was throbbing so. As I neared my door, Nurse Abrams, from Foxboro Station, exited Eloise's room. Alarmed, I asked what was wrong. She was extremely nervous. Her eyes met mine, and they were filled with sadness. "I'm so sorry", she said regretfully.

In panic, I rushed into my child's room, to my precious Eloise. She was sleeping. There was a white gauze bandage covering her right cheek. I asked Nurse Abrams what happened. She looked at my child and then at me. Bracing herself, she told me that earlier this morning Dorian instructed Dr. Williams to remove her birthmark. She told me Eloise was fine and was just sleeping off the anesthetic.

I couldn't breathe. I steadied myself, leaning hard against the nightstand. I couldn't believe what I just heard. I reached to remove the bandage, and Nurse Abrams attempted to stop me by grasping my arm. I turned and looked at her with the fury that should have been reserved for Dorian. She released me, and I removed the bandage. It was gone; the starburst was gone, and in its place was a horrible, gaping wound. I cried. Nurse Abrams insisted that I allow Eloise to rest, and she would call me as soon as my child was awake.

Back in our suite, I paced the floor, fluctuating between storms of anger and tears of anguish. I knew in my heart that my dear, sweet Dorian was now lost to me. For him to have been able to do these things, Gorza has complete control of him.

How did she do it? How could she have cast a spell that could penetrate the closed portal? Suddenly I knew how. She didn't penetrate the portal; she knew she couldn't. She has somehow gained the Knowledge of the Keepers, which is not possible but it seems that she has. Worse, she has been able to use that Knowledge to circumvent the portals. This, too, is impossible, yet she has apparently managed to do so. But how?

I felt a crushing weight in my spirit. I quickly opened the passageway and went upstairs to the Inner Sanctum. I had to contact Ashara. She must be told of what Gorza has done and the Knowledge she had obtained.

11:30 pm Thursday, December 13th:

Dorian did not come home. After dinner, I questioned Mr. Madsen as to his whereabouts. Coldly he informed me that Master Dorian did not answer to him, and that it was obvious he has been detained. With a hostile glare, he stated that Master Dorian would be home for dinner tomorrow. He gave me a perfunctory nod and left. My anger toward Mr. Madsen grows by the minute as does my mistrust of him. But if I send him packing, I fear Dorian will resent my interference and not come home at all. Should that happen, Eloise would be devastated.

I have tried contacting Ashara several times today, but still no answer. What do I do?

Friday, December 14th:

Something is gravely wrong. I have made so many attempts to contact Ashara over the past few days, and none have been successful. So much is at stake, so much will be lost if Gorza isn't stopped. I fear I have no choice but to open the portal and go to Nori. Gorza is no match for Nori's power; she both fears and hates Nori with a jealous passion. Nori will know how to break the spell. I have four hours before Dorian will return, if his message as relayed through Mr. Madsen is to be believed. Time is short.

1:30 pm December 14th:

I returned with what I need from Nori and went straight to my child's bedside. She was just beginning to stir, not yet fully conscious. I kissed her forehead and told her that I love her and to just sleep a little longer. She told me she loved me and looked up at me. Tears filled her eyes as she cried that her head hurt. I gave her a half teaspoon of the pain medicine Dr. Williams had brought. I held her hand as she drifted off to sleep, telling her how much I love her. I still am not certain how to tell her what has happened. I'm not certain I can, or should. She is too young to know; perhaps the best thing to tell her is that a growth had to be removed. That explanation will keep her love for her Daddy intact.

5:10pm December 14th:

Ashara came to me a short while ago. I told her all that has happened, and that I suspect Gorza. Also, I told her of my greatest fear – that Gorza has obtained the Knowledge of the Keepers. At first I did not think it was possible. No Keeper would ever surrender the Knowledge; they would take it to their grave. There is no spell that can be woven against a Keeper; therefore, Gorza would not be able to obtain the Knowledge directly from a Keeper. Yet somehow she has. Ashara assured me it was not so.

Inexplicable, strange things have begun to happen on other worlds, and in a multitude of realms. A very powerful, ancient evil has resurfaced, enemy to all who walk in the Light. His bonds have been broken, and Marnok has escaped his prison. Gorza, and others like her, have chosen to follow him. Their reward has been to receive power from him, temporary though it may be. However, those such as Gorza never think further than the present moment.

Ashara has assured me that she and the others will handle the matter of Gorza. I know that Gorza cannot hide from them. For all her strength as a powerful witch, she still is no match for Ashara, or any of the others, regardless of what power she may have received from Marnok.

I told Ashara that I went to see Nori, the healer, and why. Ashara was saddened that I had not waited, but she understood. I told her that Nori provided me with a potion to put in Dorian's drink to free him from Gorza's grip, and an amulet for him to wear to protect him from any further attacks. I confessed that my panic and fear for Dorian and for Eloise temporarily blinded me, paralyzing my faith. I also admitted that I acted rashly and should have waited. I told her that I have also confessed to our Lord and sought forgiveness. She smiled and nodded. She already knew.

Her words were kind, and yet there was an undercurrent that puzzles me. She told me "Do not fear; all will be as it should be." I do not understand what she meant. Before I could ask, she left.

I cannot dwell on these things any further. Now I must compose myself and ready myself for the task at hand. It will not be easy. Dorian is highly suspicious. Worse, Mr. Madsen is always hovering, watching. I must be certain that neither see what I must do. I must succeed.

11:45pm December 14th:

I am so delighted, so happy. The potion has worked. Dorian is free from Gorza.

I slipped it into his wine before he entered the Dining Hall. Halfway through dinner he became quite ill and excused himself. Mr. Madsen assisted me in taking Dorian to our suite. I instructed Mr. Madsen to call Dr. Williams, and then to wait for the Doctor in the foyer. Although he objected, he knew I would discharge him immediately if he challenged me. I made that very clear.

I placed the amulet around Dorian's neck and under his shirt, next to his skin. Mrs. Hawkins, our Head Housemistress, brought medical supplies to me. I poured the rubbing alcohol into the pan and placed the cloths in it, saturating them. I then began the process of placing and exchanging the compresses on his forehead to bring down his fever. It worked. Shortly before the Dr. Williams arrived, Dorian's fever broke. His eyes were normal again. He sat up in bed and said that he'd had the strangest dream.

Before I could speak, the door opened, and Dr. Williams entered. After examining Dorian, Dr. Williams pronounced him fit. He said it must have been a virus that ran its course. He recommended bed rest and left, promising to return in the morning to check on him.

After Dr. Williams left, I told Dorian the truth – it hadn't been a dream. I had no choice but to tell him. He would soon see the deeds he had done. He was so grieved I feared his heart would break. He had no memory of anything that has transpired the past six weeks. I told him he wasn't to blame, and I told him why. At first he thought I was joking; then he thought me insane.

I could not tell him everything; he needed first to verify with his own eyes what he has wrought because of Gorza's evil spell. Then he would be able to understand and accept what I have to say. I asked him to come with me downstairs. When we reached the landing, he saw the covered crest. He looked at me, his eyes fearful of what else lie ahead.

We entered the east Parlor first, and he saw with his own eyes the changes he procured. Every portrait had been altered, and he saw the same repeated in every portrait in the rest of the manor. He was shocked. He kept shaking his head and agonizing that he could not have done this. I held him and told him we would get through it. Then I told him he needed to see Eloise. She would be asleep by now, and it would be better for him to see her now rather than wait for the morning. Eloise did not need to see his first reaction.

We went to her room and quietly slipped inside. Gently I removed the gauze bandage and held her Faerie night lamp near her wound so that he could see.

495

Horrified, he covered his face with his hands and sank to the floor. I replaced the bandage and returned her lamp to its table. I assisted him up to his feet, and we returned to our suite. We held each other as he cried, begging me to forgive him. I repeatedly assured him he is forgiven, and that he could not help what had happened to him. I assured him our child need never know what truly happened, that we would tell her it was a medical necessity. He shook his head, not wanting to lie to her. I could no longer hold back my tears.

As I wept, I told him it was for the best. How could Eloise at her young age understand what happened, I asked him. I explained that all she would know is her Daddy harmed her. I begged him not to do that to her, but instead to allow her to keep her love for him.

His tears flowed like rivers, saying he didn't deserve her love for what he did. I repeatedly reminded him he does love her, and it was his love for her that kept Eloise alive. Gorza wanted him to kill both myself and Eloise, and he didn't.

After some time his sobbing was exhausted, and he fell silent. I told him that I had much more to explain. And I did. I told him everything. I told him who we, the Evermores, are and what we do. He drew my hands to his lips and gently kissed them. Then he kissed my forehead, my nose and then my lips. His eyes were misting with tears (as were my own), and he told me that he was right to have called me "his special angel" all these years. I laughed and told him that I am not an angel; I am a Keeper, a type of Guardian.

I asked Dorian how it was that he hired Mr. Madsen. He had no idea what I meant. I explained that he brought Mr. Madsen with him from Willington six weeks ago as his new butler, and promptly fired Mr. Jennings. He did not remember any of it, at first. Slowly a vague memory surfaced – he recalled that strange woman telling him that Mr. Jennings had to go and to take Mr. Madsen. Dorian became angry. He rang for Mr. Madsen. When he entered, Dorian immediately demanded to know how he knew Gorza. At first Mr. Madsen denied knowing any such person. But once he realized that he was exposed, he laughed – a cold, wicked sound. He told us we were fools, and that we had no idea with whom we were dealing. Before Dorian could act, Mr. Madsen ran out of our suite and from our property.

Well, enough for now. I am tired and weak. I have left Dorian sleeping in our suite, and I shall retire to it as well.

11:30pm Saturday, December 15ᵗʰ:

Today was a glorious day, both in weather and in spirit. We had a marvelous day of fun and relaxation. I sent a message to Ashara that all is well.

We will begin the process next week to restore the family portraits and to remove the carpet and table from the crest as well. Unfortunately, nothing can be done to restore Eloise's birthmark, but Ashara has assured me that it will in no way prohibit her from her destiny. I look forward to that time.

In two years and six days, she will be ten years old, and will then begin the induction into her destiny as a Keeper. Greater still will be the day she turns twelve. That will be the day she will see the Inner Sanctum and meet Ashara. I can barely contain my enthusiasm. I have seen indications in Eloise already; her spirit is strong, even stronger than my own. She will be a formidable Keeper, more so that our family has seen in many generations.

Dorian is not as enthusiastic. He worries that someone like Gorza may try again to destroy us, and he fears for Eloise. I've tried to alleviate his concerns, but it isn't possible so soon after what has happened. Although he knows Ashara has restrained Gorza, he cannot rest or trust that all will work out for the best. Not yet; but in time he will come to understand the Truth, and then he will no longer be afraid.

I tire again. I do not know why I am so weak. Perhaps I shall make tomorrow a day of rest.

11:45pm Sunday, December 16ᵗʰ:

I am extremely weakened. I can barely stand. I have a thorn scratch on my ankle. At first I thought it was an ordinary thorn from one of my roses or holly bushes. I treated it, but it has rapidly worsened.

I realized today that it was no ordinary thorn. I remembered scratching my ankle as I came back through the portal on December 14ᵗʰ. I thought it strange that I hadn't noticed the bramble bush when I entered that side of the portal, but I dismissed it due to the extreme stress I had been enduring.

Niku, a healer here, was unable to help me. I have left messages for Ashara and for Nori. I do not know if they will receive them in time to come to my aid. If not, I have told them in the message that I will not allow the portal to remain active. I will permanently close the portal until such time as a new Keeper can be assigned or, God willing, my Eloise shall take that place as is her rightful inheritance, and her destiny.

2:00pm Tuesday, December 18ᵗʰ:

The time grows near; I will soon cross over. I spoke to Ashara. The Guardians will see after Eloise and protect her. The portal will remain closed.

I do so regret that I will not be able to pass on to my daughter the Knowledge in person. I am confident that she will follow the written instructions I have left for her, and will come to know who she is, and all that she is.

I must go now. Eloise will be out of class soon, and I need to spend time with her. I do not think I will last the night.

Murielle Dara Evermore

Tears rolled silently down Susie's face, plopping onto the dust-covered floor, creating tiny puddles of mud. She closed Murielle's journal and hugged it to her heart. Several minutes passed while she struggled to regain control of her emotions. She wiped her eyes on her sleeve and then tucked the journal into the back of her waistband, pulling her clothing down over it.

As she turned to leave, a cold gust of wind swirled around her. Shivering, she glanced back at the room. She had the sensation she was being watched, that she wasn't alone. Quickly she shone the light around the room; nothing and no one was there.

Shaking her head, she mumbled, "I'm getting as jumpy as a long-tailed cat in a room full of rocking chairs." She laughed, remembering that was another one of Nana's favorite sayings.

Susie left the room and pressed the button. This time the wall moved fluidly and closed effortlessly. She turned and ran all the way back to the attic room. As soon as she had crossed the threshold, she unanchored the passageway door, closed it and returned the poker to its place in the tool stand by the fireplace. Carefully removing the letter and the journal so as not to damage them, she placed them gently in her treasure box, Nana's old trinket box. Nana had given it to her when she was eight. Susie sighed longingly at the memory.

Her hand lingered on the box containing her treasures, which now included Miss Murielle's journal and her letter to her daughter, Eloise. Part of Susie longed to give them to Miss Pritchett now, before she had the answers she sought. Part of her knew she needed to wait. Finally she decided to hide them and, when the time was right, she'd give them to Miss Pritchett. For now, there were many more questions for which she needed answers, and needed the time in which to find those answers. Gently she returned her treasure box to its hiding place.

With a heavy sigh, Susie turned and walked to the staircase, quietly returning to the Dorm Room. Nearly exhausted, Susie wasted no time getting into her pj's and diving into bed. Her head sunk into her pillow as a massive yawn released from deep within her. The last thing she saw before falling asleep was her clock – it was 4 a.m.

Chapter 24

STORY TIME CLUB

Wearily Susie awakened and began her normal routine, moving and responding as if she were a programmed robot. The girls were the first to notice, repeatedly asking if she was okay. At breakfast, Miss Hilda queried her as did most of the adults. Mrs. Coppersmith was certain she was 'coming down with something' because Susie had accompanied her to visit Mr. Coppersmith and had probably caught cold.

Susie assured them, time and again, that she was fine – just a little distracted. Miss Claire was insistent that what Susie needed was a good tonic, and that she had just such a tonic. Quick to thank Miss Claire for her kind offer, Miss Bettye reminded Miss Claire that medical conclusions were her own domain. She adamantly stated that unless Susie showed symptoms of illness, no tonics or medications were necessary. Even though Miss Claire attempted to pretend otherwise, Susie could see that she was offended at having been so summarily dismissed. Susie smiled at Miss Claire, and mouthed a silent 'thank you', causing Miss Claire's expression to brighten. Smiling and nodding her head slightly, Miss Claire's usual sunny disposition returned.

As Susie leaned back into her chair, she noticed Miss Fiona watching her. A quirky, little smile formed on her lips as Miss Fiona winked at Susie, causing Susie to giggle a little. That drew Simon's attention, beginning a round of his questions, and her attempting to stave off his curiosity.

And so the morning progressed throughout breakfast, and her subsequent kitchen duty. Susie remained preoccupied with her latest discovery, fluctuating between sadness and curiosity. It made it difficult for her to complete her tasks, but somehow she managed and was done for the day.

Her mind was plagued with the haunting words of Miss Murielle's letter and journal. She wondered where the other letters that Miss Murielle had mentioned were hidden. She kept wondering who, and where, were the people she'd mentioned – Ashara, Niku and Nori. Most importantly, why hadn't they come to Miss Pritchett to give her the letters and tell her whatever

500

it was that Miss Murielle wanted Miss Pritchett to know? Why had this Gorza attacked Miss Pritchett's father? How could she make him harm Miss Murielle and Miss Pritchett? And why didn't he fight her? What exactly is a Keeper, and what do they keep? And why had Miss Pritchett's father lied about moving all of her mother's things, and why did he close the east wing? Every thought produced another round of questions that perplexed Susie, sending her thoughts into circle after unending circle.

"Susie! Did you hear me?" came the exasperated plea. Megan was tugging hard on Susie's shirt, desperately trying to get Susie's attention. Until now, Megan had received automated responses from Susie, and most were sounds that resembled 'uh-huhs'.

"I'm sorry, Megan," Susie responded, smiling fondly at the perturbed expression on Megan's face. "What do you want?"

"Simon and Timmy won't play with me," she whined.

"Did you ask nicely?" she inquired, knowing full well Megan's approach with the boys was that of a steamroller.

Megan's full lips formed into a pretty, little pout. "I said please, but they ran away; and now I can't find them." She punctuated her disappointment with her best 'foot stomp - hands on hip' pose. Susie bit her lower lip to keep from laughing.

"I don't know where they are, Megan," Susie kindly explained. "But after dinner, they will play a game with you in the Rec Room. And don't forget, we have Story Time in the Library at four."

"Will you play with me?" Megan wheedled.

"I have something I have to do right now, Megan," Susie answered.

"Like what? You're done in the kitchen 'cause I heard Mrs. Coppersmith tell you so," Megan countered petulantly.

"It isn't kitchen duty," Susie replied. "It's just something I need to do for me."

"May I help?" Megan begged.

"No," Susie's tone was firm. "But I did hear Miss Ginger say she was looking for someone to help her with a sewing project. Last time I saw her, she was in the Lounge. Why don't you find her and see if she still needs help?"

"Okay!" Megan clapped her hands, hugged Susie and ran toward the kitchen. Susie started to remind Megan not to run, but thought the better of it. The sooner Megan was out of sight, the better. Megan was notorious for changing her mind on a whim, and Susie needed as much time as possible to prepare for her adventure tonight. She watched as Megan bounded around the corner in search of Miss Ginger. Susie turned and collided with Miss Fiona.

Merrily laughing, Miss Fiona steadied Susie and said, "Here now, where are you off to in such a rush? Afraid Megan will come back and follow you?"

Susie blushed slightly. "No, I just have things to do."

Miss Fiona's green eyes sparkled with glee. "And just what might that be?" she asked playfully.

Susie's expression clearly revealed her rising panic.

"Exploring, I would expect," Miss Fiona answered for her. "It would truly explain why you're so preoccupied this morning. You must have found something exciting to keep you so lost in your thoughts," she added teasingly.

Susie's heartbeat pounded in her ears; she struggled to not panic. Was Miss Fiona spying on her, watching as she explored? No, not possible; she's just guessing, Susie quickly reasoned. After all, Miss Hilda had told them the day they arrived that they could explore to their hearts content. So did Miss Pritchett. Apparently all the children do. Timmy and Simon have – they have a secret hiding place that they have made their club house. She scolded herself silently for succumbing to her own over-active imagination. Miss Fiona wasn't spying on her. *All* the children explore. No big deal. Susie began to relax, feeling much better. That is until the next thought struck – *But no one has found what I have found.*

Susie's expressions made Miss Fiona chuckle all the more. "It's all right, child. This is truly an amazing place. Like I said before, it's full of wonder and mystery." She grinned, tilted her head impishly and asked, "Have you noticed these paintings?" She pointed to the black horse (Gabriel) and then to the white horse (Angel).

Something inside Susie told her that Miss Fiona knew she had. Susie nodded.

"Have you now?" she inquired, her tone lilting in merriment. "Have you noticed the attention to detail?"

Susie nodded. "Yes; they're amazing."

"That they are," she agreed with a mischievous look. "They are exquisite. Did you notice the eyes?"

"Yes," Susie admitted; "I almost missed it, and then I saw in the center is a blue flame."

Miss Fiona grinned. "'Tis true; I believe it represents The Flame of Truth.....or something like that." She paused, admiring the portrait of Gabriel. Wily, she asked, "Did you notice the center of Angel's eyes?"

"No," Susie answered hesitantly. She darted to the painting, closely examining the center of the blue eyes. Now she saw it, and inhaled sharply. "Hey! ", she exclaimed, turning to face Miss Fiona; "it looks like the white centers are actually a bird in flight."

Nodding in agreement, Miss Fiona smiled. "A dove is what it is," she informed Susie; "a bird of peace."

Susie made the connections. "Pax means peace, and she painted a dove. And she painted the flame in his eyes, and Ignis means fire."

"Very good," Miss Fiona commended her.

Susie's eyes flashed with excitement and hopeful anticipation. "Do you know what the non-Latin names mean, and what the language is?"

"That I do," Miss Fiona responded, pleased at Susie's curiosity. "The language is Old Irish."

She smiled fondly, first at Angel and then at Gabriel, and translated, "Nime is 'Heaven', Chuit is 'Treasure', Chride is 'Heart', and Baile is 'Vision'. It's my understanding that the names come from the Old Irish text of the hymn, "Be Thou My Vision".

Susie smiled and whispered softly, "The names fit." She noticed that strange expression again on Miss Fiona's face and flushed a little.

"So Angel's name is Heaven Treasure Angel Dawn Peace, and Gabriel's name is Heart Vision Gabriel Truth Fire." She sighed heavily. "Wouldn't it be easier to give them just one name?"

"Perhaps," Miss Fiona agreed; "but you have more than one name, and are called by mainly just the one. Is that a problem for you, or anyone else to remember your names, or by which to call you?"

Susie laughed. "No."

"I did not think so," Miss Fiona stated matter-of-factly.

"So, Angel and Gabriel are Lacy's grandparents," Susie commented. "Are those the parents' portraits," Susie asked, pointing to the dappling grays.

"The parents are referred to as sire and dam," she responded with a whimsical tone; "and yes, those are the parents of Lacy. The sire is Black Fire Moon Silver Dancing. The dam is White Peace Shadow Sun Cloud."

Susie moved to the portraits, carefully studying each one in turn. She grinned, laughed and said, "Moon has a little, full moon painted in the center of his eyes, and Shadow has a sun and cloud painted in hers."

Miss Fiona laughed. "Yes; it would appear that Noreen had a sense of humor."

As she turned to leave, she paused and peered back over her shoulder at Susie. "Happy hunting," she teased and then strolled toward the Library.

Susie began her trek to her Dorm Room, stopped, and spun around when she suddenly realized that Miss Fiona had called the artist Noreen instead of Elizabeth.

'How did she know to use the middle name instead of the given name?' she wondered; 'and how did she know it was Noreen when the signature only shows an "N"?'

Susie fully intended to ask her; unfortunately Miss Fiona was already gone. Susie mused, "I guess I'll ask her at lunch."

———

Susie entered the laundry room and removed a pillow case from the linen closet. She opened the supply closet and removed various cleaning products, soft cloths, light bulbs, trash bags and paper towels. Her biggest need was the ShopVac – the problem, though, was how to convince Mr. Henry that she needed it again so soon. 'Well, I'll just have to do it,' she noted with an air of finality.

Leaving her cleaning bundle well hidden under her pillows, she began her search for Mr. Henry. She recalled how at breakfast she heard him tell Mr. Dale that he needed his help with the fountain in the Conservatory. She had no trouble finding them and was pleased that Mr. Henry asked no questions as to why she needed it again. He teased her about being a clean-freak and then told her that was actually a good thing. He promised to have the ShopVac in her attic room right after lunch. She thanked him and headed toward the Library. She had just enough time to take another look at that book about the fireplace that had so intrigued Miss Taryn. She chuckled and thought: 'wouldn't it be a hoot if I find the treasure before Miss Taryn does?'

———

Lunch went well – at least this time she was more attentive and didn't have that spacey look that had caused the adults to be concerned with her state of health. She had to consciously force herself not to think about the letter, or the journal or the Hidden Room.

Simon and Timmy were deliriously happy with their farm chores, and proceeded to tell Susie (and anyone else who would listen) what they had accomplished that morning. Mr. Sean had even promised them that, if they continued doing this good, they could have a baby animal of their own to care for come spring. They were so excited; they gushed and giggled.

JT gave a wink and a nod at Mr. Sean, then requested that the boys assist him during the afternoon. He had a few minor plumbing chores he said required their assistance since, as he put it, they were mature enough to help him. Their little faces beamed with anticipation and pride. Both sat up straight in their chairs and behaved themselves for the remainder of the meal. Susie said a mental thank you – this gave her the opportunity to continue exploring right up until Story Time.

After lunch, the boys rushed to JT's side, ready to start their new assignment. Susie couldn't help but giggle - they were too cute in their eagerness to be helpers.

"Susie, want to play chess now, instead of at three?"

She didn't hear Jose's approach, and he startled her. She jumped.

"Gees, what's the matter with you?" he asked.

"Nothing, just a little tired. I didn't sleep much last night," she answered, smiling as cheerfully as she could muster.

"Why not? Are you sick?"

"No, I just couldn't sleep," she shrugged, dismissing it as unimportant.

"I do that, too, sometimes," he confessed. He leaned in and whispered, "But I do it more here than anywhere else. Sometimes this place is spooky."

Although she was surprised that Jose also had sensed something odd about Glen Hollow, she perfectly masked her surprise. Instead, she attempted to soothe his fears. "It's just a big house, Jose. There's lots of drafty places and dark areas, everything that helps to play on our imaginations."

Jose smiled in earnest and nodded. 'Yeah, you're right; but it does seem creepy sometimes, you have to admit that."

Susie laughed. "It is sometimes," she admitted wholeheartedly.

"So you want to play?" he asked again, hopeful she would, as he held the chess set out to her.

She wanted to catch Miss Fiona before she began her project in the Hidden Room, but she didn't want to disappoint Jose again either. Her hesitation was fleeting, and fortunately not pronounced enough for Jose to have noticed.

"Sure, I'd love to," she answered. "How about in the Library," she suggested.

"Cool," he responded.

They headed toward the Library, discussing the ways that Glen Hollow gave them the creeps and shivers from time to time.

———

It seemed as if they had only been playing chess for a few minutes when the Munchkins came barreling toward them. Timmy and Simon were attempting to relay their plumbing accomplishments, while Megan was desperately trying to be heard concerning her sewing feat with Miss Ginger. Susie established order fast, telling them they will each have a turn in a minute, but only if they are quiet now. They waited somewhat patiently while she helped Jose put away the chess pieces and board.

"Mind if I sit in on Story Time?" he asked.

"Fine with me," she answered, turning to look at Simon, Timmy and Megan. "Okay with you?" she asked.

Expecting a barrage of dissension, she was pleasantly surprised that they readily agreed. As they entered their usual area, they found Dani and Kat already sitting on the fireplace hearth.

"Hey," Timmy scowled at the intruders; "you can't be here. We're having Story Time."

"Yeah," Simon concurred.

Before a brawl could develop, Susie intervened. "Hey guys; you've allowed Aaron and Jose to join, why not Dani and Kat?"

"Maybe we don't want to join you," Kat countered tartly.

"I do," Dani timidly said.

"You both do because you wouldn't be here otherwise." It was Aaron. He approached, and his quirky little smile said he knew something that everyone else didn't. He stood next to Susie, still smiling at Dani and Kat. "I told them about *this* Story Time. They wanted to join, so I told them it was okay."

Susie caught the emphasis on the word 'this', so she knew he had kept the secret about the other Story Time. Unfortunately Kat also caught the emphasis. Her eyes brightened, flashing with impish glee.

"'*This*'," she repeated; "so that means there's another one. I bet it's after bedtime. Am I right?"

Simon, Timmy and Megan desperately and loudly tried to convince Kat otherwise; and the harder they tried, the more convinced she was that she was right. Kat finally ended the discourse by stating all she had to do was wait until tonight and follow Susie. She gave Susie a playful, little smirk.

Susie laughed. "The jig is up guys; we're busted."

She faced Kat and Dani, hoping that they would not rat them out to the adults. "You're welcome to join us at both Story Times," Susie offered; "but the bedtime one must be kept secret."

Smiling like the proverbial cat that had caught the canary, Kat leaned back on the hearth, obviously delighted in having the upper hand with Susie. "Love to," she stated.

Dani ran and gave Susie a hug. "Thank you," she whispered before rejoining Kat.

"Let's get started," Susie told the group.

507

"What about Juls and Jared? Shouldn't we invite them, too?" Aaron's tone was adamant, leaving no room for doubt as to his opinion. His facial expression also conveyed he planned to include them.

Susie began, saying, "I think …." and then was interrupted.

The rest of the group chimed in that they had practice sessions, and it was no use to ask them. Aaron responded he didn't mean right now. Susie assured him she had understood what he meant, and she agreed with him – they should be asked if they want to join either or both Story Times. Apparently everyone wanted Jared; but no one wanted Juls, and for mostly the same reason, just expressed differently.

With Aaron's help, Susie got them all to quiet down and listen. She told them that perhaps including Juls might help her attitude to change. Reminding all of them that they didn't like to be excluded, Susie told them she was certain that Juls felt the same way, deep down. Some were concerned if Juls didn't want to come, she would tell the adults about the secret one. Susie shrugged slightly as she responded that that is the same chance she took with each and every one of them. They would also have to take that same chance with Juls.

Completely astonishing Susie was Kat's simple statement. Softly she spoke, "How will you ever know if you never give her a chance?"

After that, everyone agreed that they should both be invited. Susie said that she would invite Juls tonight at bedtime, and asked Aaron if he would do the same with Jared. He readily agreed.

Smiling, Susie told them that they now have a Story Time Club, and hopefully everyone would be a member. They all became quiet as Susie began one of Nana's short stories.

Chapter 25

ICORI LEGENDS

Mrs. Coppersmith re-entered the Dining Hall carrying a large stack of bowls. Directly behind her were Miss Thelma, Miss Elsa, Miss Fiona and Miss Taryn. Each carried a huge tub of the biggest, fluffiest popcorn Susie had ever seen. Simon's eyes popped wide open as he expressed verbally his eager anticipation of tasting the morsels. Mrs. Coppersmith was quick to inform him that, although sampling now and then of the popcorn was permitted, the popcorn was intended to make the popcorn strings. To further seal her point, she stopped next to him and gave him her famous 'do you understand me' look. Simon just beamed at her – he knew her bark was far worse than her bite.

Mr. Sean quickly spoke, telling Susie and Simon that the popcorn is a special variety, developed and grown at Glen Hollow. Jose cheerfully added that they have it on movie nights. Miss Hilda was quick to explain, for Susie and Simon's benefit, that the third Saturday of every month is movie matinee at Glen Hollow, and that the children get to select which movie is seen. Simon bounced in his chair, exuberantly announcing his choice for the next matinee. Before anyone else could speak, Juls caustically informed Simon that they took turns; it wasn't his turn because December was her month.

Simon quickly shot back at her that that was okay with him because everyone knows what he wants to see. He turned to Miss Hilda and asked when it would be his turn. Timmy graciously declared that Simon could have his turn which was in January. Simon grinned and thanked Timmy as did many others, praising Timmy for his good deed.

Timmy coyly looked down and confessed that he also wanted to see the movie, so it didn't matter whether he picked it or if Simon did. Everyone assured him that it was still a nice thing that he did. Simon beamed at Timmy, informing everyone that they were 'best buds', and that's just what 'best buds' do. Timmy concurred by loudly blurting out "'yah', and punctuating it with a sharp nod of his head. They both broke out in hilarious giggles. Miss Hilda shushed them while Miss Pritchett gave them 'The Look'. Immediately they quieted.

The ladies had now strategically placed the tubs on the table. Mrs. Coppersmith had divided her stack of bowls into four groups, placing them on the table by the tubs. Miss Thelma, Miss Elsa, Miss Fiona and Miss Taryn began the process of filling the bowls with popcorn and passing them to those in their area.

While they were thus engaged, Mrs. Coppersmith explained to those unfamiliar with stringing popcorn just how it was done while giving to each person needles that had already been threaded. Susie was glad for this convenience; the last thing she wanted to do was try to teach Simon how to thread a needle. She was also glad to see the thread was doubled – no chance for it to slip through the eye of the needle, whether accidental or intentional. Susie chuckled softly, envisioning Simon and Timmy having a contest as to how many times their needles had to be re-threaded.

Simon began to protest, demanding to know why his thread, and Timmy's and Megan's, were so much shorter than everyone else's. Mrs. Coppersmith paused ever so briefly, having just the slightest hint of a smile. In her usual no-nonsense, clipped tone, she answered it was because their arms were shorter and couldn't reach as far as the older children or the adults. He grinned at her and cheerfully agreed. As Mrs. Coppersmith continued with her instructions, Susie couldn't help but notice the little, extra lilt that was now in her voice.

After everyone had a few trial runs on stringing popcorn, Mrs. Coppersmith relinquished the floor. Susie noticed that the adults all (except for Dale) seemed very familiar with this process. In contrast, out of all the children, only Jose was familiar and proficient. Simon, Timmy, and Megan ate and crushed more than they actually strung. The rest of them, herself included, were slower than Jose and had a few mishaps.

There was a lot of teasing and banter; everyone seemed to enjoy the activity and the challenge. There were a few contests between some of the men, and that also produced a lot of laughter, some of which had nothing to do with stringing popcorn.

As everyone began to settle into their own rhythm of stringing the popcorn, Miss Pritchett asked if everyone was ready to play the Story

Game. None of the children knew this game so she explained it to them. It begins with one person who starts the story with a sentence or two. The next person repeats what was said, adding their own sentence or two. The process continues until everyone has had a turn. Simon immediately declared he wanted to be the one to start the story. Not to be outdone, Megan and Timmy both claimed the same privilege.

Delighted with their enthusiasm, Miss Pritchett assured them each one would have a turn at starting a story; but since Simon asked first, he would begin the first one. From there, the imaginations flew. Within each storyline, it alternated from goofy and silly, to scary and macabre, to sweet and fun, and a few were just plain wild. Megan's Story Game was last and, when it was over, Miss Pritchett asked if anyone had a joke they wanted to share.

"I have a question," Kat said.

"Yes?" Miss Pritchett responded.

"It's actually for Kevin," Kat stated. She smiled at him, her eyes sparkling mischievously. "You're Icori, right?" (He nodded.) "And you know the Legend that the Reverend told us?" (He nodded again.) "Well-el-el …. Do you know the name of the Spirit-Witch?"

Kevin's laugh was hearty and filled with amusement. His eyes twinkled at her attempt to be clever. "Yes, I do," he answered. "Do you want to know what it is?"

Kat answered "yes" emphatically amidst a chorus of other answers: some "yes", some "no" and some were just ambivalent. Kevin glanced at Miss Pritchett, his eyebrow raised slightly as if asking her permission. Her smile was one of amusement as she nodded her head, signaling that he indeed had her permission.

"Well," Kevin began, his voice and expression exhibiting his own mischievous nature; "her name is Shanaroosh."

"Oh, no; now she'll come get us," moaned Timmy. He had covered his ears with his hands hoping to stave off the knowledge.

Kevin chuckled. "No, Timmy," he replied. "Trust me; the mention of her name will not bring her back. She is held captive, and you are safe. She is a very powerful, evil being, but her power has limits."

"What if someone frees her?" Dani asked, her fear showing through her attempt at bravado.

511

"I doubt that will happen, Dani," he said calmly. "It would take a very powerful witch, one in league with the dark one, in order to set her free. And they still couldn't unless the Great Spirit allows it."

"Why would He do that?" asked Aaron.

"He wouldn't," Mrs. Coppersmith firmly stated. She gave a hard look at Kevin which only made him chuckle.

"Well, He might," came Kevin's swift rebuttal. His tone was light, revealing just how amused he was at Mrs. Coppersmith's unease with the legends. "If He did, it would be so we can see the strength of our faith. Icori faith teaches us that the Great Spirit already knows all things. We are the ones who cannot see until we can; and we can when He shows us. Sometimes He has to allow things that are frightening or sad so we can see just how strong our faith is."

"So where's this prison she's in?" Jared asked. His tone revealed he thought the whole thing was a joke.

Grinning, Kevin paid an inordinate amount of attention to the piece of popcorn he was currently stringing. His response had a teasing quality to it. "Well, Jared," he said as he rolled his eyes toward his cousin, Samuel; "contrary to what some people think, I've never been there, nor plan to be there." (Samuel made a chortling sound as if to say he knew different.)

Kevin shifted his position in order to face Jared. His mischievous nature was in full swing, reflecting in his manner and his voice. "According to legend, she is held in a place between worlds that has been made just to hold such creatures. It's dark, and has the stench of sulfur and death." (Susie's mind flashed to the dream she'd had and shivered.)

"Shouldn't she be dead by now?" Aaron asked skeptically.

"No," Kevin answered, slowly shaking his head. "She's a sprite. She is mortal, but not like you or me. They live thousands of years. Mere mortal weapons can only wound – but they heal so fast, that it's almost instantaneous. The only way she can be killed is by a Guardian using the power of the Great Spirit."

"So she's not super powerful?" Simon asked, hanging onto Kevin's every word. The past three days, every chance they had, Timmy and Simon had been following Kevin around, imitating his every move. Sometimes they were helping him with chores, and other times they thought they were observing him clandestinely. Sadly, their stealth abilities were sorely inadequate. Kevin, however, didn't mind being the object of their admiration, and pretended not to notice them during their 'secret missions'.

"Well, not more than our Creator, but certainly more than just us mere mortals." Kevin shrugged as if fighting such creatures were an occurrence that happened every day. "The trick is to remember it isn't up to you or me, the power belongs to The Creator. He responds to our faith, and empowers us to do the impossible by human standards."

"May we please change the subject?" Mrs. Coppersmith intoned. "I've had enough of this nonsense."

"Yes," agreed Miss Thelma. "Perhaps we can have something less frightening."

"Are there any other Icori legends?" Susie asked Kevin.

He smiled, a sense of discernment shone in his expression, "Yes, many."

"Please tell us another one," she requested. Simon, Timmy and Megan were the loudest voices in the chorus of pleas for another legend.

"Any objections?" Kevin asked.

Everyone, well most everyone, encouraged him go ahead. Mr. Dale, Miss Taryn, Miss Thelma and Mrs. Coppersmith protested. It was no surprise to Susie that Mrs. Coppersmith's objection was the loudest. She was adamant that these stories were unsuitable for the little ones.

As the others attempted to persuade Mrs. Coppersmith, Miss Claire pushed back her chair and stood. She said nothing, waiting to be heard. Everyone fell silent. Then she spoke.

"Mrs. Coppersmith; I respect your thoughts, and I know you care deeply for the children. We all know this," she said so softly.

(Mrs. Coppersmith, slightly embarrassed by the attention, shifted in her chair and tried to feign indifference).

Miss Claire smiled kindly at Mrs. Coppersmith. "However, all cultures have their stories, and many are nearly identical. This is because we all are of the human family; we share the same joys and sorrows, happiness and grief, loves and hates, hopes and disappointments. Our lives all know these things; they are common to everyone. It is these stories that show us others have experienced what we have had to endure, or yet will endure.

Through sharing these stories we have a source of strength. We also teach each other about choices, good or bad, and teach that we have a duty to each other and to our God. There is nothing wrong with that." Miss Claire reseated herself.

"I didn't say there was," Mrs. Coppersmith snapped. "I think these stories, no matter from where they come, have too much focus on the power of evil. This frightens the children, and we should tell other children's stories," she added, defending her position.

"Like what?" Miss Fiona inquired; "Grimm's Fairy Tales, Little Red Riding Hood, The Three Little Pigs, Charlotte's Web, The Snow Queen or Hansel and Gretel? They all have frightening elements, but even Megan and Timmy love these stories."

"Me too," Simon quickly added, waving his hand to make certain he was included.

Miss Fiona smiled and winked at him. "Of course you do."

"Thank you everyone; however, I think it would be interesting to hear the Icori stories," Miss Pritchett said with a voice of finality, giving Kevin a nod to proceed.

Kevin leaned back in his chair, folding his arms across his chest. He looked up toward the ceiling as he contemplated which legend to share. Samuel suggested they might like to hear about the 'Fire of Heaven', or the 'Vision Stone' or even the 'Star-Eyed Serpent'. All three suggestions received approval from nearly everyone. Kevin nodded as if he agreed, then abruptly sat upright as he declared, "No; I think the one to share would be the 'The Stone of Protection'."

Samuel's face registered his disapproval as did his sharp tone. "Are you serious? The 'Fire of Heaven' is a much better story."

Kevin shrugged. "Well, I'm going to tell the 'The Stone of Protection'. You, dear cousin, can tell the other one."

Playfully he clapped his cousin on the back. Samuel shook his head – he had no intention of sharing any legend, and Kevin knew he wouldn't.

"What are they about?" Susie asked.

Kevin grinned. "'The Fire of Heaven' is about the beginning of the line of the Guardians for the Icori. Netoshowa was a great warrior and medicine man who lived thousands of years ago. He was the eldest son of the great warrior chief, Kaiyatoba. Netoshowa became the first Guardian when he conquered a powerful demon using the Fire of Heaven. It is a weapon of immense power; and, if it falls into the wrong hands, it can be used to destroy the whole earth. A holy one, what you call angels, appeared to him after he defeated the demon and gave to him the duty of Guardian, if he was willing to become one."

"Like Swift White Eagle," Susie responded, remembering the story of Shanaroosh."

Kevin nodded. "That's right. The story of 'The Star-Eyed Serpent' is about a huge staff made of pure gold, molded and shaped like a rattle-snake. Its eyes are blue sapphires, and there's a white star in the center of each blue stone. The story tells that it has great power, and anyone who knows how, can use it to travel to different worlds. But its power can also be harnessed and used for evil."

"The story of 'The Vision Stone' is about the gift of traveling to the stars, instantly." Grinning at Simon and Timmy, he added playfully, "no need of space ships."

He laughed as the children's eyes lit up, their eager faces awaiting more details. "Its power is so great that the ancients decided it was better to hide it, and remain here rather than risk it falling into the wrong hands."

"Now, the 'Stone of Protection' is about the theft of an ancient talis-man given to the Guardians by a holy one to protect this land and all that lived in it."

"What's a talisman?" Simon asked.

Kevin grinned. "It's an enchanted object that protects you from evil. Some cultures call it an amulet."

"Let's begin," he said, settling into the affable manner of a storyteller. "My great grandfather, Kenatae, has told me the legend of 'The Stone of Protection' many, many times since I was just a little boy. The Stone pro-tected the people from many evils. It gave them good hunting, good crops and good health. Every new moon it was used in the Blessing Ceremony." (Susie's mind flashed to the story of The Cards told by Miss Claire.)

"Even though the guardian has a description of the Stone, no one really knows what it looks like," he admitted. "It hasn't been seen in about a thousand years or so because it was stolen from Spirit Mountain. Sometimes the Icori call this legend 'The Guardian and the Great Witch'."

Kevin gave them time to "ooh" and "ahh" before continuing the story, and assuring them that Shanaroosh was not the great witch in this legend. Simon squeaked, "There's another one?" to which everyone laughed. He reminded Simon (and everyone) that Shanaroosh was actually an evil sprite and not a witch. When they all quieted, he continued with the ancient tale.

"Every new moon, which is once a month, the guardian would go to Spirit Mountain just before nightfall to perform the Blessing Ceremony. He would light the ceremonial fire and would sprinkle the fire with water from the Anicaw. This made the ceremonial fire pure so that its flame would be true, sacred. When the time was right, the guardian would remove the Stone of Protection from its secret hiding place and take it to the Spirit Rock. Once set in its proper place, the Ceremony would begin."

"The tribal guardian had just removed the sacred Stone from its secret place when he sensed a presence of great power. He looked around, but saw no one. This made him uneasy; he kept looking, searching the tree line to see if anyone was hiding among the bushes and trees. He was alone."

"A strange mist, black as night," his voice dropped into a spooky timbre; "formed between him and Spirit Rock, forming a barrier. The old guardian cast a wary eye toward the mist. It was rare that a mist formed on Spirit Mountain, but he had been told of the times in ancient days when it was said to have happened. As he walked toward Spirit Rock, the mist began to thin. A woman stepped out of the mist. He was very surprised, for no one other than guardians had ever dared to step foot upon this holy place. But it was her appearance that startled him the most."

"She was like nothing the old man had ever seen. Her clothing was not made of animal skins like tribal clothing. It was oddly made, and appeared to be thick, and soft and smooth, glimmering softly in light of the fire. Though her neck was exposed, the garment formed tightly around her chest, her arms and all the way down to her waist. From there it flowed to the ground, billowing around her like a large blanket. As she neared the fire, its light revealed the deep red color of her clothing, and the gold threads that formed a strange pattern on it."

"This creature was a vision of beauty - her long hair was as black and shiny as the feathers of a crow; and her skin was as delicate as a newly fallen snow. The color of her eyes was the color of the Anicaw River on a winter morning, a pale, icy blue."

"The woman smiled and spoke softly. The sounds were strange to his ears - he did not understand her words, but her tone was gentle. Slowly she extended her left hand toward the sacred Stone he held. The old man realized she was asking him to give it to her. He tried to move, but quickly discovered that he could not. He was held in place as if bound by invisible ropes."

"She laughed softly, amused at his confusion. Her smile spread into a full grin revealing her white teeth, a glaring contrast to her blood red lips. He watched, helpless, as the Stone rose from his hands and floated into hers. Around her the mist began to form once more, swirling as it slowly thickened. He cried out to her, begging her not to remove their protection. He did not expect her to understand his words any more than he could understand hers, but he hoped she could understand what the Stone meant to his people through the anguish in his voice."

"To his bewilderment, she spoke again – this time he understood her every word. 'I'm sorry,' she spoke with great sadness; 'but all of my people will die without this. I have seen the future of your people – they will survive. Some will die, some will fall victim to the dark ones, but not all'."

"She turned to re-enter the mist, but not before the old guardian saw deep into her soul. She was a great and powerful witch in her own right; but she had not used her own power to come here, for that type of power was even beyond her ability. He saw she used the dark power to achieve this feat. He also had seen she had not yet surrendered her soul to the dark ones. But he knew that was only a matter of time. One cannot dance with them without succumbing to them, or paying with your life for refusing them."

"'Go in peace,' he said gently; 'May the Great Spirit grant you and your people the help you seek. May you seek His counsel, and not those of the dark path; and may He protect you from them.'"

"His compassion for her astonished her. She paused at the edge of the mist and turned to face him. This powerful witch, more powerful than he had ever before seen, had tears in her eyes. She nodded briefly, accepting his blessing."

"Graciously she smiled. 'Many, many winters from now, a young guardian will come,' she prophesied; 'and that one will return to you what I have taken. Until that day, behold!'."

"The witch stretched her hands upward, high over her head, and began a chant. He did not understand any of her words; but he saw strange lights in the night sky, swirling all around the mountain and the whole valley below them. Then the lights returned to the heavens and disappeared. She ceased her chant and smiled at him. It was a smile of satisfaction."

"'I have given you a little extra protection, not such as the amulet; but it will help to protect your people,' she told him."

"'I didn't use dark magic,' she retorted angrily before he had the chance to ask the question that had formed in his mind."

"She closed her eyes briefly, sighing as she opened them. 'Not all of your descendants will have your strength of faith,' she informed him. 'They will need the help I have provided. When the time is right, a young guardian will come and will return the amulet of protection to your people. Then my spell will be broken for it will no longer be needed'."

"'When will the Stone be returned?' he asked."

"'Far into the future,' she replied softly. 'I cannot tell you the exact day, but it will be many hundreds of winters from now.'"

"She stepped back into the mist; it vanished, taking with it the woman and the sacred Stone."

Kevin smiled and ended the story, saying, "And those who believe still wait for the young guardian to come and return the Stone of Protection."

"Who is he?" asked Kat.

Kevin shrugged. "We don't know."

"When will he come?" asked Dani.

Kevin laughed and repeated, "We don't know."

"Then how do you know he hasn't already returned it?" Aaron asked cleverly.

"Good question," Kevin admitted, delighting in the banter. "We know because Kenatae still performs the Blessing Ceremonies, and it has not yet reappeared."

"Thank you, Kevin, for entertaining us," Miss Pritchett said, signaling the storytelling was finished for the evening. "We look forwarded to hearing more Icori legends another time; however, it's already 9:15, and well past bedtime for the children."

A chorus of pleas erupted, begging for more time.

"We'll have plenty of time to hear more stories at another time," she insisted. "You've all done an excellent job. We have more than enough popcorn strings. And now it's time for bed."

"Miss Pritchett," Miss Hilda interrupted; "since they have done such an excellent job, perhaps tomorrow night we could have pizza and a movie as a reward."

Not only did the children approve, but so did the adults. Miss Pritchett heartily agreed, noting that for special movie nights, it was Miss Fiona's turn to choose the movie.

Instantly Miss Fiona was bombarded with suggestions from most of the children. Their frenzied zeal delighted her. She laughed, assuring them she was certain she would choose one that they all would like.

Before they could start another round of suggestions, Miss Cora and Miss Ginger intervened, rushing them away to bed and reminding them they still had to mind their manners if they wanted to see the movie. Miraculously that worked; the children went along quietly.

Lingering casually, Susie managed not to draw attention to herself, hoping all the while for a chance to speak with Miss Fiona. She left the Dining Hall after the other children, and walked down the corridor with Miss Fiona and Mr. Kevin. Susie listened as they chatted mostly about the preparations for the holiday festivities. When they reached the Library, Miss Fiona cheerfully chirped "good-night" to Susie and Kevin, telling them that she had a book or two to find, and then entered the Library. Susie was disappointed that Miss Fiona wasn't going on up to the third floor, but vowed silently that she would find a way to speak with her tomorrow.

Kevin and Susie continued down the corridor until they reached the main foyer. He told her "goodnight and sweet dreams", and she responded with "goodnight". He turned and began walking toward the south corridor as Susie was approaching the main staircase.

On the third step Susie stopped and leaned against the banister. "Mr. Kevin," she called.

Turning around, he stepped back into the foyer. "Just call me Kevin," he instructed.

"Okay, Kevin. I was wondering if your great-grandfather, Kenatae, ever visits here."

"Yes, he does. Why?" he asked.

"I would like to meet him. I think he would be interesting," Susie answered a little apprehensively. She had questions about Glen Hollow that Kenatae and the Reverend could probably answer, but she didn't want anyone to know.

"I'm sure he would love to meet you," Kevin responded pleasantly. "When I see him Saturday, I'll ask him. Maybe you can come with Miss Pritchett the next time she visits him at his home. Would you like that?"

Excitedly, though trying to be very nonchalant, Susie breathlessly answered "yes". The elation on her face, though, would not be contained no matter how much she tried. Kevin grinned at her exuberance.

After exchanging good-nights again, Kevin disappeared into the south corridor while Susie ran up the stairs and all the way to her Dorm Room. She was thrilled; her mind whirled with all the questions she wanted to ask about Glen Hollow. Finally, she was going to get some answers.

Susie entered the Dorm, bursting through the door with great energy. Miss Cora smiled, reminding her "lights out in five minutes" as she patiently waited by the door. Susie just grinned and told her good-night as she headed toward the hallway.

Miss Cora responded in kind, then asked if there was any particular reason for her effervescence. Her eyes twinkled mischievously and were as sprightly as her smile. Susie responded that there was no particular reason, she just enjoyed the evening. Miss Cora's smile spread into a full grin; she laughed and responded with "if you say so".

Susie shook her head, laughing and went quickly to her room. In two minutes, the lights went out, and Miss Cora left. Susie heard the door close with its distinctive groan, followed by its unique click.

After Miss Cora was gone, Susie hastened down the hallway and was not at all surprised to find the others already waiting just outside Juls' room. They entered together. Susie switched on the desk lamp causing Juls to bolt upright.

"What are you doing in here?" she demanded.

The girls chorused several responses, and Susie promptly shushed them.

"Juls," she began calmly; "we have a secret club, and we have all voted to include you if you want to join us."

Juls gave them a scathing glaze as she surveyed the group. "Really?" she responded sardonically.

"Yes, really," came the swift reply from Kat and Dani. Little Megan rapidly nodded her head as she said "uh-huh".

"A secret club; sounds kind of lame to me," she retorted snootily.

"It is not lame!" declared Megan furiously.

Juls laughed. "Don't be so touchy," she told Megan. "So, why is it a secret?"

The girls all looked at Susie, so she explained. "It started with just Simon and I having Story Time for him at bedtime. Then Timmy joined, then Megan, then Aaron; and today Jose, Dani and Kat all joined. We decided that we would also include you and Jared if you want to join us. Obviously we have to keep it a secret because bedtime for Simon, Timmy and Megan is earlier than for us. We meet in Simon's room right after Miss Cora leaves. So, are you in?"

Juls just stared at Susie; her expression was that of boredom. Dani, Kat and Megan pleaded for her to say yes; however Juls just rolled her eyes and shook her head no.

Megan stepped up to Juls, held her hand and said so sweetly, "Please come with us, Juls. It'll be fun. You'll see. Susie tells us her Nana's stories, and they're great. I know you'll love it; so please come. I really want you to."

Juls was totally caught off-guard by Megan. She flushed a little and then smiled. "Okay, I'm in."

Megan shouted exuberantly, "Okay, let's go 'cause we're late."

"She's right," Dani and Kat echoed. They looked at each other, grinned and raced to the door.

Megan darted after them, calling out for them to "wait for me!"

Juls laughed, as did Susie; they both dashed to the door as quickly as they could.

After checking to be certain the corridor was empty, they darted across and into the Boys Dorm. All the boys, including Jared, were waiting for them, crowded into Simon's room.

"Wow," Jared said with a grin; "you did get her to come. That's amazing."

"Oh, hush," Juls replied, pretending to be annoyed. She found a space on the bed and pulled Megan into her lap.

Megan eagerly obliged and whispered, "I like you."

Juls' face glowed as she smiled at Megan. "I like you, too," she whispered back.

"What story are you going to tell?" Aaron asked.

Susie thought for a moment; inspiration unfolded, and she grinned. "I think we will begin one of Nana's marathon stories," she told them; "in honor of us all being together. So tonight, we will begin the story Nana called 'The Kingdom of Ahnashalor'."

"Our story takes us to a place far away from here, to a land where the pastures are green with thick grass, and the whole kingdom is filled with beautiful flowers, trees and living creatures of every kind."

"Ahnashalor is a kingdom much larger than our planet, and every creature lives in harmony. That means they're nice to each other, and they help each other. The purest water starts way up in the highest mountain peak, and flows all throughout the land. It gives life and health everywhere the waters touch."

"In this kingdom, all types of magical creatures live, and work and play side by side with non-magical creatures. This is the story of how the Kingdom came to be. And it's the story of how evil tried to destroy it all."

Susie smiled at the rapt attention on each face. She delved into the story exactly as Nana had told it so many times to her, not missing one inflection, one sound or even one word.

Chapter 26

A WHOLE NEW DISCOVERY

For what seemed an eternity, Susie restlessly waited for the girls to fall asleep. Her clock disagreed with her perception, counting the time thus far as having only been forty minutes. Alternating between lying on her bed and espionage maneuvers, Susie again softy tiptoed along the hallway, listening and hoping that they were all fast asleep. Her mind wandered again to Juls, and was truly impressed with how Juls seemed to have really changed for the better. Who would have thought she would have volunteered to get Megan tucked in, and had done so cheerfully?

The memory of Megan's theatrics flashed into Susie's mind causing her to chuckle softly. Susie had gone in to give Megan her good-night hug, and found Megan bouncing on her bed after her tuck-in with Juls. Upon seeing Susie, Megan began to dance a little jig. Tossing her head from side to side, Megan had gleefully told Susie that she knew Juls would love Story Time – someone just had to tell her so.

"And I did!" she emphatically ended her victory gloat.

Her curls bounced and swayed with each animated movement. Susie had laughed, lifted Megan up and twirled her around, sending Megan into a frenzy of giggles. After several round-a-bouts (as Megan called it), Susie dropped her onto the bed amid squeals of pleasure from Megan. Susie gave her a kiss and a hug, amply reciprocated by Megan, before tucking Megan back under her covers. Susie smiled at the little cherub as they exchanged their good-nights.

Megan's countenance beamed with joy as she confided, "I'm so glad you're here, Susie. Everything's getting better."

She yawned and added sleepily. "Hazey and Mazey said you're going to make us all safe." She nodded as if that act verified what she had just proclaimed. Smiling as she gazed up at Susie, Megan's expression was as sweet and innocent as a new-born baby.

"They're always right, just like my angel," she said amidst a big yawn. Megan's eyes fluttered closed, and her head sunk deep into her pillow as she drifted blissfully asleep.

Motionless, Susie just gaped at Megan, contemplating what Megan has just said. After several minutes, Susie had shrugged and thought, 'who knows; stranger things have happened here than Megan talking to angels or stuffed animals.'

Gently she kissed Megan's forehead, then left. As she returned to her own room, she paused briefly at each doorway to say goodnight. Her greatest surprise came when she had reached Juls' doorway – Juls was waiting for her.

In a blur of motion, Juls had stepped into the hallway and hugged Susie. Tearfully she thanked Susie for including her in Story Time, divulging how much fun she'd had. Juls released Susie in a graceful motion, much like a choreographed dance. Juls smiled at Susie, and it seemed as if her smile would cover her whole face and do so permanently. Her eyes flashed with giddiness, admitting she loved Nana's story and couldn't wait for the next part.

As quickly as her excitement had risen, so now had it fallen; her expression had become somber. Juls became silent, her smile faded as she looked away from Susie. Softly Juls apologized for having been so mean to Susie. Her eyes rose to meet Susie's, and were brimming with tears. Instinctively Susie hugged Juls, telling her not to worry – they would start anew as of this night.

"Really?" Juls had asked.

"Really," Susie assured her.

Emboldened by the bond now forging, Juls confided that she never liked it here, and didn't want to be here. It was dismal, and creepy and spooky. Her plan was to act badly enough to force Miss Pritchett to send Jared and her packing. She reluctantly admitted Miss Pritchett wasn't so easy to manipulate. Everywhere else she had been had sent her packing in short order, and any other place would have done so long before now.

"But not Miss Pritchett", she had admitted, shaking her head in astonishment. Releasing a deep sigh, Juls continued her confession. Her smile was bright, hopeful even as she explained that since Susie's arrival, the place has changed – the ominous cloud seems to have lifted.

Juls laughed and rolled her eyes as she whispered that that sounded more like something Kat would say. Her expression quickly changed, becoming serious. Her voice was soft as she assured Susie she was being honest. Susie knew Juls was truthful – she could see it, actually see it (much to her own astonishment), and told Juls that she believed her.

They exchanged "good-nights" and "sleep-tights". Juls headed to her bed as Susie had scurried on to her own room, puzzled by the change in Juls.

And now, an hour later, Susie was just as puzzled. Susie pushed the thoughts away – they were better left for another time when she had the time and energy to sort through them. Besides, she reasoned, tomorrow will prove whether or not Juls has changed, or if this was just an act.

Finally the coast was clear; they were all asleep. Susie crept quietly into the Common Area and out the door, pausing briefly to make certain the corridor was empty. Running as fast as she could, Susie held the pillow case of supplies pressed tight against her body, preventing any clanging or clunking sounds. Her mind raced with thoughts of the Hidden Room, and why it was there.

Miss Murielle could have had an office *anywhere* at Glen Hollow. Why would she have it in the attic? And why did it need to be a secret with hidden doors? The questions kept popping, one after another.

Susie stepped onto the third floor landing. As she walked into the corridor, she heard the sound of a door being opened. Flooded with adrenalin, Susie darted back into the alcove. With her heart pounding hard in her chest, Susie was certain each thundering beat could be heard. She held her breath and pressed against the alcove wall, praying she would not be seen or heard. Miss Taryn passed by, heading toward the main staircase. Softly Susie exhaled and relaxed against the wall as her heartbeat slowed to its normal pace.

Chuckling silently, Susie mused, 'Apparently Miss Taryn is on another mission to find the secret niches in the fireplace.'

Although curious, Susie wasn't to be deterred; she had her own mission and was anxious to get started. Stepping out of the alcove, she had only gone a few feet when the last door at the far end of the corridor opened. Dashing back into the darkness of the alcove, and again praying she hadn't been seen or heard, Susie waited nervously as she listened to the sound of the approaching footsteps. She sneaked a peek as the man rapidly strode past the alcove.

It was Dale! He headed toward the main staircase, increasing his speed as he rounded the corner, entering the balcony walkway.

Susie couldn't resist; this was too much of a coincidence. After gently setting her supply sack on the alcove floor, Susie slipped into the corridor. Cautiously she made her way to the balcony, catching a fleeting glimpse of Dale as he ran down the stairs. Dropping to her knees, she inched her way to the balustrade and peered down into the foyer below. Miss Taryn was waiting at the base of the stairs, watching his progress from the third floor to the second and finally to where she stood.

"It's about time," she snapped at him.

"I'm right on time," he scowled. "What's your problem?"

"Never mind," she responded, her voice becoming soothing. "Do you think you can find it?"

"Of course," he answered boastfully. "If it's there, I'll find it."

Susie watched them disappear from sight into the west wing. As she stood to her feet, it dawned on her that anyone could have seen her had they entered into the corridor. Lucky for her, no one did. 'Rats,' she thought; 'I've got to be more careful.'

Snatching her supply sack, she ran to the attic door. Hastily she made her way inside and up the stairs. Setting her bundle down, she opened the passageway door and secured it. Susie took the step ladder and her supply bundle, running all the way to the secret door of the hidden room. Leaving her supply bundle and step ladder by the wall, she returned to her attic room to retrieve the ShopVac. It took longer than she had anticipated, but she had finally managed to maneuver the ShopVac into the passageway. It moved awkwardly through the passageways, much like some behemoth beast. Several times it careened against the walls, and seemed determined to remain there. But each time Susie's own fierce determination won, and they were again moving along on to the Hidden Room.

Upon arrival, Susie pressed the little button, smiling as the massive door slid open with barely a whisper of a sound. Her first order of business was to find the light switches which, as it so happened, there were only two – one by the stairwell and one by the entrance. Next task was to replace the light bulbs in all the lamps; and, now done, turn on the lights. Holding her breath, she flipped the switch by the entrance; instantly the lamps sprung to life, flooding the room with a soft glow.

Though covered in layers of dust, the room was not nearly as horrible as she had previously imagined. Granted, it would take her quite a while to clean it; but not nearly as long as what the poor light of the flashlight had caused her to believe. She began to vacuum, first the entire floor, then the desk and chair and then the oak secretary. She cleaned every nook and cranny, moving at a frenzied pace.

After finishing the oak secretary, Susie shuffled to the desk chair and plopped down into it, catching her breath before tackling the other furnishings. Her watch told her she'd been working for an hour, which gave her slightly more than two hours before she'd have to quit and return to her Dorm Room. She had to be in bed by three, she reminded herself. Susie got up and began vacuuming the remaining furnishings, finishing just slightly ahead of schedule. Next she tackled the walls. Having accomplished all of the major tasks, Susie focused on the paintings. She had vacuumed the frames when she did the walls, but dusting the actual paintings would take a little time for it had to be carefully done.

Releasing a tired sigh, Susie stood and stretched. Time was running out; she barely had an hour before time to quit. She contemplated which of the paintings she should tackle now and decided that it would be the large, life-sized one. Hoping it was a portrait of Miss Pritchett and her parents, Susie began her task, starting at the bottom and working her way up the painting. Within a few minutes, there was no doubt in Susie's mind that this was not a portrait of Miss Pritchett and her parents at all.

She had uncovered the lower portion of a lady's gown, and what appeared to be three animals. Susie continued the painstaking cleaning task until it was clean enough for her to recognize the animals were a white wolf, a white tiger and a unicorn. Well, she hadn't actually cleaned the head area yet of the one, but deduced it was a unicorn based on the other two animals. They were just like the painting in the 'Histories' book, and also the carving in the oak cabinet in the Library.

Diligently she pressed on, carefully removing the layers of dust and was rewarded. The third animal was indeed a unicorn. Excitement coursed through her like an electrical current, filling her with energy and with anticipation. Eagerly she continued cleaning the image of the woman until she had at last uncovered the face of the woman.

"It's her!" Susie gasped in astonishment. "It's the woman in my dream that woke me in time for dinner."

Staring at the portrait, Susie slowly began to realize that this woman was real, and someone had painted this portrait. With a deep sense of discernment and conviction, Susie knew the mystery woman had the answers to the questions that plague her.

"Who are you?" Susie whispered.

A cool breeze encircled Susie, playfully flipping her ponytail. The scent of lilac slowly wafted through the air while the soft, distant melody of a wind chime could now be heard.

"Okay," Susie whispered. "This is what you wanted me to find, and I found it. But I don't understand. What does this painting mean? Who is she? Is it you?"

The light breeze became stronger as it moved away from Susie, blowing the dust from the remaining portions of the painting. Strategically hidden in various places throughout the painting were images of all sorts of people and creatures. "Just like the Chapel windows," Susie noted softly.

Returning to Susie, the breeze became gentle again, lightly brushing against her face. Within seconds, it moved back to the painting, and then to Susie yet again. The third time it repeated the pattern, Susie laughed and said, "I get it; you want me to look at the painting."

Susie inched closer to the painting, not certain what portion of it she was supposed to examine. She began with the wolf. Intently she scrutinized the brush strokes, looking for anything that might reveal a hidden message. As she became absorbed in her mission, suddenly the frame began to rattle, startling Susie and causing her to jump.

A nervous, little laugh escaped from Susie. "Don't do that," she admonished.

As if to apologize to her, the breeze lightly caressed her face.

"It's okay," Susie whispered. "I'm just a little jumpy. I'm guessing you want me to look at the frame."

Susie began inspecting the frame. It was well made of thick oak planks, finely crafted into smoothly honed wood. Certainly nothing out of the ordinary, she thought. Gently she began to feel the wood, running her fingers along the edge of the frame. Within seconds, she shouted. "It's a door!"

Excited, Susie began tugging hard at the frame. Finally it gave way and popped open, revealing that it was indeed a door to yet another secret room. Snatching up her flashlight, Susie quickly switched it on as she leaned into the open doorway. Its meager light was not strong enough to penetrate the darkness and was swallowed up by it. Susie realized that the room was enormous, and she would need a much bigger flashlight or even a lantern. At that moment, she knew - this room was directly above the foyer on the ground floor.

"This is the Inner Sanctum," Susie whispered gleefully. "I found it!"

Stepping cautiously into the gaping hole, Susie stood just inside the doorway. The darkness was so thick, destroying all trace of what little light her flashlight had to offer. Susie shuddered as the image of a tomb entered her mind, of being sealed alive in the blackness and the cold. Forcefully dispelling those thoughts, Susie concentrated on the great discovery and what the room had yet to reveal. Her excitement grew with the anticipation of learning what was so important about this place and this room that it had to be kept a secret.

She decided to follow the wall on her right, hoping that this room also had a fireplace. It would make sense, she reasoned, because it would share a chimney with the Hidden Room. And both, she further reflected, obviously share a chimney with the East Wing rooms below.

Moving the flashlight slowly along the rock wall revealed wall sconces like those outside the manor except that these had wicks. Susie continued exploring and within a few feet found the fireplace. Carefully she made her way around the raised hearth. This fireplace was a little larger than the one on the other side of the wall. Past the fireplace, she came upon the side of what appeared to be a cabinet. Cautiously making her way around it, she panned the light along its front and discovered floor to ceiling shelves of books.

"How could anyone read in here?" Susie questioned; "there must be another light source."

Susie continued inching her way along the bookcase; by the time she reached its end, she realized, with a sudden jolt, that she had been in here entirely too long. Quickly as she could, she carefully made her way back to the doorway, exited and closed its secret door. She smiled at the woman in the portrait, whispering "goodnight" before rushing out of the Hidden Room and closing its secret door.

Running all the way back to her attic room, her mind raced with questions. Most would not be answered until she could actually see inside the Inner Sanctum, but her mind persisted with searching, questioning and planning. She closed the panel door in her attic room, returned the poker to its rightful place and raced down the stairwell, turning off the light as she sailed past it.

After locking the attic door, she ran all the way to the Dorm Room, mentally scheduling her day. Stealthily she made her way to her room, retrieved her pj's and hastily dashed to the bathroom. With lightning speed, she took a fast bath and then slipped into her pj's, dumping her dirty clothes and wet towels into the hampers as she darted out the door.

Quiet as a mouse, she trekked across the Common Area and slipped into her room. With a yawn of exhaustion, she dropped onto her bed, falling fast asleep just as the clock began chiming the four o'clock hour.

———

Susie awakened feeling refreshed and ready to meet the day, which was a pleasant and most welcome surprise considering how little sleep she'd had. Her conclusion was that it must have been the fast bath she took before going to bed, deciding it must have helped relax her and thus enabled her to sleep better.

She made her rounds, waking each of the girls and was thoroughly surprised and delighted that Juls was already up and getting dressed. Even more astonishing was her cheery "good morning", and Susie was hard-pressed to find an explanation other than what Juls had offered last night.

For the first time since her arrival, Susie enjoyed the morning ritual. Everyone was in a good mood and was pleasant. Miss Cora arrived on schedule; the amazement on Miss Cora's face when she saw Juls ready *and* in good spirits made them all laugh.

———

The morning flew by and Susie's kitchen duty was finished, and that was mainly because Mrs. Coppersmith shortened her duties to thirty minutes. Today was the Christmas Tree Hunt, and it was scheduled to start at ten.

Quickly she made her way up to her attic room. Initially she had planned to unpack Nana's books; but she had yawned so much during her chores, she changed her mind. Now Susie was determined to take a nap undisturbed, hoping to counter the effects of her late-night adventures. Setting the alarm for an hour nap, Susie curled up on the couch and covered herself with a couple of Nana's thick quilts. She was too tired to make a fire and decided the quilts would keep her warm. Within seconds, she was fast asleep.

Chapter 27

THE HUNT IS ON

The noise of all of the competing voices was deafening as the sounds echoed against the rock walls of the foyer. Everyone was talking at once, laughing and teasing as they dressed in their warm, outer garments in order to brave the winter cold. Even Juls and Kat, who had previously declined to participate in the hunt for the perfect Christmas tree, had been swept up in the fervor at breakfast and had decided to join the expedition. They were just as excited as all the rest, eagerly anticipating the contest and declaring that they would be the winners. A loud, spirited debate ensued among several of the children and adults as to who would actually be the winner.

Simon ignored all of this, restlessly pacing between each of the entrances to the foyer. He had been anxiously waiting for Susie, badgering Miss Ginger and Miss Cora to let him go find her. Each time they refused his insistent pleas, assuring him that she would join them soon. Simon was not at all reassured – he kept pacing and reminding them that he couldn't find her after her kitchen chores; she had just vanished.

He earnestly informed them that both he and Timmy had looked for her "real good". He explained how aliens would kidnap people, and this could have happened to Susie. They would pat his head and smile or just laugh, amused by his imagination. Finally he and Timmy decided they would sneak away, launching their own search and rescue mission. Just as they had begun to slip out of the foyer into the west corridor, Susie appeared at the top of the stairs and rapidly descended.

"There you are," Miss Ginger called out to Susie. "Some of us were beginning to wonder what was keeping you."

"I'm sorry," Susie apologized. "I fell asleep."

"Are you ill?' Miss Bettye asked.

"No," Susie hastily assured her; "I'm fine."

Simon and Timmy squirmed their way through the crowd. "Where were you?" Simon demanded. "We were going to come rescue you."

"Yeah," Timmy agreed. "We thought you'd been kidnapped."

"Kidnapped?" Susie repeated, grinning at the two characters.

Simon nodded his head. "Yeah; aliens are everywhere, so we were going to come find you."

"And rescue you," Timmy added again.

Susie laughed and hugged both boys. "Thank you; I couldn't have better detectives and rescuers than the two of you."

Simon and Timmy both enthusiastically gave her their best bear hugs amid their peals of laughter and giggles.

"Quiet down, everyone, and listen up," Mr. Sean's booming voice instructed. One by one they fell silent.

Miss Pritchett thanked him and then assigned teams, giving each team leader a colored ribbon to tie to their tree of choice. Susie and Simon were assigned to Kevin's team, and their team color was blue. Completing their team was Megan and Miss Fiona. Susie had hoped that Miss Claire would be assigned to their team, giving her an opportunity, perhaps, to ask her about The Cards, and also ask if Nini would speak to her about it when she arrived on Saturday. Such was not the case, and Susie was very much relieved that at least Miss Taryn had not been assigned to her group.

Simon and Timmy, incensed that they were to be separated, marched right up to Miss Pritchett, loudly protesting not being on the same team. After all, they argued, best buds were supposed to be together. They accentuated their displeasure with sharp nods of their heads, forcefully crossing their arms, hunching their shoulders and displaying serious looking pouts. Miss Pritchett calmly answered their theatrics by simply offering an alternative – they could remain at the manor and take a nap. Obviously they were grumpy due to lack of sleep, and that could easily be remedied, she stated. As quick as a flash of lightning, both boys assured her that they weren't sleepy or grumpy; they were just teasing. She smiled as they scampered back to their assigned teams.

Everyone left in their assigned groups, bidding Mrs. Coppersmith farewell as they hurried out the door. She reminded them all to be safe, to have fun and that she'd have hot soup, sandwiches, freshly baked cookies and hot cocoa waiting for them upon their return.

Outside, everyone climbed into the four vans except for Mr. Sean; he drove the truck that was pulling a long, flat-bed trailer. Following Mr. Sean, they proceeded slowly down the lane, past the barns a considerable distance before turning left onto one of the farms roads. They travelled a long way down the road, passing several connecting farm roads until the manor and all its out buildings were long gone from view. They reached the edge of the forest, turning onto a logging road that headed east. Several miles later, the van ahead of them stopped. Kevin followed suit, parking their van a few feet behind it.

"Everybody out," he cheerfully instructed.

Miss Pritchett gathered everyone in the center of the road, reminding them that they must stay with their assigned group at all times, and that they were all to meet back at the vans in one hour. "Good luck," she said, waving everyone off to their adventure.

Kevin grinned at his group, saying, "Come on; follow me. I know where the best tree ever is."

Grasping Megan and Simon firmly by their wrists (their mittens were too puffy), he began a brisk walk toward the forest. Susie and Miss Fiona followed, trudging through the deep snow. After a few minutes, Kevin stopped.

"The snow is too deep," he told Miss Fiona; "so how about if I carry Megan and give Simon a piggyback ride?"

Both Simon and Megan were readily agreeable as they had already begun to tire from the effort of navigating the depths of the snow. Miss Fiona offered to carry Megan, but Megan insisted that Kevin be the one. Kevin laughed and assured Miss Fiona that he was able to carry the both of them. In a swift, fluid motion, he picked Simon up, depositing him onto his back. Quickly Simon wrapped his legs around Kevin, and his arms around Kevin's neck. As if she were as light as a feather, Kevin effortlessly scooped Megan up and held her tightly against his side, resting her on his hip.

Megan giggled with glee, and Simon chortled, "Let's go!"

Kevin complied, briskly striding toward the forest, unhampered by the snow and the extra weight he carried. Susie was surprised that the deeper they ventured into the forest, the less snow there was. When Miss Fiona suggested that Megan and Simon no longer needed to be carried, they protested vigorously. Kevin just laughed and told her that they were not a problem, and it was faster to continue on the way they were. Miss Fiona disagreed, but said that if he wanted to be a pack mule, so be it. That made Kevin laugh all the more as he quickened his stride. Keeping pace with him was no easy task; but with considerable effort, Susie and Miss Fiona managed to do so. After traveling nearly ten minutes, Miss Fiona asked Kevin if he was sure of the tree's location. He laughed at her veiled attempt to suggest that they had gone too far into the forest.

"It's just ahead," he told them.

Five minutes later, they stepped into an enormous meadow, one large enough to easily accommodate a huge shopping mall. Near the center of the meadow was a small brook, winding through the meadow and back into the forest as it meandered its way to the Anicaw River. You could hear the sound of the water flowing, swirling over and around the rocks in the creek. It was a peaceful sound, giving homage to the refrain that the birds were currently singing. Several stands of trees graced the meadow, some hardwood and some softwood. Among the latter were cedars, spruce, firs and pines.

The scene that lay before them was breathtaking to behold. The vivid green colors of the evergreen trees were in perfect contrast with the stark browns and ashen colors of the bark of the other trees. The snow weighed heavily on the boughs of the trees, some branches appearing as if they might break at any moment. Capping it all was the sparkling blanket of snow that lay across the meadow, shimmering and glistening in the morning sun.

Kevin set Megan and Simon down, instructing them to stay close to him. He pointed to a grove of fir trees. "It's in the center of those," he said and began walking toward the trees.

Simon and Megan were right behind him, attempting to step in his tracks. Susie and Miss Fiona followed the little ones, amused by their euphoric antics. Kevin's stride was long, and they could not match it no matter hard how they tried. Each failure was met with boisterous squeals of delight, along with mounds of snow catapulting into the air. Gradually it changed from trying to match his stride into a contest of another sort. They began jumping from step to step and falling in the snow, purposely. This, of course, produced peals of laughter from both of them as they tried to outdo each other in the number of falls, and in the amount of snow they could launch skyward with each tumble.

After several such falls, Miss Fiona assisted Megan to her feet while Susie grabbed Simon, preventing him from taking another dive. Susie brushed off as much of the snow as possible from Simon while Miss Fiona did the same for Megan. With an impish smile, Miss Fiona encouraged them to be more careful; after all, as she so humorously said, they surely didn't want to catch their death of cold and miss all of the Christmas fun.

Although they giggled and pretended not to care, they both stopped their snow diving and quickly caught up to Kevin. Several minutes later they arrived at a grove of fir trees, following close behind him as he led them toward the center of the grove.

There it was. Kevin was right – it was the best tree ever, standing in a small clearing at the center of the grove. Perfectly formed, it rose skyward nearly twenty feet. It was so majestic looking with its crown of snow on its top, and its lush green needles lightly dusted with a gentle layer of snow.

"Well, what do think?" Kevin asked.

"It's truly a thing of beauty," Miss Fiona whispered.

Susie nodded in agreement. "It seems a shame to cut it down. Do we have to? Can we cut a smaller one down, or one that has some damage?"

Kevin smiled. "Could," he replied with an amused twinkle in his eyes; "but we're not cutting it down; not yet anyway. We're just locating a tree. After we meet back at the vans, we go to each site; then we vote on which tree wins. That's the one that gets cut down."

"But we all know that this is the one they'll choose," Miss Fiona countered.

"So let's choose a different tree," Susie suggested.

"I agree," Miss Fiona added, smiling at the tree. "This one belongs here, and we should leave it be."

Kevin laughed. "So you want to throw the contest?"

"No, just choose a different tree," Susie and Miss Fiona chorused simultaneously.

Kevin shrugged. "Fine by me. There's some that aren't as perfect closer to the road. We'll choose one of those." He winked at the girls and added in a mock conspiratorial tone, "That way no one will know about *our* tree."

"Hey, where's Simon?" Susie asked, looking around for him.

Kevin and Miss Fiona also began looking. .

"Megan, do you know where Simon went?" Kevin asked.

Megan shrugged her shoulders. "I don't know. He wanted to play hide and seek, but I didn't want to. He ran over there." She pointed toward the direction where they had entered the meadow.

"Don't worry, we'll find him," Kevin assured Susie. "Let's start looking. Spread out and keep about fifty feet between us. Just make sure we keep in sight of each other. Fiona, you take that end, and Susie will be in the middle between us."

Miss Fiona firmly grasped Megan's hand. "You'll stay with me," she instructed.

They began a search pattern, calling out to Simon repeatedly. There was no response. They continued searching for quite some time, but could not find him. Finally Kevin called Fiona to meet in the middle with Susie.

"He's gone a lot further than we thought. He's lost, but don't worry; I'll find him. He didn't come this way because I've not seen any of his tracks. Fiona, you need to take Megan and Susie back to the vans. If you hurry, you'll be on time. Have the men bring blankets and flashlights, and guide them back to the meadow."

Fiona nodded.

"No," Susie hotly countered. "I'm not leaving."

"Susie, you can't help. You don't know how to track, and you'll only slow me down," Kevin explained patiently.

"Susie," Miss Fiona spoke gently; "trust Kevin. He's experienced; he also heads the county's search and rescue team. He'll find Simon, and bring him back safe and sound."

"I'm not leaving." Susie crossed her arms, set her jaw and glared at them. "I can help you, and I will. We're wasting time," she tenaciously added.

Kevin began to speak, but Miss Fiona cut him off while keeping her intense focus upon Susie. "Very well," she responded. "I have no doubt that you will find Simon."

Before Kevin could object, she turned to him and added, "I think you'll find that Susie will not be a hindrance, but will actually be of help."

"One thing is for sure, we don't have to argue," Kevin relented. "Go Fiona; get the men and meet us in the meadow."

Miss Fiona nodded her head. "I'll do it," she affirmed. "Come Megan; we've no time to waste." Megan waved to Susie as Miss Fiona pulled her along, heading back through the forest.

Susie returned her wave, then faced Kevin.

With an encouraging smile, he said, "Let's find Simon."

She nodded. "Okay."

They rapidly headed back to the meadow. Kevin began scouting the area and quickly found Simon's tracks. He showed them to Susie, explaining that they needed to find a set that didn't return. From the tracks left in the snow, it was obvious that Simon had left and re-entered the meadow many times. After several minutes, Kevin found the one set they needed, leading back into the forest opposite of where Megan had originally pointed.

Following Simon's little footprints into the forest, Kevin watched for any sign of disturbance whether a snowy footprint, a tree limb snapped, displacement of ground items or a myriad of other clues as to where Simon had trod. Susie followed behind Kevin, amazed at how fast he read the trail. He knew exactly where to step, and what to look for as he went; that is until Simon's tracks disappeared altogether. Kevin scoured all around, but no trace of Simon was to be found. It was as if a giant bird had swooped down from the sky and lifted him up.

"Kevin," Susie called out to him. "Simon's at the meadow."

"How do you know?" he asked. "There are no tracks that show he left this spot."

"I don't know how I know. I just know. Simon is back at the meadow, and I'm going there," she replied, turning toward the direction of the meadow.

"You need to stay with me, Susie. I don't want both of you lost out here," he countered quickly.

She stopped, spun around and calmly stated, "Then you'd better come with me because I'm going to Simon."

Susie darted through the woods as swiftly as possible, mentally praying she was right. The image of Simon in her mind was so clear it was as if she was actually there watching him. Kevin quickly caught up with her. Occasionally he stole glances at her, but said nothing. He didn't need to; his expression voiced his concern quite effectively. Susie pressed on, knowing Simon was there.

They were finally in sight of the edge of the forest, and the meadow beyond. Susie raced out of the woods and into the meadow, Kevin close on her heels. Simon was there and was playing; he was bunny-hopping through the snow, all along the beginning of a grove of cedar trees. Susie ran to him, elated that he was fine, but also furious that he had gone exploring on his own.

When he saw her, he was his usual self, delighted to see her.

"Hi Susie!" he yelled as he ran clumsily through the snow to her. Throwing his arms around her, he hugged her tightly in one of his famous bear hugs. He giggled and squealed as she returned his hug.

"Hey, little man," Kevin said as he dropped out of his sprint. "You gave us quite a scare." Kevin bent his knees, bracing his hands on his thighs in order to make eye contact with Simon. "Don't ever wander away like that again. You could have been hurt."

"That's right," Susie agreed, cross with Simon's behavior.

Simon shook his head. "Nah-uh," he countered innocently; "the wolf helped me."

"What wolf?" Both Kevin and Susie asked, surprised and apprehensive.

"That one," he answered, pointing behind them.

Turning around in unison as if tethered together, they saw the eyes of a creature inside the forest, just at the edge of the clearing. Slowly it entered the clearing, never breaking eye contact with them. It was a wolf, a large, white wolf with pale gray eyes.

"See, I told you," Simon told them, gleefully. "He's my friend."

Susie moved in front of Simon, holding him behind her, just as Kevin quietly told them not to move and not to be afraid.

"I'm not afraid," Simon countered, puzzled by what Kevin said. "The wolf brought me here 'cause I was lost," he explained.

"Really?" Kevin asked.

"Uh-huh," Simon confirmed, rapidly nodding his head.

Kevin began speaking softly to the wolf in the Icori language. The wolf responded with a few sounds that were a cross between a bark and a grunt. Kevin spoke again, and the wolf again responded. Shifting its focus from Kevin to Susie, it made a chuffing sound, almost as if it were a pup just awakened and searching for its mother.

Cautiously it began moving toward them, keeping an eye on all three of them as it approached and stopped a few feet in front of Susie. The wolf slowly bowed down as if it had been trained to do so and then stood, motionless, as if waiting for something. Briefly it glanced back at the forest tree line before it began its final move toward Susie. It lay at her feet with its nose nearly touching her boots.

Stunned, Kevin stared at Susie, then at the wolf. Simon was grinning.

"See, I told you," Simon quipped. "He's friendly."

Kevin looked at the snow behind the wolf; there were no tracks. Mechanically, his head bobbed several times up and down as he pondered the reality that, while in the forest, he didn't miss the wolf's tracks because there weren't any.

Softly Kevin released a slow, deliberate breath. He knew. He now knew and understood. From his earliest childhood days, he had heard many times from Kenatae the stories of the spirit wolf. His parents and grandparents also swore the legend was true, that one was present at his birth. Always he had believed it had been just an ordinary wolf. Now he is seeing it with his own eyes, marveling that it is true.

Kevin approached the wolf, softly speaking to it again in his native language. Its ears perked, its head raised and its tail slowly began to swish back and forth across the snow, leaving not a trace. Kevin sat beside the wolf, gently speaking to it. The wolf nuzzled him playfully, then laid its head in Kevin's lap as Kevin began to gently stroke its head.

Simon had already joined Kevin in petting the wolf, and the creature responded as if it belonged to Simon.

"What did you say?" Susie asked Kevin, remaining transfixed to the same spot.

"I told him he is welcome here, and that we are honored by his presence. I thanked him for visiting us, that we are humbled he would choose us. I also thanked him for protecting Simon," he answered in a hushed tone.

Susie's mind flashed to the book from the Library she had just finished reading. It claimed that there was a special creature that took the form of a white wolf. This creature's purpose was to be the protector of the seeker. This wolf was not the same as all other wolves for this creature had the ability to travel instantly wherever it was needed, even between worlds.

Silently Susie asked, 'Could it be true? Could this be that creature?'

As if in answer to her question, the wolf raised its head until he made eye contact with Susie. A strange sensation flooded her as it had with the portraits of Angel and Gabriel. Suddenly she could see what the wolf saw, and know what he knows.

She saw Simon, playing in the meadow as they were admiring the tree. She watched through its eyes Simon as he spotted a bunny enter the meadow. She saw Simon laughing and chasing the rabbit, nearly catching it a couple of times. She watched as Simon followed the rabbit into the forest, trying desperately to catch it. She listened to his laughter and squeals of delight as time and time again he would get close, only to have the rabbit veer away at the last second in a different direction. And each time the rabbit would draw Simon deeper into the forest. She saw Simon's last dive for the rabbit, and how he quickly got up and chased it, finding himself further into the deep, dark forest.

It was at that moment Simon realized that Susie was nowhere to be seen; he was alone – and she saw the fear in his eyes, the terror displayed on his sweet face, and the abject panic in his voice that that realization brought. She watched him trying to find his way back to the meadow; the laughter gone, and the awareness that he was lost now his only reality. She heard him calling for her, screaming her name over and over, but too far away to be heard through the muffling effects of the dense forest.

She watched as a lost and frightened Simon desperately tried to find his way out of the forest. Every turn he made served only to draw him deeper and deeper into the woods, and further away from Susie. She heard him frantically calling for her, and no answer from her. She saw him crying, begging and pleading for help to find Susie. She saw him collapse onto the ground, there where Kevin found his last set of tracks. She witnessed him sobbing hysterically, leaning against the tree and begging God to help him find Susie.

And suddenly, out of thin air, she saw the wolf appear, right by his side. She watched as the wolf playfully barked, rubbing up against him, nuzzling him and comforting him. And the strangest of all things was when she witnessed the wolf pulling Simon to his feet and leading him back to the meadow. She watched the two of them playing and romping in the snow, waiting with him until she and Kevin arrived.

Susie dropped to the ground, tenderly holding the wolf's head in her hands as she continued to look into his eyes. Her eyes were brimming with tears. "Thank you for helping Simon," she told the wolf. The wolf responded with a playful bark.

Simon beamed as he continued stroking the wolf. "Can we keep him?"

"No, Simon," Kevin responded.

Simon was sorely disappointed until Kevin told him that he would see the wolf again.

Kevin inhaled deeply, exhaling slowly as he contemplated his next words. His gaze met Susie's. "You connected with him, and you are not surprised by it. This has happened before," Kevin stated quietly as he observed her.

She wasn't certain if she should tell him all that she has experienced since arriving at Glen Hollow. For now, she decided to admit to the minimum – what he already suspected. Susie nodded. "Yes, sort of ... more so, just recently. Nana always said our family has a way with animals."

Kevin's smile was one of amusement and respect. "Nayatowah is not an ordinary animal. They are spirits that come and go among the worlds to offer help whenever they are needed, wherever the Great Spirt sends them."

"Nayatowah," Susie repeated, as she gently scratched him under his chin. "Is that his name?"

Kevin shook his head. "No. Nayatowah is the Icori name for this creature. It's hard to actually translate. The closest I can come would be to say it means 'light walker'. It refers to their ability to walk between worlds, as if through light itself."

Susie's eyes widened. Helga Gretchen Von Richter's book popped into her mind again.

Kevin watched her closely, scrutinizing her expressions. "It is an honor to have these noble ones visit, and especially so if they choose to protect you," he informed her. "I have heard of them all my life. Kenatae, my grandparents and my parents have all told me of the one that was present at my birth; but I have never seen one – until now."

He paused for a moment before adding, "Kenatae will know why he rescued Simon, and why he has chosen you to honor."

"Me?" Susie asked, surprised.

Kevin nodded. "Nayatowah came to you, and lay at your feet. I have never heard of this happening before, but Kenatae may have." He smiled. "Besides, you did say you wanted to meet him."

Susie grinned. "I still do."

Kevin stood up and brushed the snow from his clothing. "Come on, kids. We need to get back. I suspect that Miss Fiona has the cavalry coming."

"Please can I pet him just a little more?" Simon begged.

"No, Simon; we have to leave now," Kevin responded firmly.

The wolf jumped to its feet and swiftly ran toward the forest, stopping at the tree line. It turned and looked back at them, pausing for just a moment. Simon bounced up and down, waved, and begged for him to "come back soon" before it vanished.

"Where did he go?" Simon asked.

"Home," Kevin responded.

"But I didn't see him leave," Simon protested.

Kevin smiled. "Yes you did. He just runs real fast."

Simon frowned as he tried to understand. He shrugged and said, "I guess so. Will he come back?"

Kevin smiled and answered, "Maybe."

"I can't wait to tell Timmy," Simon boisterously proclaimed as he bunny-hopped alongside of Kevin and Susie.

"I don't think you should tell Timmy," Susie said, hoping to persuade Simon to keep it a secret.

"Why not?" Simon countered.

Kevin intervened. "Timmy won't believe it because he didn't see the wolf. That will make him not believe anything you say, and then you won't be friends."

Simon scowled. "But you and Susie know it's true; and you can tell him, too."

"Yes," Kevin agreed; "but he hasn't seen the wolf, so he won't believe it. It's better to keep the secret for now. Maybe the wolf will come back when Timmy is with you. But until then, you need to keep Nayatowah's secret so that Nayatowah will trust you. If he trusts you, he will probably come see you again."

Simon sighed heavily, unhappy with the restriction. "Okay," he reluctantly agreed.

"Good," Kevin said. "Now, how about a piggy-back ride out of here?"

Simon perked up as he beamed at Kevin. "Okay!"

Kevin picked Simon up and hoisted him onto his back. Simon promptly wrapped his arms around Kevin's neck as Kevin hooked Simon's legs through his arms.

"Let's go," Simon decreed and off they trudged, swiftly moving through the forest and reaching its end before the rescue team had a chance to join the search.

Kevin set Simon down, reminding him that they still needed to find a tree for the contest. He pointed to a group of cedars and pines that were near the road. After several rounds of inspection, Simon chose a cedar tree that was "plenty fat and super tall" (Simon's description). Simon begged Kevin to allow him to tie their blue ribbon on the tree. He tied a lop-sided bow, but it was tied and visible, the only two requirements.

When the others joined them, Simon had to endure a round of hugs from all of the adults, and their repeated questions as to if he was all right. Kevin deftly explained how Simon went exploring, but found his way back to the clearing just as they had returned to it. Susie added that they found him bunny hopping all through the meadow. Most of the adults laughed and accepted the explanation, but with admonishments to Simon that he was never to do that again. Simon, properly contrite, solemnly promised. Susie noticed that Miss Fiona had a strange expression on her face.

Something told her that Miss Fiona did not believe their condensed version of what had happened.

Now that Simon had been found, and found unscathed, Miss Pritchett quickly convened the judging portion of the Christmas Tree Hunt. Considering they were already at Simon's tree, it was thoroughly inspected before they trekked to each of the other sites. After several rounds of voting, a tree was finally chosen – a twenty-one foot Blue Spruce. The wining team was the purple team – Mr. Henry, Miss Claire, Juls, Kat and Jose.

The men set to work to cut down the tree, taking turns using the axe. Jared and Aaron also were given turns, much to their delight. After it was cut, the men carried it to the trailer, hoisted it up onto the trailer and tied it down. They eagerly climbed back into the warm vehicles, quickly returning to the manor where hot soup, sandwiches, hot cocoa and freshly baked cookies were waiting for them.

Chapter 28

HOME, SWEET HOME

Susie leaned against the window, her breath causing little clouds of fog to condense on its icy panes. It was much colder here in the window seat, but Susie preferred writing here than by the fireplace. Whenever she pressed her face against the window, she could look up and see the stars twinkling in the night sky. Living in the city, the stars were crowded out by all of the bright, man-made lights. Nana had shown her how to use the telescope, but being able to see the entire sky in its brilliance was far better. Out here, there were no outside lights other than the porch lights by the door, allowing the velvety blackness to appear in sharp contrast to the glittering lights of the stars. She found herself looking forward to spring and thus being able to be outside for night sky watching.

Reflexively she began tapping her pencil against her journal that lay open in her lap. She had written the events of the day in her journal, yet something still nagged at her subconscious, trying to be heard and included. Just what, she didn't know.

Closing her eyes, Susie envisioned it to be spring; she was on a hillside and watching the stars dance across the night sky. She imagined the wonder of traveling among the stars, of seeing them first hand, of watching the lights disappear as she sailed past; and new ones emerge, growing ever brighter as she drew nearer to them.

Susie opened her eyes and stared at her journal, revisiting the day's events. True, she was intrigued that Kevin knew she communicated with the wolf, or Nayatowah as he had called it. But of more interest was the fact that such creatures exist, and apparently are not confined to just one continent.

"Or one world," Susie muttered as she read what she had written.

The book by Helga Gretchen Von Richter claimed that these creatures, these emissaries of the Almighty, were not hampered by time and space. They travel to wherever they are needed to assist those who are called

Seekers. Kevin had basically said the same thing, but his people gave these creatures the name Nayatowah. The book did not give them any name.

"Perhaps every culture has its own name for them," Susie reasoned. "The book could not possibly name all of the names, so none were given." Susie smiled. "It's up to the Seeker, wherever they are, to discover the protector wolf and learn its name at that place."

She read again the passage in her journal where Kevin had explained the Nayatowah to her. Now she remembered what she had forgotten to write. Kevin said that the Nayatowah had protected Simon, and had honored her.

"Does this mean Simon and I are Seekers?" she asked aloud, somewhat stunned at the idea.

She sighed, uncertain as to what any of it meant. The book did not really explain it, just told of these special creatures, their purpose and how to identify them. She quickly added in the margins of her journal what Kevin had said about the night of his birth. Now more than ever she wanted to meet Kenatae and talk to him.

"And Miss Claire's Nini," Susie added with a resolve she had not previously felt. She wrote those resolutions in the margin as well.

The next passage caused her to smile - it was about their trip home with the giant Christmas tree. Simon, Timmy and Megan were not the only ones exuberant, loud and giggly. She had never seen Kat or Juls as animated as they were this morning.

As soon as they had arrived back home, Mrs. Coppersmith was there to greet them, taking their wet outer garments from them and shooing them into the Parlor. She had set up a buffet table loaded with large soup tureens and ladles, soup cups, platters of sandwiches, urns of hot cocoa, and an assortment of straight-from-the-oven cookies. It smelt heavenly.

Simon and Timmy sped through their soup and sandwich so that they could devote more time and attention to the cookies. They tried every cookie (some more than just once), and decided that the chocolate/peanut butter ones were the best. From their cookie smeared faces and their contented looks, it was evident that all of the cookies were well received by both of them.

After everyone had ample time to warm up and enjoy Mrs. Coppersmith's delightful offerings, Miss Pritchett called for everyone's attention. Rising from her chair, she walked to the far end of the room and stood next to a large group of storage boxes.

"In these boxes are our tree decorations, with the exception of the popcorn strings; they are over there," she announced, motioning with her hand to the open boxes near the fireplace. "As soon as the tree is in place, we'll begin decorating it."

Simon jumped down from his seat and ran to her. "Miss P," he fretfully told her; "I can't reach most of the tree. It's too big."

Smiling tenderly, she agreed. "I know; it's too big for all of us, so we only decorate what we can easily reach. The rest is decorated by those that climb the ladders. Okay?"

Simon nodded his approval. "Okay."

The men took the hint to bring in the tree. Mr. Sean invited Jared and Aaron to help. They were thrilled, and scrambled up and out the door, ahead of the men. Meanwhile, Miss Cora and Miss Ginger organized the rest of the children and adults into decoration groups. Simon and Timmy were assigned with Miss Ginger (no surprise there), and Megan and Dani were assigned with Miss Cora. Juls was assigned with Miss Thelma, Jose was assigned with Miss Bettye, Kat was assigned with Miss Fiona and Susie was assigned with Miss Claire. Susie was thrilled, although she had done her very best to conceal it.

They unpacked their assigned storage boxes, removing the covers from the ornament boxes and replacing missing hangers on the ornaments as they went. Miss Hilda, Miss Pritchett and Mrs. Coppersmith sat in one of the conversation areas, drinking their hot cocoa and watching the pageantry unfold.

Susie gingerly gave to Miss Claire the last of the ornament boxes. Only two of the ornaments were missing their hangers. Susie handed the hangers to Miss Claire, and she easily replaced the lost hangers with two new ones. All throughout their assignment, Susie had tried to find a way to ask her about Nini. No opportunity seemed to present itself, so Susie decided the direct approach was necessary.

"Miss Claire," she began pensively; "I've been wondering about The Cards, and if maybe I could talk with Nini sometime when she's here."

Her eyes sparkled with delight, and her smile was warm. "Absolutely, Susie dear. I am certain Nini would very much like to meet you. She will be most pleased that you wish to meet her also."

"Thank you," Susie replied, smiling and feeling better about her quest. "I am curious; did you figure out what The Cards meant?"

"No, ma chère; unfortunately I have not. Nini has promised to interpret it when she arrives. We must be patient," she responded, smiling kindly as she gently moved Susie's hair away from her face. "Everything has its own time. The trick is to learn how to recognize this so that we are not always so impatient. Some people never learn, and repeat the same life lessons over and over, n'est-ce pas?"

Susie had grinned and nodded.

The men returned with the beautiful tree and, with a considerable amount of effort on their part, were finally able to set the tree into the stand and secure it. Quickly and easily the lights were strung on the tree, followed by garlands of dark cranberry-red beads and then garlands of antiqued gold beads. Last, they carefully draped the popcorn garlands around the tree. Afterwards, the men joined Miss Pritchett, Miss Hilda and Mrs. Coppersmith and watched the next portion of the show.

Miss Cora and Miss Ginger assigned each of the children their own area of the tree to decorate, using the ornaments and tinsel. Susie was surprised to hear that they were each allowed their own creative vision. She had thought that was not a good idea, especially where Simon and Timmy were concerned. However, they did an excellent job. The only thing questionable was their placement, or lack thereof, of the tinsel. Instead of placing it on the tree one or two strands at a time, they tossed handfuls at the tree. Some spots in their areas were overflowing with tinsel and others had none. They were exceedingly pleased with their creations, and Susie couldn't help but smile. Dancing around her, they joyously asked what she thought. She had to admit it looked pretty good, told them so and was rewarded with hugs.

Allan Roy, JT and Dale each were perched on ladders, finishing the decorating as Miss Bettye, Miss Thelma and Miss Elsa handed up to them the various ornaments and tinsel. When they finished, Miss Pritchett carefully poured water into the tree stand with a little help from Megan, and a great deal of advice from Simon and Timmy.

Miss Hilda brought out the tree skirt, carefully handing one end to Miss Claire. They laid it around the base of the tree. Rather large, it extended a good three feet out from under the tree. Simon wanted to know why it was so big. Casually Miss Pritchett had responded that Santa Claus needed that much room so that he could leave a gift for everyone. Megan, Timmy and Simon stared at her, wide-eyed; all three seemed speechless. That didn't last but just a few seconds before the Munchkins came back to life. They squeaked and squealed with delight, their faces shining with joy as they peppered her with questions. She just laughed, assuring them that Santa knows where all children are, and whether or not they have been good.

Although Susie was amused by their joyous behavior, she didn't let it distract her from taking a closer look at the tree skirt. It was beautifully embroidered. Along the edge of the skirt was a railroad track, complete with a train engine, wood car, three passenger cars and a bright red caboose. On the side of the engine was embroidered "North Pole Express" in red and white striped candy canes. The people village was in the background, just under the tree at the far right edge of the tree skirt. There was a train station with people standing on the platform, waving good-by to the people in the passenger cars.

In the front and center of the tree skirt was Santa's village at the North Pole. Several buildings were prominent - Santa's home, the Elfin Dormitory, Santa's workshop, Santa's Post Office, The North Pole Train Depot and the Reindeer Stable and Corral. All ready to go on their annual trip was Santa's sleigh with the eight, famous reindeer. In the lead position was Rudolph the Red-Nosed Reindeer.

Elves were everywhere; some were carrying large sacks of mail as they exited the Post Office, and some were carrying to Santa's sleigh stacks of gifts that were already wrapped. There were elves playing in the snow, and many other elves entering and exiting the Elfin Dormitory or Santa's Workshop. There were elves in the doorway of the Reindeer Stable, on the fences of the Reindeer Corral and elves at the North Pole Train Depot. Several elves were hiding and peeking out from behind buildings, snow piles and trees.

Megan, Timmy and Simon had joined Susie and were thrilled at the scenes displayed. They were giggling incessantly as they tried to find all of the elves, boasting as to who would find the most.

The attention to detail and the skill that created it was incredible. Nana's embroidery was very much like this. She always had a waiting list of people who wanted her to make something for them. Nana had taught her to sew and to embroider, but her own skill level was nothing compared to Nana's, or to this tree skirt. Susie had said so to Miss Pritchett.

With a radiant smile, Miss Pritchett had thanked her, telling Susie that Miss Hilda and she were just two of the people who had worked on the tree skirt. About sixty years ago, she told Susie, her great-grandmother had started the tree skirt. Smiling, Miss Pritchett revealed that her mother and grandmother also added to it over the years. As a special project, Miss Hilda and she had finished the tree skirt just before Miss Hilda had left for college.

Miss Hilda smiled, telling Susie that they have used it every Christmas since then, and that it wouldn't seem like Christmas without it.

Mr. Sean held up the last item – the star for the top of the tree. It was made of blown glass and was nearly two feet tall. The glass was clear except for the points of the star – a dusting of a gold glitter was infused into the glass. The outer points of the star were heavily gold. As the gold dusting traversed up the star's ray, it gradually diminished as it proceeded inward toward the center of the star, coming to an end about halfway up the ray. Tiny lights formed a ring around the base of the star in which the top branch of the tree was inserted.

All of the children clamored to be the one to put the star on the tree. However, Mr. Sean was quick to point out that the star was very fragile and very heavy. They were enchanted by its simple beauty, pressing around him for a closer look. Mr. Sean held it so that each one could see it and touch it, all the while repeating that it was very fragile. Miss Pritchett had sweetly thanked all of the children for wanting to help, assuring them that when they were a little older, they would be allowed to take turns placing the star on the tree. Though disappointed, they all readily agreed.

Miss Pritchett then asked JT if he would do the honors since it was his turn. He grinned and then climbed the ladder. Mr. Sean handed the star up to him, and JT placed it securely on the top of the tree before carefully descending the ladder.

"Lights, please," Miss Pritchett said after JT had moved the ladder away from the tree.

Miss Hilda had slipped away to the door and was standing by the light switch. She smiled and flipped the switch, casting the room in darkness.

A few seconds later, the tree burst into a wonder of light as it seemingly came to life. The tree sparkled and shimmered like a rainbow jewel; but the most beautiful sight was the star, shining brightly and glimmering with just a touch of a golden hue.

The children's comments were an assortment of appreciation along the lines of "wow-wee" and "awesome" and "neat-o".

"It looks like the Star of Bethlehem," Susie whispered.

"Yes, that is what the artisan called it," Miss Hilda agreed, a hint of awe resonating in her tone. She had joined them, but Susie had been so engrossed with the tree that she hadn't noticed. "Miss Pritchett had this one made about twenty years ago when the old one broke," she added, finishing her explanation.

Softly the strains of "Silent Night" floated in the air as Miss Cora quietly began singing. One by one they all joined in, softly singing the old Christmas Carol. When the last note had been sung, they all stood silently for a few minutes just enjoying the amazing beauty of the tree. The room brightened with the sudden burst of light from the chandeliers, and the magic spell that the tree had woven was broken.

The grandfather clock had begun chiming, announcing it was now three in the afternoon, causing everyone to wonder what had happened to the day. Miss Pritchett thanked everyone for all of their hard work. Addressing Miss Cora and Miss Ginger, she reminded them that it was naptime for Megan, Timmy and Simon. Although they weren't happy about it (as was evident by their frowns), they didn't argue. With great sighs, they began shuffling toward the door where Miss Cora and Miss Ginger were waiting.

Miss Pritchett's eyes were twinkling far too much, so Susie had known that there was more to come. Sure enough, when they reached the door, Miss Pritchett called out to them, reminding them that they would be up late tonight, and would need the nap in order to stay awake during the movie. "Or have you forgotten that this is special movie night?" she asked nonchalantly.

Surprise was the first reaction that registered on their faces – they had forgotten. It was replaced nearly instantaneously with joy as their faces glowed. They bounced up and down, clapping their hands.

Miss Fiona chimed in, her voice impish and teasing as she announced that she had chosen one of their holiday favorites.

"'The Woganoks Save Santa'?" both Timmy and Simon squealed in hopeful anticipation. Clasping her hands in a prayer pose, Megan's blue eyes opened wide as a gleeful smile spread rapidly across her sweet face.

"That's the one," Miss Fiona confirmed.

The boys exuberantly burst into their victory jigs; Megan ran to Miss Fiona and hugged her.

Miss Ginger quieted the boys, and Miss Cora called Megan back to her. Cheerfully (for the first time) they went to take their naps.

Afterwards, Miss Pritchett excused the other children to their chores or free time, reminding everyone that tomorrow they would all be helping Miss Taryn and Miss Elsa with the other decorations. Company would be arriving soon, and everyone's help was needed.

The next portion of her account of the day brought a happy, contented smile to her face. Susie had stayed behind and helped to restore order to the Parlor. Afterward, she slipped away to the Library.

On a whim, or instinct (she wasn't at all certain which), she changed her mind and went instead to the Music Hall. It had been months since she'd played the piano – not since Nana had passed, and she and Simon went to live with Mrs. Crenshaw. Oh, Mrs. Crenshaw had offered to rent a piano, but Susie knew there was no place really to put one in her little cottage. Besides, Simon needed her more than she needed to play, or so she had thought at the time. For some strange reason, she now felt an overwhelming urge, a need really, to play but only to do so in private.

Slipping into the Music Hall, she sprinted to the piano. Simon and the others would be in the Library within the hour for Story Time, so she decided to use this precious, little time to soar again. That's what playing the piano had always seemed like to her. She would close her eyes, allowing her spirit the freedom to just play. Of course, she always thought she was alone; but most of the time Nana was nearby. She'd wait until Susie was finished before revealing herself, her eyes brimming with tears as she would hug Susie, telling her she needed to start recording the music so she could transfer it to grand staff paper. Susie always tried to explain that the freedom would be lost, but Nana didn't understand. Susie loved playing printed music; but what she called her "spirit music" was not meant to be repeated, nor confined to print.

Quietly, reverently, she had seated herself onto the piano bench, remaining very still for some time. With her eyes closed, her fingers lightly moved over the keys. Back and forth, little by little, her fingers brushed gently across the keyboard as her body began to feel the music within and all around her. She had inhaled deeply, slowly, and released her breath just as slowly, allowing her body and her mind to connect with her spirit. The connection came, the room melted away, and her fingers began pressing the keys. The spirit melody captured her; once again she felt that soaring sensation as if she was an eagle, flying high in the heavens above the earth.

Smiling, Susie nodded at the words she had written. Soaring was the perfect word to express how she felt while "spirit playing". She continued proofreading her entry, making certain nothing important had been omitted. That nagging feeling just wouldn't go away. She sighed. Maybe she'd figure it out by the time she finished reading.

She had noted in her journal that, for the first time, Simon had deferred his turn to choose a book in favor of Megan choosing one. Knowing that she very much wanted the book, "The Tale of the Singing Dragon" to be read, Simon had smiled at Megan, giving her his turn. Susie also had written that she was so proud of him, and that she had told him so. Megan hadn't expected such generosity and was elated, spending several minutes profusely thanking him. He had even tolerated Megan hugging him, but only for a few seconds.

Susie smiled as she mulled over the changes in Simon since they came to Glen Hollow. Her amusement deepened as she also realized that she, too, had changed. Much had happened and in a short period of time; most of which she still didn't understand, and had more questions than answers.

Suddenly she realized what it was that had been nagging her. "Home." She had written that word to describe Glen Hollow. She laughed softly.

'For some strange reason, it feels like home; and not just here in the attic,' she thought.

In spite of all of its quirks, oddities and mysteries, Glen Hollow had found its way into her heart, just as Miss Fiona had predicted. "It is home; I am home," she said aloud.

Susie closed her journal and returned it to its hiding place. There was a bounce in her step as she crossed the room, heading to the stairwell.

As she locked the door, she realized she was humming the song Nana had taught her two years ago. With a light-hearted laugh, she skipped all the way to the main staircase. Descending the stairs two at a time, she landed with a soft thud on the second floor landing, running the rest of the way to the Dorm.

Quietly she changed into her pj's and slipped into bed. She ran through her litany of prayers, yawned, and fell sound asleep as the clock chimed the two a.m. hour.

Chapter 29

TEAMWORK

The hanging of the evergreens and the decorating of the manor went well, just as the entire morning had. There seemed to be an aura of liveliness in the air, infusing everyone with a sense of excitement, anticipation and wonder. Breakfast found all, young and old alike, vibrant and chatty. Thoroughly discussed was the decoration plans for the manor, and the list of things yet to be done prior to the arrival of the family members and guests. Miss Taryn asked for additional help with the decorating, specifically she needed a couple of the men to assist with the heavier items and in climbing the ladders. Kevin and JT volunteered.

With a firm look at Juls and then Kat, she told them that she still expected their help. Juls seemed surprised, but Kat nodded her head in agreement. Juls shot Kat a quizzical look; Kat grinned. Juls knew what Kat had done. Although she really didn't want to work with Miss Taryn, Juls figured she and Kat would find some way to have fun. She smiled at Kat.

Miss Taryn had informed everyone that the transformations of the Foyer and the Music Hall into a holiday wonderland were scheduled for immediately after breakfast. The Parlor and the Dining Hall transformations were slated for after lunch. She was quite emphatic that no one was to enter any of the areas until the great unveiling, which would begin with the Dining Hall at dinner. Afterward, Miss Taryn had informed them, they would all proceed to each area. She wanted it to be a surprise for those not working on the decorations. Miss Pritchett pleasantly assured her that everyone would wait for the unveiling and would not spoil the surprise. Then, beginning with Simon and Timmy, she had cast a warning glance at each of the children, leaving no question in any of their minds as to whether or not obedience was optional.

'If it turns out to be half what Miss Taryn has hinted,' Susie thought; 'it'll be awesome.'

After breakfast, the volunteers followed their team leaders to their designated stations for their decorating tasks. Susie proceeded to the kitchen for her daily kitchen duty.

Upon completing her tasks, Mrs. Coppersmith asked if she would mind helping her in the kitchen all day since she had lost both Miss Taryn and Miss Elsa to the decorating committee. Although Susie had planned to start investigating the Inner Sanctum, she knew it would still be there when she could slip away later. Smiling, she told Mrs. Coppersmith she didn't mind. Mrs. Coppersmith grinned, hugged Susie and thanked her.

Handing Susie an apron, she commented; "then let's get cracking." Mrs. Coppersmith set her to work making cookies; dozens of cookies each of several varieties were to be made. She gave Susie a list, instructing her to start at the top and check them off as she completed each batch.

Stunned, Susie meekly stammered, "All of these today?"

Mrs. Coppersmith's laugh rang loudly throughout the kitchen. "Dear me; no. It would be nothing short of a miracle if you alone could accomplish that feat, Susie dear. But we do need to have them all baked by tomorrow noon. You'll have plenty of help later this afternoon. Miss Fiona and Miss Elsa will be joining us after lunch."

"Okay," Susie said as she reached for the flour. "I'm ready."

Mrs. Coppersmith left her to it, proceeding with her own tasks of preparing the food for the mid-day meal in addition to desserts for the holiday week.

The morning flew rapidly past. Miss Elsa and Miss Fiona arrived to help serve lunch. They took one look at Susie and laughed; she had little puffs of flour on her face, in her hair and on her sleeves. The apron, fortunately, had protected the majority of her clothes from receiving the same dusting. Miss Fiona cheerfully picked up a towel and began dusting the flour off of Susie.

All during lunch, the main topic was the decorating project. Even Simon, Timmy and Megan had been given "important jobs" (according to the Munchkins). Excitedly they recounted in great detail what they had to do. Susie was grateful that Miss Taryn had given them something to do that made them feel important.

With much work to be done still ahead, lunch time was shortened. Everyone dispersed to their assigned tasks with Miss Taryn's shrill reminder that everything had to be finished before dinner time.

Breathing a little sigh of relief, Susie was glad that Mrs. Coppersmith had asked her to work all day in the kitchen. Not only was Mrs. Coppersmith more pleasant, but Susie had the added bonus of the wonderful aromas and the sampling. While she was baking cookies, Mrs. Coppersmith was also baking cakes and pies. This afternoon and tomorrow they would be baking holiday breads and making candies, including sugar plums. Susie sighed contentedly.

Miss Fiona and Miss Elsa were busy tackling the dishes when she entered the kitchen. She offered to help, but they declined. Miss Fiona smiled and winked at Susie, telling her that there would be plenty of dishes over the next week that she'd have a hand in cleaning. That made Susie laugh.

Grabbing her apron, Susie quickly started the next batch of cookie dough. Soon she was joined by Miss Elsa and Miss Fiona, and they promptly started their own batches. One by one they checked cookies off of the list until they were finished. Just as her last batch came out of the oven, Mrs. Coppersmith told Susie she'd done enough for the day.

"Besides," she added; "Simon and the others will be looking for you soon. It's nearly Story Time, so off with you."

"You know about Story Time?" Susie asked, surprised.

"Well of course, child," she replied, grinning. "Everyone does. If it was meant to be a secret, it's a poorly kept one."

Susie shook her head. "No, it isn't a secret."

Mrs. Coppersmith chuckled. "Most of us have listened in a time or two. You've a real knack for it, child; and that's a rare thing."

Miss Fiona chimed in, "'Tis true; you have a gift for it, and it's a wonder to hear and to see." Her smile was mischievous. "Mrs. Coppersmith is telling the truth; we've all sneaked a peek and a listen, and have been the better for it."

"It is a nice thing you do for all the children," Miss Elsa nodded in agreement. "You've helped them to become family, with each other and with us."

Mrs. Coppersmith's eyes glistened as she said softly, "Like I told you before, Susie dear; we are a family. We look out for each other, and care for each other. Now, go tend to the little ones."

Susie smiled, nodding in agreement. Removing her apron, she glanced at the clock; it was three-thirty. Susie thanked Mrs. Coppersmith, Miss Fiona and Miss Elsa, hugging each of them before rushing out the door.

———

Sitting in Simon's chair, Susie yawned and stretched. She felt sleepy all of a sudden and wished she could take a nap. Unfortunately, Simon and the others would be arriving in about fifteen minutes. She yawned again as she rested her head against the chair. 'Simon is right – this chair is comfy-cozy,' she thought as she closed her eyes.

"Susie," the familiar voice called out to her. "I have missed you so. You've been so strong, and have been so good with Simon and the other children. We are very proud of you. There are many things I need to show you, but you will need to finish unpacking. And Simon needs his toys and his books."

"Nana?" she responded a bit dazed. Opening her eyes, she saw the old, familiar face. Tears streamed down her cheeks, spilling onto her shirt. "Nana!" she cried out, a mix of anguish and delight in her voice. Her arms reached out to Nana.

"Susie! Are you okay?" "Are you sick?" "Do we need to get Miss Pritchett?" "No," another voice said; "we need to get Miss Bettye." Still another voice insisted that they should probably get both of them, and Miss Hilda, too.

Susie's eyes opened to the worried looks upon their faces, realizing that she had only dreamed she was with Nana.

Simon crawled into Susie's lap. Anxiously he said, "Please don't be sick. I don't want you to be sick." He buried his face into her shoulder and started crying. Timmy and Megan both began crying, insisting they also did not want her to be sick. Quickly they crawled up into the chair with her and Simon, crying and begging her not to be sick.

She gave the Munchkins a group hug, insisting she is fine.

"Really?" came the worried reply from Kat as she leaned down, peering intently at Susie.

"Something's wrong," Juls flatly stated.

"So what is it?" asked Aaron. "You should tell us."

"I just fell asleep for a minute," Susie protested.

Simon looked at her skeptically. "You never used to take naps, and now you fall asleep all the time," he charged.

A quizzical look spread across Juls' face. "Have you been doing my chores? Someone has been emptying the laundry hampers morning and afternoon every day this week. And someone has been folding all the linens assigned to me. Is it you?"

Susie nodded. "Yes, I've been helping."

"Why?" Juls asked.

"Because you need the extra time to spend preparing for the Dance Recital," she answered. "You've been working hard on it, and coaching our little Munchkins here, so I thought I'd help. It only takes a few minutes."

"Thank you," Juls replied, her voice catching in her throat. She felt so humbled and amazed that Susie would just do her chores for her and not say a word.

"So that's why you're so sleepy," Megan touted.

"But you were crying," Jose softy spoke.

"And calling out to Nana," Dani added.

"What gives?" Jared adamantly said. "You were asleep, crying, calling out to Nana and reaching out to her. Something is bothering you, so tell us and maybe we can help." He paused, let out a short, forced breath and added softly, "We are a team, a family I guess. So, spill it."

Susie looked from face to face; their concern was genuine. They were frightened that she might be sick, giving them reason to worry that they might lose her, too. Suffering another loss was something none of them wanted to even remotely consider. She smiled in an attempt at bravado, and again repeated that she is fine; they had no reason to worry.

"I dreamed that Nana was here," she spoke with a sigh. "I miss her. I guess I've not unpacked our things in the attic because I didn't want the reminder that she's gone."

She smiled tenderly at Simon. "And that is unfair to you, Simon; and I apologize. Your toys and books are still packed, and you should have them."

"What if we all help you?" Jared offered. "That way, you're not alone."

"And it'll go much faster," Juls added.

Susie nodded, choking back the tears as a feeling of relief washed over her. "Thanks," she sniffled; "I'd like that."

"So, let's get started," Kat insisted, lifting first Megan, then Timmy and finally Simon from the chair. She extended her hand to Susie. "Let's go."

Grinning, Susie took her hand, and Kat pulled her out of the chair, surprising Susie at the strength Kat possessed.

Once Susie was out of the chair, Dani called for a group hug. Simon, Timmy and Megan quickly wrapped themselves around Susie's legs. The others gathered around in a huddle, sealing their unity, their family status with a group hug.

"All right," Susie said with a laugh; "as Mrs. Coppersmith would say, 'enough blubbering'. Let's go to the attic. We still have nearly two hours to get some unpacking done."

The Munchkins squirmed their way out of the huddle and ran to the Library doors, laughing and cavorting all the way. Kat, Jose and Dani grinned impishly before darting down the aisle in fast pursuit.

"Last one to the door has trash duty all weekend," Jared pronounced as he ran behind them. Aaron took off running, hot on his heels. Susie and Juls looked at each other and laughed.

"After you, "Susie said. Juls grinned and trotted toward the door with Susie just a step behind her.

Jared, as it turned out, was a great organizer. He quickly separated the boxes into three categories; Simon's, Susie's and the non-specified boxes. Next he further grouped each category, placing the 'fragile' marked boxes into a separate group. When finished, he assigned Simon, Timmy and Megan to unpack the non-fragile boxes bearing Simon's name. Grinning, he added that Juls would help them.

The Munchkins excitedly began attempting to open boxes, each one grabbing their own box, pushing and tugging at the sealed top. Juls stopped them, telling them they would open one box at a time. When everything was put away, then they would open the next box.

"Nah-uh," Simon protested.

"Yes, Simon," Susie intervened. "Juls is in charge of your group, and she is right. You need to make certain nothing is damaged or broken. You can't do that if you're pawing through without checking."

"Okay," Simon quickly agreed, smiling at Juls; "which one first?"

Juls returned his smile. "The one in front of you will do."

He inspected the seal, and then looked up at her. "How do I get it open?"

"With this," she said holding up a box cutter. "I'll open the boxes, and the three of you will be the inspectors. Okay?"

"Okay!" declared three happy voices in unison.

"Come on the rest of you," Jared said. "Dani and Jose can start unpacking the non-fragile generic boxes. Kat and Susie can unpack everything marked fragile. Aaron and I will handle the heavy boxes. I'm guessing those are books."

"Most likely," Susie acknowledged cheerfully.

Working carefully over the next hour and a half, they had successfully unpacked all of the boxes with the exception of one of Nana's boxes. It had been labeled 'very fragile'. Susie was in the process of gently emptying it of its delicate items. Nothing had been broken or damaged in any of the boxes.

After everything had been stored neatly onto the shelves, Susie considered asking Simon if he still wanted to donate some of his toys to charity, but decided to wait until they were alone. Instead, she had Simon choose a few of his most treasured toys to take to his room. He was very insistent on taking all of his things. However, Susie reminded him that there wasn't enough room, but offered to ask Miss Pritchett if they could all come to the attic room with her sometimes.

"That way, she said encouragingly; "we can all share in the toys and the books."

Simon readily agreed.

Kat wasn't so sure Miss Pritchett would allow it and said so.

Susie shook her head slowly. "A week ago I would have agreed with you, but I don't think so now. I think she will let us. Whatever time she allows, we'll honor it; and then maybe she'll allow us to come here whenever we want."

"I agree with Susie," Jared spoke firmly. "Miss Pritchett has always been reasonable. I think if we prove we're responsible, she won't have a problem with us coming here."

"Well," Kat said slyly; "does that include our being here now without permission, or our breaking the rules by having Story Time at bedtime?"

Jared laughed. "No, I suppose if she knew about either one she might not think we're responsible enough."

"I disagree," Susie quickly countered. "I think she would be pleased that all of you wanted to help me, and did help me, giving up your own free time. And as to the bedtime Story Time, I don't know." She paused. "Maybe knowing that everyone enjoys the Story Time before bed will make her decide to allow it. Then it wouldn't have to be in secret."

Everyone agreed, offering their own sentiment as to how Miss Pritchett should be told and who should be with Susie. It was finally decided that they all should go with Susie.

Juls began grinning mischievously. "You know, I kind of like the secret Story Time. It's fun. I mean I love the stories, but sneaking around .... I don't know. It just seems to make it more fun."

Kat thoroughly agreed, her eyes flashing with glee. "I'm so-o-o glad to hear you say that. Let's vote. Do we tell Miss Pritchett about both, or just the attic and ask permission for all of us to be here?"

Instantly the others sprang to life, voting to keep the Secret Story Time a secret. Susie shrugged. She retrieved the last item out of the storage box. It was heavy, rectangular and wrapped in a thick packing paper. Placing it gently upon the couch, she proceeded to unwrap it.

"What is it?" asked Dani.

"I know," Simon declared. "It's Nana's puzzle box."

Susie nodded, continuing to unwrap it. The oak box was an antique; according to Nana, it had been in the family for many generations. A beautiful carving of a unicorn decorated the center of the lid, much like the one on the cover of the Unicorn book. Funny, Susie thought, she had forgotten about it. Looking at it now, she remembered it well, and especially all the times she asked Nana to show her how to open it. Nana would always chuckle and tell her that, at the right time, Susie would know how to open it. Until then, she would not see the contents.

"It's beautiful," Juls whispered.

"Awesome," agreed both Dani and Kat.

"What's inside?" asked Megan.

"I don't know," Susie answered with a shrug, looking up at them. "Nana said I'd have to figure out how to open it if I wanted to see inside."

Simon forcefully nodded his head. "That's why Nana called it a puzzle box," he repeated.

"We don't have time now," Jared interrupted; "it's five-thirty. We'd better get going."

Immediately they all ran to the stairs, climbing down them as fast as they could, and sounding like a herd of elephants in the process. Susie carefully placed the puzzle box on a shelf high enough that would prevent the little ones from reaching it. Then she ran after the group, catching up to them in short order.

———

Jared and Susie were the only ones not surprised that Miss Pritchett so readily agreed to allow all of the children permission to be with Susie in the attic room. The only caveat she imposed was that it could only be on the weekends, and only after chores were completed.

The whole group excitedly and profusely thanked her, promising that she'd never regret it. They also hugged her numerous times before she laughed and told them, again, that they were welcome. Finally, she called their attention to the grandfather clock. They had less than ten minutes to get to the Dining Hall. They scurried out the door like rats deserting a sinking ship.

Susie remained behind.

"Is there something else, Susie?" Miss Pritchett inquisitively asked.

Tentatively, Susie answered. "Yes, I feel I need to talk with you about something, but the others will be upset with me if I do."

"Why would they be upset with you?"

Susie sighed. "Because they think you won't allow us to continue it, but I think we should tell you, and ask permission."

"I see," she responded casually. "And just what is it you want permission to continue doing?"

"I'm sorry that we've broken the bedtime rule," she answered repentantly. "At first it was just Simon and me at bedtime. Then Timmy, and then Megan and then Aaron found out and joined us. One by one they all found out and joined us; so we've been having Story Time in Simon's room every night. "

"Really," she commented calmly.

Susie nodded. "Yes, and it's really been good for all of us, not just Simon."

Miss Pritchett's smile made her face glow as her expression was one of tenderness and understanding. "I agree; it has been good for all of you."

Surprised, Susie replied, "You knew?"

She laughed a light-hearted chuckle as her eyes lit up with joy; "Yes, dear, from the very first night."

Susie was confused. "I thought we could only have Story Time in the Library in the afternoon?"

"I knew you misinterpreted what I said, just as you did with your morning assignment," she replied kindly. "You thought it through and discovered what your morning assignment actually is. Problem solved. However, the Story Time issue has been different. I suspect it's because you thought you needed a special bonding time with Simon, something separate from everyone. In reality, you have discovered that having this special time with all of them has been what you, Simon and they needed all along. Don't you agree?"

Susie smiled and nodded slowly. "Yes, it has made a big difference."

"Good. You certainly may continue to have Story Time at bedtime. It is entirely up to you if you tell the others that it isn't a secret."

Susie thought for a moment. She grinned. "I think I'll let them think it's still a secret. Some of them like the danger aspect to it being a secret."

Miss Pritchett laughed lightly. "Good enough. Let me know when you decide to tell them. Now you need to go on in to Dinner. I'll be there shortly."

Susie hugged her. "Thank you for everything," she whispered.

"You're welcome," she replied, returning Susie's hug.

"Miss Pritchett, is it all right if we continue having it after eight o'clock? If I change the time any earlier, they will know it isn't a secret," Susie requested with a hopeful lilt teeming in her voice.

Smiling, Miss Pritchett agreed. "It seems as if the later time hasn't adversely affected any of them. So, yes, Susie. As long as they are in bed, and lights out by 8:30."

"Thank you, Miss Pritchett," Susie gushed, thrilled that Miss Pritchett was so amiable.

Susie left Miss Pritchett's office, darted across the waiting room and out its door, swiftly making her way to the Dining Hall. Rounding the corner, she ran into Jared, who had obviously been waiting for her.

He grinned. "Told her, didn't you?" he asked non-judgmentally. "It's who you are, honest to the core. I respect that. So what did she say?"

"She already knew," Susie answered. "She said we could continue; she approves."

"See, I told you."

"You did."

"You going to tell the others?" he asked.

Susie laughed. "No; why spoil their fun. I'll tell them later."

Jared grinned. "It'll be our secret," he whispered, his eyes twinkling at the thought of a shared clandestine mission.

"Absolutely," she agreed.

They entered the Dining Hall together, both grinning from ear to ear.

Chapter 30

COMPANY'S COMING

"Company's coming, company's coming!" The Munchkins sang out, chasing each other and then finally tempering their exuberance by merely jumping up and down and clapping their hands in excited anticipation. Miss Ginger and Miss Cora tried once again to curtail their enthusiasm (but with little success) as they slowly guided the boisterous three out the door. They had another fitting for their recital costumes, and apparently were not the most cooperative of "mannequins".

Everyone could feel that little extra, special energy permeating the air, all due to the impending arrival of so many new faces. Simon, Timmy, and Megan were just a little less restrained in their jubilant expressions. Susie choked back a laugh. Encouraging them would not bode well for them or for her.

Having already given Simon, Timmy and Megan their hugs and her solemn promise to meet them for Story Time, Susie dashed out of the Dining Hall and ran to the kitchen. Several times during breakfast Mrs. Coppersmith made it abundantly clear that she expected Miss Taryn, Miss Elsa, Miss Fiona and Susie to be punctual.

"We've a hard morning ahead, lots of baking still to do," she had reminded them.

Most of the conversation that morning centered around two things; the company that was to arrive at two, and the amazing decorations. Everyone had already complemented and thanked Miss Taryn several times last night. And rightly so, Susie had thought at the time; she had been enthralled when she walked into the Dining Hall at dinner. That was just the first of the surprises. Each room had a different theme, and was absolutely astounding. Miss Taryn truly deserved the high praises – her talents are awesome, and Susie had told her so. Everyone did, even Mrs. Coppersmith.

Susie hurriedly entered the kitchen which was already a den of noise and a flurry of motion. As usual, Mrs. Coppersmith was handling several projects at once, and all the while barking out instructions to the rest of them.

"Good of you to join us, Susie," Miss Taryn intoned sarcastically, observing Susie's late arrival of a whole three minutes.

"I'm sorry," Susie responded.

"Don't worry, child," Mrs. Coppersmith told her. "You do enough work for two. Now get your apron, wash your hands and finish your cookie list. When you've done with those, you can start on the cupcakes."

Susie grinned. "Chocolate?"

"We'll see," Mrs. Coppersmith answered with a hint of a gruff tone, but her joyful expression completely belied her words. There would definitely be chocolate; knowing Mrs. Coppersmith, there'd be several kinds. She knew Susie loved any kind of chocolate; and, here lately, they were having the delectable treat more often.

Miss Pritchett made mention of it just yesterday when dessert was served. She marveled at the German chocolate cakes, the chocolate fudge pies, the Bavarian chocolate cakes and the Chocolate-caramel Turtle cheesecakes that Mrs. Coppersmith had so expertly made.

"Mrs. Coppersmith, your confections are the best; there is no question," she had said with a gleam in her eye. "However, I don't think I've ever seen so many chocolate desserts at one time." Adding quickly, she said, "Outside of our Homecoming."

In spite of herself, Mrs. Coppersmith had grinned, and her brown eyes twinkled. "Well, everyone likes chocolate; none more than me, except for perhaps one of us."

She had briefly glanced at Susie and winked. No one had apparently noticed, but Susie did. It had thrilled Susie that Mrs. Coppersmith had noticed her penchant for the heavenly confection.

Susie's reminiscing was interrupted. The noise in the kitchen was nearly deafening with the different timers sounding, the clanging of pots and pans and the array of cooking sounds. The ladies laughed and teased and shared information. And above all of this, Mrs. Coppersmith could be heard bellowing instructions, followed by quick and, sometimes, humorous replies.

Interspersed among the clamorous fray were the stories of years past, making Susie feel as if she had been part of the experiences. Mrs.

Coppersmith, having been here the longest, knew quite well those who were coming. Elsa, Joe and Taryn were raised at Glen Hollow, but so were Jason, Kyle, Zoe, Chad and Erin. This was a homecoming for them, and the stories bandied were hilarious and heartwarming.

All too soon it was time to serve lunch. Not wanting the camaraderie to end, Susie saw an opportunity when Mrs. Coppersmith handed her baskets of rolls to place on the food carts. Quickly she volunteered to help after lunch. Mrs. Coppersmith beamed with pride, thanking Susie for her kind offer. Unfortunately she firmly refused, citing that Susie needed to spend the time on her own pursuits. Noticing the disappointment on Susie's face softened Mrs. Coppersmith's approach; she hugged Susie tightly, patting her back lightly several times before releasing her.

Gently cradling Susie's face in her hands, Mrs. Coppersmith explained; "Susie dear; you'll have plenty of time to work when you're grown. Take the time to be a child. Enjoy the time you have. Now, if you want to spend your afternoon in here with us, you're more than welcome to do so. We'd love to have you. But you don't have to work to be with us. Just keep us company. Okay?"

Susie nodded.

"It's my considered opinion, such as it is, that you should spend the time on one of your hobbies. You've had precious, little time to yourself. And the others will be expecting you for Story Time at four," she continued in her motherly tone. "It's your decision, child," she added, smiling warmly; "you're welcome in here anytime."

Susie smiled. "Thanks, Mrs. Coppersmith; but I think I'll go to the Library after lunch."

"Good girl," Mrs. Coppersmith responded, giving Susie a brief, heartfelt hug before leading the procession of carts to the Dining Hall.

———

Susie sat quietly, watching the dark clouds move across the moon-lit sky. Every now and then the moon and stars would peek between the billowing storm clouds, granting a few moments of light against the veil of black. The long, thick branches of the oak tree swayed gently as the wind currents sailed all around it. Strong and sturdy, it was able to withstand much stronger forces than what was currently railing against it. The old behemoth appeared stark and lifeless without its covering of leaves, casting elongated, twisted shadows with each movement. Most of the movements were gentle and fluid, creating the image of an intricately, choreographed dance as the branches slowly fluctuated. A few movements were more forceful, as if the dance had become a duel, sword clashing violently against sword.

Susie watched as the wind renewed its rage against the old tree, and witnessed again its staunch defense. Smiling contentedly, she reflected on how the day had gone.

Nearly all the guests had arrived at two o'clock that afternoon. Mr. Henry, Mr. Sean, Sam and JT had taken two of the vans to Foxboro Station in order to transport to Glen Hollow those guests arriving by plane or train. Miss Pritchett had the remaining members of Glen Hollow waiting in the foyer for their arrival to give them a proper welcome. With each passing moment, the excitement and suspense increased, matching the rising sound of the voices in fervor and intensity.

At long last the vans arrived, and one by one the visitors quickly entered the manor, grateful to leave behind the frigid December air. Introductions were made as they entered, first the adults and then the children. Afterwards, family members gravitated to each other, hugging and kissing each other, and recounting their various travel stories.

A shrill, and very loud, whistle sounded, echoing harshly against the stone walls. It was Mr. Sean. "Now that I have your attention," his smile turned into a grin, deepening the wrinkles around his eyes; "Miss Pritchett has something to say."

Her smile was one of amusement as she nodded slightly and responded, "Thank you, Sean."

Looking from face to face, she welcomed them with a countenance that joyfully glowed. She smiled happily seeing all the familiar faces. "Welcome everyone. Thank you for spending the holiday here with us. The men will take your luggage to your suites. Mrs. Breslin, Ginger will show you to your suite, and I'm certain Aaron and Timmy will love to assist you. Claire, if you would be so kind as to show your family to their suite, that would be most appreciated. The rest of you know where your rooms are; they haven't changed. Please make yourselves at home. Dinner will be served at six."

Giving a little nod of her head, she signaled her welcome speech was over. The men began the process of carrying the luggage to the elevator, their owners following close behind.

Miss Ginger had quietly crossed the foyer during Miss Pritchett's speech, joining Aaron, Timmy and their Grammy. Grammy was quick to insist that Miss Ginger call her Grammy because everyone calls her Grammy. With a little assistance from Aaron and many eager suggestions from Timmy, Miss Ginger did manage to escort Grammy to the elevator and to her suite on the second floor. Timmy chattered nearly non-stop all the way, telling his Grammy everything about everything that is Glen Hollow.

Simon, feeling a little blue, looked up at Susie. His sadness nearly made her cry. "Simon; would you like me to read to you from your 'forever favorite'?" she asked.

He shook his head slowly.

Susie pulled him to her and hugged him. "Simon, I'm sorry Nana isn't here," she whispered, choking back her tears. "Timmy is still your best bud; he just needs a little time with his Grammy."

Simon returned her hug. "I know," he whispered back.

Simon's half-hearted smile slowly spread into a full grin. "You really want to read 'Maury Mouse and Carrie Cat: The Circus Comes to Town'?"

She laughed. "No, but I will."

Simon shook his head. "That's okay. Where's Megan?" he asked, just noticing she wasn't in the foyer.

"She left with Miss Pritchett a few minutes ago."

The crowd had dwindled down to just a few when Susie noticed Miss Claire was heading her way. With her were three elderly ladies.

"You are Susie. Oui?" the eldest of the three visitors asked.

Susie nodded slowly. "Yes."

"Ah; so I thought," she replied, standing nearly nose to nose with Susie, giving Susie an intense, perceptive scrutiny. "I am Anais Benoit, but you may call me Nini." Turning to the lady on her right, she stated, "This is my daughter, Lisette. You may call her Mimi."

Susie said hello, as did Mimi.

Next Nini turned to the lady on her left, stating, "This is my grand-daughter, Claire's mother. Her name is Michele, but you may call her Mema."

Again, Susie said hello, and so did Mema.

Leaning heavily on her cane, she raised her left hand to Susie's face, touching Susie's birthmark with her gnarled, bony finger. A smile slightly formed on her lips as her eyes flashed with delight. Gently she patted Susie's cheek. She repeated the same gesture with Simon, causing him to flash her one of his famous grins.

"I hear you wish to speak to me, to ask me some questions, n'est-ce pas." Nini stated.

Susie nodded. "Yes."

"Bon; I am most looking forward to it. We will have many opportuni-ties in the coming days, but for now I must rest. Come, Claire; show us to our room."

Miss Claire smiled appreciatively at Susie before turning to her great-grandmother. "Yes, Nini," she answered, leading the way to the elevator with Mimi and her mother (Mema) assisting Nini.

Simon had begun tugging on Susie's shirt, insisting that they go to the Library, and so they did. Curled up in his favorite chair, Susie decided that now would be a good time to begin having remembrance stories, starting with Nana. She began by asking him if he remembered his last birth-day. He did, launching into his animated and unique version of that day's events. They had laughed together as they shared their memories of that day, and the many other times spent with Nana.

All too soon, the Story Time Club members began arriving, ready for their next story. Susie got out of the chair and moved to the hearth, pick-ing up the books she had left on the coffee table for today's choices as she went. She sat down on the hearth, waiting for the rest of the members to join her at the fireplace.

Timmy ran to greet Simon, excitedly telling his best bud that he got Grammy to come to Story Time. He giggled, confessing that Aaron helped a little when Grammy gave him that "knowing" look of hers. Simon insisted that Grammy sit in his chair because it was the most comfy-cozy one. Susie was so proud of him.

Thanking Simon for his kindness, Grammy patted his head as she slowly shuffled to his chair and settled herself. Timmy rushed into his Grammy's lap, snuggling down and holding onto her as if she would vanish at any moment. She kissed the top of his head, lightly patting his back before moving him to the right side of her lap.

Looking up at Simon, Grammy smiled and held out her hand to him. "Come, Simon; there's room enough for you," she encouraged him, her eyes twinkling as brightly as her smile.

Simon didn't need to be asked twice; in a flash he was snuggled up to her, his grin as wide as the one on Timmy's face. A happy, contented look settled over Grammy as she closed her eyes and rested her head against the chair, each boy tucked gently under an arm. Aaron sat on the floor, resting his head against her right knee.

Quickly the others joined him. Dani moved the fastest, claiming the floor by Grammy's left knee, leaving the others to scramble for a place on the floor in front of Grammy. The ensuing scuffle caused Grammy to open her eyes and chuckle. She told them that she would be here a while; they would all have a turn sitting next to her, or in her lap.

With this assurance, Megan's forlorn look quickly was replaced with her usual sunny smile, and she sashayed her way to Susie.

"I want to sit in your lap," she insisted, then quickly added, "please."

Susie smiled, amused by Megan's sudden attitude change and responded; "Okay, but we're going to sit on the coffee table. The hearth is too far away."

Megan slipped her hand into Susie's as she tugged Susie toward the group. Susie moved to the coffee table and quickly slid the table a little farther from the chairs, giving ample room for those on the floor to spread out and get comfortable. She seated herself, and Megan climbed into her lap, barely giving Susie time to settle. Susie repositioned Megan, and smiled at their Story Time Club members. Laying the books aside, she told them she would tell one of Nana's short stories.

"Today's story happened a long, long time ago in a world far away from us," she began in a soft tone. "The kingdom of Daekatear was surrounded by a great, big sea filled with dangerous, gigantic sea monsters. The only way to get there was by magic."

She was pleased to see the mesmerized expressions on their faces, and their eyes sparkling with anticipation.

Grinning at the memory, Susie rested her head against the window pane, recalling how each of them had been captivated by the story. When she had reached the conclusion of the story, Megan, Timmy and Simon clapped and cheered the loudest of the group. Even Grammy had liked it.

Susie sighed happily, remembering how Grammy had thanked her for sharing it, and had said that it was a great story. Simon had proudly told her that it was one of Nana's stories. Grammy had playfully pulled at his nose, telling him that Nana had great stories. Simon had giggled, his eyes shining with joy.

Yawning, Susie closed her eyes as her mind reflected back to the Dining Hall, and her heart raced anew.

After Story Time, they all had walked together to dinner, which took a good deal of time since Grammy wasn't able to walk very fast. It was a few minutes after six when they arrived. As she had entered the Hall, Susie saw him. ... Kenatae. ...

Without being introduced, Susie had known it was him. He, Miss Pritchett, Reverend Tillman, an elderly couple and two other couples were standing by the fireplace. It was obvious that they were all well acquainted. As she entered, Kenatae had turned and looked at her; their eyes met, and she knew.

Simon and Timmy were pulling at her, wanting her to help them find where they were supposed to sit. The cause of their distress was that the tables had been changed. The normal dining tables had been placed further toward the windows, forming a long line, and were covered in crisp, white linen tablecloths. Serving now as buffet tables, they held a variety of meats, vegetables, salads, breads, desserts and beverages. The first table held the plates and glassware.

Seven large, round tables were stationed in place of their normal table and the majority of the space that the other tables had occupied. Forming a half circle, the tables were covered in satin cloths, embroidered with poinsettias. The table centerpieces were beautiful and elegant - a clear glass plate held a holly wreath (complete with red holly berries) and a large, red pillar candle in the center of each wreath.

574

A smaller table (obviously for the children) was placed in close proximity to the middle of the larger tables, forming an "e" shape. The cotton tablecloth was embroidered with all types of Santas, his elves, Mrs. Claus, the reindeer, Santa's sleigh, wrapped presents and Christmas trees.

Susie smiled; Miss Taryn had outdone herself again – everything looked picture perfect.

The ringing of the bell had broken through Susie's critique, and the room fell silent as everyone's attention was drawn to Miss Pritchett.

"Thank you everyone. If you have not yet met our newest arrivals, please allow me to introduce them. We have with us Reverend Tillman, Chief Standing Bear, his wife Spotted Deer, Kenatae, Running Wolf and Little White Dove who are Kevin's parents, and David Burgess and Dancing Sky Dove who are Samuel's parents. We are delighted that they are spending the Holidays with us again. After the Blessing, we will serve ourselves. The food tables are arranged so that we can have a double line to make the process faster. Our elders and our guests will be first, the children will be next and the rest of us will follow."

Miss Pritchett smiled and turned to Kenatae. "Kenatae, will you ask the Blessing?"

The elderly man nodded and said," It would be my honor."

For a brief moment the elderly man closed his eyes and placed his hands over his heart. Opening his eyes, he turned his face toward the heavens as he raised his hands upwards in a humble gesture.

"Great Spirit, we thank You for the many blessings that You have given. From Your abundance, You have given us this food. We ask that You bless this food so that it may fill us and nourish us. We thank You for the blessings of family and of friends. We ask that You bless this time of sharing so that our souls are filled and nourished as well as our bodies."

Everyone said "Amen" when he finished, and Miss Pritchett thanked Kenatae.

The Hall took on the atmosphere of a carnival. The flurry of activity, the wonderful aromas, the sounds of laughter and the various decibel levels of so many different conversations being held concurrently helped to foster that feeling. The very air seemed to be powerfully charged, filled with an exhilaration that infused everyone with a sense of elation, of exuberance.

Sorting through the pandemonium, Susie searched for Simon and finally spotted both Simon and Timmy. Quickly she crossed the Hall and snared them as they tried to stack their plates with nothing but desserts. They were a little unhappy that their planned menu was thwarted; however they were easily placated with her promise of desserts to their heart's content, but only after a proper dinner. Aaron suddenly appeared at her side, grinning. He had helped Grammy to a chair at the table and was now getting her dinner. He reminded Timmy to behave, telling Susie he would be back to help. True to his word, Aaron returned in time to assist Timmy to the table with his plate and drink while she carried Simon's.

As the meal progressed, the Dining Hall became so loud at times that it was difficult to hear the person next to you. There were a lot of stories, laughter and teasing bandied about, and Susie couldn't help but wonder if some of the tales were just a little exaggerated.

Near the end of the evening and long past the children's bedtimes, Chief Standing Bear rose slowly to his feet. Little by little the noise decreased as each one noticed him and became quiet, waiting to hear what he had to say.

As soon as the room was silent, Chief Standing Bear spoke. His voice was soft but strong, resonating with the strength of a true leader. "For many generations the Icori and the people of Glen Hollow have been friends. We have shared with each other the bounty of the earth provided by the Great Spirit. We have celebrated together and mourned together many times, here and at the Icori Tribal Lodge. The people of Glen Hollow have always had the same spirit as the Icori the spirit of sharing, of giving, of protecting the people and the land. My ancestors recognized this in your ancestors, and that began a great bond between our two peoples."

The elderly chief smiled fondly at Miss Pritchett. "An old Icori wisdom says, 'Wyee shona echee sotu naahkaho achi naiya achi daena. Kaiee tonah.' It means, 'One soul can change the world for good or for evil. The choice is theirs.'

He had paused for a moment, allowing the message to be absorbed by each person. "You, Eloise, have done just that. I have known you since the day of your birth. You have been the daughter of my spirit, and a daughter of the Icori. You and those who live here have changed for good the lives of many that have come through these doors. Like your ancestors, you are also a kindred spirit of the Icori. It has been my honor to know you."

With a quick nod of his head, he signaled he had finished. With considerable effort, he lowered himself back into his chair. As she watched him, Susie had realized that he was probably the same age as Reverend Tillman, maybe a little older. And like the Reverend, he had known not only Miss Pritchett but her family as well. Susie's heart had leapt with hope and anticipation – here was another potential source of information.

Blushing faintly from his praise, Miss Pritchett had thanked Chief Standing Bear for his kindness, and for all of their goodness to Glen Hollow down through the years. She affirmed that he and the Icori were not just friends of Glen Hollow, but were family. His smile spread across his peaceful face as he nodded in agreement.

Miss Pritchett had then turned her attention to the children, announcing that it was past their bedtime. And it was – it was nearly ten o'clock. Intrigued as they were with the Icori visitors and wanting to hear more stories, none had complained, quickly saying their goodnights. Of course, the fact that Chief Standing Bear promised many more stories in the coming days had helped considerably to circumvent any such whining.

—

Susie softly released a long sigh. The warmth of her breath caused the window pane to fog again, so she quickly rubbed an area clear. Outside the wind was still howling, yet the old tree was as strong as ever, seemingly unaffected by the onslaught of the blustery weather. That made her smile. It was a comfort to see that regardless of its circumstances, it remains unmoved, secure and steadfast in its place.

Absentmindedly, she began to write on the fogged pane beside the spot she had cleared. She wrote Nana's name, her mother's and father's names, then Simon's and finally her own name. She drew a heart around the names, encompassing them in the center of the heart. Closing her eyes, she rested her head against the cold pane.

Susie felt restless but didn't know why. As the icy cold began to numb her face, the realization came. She missed the bedtime Story Time. Funny, last night when they all had agreed to suspend the bedtime session, she had welcomed the reprieve. Now that it was a reality, she found she missed it and missed being with the others.

Yawning, she mumbled; "It's for the best."

They had all reluctantly agreed that having the Story Time at night would cause them to be caught. There wouldn't be any way to keep it from the visiting children. And if they knew, the adults would soon know. What Susie didn't tell them was that it wasn't actually a secret, the adults had always known. Jared had given her 'the look', as if to say it was time to tell them. She couldn't bring herself to do it; they liked it being a secret. The clandestine atmosphere and the camaraderie that it added lent an extra excitement that they all seemed to need.

After a few moments of contemplation, she knew what she had to do. Jared was right, she decided. She smiled; Jared was smart. And he was right.

"We'll start tomorrow – make that tonight", she corrected herself. Jotting down one last note in her journal, Susie closed it and returned it to its hiding place.

She hurried out of her sanctuary, to her Dorm and the welcoming warmth of her bed. Hearing the clock strike the two o'clock hour, she drifted off to sleep.

Chapter 31

SURPRISE, SURPRISE

"Wake up sleepy head," the words broke her dream, forcing her into the conscious world. Susie sleepily opened her eyes. Megan's face was the first thing she saw. She had crawled next to Susie and was nose to nose with her. Juls, Dani and Kat were all sitting on her bed. Panic overwhelmed her, thinking that she had overslept. Bolting upright, Susie sent poor, little Megan tumbling. Fortunately Juls was behind Megan, catching her before she fell from the bed.

"What's the matter?" asked Dani teasingly.

Kat grinned, thoroughly enjoying seeing Susie caught by surprise. "Did we scare you?" she asked mischievously.

"No, I wasn't expecting a group wake-up call," she answered as she tried to suppress a yawn. "I'm sorry I overslept. What time is it?"

"You didn't oversleep," Juls told her. "It's five o'clock." She had just settled the squirming Megan back to her position next to Susie.

"What are you doing up so early?" Susie asked, uncertain whether to be shocked that they could get up at five, or aggravated that they did.

Megan shrugged her shoulders as she tossed her head from side to side. "I just woke up all by myself. Juls had her light on, so I went to see her. She was practicing, and she showed me how to do ballet," she answered in her 'I'm-in-a-good-mood' sing-song manner. "And you know what?"

"What?" Susie responded, beginning the "itsy bitsy spider" tickle game they played every morning.

Megan giggled and wiggled. "It is fun," she declared amid squeals of laughter.

"Yeah, must have been," Kat admitted, feigning annoyance. "She and Juls sounded like a couple of hyenas. I can't believe you slept through it."

Dani nodded her head in agreement. "You were out like a light."

"I guess I was because I didn't hear anything," Susie admitted. "Hey," she said to Juls; "since when do you get up at five?"

Juls grinned, and her eyes flashed with devilish amusement. "Actually, I always get up at four to practice. I went back to bed just to annoy you. Well, to be honest, first it was to annoy Miss Cora." She shrugged. "And then you got the job to wake us all up. Lucky you," she added light-heartedly.

She laughed at the expressions on their faces. "Oh, come on; you guys know that's all over with now."

"That's right," Megan chimed in, defending Juls. She leaned forward, giving Juls a big hug. "You like us now."

Juls returned her hug. "I always did, sweet pea; I just didn't want to be here. Now I don't mind so much. I think I'm starting to like it here."

"Me too," Dani said with enthusiasm. "What about you, Kat?"

A clever grin spread across her face as she contemplated her answer.

"Well," Susie asked; "what's your answer?"

"Yeah; I guess it's okay," she responded, attempting to be non-committal.

Juls playfully popped Kat with one of Susie's pillows. "You know you like us, and you like it here," she challenged as she laughed.

Kat picked up a pillow.

"All right, no pillow fights," Susie intoned.

The girls looked at each other and grinned. The pillow fight began with Susie being pummeled by all of the girls.

———

Although the tables were positioned the same as the night before, the organization for meals was back to normal. Place settings were already on the tables, along with serving dishes ladened with the various foods prepared. Mrs. Coppersmith, with the help of Miss Taryn and Miss Elsa, brought in the pitchers of milk and urns of coffee. Miss Cora and Miss Ginger served the food for the children, setting their filled plates and glasses of milk in front of them prior to taking their seats at the adult tables. Apparently, this would be the new normal while all the company was visiting. But that was okay with Susie. It was actually better this way, she thought; they could see and hear each other better than at the long table.

It wasn't as chaotic a scene as dinner had been, nor was it quite as noisy. When everyone had settled in their seats, Miss Pritchett asked the Blessing. Afterwards, the Hall filled with various sounds: the clinking of serving utensils, flatware and glasses intermixed with laughter and conversation. Spirits were high, and the conversations, laughter and banter wholly reflected it.

Simon and Timmy had concocted a scheme in which to get their 'best buds' favorite book chosen for Story Time. Simon casually mentioned the book several times between mouthfuls of syrup-laden pancakes. Each time, Timmy would pretend he had never heard of it, but might possibly be interested in it. Timmy's efforts to refrain from smiling were laudable, but were completely unsuccessful. Coupled with their constant winks at each other, their ploy was obvious and comical.

Susie repressed the urge to laugh, choosing to smile instead while praising their desire to read. Aaron chuckled several times while watching their attempts at being covert. She noticed that he was in a particularly good mood this morning. Having Grammy here seemed to make all the difference.

'Nana would too,' she thought wistfully.

Her eyes focused, and she saw that Jared was watching her. His eyes showed his concern as he mouthed, "You okay". She smiled and nodded her head. He smiled back, then returned his attention to Mary, Miss Hilda's eight-year-old granddaughter. She had maneuvered her way to sit next to Jared, and was a little perturbed that his attention was on Susie and not herself. Her demeanor quickly improved the second he smiled at her.

"Susie, will you read it?" Simon insistently implored her.

"Please?" Timmy sweetly begged. He tilted his head slightly as he gave her a big smile, comically fluttering his eyelashes at her.

"Sure," she answered, smiling at them both; "unless Reverend Tillman or Chief Standing Bear is telling a story after lunch."

"Oh yeah," the boys eyes widened in surprise. They had forgotten about the promise of more stories.

Susie laughed. "I'm sure they'll let us know at lunch time. But you'd better finish eating. It's almost time for chapel."

The best buds gawked at each other, grinned and quickly began devouring the remaining portions of their breakfast.

Decorations in the Chapel were sparse in comparison to those in the manor. Nevertheless, they were elegant and beautiful in their simplicity. Evergreen boughs draped the sides of the pews, held in place by large, burgundy bows at each end. Garland strings of dyed wooden beads were artistically intertwined throughout the boughs. The rich hues of the cranberry, gold and silver beads cast a dramatic flair against the deep color of the evergreens.

Chapel had been really different this time. Reverend Tillman asked each of the children to select their favorite Christmas song, and everyone would sing along. Although most were traditional carols, there were a few non-traditional selections.

Kat started that ball rolling when she impishly requested, "All I Want for Christmas is My Two Front Teeth'. Simon asked for 'Rudolph the Red-Nosed Reindeer' and 'Away in the Manger'. Not to be outdone, both Timmy and Megan also asked for two. Timmy requested 'The Little Drummer Boy' and 'We Three Kings'. Megan's choices were 'Santa Claus is Coming to Town' and 'Joy to the World'. Grant and Mary insisted that they be allowed to choose a second song, too. Reverend Tillman's bountiful smile increased even more so, and the joyful glow on his face seemed to become just a little brighter. He wholeheartedly agreed, and extended the invitation to the other children and adults who had thus far only given one selection. As a result, the song service lasted nearly ninety minutes; but it was a great deal of fun, and everyone enjoyed it immensely.

Afterwards, the Reverend read several portions of Scripture. When he finished, he asked Kenatae to lead them in prayer. As soon as Kenatae had returned to his seat, the Reverend spoke about true Peace and everlasting Love, the reason why we celebrate Christmas. His message was simple, eloquent and resonated deep within each spirit. 'Waters deep enough that an elephant can swim, yet shallow enough that a baby can wade' - one of Nana's sayings drifted into Susie's mind while listening to the Reverend. A smile formed on her lips.

When service ended, everyone quickly made their way back to the warm comfort of the manor. Snow had fallen again during the night, covering everything with a thick, fluffy blanket. Susie had heard Mr. Sean say it was at least four feet, not a record but close. She also heard the men discussing the unexpected cold snap the morning had brought, and the scramble to prepare the barns for the onslaught of harsh winter weather. Already the temperature had rapidly fallen and was to drop down to twenty degrees by late afternoon, plummeting to near zero come nightfall.

Simon, Timmy, Megan, Mary, Grant, Dani and Jose had left the pergola and waded into the deep snow drifts that had accumulated in the east garden. Currently, they were in the midst of a grand snowball fight. No sides; it was everyone for themselves. They were all covered in snow; their laughter echoed, mingling with the plopping sounds of each direct hit of a snowball. Their romp didn't last long; Miss Cora, Miss Ginger and Miss Bettye curtailed their adventure, dusting the snow from their clothes and faces before hurrying them inside the manor.

Susie turned away from the window, sprinting to the Cloak Room. She put away her outer garments and quickly made her way to the Library.

Before service had begun, Miss Cora and Miss Ginger had stood on each side of the Chapel's interior doors, smiling and greeting each of the adults that entered. However, as each child approached, they leaned down and whispered, "All children are to meet in the Library reception area immediately after service".

After they were seated in the pew, Simon had asked her "what for?" Susie admitted to him she didn't know, but it must be an important secret since none of the adults received the message. His bright eyes had twinkled, dancing with glee at the idea of a secret. His smile widened into a big grin as he pressed his index finger to his lips, assuring Susie that he'd keep the secret.

Entering the Library she found the others were already there; everyone that is except for those involved in the snowball fight. Those already waiting had hoped that Susie knew why they were meeting here. She had told them she didn't know, but her hunch was that it had something to do with Miss Pritchett's birthday.

"It is today," she told them. No one thought to ask her how she knew, and she was glad that they didn't.

The Library doors swung open, and the stragglers were herded inside by Miss Cora and Miss Ginger.

Miss Ginger wasted no time, especially since they had very little of it before lunch was to start. "Children, today is Miss Pritchett's birthday. When Mrs. Coppersmith, Miss Taryn and Miss Elsa bring in her birthday cake, I want you to stand and start singing 'Happy Birthday'. The adults will all start singing with you. Okay?"

A chorus of responses including "okay", "sure", "no problem", and "awesome" were eagerly bandied by the group.

"Thank you for helping," Miss Ginger said, smiling appreciatively.

Miss Cora beamed; so proud of their children was she that she could hardly contain her enthusiasm. Removing a pitch pipe from her pocket, she played a note. "Quiet down and listen. I'll play it again and then start singing." She did, and they all began to sing. When they finished, both Miss Cora and Miss Ginger praised the group.

"All right everyone; let's go to lunch. And remember," Miss Ginger reminded them; "when they bring in the cake, stand up and start singing."

"And don't tell anyone. It's a surprise for Miss Pritchett," Miss Cora added hastily as the children began exiting the Library.

———

Susie was amazed that Miss Pritchett hadn't realized that something was in the works. All through lunch, Simon, Timmy, and Megan giggled and snickered, wiggled and squirmed like they all had ants in their pants. They kept stretching and peeking at Miss Pritchett, bouncing jubilantly in their chairs. It didn't matter how many times they were told to be still and to hush; eventually it started all over again.

Apparently there was enough noise and conversations that she didn't notice the oddly exuberant behavior displayed at the children's table. Or if she did, she had decided to ignore it. Either way, she seemed truly surprised when the cake was brought in and the children all stood, singing 'Happy Birthday' to her. The adults all quickly joined in the acapella rendition; when the last note faded away, they all began to clap. There were a few whistles and cheers from several of the men as well.

Happiness radiated from her as she smiled and thanked everyone. Rising from her chair, she rushed to the children's table, hugging each one of them for their wonderful rendition. As she returned to her chair, she also thanked Mrs. Coppersmith, Miss Taryn and Miss Elsa for the delightful cake they had made. "How in the world did you make one so big?" she asked.

Mrs. Coppersmith grinned playfully as she responded, "That is a secret."

Everyone laughed, and Mrs. Coppersmith handed Miss Pritchett a knife. "Will you do the honors?" she asked.

"I'd be delighted," Miss Pritchett responded, taking the offered instrument and beginning to make the first cut.

"Before you get too far into that, you might want to look at this," Miss Ginger advised as she and Miss Cora approached from behind her.

Miss Pritchett turned around. They were carrying a very large package, wrapped in the prettiest pink paper. It was trimmed in a purple satin ribbon with a huge purple bow. She began to laugh, delighted and completely surprised. "What in the world?" she said.

"This is from all of us, and I do mean all of us," Miss Ginger told her.

"You'll see as soon as you open it," Miss Cora added, responding to the puzzled look on Miss Pritchett's face.

The children began chanting for her to open it, and soon the adults joined in the chorus. Mr. Sean had risen and quickly retrieved the folding table, currently leaning against one of the sideboards. He placed the little table in the middle, ensuring a clear view of the present. The ladies set the present on the table and stepped back so as not to block anyone's view. Miss Pritchett carefully opened the paper, keeping it in tact as much as possible. Most of the children kept encouraging her to just rip it open. Smiling at them, she continued her efforts to not destroy the beautiful wrapping. She succeeded and opened the box.

Immediately tears sprang to her eyes, she inhaled sharply and her hand covered her mouth. "It's wonderful," she exclaimed; "It's absolutely wonderful."

Gently she picked it up, extending it to Miss Ginger and Miss Cora for assistance in holding it so that everyone could see it. It was an enormously large picture quilt of the staff and residents of Glen Hollow, past and present. There was one quilt block for each person. All staff (past and present) and all previous residents had two pictures in their blocks, one picture from when they first came to Glen Hollow and a current picture. Current residents, of course, had only the one picture. Each block displayed a handwritten message from the individual to Miss Pritchett in the bar across the bottom of their quilt block.

"How ever did you do this?" Miss Pritchett asked breathlessly.

Miss Ginger's eyes lit with joy as she responded, "With a lot of help from everyone. First we set the blocks for the message portion of the transfer fabric. For those that don't live here, we mailed it to them with instructions on how to write in the message block. We also requested that they return it with a current picture. After they had returned the transfer fabric and picture, we had all of the pictures transferred to the fabric blocks. Then it was a matter of choosing for each one the right fabric to become the frame for that particular block. After that, we pieced it together. And, by "we", I mean every one of us has had a hand in making this. Some helped with the layout, some selected the fabrics, some cut the blocks, some cut the strips, some did the piecing, and some helped with the batting or the final quilting and binding."

"This is truly the best gift ever. I am so amazed ... so ... just thank you all so very much," she said amid tears.

"Hey, that's me," Simon told her, pointing at a block on the quilt. He giggled. "And that's what I wrote. See, that's my name; and that is Binky."

He had slipped away from their table unnoticed and had maneuvered next to the quilt for a better view. Simon's fabric block was done mainly in his favorite colors (purple and lime green) in honor of his favorite stuffed dinosaur, Binky.

Miss Pritchett knelt down. Hugging Simon, she thanked him and told him he had done an excellent job. That opened the floodgates; all of the other children descended upon her, and Miss Cora and Miss Ginger. They all wanted Miss Pritchett to see what they had done. Each one received high praise and a hug from her.

"Cake and ice cream are now served," Mrs. Coppersmith announced. "Please take your seats because if we wait much longer, it'll be cake and cream that we'll be eating."

"Of course, Mrs. Coppersmith," Miss Pritchett readily agreed. The ladies assisted Miss Pritchett in folding the quilt and laying it onto the little table.

Conversations and laughter filled the room once again as they consumed the marvelous dessert. Everyone was happy; excitement seemed to flow all around, imbuing them with a sense of hopeful anticipation. Everyone except Kat.

Susie saw a strange, look come over her. Staring at the fireplace across the room, Kat appeared as if she had fallen into a trance. Susie's eyes slowly gravitated toward the fireplace. She saw nothing. She turned back to look at Kat, thinking Kat was just playing those stupid games again. Her stance was unchanged; her focus was locked onto the east fireplace. Ever so slowly her lips formed a slight, cunning smile, reminiscent of a predator finding its unsuspecting quarry. Hesitantly, and with rising apprehension, Susie forced herself to focus on the fireplace.

Movement! Something moved. Like a shadow, but not a shadow. It was translucent, but not invisible. Susie's heart pounded as adrenaline poured into her blood.

'What was that?' she asked herself. 'Did I really see anything? Maybe I imagined it. Kat set me up with that goofy act of hers. That's what it is,' she chastised herself as she turned to vent some of her frustration onto Kat.

Susie froze. Kat wasn't playing games. Nervously Susie watched as Kat glared at the specter, narrowing her eyes in a fierce stare as if in an attempt to intimidate whatever it was. Suddenly Kat turned her head, facing Susie. Avoiding Susie's gaze, Kat focused on her cake and ice cream.

Quickly Susie's eyes darted around their table, attempting to ascertain if any of the others had noticed. They hadn't. They were all laughing and challenging each other to snowball fights, snowman building contests and the like. Susie looked back at Kat, her countenance now cold and impenetrable. Susie mouthed, 'Talk to me.' Kat turned away, choosing to watch the adults.

A shiver crept down her spine, causing Susie to involuntarily shudder. Without reason, she turned and looked at Kenatae. He was watching her. His eyes darted to the fireplace and then returned to her. Ever so briefly he tilted his head in a nod so slight in movement that it was imperceptible to everyone except Susie. All the while his gaze remained focused on her.

Without thinking, she mouthed, 'Did you see it?'

His response was a fleeting smile before returning his attention to Nini, and her discourse on healing potions.

———

After lunch, everyone had gathered in the Parlor for a Story Time. True to his promise, Chief Standing Bear was ready to tell the Icori legend of how the Great Spirit had brought the Icori people to this area.

Simon was preoccupied with Timmy, and they both were determined to sit next to Chief Standing Bear, or directly in front of him at his feet. Their persistence was rewarded. Taking the opportunity granted to her, Susie wove her way around the adults and sat next to Kat.

"Kat," Susie whispered; "I want to talk to you about what you saw in the Dining Hall."

Indifferent, Kat kept her focus on Chief Standing Bear. "I don't know what you're talking about," she responded dismissively.

"Yes, you do because I saw it too. I just don't know what I saw," Susie insisted.

Kat ignored her initially. She waited a few seconds before coldly replying, "Leave me alone. I want to hear his story."

Astounded, Susie just stared at her. Kat didn't even look at her; never even gave her that courtesy. Anger started to build within Susie.

'What is with her?' she asked herself. 'She's the one who whines that no one believes her. Here I am trying to make sense of it, and she blows me off. What is wrong with her?'

Steaming mad, Susie's jaw tightened. Every now and then she would peek at Kat from out of her peripheral vision. Kat was unchanged - her entire focus was on Chief Standing Bear.

Susie sighed. 'I'll never understand her,' Susie mused silently, turning her attention to Chief Standing Bear.

She began to listen to the Chief's story. He was good. She enjoyed listening to him, and found that she had begun to relax. Soon she realized that her anger toward Kat had vanished.

'Perhaps Kat can't allow herself to talk to anyone,' Susie reflected. 'Maybe after all that's happened to her, she just can't trust anyone,' Susie thought, realizing that Kat needed to know she could trust Susie. 'And that level of trust takes time', she noted to herself.

Susie smiled; she would give Kat the time. In the interim, she would speak with Kenatae and with Nini. Somehow she knew they had some of the answers she sought.

———

Susie found herself with a little free time after Chief Standing Bear had finished his story. Simon, Timmy, Megan, Dani, Kat, and Jose had gone with Juls to the Music Hall to rehearse for Wednesday's performance. Juls had even persuaded Mary and Grant to participate. She was impressed that Juls had convinced them all not to reveal any details of the recital. When anyone asked, they would giggle, shake their heads and recite, "It's a surprise".

She had a good two hours before needing to be in the Library for their Story Time Club, and she had decided that she would confess to them that the nighttime session was not, and had not been, a secret. That way, they could also include Grant and Mary, which Susie (and Jared) thought was a good idea.

'Inner Sanctum, or Attic or the Library,' she mused. She smiled. None. Lacy was her decision.

Susie sped to the kitchen. It was empty as she thought it would be; it was a little early yet for Mrs. Coppersmith to start the final preparations for dinner. She dashed to the refrigerator and quickly removed two dozen carrots and a dozen apples. In short order she had cut them into bite-sized pieces (bite-sized for a horse, that is) and placed them into a sack. She washed the knife and cutting board, placing them into the rack to dry before leaving.

Walking at a fast past, she darted down the corridors to the Cloak Room where she hurriedly donned her coat, hat, scarf and gloves. Slipping

into the south corridor, she ran to the door. Although she knew it was
cold, her body was still unprepared for the reality of it. She drew in a
sharp breath as its bite seared through her coat. The outdoor thermometer
revealed that it was fifteen degrees; the howling wind made it much colder.

Susie covered her nose and mouth with her woolen scarf, carefully
making her way to the horse barn. She wasn't certain how the men had
managed to clear the walkways, but she was awfully glad that they did.
What little snow remained, though, had now formed into ice, making her
journey a little more difficult than she had anticipated. But that didn't matter. She was determined to visit Lacy and the other horses. They would
appreciate it, she hoped; but she knew they would really appreciate the
treats.

By the time she reached the barn, Susie's feet and hands felt numb; the
bitterly, frigid air pierced through her gloves and footwear as if they were
but a thin gauze. She stepped inside; immediately the warm air greeted
her, wrapping around her like a cocoon. It was a balmy 60 degrees in here
according to the thermometer outside the tack room door. Susie grinned,
removed her outer garments and laid them over the first empty stall.

Quickly she went to each stall, greeting the horse by name, giving it
some carrots and apples. She gently stroked each one, whispering words
of encouragement and affection. The image of Saint Nicholas popped
into her mind, of him visiting the children of the Netherlands and offering treats to all who had been good. Feeling uplifted, she chuckled and
continued on with her mission, saving Lacy for last.

Waiting patiently for Susie, Lacy was at the door of her stall. Like seeing a long-lost friend, Susie felt that same type of joy rise within her spirit.
Lacy nodded her head several times as Susie approached, welcoming Susie
before placing her forehead up against Susie's shoulder. Susie felt humbled
that such an amazing creature would befriend her so quickly.

'That is it,' Susie realized with wonder; 'I feel as if she is my friend.
How awesome is that?'

Lacy nudged her as if to agree. Susie laughed and pulled from the sack
some carrots and apples, feeding them to Lacy. Gently Lacy removed the
treats out of Susie's open hand, her velvety muzzle tickling her hand each
time. As with the others, Susie also whispered words of encouragement

and affection. All of the horses were sweet, and had garnered a spot in her heart; but there was something special about Lacy. Susie knew it the minute she first met her.

Now that she had seen the portraits, she was even more convinced. Thinking of the portraits caused Susie to realize something that she hadn't thought of until now – there wasn't a portrait of Lacy. Granted, Miss Elizabeth had passed on long before Lacy was born, but surely Miss Pritchett could have found someone to paint Lacy's portrait.

"Don't worry, Lacy," she whispered. "I'm not as good as Miss Elizabeth, but I'll paint your portrait. I just wish I could have had it done in time for your birthday."

Lacy snorted affectionately and nuzzled Susie's hair, blowing kisses along Susie's neck as her head moved down to Susie's shoulder and came to rest upon it. Susie reached up and patted her neck. "Thank you, Lacy," she whispered.

They stood there for several minutes, just enjoying each other's company. Finally Lacy pulled back and faced Susie. Tossing her head a couple of times, she blew a few kisses at Susie and moved deeper into her stall. Apparently it was nap time. Susie told her good night, returning to where she left her outdoor garments. Bundling up, this time she made certain that her scarf covered her nose and mouth before stepping outside.

———

The Story Time Club went rather well, all things considered. Grammy had joined them again, and this time Timmy and Simon had kindly relinquished their spots on Grammy's lap to Megan and Mary. The girls were pleased, of course, and wasted no time in scrambling into Grammy's lap, nestling up close against her. Grammy gave both boys one of her winning smiles, praising them for their generosity. They puffed up and strutted like little peacocks, thrilled at the attention not to mention the accolades.

As soon as everyone was settled and quiet, Susie told them the truth about their 'secret Story Time'. Although the group was a little disappointed that their attempts at a covert operation were not so covert, they were still delighted that Miss Pritchett approved of the nighttime session.

First, the Attic Room permission was granted, and now the night session of the Story Time Club. Things were definitely looking up, and their faces revealed their hopeful anticipation of better things yet to come.

Since it was no longer a secret, Susie proposed that they start holding it in the Common Area of the Boy's Dorm at 7:45 p.m. sharp. She was met with staunch opposition – they liked the later time. Adamant that they needed to comply with Miss Pritchett's extended deadline of 8:30 for the younger ones, Susie finally won them over. Beginning with tonight, they would start their new session, and in the open.

Grammy sat quietly smiling during their discussion. When they were finished, she spoke. "I am very proud of all of you," she commented. "You are showing yourselves to be fine, upstanding young people. I am very proud; yes indeedy, very proud."

Amid the giggles and ecstatic utterances, were the 'thank yous" from the older children, followed quickly by 'yeah, thank you' from the younger ones.

It was Dani's turn to choose a book, and Susie asked her what she wanted. Grinning, she said, "I think Mary should choose since she'll only be here this week."

Pleasantly surprised by Dani's generosity, Susie agreed, and asked Mary if she had a preference. Mary shook her head, stating that whatever Susie wanted to read was fine with her. Grammy suggested that Susie tell one of Nana's short stories which elicited applause, cheers and a little victory jig from both Simon and Timmy.

Laughing at their antics, Susie told them to settle down, and they dropped back down to the floor with a dramatic thud. She thanked Grammy for her wonderful suggestion. As her mind whirled around what story to share, her eyes rolled from side to side as her mouth wiggled in tandem. Simon and Timmy pointed and snickered, telling Susie (and everyone) that she looked like a bunny rabbit.

Everyone laughed, including Susie. Inspiration came in a flash, and she knew what story to share.

———

Dinner was over and Simon, Timmy and Megan had left, escorted by Miss Ginger and Miss Cora. For once, they truly didn't seem to mind bath time. Susie waited a few minutes hoping to catch Nini or Kenatae alone, just for a moment. Such was not her luck. After fifteen minutes of waiting, Susie realized that she was drawing attention to herself, so she slipped out of the Dining Hall and headed for the Rec Room. The others would be there.

She bounded around the corner, slowly jogged to the foyer and took the stairs two at a time. Upon reaching the landing, she caught the faintest essence of lilac. She paused. Automatically her body inhaled deeply, holding her breath to shore up her nerves. Looking to her right (west wing) and then to her left (east wing), she saw nothing. No one was present, yet the scent remained.

Susie waited briefly, expecting to hear the wind chimes or the music, but neither happened. Now the scent was gone. With relief she exhaled, and the tension that had arisen within her seemed to flow out of her body along with her breath. A sense of urgency began to compel her to return to the Inner Sanctum. Shaking her head, she said aloud, "Not tonight."

Rapidly, Susie strode to the Rec Room, determined not to allow anything, or anyone, to impede the first official bedtime Story Time. Stepping inside provided a welcome relief; everyone was in a good mood and playing a game of "Go Fish". They invited Susie to join them, and she wholeheartedly did. The time passed quickly, and the fun they had pushed the spooky events of the day from her mind.

It wasn't long before they were joined by Simon, Timmy, and Megan, fresh from their baths and in their pajamas. Miss Cora and Miss Ginger followed them into the room. Their eyes sparkled and danced; their smiles couldn't have been any broader had they tried as they announced that it was time for the bedtime Story Time. (Obviously Miss Pritchett had shared the new rule.) Miss Ginger quickly reminded them that the little ones had to be in bed by eight-thirty. The whole group thanked them, promising that they would keep the new bedtime rule. As they left, Miss Ginger and Miss Cora gave fair warning that they would return at 8:30 for a bed check.

Kat scooped up the cards, deftly getting them back in order. Jared, Juls and Aaron had begun shepherding the rest of the group to the Boys Dorm while Susie waited by the door for Kat. It wasn't a long wait, all of maybe a minute or two, then they strode to the Boys Dorm together.

———

In honor of it being the first open Story Time at night, Susie chose one of Nana's mini-marathon stories. Grinning, she told them that this particular one would take three nights. That seemed to please them. Although they loved all of Nana's stories, they loved the marathon ones the most, just like she and Simon. Simon began calling out names of stories, but each time Susie would tell him it was not the one. After several attempts to guess, she and the others finally convinced him to be quiet so she could tell the story. With a scrunched expression and huffy sigh, he fell quiet. His countenance quickly changed to delight once she began the tale.

"This story takes place on another world. It's very different from ours. There aren't any oceans or lakes. There's only one, gigantic river, and it winds all around the planet like a great, big ribbon," she told them. "This is a very special world, where time stands still, and everyone lives in harmony."

———

Quietly Susie laid in bed, staring at the ceiling. She was so very tired, but she wanted desperately to continue exploring. She had yet to do so with the Inner Sanctum. That urge had now returned, compelling her to get out of bed and go there. Her body refused. Her mind did not want to accept that her body needed rest.

She yawed. Closing her eyes, Susie ran through her litany of prayers. She yawned again, this one much longer and deeper than the first. Decision made – she was going to sleep.

She sent a quick missive to Heaven, praying that she would be granted a good night's sleep - one that would allow her to be refreshed and re-energized come normal wake-up time. Within seconds of her arrow of prayer, Susie was fast asleep.

Chapter 32

IT'S BEGINNING TO FEEL A

LOT LIKE FAMILY

Susie awakened two minutes before her alarm sounded. Smiling, she reached over and shut off the alarm button. She had slept the entire night through; no weird noises, fragrances, music or anything else spooky or nerve rattling happened.

'Well, if it did,' Susie grinned; 'I didn't know it. I slept great.' She bowed her head, saying a quick prayer of thanks to God for answering her prayer.

Bounding out of bed, she headed down the hallway, and was most pleasantly surprised to find that the girls were already awake. Even more amazing, they all were in the Common Area receiving ballet instructions from Juls. Apparently the expression on Susie's face must have been comical. Juls burst out laughing when she noticed Susie standing at the edge of the Common Area. That led to the other girls turning to look, and they also began laughing.

"Are you really that surprised to see them learning ballet?" Juls teased. "Or are you just surprised to see me teach?"

"No," Susie responded good-naturedly. "I'm surprised that everyone is awake so early."

Megan came running to Susie, throwing her arms around Susie for her good-morning hug. Susie readily complied, picking her up and twirling around with her before gently setting her down.

"We need the practice," Megan informed her, repeating what Juls had apparently told them sometime yesterday.

"Yeah; some of us aren't as co - or – din - a - ted as others," Kat grinned, her teasing meant for Dani.

"Well, some of us have other talents," Dani tossed back to her.

Susie seated herself on the couch, waiting to watch their lesson. Megan followed her, promptly crawling into Susie's lap.

"You can't watch," Juls informed her. "We're practicing."

"Practice is over," Susie answered pleasantly. "It's time to get dressed. Miss Cora will be here soon."

That was all Dani and Kat needed to hear. They ran out of the Common Area as if running for their lives. Juls gave Susie a perturbed look, but it quickly dissipated into a grin. Sashaying to the couch, she gracefully settled herself next to Susie.

"They'll never be ballerinas," Juls confessed; "but they are trying to learn. I really do appreciate their effort." Her tone was soft, and Susie detected a hint of affection.

"Why wouldn't they, Juls? They want to help you because they know it's important to you," Susie gently replied. "Jared is right; we're family; and Mrs. Coppersmith is right, too. Remember when she gave us the ice cream after Megan was hurt? She said we're family, and that we're to care for each other and look out for each other."

"And that is what they're doing for you," Susie added as she shifted Megan from her lap and stood.

Juls' smile broadened, lighting up her face, "Thanks, Susie."

"You're welcome," she responded as she turned her attention to the fidgeting Megan. "Come on, Megan; we need to get you dressed."

"I'm a big girl now, Susie. I can pick out my own clothes," Megan answered with a perky toss of her head.

Though forcing a smile, Susie wasn't able to hide the downhearted look that suddenly clouded her face. She would miss those fun moments with Megan. Her mind flashed to her first night here when she essentially told Miss Hilda the same thing, and the ensuing look of sadness on Miss Hilda's face. "Okay, Megan," she responded softly.

Megan saw her sadness. Her angelic face filled with remorse. "I didn't mean to make you sad, Susie. I'm sorry."

Susie hugged her. "It's okay, Megan; really it is. We all have to grow up sometime. You are getting to be a big girl, and I'm proud of you,"

Megan's countenance brightened. "I love you, Susie," she gushed, throwing her arms around Susie.

"I love you, too, Megan," she replied affectionately, returning her hug.

Megan began to dash away to her room, stopped and spun around. "I still need help with my hair," she announced. "I'm not that big yet."

Susie laughed. "Okay Megan. You just let me know when you need help, whatever it is, and I'll help."

"Okay," Megan agreed enthusiastically and ran to her room.

———

The rest of the day was busy, filled with Holiday preparations. Except for a short, two hour stint assisting Miss Hilda with folding towels, Susie spent most of her day in the kitchen with Mrs. Coppersmith. What free time she did have did not coordinate with Simon's free time.

Susie decided to use her time to write a letter to her best friend, Molly. It had been two weeks since she and Simon had arrived at Glen Hollow. Having left Mrs. Crenshaw's so abruptly, she didn't have a chance to write Molly beforehand and let her know where she was being sent. She had been so preoccupied with Simon and with settling in here, she hadn't had time to write, nor thought about it.

The words flowed onto the stationery, detailing Mrs. Crenshaw's search for a foster home and in the selection of Glen Hollow. She described Glen Hollow, relaying to Molly its amazing features such as the Library, the Chapel, the Conservatory with its awesome waterfall and goldfish pool, the Dolphin fountain and the Unicorn statue. She omitted the more unusual details and happenings; those were better left for personal experience, especially since it would sound as if she'd lost her mind. She chuckled softly, remembering all the sleep overs they had with their make-shift tents, flashlights and spooky ghost stories.

Going into great detail, she told Molly all about the other children. Well, not all – she kept the details positive, revealing just the best. Deciding she needed to save something for her next letter, Susie mentioned only a few of the adults, but telling her how many were actually living and working here.

Susie told her of Simon's reactions to the farm animals and the many trees at Glen Hollow. Knowing how much Molly loves horses, Susie told her about Lacy. She was certain that Molly would love it here, inviting her to spend some time at Glen Hollow during the summer break. She added how much fun they could have riding the horses, and maybe even going on picnics like Miss Pritchett and Miss Hilda had done so many years ago.

Most importantly, Susie told Molly, their plans to have a fashion house together is just as viable now as it had been this past summer. (She had spent consider time reflecting on what Mrs. Coppersmith had told Miss Taryn.) After all, she reminded Molly, they could spend summers visiting each other, and were going to be together at college in a few years. Until then, they would correspond by mail.

A smile graced her lips as a thought flashed into her mind - Miss Pritchett might occasionally allow her to call Molly, or even use the internet to email each other their designs and pictures of finished items. The thought was quickly penned, conveying the hope that had risen in her that this time at Glen Hollow would be nothing more than just a minor inconvenience.

Encouragement swelled within her as Susie shared with Molly that she had some new ideas and would include sketches in her next letter. Susie finished the letter, folded it and then carefully slid it into the envelope she had prepared. After sealing the envelope, she sat quietly, just holding it in her hands.

They had dreamed big dreams together, she and Molly; and they'd had so much fun planning everything from the pre-college days, then college and finally the ultimate dream – their own fashion house in New York City. Closing her eyes, Susie prayed that their plans would still come true. And she fervently prayed that Molly would come to Glen Hollow to visit.

"Please," Susie whispered aloud.

With a peaceful sigh, she opened her eyes. Everything seemed a little brighter, as if suddenly a light was now seen that had previously been obscured.

Susie left the Dorm, taking the precious missive down to Miss Hilda's office to where the outgoing mail bin was kept. She hadn't realized that there was a skip in her step, or that her face glowed, reflecting her happiness. Nor did she realize that she was humming.

Susie arrived several minutes early for the Library session of Story Time, and was very surprised to see that they had a much larger audience this afternoon. Grant and Mary's parents (Mr. Kyle and Miss Alice), Kenatae, Chief Standing Bear and Spotted Dear (his wife), Running Wolf and Little White Dove (Kevin's parents), Mr. David and Dancing Sky Dove (Sam's parents), Grammy, Miss Claire, Nini (Miss Claire's great-grandmother), Mimi (Miss Claire's grandmother), Mema (Miss Claire's mother and, of course, Miss Taryn's grandmother), and Reverend Tillman were all seated and waiting for her.

Strategically arranged were three comfortable love seats, several chairs from the Music Hall, and a dozen plush floor pillows from the children's Media Room. Reminiscent of the seating in an amphitheater, the floor pillows comprised the first three rows, followed by three rows of chairs, culminating in a final row with the three love seats placed side-by-side. Even a soft cushion had been placed on the hearth for her to use. A cheery fire had been made in the fireplace, creating a cozy ambience for their Story Time Club. Someone had gone to considerable effort, and Susie was certain Miss Hilda and Miss Pritchett had seen to it.

Simon was the first to see her. He jumped up from his pillow and ran to her. Bubbling with joy, he threw his arms around her.

"Susie," he squealed with delight; "look at what someone did!"

"I see," she smiled, returning his hug.

Not to be overlooked, Megan and Timmy came running, chattering ecstatically the entire trek to her about how surprised everyone is, and nobody knows who did it. They quickly showered her with hugs, vying for her attention. Susie hugged them both, thanking them for their great hugs as she guided them back to the fireplace.

Everyone greeted her as she approached, stating they all hoped she didn't mind their joining the session. Having heard of Nana's stories, they all wanted to hear one first hand. Their excitement and eagerness helped to fuel the lively antics of the children. Susie couldn't help but grin – she'd never seen such animation from Aaron, or Kat or even Jared.

Assuring the newcomers that they were all welcome, Susie then instructed Simon, Timmy and Megan to take their seats. Simon and Timmy darted to their pillows (which they had pushed together to form one, giant-sized pillow) and plopped down onto them. They stretched out onto their tummies, their elbows burying deep into the plush pillows and cradled their chins into the open palms of their hands. They were ready.

Megan wasn't. She kept trying to crawl into Susie's lap, ignoring Susie's requests for her to sit on one of the pillows. Mary had taken Megan's pillow when Megan left it to greet Susie. It was positioned directly in front of Susie, and it was obvious that Mary had no intention of surrendering it. The only available pillow was in the last of the pillow rows. Megan buried her face into Susie, beginning a plea to be held. Susie tried again to coax her into taking the remaining available pillow, but Megan just shook her head. Susie sighed as she turned Megan around, pulling her into her lap.

"Come sit with me, Megan," Grammy called out to her as she patted her lap. "Come on, child; keep me company, and make this old woman happy." Her grin told Megan she meant it.

"Is it okay if I sit with Grammy and not you?" Megan asked in a loud whisper.

Susie whispered back just as loudly, "Yes, it is." She smiled and kissed the top of Megan's head.

"Okay," Megan responded cheerfully, giving Susie a fast hug. "I'm coming, Grammy," she yelled as she jumped down and ran to Grammy, her curls bouncing with each step.

The adults laughed cheerfully, amused by Megan and her joyous antics.

After Megan was contentedly settled on Grammy's lap, Susie realized it was quiet; so quiet that the soft crackling sounds of the fire behind her sounded more like the popping of firecrackers. Everyone was looking at her. All of a sudden she felt nervous. Until she remembered why they were all here; they all came to hear Nana's stories because they were intrigued by what they had been told. That pleased her; and, strangely enough, calmed her.

She smiled, briefly looked at each face one by one, and began.

———

All through dinner Susie was happy with that bubbly kind of happy that makes you feel as light as a feather. During Story Time, she had watched their faces as she wove the chosen tale. The listeners all seemed spell-bound, their faces clearly revealing just how much they truly loved the story. It was a wonderful feeling to be able to brighten everyone's day a bit, even with just a story. Nana's stories were the best; Susie had always known that, but today served to prove it to her. As she spun the tale, most of the household had slipped into the Library at one time or another, listening for a little while before returning to their duties. It made Susie immensely proud of Nana. And she had to admit to her listeners that this tale is her all-time favorite.

Most of the conversation during dinner centered on the story that Susie had chosen, especially after Susie revealed that this particular story was one of a few for which Nana had created subsequent stories. Apparently, Susie confessed, when she was much younger, she had asked Nana a great many questions about the people in the story, so Nana developed little side-stories to answer those questions. Susie wasn't certain whether the adults or the other children were the loudest in their pleas to hear these stories as well. She grinned, agreeing to tell the three sequels.

Realizing that he and Mary would miss the last two sequels since they would be traveling home on Saturday, Grant asked if they could have all Friday afternoon as Story Time. Susie told him she didn't think the little ones could sit still that long. Miffed at the possibility of not hearing the complete story, Mary petulantly added her opinion, agreeing with her big brother that Story Time should be all of Friday afternoon because it wasn't fair that they had to miss the last two.

Miss Pritchett intervened, suggesting that beginning with tomorrow, the evening Story Time could start the first of the sequels with the second and third on Friday afternoon and Friday evening. She also suggested that they hold the story sessions in the Parlor since it would accommodate any-one, and everyone, that might wish to attend. Her final suggestion was to change the evening session to right after dinner, adding that the little ones would have bath time immediately after Story Time, after which they would proceed to bed. Everyone was in agreement, offering varied comments about how much better that schedule would actually be.

The only two dour faces were those of Miss Taryn and Mr. Dale, not at all a surprise to Susie. Eventually Miss Taryn managed to steer the conversation to her impending wedding. Once again the center of attention, Miss Taryn reveled now that the focus was where it belonged, at least in her opinion. The icy glare she gave Susie made it quite evident Miss Taryn had no intention of sharing the spotlight.

But, alas for Miss Taryn, the subject changed and with it the spotlight. Juls announced that she needed to meet after dinner with Jose, Kat, Dani, Mary and Grant. Surprising most everyone, Juls thanked all of her performers and her helpers for being part of the recital, for working so hard and for being so willing to suspend Story Time for the dress rehearsal. Quickly she added that dress rehearsal was to begin promptly at two tomorrow and needed all of them thirty minutes beforehand.

Juls sat down, immediately popping back to her feet. Simon and Timmy giggled, spouting that she looked like a jack-in-the-box. Everyone laughed, even Juls. Waiting patiently for the laughter to subside, Juls stood quietly. When the Hall had become fairly quiet, she reminded everyone that only those participating or helping were allowed in the Music Hall during the dress rehearsal. She thanked everyone for listening to her and gave a modified curtsey, one that Susie was certain Juls had practiced for curtain calls, whether for now or for when she was a prima ballerina. Susie smiled warmly; she actually could envision Juls performing as a prima ballerina. Deep in her spirit, Susie prayed a quick prayer that Juls would have the desire of her heart.

A round of applause broke out as most of the adults clapped for Juls their approval. Miss Hilda spoke loudly in order to be heard, saying that she and the others were so happy that Juls had chosen to perform, and to do so in a production. Miss Hilda showered Juls with praise for all the hard work Juls had done, from choosing and writing the program, to teaching the others, to designing the props and the costumes. Her eyes misted slightly as she concluded, saying that Juls choosing to include the others, whether performing or helping, was a wonderfully selfless act, and they were all most especially proud of her.

A few approving whistles and various accolades erupted from among the adults, culminating in another round of applause. Juls flushed, slightly embarrassed by all of the attention, and quickly rose to her feet. In an elegant sweep of her arms, she motioned with her right arm (the other performers) and then with her left arm (the helpers), signifying that they all be included.

Gracefully Juls tilted her head slightly, slowly bowing her head ever so dramatically, acknowledging and accepting their high praise on behalf of all of the recital members. And, just as gracefully, Juls performed a full courtesy before returning to her seat. To the delight of the children, the applause, cheers and whistles continued for several more minutes, echoing and swelling into a grand crescendo before finally subsiding.

Although her eyes twinkled mischievously, Miss Pritchett quite casually asked Juls what the program was for Wednesday. Juls was quick to respond, "The details are a secret; and yes, we will be ready. Our performance will start at three o'clock sharp, so everyone needs to be in their seats before three."

Naturally, the mere mention of the word 'secret' was the equivalent to throwing down a gauntlet. It became an undeclared contest, but a contest nevertheless, to see who could glean the prized information from one of the performers, or from any of the helpers. Everyone joined in the teasing and bantering, especially Simon and Timmy. They were in an exception-ally great mood. Their boisterous laughter, squeals and giggles were as energetic as their continuous assertions that they would never tell – no matter what, punctuated by equally vivid descriptions of the types of hor-rid atrocities which could not force them to tell.

All too soon dinner time had come to an end, and it was bath time for Simon, Timmy and Megan. Miss Cora and Miss Ginger made their way to the doors and waited patiently for them. They didn't have long to wait. Though not exactly thrilled, all three offered no resistance. Smiling up at the ladies, they marched past them and into the corridor.

———

As Juls and her performers quickly left for the Music Hall, Aaron chose to finish a model he had started and Jared headed to the practice room for a little sparring time with Kevin. The majority of the adults had gravitated to the Parlor for coffee and conversation. Susie decided to slip away to her attic room. She needed some time to think, to sort through her exploration activities that were currently, and temporarily, being delayed.

She needed a plan of action, and it came to her as she climbed the attic stairs. She would take Nana's battery lanterns to the Inner Sanctum.

There were only nine, but Susie was certain, if placed properly, they should provide enough light. Once in place, she would be able to see what the room actually is, and just what, if anything, needed to be done.

It required four trips, but she now had them all outside the secret panel to the Inner Sanctum. She held her flashlight so that she could find the switch in order to light one of the lanterns. It lit the wall portrait fairly well. Susie turned off her flashlight and turned on two more of the lanterns. She picked up two lanterns and carried them into the Inner Sanctum, holding them out in front of her.

The light from the lanterns illuminated a broad swatch in front of her, but not nearly enough to do a proper sweep of the room. Sadly, she did not have the time to explore tonight, let alone try to discern the most strategic place for each of the lanterns. She set the lanterns down just inside the door. Quickly she retrieved the other lanterns, placing them also just inside the door of the Inner Sanctum.

Turning her flashlight on, she proceeded to switch off the lanterns, stepped back into the Hidden Room and closed the door to the Inner Sanctum. Shivering from the cold, Susie darted across the Hidden Room and out into the passageway. Her fingers were so cold, she could barely feel the button as she pressed it to close the door. She turned and ran all the way back to the attic room.

After returning to her attic room, Susie wished she had taken the time to build a fire when she had first arrived. Even a small one would have been a welcome relief right now. But she hadn't, so she hurried out of the attic room and down to the Dorm. There she could get under her bedcovers and get warm before she had to meet the others in the Rec Room.

—

After Story Time, Susie continued the new bedtime ritual – a Hug Fest first with Simon and Timmy, followed by one with Megan.

Miss Ginger also had to continue her ritual as well; both boys were insistent that they needed their hugs from her and from Susie. It was quite evident that Miss Ginger loved the boys, and loved the bedtime ritual as much as they all did. Next the ritual continued with Susie listening to them say their prayers, and then tucking each one in bed. Of course, that also entailed their sharing secrets with Susie, or asking her for a favor of some kind.

After finishing with the boys, it was off to her own Dorm, and the same bedtime ritual with Megan – hugs, listening to her prayers and tucking her in bed. Miss Cora would patiently wait, having already performed their ritual while Susie was with the boys.

There was no doubt Miss Cora loved Megan, and Megan was very vocal that she needed both bedtime tuck-ins in order to sleep well. After Megan's prayers and tuck-in, Megan also would share secrets with Susie. Most of the time it was about Hazey and Mazey, but sometimes she had other things she wanted to tell Susie. Invariably, Miss Cora would have to cut it short – Megan was a chatterbox and had a very fertile imagination. Megan's eyes would sparkle as she would tell Susie "good-night", give Susie one last hug, whispering she'd tell Susie the rest later. Susie wouldn't miss either ritual for anything.

Normally, Susie would read afterwards (or do homework, or explore), but tonight Susie decided she was going to bed early. She needed sleep. To prevent Miss Cora from worrying, Susie told her she was a little tired, and just needed a little sleep. Miss Cora had smiled and nodded, telling Susie she'd make certain that the other girls did not disturb her when they came to bed.

"Miss Cora?" Susie began as Miss Cora turned to leave.

"Yes, Susie?" she responded, turning around.

For a moment, Susie hesitated, then smiled. "I just want to say thank you for all you do for us … for me. I really do appreciate you."

A surprised and pleased Miss Cora smiled brightly as her eyes began to mist. "Thank you, Susie."

Impulsively, Susie hugged Miss Cora. Though somewhat astonished, Miss Cora returned her hug.

"Are you okay?" Miss Cora asked, carefully searching Susie's face.

Susie nodded. "Yes; I just… sometimes … I guess I need hugs, too."

Miss Cora smiled affectionately as she moved Susie's bangs away from her eyes. "We all do, Susie. We never outgrow hugs. Now, get some rest. I'll see you in the morning."

Susie smiled. "Good-night, Miss Cora."

"Good-night, Susie."

The morning brought with it a renewed sense of hope, peace and strength as Susie awakened, refreshed and full of energy. Inhaling deeply, Susie released it slowly, centering herself and readying herself for whatever the day might bring. She felt more like her old self, back to when she and Simon lived with Nana. Sitting quietly, her thoughts drifted to Nana. She smiled, and then began to chuckle.

"Nana would love it here," she admitted, amused by visions of Nana exploring the old manor.

Suddenly a thought occurred to her – if Nana hadn't contacted Mrs. Crenshaw and made arrangements with her, they would not have been sent to her in Willington. Instead, they would have gone to Child Services in Stonebridge, and would never have been sent to Glen Hollow.

And, she realized with a shudder, she and Simon probably would have been separated. "Thank you, Nana," she whispered, amazed and grateful that Nana thought of everything.

The day flew by for Susie. It seemed as if it had barely started when it was nearly over. After breakfast, she had volunteered to assist in the kitchen, doing dishes, sweeping the floor, making cookies and peeling potatoes and onions. She hadn't realized that she was humming, and laughing and being overly chatty until Miss Taryn had snidely remarked that perky people were annoying.

True to her nature, Miss Elsa tactfully stated that she thought it uplifting to be around happy people. Her smile reinforced her words. To Miss Taryn's ultimate dismay, Miss Elsa asked Susie to pick a song, and they'd sing while they worked. After several titles, they landed on one they both knew and launched into a rousing duet.

Within seconds, Mrs. Coppersmith entered the kitchen from the larder, belting out the song in her alto voice, and in perfect harmony. Afterwards, they laughed and laughed, and Mrs. Coppersmith said she hadn't done that in years.

Miss Taryn ignored them, continuing to ice the strawberry cake. Mrs. Coppersmith walked over to her, put her arm around Miss Taryn and gave her a quick hug. Completely taken by surprise, a stunned Miss Taryn jumped, slinging the icing from her spatula.

Mrs. Coppersmith just laughed, her eyes crinkling with delight. "Here now, child; since when have you been afraid of a hug?" she teased. "Join us in song," she coaxed; "you've a lovely voice, and it's a shame to hide it."

Wiping the icing from the table, Mrs. Coppersmith added softly, "You choose, Taryn. Pick a good one that we can really let loose on and make the rafters rattle. You know; like we did when you were just a wee slip of a girl."

Taryn's sour expression slowly turned into a reminiscent one, and a genuine smile actually formed. With a silly grin, she began to laugh light-heartedly. "I'd forgotten about those times," she confessed.

"I haven't," Mrs. Coppersmith said fondly. She paused ever so briefly. She laughed as she remembered, saying, "You used to use a meat mallet as your pretend microphone. You would dance all around here, sliding this way and that, spinning and twirling all around."

Still grinning from ear to ear, Miss Taryn looked first at Mrs. Coppersmith and then at Miss Elsa. She laughed happily, and her eyes lit up like sparklers. "Yes I did, and it was fun. So … you know the one I want," she said with a cheerful lilt in her voice.

"Susie may not know it," Miss Elsa tendered.

"Then she can learn like I did," Miss Taryn responded gleefully with a nod toward Mrs. Coppersmith.

"'Tis true; I taught it to the both of you; so if she doesn't know it, she can learn the way you both did," Mrs. Coppersmith agreed.

"What song is it?" Susie asked.

All three grinned at Susie, answering in unison, "'Old Time Rock and Roll'."

Susie laughed. "That was one of Nana's favorites."

"Hit it," Mrs. Coppersmith said, and they launched into the song, singing and dancing all around the kitchen, using various kitchen tools as their make-believe microphones.

Lunch time was better than ever. An element of excitement filled the air with tomorrow being Christmas Eve. The dress rehearsal was on for this afternoon, and once again several of the adults attempted to persuade the troupe to at least give a hint. They remained united and steadfast that they would not spoil the surprise.

Everyone had noticed the cheerful mood of Miss Taryn. She was pleasant and complimentary, most unusual. However, Mrs. Coppersmith, Miss Elsa and Susie knew why, and Susie felt a surge of hope that she and Miss Taryn could be friends after all. One of Nana's sayings popped into her head: 'a leopard doesn't change its spots'; but she pushed that thought away, determined to remain positive. However, the real surprise came when Miss Taryn volunteered to assist Miss Ginger with the costume alternations for the dress rehearsal. It was almost as if someone had cast a spell, freezing them all momentarily. Miss Ginger quickly recovered, smiled graciously and told Miss Taryn she'd be delighted to have her assistance.

Miss Pritchett announced that since time was of the essence, Megan, Timmy and Simon would have their naptime in her office. Their mats had already been placed near the fireplace, and she would be there with them to allow Miss Cora and Miss Ginger to attend to the dress rehearsal preparations. The Munchkins were delighted, and their exuberance was met with laughter.

As soon as lunch was over, Miss Pritchett escorted Simon, Timmy and Megan to their temporary nap room. Their ecstatic voices could be heard long after they had left the Dining Hall, giggling and laughing while telling Miss Pritchett all about their plans for the snow people and snow village they were going to build come the first really big snow. By the list of names that could be faintly heard, they had enlisted several of the men to help with this project.

Susie chose to stay and assist Miss Thelma in rounding up the table linens since Miss Elsa, Miss Fiona and Miss Taryn were occupied with the rehearsal. After dropping the linens into the laundry bin, Susie went to the kitchen, helping with the dishes and in putting away the leftovers. It took a little longer with just the three of them; but, afterwards, Mrs. Coppersmith rewarded them with a mug of her special, dark chocolate hot cocoa, topped with a large spoonful of marshmallow crème. It was great!

———

Susie left the kitchen, strolling aimlessly toward the foyer. She was tempted to change directions and stand outside the Music Hall to see if she could hear anything, but decided against it. She would give Juls her due and not try to circumvent the surprise. Instead, she decided that she would go to the Library and find a book or two for her own reading pleasure.

However, she changed her mind as she approached the Library, deciding instead to start sketching Lacy. After all, she told herself; if she was going to paint Lacy's portrait, she'd better get it started. With dinner nearly three hours away, she headed upstairs to her attic room.

Grabbing her sketch pad, gum eraser and pencils, she settled herself onto the window seat and leaned against the wall. Closing her eyes, she allowed herself a few minutes to focus her thoughts, her energies, before attempting to create Lacy's image.

Her pencil moved furiously over the sketch pad, creating lines and shading until finally she had a fairly decent likeness of Lacy. Susie smiled at it, thinking that Lacy would approve. Even though it didn't have the same pop or vibrancy as that of Miss Elizabeth's portraits, it was still a good drawing. Next step was to pick a canvas, mix the paints and paint the portrait. She set her pad and pencil down on the window seat as she stood.

Susie stretched her muscles, attempting to relieve the ache that had developed from sitting so cramped in the window seat. "Definitely need a better place to sit," she thought as she walked to the shelves. Glancing at the clock, more out of habit than anything else, Susie did a double take.

"That can't be right!" she exclaimed. She ran to the clock. It hadn't stopped. It was working; and according to it, Susie had ten minutes to get to the Dining Hall, or be late for dinner.

Moving like a house afire, she ran down the attic steps, slamming the door shut as she tore past the threshold on her way to the circular stairwell. She took the stairs four at a time, jumping as she went and hoping that she didn't break a leg, or her neck, in the process. Landing on the first floor, she raced down the side hallway, rounded the corner into the west wing corridor and ran with lightning speed to the Dining Hall. She entered just as Miss Pritchett was about to ring the bell.

Miss Pritchett smiled at her, and graciously waited for Susie to take her seat prior to ringing the bell.

———

Simon's furled brow and Timmy's pouty expression had told her that they weren't at all happy that she was so late in arriving. Petulantly they informed her that they wanted to go find her, but Miss Ginger had said no. Megan, thoroughly cross with both boys for excluding her, hastily added that she had asked to search for Susie, too, but was also denied. All three began peppering her with questions; she quickly calmed their fears by telling them she had been drawing and just lost track of time.

Remembering his little debate with Miss Pritchett regarding tardiness, Simon's eyes danced with impish glee as he grinned at his big sister. "I thought you knew how to tell time."

Susie kissed his cheek and laughed. "I do, silly. And I wasn't late."

"You would have been if Miss Pritchett had rang the bell on time," Jared commented. His tone was flat and well controlled, but his eyes revealed the truth; there was definitely a mischievous shimmer in them.

Susie laughed, "Maybe so."

"Looks like we have a teacher's pet," Kat teased.

"Miss Pritchett's not a teacher," Dani challenged.

Kat shrugged. "Same thing. It just means that she's given special treatment. And I'm just kidding, so chill," she added before it turned into a hot debate.

"I think we all know that, Kat," Susie acknowledged cheerfully.

The rest of dinner went smoothly with plenty of light-hearted banter. Susie was pleased to see that all of the children were having a good time. It felt as if they had always known each other.

Even Grant and Mary seemed to fit right in with the rest of them. In some ways it was strange, and yet it felt as if it was perfectly normal. It was a good feeling, and Susie found herself smiling as she dwelt on it. And then she knew what it was. The thought struck, coursing through her mind as quick as lightning flashes across the sky.

"It feels like family," Susie whispered, awe-struck at the revelation.

Chapter 33

LOVE COMES FULL CIRCLE

Christmas Eve! Susie was excited and apprehensive. She lay quietly, listening to the "tick-tick" of her alarm clock as it steadily counted the minutes, fast approaching the time to awaken the girls. She had been awake now for just over an hour. Curiosity had gotten the better of her when she had first awakened, so she had slipped down the hallway just to see if Juls really did practice every morning at four.

As it happened, Juls was indeed practicing. Susie was amazed at her agility and her strength. Juls could hold a pose for what seemed an eternity, making it appear to be completely effortless on her part as if she were floating on air, not at all constrained or hindered by gravity. Slowly and gracefully her body shifted from one pose to the next in a seamless, elegant fluidity of movement.

Susie was in awe; it was no wonder Miss Kessler had agreed to teach Juls. What little she had previously seen, Susie had thought Juls was really good; but now … now Susie had to agree – Juls truly was gifted. And not just because of the physical movements she had just seen.

The cheval mirrors perfectly reflected her countenance as she danced, allowing Susie to witness the transformation of an ordinary girl into the ethereal dancer. Her passion and love for the dance sprang from a source deep within her being. Rising from the very depths of her soul, the sublime emotions burst forth, filling her countenance with joy and serenity as Juls lost herself in the spirit of the dance.

Quietly Susie had slipped back to her room, making certain not to disturb Juls. In her heart, she prayed that Juls would be the prima ballerina that she desired to be, enabling her to share her gift with the world. Susie smiled as she thought how great it would be to see her perform in all the major cities.

"Even better," she whispered into the air; "maybe Molly and I will design and make her costumes. That would be so awesome."

Her thoughts shifted to Simon. Today will be tough for him but not as difficult as Christmas. Their first one without Nana. Susie fought back the

611

tears that began coursing down her cheeks. She wiped them away, refusing to yield to them.

"I have to be strong for Simon," she chided herself. "Simon needs to have a happy Christmas, and I'm going to make sure he does. So no more tears. Be strong, no matter what."

Reaching over, she shut off her alarm and put on her slippers. The girls technically had five more minutes, but Susie decided to get the day started. As she headed for Dani's room, an idea burst into her mind. She would make Simon a photo scrapbook. She would ask Mr. Henry to help her make duplicates of some of Nana's pictures, especially the picnic one. Since his hobby was photography, he would know how to do it. He had volunteered to take the pictures of the dance recital and would be developing them. Susie felt a surge of energy flood through her, and she knew that this would be a good thing for Simon.

"And I'll leave plenty of room for pictures from the recital and Christmas," she decided.

———

There were all types and varieties of breakfast breads, doughnuts and other marvelous pastries available for their choosing. The serving table was so laden with the scrumptious morsels that there wasn't any space available for plates. A rather tall plant stand had been temporarily conscripted to serve as a table for the plates.

Like a magnet, the wonderful aromas and festive sights of the treats had drawn the children. Nearly drooling with anticipation, they all gathered around the pastry table, just aching to sample each and every one. Mrs. Coppersmith kindly reminded the children that first they had to eat the "real food" (as she had said) before they could devour the treats. The "real food" was more than welcome; Mrs. Coppersmith had made Belgium waffles with butter and hot maple syrup, scrambled eggs, ham, bacon, crispy potatoes, biscuits, gravy and a fruit compote.

"Did your Nana cook like this?" asked Mary. She wasn't trying to cause Simon any pain; she was truly curious what type of life he had before he came to Glen Hollow.

Simon's expression shifted from one of sheer bliss (he had been eyeing the waffles) to a scowl. Next it shifted to one of sadness as his eyes focused on Susie. She saw the beginning of tears. Quickly she hugged him, whispering that it's okay if he misses Nana. She admitted to him that she does too, and told him that Nana wants him to be happy. He looked into her eyes and could see she meant what she said. His smile was faint, half-hearted at best; he wiped the tears from his eyes as he rested his forehead against Susie.

"I'm sorry if I said something wrong," Mary contritely apologized. "I didn't mean to, honest."

Susie smiled at her, forcing her voice to sound normal. "We know that; right, Simon?" Simon nodded, keeping his face buried into Susie. "Come on; let's eat some waffles, and then we can pig out on the sweets."

Simon gave her a dubious look; he knew she was just trying to make him feel better. Suddenly he realized, he did feel better. He grinned, giving his big sister one of his famous, super grins. Grabbing her hand, he escorted her to their table, strutting like a little peacock all the way.

———

After breakfast, the entire recital troupe headed to the Music Hall for one last rehearsal. Although Susie had kitchen duty, she just had to speak with Mr. Henry. Hurriedly she wove her way through the adults, barely catching up with him as he exited the Dining Hall.

"Mr. Henry?" she called out to him.

He stopped and turned around. "You need something, Susie?" he asked pleasantly.

She nodded. "I'm making a photo scrapbook for Simon. I want to include old family photos, and photos from his life here. I need to make duplicates of the old photos."

His broad grin deepened the laugh lines on his face. "I think that is a really nice thing you're doing for him, Susie. I'll be glad to help. I'll be in my office. Bring me your pictures when you're done with kitchen duty."

"Thank you, Mr. Henry," Susie bubbled with joy. Without forethought, Susie quickly hugged him. "Thank you so much."

"I'm more than happy to help," he said, returning her hug. "Now run along. We both have work to do," he added, his tone as gentle as his smile.

She grinned. "Yes, sir," she replied, then walked as fast as she could to the kitchen.

———

The Munchkins were down for their nap, but they weren't the only ones. Juls had insisted that all of the performers rest after lunch, and meet in the Music Hall at two o'clock sharp. And to accommodate this schedule change, lunch time had been moved to eleven. Susie couldn't help but smile – Juls really was a commanding presence when she chose to be.

Mrs. Coppersmith had given Susie a respite from afternoon kitchen duty. She, too, thought Susie's photo scrapbook for Simon was a really good idea, and had fiercely hugged Susie for being such a good sister. Susie had tried to assure Mrs. Coppersmith she could do kitchen duty after lunch and still have plenty of time to put the scrapbook together, but Mrs. Coppersmith would not hear of it. She insisted, saying that her mind was made up and no use to try to change it. That made Susie laugh, and had made the morning kitchen duty seem shorter than ever.

So, after lunch, Susie first went to Mr. Henry's office. He had told her at lunch that the pictures were ready and on his desk – she could pick them up any time. And they were - the pictures were waiting for her on his desk in a big, brown envelope with her name on it.

Carefully she removed them. He had done a great job, not that he wouldn't. After returning the pictures to the envelope, Susie picked up a pen and wrote a thank-you note to him. She hurried out the door and headed to the attic room at as fast a pace as possible, just shy of what could be deemed running.

Spreading the pictures out on Nana's coffee table, Susie began the process of placing them in order, beginning with a picture of all four of them. Next she chose a series of pictures of Mommy during various stages of her pregnancy with Simon, some she was in and some Daddy and Nana were also included. These were followed by the pictures of Simon's debut at the hospital and several pictures shortly after his birth. Culminating this series was the picture of the picnic. Now she chose a series of pictures portraying special times in their life with Nana; birthdays, day trips, New Year's Day, Valentine's Day, Easter, Fourth of July, Halloween, Thanksgiving and Christmas. Finally she chose a series of candid pictures that captured their everyday life with Nana.

Slowly a smile adorned her face as she reviewed her handiwork. Gently her fingers touched the images of Nana and her parents. Tears flooded her eyes. She missed Nana, and she missed Mommy and Daddy. Digging through Nana's photo albums, and searching for the right ones to include in his scrapbook had proven to be a daunting task for her both physically and emotionally.

Now that she had actually sorted through the chosen ones and placed them in a timeline, her mind was forced to remember many things long forgotten. She now could actually remember the faces of her parents, the sound of their voices and of their laughter. Mommy loved to sing and dance, and Daddy loved to make them laugh. She could remember all of the games they played, the stories they told and how much Mommy and Daddy had loved them. Her tears flowed fast and hot, streaming down her face in a salty torrent.

"Why now?" Susie asked between sobs, the sound of her voice filling her sanctuary.

"Why couldn't I remember before? Why now when I need to be strong for Simon? He can't see me cry. He needs to be able to depend on me!" she shouted.

Grabbing Nana's afghan, Susie buried her face into it, relinquishing herself to the sorrow she had kept buried for so long. Finally the crying ended as the overwhelming sense of grief subsided, leaving her with a wretched case of the hiccups.

"Great," she sighed between hiccups; "just great."

Several minutes later, her hiccups abated, and she felt so very tired. Susie breathed deeply and slowly exhaled, trying to regain her energy. She stared into the fire, now just a scattering of dying embers. Nana loved this stage of a fire. To her, the embers were the prettiest stage due to the different colors of red, and yellow and blue of the flames coupled with the various grays of the ashes. Nana would smile at the dying embers, and just watch them for the longest time before adding another log or extinguishing the fire altogether.

Another memory now surfaced. It was of Nana begging Susie not to shut her out, to allow her to help Susie grieve the loss of her parents. But Susie, at just seven, did not understand the need to grieve. All she knew at that time was that Mommy and Daddy were gone. She didn't want to talk about it; she didn't want to hurt anymore. She wanted the pain to go away, and she found a way to do just that. She walled everything deep inside her soul, refusing to remember. And the pain went away. Until now when the wall broke, and the memories all came pouring out, flooding her conscious mind.

Bittersweet was the smile that graced her lips. Nana had tried to help. She should have listened to Nana. "Thank you, Nana," she whispered as her tears flowed silently. "Thank you for all that you did for me and for Simon. I'm sorry I never understood how much you really did for us. I'm sorry I never got to tell you how much I love you."

Suddenly her mind envisioned all of the happy moments with Nana, of the hugs and laughter, of the games and playtime, of the cuddling and the diving into Nana's bed for comfort and security during thunderstorms. Susie remembered all of her secrets shared with Nana, of her hopes and dreams told to Nana over milk and cookies. Vivid recollections flooded her mind of piano lessons with Nana, of cooking and baking with her and of their many shopping trips. Susie remembered the endless patience and of the hours of Nana teaching her to sew, to embroider, to knit and crochet. She remembered all of the "I love you" she had said, and of those that Nana had said to her. Susie began to laugh, light-hearted and carefree, as a sensation of being hugged enveloped her.

"Thank you, Nana," she giggled aloud. "I needed that."

Her smile broadened as she realized something else. "Simon needs this," she spoke softly, looking at the photo scrapbook. "He needs to remember you, Nana; and he needs to learn of Mommy and Daddy, and to make good memories of this place. Thank you, Nana; help me to help him."

Susie wrapped her gift to Simon. She had chosen from Nana's stash of supplies white tissue paper, and had carefully drawn images of Binky all over it. She finished it with a purple bow and a lime green ribbon, also retrieved from Nana's stash. As much as she wanted to give it to him for Christmas, she knew she couldn't. Out of consideration for the others, it would have to wait until her birthday. That would please Simon to no end – his receiving a gift from her on her birthday.

As she wrapped his gift, she had kept a close watch on the clock. She absolutely did not want to be late for the recital. She had asked Simon once during the bedtime tuck-in ritual what the recital was going to be. He remained true to his promise to Juls, slowly shaking his head and telling Susie it was a secret he could not share. He seemed a little sad so Susie had smiled, telling him not to worry: it was okay to keep this secret. His eyes sparkled, and he fiercely hugged her. Then he had confessed that he really was having fun, and that he couldn't wait for Susie to see it.

Quickly she descended the stairs, making her way to the Music Hall. There was still plenty of time, but she definitely wanted to be front and center so that Simon would see her.

When she entered the Music Hall, Susie was surprised to see that everyone was already seated. Fortunately, Jared and Aaron had saved her a seat. They, too, made certain that they were front and center, desiring to show their avid support for the recital troupe.

The room was abuzz with conversations reminiscing about the many pageants and recitals of yesteryear. The anticipation of what was to come filled the air with an energy that swept everyone up in its wake. Apparently, though, this was the first in the history of Glen Hollow in which the audience did not have advance knowledge of what the Program was, creating an air of mystery, suspense and curiosity among the audience.

Overhead the lights began to flicker, signaling to all that the recital was about to begin. Everyone quieted, waiting eagerly for the entertainment to commence. Miss Pritchett announced that in order to save time, Juls had requested that everyone hold their applause until the end of the recital. Then she lowered the lights to just a dim glow, giving to Miss Ginger her cue. In the center of the stage, Miss Ginger stepped out from behind the curtain. She carried a very large scroll, very much like the town criers carried centuries ago when announcing a royal proclamation.

Waiting until all eyes were focused upon her, Miss Ginger unfurled the scroll and began reading. "Hear ye, hear ye. Come one, come all, and give an ear to the story of old. See how love, and mercy and peace does unfold." She bowed, and stepped back behind the curtain.

The house lights completely darkened, and immediately gentle strains of music from the harp floated in the air, peaceful and uplifting. A few minutes later, the piano softly accompanied the harp, uniting with its heavenly sound. Several minutes later, the pleasing sound of a flute could now be heard as it quietly blended with the harp and the piano. Together they created a sense of harmony and serenity as the music slowly intensified before ebbing to a point where it was barely audible.

As the curtain drew back, the voice of a narrator was heard. It was Mr. Sean. He began reading a passage from Scripture. First he read several portions of the Old Testament. Next he read the beginning of the passage when the Angel Gabriel came to visit Mary.

A spotlight penetrated the darkness, illuminating the far right corner of the stage. Gabriel (Jose) was standing on a "boulder" (a plywood cutout painted to resemble a boulder), and below him was the young Mary (Kat). Gabriel recited his Scripture words to Mary, and Mary recited her Scripture words to him. Afterwards, the spotlight narrowed, hiding Gabriel from view. Mary turned toward the audience, but her face was turned upward to Heaven as if in supplication. She continued with her lines, reciting the passage called "Mary's Song". When the passage was done, the light disappeared.

Mr. Sean read the next passage; Mary and Joseph en route to Bethlehem. As he read, the spotlight again flashed onto the stage, revealing Mary (Kat) on a "donkey", and being led by Joseph (Grant). Actually, the donkey was a wooden cutout, painted very realistically, being moved along by Kat as they progressed across the stage. The backdrop had Bethlehem painted in the distance, simulating that they had a long, hard journey ahead.

The spotlight again disappeared, and Mr. Sean moved on to the next passage – no room at the inn. When next the light burst upon the stage, it revealed the little town of Bethlehem, and the inn where Joseph and Mary had sought lodging for the night. JT served as the innkeeper, and that produced a chorus of laughter. First turning the young couple away, the innkeeper felt remorse and relented. He offered them shelter in his manger and led them to the humble shelter. Once again, the spotlight vanished, leaving the stage in darkness.

Mr. Sean read a short narrative about the young couple, of their preparing the manger for their stay and for the baby Jesus. The spotlight came on again, illuminating one small scene – the manger. The backdrop revealed a small wooden stall with hay on the floor all around them, and with the animals in the stalls on either side of Mary and Joseph. The baby Jesus (one of Megan's dolls) was wrapped in a rough looking cloth, being held by Mary (Kat) as Joseph (Grant) lovingly looked upon the child. High above the manger in the night sky was the Star of Bethlehem. As Mr. Sean read the next portion of the passage, Mary placed the child into a small feed trough, being used as a makeshift crib. The spotlight ceased, and the stage fell back into darkness.

The next passage told of the shepherds in the fields nearby who were watching their flock, and of the visit by the choir of angels. The spotlight flared with a wide angle, lighting most of the stage. The upper backdrop was of a starry night sky, dark as ebony with twinkling little stars (ornamental lights) that glistened as brightly as diamonds. In the center of the night sky was an amazing portent. Bursting through the darkness was a brilliant, white light, revealing a throng of angels, painted to appear as though singing praises to 'God in the Highest'.

In the midst of the painted angels was one particular angel that looked very familiar. It was Megan; she was perched on a platform which had been cleverly disguised as a cloud. In the field below (the main backdrop), shepherds were tending their sheep. The shepherds were Simon, Timmy and Dani. The sheep were plywood cutouts, and were covered in cotton balls; they had black button eyes, pink button noses, black socks for hooves and black felt lines for the mouths.

The light intensified around the shepherds; they fell to their knees, showing great fear of the heavenly sight. That gave Megan her cue; she shouted out her lines, quoting the Scripture passage. The light dimmed a little from the shepherds, intensifying onto the choir of angels around Megan. A trio began singing the scripture passage ascribed to the angelic choir. Susie readily identified the voices as being those of Miss Fiona, Miss Cora and Miss Taryn. The light disappeared from the angels, reappearing onto the shepherds. Dani quoted the Scripture passage as Simon and Timmy vigorously nodded their heads in agreement to go to Bethlehem. Again the stage went dark.

Mr. Sean read the next portion of the passage; the shepherds' visiting the manger, and of their witnessing to all of the townspeople regarding the events of the night. The spotlight once again shone brightly, revealing the three shepherds in the manger visiting Mary, Joseph and baby Jesus. The spotlight followed them as they left the manger, entered the town and ran from person to person (painted plywood cutouts), spreading the good news. Slowly the light dimmed until the stage was clothed in darkness.

The final passage read was that of the visit of the Magi. The light flared again to one small section of the stage - the humble abode of Mary and Joseph. The Magi were Sam, Kevin and Jason, producing several loud guffaws and chuckles. Upon seeing the child (also a plywood cutout) with Mary (Kat), the Magi bowed down and worshipped him. They rose to their feet, presenting to the child their gifts of gold, frankincense and myrrh. The light disappeared, leaving the stage in utter darkness.

The music began to gradually increase its volume and, ever so slowly, bringing the spotlight with it, casting a faint light upon the stage. When the music reached its crescendo, the spotlight suddenly opened in full, flooding the entire stage with a brilliant white light as if it was the noonday sun. All of the children were dressed in angel costumes, complete with gossamer wings and golden halos. As the trio began to sing the hymn, 'Gloria in Excelsis Deo', the children performed a beautifully choreographed ballet of praise.

When the song ended, the children quickly formed a line along the front portion of the stage, and the stage curtain closed behind them. The spotlight became a wide angle light again, but the light was now diffused. Softly, the music changed to another tune, and the children sang, 'C-H-R-I-S-T-M-A-S'.

As the last note faded away, so did the spotlight. The house lights came up in full, and the children were joined on stage by all of the other performers and helpers. They received a standing ovation, cheers and whistles among which was shouted "bravo" and several other accolades. The children bowed to the audience, returning for three curtain calls. Each time, Juls would gracefully motion to the others, both cast and crew. The girls would curtesy, and the boys would bow. After the third curtain call, Juls performed the same ritual as did the cast and crew. However, after they had finished, no one moved for several seconds. Juls, in elegance and grace, slowly stepped forward. With all the agility and eloquence of a far more seasoned ballerina, Juls performed a deep curtsey and held it. The ovation burst forth from the audience, building rapidly into a crescendo that echoed throughout the Music Hall. Rising ever so slowly and perfectly, Juls again gracefully motioned to the cast and crew to receive the accolades.

Miss Pritchett had joined the cast and crew on the stage, hugging them and thanking them. She began motioning for quiet; and after several more minutes, the audience began to cease their fervent and rousing cheers. When the Music Hall had become quiet, Miss Pritchett announced that refreshments had been set-up in the Grand Parlor. She asked everyone to meet there to congratulate all those that participated in the recital, and to celebrate such a fine performance. As the children came down from the stage, they received hugs from everyone. It was truly a time of celebration, spilling into the corridor as they meandered into the Grand Parlor, continuing with the festivities until it was time for dinner.

Even Mrs. Coppersmith lost track of time, realizing that dinner would now be a few minutes late. Everyone laughed, assuring her that the world would not come to an end. Grinning, she called on her kitchen staff to come and lend assistance in getting dinner to the table. Those in costume had to remain so – there wasn't time to go change. Jared, Aaron and Susie were the only ones not dressed in costume, so they assisted the other children in shedding their wings. Megan, Timmy and Simon insisted on keeping their halos.

As he passed by them on his way out the door, Mr. Dale unkindly remarked that all of the children should have been dressed in red suits, wearing horns and carrying pitchforks. Unfortunately, none of the other adults heard him. Susie managed to calm down the older children as the younger ones wanted to know what he meant. She convinced them to ignore what he said, reminding them that mean people are mean because they are so unhappy and miserable.

Jared, Juls, Aaron, Jose, Grant, Kat, Mary and Dani wanted to get even, and began launching a series of possible practical jokes to play on him. Susie shook her head, telling them that it wouldn't be worth the trouble because it could come back to haunt them. She grinned as she told them he would get his come-uppance without their having to do anything.

"Is this another one of your Nana's sayings?" Aaron asked.

Susie nodded. "Yes, and it's true. Let's go; we don't want to be late for dinner."

They scurried out the door, race-walking their way to the Dining Hall. It was then that Susie noticed Simon wasn't with them. She turned around, ran back down the corridor and into the Parlor. Simon was sitting in front of the Christmas tree. She strode across the room, smiling at his enthrall-ment of the tree.

"Come on, Simon," she said jovially; "we have to go to dinner."

Simon shook his head; he kept staring at the tree with his back to her.

"Simon, come on. Let's go," she repeated, a little more firmly.

Again, he shook his head. He just kept staring at the tree.

Susie sat down beside him, wrapped her arm around him, hugging him tight against her body. "What's wrong, Simon?" she whispered softly.

He buried his face into her, sobbing uncontrollably. She pulled him into her lap and gently rocked him, stroking his hair as she kept telling him it's okay to cry. Finally he stopped crying and hugged her tight, holding onto her for dear life. She continued rocking him until she felt him relax; then she shifted him so that she could see his face.

"Simon, please talk to me. What's wrong?"

Tears sprang up again, coursing down his chubby, little cheeks. "I miss Nana," he cried; "I miss Nana." He fell against her, sobbing in gulping gasps, his little body heaving and jerking with each one.

Susie held him tight, rocking him slowly as she gently rubbed his back. "I know, Simon; I know. I miss her, too. It's okay to miss her because we love her. We'll see her again someday. Remember the stories Nana told us about Heaven, and how we'll all be together?

Simon nodded, still crying and pressing closer than ever to Susie.

She set him back again. She looked into his eyes. "Simon, it's true. Someday, I don't know when, but someday we will be with Nana, and Mommy and Daddy again. You can believe it because Nana believed it. And she believed it because it is true. Okay?"

Simon nodded, his tears now reduced to an occasional trickle. He sighed, and his eyes were so sad. "I miss her so much my heart hurts," he told her amid sobbing gulps with each intake of breath.

Susie nodded. "Mine too, Simon. But you know what?"

He shook his head no.

"That bad hurt goes away. We'll always miss her, and want to see her; but the bad hurt will go away. The more we talk about Nana and remember her, the less it will hurt that she's in Heaven and not here," she explained.

He gave her one of his 'that's crazy' looks. "You sure?"

"Yes," she answered confidently. "I'm positive. It takes time, but it will stop hurting so much if we keep her memory alive. We do that by sharing our memories of Nana."

Smiling tenderly at her little brother, she wiped away a tear from his cheek, adding, "And we've already started keeping her memory alive by sharing with everyone the stories she used to tell us."

Simon smiled at her. "Okay," he agreed with a heavy sigh.

"Feel better?" she asked.

Simon gave her a full, toothy grin as he nodded his head. "Yes."

"Good," she replied. Giving him one last hug, she told him, "Let's go to dinner."

Simon helped her to her feet, and they walked arm-in-arm to the door, nudging each other.

"Susie?"

"Yes, Simon."

"Nana was going to take us to the Zoo Sleigh Ride for Christmas," he said with a sigh. "Now we'll never get to."

"Not with Nana," she agreed; "but that doesn't mean we'll never get to do it."

He grinned up at her. "Really?"

"Really," she answered.

He stopped walking and gave her one of his bear hugs. "You're the best, Susie. I love you."

"I love you too, Simon," she responded, returning his hug. "Now we really do have to hurry, or we'll be late."

He giggled. "No problem," he assured her, linking arms with her and strutting toward the door in a fast peacock walk.

Unknown to Susie and to Simon, Miss Hilda and Miss Pritchett had followed Susie. They had just left their office suite when they saw her

running back into the Parlor. Concerned, they followed and were just outside the door. They witnessed the exchange by the tree and the one nearer
to the door, moving both ladies to tears.

"She truly is a marvel," Miss Hilda whispered to Miss Pritchett.

"Yes, she is," Miss Pritchett agreed. "Come, let's go."

Both ladies quickly returned to their office suite, allowing ample time
for Susie and Simon to pass by on their way to the Dining Hall.

Chapter 34

ANGELS AMONG US

Cradling her head in her clasped hands, Susie just stared up at the ceiling. Though she was very tired, the much-needed sleep persistently eluded her. Her mind whirled, flitting from one thought to the next, unable to focus on any one in particular. So much had happened in the past few days, she wasn't certain just what to think of it all. It was as if everything was in reality just a huge puzzle, broken apart and the pieces jumbled and scattered.

Adding to her dilemma was the fact that tomorrow was Christmas; actually, she reminded herself, in ninety minutes it would technically be Christmas. That brought a whole bevy of angst with it. She missed Nana, and tomorrow would be terribly difficult; not just for her, but also for Simon. It would be their first Christmas without Nana

Tears rolled from the corners of her eyes, saturating her pillow. She had fought the tears all day in the hope that her bravado would keep Simon from being sad. It had worked, for the most part – he missed Nana, too, but she was able to distract him somewhat with all of the activity Glen Hollow provided. Plus, Grammy being here was a great help. Simon had taken to Grammy as if he had always known her; and Susie was thankful and grateful that Aaron and Timmy didn't mind sharing her.

Having that little talk with him just before dinner certainly helped, but Susie was concerned that Christmas Day would bring to the forefront memories of Nana. It could spark another round of grieving. She prayed that would not be the case. Thinking of dinner, she realized that both Miss Pritchett and Miss Hilda had arrived late, even more so than what she and Simon had. No one seemed to know what kept them, and they offered no explanation when they did arrive. It was curious, Susie decided, because they seemed in an especially good mood, even more so than after the recital.

The thought of the recital revived the memory of how excited Simon had been. He loved the stage, loved performing and loved the accolades.

She began chuckling to herself. He was very much like Mommy, and like Nana. She, on the other hand, was more like Daddy.

Susie smiled as the memory resurfaced of how thrilled and happy Simon had looked earlier this evening. After dinner, everyone had gathered in the Parlor to share their favorite holiday memory, followed by a reading of the poem, 'Twas the Night Before Christmas'.

By the time Miss Pritchett finished the reading, it was 9:30 and well-past bedtime. With all of the excitement of the evening bubbling inside, they didn't want to sleep. And, with ecstatic utterances, they pleaded for just one more story. However, when Miss Pritchett reminded them that Santa won't visit if the children aren't in bed and asleep, they scrambled to their feet, eager to comply. Megan, Timmy and Simon elatedly ran around the room, hugging everyone good-night and promising to "go to sleep real fast so Santa will come".

Susie's smile broadened recalling how their wondrous delight and their passionate hugs had made all of the adults even more cheerful, whether resident or visitor. She had to admit that even her spirit was buoyed when she tucked Simon in bed during their regular good-night session. He radiated such joy looking up at her. His eyes sparkled, gleaming with hope, and contentment and happiness.

Closing her eyes, Susie sighed and thought, 'He'll miss Nana at some point tomorrow; something is bound to make him think of her. But with so many people here, maybe that will help ease the loss. Maybe tomorrow won't be so bad. I hope so.'

Her thoughts shifted once again to Nana and caused tears to flow anew, streaking her face with little rivers. Grabbing her pillow, she buried her face into it, hiding the sound of her grief as she relinquished herself to the sorrow that ached within her heart. Several minutes later, after all her tears were spent, she released a deep, cleansing sigh into the pillow then placed it back under her head.

Turning to look at her clock, she was glad to see it was only a quarter to eleven. "Maybe I can get some decent sleep after all," Susie mumbled to her clock.

As her body began to give way to the encroaching delight of sleep, she yawned, a big, long relaxing one. Just as she snuggled down, readying herself for sleep, something in the hallway caught her attention. Whatever it was, it had moved quickly. Darting past her doorway, it was nothing more than a brief shadow amid the darkness.

Curiosity rising, Susie threw back her covers and jumped into her slippers. Grabbing her robe, she struggled into it as she ran into the hallway. It was empty, but Susie heard the distinctive click of the Dorm Room door. Someone had just left.

Susie ran to the door, opened it and peered into the corridor just in time to catch the briefest glimpse of someone entering the spiral staircase. She hastily followed, waiting at the top of the stairwell until she was certain the person had exited below. As she reached the bottom of the stairs, Susie heard the closing of the door that led to the pergola.

Running as fast she could, she arrived within a minute of it closing. She pulled the door open and immediately regretted her impetuous reaction. The frosty air cut through her robe and pajamas as if she had nothing on at all. Hastily she closed the door, shivering and rubbing her arms as she held them tight against her body.

She had to know who left and why. Running back down the corridor, she entered the Cloak Room and retrieved her winter coat and boots. As she ran back to the door, she buttoned her coat, put on her knit cap, gloves and scarf. Now she was ready to brace the winter night air.

Outside, she realized that she very much needed her woolen pants and socks, but she didn't have time to go back to the Dorm. She ran along the pergola, making short the distance between it and the portico in front of the Chapel. She hesitated, trying to decide which way she should go.

Did the person go to the left, which would lead to the garage and to the cottages; or did the person go to the right, which would lead to the cemetery or back to the kitchen? Susie decided it must be the left path, and the destination must be the garage or the cottages. After all, Susie reasoned, there was no need to come out here to go to the kitchen; and no one would go to the cemetery this late and in this weather.

She headed down the left path and stopped. A faint light streamed gently through the stained glass windows. The person had gone inside the Chapel. Susie turned and ran back to the Chapel doors. Quickly she pulled it open and stepped inside. Giving scant consideration to both the bell tower and the basement options, Susie gently eased open one of the sanctuary doors just enough to peek inside. At first, she didn't see anyone, but instinct was telling her someone was there. She waited, and her patience was rewarded.

It was Kat! Apparently she had been resting on the bench. Now she sat upright, her arms laying on the back of the bench in front of her. She bowed her head for a few minutes before resting her forehead on her arms. Susie could completely understand why Kat would come here; she also felt drawn to his place. She decided to leave, giving Kat her privacy. Granted, Kat was technically breaking the bedtime rule; however, Susie couldn't imagine anyone objecting to her spending time in the Chapel.

"Come on in, Susie," Kat called out to her.

Embarrassed at being caught, Susie's face flushed.

"You might as well come in. I know you're here," Kat repeated, turning to face Susie.

Susie stepped inside. "I'm sorry I disturbed you, Kat," Susie apologized. "I didn't know who was up, so I followed. I just was going to leave when you called out."

Kat shrugged. "Don't worry about it."

"Don't stay too late," Susie advised in a gentle tone. She turned to leave when the thought struck her that Kat had known she was here without seeing her.

"How did you know I was here?" Susie blurted out, surprise and confusion competing for dominance in her voice.

Kat smiled - that eerie, half-smile of hers before turning it into a full grin. She didn't respond, just kept smiling. Her eyes danced with an impish gleam, apparently delighted that she knew something that Susie didn't. Kat turned back to face the front of the Chapel, laying her forehead once again on her arms.

Susie's curiosity was in full bloom. She had to know. She had been so careful – Kat couldn't have heard her, or seen her. But she must have.

Susie trotted to the bench and sat next to Kat. "How did you know?" she pressed. "When did you see me, or hear me?"

Kat flashed an amused smirk at her as she turned her head sideways and laughed. "I didn't see you, and I didn't hear you."

"So how did you know?" Susie pushed for an answer.

Grinning mischievously, she replied, "You know."

Slightly irritated, Susie retorted, "No, I don't. You keep saying that every time I ask you anything. It's really annoying, Kat. Why don't you just answer?"

Kat shrugged, closed her eyes and turned her face back to her arms. Several minutes of awkward silence had passed before she spoke. Her voice was soft and filled with pain.

"I came here tonight with the same prayer I always have. Every Christmas Eve, just before midnight, I find a church somewhere and specifically ask for one thing, and only one thing. Every year it's the same, no answer."

She sighed heavily. "Why is that?"

Compassion flooded Susie as she reached her arm around Kat. "I don't know," she answered honestly. "What do you ask for?"

Kat chucked softly, her forehead still pressing onto her arms. Turning slowly to look at Susie, a sly grin spread across Kat's face, and a devilish glint sparkled in her eyes. "Do you *really* want to know?"

Susie abruptly removed her arm and sat back against the bench. Part of her wanted to throttle Kat, and part of her wanted to help her. Kat could be so infuriating. Susie closed her eyes, slowly counting to ten. When she opened her eyes, Kat was still watching her; only this time, her expression was one of curiosity, and not that morbid, spooky one she usually touted.

All of sudden the realization dawned; what Kat needs is a friend, something she has never had. She needs someone to listen to her, regardless. She needs someone to accept her as she is, without criticism and without judgment. She needs a friend. 'We all do,' Susie thought. Susie's demeanor changed with her new-found understanding. Kindness replaced irritation and impatience

"Kat," Susie began gently; "I really do want to know because I am your friend. I want you to be my friend, too. It doesn't mean we'll always agree on everything; but you can talk to me, and tell me anything. We're friends."

Pressing her lips tightly together, Kat immediately sat upright, folding her arms tightly against her body. She slumped back against the bench, shoulders hunched forward, and with her head hanging so low that her chin nearly touched her chest. Kat slowly shook her head back and forth as if sifting through a chaotic jumble for just the right words.

Her motion ceased. She remained still for several minutes, just staring at the bench in front of her. Rapidly she turned her body to face Susie, sitting cross-legged on the bench. Her eyes were cold again, like they were the very first time Susie had seen her. An uneasy chill rippled through Susie, but she didn't turn away. Susie met that gaze firmly, waiting for Kat to decide whether or not to trust her. Several minutes ticked by before Kat sighed, more in resigning herself to what she perceived as inevitable rather than out of sadness.

"You won't believe me; you haven't so far," she stated. There was no hint of accusation, or of disappointment in her tone; it was merely a statement of fact. "You should," she added.

Kat began to laugh and quickly tried to squash it. "I'm sorry, but it is funny."

"What is?" Susie asked.

"You used to know these things, same as me and Megan. Even Simon," Kat responded.

"Know what?" Susie pressed, trying to maintain a sense of calmness. She felt ill at ease broaching what she guessed Kat would say next. But she truly wanted to help Kat, to be her friend.

Exhaling sharply, Kat nodded and said, "Okay. You really want to know. Here it is. Every year I ask that this ability I have stops. I used to ask that it stop for only the bad ones. Since that prayer was never answered, I figured that meant it had to be all of them. So two years ago I started asking that it stops for all of them. I'll miss seeing and talking to the good ones, but I can live without it if that's what it takes."

"Only problem is," she added dryly; "that prayer isn't answered either."

Reflecting for a moment, Susie gently requested, "Tell me about the good ones."

Sensing her interest was genuine, Kat smiled and relaxed. "Okay. Most are angels, some are fairies, some pixies and some … well; I'm not sure what they are. But they're really neat, and a lot of fun. My angel chases away the bad ones. There have been a few times that the bad ones were super powerful, so he had to call for help from other angels. They always chase away the bad ones. They always tell me not to be afraid."

"Since they chase away the bad ones, why are you so afraid?" Susie asked.

Kat's eyes narrowed as she studied Susie, uncertain if Susie was naïve, or being sarcastic. Within a heartbeat, Kat decided it was Susie's lack of experience and not an affront.

Softly, coolly Kat responded, "Because the bad ones can be really, really bad. It's not just the way they change form; it's what they say, and how they say it. And they're constantly telling me what they'll do to me if I don't choose their side. They never shut–up."

"Have they ever done anything they said?" Susie inquired.

Kat's brow furled as she mulled it over. "No."

Susie smiled encouragingly and reminded Kat, "Because your angel stops them; right?"

Kat nodded, puzzled.

"So," Susie rationally construed; "your angel keeps telling you not to be afraid because your angel will protect you. And your angel does. Has your angel ever failed?"

Kat shook her head no.

Placing her hands firmly on Kat's shoulders and looking her in the eye, Susie smiled and added; "So then you don't have a reason to be afraid."

Sheepishly, Kat chuckled. "I guess not; but I'd like to see *your* reaction to some of these bad boys."

Susie laughed. "I'd rather not; I'll take your word for it."

Kat began to laugh, a full, hearty, rolling laugh. She could just imagine Susie's reaction, and said so. Susie agreed, laughing with her. They bantered good-naturedly back and forth, laughing and bragging on what they'd do to the bad ones if given a chance.

As the laughing subsided, Kat's expression became somber again. "Why do you think I see and hear them?" she asked quietly. "Other people get to quit, why not me?"

Susie shook her head. "I don't know, Kat. Maybe there's a reason for it. Maybe someday it'll be necessary that you know what's happening," Susie suggested.

Kat frowned. "So why did you and Simon get to quit?"

"What?" The implication of Kat's question astonished Susie. She felt a rising tide of panic within herself and struggled to hide it.

"You heard me. Simon used to see and hear them, and you did too. Your Nana was able to make it stop for him. But *you* were able to stop it yourself. Why?"

Susie was thunderstruck. She didn't know what to say. Her mind raced, wondering how Kat knew about Simon and his imaginary people. Why did she say Nana stopped it; and why would Kat think she had ever seen any imagined people?

Kat laughed, amused by Susie's reaction. "Chill, girl," she advised; "it's no big deal."

"What makes you think we have?" Susie hesitantly countered.

Her eyes sparkled and danced with glee. "Because my angel told me so," she answered spritely. "And because your angel told me so."

"Really." Susie's tone was pensive.

"Oh, yeah," Kat gleefully answered, nodding slowly. "My angel's name is Nahriel. Simon's angel's name is Chakahel. Megan's angel is Rhikael, Dani's is Triyunel, Juls' is Mirinel, Jose's is Phentuel, Timmy's is Roehnuel, Aaron's is Lehtolel and Jared's angel is Jahnighel. There are more, but I don't see the point in telling you because you don't believe me."

"I don't know what to believe," Susie replied.

"How would I know about you and Simon?" Kat asked gently. "I can tell you more. I can tell you things that only you would know. Will that help you? I don't know why, but I know it's important that you remember."

The earnest tone in her voice, and the pleading in her eyes clearly revealed to Susie that Kat was not playing games. And it was clear to Susie that either Kat spoke the truth, or she was mentally unstable and believed her own delusions. Breaking her reverie was the sound of light-hearted giggles rolling out from Kat.

"What's so funny?" Susie asked.

Kat's face lit up, and her eyes sparkled with the excitement that comes from knowing a secret, a really good one. "It's one thing to say you believe me; it's another to know that it's true. For instance, I know that Nana gave you a very special pin on your tenth birthday. I also know you are supposed to wear it on your birthdays and only on your birthdays. And I know that

632

Nana gave you that silver pendant you're wearing now, and told you to always wear it," she cheerfully informed Susie.

"You couldn't know …. How do you know?" Susie stammered.

"Because Tahlranel just told me," Kat replied softly as she reached over and held Susie's hand. "Don't you remember Tahlranel?"

Susie shook her head, attempting to clear the fog swirling in her mind. "No, I don't… I don't think… Wait, I … I do know that name. … How do I know that name?"

Panic began to rise within her, overwhelming her as she struggled to maintain her composure. Her breathing quickened as her heart pounded in her chest.

"I … can't … breathe," she cried, hyperventilating. Dizziness overcame her, causing her to sway.

"Are you okay?" The alarm in Kat's voice raised the normal timbre of her voice at least an octave.

Susie shut her eyes tight, and she covered her ears with her hands. Tears cascaded down her face as she fought against the flood of memories. Kat slid next to Susie, hugging her tight until the sobs subsided.

"I'm sorry," Kat whispered; "I'm so sorry."

"It's okay. … It's okay … Really, it is," Susie assured her, returning her hug. "It's better to know the truth than not."

"Hi, Tahlranel," Susie said to her childhood friend and protector. She stood, leaned over the bench and gave the angel a hug.

"Hello, my little one," Tahlranel responded, wrapping his arms around her.

"I'm so sorry for the way I treated you," Susie told him amid her tears.

"You do not need to apologize," he lovingly told her.

"Yes, I do. I remember now." Susie looked at Kat and explained. "We played together all the time. We had the most fun. When Simon was born, I saw his angel enter the room. That's when Tahlranel knew I could see all other beings. He began to prepare me for the bad ones. When Mommy and Daddy died a few weeks later…"

Susie paused as she choked back her tears. "I was angry that Tahlranel did not bring them back. I was so mean to him. I screamed and screamed at him, and told him that I didn't want him here if he wouldn't bring back

Mommy and Daddy. I just kept screaming until I fainted. When I woke up, Nana was holding me and crying. She asked me who I had been talking to before I fainted. I didn't know. My memories were gone. Tahlranel was gone. I'm glad you're back," she told him as she hugged him again.

He gently wiped away her tears, and then kissed her on her forehead. "I never left," he assured Susie; "and Chakahel has always been with Simon."

Susie looked to where he had gestured. It was Chakahel. She ran to him and hugged him. "Thank you for watching over Simon," she earnestly told him.

He returned her hug. "It is what I am to do. It was good to speak with you again Susie, but now I must return to Simon." No sooner had he finished speaking than he was gone. He was there, and then he wasn't.

"Susie," Kat interrupted her trance; "this is my angel, Nahriel." She had left the bench, hugged her angel and was now standing next to him.

"Hi, Nahriel," Susie greeted him.

"Hello, Susie," he responded cordially.

Susie turned to Tahlranel. "Why didn't you show yourself to me?" Susie asked him, curious as to why he waited until now.

Tenderness and compassion emanated from him as he gazed upon his charge. "I tried many times over the years, but your defenses were strong. To break them when you were not ready to remove the barrier could cause harm to you. Simon's ability was masked for him in order to protect him and to protect you as well. Much has changed, and there are more changes to come. You and the others have been brought here for a purpose."

"What purpose?" Susie and Kat asked simultaneously.

Tahlranel smiled. "I do not know, but the time for the message to be delivered grows near. You must wait."

"May I ask a question?" Susie asked.

"Yes," he answered.

Susie grinned. "I'm just curious. Why don't you have wings?"

The angels smiled at each other, amused at her inquisitive streak. "We are in veiled form," Tahlranel explained. Instantaneously they radiated a flash of light resembling that of a starburst. The flash was so quick it was gone within a second of its appearance.

Standing before the girls were two of the most beautiful creatures they had ever seen. The angels glowed with a light that shone from within; their eyes pulsated with a blue radiance. They were soaring in height, and their skin sparkled like sun-lit water. Arcing well above their heads, their wings unfurled, revealing wingspans that were easily more than double their height. Their feathers were unlike anything Susie had ever seen, opaque yet translucent, reflecting the glowing brilliance that surrounded the celestial beings.

Susie gasped in amazement. Kat uttered softly, "awesome." (Kat had never seen the true form of her protector either, nor had it ever occurred to her to ask.)

The angels lifted their faces heavenward as they slowly extended their hands upward in a pose of supplication. Tahlranel and Nahriel began to glow brighter and brighter, receiving and emanating Divine Love. As the Light intensified, Susie and Kat had to shield their eyes.

The angels ceased their prayers, and the Light began to dissipate enough so that the girls were able, once again, to look upon the angels. Turning their focus to their charges, Tahlranel and Nahriel smiled devotedly as they opened their arms wide to receive them. Without hesitation, the girls rushed into those loving arms.

As Tahlranel's wings closed around her, Susie was almost certain she could hear the choir in heaven singing, and its music reverberating through him. She told herself it wasn't possible. Then she laughed, hugged Tahlranel and told herself, 'Everything is possible where God is concerned.'

She focused on the music, and the angelic voices singing praises. She felt all of her anxieties, all of her fears and all of her sorrows just melt away. Love, Joy and the deepest, greatest Peace flowed into her.

"It is time for you both to return to your Dorm," Tahlranel spoke as he unfurled his wings. Susie noticed that Nahriel had done the same.

"I have so many questions," Susie began.

"Me, too," Kat was quick to interject.

Tahlranel shook his head. "Now is not the time. Soon you will have your answers."

The angels looked at each other and then at their charges. "Sleep well," they said gently.

Both Susie and Kat awakened Christmas morning, in their own beds, well rested and humming the same tune – the heavenly strains they had heard resonating through the angels. Neither remembered walking back to the Dorm; neither remembered anything past being told to "sleep well".

Chapter 35

CHRISTMAS IS HERE,

BRINGING GOOD CHEER

Susie heard them coming long before they reached her doorway. Their attempt at covert operations left much to be desired. A pack of coyotes being chased by a herd of buffalo would have been less conspicuous, and much quieter by far, than the thunderous cacophony of footsteps she had heard. Their voices, a mix of loud whispers, shushing sounds and giggles also revealed their presence long before they arrived.

"See, I told you she'd be awake," Simon declared victoriously, running and jumping onto her bed. He threw his arms around her, giving her his best bear hug and a 'good-morning' kiss on her cheek. She couldn't help but laugh, returning his hug and kiss.

Megan and Timmy had both firmly planted themselves onto her bed, trying their best to dislodge Simon from Susie, each demanding it was their turn for a hug. Susie opened her arms, and they wiggled and squirmed their way next to her with Simon firmly entrenched in the middle. Juls, Kat and Dani hopped onto her bed, quickly followed by Jose, Aaron and Jared.

Susie smiled. "Good morning. What's going on?"

Juls smiled. "Don't you mean ..." - and in unison they all said (using their outdoor voices) "Merry Christmas!"

Susie laughed. "Merry Christmas to you, too. Why are you up so early? It's only four o'clock."

She was bombarded with simultaneous responses: "It's Christmas!", and "I couldn't sleep", and "I want to see if Santa came", and the crowning jewel was "I want to see how many presents Santa left me," which was quickly followed by several who parroted, "Me, too".

Laughing and shaking her head, she responded, "We can't go down until it's time for breakfast."

"Said who?" Kat challenged, receiving accolades from the others, voicing their support.

"It's the rule. We're supposed to wait and go to breakfast together," she answered.

"It's *CHRISTMAS*," Kat repeated loudly, leaning toward Susie to further emphasize her point.

Jared grinned. "She's got you there. No one said we couldn't."

"Yeah; I think they probably expect us to," Aaron agreed, grinning like the proverbial cat that caught the canary. Raising his eyebrow, he shrugged and gave her a little wink as he added, "And we wouldn't want to disappoint them, now would we?"

"Fine with me," Susie acquiesced. "But no one touches any of the presents. Agreed?"

"Agreed," they all shouted in unison as they stampeded to the door.

Susie shouted after them, "And be quiet!"

But it was too late; they were already out the door, and running as fast as they could to the Parlor. Susie put on her slippers, grabbed her robe and dashed after them, catching up to them before they made it to the west wing.

Susie slipped in front of the group, blocking the doors. "Don't forget your promise. No one touches the presents," she reminded them.

"We know; we know," they all agreed, trying to get past her.

"All right, then," Susie acquiesced, stepping aside.

Jared and Aaron pushed the doors open, and they all rushed into the Parlor. To their complete and utter astonishment, the entire household, residents and guests alike, was gathered there, calling out in unison, "Merry Christmas!" as the children burst into the room.

Too stunned for words, all of them just stood there, staring. The room was brightly lit, and the fireplaces were blazing away with massive yule logs in each one. Someone had the forethought to place some cinnamon sticks on the fire, delightfully scenting the room. Adding to the cinnamon fragrance, there were the heavenly aromas of food and drink. The lights on the Christmas tree and on its Star of Bethlehem created the illusion of a Divine Aura around the tree. Christmas stockings hung all along the mantles of the fireplaces, stuffed and nearly overflowing with miniature toys, trinkets and candy. Each beautifully embroidered stocking bore the name of a resident or of one of the guests. It was an amazing sight to see.

Mrs. Coppersmith approached swiftly, her eyes merrily twinkling like the stars in the heavens. "What took you so long? We were certain you'd all be down an hour ago. There's hot chocolate, and you can have marshmallows or the marshmallow crème." She winked at Simon as she patted his head – she knew he loved the mini marshmallows.

She gave each child a hug prior to herding them further into the room. "And there's sausage biscuits, ham biscuits and some doughnuts to tide you over until breakfast," she added with a wink.

"Merry Christmas, everyone," Susie found her voice at last

The other children joined in, wishing everyone a Merry Christmas. The adults met them in the center of the room, exchanging hugs, "good mornings", laughter and joy. Mr. Henry's eyes crinkled with delight as he told Susie that he captured their moment of surprise with a great group photo.

He added in a conspiratorial whisper, "And it'll be a good addition for you know what." She grinned and nodded, thanking him profusely. "My pleasure," he responded.

"He came! He came! Santa came!"

The jubilant squeals were pronounced by Megan, Timmy and Simon. All three had just noticed the tree now that the adults had moved away from that area, enabling them to see the base of the tree. Actually, what they saw was the mound of presents that protruded far beyond the base of the tree.

"Now that everyone is here," Miss Pritchett began, speaking loud enough to be heard over all of the excited voices; "we will begin opening presents. As you can see, we have cleared the furnishings from this whole area in front of the tree. You children will sit on the carpet and form a circle."

Her smile was as bright as the joy with which her face glowed. Gazing lovingly upon each child, one by one, she continued; "This way, we can all see you open your presents because the adults will be sitting on the sofas behind you. And it will allow Mr. Henry to get some good photos of everyone. So, please find a place to sit."

The children needed no further encouragement. Susie was impressed that the older children did not have to be reminded to allow the younger ones first dib's for a place to sit. In fact, Juls and Kat went out of their way to ensure that the youngest ones were seated first, followed by Mary, Dani, Grant and Jose. Taking a cue from the girls, Jared and Aaron deferred choosing until after Juls and Kat had done so. Both boys then turned to Susie, made an eloquent sweeping bow, suggesting that it was now her turn. She laughed and curtsied. Juls patted the floor next to herself at the same time that Kat had done so. Juls and Kat exchanged glances and laughed. Sliding apart, they compromised, making room for Susie between them.

Opening presents took nearly four hours to finish. The adults had one gift each under the tree, and it was from Santa. All of the visitors also received a gift from Santa, just like the adult residents of Glen Hollow. Susie hadn't thought of it previously, but she was glad that someone had, and had so kindly included the guests. However, each of the children had three; one was from Santa, one was from all of the adults at Glen Hollow and one was from a Secret Santa.

Miss Pritchett explained that, this year, Secret Santa was done a little different. Since several of the children were late arrivals, it was decided that the adults would divide into groups and each group would be a Secret Santa for one of the children. The only stipulation is that the gifts given by Secret Santa must be hand-made, not purchased. Next year, she added, the Secret Santa would return to its more traditional form, but the hand-made-only rule would still apply.

The children, including Grant and Mary, were enchanted and thrilled with each of their presents, but especially the one from Santa. Each child had marveled at how Santa knew exactly what they wanted. Megan, Timmy and Simon squealed with delight, their little faces shining with joy at the miracle of receiving what they had asked Santa for in their prayers.

Susie smiled and laughed as Simon's eyes widened in surprise when he opened his gift from Santa. His mouth flew open, astonished and captivated at the miracle he beheld. Clutching the box tightly against his body, he began jumping up and down, thanking Santa over and over again. It was comical to see – the box was large and bulky, causing Simon to stumble, but that didn't damper his enthusiasm. Awkwardly he ran to Susie as the box bumped against him and dragged along the floor. Holding out the box for her to see, he grinned and giggled. He radiated such happiness, Susie's heart was profoundly touched. She could barely keep the tears at bay.

"Look Susie," he gushed; "look what Santa gave me."

"I see," she responded with a smile.

His face registered elation, surprise and wonderment all at the same time. "I was afraid that Santa would forget me, but he didn't."

Puzzled, Susie asked, "Why did you think he would forget you?"

He gave her that look of his that clearly suggests you have just asked the dumbest question ever, and answered; "'cause I didn't get to sit in his lap at Macy's. Don't you remember? We have to *go* and tell Santa what we want. I didn't get to do that this year," he reminded her, slowly moving his head back and forth. Within a fraction of a second, his happy, little grin returned. "But Santa knew I was here. I bet he heard my prayers 'cause that's how he knew I wanted a Junior Binky and his best friend, Rocko."

He had the mystery all solved – no need to confuse him with facts. All he knew was that his prayers were answered; he had his Junior Binky and best friend, Rocko, complete with skateboards, roller blades, ball caps and denim outfits. Susie smiled, as she viewed his treasure, remarking how great it was because the skateboards and roller blades really work. Pointing to the information, she read to him the entire promo printed on the box. Susie was delighted to see his joy increase so intensely. The sheer magnitude of his emotion was such that his laughter created a joy in her own heart. As she quickly glanced around the room, she noticed the same effect reproduced on the faces of the others as they watched him and listened to the enrapturing sound of his laughter. Simon hugged her profusely and kissed her cheek before running back to his spot in front of the tree.

Following Simon's example, Megan and Timmy also ran to her, showing her what they received from Santa. Megan received her first-ever, real china tea party tea set, Old Country Roses. The diminutive set was in a box larger than Megan could carry, requiring assistance from Jared. Although Susie offered to come to her (the same suggestion was made by some of the adults), nothing doing - Megan was adamant that the tea set be brought to Susie, just like Simon did with his present. So Jared, with an amused grin, offered his assistance.

Megan's smile filled her face with joy as she bubbled at how she couldn't believe that Santa knew exactly what she had hoped for because she didn't tell anybody except for Susie. Susie laughed, telling her that Santa must have been listening. Megan threw her arms around Susie, hugged her tight and kissed her cheek.

The miniature set looked just like the real china, from the fine bone china to the perfectly painted roses and the elegant gold trim. It was a complete tea service for twelve, including a dainty 3-tiered serving dish, and had the cutest, little teapot, sugar bowl, tongs and creamer. Susie made a fuss over the exceptional quality and beauty of Megan's new, real china tea set, assuring Megan that it was without question what a fairy princess would use when entertaining her guests. Susie added that to have such a tea set made Megan very special, and that she was positive that Hazey and Mazey and all their friends would love to come to Megan's tea parties.

Megan's countenance just glowed as she asked "Really?"

Susie nodded and answered. "Yes; there'll be so many that want to come, you'll have to have a waiting list."

Squealing with delight, Megan bounced up and down, clapping her hands and promising that everybody would have a turn coming to her tea parties, even her people friends. Susie was almost certain that she heard a slight moan from Dani and from Kat. That made Susie smile all the more.

Jared, bless his soul, asked Megan if he was included in her invitation. She looked up at him with the sweetest expression; she absolutely adored him now more than ever. Nodding her head fervently, she answered, "Oh, yes!"

"Good," he responded, accepting her open invitation; "now let's put this where it won't get broken, and I'll take it to your room later."

Megan told him to follow her, and he did. She chose a corner of the room, far removed from any chance of it being broken. They returned to the circle, Megan's tiny hand in his, with Megan chatting up a storm all the way back about her plans for a tea party. Jared gave Susie a wink as he settled himself once again beside Aaron. She smiled and mouthed "thank-you". He nodded.

Timmy's gift from Santa was a treasure he thought he would never see. He had whispered it to Santa at the mall the past two years, but it never materialized. This year, he included it in his prayers at night, hoping and praying that Santa would hear. And, miracles of miracles, he did. Greater still was his amazement that Santa gave him one that was bigger and better than the one for which he had asked.

"I didn't even know about this one," Timmy's voice cracked with emotions of joy and of wonder

It was a complete, deluxe, special edition, Lionel train set, containing engines, fuel cars, water cars, cargo cars, cattle cars, passenger cars, sleeper cars, dining cars and cabooses. It also contained a considerable amount of track, trestles, bridges, switching towers, water towers and railroad crossings.

As Mr. Sean pointed out to Timmy, he could set it up as one big train, or have two smaller ones running the track. Timmy's expression was heartwarming. His joy was so overwhelming that tears had formed, rolling down his little chipmunk cheeks. Wrapping his arms around the box as much as he possibly could, he laid his head on it and kept repeating over and over, "Thank you, Santa".

His box, also, was a little too big and too heavy for him, so Aaron carried it to Susie for Timmy. Susie "oohed" and "ahhed" over it, thrilling the budding train engineer to no end. She marveled at the incredible detail of each and every piece, assuring Timmy of the great amount of fun he would have with such an awesome train set. Timmy enthusiastically hugged her, kissed her with a quick peck on her cheek, and then rushed back to the circle for the next round of presents.

And so the morning progressed until all the presents had been distributed. To Susie, she had already received the greatest gift that she could ever receive: to see Simon so happy, so content, so safe and so loved. Tears filled her eyes, but these were no longer the tears of sorrow, of loss and of fear. These were tears of love, of joy, of peace and of hope.

Chapter 36

SO MANY QUESTIONS, SO LITTLE TIME

Quietly Susie lay listening to the sound of the grandfather clock in their Common Area. It had just begun chiming the eleven o'clock hour. She had so many thoughts whirling through her mind, it made her restless. Not from fatigue, or worry or even fear; this restlessness was more due to the excitement, nay the elation, she had felt within her heart all day long. She had tried several times to clear her mind and go to sleep; she just couldn't sleep.

Mostly, she supposed, the reason she couldn't sleep was due to the fact that she now knew and understood that she and Simon are exactly where they are supposed to be. Today proved to her that Simon needed Glen Hollow, and so did she. How Nana knew this, she couldn't fathom; but she trusted Nana.

The images of Simon's face while opening his presents and of stuffing his face with all the different treats Mrs. Coppersmith had provided flooded her mind. It made her smile. Simon made her smile. He was the most loving soul, the gentlest being; it humbled her to know how much he loved her and trusted her. He was able to read her and know that she is happy here, belongs here and wants to be here. That knowledge helped to spur in him the acceptance of Glen Hollow as his home. Then again, it certainly didn't hurt that somehow they knew just the right presents to give him, and all the other children, too, for that matter.

Nevertheless, Simon's main character flaw (if you could call it that) was that Simon had never met a stranger. He loved all people, choosing to see them as friends he just hadn't met yet. That had worried Nana some, and herself as well, but it never seemed to faze him their urging him to be cautious. Here, at Glen Hollow, he is safe, loved, well provided for and protected; she didn't have to worry. Other than perhaps Mr. Dale and, on occasion, Miss Taryn, the love and affection that each of the people here had for each other and for the children was a solid foundation and a fortress.

'We are home,' she realized, still gazing at the ceiling, and that sentiment filled her spirit with joy and peace.

She thought about Lacy, and her visit this afternoon to the animals.
After the lunch dishes were cleaned and the kitchen was quiet, Susie slipped
into the kitchen again and prepared another round of treats for the horses.
This time, in addition to the carrots and apples, she also included oranges.

Susie had exited the south wing sight unseen, hurrying along the pergola. During lunch, Mr. Sean had said that the temperature was only twenty
degrees outside, and that it was dropping fast. Bundled up in several layers
of clothing (including two layers of thermals), she thought it would be
enough to keep her warm; but the harsh winter air still penetrated, causing
her to shiver and her teeth to chatter. She took solace in knowing that the
barns would be warm; she told herself that she could endure the slight
discomfort of the jaunts between the barns and the manor.

As she left the path at the edge of the east wing where it connects to
the path that leads to the garage, she ran into Kevin – literally. He was
running toward the manor.

"What are you doing out here?" he asked, steadying her.

"I'm going to visit the animals," she told him.

"Why?"

"It's Christmas. I brought treats for the horses. For the other animals,
I thought I would use the grains in the barns as their treats," she answered,
opening the sack so he could see the fruit pieces.

He laughed, slowly shaking his head. "Only you," he said; "would
venture out in weather like this."

"You're out in it."

"That's different. Come on; I'll help you. You don't need to be out
here alone; and you'll need someone to tell you what to feed them, and how
much," he told her, grinning. "Where do you want to go first?"

Susie thanked him, telling him that she planned to start with the chickens and work her way back to the manor. He nodded in agreement, and
they quickly began walking toward the barns.

The chickens flocked around them as they had when Miss Hilda had
given Simon and her the tour nearly three weeks ago. Susie petted a few,
until Kevin laughingly told her they couldn't spend all day in here. He

645

measured out the grain in a bucket and handed the bucket to her, instructing her into which feeders to place the grain. He grinned, adding that if she really wanted to give them a Christmas treat, she'd give them some of the worms from the terrarium. Her grimace made him laugh. But she decided he was right and said so; she told him to show her what to do. At first he thought she was joking; then he realized she was serious.

She grinned, remembering how surprised he was. It was her turn to laugh; and he chuckled as well, opening the door to the terrarium room. Together they harvested a considered number of worms into the containers. Then, roost by roost, they placed a couple of worms into each feed cup. After washing her hands thoroughly (and amusing Kevin at her revulsion to icky, slimy things), they left the chickens.

Entering the pig barn, Susie spent a little time petting them, wishing them a "Merry Christmas" before gathering the grains and nuts for their treat. Kevin told her exactly how much of each one to put in the buckets, and each variety was a different amount. She asked why, which surprised him; but he patiently explained to her the different nutrient values of the grains and the nuts.

Carefully she poured the contents of the buckets into the feeding troughs. Both the Tams and the Choctaws thoroughly enjoyed their treats.

Next they quickly headed to the dairy barn where Susie repeated her "Merry Christmas" greeting to the cows, which took considerably longer. Kevin didn't seem to mind that she took the time to greet each and every one. Afterward, he told her how much of each grain to mix together, and how much to put into the troughs. Given the fact that there were so many cows, Kevin had insisted on helping her – otherwise, he had said, they'd end up missing dinner. She laughed, accepting his assistance.

They left the cows to their treat and headed rapidly to the horses. Inside, Susie picked up a bucket and poured half of the treats out of her sack into the bucket. She handed the bucket to Kevin and smiled. He shook his head, telling her to go ahead since she thought of it. She insisted. He relented, took the bucket and began distributing the fruit pieces.

Susie went to Lacy first, wishing her a "Happy Birthday" in addition to a "Merry Christmas"; next she proceeded to the other five horses on her side of the aisle. She wished each a "Merry Christmas", and then did so with the other six horses that Kevin had fed.

When she asked if they could give the horses a little extra grain also, Kevin just laughed. But he agreed, again instructing her how much of each grain to mix, and the quantity to put into the troughs. She followed his instructions and distributed the treat to each one. Lacy gave her another round of nuzzles for this treat, followed by leaning her head against Susie.

Kevin had walked over, telling her they needed to return to the manor. He greeted Lacy, who had already shifted her position, stretching out her head for a pat or two from him. He gently stroked her neck and mane, affectionately speaking to her. She leaned her head against him, enjoying his attention. With a final whisper and gentle stroke of her neck, he told Lacy they had to go. Susie patted Lacy one more time, told her "good-night" and kissed her on her nose. Reluctantly, Susie walked to the door where Kevin was patiently waiting.

It was definitely colder now than when they started this 'Merry Christmas' venture. The bitterly frigid air seemed to penetrate deep into her bones, making her feel as if she was just a hair's width away from becoming frozen solid. They moved quickly, at a fast trot, until they reached the manor. Its warmth was a most welcome change from the outdoors.

As they put away their outdoor clothing in the Cloak Room, Kevin had asked her if anyone knew she was going to the barns. Hesitantly, Susie had said no. His look was somber, as was his tone, when he said she must always let one of the adults know that she is going outside and where she is going, especially when the weather is bad. Susie promised that she would. He had smiled and said "good enough".

They had gone their separate ways; she to the Dorm, and he to the Parlor where the adults had gathered for coffee, tea and a little conversation.

Susie shifted her position again, hoping that this time it would aid her in her quest for sleep. Apparently it was not meant to be. Her mind would not allow her to sleep. It had too many things that needed pondering. For instance, Nini had requested her company for tea tomorrow at two. They were leaving for New Orleans early Saturday morning and would not return until just shortly prior to Miss Taryn's wedding, five weeks away. Nini told Susie she had questions for Susie, but that she also had some answers for which she believed Susie was searching.

Nini had patted Susie's cheek affectionately, telling her that Simon would be busy with his new toys and also with Timmy, so Susie needn't worry that he would miss her for an hour or two. Susie readily agreed, for she had quite a few questions for Nini. Simon would not be a problem – she already knew that he and Timmy planned to play with the train set all day tomorrow. She was definitely free for tea at two.

An hour or so later, Kevin asked her if she still wanted to talk with Kenatae about the Nayatowah. Her breathless "yes" thoroughly showed just how much she did want a meeting with him. Kevin grinned and chuckled. His eyes danced with a mischievous light as he told her Kenatae would be pleased, especially so if he chooses her to be a student.

That surprised her; she hardly expected Kenatae to devote any real time teaching her about Glen Hollow or the Icori customs. She was immensely pleased. Kevin smiled warmly, telling her that Kenatae had said he would meet them at nine o'clock Saturday morning in the meadow where they met the Nayatowah. Susie was thrilled and exuberantly said so. Kevin laughed, telling her that Kenatae tended to be a little long-winded, so she was not to encourage him too much. That made her laugh; somehow she had the distinct feeling that Kevin hung on every word from Kenatae - always did and always would.

Now that she had meetings set with Nini and Kenatae, she was so glad that Mrs. Coppersmith had given her the rest of the week off from kitchen duty. Susie had protested initially, insisting that she wanted to help. Mrs. Coppersmith was firm (like trying to convince a brick wall to pick up and move on its own accord), telling Susie she needed time with Simon, time with the other children and, most especially, some time to herself. Mrs. Coppersmith had hugged Susie gently, then cradled Susie's face in her hands as she looked affectionately into Susie's eyes. Softly she urged Susie to take some time to be a child because it goes by so fast, that Susie would be grown before she realized it. Then, with a quick hug, Mrs. Coppersmith told her to "skedaddle and have some fun". The memory caused Susie to laugh softly.

Susie sighed and rolled over yet again. "Eleven fifteen," she mumbled, looking at her clock. Throwing back her covers, Susie sat upright. "That's it," she decided; "I'm going to the Inner Sanctum. I can get the lanterns placed if nothing else."

Bundling up in several layers of clothing, including thermals and three pairs of heavy socks, Susie headed quietly to her destination.

It took some doing, but Susie finally had the lanterns positioned in such a way as to illuminate most of the Inner Sanctum. Her heart sank a little as she surveyed the enormous room. It was going to require a lot of work to clean it up, especially all of the cobwebs. Susie shuddered at the thought of encountering the horrid creatures.

An idea danced its way through her mind, giving her reason to smile. "No problem," she told the room, using Simon's mantra. "I think it's time to enlist the others. If we all pitch in, we can have it done in two or three hours. Plus, Jared and Aaron can get rid of the creepy-crawlers."

Susie giggled as an image of the two of them chasing spiders popped into her head. One by one she turned off each lantern and then exited the room, closing the panel door behind her. Quickly she crossed the Hidden Room to its secret door and exited, pressing the button to close that door as well. She ran all the way back to the attic room, her sanctuary. Once inside, she closed the secret door and dropped into Nana's chair.

Writing just the briefest of notes (an outline, mainly) in her journal of the day's events, she set the journal down and closed her eyes. She had considered actually writing in her journal, but decided against it. It was late and the outline would do for now. Besides, she rationalized, she would have more to add after her visits with Nini and Kenatae.

Susie smiled. She made one more, quick note in her journal – Saturday, I will ask for their promise to keep everything I tell them, and show them, a secret. Then I will tell them of the secret passageway, of the Hidden Room and of the Inner Sanctum. I will get them to help me to clean the Inner Sanctum.

Susie yawned several times before it dawned on her that she had even done so. She chuckled lightly. It would seem that she was now ready to sleep. She rose to her feet and headed down the stairs. As she locked the attic door, she realized something with a twinge of sadness – it would no longer be her sanctuary once the others started helping. True, Miss Pritchett had put limits on their usage of the attic room, but the more they knew what she knew, the more they would want to be here with her.

"And maybe that's a good thing," she whispered.

Susie awoke feeling a little tired, but then she could hardly expect any-thing else on just three hours of sleep. Stretching her arms high above her head, she slowly moved her muscles from side-to-side. When she felt sufficiently limber, she swung her legs off the bed and slid her feet into her waiting slippers. She was in good spirits though; first, she had meetings with Nini today and with Kenatae tomorrow. Second, she had a plan to get the Inner Sanctum clean so that she could continue exploring. Granted, she would have to include the others, but she was okay with that. And she would have to wait until after Grant and Mary left before she could reveal its existence. The only potential problem that she could foresee would be if the Munchkins accidently revealed the secrets. That would not be good.

"Can't be helped," she conceded; "it's too much work for just me."

Reaching for her robe, she gave a quick look at her alarm clock. "Oh rats," she moaned when she saw the time. She checked the clock – the alarm was off. "I know I set it. I know I did," she puzzled.

Jumping up, she struggled into her robe as she turned to leave. Before she reached the doorway, the girls all popped into her room. "Good Morning," they chimed in unison.

Very much surprised, Susie laughed, delighted that they were already up, dressed and ready for Miss Cora. "Good Morning to you, too," she responded as Megan gave her a big 'good morning' hug.

"You were sleeping so soundly, so I shut off your alarm and gave you a few extra minutes," Juls confessed. Her eyes danced with joy at having done something nice for Susie, and her smile spread from ear to ear. "I'm already up, so I thought I'd give you a break and wake everyone."

Susie's grin matched that of Juls'. "Thanks Juls," she said, giving her a hug which Juls readily reciprocated.

"I'm not going to do this *every* day," she said, feigning her prima-donna attitude; "so don't expect it."

Susie laughed. "I wouldn't dream of it."

Dani hugged Megan, then Juls, then Susie and finally Kat. Susie was surprised that Kat didn't instinctively back away like she usually does. Dani grinned as she moved her hand in a sweeping motion, pointing her index finger at each one of them.

"I think a 'good morning' hug is the best way to start a day. Mommy and Daddy always gave me a hug every morning and every night," she shared. Softly she added, "I miss that. Maybe you do, too. Maybe if we start and end our days with hugs, we'll all feel better."

Megan nodded rapidly, sending her curls into a bouncing frenzy. "It does," she testified; "Susie and I share hugs every day, and I feel great!" Her perky expression made them all laugh, even Kat.

Susie agreed. "I'm game."

"Me, too," echoed an enthusiastic Juls and Megan.

Kat rolled her eyes, endeavoring to pretend that she wasn't interested. However, the sparkle in her eyes clearly said otherwise. Kat shrugged her shoulders and sighed. "I guess I am, too."

Dani yelled, "Group hug!"

They did; and it was fun, especially since Megan really didn't understand the concept of a group hug yet. She ended up inside the group hug, giving each one of them a separate hug. They laughed and explained to her just how a group hug works.

Grinning profusely, Megan shrugged her little shoulders and responded quite unequivocally; "I like my way better." It was decided that they now have a new way to do group hugs.

"Susie, I think if you don't hurry," Juls began teasingly; "Miss Cora will be here in a few minutes, and you won't be ready."

"Oh rats," Susie responded. She had completely forgotten.

"Don't worry," Kat added gleefully; "we'll keep Miss Cora busy."

Kat's idea caught fire with the girls, creating an impish conspiracy as they laughed and headed to the Common Area while Susie hurriedly got dressed.

———

All through breakfast Susie listened to Simon and Timmy sharing with her their plans to build their train world of which Binky, Jr. and Rocko were now an integral part. She considered telling them that the stuffed animals were too big to ride the train cars, but decided against it. They would see for themselves and, knowing them, find a way to make it work. Their plans also included using the Legos and the Lincoln Logs to construct towns, roads and farms.

When she jokingly asked what they were going to use for people, they were momentarily stumped. She laughed, telling them she was only kidding, that they didn't need people. The boys were quick to inform her that they did because you have to have people. Undaunted, Simon dismissed the problem, stating they would come up with something. Timmy nodded his head in agreement, grinning as he swayed and bounced in his chair, eagerly anticipating the plan they would hatch.

Megan, of course, announced that she was going to have a tea party Sunday afternoon and wanted every one of the children to attend. Susie cut short Simon and Timmy's refusal, thanking Megan for her gracious invitation and accepting on behalf of all of them. Jared and Aaron quickly agreed with Susie, telling Megan how honored they were that she chose them to be the first to use her new tea party set. Megan just glowed; her bright eyes sparkled vibrantly as she giggled and clapped with glee.

Susie smiled appreciatively at both Aaron and Jared. They grinned at her, and it was at that moment Susie realized they had taken little Megan to heart – she was indeed their little sister.

———

After breakfast, Mr. Sean accompanied Simon and Timmy to the Rec Room to begin construction of the train set. Their high-pitched chatter as they left the Dining Hall clearly revealed how excited they were. Mr. Sean patiently reminded them to use their inside voices. Susie smiled and laughed inwardly – he was going to have his hands full with the two of them. Susie wondered why he didn't put it together himself before the boys got up this morning; it would have been much easier and faster. It wasn't until she saw Megan ask for Mrs. Coppersmith's help in washing her new china that she understood why Mr. Sean waited. Mrs. Coppersmith's face brightened; she hugged Megan, telling her she would be honored to help Megan wash her special china.

It is love. Love for the children, love of the interaction with them, of building a relationship with them and helping them any way that they could. She smiled. This really is home, she thought.

———

Susie sat back, leaning against her desk chair. With the others all preoccupied, she slipped away, deciding to spend some time formulating her thoughts and questions regarding Glen Hollow. She wouldn't have much time. Story Time was at four; at best she would have a little more than an hour with Nini. Nini had said she had questions for Susie as well. That puzzled her; what possible questions could Nini have? She didn't really know anything about Glen Hollow; at least nothing she could share just yet. Besides, Miss Claire and Miss Taryn have lived here for a long time; surely they have told Nini all about this place. Susie grinned and laughed. Well, maybe not all about it, she mused.

Next Susie focused on her questions for Kenatae. It began with the Nayatowah and progressed to all of the same questions she had for Nini, with a few additional ones regarding the Icori and the earlier residents of Glen Hollow.

Pleased with her questions lists, Susie slid the papers into her desk drawer. As she closed the drawer, her mind flashed to one more. Quickly she retrieved the papers and added the author, Helga Gretchen Von Richter, to both lists. Returning her lists to the drawer, Susie closed it and started downstairs for lunch.

———

After lunch was over, Susie decided to pass the time in the Library while waiting until time to visit with Nini. As she approached the connecting hallway, she stopped. A heated disagreement was brewing again between Miss Claire and Miss Taryn.

"Why not?" Taryn demanded of her mother.

"Because Nini said no," was her mother's patient response.

"That isn't a reason," Taryn retorted. "I want a plausible reason."

Even from around the corner, Susie could feel the tension between them. She could hear the sadness in Miss Claire's voice.

"Oh, ma petite Cœur; must you always be so disagreeable? It is enough that Nini has said she wishes to speak to Susie alone. Why can you not be respectful?"

Haughtily, Taryn snapped, "Respectful? What about respect to me? I asked for time off so I could attend this little tea party of hers. Does she respect that? She is *my* great-great-grandmother, not Susie's. Anything she has to say to that brat she could say in my presence."

"Taryn," Claire's voice now had a harsh edge; "do not ever speak in such a manner again. First, you will show respect to your elders for that is their due. Second, you will never again call anyone a bad name. Third, the matter is closed. Do not try to circumvent Nini's wishes. You will not like the consequences. Now, go to the Chapel, and stay there until I come for you. Whether you pray or sleep is your choice; but you will go, and you will wait for me there."

Fortunately for Susie, Miss Taryn stormed down the inner corridor toward the foyer instead of returning to the main corridor where she currently was standing. She heard Miss Claire sigh, followed by the sound of her climbing the circular stairs.

Susie waited a minute before proceeding to the Library. She mulled over what she had heard, trying to understand Miss Taryn. "I thought everything was better," Susie contemplated, remembering the last few days. "What is her problem? " Susie shook her head, deciding she had neither the time nor the energy to waste on it.

She entered the Library, and made her way to the far corner of the East section. The fireplace had a small fire blazing away, creating a little pocket of warmth and an atmosphere of serenity that Susie desperately needed at this moment. She curled up into one of the wing chairs, resting her head against the chair. As she watched the fire dance around the logs, she began to relax. Closing her eyes, she smiled. A peaceful, tranquil feeling began to settle over her.

All too soon, the mantle clock chimed the quarter hour. She jumped up and ran to the door. She didn't want to be late.

"Would you prefer milk or juice instead of tea?" Nini asked.

"Tea is fine," Susie assured her.

Nini smiled. "Très bien; and how do you take your tea?"

"With a little milk and sugar," Susie replied.

Nini nodded approvingly. "I see you have been taught how to properly take afternoon tea."

Susie smiled. "Nana always had afternoon tea. Sometimes she would fix a cup for me."

Nini finished pouring the tea, first for Susie and then for herself. Next, she removed three little cookies with raspberry filled centers (she called them tarts) from the server, placed them on a dessert plate and handed the plate to Susie. Then she repeated the process for herself. Susie used the time to examine the delicate napkin Nini had given her. It was made of a fine linen, ice blue in color, with matching lace. A bouquet of violets was beautifully embroidered in one corner. The ribbon that held the bouquet together wove its way along the edging, creating a vine-like pattern as it encompassed the napkin.

"Pretty isn't it? Do you know how to embroider?" Nini asked.

The question had surprised Susie, startling her out of her examination of the napkin. "It's beautiful," she responded. "Nana started teaching me, but I couldn't do anything like this."

"Not so," Nini told her. She leaned slightly toward Susie, her eyes sparkling with amusement. "All that is required is practice, lots of practice."

She sipped her tea and ate one of the tarts. Susie followed her example, relishing the delectable treat. Nini made small talk while they shared tea. Mostly, Nini wanted to know where Susie had previously lived, what she liked about those places, what Susie thought of Glen Hollow and if she and Simon were happy here. Susie answered all of Nini's questions, and most assuredly answering that she and Simon were very happy here. Nini nodded her head, listening as Susie mentioned Simon's penchant for animals and for trees.

Nini chuckled, sharing a memory from Taryn's childhood when Taryn was about seven. Nini was visiting, and Taryn wanted to show off her new-found skill of tree climbing. She had practiced on the smaller trees in the gardens, and had thought that the old oak tree would be no different.

So she climbed it. After several hours of hunting for her all through the manor and no one could find her, it was decided she must have gone outside. It was Mr. Sean who had found her. She had climbed about a hundred feet up the tree, and was too frightened of falling to climb back down on her own.

"Oh, how that child cried and wailed when he told her he had to leave in order to get the proper equipment. Never have you heard such screams. By then, most of us had gathered at the base of the tree, reassuring her she'd be fine. She moaned and carried on so, demanding that someone climb up and get her. Well, that was not happening, I can tell you. It wasn't long until Mr. Sean arrived in the bucket truck and got her down safely," Nini told Susie.

Nini laughed as she next relayed that Taryn had wrapped her arms around his neck so tightly that she nearly choked the poor man to death. "But," she added with a wink; "we never had to worry about her climbing any more trees."

"Didn't any of the other children know where she was when you were searching for her?" Susie asked.

"Oui, they did; but they were a little pleased to see her in such a state," Nini confirmed. She sighed a little sadly, but also with a resignation and acceptance of what is. "Taryn never got along with other children. She was not willing to share her parents with anyone."

Nini straightened as she asked if Susie would like some more tea. Susie shook her head, and told her, "No, thank you."

"Bon," Nini responded. "You have questions for me, yes?"

Susie nodded, "Yes, ma'am."

"Please, call me Nini."

Smiling, Susie answered," Okay, Nini."

Now that the moment was here, Susie felt a little apprehensive. What if Nini wouldn't answer her questions? Or, what if she couldn't answer her questions? Even worse, what if Susie didn't like the answers? What if … Susie stopped her mind from whirling, willing herself to focus on Nini who was closely scrutinizing the expressions on Susie's face.

Nini smiled graciously. "Ask what you will, Susie. I am here to help."

There was a comfort in that smile, a familiar feeling. Something that Susie couldn't explain; but it was there nonetheless, giving her the sensation that Nini could be trusted like she had trusted Nana. Susie relaxed and found that her moment of panic was gone. She is ready, regardless of what the answers are.

"Miss Claire told me a story about The Cards. Simon and I saw her with them in the Library. Simon asked to hear the story, so she told us. She had me mix them up in the bag and place them on the table, one at a time. It's just a game, I know; but the way she looked, she seemed upset. She said she had to ask you about it. When I asked her later what you had said, she told me that you were coming here and would tell me. I have to admit, I am pretty curious about it."

Nini smiled, but the smile was more of one that suggested she knew something that Susie did not. It was the smile of a wise, old sage. Nini shrugged one shoulder as if to dismiss what Susie had said. "You say it is but a game, of no importance. Why should it matter to you? Why have you given thought to it at all?"

This surprised Susie; it was not at all what she expected. "I don't know. It just … I mean … I'm just curious why Miss Claire reacted the way she did."

"I see. So this curiosity you have has led you to me, to learn, n'est-ce pas? Nini asked, smiling playfully.

Susie grinned. "Yes."

"Bon," she replied with an air of satisfaction like a cat who has filled its tummy with warm cream. "We shall begin. Let us join hands and pray," she instructed, extending her hands to Susie.

Susie gently clasped the elder lady's hands in her own. She bowed her head and closed her eyes, waiting for Nini to begin. And waited… and waited. Just when Susie began to wonder if Nini had fallen asleep, Nini began to pray. The power of this woman's prayer was very much like Nana's, Susie immediately realized. She felt that same surge of power as she did when Nana prayed. Nini was a prayer warrior just like Nana.

Nini prayed, asking that she would receive the message clearly and to be able to relay it to Susie accurately. She prayed that Susie would understand and receive the message, treasuring it in her heart. She prayed for strength for Susie, that she would remain true to the Almighty regardless of where her path might lead. She ended her prayer with thanksgiving for all that God has done, is doing and will do.

She smiled, a radiant smile, as she placed the photograph on the table in front of Susie.

Her voice was soft, full of wonder and awe, as she began to explain. "This is your path. Where you are in life at this moment is here. As you can see it soon splits and forms two, completely separate paths. This mean you have a choice to make; you must choose one. This path is one that is ordinary, but is a life path filled with many accomplishments and much joy."

"But this path is very different. It is a path of power, great power. Not of your own, but because of who you are, your lineage, and because of the Almighty. It is a path that can do great and wonderful things, accomplishing much for the Kingdom of Light. But it can also be a path of great and terrible destruction, filled with darkness, if one is not very careful and very strong in their faith."

"Look here; see how the lines in this path connect, one to the other and overlapping at times. It shows the many places that this path will take you, sometimes more than once. This path will take you places that are far beyond your understanding, or even mine, at this time. When reading this pattern and sequence, I have seen images I do not understand, though I have sought understanding."

Tears filled her eyes, causing them to shine like a glassy sea; her beautiful smile radiated the joy that filled her soul. "The Holy Spirit has told me it is not mine to understand, but to pray for you. Knowledge and understanding will be revealed to you when the time is right. It is my honor and my privilege to uphold you in prayer."

"There is a great evil brewing, far greater than what is already here," she continued somberly. "It desires to control this world, to enslave it and is soon coming. It will descend on this world like a plague, and will bring strife, chaos, fear, hatred, sickness and death. Those that stand against it, it will seek to destroy. But the Almighty is greater than all of evil combined. He is your Strength and your Song. He will be your Rock and your Shield if you seek Him, if you trust Him. The battle is His, and is won through faith and trust in Him."

Placing her right hand on Susie's head and raising her left hand to Heaven, she began to pray. She asked for God's blessings on Susie, to protect her and to guide her, to strengthen her and to encourage her heart to follow Him. Then she prayed the blessing from the Book of Numbers.

Somewhere deep inside her spirit, Susie heard a still, small voice that gave a resounding "Amen!" when Nini finished her prayer. She felt a power that seemed to imbed itself in her spirit, giving her a sense of strength that she had not known before. She remembered that the angels had told both she and Kat that they were here for a purpose.

Opening her eyes, she found Nini smiling at her. Susie could sense that Nini knew Susie was now different. Something had happened deep within her being just now, and Nini knew; Nini understood. She hugged Nini tightly and began to cry. She didn't even know why she was crying. It seemed to be a powerful force within her, welling up from the deepest recess of her soul; and she could not stop its flow.

Nini held her, gently rocking her back and forth as she repeatedly whispered, "All is well, ma petite Cœur. All is well, come what may."

For the longest time, Nini just held her, rocking her and humming softly. As her tears subsided, Susie realized that Nini had been humming the same tune she had heard coming from the East Wing. She looked up at Nini and asked, "What song is that?"

Nini smiled as she answered, "I do not know, Susie. I heard it many years ago. A lady that came into our shop was humming it. It captured my soul from the moment I heard it."

"You didn't ask her?" Susie queried, her tone incredulous.

"No, I had another customer to assist. I had hoped that I would be able to ask her but," Nini shrugged her shoulders and sighed. "It was not meant to be. It is enough that I have the beautiful music that fills my heart."

Susie wanted to tell Nini about the East Wing, but she wasn't sure she should. Then she wondered if she should tell Nini about the angels. Again, she wasn't certain what she should do. Silently she asked Tahlranel for help.

She giggled; Tahlranel was there.

"What is it that makes you laugh so cheerfully?" Nini asked. "I am delighted to see this happiness; but it is sudden, n'est-ce pas?"

There was a keen understanding in her eyes; Susie could see that Nini's spirit sensed the presence of the angels.

Tahlranel spoke, telling Susie what she could say.

"Do you believe angels exist?" Susie asked.

"But of course. They are servants of the Almighty God. Sometimes they bring to us messages from Him; sometimes they are to protect us from harm, or to deliver us from harm that has befallen us. Sometimes they bring healing or comfort, and sometimes they bring to us visions or dreams, or the interpretations of visions and dreams. Why do you ask?" she answered with a perceptive look.

"Have you ever seen one?" Susie pressed, grinning and fairly nearly ready to burst with excitement.

Nini's expression was a cross between puzzlement and curiosity. "No, I do not know that I have. I have felt their presence, and have heard their whispers from time to time; but cannot say that I know I have seen one. I do believe, as the Good Book states, we attend angels unaware at times. Why do you ask?"

Susie grinned. "I have seen them." She paused waiting for a shocked reaction from Nini. No such reaction happened. That thoroughly surprised Susie. "Did you hear me? I said, I have seen angels."

Nini's laugh was filled with joyfulness. "I heard you, ma petite Cœur; I heard you. However, the Spirit of God told me this morning not to be surprised by anything you would reveal to me today."

Susie shook her head, chuckling. "Well, it's true. I have seen and spoken with angels. So has Simon, and Megan and Kat."

Nodding as if in agreement with Susie's declaration, Nini sipped her tea, inwardly praying a brief missive for Susie, for Glen Hollow and for Miss Pritchett. Although Nini had always felt as if there was something familiar about Miss Pritchett, it was this trip that she recognized Miss Pritchett from all those years ago. This time, Miss Pritchett was not covering her scar as she had what few times Nini had been to visit Glen Hollow. Nini would never forget the scar on that young girl's face, and now Nini knew. She knew that Glen Hollow was at the epicenter of a great spiritual war, and it was about to come to a bursting point.

Nini looked upon Susie with such love and compassion, reminding Susie again of Nana. There was a wisdom, an understanding, in her eyes that Susie had also seen every day reflected in Nana's eyes.

"Little one," Nini spoke softly; "you are where you are meant to be. Dark forces have been trying to destroy this place for a very long time now. A battle will be waged here. I do not know when, but I now know that you are here for this purpose. I am delighted that you see and hear these special beings. It does my heart good to know this."

Silently Susie asked a favor of Tahlranel. At first he denied her request. She asked again, telling him she really needed him to grant the favor. He smiled and nodded. A bright flash of light filled the room and instantly subsided. There in its place was Tahlranel.

He smiled at Nini saying, "Do not be afraid. I am a servant of the Almighty One. I am Tahlranel. I am the one who watches over Susie."

The old woman smiled so sweetly, so contentedly. Her eyes brimmed with tears of joy as she witnessed the presence of the angel.

"Behold," he said as he pointed to his right. Another flash of light appeared resembling a starburst before it dissipated. Standing next to Tahlranel was another angel.

"Do not fear. I am a servant of the Almighty One. I am the one assigned to you. I am Shonrohiel."

Tears of joy flowed down her wrinkled face as she nodded her head. Her countenance glowed with a peace and a joy that flowed from the deep recesses of her spirit. "Thank you for revealing yourself," she said softly. "It is good to see you."

He smiled lovingly as he gazed upon his charge.

Tahlranel spoke to Susie. "Now it is time for you to meet with Simon and the others."

He was right. Nini's clock showed she only had ten minutes to get to the Parlor for Story Time. The time had just flown by, and she still had so many more questions to ask. "Okay," Susie responded reluctantly.

"We will talk again when I return for the wedding," Nini assured her.

Susie quickly hugged Nini, waved good-by to the two angels and darted out the door.

Tahlranel appeared suddenly in the corridor.

"Someone will see you," Susie whispered.

He shook his head. "Only you can see and hear me. You must keep what she has told you in your heart; tell no one," he instructed.

Susie nodded. "I wanted to tell Nini a few things about Glen Hollow, and I still have more questions."

He smiled. "For now, you have what you need. Go to Simon. He waits for you." And then he was gone.

"Hmm," Susie replied. "I guess it'll have to be enough where Nini is concerned. But I still have my meeting with Kenatae tomorrow. I'm sure he has some answers for me."

Story Time was another success. Susie had deftly told the second of the three installments and finished barely in time for dinner. The only ones missing from Story Time were Miss Taryn and Mr. Dale. Nini had arrived just seconds before she had begun the story. Susie delayed the starting of it, hoping Nini would arrive. And she was glad that she had waited

Nini entered the Parlor accompanied by Miss Claire, Mimi and Mema. They were all in high spirits. The way they waved to Susie told her that Nini had told them something positive of the visit, but not what was said or had transpired. As they entered, Nini quite deliberately placed her index finger to her lips, holding it there for several seconds as she made eye contact with Susie. It was to be kept a secret between herself and Nini. Susie understood; smiled and nodded. Nini grinned.

Everyone chatted about the second installment, wanting hints about the final installment. Susie kept repeating they would have to wait until after dinner. Inwardly, she couldn't help but laugh. She remembered the many times she would beg Nana for hints, and she was told the same thing: you must wait.

Dinner time seemed to go by much faster than usual, and Susie found herself swept along with the excitement of the others. She had answered many questions about Nana's stories, such as, how many are there (she had never counted them), do you remember them all (she wasn't certain, but thought so), how many serial stories are there (don't know, but there are more of them than the individual ones), and did Nana create them all, or were they told to Nana (don't actually know, but pretty sure they are all from Nana's mind).

After the questions had ceased, Miss Pritchett asked one of her own. With a look of impish joy, she asked if Susie would be willing to permanently have the after dinner Story Time in the Parlor, and continue with Nana's stories each time. She explained that the adults also enjoy them very much, and would love to be able to hear more. Miss Pritchett also suggested that the afternoon session remain a book reading session as a means to keep the younger ones interested in reading books.

Everyone, well nearly everyone, begged and pleaded for her to say yes. How could she not? Besides, she found that she loved telling the stories just as much as Nana had. She agreed, and received a rousing round of applause and whistles. It was a good feeling. Sighing contentedly, she silently thanked Nana.

After Miss Pritchett rang the bell, signaling that dinner was over, Mrs. Coppersmith informed everyone to just leave the dishes. "They'll keep," she said; "let's go hear the rest of the story."

It was almost like a stampede the way everyone quickly moved away from the tables, left the Dining Hall and headed for the Parlor. Simon, Timmy and Megan moved the fastest and were gone before anyone else had a chance to leave. Susie laughed, thinking it was just another one of their contests to see who could get there first. She noticed that Jared, Aaron and Jose were also grinning, so she had assumed that they also deduced the Munchkins had another contest going.

What she didn't know, until much later, was that it was an entirely different type of contest. So far, Mary had usurped Megan's spot at Story Time every single time, usually with the assistance of her brother, Grant. Megan was determined that it would not happen tonight.

She had asked Simon and Timmy to help her. Jared, Aaron and Jose had overheard her, and helped the Munchkins devise a plan to aid Megan in her quest for a prime spot at Story Time. The plan was simple: as soon as Miss Pritchett rang the bell, the Munchkins were to immediately run as fast as they could to the Parlor. That would give them a head start. Jared, Aaron and Jose would delay the arrival of Grant and Mary, ensuring Megan a place in the front row, along with Simon and Timmy.

Susie had noticed at the time that Jared, Aaron and Jose were walking together, joking and kidding with each other. That in itself didn't ring any bells; however, she did think it a little odd that they were moving a little slower than normal. Grant and Mary were walking directly behind them, clearly wanting to get around the boys. Every time they tried to pass, Jared, Aaron and Jose would thwart their attempt. Much to their credit, they managed to make it appear each time as accidental; but it wasn't. Although Susie would have preferred that they resolve it a different way, she couldn't help but laugh and be thrilled that the guys were looking out for Megan.

———

Susie finished tucking in Simon and Timmy, listening to their stories about Train Town (that's what they named it), and how Mr. Sean was the best. He had patiently spent most of his day helping them to construct the train tracks. Mr. Henry had graciously built a table to house this endeavor. They prattled on about how big it was, and that it was just the right height for them. They could stand and play, or they could sit on the benches that he also had made.

Next they informed her that Mr. Sean was going to help them tomorrow build the town, the roads and the farms. Mr. Henry had promised to make all signs for the buildings, the town and the railroad crossings. JT had volunteered to make a water tower for the town and a river, complete with a waterfall. Joe told them he would make some fences, light poles, trees and park benches out of some scrap wood. Allan Roy was going to make an electrical station for the town (they had to ask what that was) and give it working lights. Sam and Kevin had promised to carve some town animals and some farm animals. They were so excited; their angelic faces just glowed with happiness, and their eyes glistened and sparkled with joy.

She had to tell them several times to settle down and go to sleep. Much had happened in the past two days to make them happy, especially with tonight being the first night of their new, shared living space. How they convinced Miss Ginger to allow it, she had no idea. But they did, so they are.

Susie smiled as she told them it made her happy to see them so happy. (This produced another round of giggles and wrestling). However, she reminded them, Miss Ginger had said that if they didn't sleep, they would have to go back to having separate rooms. They calmed down considerably, but Susie could easily see that it would be awhile yet before either of them fell asleep tonight.

She tucked Simon's old Binky under his arm, and Timmy's Fu-Fu (stuffed panda) under his arm. Giving both of them one last 'good-night' kiss, she turned the night light on and turned off the overhead light, waving to them as she left. She hadn't gone two feet when she heard loud giggling and snickering. She popped her head back inside and found them wrestling. They froze, staring at her with that 'uh-oh' look she had seen so many times.

"If I had been Miss Ginger, you'd be sleeping in separate rooms right now," she admonished, struggling not to laugh.

"I'll be asleep in one minute," Timmy announced, closing his eyes as his head hit his pillow.

"Me too," Simon heartily concurred, following Timmy's example.

"Good night, boys," Susie called out, desperately suppressing the urge to laugh.

"Good night, Susie," they sweetly responded in sing-song unison.

She left and had taken only three steps when she heard muffled giggles and the sound of them repeatedly telling each other to "hush and go to sleep", and "no, you hush and go to sleep". Covering her mouth in an attempt to contain her laughter, she ran as fast as she could and exited into the corridor. She leaned against the wall, laughing until her sides ached and the tears rolled.

———

After Megan's tuck-in, good-night hugs and kisses, Susie hurriedly went to her sanctuary. Retrieving her journal from its hiding place, she began entering the events that had happened, beginning with Christmas Eve and culminating with today's events. Her hand was aching from the stress of so much writing, and her neck felt stiff and sore. She stood and stretched for a few seconds, determined to finish what she had started. She returned to Nana's chair and continued writing. She had several questions in the margins, things that she wanted to remember to ask Nini about when she returned next month.

She put her journal away, extinguished what little remained of the fire before leaving the attic and quickly went to bed. It was much later than she had planned to be, but she was glad that she had taken the time to catch up her journal. She chided herself about being so lax; she really must be more conscientious about writing every day, she admonished herself.

Crawling under her covers, she gave a very condensed version of her usual prayers. She heard the clock chiming the two o'clock hour as she faded into a deep sleep.

———

Morning is truly a glorious time of day, and this one promised to be just that. Susie awakened feeling invigorated despite having had such meager amounts of sleep here of late. She bounded out of bed, cheerfully told Juls "good morning" on her way to awaken Dani, Kat and Megan. Each received a "good morning" sing-song cheer, with Megan also receiving her usual hug and 'itsy-bitsy spider' routine. Afterwards, Megan beat her to the hallway where she loudly yelled, "group hug time, group hug time". Within seconds, Dani, Juls and Kat appeared, and they shared a group hug before getting their day started.

They were ready long before Miss Cora arrived.

———

After breakfast, Megan was preoccupied with Mrs. Coppersmith, planning for tomorrow's tea party. Mrs. Coppersmith was determined that the inaugural tea party had to be spectacular. Megan clapped ecstatically with each treat Mrs. Coppersmith suggested. Susie chuckled – it would be a long, long planning session if the decisions were all left to Megan.

Simon and Timmy had already left with Mr. Sean, making suggestions to him as they headed to the Rec Room. He had a very busy morning ahead of him building Train Town.

Aaron, Jared and Jose had left the Dining Hall shortly after Simon's and Timmy's departure with Mr. Sean, whereabouts unknown.

Dani, Kat and Juls had enthusiastically discussed all through breakfast that they should have a day of pampering, making today a day of beauty. Excitedly, they laughed and chatted, going into detail about hair styles, nail polish and such. Miss Cora had already offered to help, as did Miss Ginger and Miss Elsa. They had tried several times to get Susie to agree, but she had dodged the bullet each time, usually answering a fortuitously timed question hurled at her by one of the Munchkins.

Now that breakfast was over, the girls ran to the beauty consulting volunteers, chatting away and finalizing plans. She heard her name called several times by Dani, Kat and Juls. Fortunately, there were several adults blocking the line of sight between her and the girls, so Susie was able to slip away without being seen.

Arriving at the Library, Susie pushed the door open; quickly she realized that this would be the first place they would look for her. Changing her mind, Susie headed to the last place that they would ever think of to look for her – the classroom. She giggled as she trotted down the corridor, rounded the corner and ran through the foyer into the southwest corridor. Once inside the classroom, she sank into one of the chairs, waiting for the time to meet Kevin.

———

They trudged through the snow, and Susie was so glad that she had decided to go back upstairs and put on warmer clothes. In addition to the thermal pants and shirt, she was wearing two sweatshirts, knit pants and a pair of sweat pants, three pairs of socks (two thermals and one woolen), her wool scarf, gloves, heavy winter coat, ear muffs, a knit cap and wool-lined boots. She looked like an Eskimo and movement was a bit cumbersome, but she was warm. Kevin had laughed when he saw her outside the Cloak Room, asking if she was planning an Artic outing. She teased back, telling him she wasn't the one that would be freezing and turning all shades of blue.

Upon arrival at the meadow, Susie was surprised to see that a tepee had been erected not far from the tree they had decided that they would not enter in the Christmas tree contest. A thin spiral of smoke wafted up and out of the top of the tepee.

Kevin called out a greeting in Icori. The flap of the tepee opened, and Kenatae emerged. He smiled at them, greeting Kevin with the same greeting (or so it seemed to Susie) before telling her that she was welcome. Kenatae gave them both a hug just as Little White Dove and Running Wolf emerged from the tepee. They hugged their son, greeting him and then greeted Susie, inviting them both into the warmth of the tepee.

Susie was very surprised at how warm it was inside. Within a very few minutes, she began to feel as if she was roasting. She was quick to shed the outer layers as Kevin just smirked with that 'I told you so' look. Little White Dove offered her some hot herbal tea, which Susie eagerly accepted.

"Kevin tells me that you have seen and have talked with Nayatowah," Kenatae began.

Susie nodded. "Yes, sort of. We saw him and pet him, but I didn't talk to him. I just saw through his eyes what happened to Simon."

Kenatae's smile was a patient one. "That is a form of communication, same as talking. Talking with your mind is more complicated. Very few can actually do this. When did you first notice you could?"

Susie was a little confused. She thought she was here to learn about the Nayatowah and Glen Hollow, but all Kenatae was doing was asking her questions about herself. "I don't know. I've always had a connection with animals, most animals anyway. It's only been recent that I've had other experiences." She took a sip of the tea; it was delicious.

Kenatae nodded slowly, studying her. "When did you first learn of Nayatowah?" he asked softly.

Startled, Susie looked up at him. "I saw it the same time Kevin did," she answered.

"That is not what I asked you," his tone was firm. His eyes narrowed as he watched her closely.

Susie glanced over at Kevin. From the expression on his face, she knew not to side-step any more questions. Slowly, deliberately, she sipped her tea, trying to determine just what and how much she should share. Her heart began racing as her mind whirled. She quickly decided it couldn't hurt to tell him about the book. After all, it had nothing to do with anything else that had happened. She took one last sip. She smiled at Kenatae.

"I found a book in the Library. It's called 'Wolves: Protectors of Seekers'. I read the book just a few days before we saw it. The book didn't give it a name, and I didn't think they were real until that day," she answered.

Kenatae nodded. "Your words are true," he stated. He picked up a stick, and began stirring the embers with it. He tossed the stick on top of the newly formed flame that had arisen around the branches. He looked at her; and in that gaze, she felt as if he could see into her soul, know all her thoughts and see all her memories. She shivered, but she met his gaze without flinching or looking away.

He smiled. "What is it you wish to know?" he asked.

Relieved that she had apparently passed some kind of test (although just what, she had no idea), she answered, "I want to know about the Nayatowah; and I have so many questions about Glen Hollow and also the Icori. I've been told that you were friends with Miss Murielle," she began, but stopped when she noticed the sadness that had surfaced on his face.

"Yes, we were friends," he admitted. "Why would you have questions about someone you've never met?"

"If I had met her, I wouldn't need to ask questions," Susie countered.

He laughed, amused by her attempt to be clever. "Possibly. What is your question?"

"Do you know what happened to her?" she asked, her voice barely above a whisper.

The silence was deafening, enveloping them like a shroud. No one moved. The only sounds were those of the fire crackling and popping as it consumed its way toward extinction. Several agonizing minutes passed as they listened to the fire, watching it dance its way into oblivion.

"Do you?" came the quiet response from the old man. He ceased staring at the fire and looked at her.

The shock wave of that question volleyed to her sent a ripple through her. What should she say, she wondered? Should I tell him? If I do, he'll want to know how I know. If I tell him that, will he tell Miss Pritchett? Does he already know? Is that why he's asking me? To see if I'll be truthful or not?

His lips began to slowly spread into a grin as he watched her inner turmoil. "You want me to trust you," he spoke without inflection; "but you do not want to trust me. You must choose."

The old man sighed and looked first to his grandson, then to Little White Dove and finally to his great-grandson, Kevin. He closed his eyes, waiting for her decision.

"Yes, I know what happened to Miss Murielle. I know how she died, and who caused her death," she told him.

"And you know this how?" he asked, his eyes still closed.

Susie took in a deep breath, and slowly released it. She felt as if she were about to fall into a bottomless pit. What if he doesn't know all the details, she thought? What if he's fishing just like I am? But if he does know and I don't tell the truth, he will not ever speak to me again, or answer any other questions I have, she reasoned.

Susie sighed; she made her decision. "I know because I found her journal and read her last few entries."

The only indication she had that he had heard her was the smile of satisfaction that momentarily formed on his lips. His position remained unchanged, and his eyes remained closed.

"What is the name of the person who caused her death?" he asked.

Nana had always said, 'in for a penny, in for a pound', so Susie decided there was no reason to withhold anything now. "Her name is Gorza."

"So you do know," he stated matter-of-factly. He opened his eyes and smiled at her.

"How did you know her name?" Susie asked.

The sadness returned to his countenance, and he looked away, back to the fire. "As I said, we were friends. As soon as she suspected Gorza, she came to see me. I could find nothing to reveal that Gorza had come here, or was even responsible for what had happened. At least, not at first. By the time I found out what had actually happened, it was too late. She had been poisoned, and it had already done its damage."

"How was Gorza able to come here?" Susie asked, concerned it could happen again.

He shook his head. "She didn't. That was her plan – to trick Murielle to come to her world. Gorza had sent one of her minions. She pretended to be Gorza to get Murielle to come after Gorza. Although that is not what Murielle did, the end result was the same. Murielle went to see Nori, who just happens to live on the same world as Gorza."

He shrugged. "Had Gorza been here, Murielle would still be alive. Gorza felt the force of Murielle's spirit the moment Murielle entered her world. When she discovered that Murielle had not come for her but sought the aid of Nori, Gorza cast a spell that created the poisonous plant."

He paused, turning to face Susie. She could see the great sadness in his eyes for the loss of his friend. "Murielle blamed herself for not noticing the plant when she entered that world, thinking she could have avoided it when she left had she noticed. But it wasn't there when she entered. The spell was cast so that the plant would attack her; Gorza left nothing to chance. Had she tried to avoid it, she could not have. The plant was meant for Murielle, and only Murielle. To destroy the plant, Murielle would have had to know of its existence and sought aid from Ashara, not Nori. I knew Murielle well; well enough to know how observant she was, how intuitive she was and how strong she was. That is how I know the plant was not there when she entered."

"Why couldn't anyone help her?" Susie asked, her own anguish beginning to seep into her voice.

Kenatae shrugged. "I do not pretend to know the mind of the Great Spirit, nor do I presume to answer for Him. What I do know is my friend chose to put herself out of the path she was to walk. Sometimes the consequences are devastating, sometimes not."

"Why didn't you tell Miss Pritchett about her mother?"

"What should I have said?" he asked softly.

In that moment, Susie now understood there was nothing he could have told Miss Pritchett when she was a child. As the years passed, he could not tell her without possibly destroying any good memories she might have of her father, a risk he wasn't willing to take. "What about now? Why not tell her now?" Susie asked him.

He smiled at her, and she could see in his eyes that he was pleased at her questions. Suddenly she had the distinct impression that he was leading her to ask what he wanted her to ask. She glanced at Kevin. Like his parents, his face was expressionless, well-guarded; unlike his parents, his eyes were twinkling. So ... they also knew that Kenatae was guiding her to ask certain questions; Kevin just wasn't as practiced yet at hiding his thoughts. She wasn't certain whether or not to be irritated with Kenatae. Why not just tell her what he wants her to know?

Kenatae began to chuckle as he observed her, seeing her thoughts displaying on her face as clearly as if watching fish swim in the crystal waters of the Anicaw. His golden brown eyes began to dance with amusement as he witnessed her struggle.

"You have a sharp mind," he told her; "and you seek to find logic and reason in all things. That is neither good nor bad. What you do not understand is that not everything can be defined or understood by logic and reason alone. Most things defy logic and reason, and must be seen through eyes of faith and trust in the Great Spirit. It takes wisdom to know which is required."

Susie began to speak, but Kenatae held up his hand, stopping her.

"And you need to learn when to be silent. If you are constantly speaking, you will not hear the small voice of the Great Spirit. He speaks to your spirit, but He will not compete with other voices. If you choose poorly, you will miss His words to you."

He sat quietly, looking intently into her eyes. At first, she was ill at ease. His gaze was a little disconcerting; it had once again become piercing, as if to scour the deepest recesses of her soul. Slowly she began to relax when she realized that such a gaze also left that person open for intense scrutiny. She smiled, returning his scrutiny with her own.

A low rumble began, developing in a full, hearty laugh. Kenatae nodded his head as he laughed; his eyes were laughing as well. "You learn quickly for one so young. Your spirit is strong," he told her.

Susie laughed with him, pleased that she had again passed some undeclared test.

"What do you want to know about Nayatowah?" he asked her.

"Whatever you can tell me," she answered.

His smile was one of approval. "Nayatowah is the name given by the Icori to the spirit wolf," he began in a soft, almost sing-song tone. "They are creatures of Light. They travel among the worlds by walking on the Light and in the Light. I do not know how they do it," he added in anticipation of the question she was about to ask. "What I do know is that the Great Spirit sends them. Wherever He sends them, they go. Whomever they are to protect, they protect."

He stopped speaking and just smiled at her.

She waited, but he didn't resume. 'It's almost as if he's waiting for me to ask a question,' she thought. Then she realized he was doing just that. 'What in the world does he want me to ask?' she pondered silently. She smiled.

"Why was the Nayatowah sent to protect Simon?" she asked him.

His grin spread rapidly across his face. "That is a good question, what we all seek an answer to," he told her.

"You don't know?" she shot back, stunned and surprised.

His chuckle reminded her of Nana, of the times whenever she had asked Nana a question that the answer seemed obvious to Nana as an adult, but was not so obvious to Susie.

His smile was kind as he answered. "What I know is that Nayatowah was sent to protect Simon, but Nayatowah do not communicate the why. They are servants of the Great Spirit; they do not ask why. They just go and do as they are commanded. What I think is Simon has a purpose here that has not yet been fulfilled. The dark forces lured Simon into chasing the rabbit into the woods where he became lost and would have died from exposure. They sought to stop whatever purpose Simon is to fulfill. Nayatowah was sent to undo what they had done, to protect him until others arrived to do so. You and Kevin were the ones for whom Nayatowah waited."

He paused again, his eyes merrily dancing.

"What is Simon's purpose?" she asked. The look on his face told her she had asked the wrong question, and she hated that.

"Who is to say? Whatever it is, it could be today or in a hundred years," he responded with a shrug. "Simon may never know what it is; it may unfold naturally as part of his life path. That is in the mind of the Great Spirit; He chooses to reveal what He chooses to reveal."

Susie nodded. 'Get a grip,' she told herself. 'Think; ask the right questions,' she mentally chided herself. She glanced at Kevin. He grinned and winked. And she knew.

"Kevin said that Nayatowah honored me when it lay at my feet. What did he mean, and why did Nayatowah do that?"

A look of sheer pride radiated from Kenatae's face. She had asked the right questions. "Nayatowah recognize those in whom the spirit is strong.

It is said that in days of old, there were those among men who had such strong spirits and strong faith in the Great Spirit that Nayatowah would obey their commands. Nayatowah cannot be tricked. They can see the truth in one's spirit, and know whether or not your words to them are from the Great Spirit. No one has ever seen anyone do such a thing, but it is a legend from the earliest days of Icori history.

He smiled at her. "Nayatowah honored you for a reason. Perhaps it is because your spirit is strong. It may be that Nayatowah knows something about you that you do not. But it may also be that Nayatowah did so in order to speak with you, to show you what happened to Simon."

He paused briefly, studying her. "It may be all these things, some, or none of these," he added and then fell silent.

"Is there anything else you can tell me about Nayatowah?" she asked softly, hardly above a whisper.

"Only that I have never known of anyone that has spoken with Nayatowah, nor of anyone Nayatowah has honored."

He paused briefly before adding with an amused chuckle, "And I have never known anyone to actually pet Nayatowah, until now."

He shook his head and laughed. "When Kevin told me that he sat beside Nayatowah and petted it; and that Nayatowah laid its head in his lap as you and Simon also petted it, I had to wonder if it had been a dream or a vision. But Kevin assured me that it is real. And so it is." He returned his attention to the fire, dancing and twisting along the branches.

Susie smiled. She glanced again at Kevin and his parents. Amusement was the best way to describe Kevin's expression. His parents, however, gazed upon their son with pride, love and admiration.

All of a sudden Susie realized something Kenatae had said that he couldn't possibly have known. Without forethought, Susie asked, "How do you know Simon chased a rabbit into the forest?"

"That is a good question, little one," he answered. Slowly he turned and faced her. "How do you think I know?"

Perplexed, Susie slowly shook her head, shrugging her shoulders. "I don't know."

There it was again – that stare of his that inevitably carved deep into your being. Softly, he asked, "Who else was with you?"

Dumbfounded, Susie turned and looked at Kevin. He just grinned and winked.

"You?"

He nodded.

"But you didn't say anything."

He shrugged. "Nor did you."

Kenatae laughed softly, amused by her confusion. "You are not the only one with spiritual gifts, little one," he told her.

Susie nodded, a little chuckle escaping as she realized the veracity of his words. She noted to herself that she would discuss this later with Kevin. She also planned on asking Tahlranel why Chakahel had not rescued Simon, a thought that had not occurred to her until just now.

They sat in silence, sipping herbal tea and watching the fire as it flared and danced along the branches. Strangely enough, the crackling and popping sounds mingling with the scent of the burning wood gave as much comfort to her soul as its warmth did to her body. A sense of completeness seemed to float from the fire, cocooning them in its sweetness.

As she sat enjoying the fire and the tea, Susie kept trying to find the right way to broach the subject of Glen Hollow and its history. She didn't want to stir any sad or painful memories for Kenatae. Nor did she want to wade into areas that might be considered off-limits to her. Finally she had an idea, and her quiet voice broke the stillness.

"Kenatae," she began; "Reverend Tillman told us of the Icori Legend, 'The Witch of the Mist'. I believe it to be true. Is the Bride Miss Pritchett's ancestor?"

Shock waves rippled through the tent as Kevin's parents reacted to her question. They were obviously unprepared for her leap of faith or logic, depending upon one's point of view. Kevin just continued to be amused. He winked again at Susie. Kenatae, however, showed no emotion, no visible reaction whatsoever. Several minutes more passed in silence. Susie was just aching to repeat her question, or ask another one but kept still, remembering what Kenatae had said earlier.

When Susie thought she could no longer endure his silence, he spoke. His voice was soft. Staring into the flames, his countenance held a distant look as if he was no longer with them. His answer was so soft, she almost missed it. '"Yes."

Elation! Excitement! Jubilation! Triumph! All these emotions and more surged through Susie as she rejoiced in hearing that one, little word. Never could she have imagined how one, small word could have so much meaning. Tears of joy and of happiness, of victory and of relief all flooded her at once. She laughed, and she cried. Before she knew it, they had surrounded her and hugged her.

Kenatae simply said, "Welcome to the real world, little one. You have much to learn. I have much to teach you."

Wiping away her tears, Susie grinned and asked, "When can we start?"

"You already have. Today was your first lesson," he answered with a laugh.

"Okay; when is my next lesson?" she asked eagerly.

"With the new moon," he responded. He smiled for he could see that she did not understand. "January 26th," he told her.

"Why not now?" she argued.

His expression was that of which a parent would have toward an obstinate child, determined to have its own way. "There is an order to all things, and in all things. The order must be followed."

Susie sighed heavily. Her disheartened expression softened his stance.

"Do not be in a hurry to wade into waters you do not know, nor ones where you cannot see the bottom," he said gently. "That can prove to be a fatal error in judgment."

Remembering Miss Murielle, Susie's eyes raised to meet his. He could see she caught the reference and understood.

Susie nodded. "Okay."

"Store these things in your heart," he instructed. "Do not repeat what you have learned to anyone other than those here today."

"I promise," she vowed.

He smiled and hugged her. "Kevin will escort you back to the manor."

Kevin's parents hugged them both, waving good-by to them as they left the meadow and the teepee behind.

Chapter 37

CHANGES

Susie had wanted to spend a few minutes visiting with Lacy, but had to forego the pleasure after Kevin checked his watch. It would be a close call for them to be punctual for lunch even without making the detour. Kevin had grinned, teasing her that the time it would take her to shed her Artic outfit might make her a few minutes late. He winked and told her not to worry; he'd find a way to keep the bell from being rung until after she arrived.

She laughed. He was so funny, and somehow always knew what to say to make her laugh. He was one of those people who had a light-hearted view of life, no matter what happened. His positive approach and his sunny disposition made it easy to be around him. They bantered back and forth on a variety of subjects, lapsing into a pleasant silence as Kevin maneuvered the truck toward the stone garage.

Susie mulled over what Kevin had told her about Nayatowah in answer to her question. Scarcely had they begun traveling down the farm road when Susie launched it. She really wanted to know. He laughed, telling her that he had always been able to connect with animals – he never knew a time that he couldn't.

"People, on the other hand, are a little more difficult. Some anyway," he said jovially. "But," he continued a little more serious; "to read a person, knowing whether or not they can be trusted, is one thing. To misuse your gift by invading their thoughts, their spirits, is another. Though you will be tempted, do not walk down that dark path."

Susie nodded.

"Kevin," she began, just realizing something; "Kenatae didn't answer my question when I asked why he doesn't tell Miss Pritchett now about her mother. I do understand why he didn't when she was a child, or even a young adult; but what about now?"

Kevin turned his head slightly toward her, his eyes flickered her direction before quickly returning to the farm road. "Perhaps an answer isn't warranted," he responded noncommittally.

Susie turned to face him and tilted her head slightly as she gave him 'the look', relaying she wasn't buying that answer.

He chuckled. "Why do you think he didn't answer?" he asked.

"I don't know. Probably because it's none of my business," she answered bluntly.

Kevin's laugh rolled out good-naturedly. His dark eyes flashed with glee at her answer. "Well, that's definitely a possibility," he commented. "However, I would venture to think it's more likely he's saving that for another time."

Susie grinned. "Like on the new moon?"

"Maybe," he grinned at her; "I don't know."

"Did he ever tell you?" she asked softly.

"Nope," he winked at her. "But then, I didn't ask." His eyes just danced with amusement.

She grinned, eagerly anticipating her next lesson with Kenatae.

Exiting the truck they hurried out the backdoor of the garage, entering the pathway that would lead them back to the pergola and the nice, warm manor. When they reached the door, Kevin held it open for her, grinning as she lumbered across the threshold. Susie began peeling the outer layers, waddling her way to the Cloak Room. Kevin waited at that door as well, holding it open for her. Within a minute, he had his things put away.

Conspiratorially he whispered, "Lunch is in ten minutes. I figure you need at least fifteen. I'm off to circumvent the ringing of the bell," he winked.

She laughed. "Thanks."

And he was gone.

———

True to his word, Kevin had indeed found a way to delay the ringing of the bell. Susie had just entered the Dining Hall when Miss Fiona found it. Somehow it had miraculously developed the ability to fly, alighting itself in one of the nooks in the fireplace columns. Even more miraculous was that it found the perfect hiding place behind a figurine of a group of fairies. Everyone had been involved in the hunt for the bell, searching high and low for the missing item.

Miss Fiona merrily brought the bell to Miss Pritchett, her eyes twinkling and sparkling as she surrendered it. Miss Pritchett laughed as she received the bell, commenting that she loved a practical joke as much as anyone. Mrs. Coppersmith, however, was quick to inform them such a practical joke was not a good idea since the ten-minute delay was causing their food to get cold. Miss Pritchett agreed, reassuring Mrs. Coppersmith, that whoever the prankster is, she is quite certain it won't happen again. With an amused smile, she advised everyone to be seated.

Susie quickly slid into her chair, motioning for the others not to ask her any questions. She received pouty looks from the Munchkins, a smirk from Kat and curious looks from the others.

The bell rang, and Miss Pritchett calmly stated, "Kevin, I do believe it's your turn to lead us in prayer."

Susie noticed the knowing, little grin and fast nod of her head that she gave to Kevin. It made her wonder if Miss Pritchett knew that Kevin was the culprit. Kevin noticed it too; he flushed slightly, and immediately launched into the Blessing.

To make it up to the girls for having disappeared on them, Susie spent the afternoon with them in the Rec Room playing Monopoly. It wasn't long until they were joined by the guys. Just as the game was really getting interesting, the Munchkins appeared, fresh from their naps and full of energy. Mr. Sean was occupied with necessary farm chores, so Mr. Henry had volunteered to assist them in his stead. One by one their Monopoly game lost the boys, then Dani, and finally Kat to the lure of Train Town.

Juls shrugged. "If you want to keep playing, I will," she offered; "but I'd rather go practice."

"Go practice," Susie told her. "When you are the world's foremost prima ballerina, I can say I knew you when you were just a kid; and even then I knew you were going to make it."

Juls hugged her. "Thanks Susie," she beamed.

"Just remember; I get free tickets to all your performances."

"No-o-o problem," she tossed back at Susie as she sashayed out the door.

Susie joined the others at the train table. It was an awesome work in progress. Mr. Henry had to stop the trains periodically to place a building, or tunnel or some other item. He had tried to convince the boys to first build the entire set, then run the trains.

However, as Simon so pointedly stated, "real trains don't wait just 'cause you're building something." Mr. Henry yielded, working around the train schedule unless there was no other option.

Susie watched with them for a while, enjoying the fervor that all the participants had for Train Town. It was incredible to her that something so simple as a train running round a track could create so much joy and such a bond between them, from the youngest to the oldest. Enthusiastically they all made suggestions for more additions to Train Town with Simon and Timmy laughing and high-fiving each one.

Susie quietly slipped away, heading straight for her sanctuary. She needed to include her visit with Kenatae in her journal and her subsequent conversation with Kevin while they were still fresh in her mind, and to ask Tahlranel her question about the incident in the woods.

———

"Tahlranel," this time Susie called aloud. "I know you can hear me. Please stop ignoring me. I really need to talk with you."

Silence.

"Tahlranel?" She repeated his name in sing-song fashion.

No response.

With a sigh of aggravation, Susie rose, put her journal away and returned to Nana's chair, wrapping the afghan around her body for a little warmth. The fire she had made when she first entered her sanctuary was nearly gone now, just a scattering of embers remained. Since she had to leave in less than ten minutes for Story Time, there was no point in adding any more kindling or wood to the fire.

She sighed again, a little louder this time. "Tahlranel, please come talk with me," she requested with just a hint of irritation in her voice.

A few minutes later, he appeared. "Hello, little one," he greeted her with a tender smile. "Why are you so petulant today?"

Surprised, Susie responded, "I am not petulant. I'm concerned."

Tahlranel's smile increased, amused by her repartee. "And what is it that causes you to be concerned?"

Susie's eyes narrowed slightly, a little perturbed that he was apparently placating her. "I *know* you know Simon was lost in the woods. What I don't know is why Chakahel did not protect him. Why did he leave Simon alone? And why didn't you tell me when he ran into the woods? I would have gone after him."

Compassion permeated his expression and his voice. "Yes, and that is why I was not to tell you. Simon was exactly where he was meant to be. He has learned at least two things: one, not to leave without having you or another with him; and, more importantly, he has learned that the Almighty One does answer *his* prayers. Chakahel was there with him, and no harm would have befallen Simon."

"So, Chakahel sent the rabbit?" Susie asked, baffled by this development. Kenatae had said that it was the work of a dark one.

Patiently Tahlranel explained. "No, Susie; a dark one lured Simon into the woods by sending the rabbit to entice him, knowing Simon would not be able to resist playing with the rabbit. The dark one meant to kill Simon, but God meant it for good. The spirit wolf, Nayatowah to the Icori, was sent to Simon as an introduction for what later will be revealed to Simon in preparation of his future path."

Embarrassed now by her assumptions and attitude, Susie contritely apologized. "I'm sorry, Tahlranel. I need to apologize to Chakahel, too."

"No, little one," he responded lovingly. "You do not need to apologize to either of us. You need to ask your Heavenly Father for forgiveness in judging His methods, and to ask Him to increase your faith in Him and your understanding of His ways."

Susie nodded, closed her eyes and began praying. Immediately her spirit was renewed, and she felt the cleansing of her soul. She opened her eyes and smiled.

Susie darted into the Library just as the clock chimed four. She'd hoped she could get here without being late, a habit here of late that she had developed which she wasn't too keen on continuing.

Before they could pepper her with questions, she apologized. "I'm sorry I'm late. I was writing in my journal and forgot to watch the clock. I will do my very best not to be late again."

"That's okay," the Munchkins chimed in unison. "We just got here, too."

"Really?" Susie asked as they all burst out laughing.

"If you'd given us a chance, we'd have told you," Jared intoned.

"Yeah; you're getting awful bossy here lately," Aaron teased, causing the rest to join in with a spontaneous roast of Susie.

She laughed along with them as they teased her. She returned their wisecracks and one-liners with some of her own. She was impressed at how good both Aaron and Jared were. They both were funny, worked well in concert with each other, thought fast on their feet and had great timing. They had all of them rolling with laughter.

Finally Susie told them they had to stop if they wanted to have time to find a book and then read it. She was quickly informed that they had already picked a book. Simon presented it to her. She laughed. It was 'The Magical World of Mr. Wedgilwog'.

"You've already read this one," she reminded Simon.

"But we haven't," came the reply from the rest of the group.

"Okay then," she said; "let's get started."

After she finished the book, she told them she had something important she wanted to tell them.

"Can't it wait?" Jared asked.

Aaron added, "Yeah; we don't want to be late for dinner."

Susie shook her head. "No, it can't. It's really important."

Jared and Aaron exchanged a quick look before shrugging their shoulders and sitting back down. The others followed suit amid a series of questions.

Susie stood and strode rapidly to the main aisle, checking to be certain that they were alone. They were. She returned to the group and sat down on the hearth. They were looking at her as if she were possessed. Inwardly she laughed for in a way she was – possessed with determination to find all the secrets Glen Hollow held, and not just a few. Patiently she waited for them to be quiet and listen. Jared and Aaron caught the drift, immediately calling for everyone to settle down. She smiled and laughed. 'Amazing,' she thought.

"What I'm about to tell you is a big, big secret," she began; "and what I will show you is an even bigger secret."

That elicited "oohs", "ahhs", "oh boys", "all right; secrets", and a few other cheers thrown into the mix.

Susie waited until they became quiet again. Her face was somber. "No kidding around, guys. This is a really super, big secret. You can never tell anyone. Not anyone. And I mean no one."

Her stance was forceful. They could see that something was very different about her; and they recognized that, whatever it is, it is very important. Even the Munchkins' demeanor changed appropriately. Assuring her that she could trust them to "forever keep the secret", they all asked her to just tell them.

So she did. Susie told them of the secret panel door, and how she found it when she lost her hairpin. Susie told them of the passageway, and that it led to a Hidden Room. She told them of the greatest secret of all – The Inner Sanctum. Their faces were lit with a fire of enthrallment, captivated by what they heard and could imagine. Susie admitted she needed help to clean the Inner Sanctum because it was far more than she could do alone. She asked if they would help her clean it. Eagerly they all jumped to their feet, ready to start the cleaning process.

"Wait just a minute," she said, motioning them to be seated. "We have to go to dinner, remember?"

They groused a little, returning to their seats. "You can't just drop a bombshell like that and expect us not to want to go see it," they all clamored.

"Please listen to me," Susie pleaded. "The next few days are going to be really busy with all of the extra chores of removing decorations, taking down the tree, the extra laundry ..."

"And don't forget having to help break down the sets and store them," Juls interjected.

"That's right," Susie agreed. "I didn't see any good time to tell you except now. Please try to pretend you don't know anything."

"Well, I guess we really don't," Jared remarked with a grin. "We haven't seen it, so we really don't know it's true." He shrugged. "For all we know, it isn't any different than one of Nana's stories."

"I agree," Juls and Aaron spoke simultaneously. It was settled. They all agreed: until they actually saw it, Susie had just told them a story – just like Nana's.

She smiled. "Thanks, guys."

"Now, when do you plan to let us see the proof?" asked Jared.

"And when are we going to help you clean?" questioned Dani.

"Well … since you asked," Susie began, grinning like the Cheshire cat; "if you will agree, we could start cleaning early tomorrow morning. If we all get up at three, we can get the room clean before we have to get ready for breakfast. Then it will be ready for exploration. You game?"

"We're game!" they all shouted in unison.

"Great; we have a plan," Susie said.

"Yeah; now let's eat. I'm starving," Aaron added as he began a fast trot toward the door.

Amid a stream of giggles, squeals and laughter, the other children were right on his heels.

———

Now that nearly all of the company had left, Susie would miss the fun that they had at their own table. As they neared the Dining Hall, she wondered if she should ask Miss Hilda to allow Simon and Timmy to sit together at the big table. That would at least help a little, she thought.

All of them were surprised that the Dining Hall had not been returned to its normal state. The long tables were placed further toward the unused side of the room. The unneeded round tables were removed, leaving two of the large, round tables with the smaller round table between them.

Miss Hilda laughed when seeing their expressions. "The round tables seemed to work so much better than the long ones that we decided to keep them. What do you think?"

She was immediately inundated with all types of positive, effervescent cheers and comments from them. Susie just smiled.

———

The after dinner Story Time seemed a little strange now that Grammy and Reverend Tillman were the only remaining company. Grammy would be returning home tomorrow after lunch, escorted all the way by Reverend Tillman. The children were all down in the dumps that she was leaving, and had been ever since they learned at dinner that it was so. Timmy had cried, as did Megan and Simon. Aaron was quiet, even for him. But then, they all were. No one wanted Grammy to leave, but she insisted it was time. She also assured them she would come back for another visit real soon. It did not have the desired effect; they all remained very much saddened that she was leaving.

Susie searched her memory for a story that would help buoy everyone's spirit. She wanted something special, something that would work for everyone. Finally, she knew just the right story.

Closing her eyes, she centered herself. Slowly she breathed in deeply and just as slowly she exhaled, pushing away the trauma and drama of the day. Focusing her energies on the story, she allowed its message to infuse itself once again into her memory, into her soul.

She opened her eyes, and her smile radiated a light from within as she began the tale.

———

Tuck-ins, bedtime hugs, secrets and kisses went far more quickly tonight than ever before. In record time all three Munchkins were down for the night, happy and content, singing and humming the little ditty from the story she had told after dinner. Inwardly she thanked Nana, for it was Nana's story that had given them this happiness.

Susie decided to go to her sanctuary and make a list of everything that needed to be done. She could plan the cleaning project ahead of time, hopefully enabling them to get it done more quickly.

As she entered the west wing, she saw Grammy walking toward her room. Susie ran and caught up with her.

"Hi Grammy," she called out to her.

Grammy turned around, and her smile lit up her face. "Susie, dear," she said as she hugged Susie.

Susie returned her hug. "Grammy, is there any reason you don't want to live here?" she asked tentatively.

Grammy just chuckled. "Did Miss Pritchett put you up to this?"

"No, Grammy," Susie answered; "she didn't."

"Uh-hum," Grammy responded, giving Susie one of her all-knowing looks. "Well, I'll tell you same as I told her: I can't stay. As much as I love my boys, I can't stay."

"But why?" Susie pleaded. "Aaron said you don't have any other relatives. Why can't you live here?"

Compassion filled her heart, flooding her face as Grammy gently patted Susie's cheek. "Child, what is it? Why are you so distressed?"

"I don't' know. .. No, wait; that's not true. I do know," Susie answered, fighting the emotions welling within her. "We all love you, and need you, and want you to live here. But most of all, Aaron and Timmy really need you to be here. Don't you see that?" she asked as her tears began to roll. "How can you leave?"

"Oh, baby girl," Grammy cooed as she hugged Susie, holding her tight. "There, there baby girl. Let it out; you'll feel better."

Grammy held her until the sobbing had ceased. She wiped away Susie's tears, and her own. "Child, if I thought they really needed me, I would stay. They have so many here who love and care for them. I would be in the way. My health is not good, and there isn't much I can do."

"Love them. Love us. Be here for them and for us; that's all you need to do. That's all we need. No, we also need to be here for you. You need us just as much as we need you. Please stay?" Susie pleaded, ending her oratory.

Grammy chuckled softly. "It's hard to fight logic like that. How did you get so smart at such a young age?" she said approvingly.

She patted Susie's cheek again, smiling tenderly at her. "I will speak to Miss Pritchett in the morning about staying."

"Why wait? Why not right now?" Susie countered, grinning. "Nana always said, 'there's no time like the present to get a thing done'."

Grammy laughed, her eyes lighting like little beacons. "I think when I finally get to meet your Nana, we will get along famously. Come on, child; walk with me to Miss Pritchett's office."

Susie grinned. "I'd love to," she responded, linking arms with Grammy.

———

Susie wrote in her journal about the remaining events of the day, culminating with Grammy agreeing to live here. Miss Pritchett had been very surprised, but very pleased, that Susie had persuaded Grammy to change her mind. Susie had left them to work out the details, continuing her trek upstairs.

Elation coursed through her. First, because they had all kept the secrets. Not one of them gave any inkling at dinner, or at Story Time that they knew something that the adults didn't. Second, she was going to have help cleaning the Inner Sanctum. And third, Grammy was staying. She giggled happily as she envisioned the surprised and happy faces, especially Timmy's and Aaron's. It was good for Grammy to be here; good for everyone, herself included, she noted in her journal.

Susie could barely contain her excitement. Tomorrow was going to be a fantastic day. She just knew it, and she wrote that in her journal, too.

Closing her journal, Susie sat quietly, eyes closed and absorbing the peaceful tranquility of the fire. Its warmth barely kept the chill at bay, but it was enough. She loved the way it crackled, sizzling at times, as it slowly consumed the wood and kindling. It was so peaceful here, so relaxing. She could almost see Nana in her chair by the fire, afghan across her lap or wrapped in it, depending upon the chill in the air. She wondered if the others would ever come to love this room as much as she.

'Doubtful; my memories of Nana is why it's so special to me,' she mused silently. Slowly she now realized what she needed to do. "We'll make our own memories together. That will make this place special to them and a safe haven, just as it is for me," Susie whispered.

She sat quietly watching as the fire slowly died, leaving but a few embers that faintly smoldered. Rising, she moved to the fireplace and extinguished the embers, making certain that all of the fire was gone. Carefully she folded Nana's afghan and draped it gently across the back of the chair. Smiling at the picnic picture, she said good-night to the room and headed down the stairs. As she locked the attic door behind her, she yawned.

She yawned just about every other step on her way to the main staircase. "At least I'm finally getting to bed by eleven," she mumbled, descending the stairs to the second floor.

As she stepped onto the landing, she realized she should have chosen the back way, using the circular stairwell. If she was caught breaking the rule, Miss Pritchett might suspend her attic room privileges for a while. Looking around, the corridors were empty – she ran all the way to the Dorm.

Quietly she crept to her bed, being very cautious not to wake anyone. While changing into her pajamas, she checked to make certain the alarm was set for 2:45 (it was) and glided into bed. Quickly she recited her prayers, yawned and dropped off to sleep.

———

Susie bolted upright. She listened. Nothing. Something woke her, but what? Still nothing. She sighed and fell back onto her bed, her head crashing into her pillow.

"I must have dreamed it," she yawned. She glanced at the clock – 11:40. "Rats," she fumed, rolling over in an effort to ignore it and its steady "tick-tick" sound.

She closed her eyes and immediately reopened them. Holding her breath, she listened intently. Nothing. "I know I heard it again," she whispered, sitting upright.

"Tahlranel, where are you?" No answer.

"Tahlranel?" Still no answer.

Shaking her head, she scolded herself, saying, "Stop being a baby. You can't freak out every time you hear a noise."

Settling back under her covers, Susie closed her eyes again as she waited for sleep. It wasn't coming. She heard the noise again, this time louder than before. Susie got out of bed, put on her bedroom slippers and her robe. Striding rapidly, she checked all the girls – sound asleep, each and every one. She hurried to the Common Area – empty. Next she checked the bathroom – also empty.

"What in the world?" she asked, returning to her bed. It was there again, taunting her before she even kicked off her slippers.

"What is it? Tahlranel; where are you?" she whispered into the air. Still no answer. Susie exhaled sharply. "Okay; so this is some kind of test, I guess; and you aren't allowed to help," she fumed.

Softly she began to laugh. "It would make things a *whole* lot easier if you would just tell me what I need to know," loudly she whispered in a teasing tone.

Tahlranel appeared, smiling at her. "It isn't my purpose to make things easier for you, little one. My purpose is to guard and to protect you from forces that seek to alter your purpose. But you know these things already."

"And my purpose is …?" she inquired playfully.

He laughed. "The Almighty One will reveal that to you when the time is right to do so," he replied. "You also know this."

She sighed, feigning a pout. "So I have to figure out on my own what that noise is?"

He smiled at her attempt to out-maneuver him. "If you heard a noise, then yes. I do not know what you heard, or if you heard anything."

Her eyes narrowed slightly, her head tilted just barely as she pressed her lips together and crossed her arms, thinking what her next questions should be.

Delighted, Tahlranel laughed. "You have not changed, little one. You still pursue counter moves when it would be just as easy for you to do what you avoid."

Surprised, Susie stared at him, and then shrugged. "I guess I do." She laughed, amused by his analysis. "Care to give me any hints as to where I should start looking for the noise?"

He smiled. "Happy hunting or sleep well, whichever you choose, little one," he answered and vanished.

Susie giggled. "Can't blame me for trying," she whispered.

Silently she sat on her bed, thinking about the sound she heard. She really wasn't certain what she heard, to be honest. She inhaled deeply and slowly exhaled, clearing her mind.

There it was again! 'Third floor, maybe?' Susie pondered silently.

"Wait a minute," she whispered aloud; "this wing doesn't *have* a third floor."

Susie smiled. 'Or does it? Just because Miss Pritchett was told there isn't one, doesn't mean there isn't,' she thought, remembering the truth regarding Miss Murielle's things and about the East Wing.

Susie bolted off her bed, hurriedly donning warm clothing. The only way to get there would be through the passageways in the attic and work her way down. Then she could locate a secret panel that would give her access from the second floor. She felt the adrenaline pumping through her, racing through her veins. Her heart beat faster and faster as her mind whirled through the endless possibilities of why there was a secret floor.

Peeking into the corridor first, she eased the door open and softly closed it behind her. She ran all the way to the foyer entryway, darting along the balcony to the circular stairwell and climbing the stairs as quickly as she could. Pausing at the third floor landing just long enough to make sure no one was about, she scurried down the corridor to the attic door.

She really hated having to take the time to lock and unlock the door each time. Now that the others had limited permission to be here, maybe she wouldn't have to lock it anymore.

'No, it still has to be locked; they're only allowed here if I'm here,' she reminded herself.

She took the attic steps two at a time, carefully holding onto the railing as she climbed. She didn't dare turn the light on in the stairwell; that would be difficult to explain should the light be seen by any one of the adults that happened to get up early. Fortunately the light from the moon was more than ample, streaming through the windows and casting the room in a pale, silvery hue of illumination.

Susie opened the secret door, securing it with the fireplace poker. Retrieving her flashlight from the shelf, she grabbed the fireplace shovel (you never know; be prepared was her mantra) and entered the passageway. She ran along it until she came to where she thought the south wing should be. Nothing but a wall. She walked back and forth along the passageway between the east and west wings. It appeared to be a solid wooden wall.

"It has to be here," she said, staring at the wall. She smiled. "It's just like the other wall. I bet you're a door, too," she said to it. Carefully she began examining the wooden support beams. No button.

"This doesn't make sense," she said to the wall. "Oh, rats!" Susie exclaimed, shaking her head. "Of course there's no door *here*."

Remembering from her first escapade in the passageway, Susie quickly walked over to the alcove near the east wing and looked down into the stairwell. She sighed. "I'm not cleaning that out tonight," she decided. She turned away and headed back toward the west wing. She stopped and looked down the alcove stairwell. It, too, boasted a thick covering of cobwebs.

"Rats," she murmured, turned and headed back toward her attic room. As she approached, the beam from her flashlight fell on another stairwell entrance, the one against the rock wall, just past her attic door. She had forgotten about it.

Susie's heart skipped a beat, anticipation building. She stood in front of it, said a quick prayer and shone the light down the stairwell. No cobwebs. None at all.

'Easy to figure,' she thought as her teeth began to chatter. 'It's much colder over here than back over there.' She hesitated, trying to decide whether or not she should wait until she had another layer or two of clothing.

"I'm going," she decided, fastening her flashlight's clip to her belt loop.

As she began her descent, the beam of light bounced and swayed, illuminating very little directly below her. She reached the third floor, unclipped her flashlight and began moving along the passageway toward the south wing. Along the way, she noticed levers just like on the floor above.

'I knew it,' she silently congratulated herself; 'all the rooms have a secret door.'

She moved quickly along the passageway, arriving shortly at the fork: left would take her eventually to the east wing, and right would continue along the west wing. She veered left and paused a short distance later in front of a large, wooden wall. As she stood in front of what she knew had to be the way to the south wing, it suddenly occurred to her that she wasn't as cold as she had been. True, it was still freezing, but not as intensely as it had been.

"Oh yeah," she whispered; "the heating system has hot water pipes that run all through the third floor." She was thankful that some of the heat managed to find its way to the passageway.

Susie began her search along the wall for any sign of a lever or a button, but didn't find anything. She stared at the wall, wondering just where she would put it if she was trying to disguise it. And then it came to her. She laughed. She had stared at it, and had passed over it time and time again.

"How clever," she taunted; "but not clever enough." Quickly she pressed on the knot in the center of the wood beam. A groaning was heard as the door began to shudder, slowing sliding inside the wall. Susie's eyes sparkled, delighted and thrilled at her new discovery.

Standing in the threshold, she shone the light into the room. "Good grief!" Susie exclaimed.

Obviously intended only for storage, there were no walls to divide the floor; it was one, gigantic room. The ceiling wasn't very high, maybe about seven or eight feet, Susie guessed. There were several light fixtures in the ceiling, and it looked as if the items had been stored here a long time. Just like the East Wing, everything stored was protected by dust sheets, necessary because a heavy layer of dust covered the dust sheets and the floor. Slowly panning the room with her light, Susie could see that many of the covered items were paintings, some furnishings and some boxes.

With caution, she began moving toward the area that would be directly above her bed.

No one had walked in here – not in a very long time, and absolutely not tonight. Hers were the only footprints in the dust. She looked around, trying to find anything that would account for the noise she had heard. Nothing was out of place; no dust had been disturbed.

"This is really weird," Susie admitted; "but someone had to have been in here."

She kept walking, looking for another way in or out of the secret floor.

"If I wanted an easy access to this room, where would I put a secret staircase?" she asked herself. She thought about it for a minute. "Oh yeah," she said with a hint of triumph in her voice.

Hurriedly she made her way to where the laundry room would be on the floor below. During Miss Pritchett's childhood, it would have been part of the linen room which is now the laundry room. She found it. Squatting down, Susie shone the light into the stairwell. Clear as a bell. Rapidly she descended, arriving at the bottom which was a small, enclosed room, not more than three feet by three feet. She shone the light on the wall facing the entrance of the stairs. To her absolute delight, she saw the button. She pressed it, the door slid into the wall, and she stepped out into the laundry room.

Susie was elated! Now she had another way to the attic room, sight unseen. She peeked back into the hidden alcove, studying the position of the button and compared where it should be on the laundry room side. She started laughing.

"How very clever," she mused. The button was very well disguised as one the "beads" in the beaded wainscoting that formed the horizontal decorative panel around the wall.

Re-entering the alcove, Susie pressed the button, closing the panel door. She climbed up the stairs, making her way back to the passageway entrance. Curiosity got the better of her, and she peeked under one of the dust cloths. She had assumed it was a painting, and it was.

It was a portrait of a little girl, maybe two years old. She was captivating with her pink cheeks, her cute, little baby teeth, and her crystal clear, dark blue eyes that were fringed with thick, black lashes. She was laughing, looking up and reaching for a butterfly. A radiant glow filled the child's face as she watched the butterfly with wondrous fascination. She looked so real, you could almost hear her laughter, her squeals and giggles of delight and joy. At any moment you expected to see her turn and look at you, or come running to you.

"Awesome," Susie whispered.

The ordinary act of reaching to drop the cover back over the painting gave Susie another look at the detail. Her light shone brightly upon what she had assumed was part of the pink cheeks. It wasn't. It was a little starburst.

"Oh no," she mumbled as dread began to rise in her heart. Her eyes fell to the bottom of the portrait. It was signed 'Murielle D. Evermore 1950". The name plate read: Eloise Noreen Evermore.

Susie's heart sank. "So this is where her Dad stored everything from the attic studio," she sighed. "At least he didn't get rid of it."

She stared at the portrait. Miss Pritchett had said her mother was truly gifted, and Susie agreed that she was. Sadness filled her as she looked at Miss Pritchett's face.

"She was so happy. Why did it have to happen?" She felt her blood boiling, anger swelling within. "Someone needs to find that Gorza, and punish her for all the hurt she's caused."

The little toddler in the portrait was oblivious to anything other than the joy of that moment, captured forever on canvas. Susie felt her anger subside as she focused on the little girl. She smiled.

"Miss Pritchett is still happy, just in a different way," Susie realized, puzzled by it. "But Gorza still should be punished for what she did," she adamantly declared.

She sighed deeply as she turned to leave. She froze. Hastily she shone her light on the butterfly.

It wasn't a butterfly. It was a fairy! "Good heavens," she exclaimed; "it looks like Miss Fiona. And that firefly looks like Annie from the Diner."

Susie backed away from the portrait, allowing the cover to fall back over it. "Boy, I am really tired if I'm starting to see things."

With haste she sprinted across the floor, exiting into the passageway. She closed the door and returned to the stairwell, wasting no time in returning to the attic level and to her attic room. She closed the panel door, darted across the room and down the stairs. After locking the door behind her, she ran all the way to the main staircase, down the stairs and then all the way to her Dorm.

She shed her clothes and got into her pajamas faster than she ever had. Diving under her covers, she peeked at her clock – it was 1:30. She groaned.

"Only an hour of sleep left. I sure hope I can wake up when the alarm sounds." She yawned. "I really need to get that room cleaned."

She yawned deeper and longer this time. "I know one thing for sure," she mumbled. "I'm taking a nap after breakfast," she vowed, and then promptly fell asleep.

Chapter 38

THE INNER SANCTUM

"Hey Susie; look at this!" Kat yelled.

Susie stopped cleaning the work table and looked up at Kat. "What is it?" she asked.

"It's a letter," she began and was promptly interrupted.

"You're supposed to be cleaning, not reading," Dani tersely snarled.

"I am!" she hurled back. "This book fell off the shelf, and the letter slid onto the floor."

"Yeah, right," Dani countered, cynically. "It just happened to fall, all by itself."

"It did!" Kat protested vehemently.

"Stranger things have happened," Susie commented as a peace offering between them. Smiling at both girls, she headed toward Kat.

"Yeah, especially in this place," Jose agreed apprehensively.

"Enough with the creepy talk," Jared insisted. "We all agreed not to let our imaginations run wild. Keep working, and you won't have time to be scared."

The others returned readily enough to their tasks, but with a considerable amount of side-ways glances, snickering and a lot of whispering. Susie chuckled silently as she pictured Jared encountering some of the experiences she had had of late, and how quickly he would change his tune. But, for the sake of the others, she wasn't about to tell him. For now her mission was to root out the secrets that this place held, and to keep her promise of help to her new-found, ethereal friend.

"What does the letter say?" Susie asked as she approached Kat.

"It's really weird," Kat responded, handing the letter to Susie while still holding the book that had previously safeguarded the letter. Her fingers automatically clasped the sterling silver bookmark, and the book easily fell open to its intended page. Kat began silently reading while Susie read the letter.

"What does it say?" Juls asked, noticing the look on Susie's face.

"Kat's right; it's weird," Susie slowly responded, still focused on the stationery, now yellowed with age.

"Read it," was the insistent pleas from everyone. They, too, had noticed her expression. Their curiosity having gotten the better of them, they all left their assigned tasks and joined Kat and Susie.

"Okay," Susie agreed. "The letter is from Edgar Allan Poe…."

"*The* Edgar Allan Poe?" chorused Aaron, Jared, Juls, Jose and Dani.

"Yes," Susie answered, slowly nodding her head while she remained focused on the fragile page she gently held. "The letter is dated September 23, 1849. It was written to Mrs. Josephine Lee Evermore. It says:

Mrs. Josephine Lee Evermore
Evermore Estate
c/o Foxboro Station

Dear Mrs. Evermore,
    I have enclosed a poem I wrote entitled <u>Annabel Lee</u>. Yes, I named it for her and the love that was, and is, ours. I want you to know that I will publish this poem as a testament to our love.

    The world will know how beautiful she was, physically as well as spiritually. She was the most loving, the most kind, and the gentlest soul that has ever graced this earth. I also want you to know that my lectures will now include this poem and the whole truth regarding Annabel Lee, from the moment we met when we were at the tender age of eleven to her death at fifteen because of you.

    Did you truly think that you could hide her resting place from me? Did you think that I would never find where you hid her sepulcher? I have been there many times and have spent hours there grieving, mourning the loss of the one who was to be my bride. And yet she was, and is, my bride, for her soul and mine were united that fateful day in 1820. In your eyes we were merely children, unable to know what love is. But you were wrong - our love was stronger than any love this world has ever seen.

Though a number of years have passed between my visits to her, my last visit on March 15ᵗʰ of this year is when the poem came to me, pouring into my soul as if from the very soul of my Annabel Lee. I realized then how fitting was the choice you made for her tomb; she must have told you of the holidays taken at the sea, and how she loved it so. It was one of the many things we shared; our love for poetry, for literature and for the sea with all its many wonders and mysteries.

As her mother, I have no doubt you did grieve the loss of your child; but that grief is not greater than my own, nor does it equal the loss I have endured and continue to endure. Neither has my grief diminished with time. Though I have allowed myself to love others, none have ever captured my soul as did my beautiful Annabel Lee.

Our souls were united; nothing and no one will ever change that. I know she waits for me. Until I am reunited with her, I will immortalize her and our love through this poem.

Edgar A. Poe
September 23, 1849

Susie added in a soft tone, "The next page is the poem."

At first no one spoke. The silence felt heavy, weighing down on them like an anchor.

"Oh ... my ...," Kat whispered as tear drops began rolling down her face.

Everyone looked at Kat. "What's wrong?" Susie asked.

Kat slowly shifted her focus from the journal to Susie and then to the concerned faces of the others. Struggling to keep her composure, Kat's voice cracked with the strong emotions surging through her.

"It's so sad; she died trying to get away from here," she gulped between sobs. "They were so cruel to her. How could they do that?"

Her pleading eyes gripped Susie's heart, causing her to desperately want to find the answer that would ease Kat's pain. Whether consciously or unconsciously, she knew that Kat had drawn a parallel between her own experiences and that of Annabel Lee's.

Susie took the journal from Kat and quickly read the passage. Tears sprang to her eyes as she read, and her head slowly moved back and forth in disbelief. 'How could they,' she thought?

Aloud she said, "I don't know." Her voice was soft, barely that of a whisper as she tried to make sense of it.

Kat began shaking her head rapidly - anger replacing the sadness she had felt. "They locked her in her room. They nailed her window shut. They guarded her like she was a criminal; and all because she loved him, and wanted to marry him when she was eighteen. It wasn't like she wasn't willing to wait. They did this! They locked her up! They thought they could change her by making her a prisoner!"

Kat was shouting by the time she finished, her words echoing off the stone walls. Her voice was racked with anger, fear and grief. Her face had contorted with every one of the powerful emotions that compelled her outburst.

"Who did?" Jared asked Kat.

"What happened?" Juls' query was directed to Susie.

"Are you okay?" Susie asked Kat. "I know this brings back some bad memories for you, and I'm sorry."

Kat folded her arms against her chest, swallowed hard a few times and forcibly exhaled before answering. Brusquely, she said, "I'm fine."

"Are you going to read it to us, or tell us what it says?" Aaron asked impatiently.

Susie looked at Kat. "What do you want to do?"

Kat shrugged, feigning indifference. "Doesn't matter; read it if you want."

Susie began reading aloud the entry dated September 27, 1849.

"I received a letter today by special courier from EAP. I had not heard from him in 25 years; the audacity of that man to purport that his grief outweighs my own. I struggle with her loss constantly. Had I even the smallest inkling she would have broken the window, I would have had the window barred and boarded. In time, she would have understood and accepted our choice for her. I know it.

At first I had blamed the Academy for not properly supervising their charges, thus allowing the circumstances in which she and EAP were able to meet outside of proper social functions. The fact that none of the Academy's staff had noticed the developing relationship at chaperoned functions, from cotillions, to picnics to sea shore holidays, caused me to believe that their exceptional reputation was at best a farce.

Ever the placid one, Horace preferred to handle it through dispatches with the Head Mistress. I wasn't willing to be that patient. We left immediately for the Academy, officially removed her from residence and brought her home. I was certain that the embarrassment she felt at being whisked away so abruptly would diminish once she was home. Bringing her home in November, prior to the Holidays, seemed the proper avenue – after all, with Annabel here that would be the end of it. Or so I had thought at the time.

Next I had blamed her friend, Lucy Abernathy, for being a conduit between them. I caught Lucy just after New Year's with a letter from him that she was attempting to deliver to Annabel. I stopped all visits and correspondence between the girls. Our minister helped me to see that Lucy was just a child, as was my Annabel. They were two, love-struck girls with a romanticized notion of what love is. With proper discipline, supervision and time, they would both pass through this phase and blossom into the respectable ladies that they have been taught to be.

After two months of isolation, I relented and allowed Annabel to have supervised visits with Lucy. I truly thought Annabel was improving, that she understood why we would never approve of marriage to him at eighteen or at any age. I had no idea what she was planning until that morning when we found her room empty.

The window was broken; snow had blown inside; and the room was cold enough to store blocks of ice. We had everyone out searching for her. Hours later, we found her. Annabel was in her favorite place in all of Glen Hollow – the cave by the rapids. She told me once it was her favorite spot because the sound reminded her of the sea shore. She was unconscious and barely breathing. Her lips had turned blue, and her pallor was that of ash. We wrapped her in blankets and quilts and hurried home. Dr. Langston had already arrived just prior to our own arrival.

The next morning she regained consciousness briefly. In those few moments, she smiled and told us she was sorry. She cried as she told us she loved us, but she also loved him. I told her not to worry, to rest and get well for that was all that mattered. We told her how much we loved her. She smiled, one of her radiant smiles; and in that moment, my Annabel was back with me. We got to hug our baby, kiss her and spend a few minutes with her before she lapsed back into unconsciousness. She passed two days later, never regaining consciousness.

I know that she loved him with that "first love" syndrome; but I do know she would not have remained with him. They were worlds apart, and she would have eventually seen this. Lucy did. Three years later, Lucy came to me the day before the formal announcement of her engagement. She apologized to me for her role that led to that night, and asked my forgiveness.

How could I withhold forgiveness? Through much prayer, I had, long ago, come to terms with the circumstances and had forgiven Lucy. But she needed to hear it from me in order to move forward. She was marrying the young man whom her parents had chosen years ago. She, like Annabel, had a "first love" with an entirely unsuitable young man, who was imprisoned for horse theft shortly after Annabel's passing. Time, discipline and supervision helped set Lucy on the right path.

It is bittersweet that Lucy named her daughter Annabel Lee as a tribute to my child. Over the years I have been privileged to be a part of their lives as if this Annabel was my grandchild. Now she is grown, has married well and has just given birth to her first child. Annie has asked my permission to name her daughter Josephine Lucille after myself and her own mother. Although my daughter has been lost, yet she has been restored through Lucille and through another Annabel Lee.

I don't know what disturbs me the most regarding his letter; the fact that he has trespassed, or that he has some vengeful agenda that he intends to launch against us. Horace will know what to do. Perhaps it is time to offer an olive branch. Perhaps if we have a memorial service for her at her sepulcher, and allow him to attend, then that will enable him to find the peace that has eluded him. Horace had urged me to include him when preparing for her burial; but I blamed EAP at that time for her disobedience and death, and could not abide even the thought of his presence.

Time has helped me to see that he, also, was merely a child of fifteen then, and was smitten with "first-love" syndrome. He, for whatever reason, has not been able to move past it. I don't know what will bring him peace where Annabel is concerned, or if he will ever find it.

I do think if we hold a memorial service we should have it on her birthday, March 1st, as a celebration of her life instead of mourning her loss on the anniversary of her death. I will ask Horace to contact EAP regarding such a service.

Perhaps I should have Annabel's trunks brought down from the attic. The servants packed her things for me, and I have never had the heart to go through them. Her journals will be there, and they may well be the healing balm that is needed. Horace had thought so upon her passing, but I just did not have the strength to see her things, let alone read her journals. My own journals from that time have been locked away since shortly after her funeral. I did not want to be reminded of any of it. Perhaps I should read her journals and mine together – doing so may well prove to be the balance needed for the healing equation. Perhaps Horace was right after all.

It has been twenty-five years since my baby passed, but it feels like yesterday.

Josephine Lee Evermore

A hush had fallen over them, broken only by the sounds of sniffling as each one struggled with the words that recounted the tragic event. Time seemed to stand still; they were frozen in that moment as they stared at one another, overwhelmed by the sadness that permeated the room.

Jared cleared his throat, breaking the silence. "I think they regretted what happened," he commented, his voice was soft, contemplative. "At least the mother did. She thought he was bad for her. I feel sorry for both he and Annabel, but not as much as I feel for her Mom and Dad. They must have felt awful until the day they died. You know they did."

Aaron slowly nodded his head in agreement. "It's really sad, and bad, that she died, but they did love her. Her mom's journal shows they did." He shook his head, trying to sift through his next thoughts. "I think they were wrong to lock her up," he shrugged; "but she was wrong to break the window and run away."

"She didn't deserve to die," Kat hissed.

"No, she didn't," Susie agreed; "and no one said she did. It was a tragic accident, Kat. Her parents didn't want her to die."

"That's right," Juls echoed. "She wouldn't have if she hadn't run away in a snow storm."

"Why did she?" asked Jared, clearly puzzled by Annabel's escape. "Why would she run away in a snow storm? That doesn't make sense."

"It probably started snowing after she left, so she hid in the cave until it stopped," Susie suggested.

"Hey, do you think we can find it?" Juls asked, her eyes sparkling with excitement.

They all exchanged stunned glances – no one had thought to hunt for the tomb until now. As if by some telepathic link, they all quickly shouted "yes". It was decided that they would have to wait until springtime to actually start the hunt. Jared, Aaron and Jose were assigned the task of obtaining a map of Glen Hollow from Mr. Sean, and do so without revealing their mission. Once procured, they would study the map to narrow the search area.

"We could read the Journals that Josephine wrote," Juls stated firmly. "They have to be here somewhere," she added, dramatically gesturing with a sweeping wave of her hand.

"I don't think her personal Journals would be stored in here; at least not those. From what I've seen so far, these books are sciences, medicine, languages, literature, horticulture and botany," Susie commented.

"Which sort of explains all of the shelves, and drawers, and jars of stuff and all of the dried hanging plants," Jared agreed.

"You think they made their own medicines?" Jose asked.

"I don't know," Susie responded; "but their Journals might tell us. Probably one of the attic rooms would have the Journals. We could start searching in those rooms after we finish cleaning in here."

"Well, let's get to it; we're almost done," Jared abruptly stated. He grabbed his broom and headed back to the area he had been sweeping.

Everyone quickly resumed their tasks; Juls took on the added chore of supervising the Munchkins, more in an effort to keep them occupied than anything else. Fortunately, they seemed to enjoy her attention as much as she enjoyed being a mother hen. An hour later, the entire Inner Sanctum was clean.

"What do you think it is?" Jared asked. He had approached silently and stood next to Susie.

She had just been contemplating that very question. The "it" in question was a circular structure. It was positioned dead center of the room and directly above the seal in the foyer below, currently covered by the plush, green carpet. Miss Murielle's journal had made mention of the seal being covered during her absence, and how distraught she was that it had been done. The seal was apparently important; but Susie still didn't know why, so she had not yet told the group about everything she had found. Every discovery seemed to lead to more questions, more secrets. And this new discovery seemed to be the biggest secret of all.

She looked at Jared and smiled. "I don't know, but there are parts of it I recognize," she answered.

"Like what?" he countered inquisitively.

Susie scanned the object before answering him. Twelve pillars, evenly spaced, formed the outer ring. The interior of the circular structure formed an interconnected web, much like that of a spider's web, with each of the vertical lines connecting to the base of the pillars and also to the center of the structure. Adorning the center of the structure was a granite pedestal that appeared to be made of the same granite as that of the unicorn statue in the East garden. The "web" was actually channels cut into the wooden floor and filled with a shiny, silvery gray metal. A symbol was carved in the center of each "web block" and appeared to be of the same poured metal as in the channels. Each symbol connected to the web above and below it. Every pillar contained a three-inch round imprint in its center, facing the pedestal; but what was to be placed in those imprints, Susie had no idea.

"Well, these are some of the symbols I've seen in the Chapel windows and on the foyer floor. And these are symbols I've seen in Nana's books."

Susie paused briefly, debating whether or not to mention that some were also symbols she had seen in the "Histories" volumes she had found in the Library. She decided that was best left to another time.

Pointing to another group, she continued, "These symbols are our constellations, so those are probably constellations, too. This is our solar system, this is our Milky Way galaxy, and this one is the Andromeda galaxy; but I don't know what these are. I'm guessing galaxies and solar systems since they're grouped together like ours. These are nebulas - the Horsehead, the Swan, the Eagle, the Cat's Eye, the Dolphin, the Heart, the Wizard, the Witch's Broom, the Witch Head and the Pillars of Creation. I bet these over here are nebulas too, but I'm just guessing."

Aaron grinned at her. "How do you know all that?"

Susie laughed. "Nana was very much a star buff."

"Sounds like it," Jared agreed.

"There must be thousands of symbols here," Dani observed, slightly overwhelmed at the idea of identifying each of them.

"Actually," Jose corrected Dani; "there are 288 symbols; 300 if you count the pillars." He grinned at the scowl Dani gave him and explained. "I counted the number of columns and multiplied it by the number of horizontal lines, which is 288 symbols. Add to that the twelve columns, and the total number is 300."

"How are we going to know what they all mean, smarty pants?" Dani said snappishly.

"There must be books here somewhere," Susie answered. "Whoever made this had to learn about them in order to make it."

"Yeah, but what is *it?*" pressed Juls.

Susie shrugged. "I don't know. Aaron, you're the space guru. What do you think?"

Aaron scowled somewhat. "I'm not a guru. My interest is in designing aircraft and spacecraft."

He exhaled abruptly, as if shedding whatever thoughts had antagonized him and added, "I do recognize some of these symbols, so I think all of them must be symbols that represent the star systems."

"Really," quipped Kat a little caustically; "so what's it for?"

"I don't know," Aaron responded, somewhat irritated with Kat; "but someone went to an awful lot of trouble to make it."

"You're right," Jared agreed as he rose to his feet. He had been examining the metal. "This was no easy job. Not only are the carvings precise, but this is poured platinum. That means they had to heat it to the melting point, and then pour it into the channels and into the carvings. How they did it, I don't know; but it's awesome." The expression of appreciation on his face was accentuated by the reverent tone carried in his voice.

"Susie's right, guys" Juls stated. "There has to be at least one book that tells what it is, and what it's for. So let's look for it."

"But where?" Dani huffed in an exasperated tone. "Look at all these books! We'll never find it."

"Not with that attitude," Susie challenged. "It has to be here, and we will find it."

Dani released a forceful sigh, clearly registering her disdain for such a monumental task. "Don't you ever get tired of being so positive?" she asked, whining.

"No," Susie responded cheerfully, sauntering to the first bookcase.

Everyone scattered, choosing their own bookcase in which to start the hunt.

———

"Hey!" Susie yelled, excitement inadvertently raising her voice an octave. Quickly clearing her throat, she added; "Look what I found!"

Everyone stopped their searches, rapidly crossing the room while responding with "What is it?" and "Did you find the book?"

Susie shook her head, answering, "No, I didn't find the book; but I think I found something more important."

"What?" and "What is it?" were the general responses; however, Simon, Timmy and Megan had pushed through the crowd and were demanding to be shown what she had found.

Susie had already closed the secret drawer, waiting until they all had arrived so that she could reveal it to them at the same time. After everyone had gathered around, Susie pressed firmly the carvings on each end of what appeared to be the base of a shelf in the bookcase. Gliding without effort, the drawer slowly opened.

"How did you find this?" Jared asked.

Susie smiled. "Well, this shelf base is a little deeper than the others, so I thought it could be a secret drawer. And it is."

705

"Now," she proclaimed, thrilled at the find; "look!"

She removed the velvet cover, revealing twelve, round blue diamonds. "I think this is what goes into the column spaces," Susie gushed, her eyes sparkling with excitement.

For a moment, all of them stood spell-bound by what lay in front of them. The hue of the blue was perfect; the clarity was unimaginable – though the stones were blue, they were transparent, allowing the velvet lining on which they rested to clearly be seen. The stones had been well cut and polished, glimmering as they reflected the light.

"I think you're right," agreed Jared.

"Let's find out," Kat said, snatching one of them from the drawer.

Not to be left out, everyone grabbed a stone and ran to the columns. Unfortunately, Jared was the only one tall enough to reach the space. One by one, he placed each diamond in the crevices. They fit perfectly.

"Now what?" Juls asked.

Susie shrugged. "I don't know."

They stood staring at the columns, waiting for something to happen. Nothing did.

"Maybe they have to be placed in a certain order," Jose suggested.

"Maybe," Jared agreed; "but the columns would be numbered if that were the case."

"Maybe not," Kat disagreed. "Everything about this place is secretive. Maybe they didn't number them deliberately so that only the right people could use it."

"Or," Susie interjected; "maybe there is more to it than just putting in the stones. We're missing something."

As she spoke she began wandering through the web, looking at the various symbols she passed. When she reached the pedestal, she smiled. "Come look at this," she instructed.

Immediately the others ran to her, vying for a prominent position in which to see what she had found.

"Look," she told them. "The channels run from the pillars and all the way up to the pedestal." She paused a minute to give them a chance to see for themselves.

"What does that mean?" Aaron asked.

"I don't know, but it must be important," Susie answered. "See. Here. Each pillar has two channels until it reaches the base of the pedestal. Then they merge into this ring that surrounds the pedestal. Only one channel per pillar emerges, runs up to the top of the pedestal where they funnel into this channel. This channel connects to these symbols."

Susie gave them time to inspect the channels, the pedestal and the platform of the pedestal with its twelve unique symbols.

"What do you think they are?" asked Jared, pointing to the symbols.

"Best guess," Susie began; "is that it's a language of some kind, maybe like a type of shorthand."

"Or a secret code," suggested Simon. His eyes sparkled with excitement at the thought of it. After all, he and Timmy had their own secret code, so this could be one too.

"Yeah-ah-ah," Timmy echoed, equally as enthused as Simon.

"Could be," Jared agreed, grinning at the boys.

"What's this one?" Kat asked, directing their attention to one, lone symbol. Carved into the granite was a twelve-pointed starburst in the center of the pedestal.

Susie just shook her head. "I don't know. It's different. These all appear to be a language of some sort, but this one is just a starburst."

Silence grew as each one became engrossed in discovering just what the code could be, determined to be the one to solve the mystery.

Aaron broke the silence. "Let's find the book, if there is one. Otherwise, we'll never figure out what this is."

Intuitively Susie's hand glided to the starburst, hovering just above it. The starburst began to glow. A soft click was heard. A little opening slowly appeared. Rising from inside the pedestal was a slender platinum stand. The inward prongs of the stand suggested to Susie that it was obviously meant to hold something suspended over the starburst. After the stand locked in place, another opening appeared. It was shallow and held another blue diamond, only this one was cut in the shape of a triangle.

Mesmerized, the group stared in wonder at this latest development.

Without hesitation, Susie picked up the stone and anchored it between the prongs of the stand.

A brilliant flash of white light filled the room. Shielding their eyes yielded no relief; they could not see anything. The sounds they heard were loud and frightening at first, resembling a blend of the cry of a screech owl and that of metal scraping against metal. Dizziness struck them, disorienting them and causing them to stagger and sway, much like being aboard a tiny boat in the midst of an angry sea.

It seemed like an eternity had passed before the sounds finally dissipated, the dizziness vanished and the brightness dispersed. When at last their faculties had returned, Susie discovered that Simon, Timmy and Megan were frantically clasping onto her. Around them, pressing as close to Susie as possible were the rest — Dani, Kat Jose, Juls, Aaron and even Jared.

"Everyone okay?" Susie asked.

Comments varied, but the general consensus was that they were all right. Shaken and frightened, but no harm was done.

"Where are we?" Dani asked, her tone a fusion of surprise and trepidation.

Immediately the others began looking at their surroundings. They were no longer in the Inner Sanctum; and, Susie surmised, no longer at Glen Hollow.

"Good question," she responded, inspecting their new location.

Looking around, it was plain to see they were on a small island in the middle of a wide river. The crystal clear water swirled around the island as its current flowed rapidly downstream. There were very few trees, but it did have a thick carpet of green grass and beautiful flowers growing everywhere. A small cottage stood not far from them.

The sun was bright and high overhead, but not hard on the eyes; its gentle warmth blanketed them, comforting and relaxing. The crisp, cool air was invigorating, instilling the desire to run and play, yet competing with the yearning to sleep in the sun.

"This is awesome!" Juls proclaimed. Her pronouncement was quickly mirrored by nearly all of them.

Something was nagging at Susie; something that she couldn't quite comprehend. It was there, just beyond the reach of her memory, desperately trying to surface. Brushing it off, Susie decided to concentrate on their more immediate problem – how to find out where they are; and, more importantly, how to get home. The sounds of humming and laughing caught her attention.

The Munchkins had begun playing, chasing each other, laughing and squealing as they tumbled and rolled in the grass. Juls and Dani had begun picking wildflowers, placing them in their hair as well as starting a flower chain braid. Kat had positioned herself on the porch, warily watching, eyes scanning as if she expected trouble at any moment. Jared, Aaron and Jose were staring at Susie, waiting for an explanation. She had none to offer.

"Come on, everyone," Susie called out; "let's knock on the door and see if we can find someone who can tell us where we are."

"And how to get home," Jared added.

Quick as ever, the Munchkins raced to the porch, followed closely by Dani, Juls, and Jose. Jared and Aaron gave Susie a dubious look as they passed by her and climbed the porch steps. Susie sighed, wishing she could remember whatever it was that was currently just beyond her consciousness. Some sense within urged her that it is important. Susie stepped onto the porch, walked to the door and knocked.

No answer. She knocked again, a little louder this time, and still there was no answer.

"Just open it, Susie," the group insisted.

Hesitantly, Susie turned the doorknob and slowly opened the door. "Anyone here?" she called out loudly, hoping someone was home. No one was. The place was empty.

The group pushed passed her, rushing into the center of the barren room. A rock fireplace encompassed most of the wall to her left, shared with the bedroom on the other side of the wall. The kitchen, small but functional, was to her right and housed a cast-iron cook stove mid-way on the right wall. More than likely, Susie surmised, it also functioned as a secondary heat source in winter. Instead of cabinets, four open shelves lined the back wall near the stove, providing barely enough space for the most basic of food items.

Jared announced that he and Aaron would check out the basement, a task that Susie was more than happy to allow them to handle. He assigned Jose, Juls, Kat and Dani to check out the attic. Juls wasn't overjoyed at the prospect; however, when Jared graciously offered to switch places with her, she quickly declined. Susie chuckled.

Simon and Timmy begged to accompany Jared. They wheedled, whined and pleaded, but to no avail. Jared was firm, telling them that they needed to remain with Susie and Megan, just in case.

"In case of what?" Simon pouted.

Leaning down, Jared whispered in his ear. Whatever he said, it worked. Simon beamed and began to strut around the living room. Scowling and offended to have been left out of a secret, Timmy grabbed Simon's arm as Simon made his loop around the room, demanding to know what Jared had said. Simon stopped walking and looked at Jared.

Jared grinned and nodded; so Simon whispered in Timmy's ear, passing the message to his best bud. Timmy giggled and vigorously nodded his head. Like miniature soldiers on sentry duty, they began marching around the room in opposite directions. As they met, they saluted each other and Susie.

Susie looked at Jared, her expression one of puzzlement and curiosity as to what he could have told them. He laughed and winked. "We'll be back in a minute," he told her. Looking up at the quartet on the stairs, he advised them to get moving. In a flash they scrambled up the stairs with Kat leading the way. Aaron reluctantly followed Jared down the basement stairs.

"Susie!" shouted Jared.

"Come here quick!" was the equally frantic voice of Aaron.

Running to the basement staircase, she ordered the Munchkins to remain behind. They shook their heads rapidly, begging her not to leave them. She didn't have a chance to respond. Horrific screams emanated from upstairs, and were immediately followed by shouted requests for Susie to help.

Susie ran upstairs while struggling to remain calm, knowing that panic is always your worst enemy. Taking the stairs two at a time, Susie's imagination had envisioned an array of creatures from which to defend them, whether a gigantic spider, a snake, a rat or a bat or even something as small as a mouse.

No imagination could have prepared her for what she saw as she bolted through the attic door. It stopped her cold, frozen in her tracks. Menacingly standing near the door of the attic and barring the quartet's exit was an enormous white tiger.

Juls had positioned herself between the white tiger and the others, shielding them as much as possible. Terror gripped her face, and her eyes revealed the depth of her fear; yet Juls remained firmly planted between the other children and the tiger. Armed with nothing but an old mop, she held it as if it were the mightiest of swords. Tears were beginning to well in her eyes, her breathing was shallow and rapid, but she remained steadfast at her post.

Kat held Dani behind her, using her own body as a potential shield for Dani when the tiger got past Juls. Dani was crying, begging Susie for help. Kat's face was resolute, almost as if she knew what the outcome would be, and was ready for it.

At the far end of the attic, Jose had chosen a broom as his weapon, and was vigorously trying to prevent another tiger from entering the attic through what appeared to be a swirling, foggy cloud in the back wall of the cottage. Each time its head came through the mist, Jose would whack it as hard as he could. It would pull back and try again, only to have Jose repeat the process.

As Susie burst into the attic, the tiger turned its huge head and snarled at her. Her heart raced, pounding like the beat of a drum signaling danger. The magnitude of death that this creature possessed struck terror deep within her. Susie inhaled sharply, reacting to its threat.

Behind her, she heard the Munchkins screaming. They had followed her.

Without taking her eyes from the tiger, Susie firmly told the Munchkins to run outside and stay there until she came for them. Seconds later, sounds akin to that of elephants stampeding clearly revealed that they had done as she instructed.

The tiger's intense focus made her skin crawl. Its eyes never wavered and never blinked. Every snarl prominently displayed its huge, razor-sharp fangs. It moved backward to the side of the attic, cautiously, deliberately, as it shifted its watch to encompass both Juls and Susie.

All of a sudden Susie knew what was familiar about the river, the island and the cottage. It was a scene straight from the book by Helga Gretchen Von Richter, 'White Tigers: Guardians of the Realms'. Now she realized that the object at Glen Hollow was a portal, and somehow they had opened it. Miss Murielle had written in her journal that she had permanently closed it, and would require another Keeper to open it. The thought flashed through her mind – 'Am I a Keeper?'

The tiger began emitting a low, rumbling growl. Its eyes flashed with its hostile intent. Susie knew what to do. In a hushed tone, she told the tiger they were here by accident and would leave.

"Juls, listen to me," Susie called out to her softly. "I want all of you to slowly come toward me, but come around by this side."

"We can't," she responded fearfully.

"If I leave here," Jose shouted to Susie; "it'll come through. You get the girls out of here."

"No, Jose," Susie adamantly countered. "Listen to me, all of you. Do exactly what I say, when I tell you, and you will all be okay."

"Really?" asked Dani as Kat asked, "Are you sure?"

"How do you know?" asked Juls.

"Please trust me. Please?" she asked gently. "Jose, put down your broom. Juls, you need to put down your mop; all of you come to me now. Come around to the side and make a wide berth. Don't make threatening moves or gestures."

Jose looked over his shoulder at her. "I do trust you," he stated emphatically.

After taking one last swipe at the emerging tiger (and nailing it), he ran to Dani and Kat, dragging them with him to Juls. He positioned all three behind him as they slowly maneuvered their way toward Susie, walking crab-style. During the entire trek across the attic, Jose kept a watchful eye on the wall, and on the tiger currently near their only escape route.

Moving a little closer to the tiger, Susie began speaking to it, assuring it that they meant no harm. As she did, the tiger began to walk away from her and toward the center of the attic. Its stalking movements and its snarls did little to reassure her or the others that no harm would come to them. But it continued its movement away from her and, more importantly, away from the door.

After Jose and the girls ran from the attic, Susie backed slowly to the door. Again she gently repeated that they meant no harm, and were sorry if they caused any trouble. The tiger tilted its head slightly. Susie wasn't certain if it was in contemplation of what she had said, or in what its next move should be.

In a blur of motion the tiger that Jose had kept at bay leapt through the mist, landing beside the first tiger. Their eyes met and exchanged what Susie could only surmise was a greeting before turning their attention to her. The power that exuded from their gaze caused shivers to crawl up and down her spine. She shuddered. Both beasts began to approach her in a slow, deliberate and precise motion, their eye contact never wavering.

Instinctively Susie jumped backwards, slamming shut the attic door. Seizing a piece of rope, she anchored the door closed before turning and running downstairs as fast as she could. Before she could reach the bottom of the stairs, she heard Jared and Aaron yelling for her, wanting her help and asking what was taking her so long.

As she sprinted to the basement staircase, Susie told Jose to get the others outside and stay there. Not waiting for his answer, she descended rapidly, knowing what had to be the cause of their distress.

The scene was all too familiar – in the middle of the floor was another swirling, foggy mist. Aaron was using an old board as a means to prevent another tiger from entering the basement. With a crowbar held tightly in his hand, Jared was attempting to defend them from the tiger that had made it through. Currently the tiger was backed against the concrete wall and not in a particularly good mood.

"Where have you been?" shouted Aaron, struggling not to appear as frightened as he truly was.

"Have you found any weapons we can use?" Jared asked while keeping his focus on the enormous tiger currently toying with him.

"No, and you don't need any," she answered. With considerable difficulty, she managed to keep her voice calm.

"What?!" both boys shouted.

"Trust me," she responded soothingly. "We just dealt with this in the attic. Everyone is outside. The tigers want us to leave. Let's go."

"Are you crazy?!" Aaron scolded her. "They'll kill us when we try to leave."

"Do you really think you can win with a board and a crowbar?" she asked, appealing to his logical nature. "They want us to leave. Put down your weapons and get outside."

"She has a point," Jared agreed. "Let's go."

Aaron shrugged, dropping his board as he ran to the stairs and quickly ascended, taking them three at a time.

Jared followed suit, dropping his crowbar. "Come on, Susie, let's go," he urged, darting past her.

"Go on," she replied, facing the snarling tiger. "I'll be right there."

"Susie --," he began.

"Go, Jared," Susie insisted. "Get everyone together on the porch and keep them there. I'll be right there." Briefly, she turned her head and smiled at him as reassuringly as she could manage. "I promise."

Jared's concern for her was obvious, but he deferred to her good judgment. He nodded once before racing upstairs.

Susie turned once again to face the tiger which now had been joined by two others. More were coming through the mist.

"I'm sorry we came here. It was an accident," she whispered as she slowly backed her way to the stairs.

They just stared at her, unwavering and menacing in their stance.

"Okay, then," she said, struggling to remain calm. "We'll leave."

Abruptly turning, Susie ran up the stairs and slammed the basement door shut behind her. She leaned against it and gave a sign of relief. It was short lived.

Screaming, the others ran inside the cottage.

"Outside ... now!" Susie ordered as she ran to them.

"We can't!" all of them yelled.

"Look outside," Jared told her.

Susie did. Her heart sank. Swimming across the river from all directions were dozens and dozens of white tigers.

"Susie!" The Munchkins began screaming.

The tigers were descending from the attic, and were being joined by the ones coming up from the basement.

"Outside! Now!" Susie yelled at them. She grabbed the Munchkins, shoving them toward Jared. "Take them and get out! All of you, now!"

Jared picked up Megan, handing her quickly to Juls before firmly grasping Simon and Timmy as he pulled them to the door. Susie was the last to leave, gathering everyone together on the porch. Positioning the Munchkins up against the wall, Susie placed Dani and Kat in front of them, then layered Jose and Juls next, followed by Aaron and Jared just to the side so to protect from each direction. At the front of the group, Susie took point, steeling herself for whatever was to come.

Within minutes they were completely surrounded by a sea of huge, white tigers, all snarling and growling. Slowly a ripple effect appeared, growing ever closer, as the tigers moved aside and back again, allowing for one tiger to come to the front. He was the largest of them all.

With each purposeful, calculated step, their leader moved with precision up the steps and stopped when he reached the porch. His fierce glare had remained on Susie the entire time. His followers moved in closer. There was no escape; nowhere to go, nowhere to hide.

He tossed his head upward as he vocalized what Susie could only ascertain was a command. The sound was petrifying as it reverberated through the air, and its shock wave seemed to penetrate their bodies, deep into their bones. Immediately all of the tigers became quiet, but their ferocious expressions were more than enough to convey the message that the children were uninvited, and had broken some rule that they did not know or understand.

The leader moved in closer, ceasing his advance a few feet from Susie. Moving his head slightly to one side, the tiger jerked his head upwards as he bellowed a series of terrifying sounds. He swung his head back around, staring at Susie for a few seconds before sitting in front of her as if in judgment of her. She was eye to eye with this powerful and terrifying creature. Looking into his eyes, she knew that death was certain unless she could somehow convince him to let them go. There was no compassion in those eyes, only the sense of duty to protect this Realm.

"Please try to understand," Susie spoke, hoping to elicit some sense of understanding in the creature. If the book was right, he would understand her; and where there is understanding, there is the possibility for peace. "It was an accident that we came here. I didn't understand what we were doing. I don't know how to get us home. I have read the books, all of them. I know you have to protect the Realms, but we aren't going to hurt you. We didn't mean to come here. Please help us go home."

Her plea was met with an angry growl, rumbling menacingly like the sound of a horrific storm in the distance.

"Don't punish them; punish me. It's my fault we're here. Send them home, please?" she entreated him.

His lips curled, fangs glinting in the light as he shifted to a standing position. Judgment now passed. His head jutted forward slightly as his body tensed for action.

A dazzling flash of light illuminated the area, as bright and as blinding as a field of snow in the noon-day sun. The light dissipated quickly, and in its place was the woman from Susie's dream, the one in the portrait in the Hidden Room.

The tigers bowed. She smiled and lovingly placed her hand on the leader's head. "Hello, my old friend," the woman said tenderly.

Susie knew that voice – she'd heard it in her dream. Then again, it couldn't have been a dream.

The woman smiled at Susie. "I am an angel, a servant of the Almighty One. My name is Ashara; and yes, we have met, although you perceived it as a dream."

She motioned to the lead tiger as she continued, "Susie, this is Roktur. Roktur, this is Susie, and the others are Jared, Aaron, Juls, Jose, Kat, Dani, Megan, Timmy and Simon."

Stunned, the children began all talking at once. Ashara raised her hands, making a gentle motion for them to be silent. They fell quiet.

"They will not harm you," she told the children; "because I am here, and they must obey my instructions. They protect the Realms from intruders, and they do it very well."

"They are intruders," Roktur growled in deference to Ashara's statement.

"You can speak," Susie said, astonished at this new twist.

"What are you talking about?" Jared asked her.

Ashara smiled. "Your abilities are growing faster than anticipated, Susie. They only heard the rumbling sound. I will allow them to understand him as well."

Roktur seemed both curious and puzzled. "They are not intruders? How can this be? They were not expected – that makes them intruders."

"Usually true, my friend," she agreed patiently; "but this shows the innate strength that Susie possesses. Without any knowledge, without any training and without prior permission of access, she managed to open a closed portal, and to come here, of all places. This isn't her first visit here either. She came here by the sheer will of her spirit, a feat that has never happened."

Roktur looked at Susie with a new-found respect. "That was her? Who is she?" he asked.

"She is the daughter of Liana, the granddaughter of Arielle and the great-granddaughter of Sophie Tremont," Ashara responded. Her smile lit her face with immense joy as she spoke each name.

A reverent hush rippled among the tigers as they reacted to this news. Roktur's eyes widened. He bowed his head in acknowledgement of her lineage.

"I know them well," he spoke in an awed tone. "They are great warriors. It is my privilege to know them, and my honor to be their friend."

"You knew them?" Susie responded, stunned and confused.

"Still do," he asserted.

"How? They died," Susie countered.

Amused, Roktur cast his eyes toward Ashara. "She doesn't understand," he simply stated.

"Not yet," Ashara agreed; "but she will."

"What do you mean?" Susie asked.

"You already know that the physical body has perished. You also know that their spirits continue to live. The Realms in which they now serve, they serve at the direction of the Almighty One, just as I do and as Roktur does. That is all you need to know for now."

Ashara held up her hand, stopping Susie's question before she even vocalized it. "I cannot tell you more than that at this time."

Turning to Roktur, Ashara cradled his face in her hands and gently kissed the top of his head. She smiled. "Stay vigilant and well, my old friend."

The old tiger rubbed his cheek against her face as he responded, "And you, my old friend."

Another flash of white light blinded their vision. In the blink of an eye, they had returned to the Inner Sanctum. Megan rushed to Ashara, throwing her arms around her. Simon and Timmy joined her in giving the angel a thank-you hug. One by one, each of the others joined in the group hug.

Ashara laid her hand upon each one, telling them they have nothing to fear as long as they stay away from the portal. With a wave of her hand, Ashara removed the crystal from the pedestal and those that were in the pillars.

"I have returned them to where you found them," she told the children; "do not use them again."

Each of them solemnly promised never, ever, to go near it.

"We have one more matter to discuss," she began, shifting her tone to one much more serious. "You must never tell anyone about what you found here, or what happened. There may come a time in the future that Miss Pritchett will need to know. Should that day come, I will tell you. Do you understand?"

Again, they all swore that they would keep the secret forever. Simon and Timmy enthusiastically began the 'cross my heart' chant, and was quickly joined by Megan and Dani.

Ashara smiled. She knew they meant it, at least for this moment. She also knew, human nature being what it is, they would not be able to keep their promise. It was inevitable that they would tell someone, especially the younger ones.

"Guys, it's 6:30; we're never going to get back to the Dorms in time," Jared announced with a hint of doom in his voice.

"You needn't worry," Ashara calmly told them, squelching the rising panic among them.

"How are we going to get there without being seen?" Juls asked.

"Your angels will take you," Ashara answered.

Before any of them could ask 'what angels?' they were enveloped in a dazzling array of lights, flashing and filling the Inner Sanctum. When the lights subsided, an angel stood beside each of the children. Only Megan, Simon, Kat and Susie were not surprised.

Megan squealed with delight. "My angel!" she ecstatically cried. Quickly she hugged the celestial being, then turned to face the others. "She's the one I told you about!"

Simon, staring up into the lovely face of Chakahel, grinned. "I know you," he declared softly. "You're the one who chased away the bad ones."

Chakahel nodded, returning Simon's smile. "Yes, little one."

"You're the best," Simon told the angel, hugging his defender.

"It's time," Ashara stated.

The angels responded with a brief nod, placing their hands on the shoulders of their charges. And then they were gone. Only Susie, Tahlranel and Ashara remained.

"What's happening?" Susie asked.

"I need to speak with you, Susie," Ashara explained. "Tahlranel will take you to your Dorm when we are finished."

"Why do you need to speak to just me?" Susie queried, guardedly.

"Your abilities are strong, much stronger than anticipated," Ashara spoke admiringly. "And because of this, the sequence of introduction has been altered."

Ashara smiled reassuringly. "This is good that you possess such strength. Soon you will see and understand that this is so. I do not know why your preparation for your twelfth birthday was interrupted. Perhaps it was to allow you the chance to see your own strength. What I do know is that all of you were brought here for a purpose. Your paths will merge for a time, some longer than others. For now, you and you alone are to know of this place."

Her demeanor and tone changed, becoming solemn. "The memories they have of the Inner Realm, of all that is related to this room and to the Evermore family have been removed. They will awaken shortly, refreshed and without knowledge of any of this – not even as a dream. You will not mention this to them."

Softening her stance, Ashara continued, "On your twelfth birthday you will have a visitation. At that time, much will be explained. Should you choose to follow this path, your training will begin."

"What happens if I don't?" Susie asked, her voice now revealing a slight tremor.

With a kind smile and in a comforting tone, Ashara answered. "Nothing, Susie. Your memories will be removed. You will not find any of this again. You will continue to live here, and grow up as any normal child. Another will be chosen."

"Chosen for what? I don't understand," Susie retorted. "Am I a Keeper?"

Ashara paused, but momentarily. "Since the order of revelation has already been altered, I have been instructed to answer. You are not a

719

Keeper, although Keepers are a type of Guardian. They prevent certain beings from entering this world through portals, and they keep certain beings from leaving this world through portals. You are a Guardian, but not a Keeper. You, like those before you, are a warrior should you so choose to follow in their footsteps."

"Doing what?" Susie asked, frightened and confused by so much that made no sense.

Patiently Ashara answered. "That will be revealed to you when your training is complete. Give no more thought to this. Await the visitation on your birthday."

"How can I just wait? I have a million questions," Susie pressed.

"Perhaps you should examine again the puzzle box Nana left you," Ashara stated. Her tone held a slightly amused quality to it.

"Why?" Susie asked; "what's in it?"

"Open it and see," was her response.

Peevishly Susie retorted, "I have tried, but I can't open it. Nana wouldn't show me. She said when I was ready, I'd know how."

Nodding in agreement, Ashara answered, "She is correct. When you are focused, you will see how to open it. You need to open it. Do so soon."

Ashara signaled to Tahlranel, and Susie felt the weight of his hands as he placed them on her shoulders. The room disappeared in a bright explosion of light.

Chapter 39

PERSEVERANCE PAYS

Grammy did announce at breakfast that she was staying at Glen Hollow, but she did so quite ingeniously. First, she sweetly shared how much she loved being here, and being able to spend the holiday with her grandchildren. She told them how much she had come to care for them all, and especially enjoyed being a part of a large family. Then she said how much she would miss everyone when it was her time to leave. That confused Susie a little since she had thought that Grammy was staying, until she saw the twinkle in Miss Pritchett's eyes, and the grin on the Reverend's face. Miss Pritchett and the Reverend were obviously involved in her little ruse.

The Reverend casually asked what time Grammy thought they should leave for the station. That's when Grammy, smiling as big as big could be, very calmly stated it wouldn't be necessary now that she was remaining at Glen Hollow. Stunned faces soon melted into surprise, followed by sheer delight as each one realized what she had said.

The adults all laughed, welcoming her to the Glen Hollow family. The children, however, were a little more demonstrative – they began a rousing chorus of yells, cheers and laughter, leaving their table to give Grammy a hug. Aaron actually had tears in his eyes. He held on to Grammy for the longest time as she just patted his head, telling him "everything's all right now". She finally convinced them all to finish their breakfast before it became cold.

During the course of breakfast, Susie yawned several times, drawing curious looks from Miss Cora, Miss Ginger, Miss Hilda, Miss Bettye and Miss Pritchett. Forcing herself to appear as alert as ever, she did her best to convey nothing was amiss. It wasn't until Megan cheerfully reminded the group that her tea party was at three that Susie realized she had forgotten. She groaned inwardly as she realized that, not only would there be no nap after breakfast, but only a very short one after lunch. Unless ...

"Megan, I just had a great idea for your tea party," Susie told her. "If we have your tea party at four, I can read a book while everyone enjoys their tea and treats. It'll be entertainment, like having snacks during a movie."

Relishing the idea, Megan began clapping her hands. "I like it; I like it," she giggled approvingly. "I'll tell Mrs. Coppersmith." Suddenly her angelic face clouded as her brow furrowed. Her lips formed a pretty, little pout as she declared, "We can't, because we can't have food in the Library."

Susie smiled. "But we can have food in the Parlor," Susie reminded her.

Megan's eyes flashed with glee, "Oh yeah," she giggled joyously. "I'll tell Mrs. Coppersmith that too." She gave a cute, little nod of her head, formally signaling that the matter was resolved.

Susie chuckled. She felt a little guilty that she had manipulated Megan into changing her tea party time so she could have a nap, but it really would be better this way.

The bell rang, breakfast was over, and everyone began the process of clearing the tables and then proceeded to chapel.

———

For the first time during chapel service, Susie could see all of the angels that were around them, witnessing their worship in conjunction with the members of Glen Hollow. Their voices were raised in the most wonderful harmony as they sang together with the congregants, filling the little Chapel with the heavenly strains. For some reason it seemed as if the instruments today sounded a little sweeter, and today the Reverend had been exceptionally inspiring. To her surprise and delight, the fatigue she had felt seemed to disappear completely during the worship service.

Getting through lunch had been a little difficult. Several times she zoned out enough to where even the other children noticed. She managed to convince them she was just a little preoccupied, trying to think of a book to read for the tea party. The Munchkins offered several suggestions, as did Jose, Dani and even Kat.

When lunch was finally over, Susie slipped away to her sanctuary before anyone had realized she was gone. It was the only place she could go where she would not be disturbed. Well, at least not by corporeal beings. She set the alarm to awaken her at 3:30; that should allow her ample time to be punctual for the tea party. She pulled from the shelf one of Simon's favorite books from ages ago, "The Little Engine That Could". She would read this one – a little fitting since they had apparently hit a snag in building Train Town. Settling into Nana's chair, Susie covered herself with Nana's afghan and dropped into a deep sleep.

———

Contrary to what most of the children had feared, Megan's tea party turned out to be fun and a big hit. Mrs. Coppersmith had prepared wonderful tiny, little, crust-less sandwiches: peanut butter-and-jelly (cut into triangles), chicken salad (cut into squares) and pimento cheese (cut into circles). For sweets, she had prepared several dozen micro-mini pies, each one just about the size of one bite for those older than the Munchkins. They had a choice between strawberry, banana cream, chocolate, cherry, apple and peach.

The book she read was also well received; so much so that Jared, Aaron and Jose all convinced Simon and Timmy that their Train Town problem would be solved before bedtime. Simon and Timmy cheered and clapped, their little eyes just dancing with joy. Susie had looked at the older boys with an 'are you sure you know what you're doing look'. They had all three given her a nod that left no room for doubt – they would solve the problem. And they did – it required the help and experience of the men; but they solved it, giving much joy and happiness to Simon and Timmy. Susie had noticed that it also buoyed the spirts of the men, and especially of Aaron, Jared and Jose.

———

The day was over; Susie reviewed what she had written in her journal. She smiled. It had been a good day, a really good day.

Starting with the Inner Sanctum, she wrote about the cleaning project, and how quickly everyone had pitched in and done a fantastic job. Next she recorded what had happened, how she had accidentally opened the portal, transporting them all to the Inner Realm. She included the stand-off with the Guardians of the Realms, the White Tigers. If Helga Von Richter is to be believed, they are very fortunate that Ashara came when she did. She rescued them from certain death. She included what Ashara and Roktur had said about her mother, about her grandmother and also about her great-grandmother, Nana.

Now she had even more questions, including, what did Ashara mean when she said her training in preparation of her twelfth birthday had been interrupted? What did she mean her lineage are warriors? Susie's head ached from the questions swirling around in circles. Each one spun another three, and all were spiraling out in different directions.

"No matter," she told herself. "Ashara promised that all my questions will be answered. I guess I have to wait." She chuckled when she thought how waiting had never been easy for her. She finished writing about the Inner Realm experience, and what Ashara had told her individually.

Dinner time had been fun, though much quieter now that all the company had left. It seemed a little strange, but it would be good to get back into a normal routine. Susie chuckled as she read what she had written.

'Normal – here?' she mused. 'Glen Hollow is anything but normal … but I guess it all depends on what your definition of normal is.'

She had begun a new serial for the night session of Story Time, one that would take three nights to finish. It happened to be one of Nana's favorites, and she had shared that knowledge with the others. Simon's face lit up, and she noticed that everyone, especially the adults, was even more attentive than ever. Perhaps they hoped to see something of Nana through the story, to learn more of her through the story that she loved most. Susie nodded as she read what she had just written.

Susie made an entry regarding the Munchkin's usual bed time routine, and how much fun they had had today. She loved how their every thought and emotion displayed so clearly on their sweet faces.

Sadly she noted that none of the others remembered anything about the secrets she had shared, nor the Inner Sanctum, nor the trip to the Inner Realm or the return trip back to the Inner Sanctum. Ashara had thoroughly removed their memories, just as she said she would.

Nevertheless, it had been a good day. Tomorrow will also be a good day. I know it, she added to her journal.

———

Susie awakened in the morning refreshed and invigorated. She had slept the night through undisturbed. She arose with a song in her heart, beginning the series of wake-up calls followed by their "good morning" group hug.

Breakfast seemed back to normal with the conversations centering on Miss Taryn's forthcoming wedding, necessary repairs, animal care and the like. After breakfast, Susie had morning kitchen duty again, a chore that really wasn't at all a chore. Afterwards, she spent a little time in the Library, reading by the fireplace in the east section.

Her mind kept wandering to the Hidden Floor. It just seemed so odd that Miss Pritchett's father would choose to hide everything that way. There were plenty of storage places in the attic; it didn't make sense to build an entire floor that you kept hidden. As much as she would like to explore that room too, her first priority was to explore the Inner Sanctum. After that, she'd continue exploring the East Wing and the Hidden Floor. She wished she could share her discoveries with the others. It saddened her to think that it had to be secret from them as well.

"At least for now," she corrected herself. She remembered that Ashara did mention a time would come when their paths would join; at that time, they would be told about the Inner Sanctum.

Lunch came and went quicker than Susie expected. Somehow it seemed as if they had just sat down, and now it was time to go. The Munchkins all gave her a kiss and a hug as they paraded toward the door on their way to naptime. Kat and Dani had left together, concocting some secret plan that kept them snickering all through lunch. Juls had left for a practice session. Jose and Aaron were playing chess, while Jared was assisting Kevin and Sam on a project.

The Dining Hall was empty except for Miss Fiona and herself. Susie had decided to stay and lend a hand in collecting the table linens. She began with her table.

"Well, aren't you a treasure?" Miss Fiona said teasingly. "You could be doing any ol' thing your wee heart desires, and here you are helping me."

Susie laughed. "True, so obviously my wee heart desires to help you," she teased back.

Miss Fiona burst out laughing, long and loud. "If I didn't know better, I'd swear you've kissed the Blarney Stone."

Her eyes twinkled with delight. "You've come a long way in a short time, wee lassie," she playfully bantered, intentionally increasing her slight Irish accent to a heavy brogue. "It does me wee heart good to no end," she added; "to see how you've blossomed in such a way as ye have."

Susie laughed; Miss Fiona had such a carefree spirit, she made everyone feel better. "I'm thrilled you approve," she responded lightly. Susie's eyes flashed with amusement, tossing the linens she held on top of those on the adult table.

Still grinning and eyes twinkling, Miss Fiona softly replied, "Aye I do, Susie girl; I surely do. Now, let's get to it, so you can go do something fun."

And it short order, the linens were removed. Miss Fiona took them to the laundry, and Susie headed upstairs to her sanctuary. She had decided what she was going to do.

———

Susie ceased her attempts to open Nana's puzzle box. Frustration was beginning to overwhelm her. At this moment Susie could not understand how Nana had been so certain that she could open it. "Ashara, too," she mused. So far, the score was puzzle box, 7; Susie, 0.

Gently placing the carved box on the window seat next to her, Susie leaned back against the wall. She sat cross-legged, just staring at it.

"So, what is the secret?" she asked of it.

Again, Nana's words returned to her, "When you are ready, you'll know how to open it."

"I am ready, Nana," Susie whispered; "but I don't know how to open it."

She again heard Ashara's words echoing in her mind; "She is correct. When you are focused, you will see how to open it."

Susie stared at the box. "I will open you," she told it. "I am determined. I have to go to Story Time now, but I will be back tonight. I will open you.

Picking up the box, she strode across the room, returning Nana's puzzle box to its place on the shelf and left her sanctuary.

———

It was Megan's turn to choose a book, and her choice caused groans and moans from all of them. Susie had laughed, reminding them that their turns were coming, and Megan would have to sit through those as well.

The little book was entitled 'The Fairy Princess Tea Party Extravaganza', complete with beautifully illustrated pop-outs. It was definitely a 'chick' book, make that 'a little chick' book, but that was okay. When they finally settled down and accepted the inevitable, Susie began reading. Megan was enchanted; her starry eyes rarely blinked as she focused intently on the book. The story was really quite good, and Susie noticed that the others were engrossed in it nearly as much as Megan.

Afterwards, they were kind enough to admit it to Megan, which pleased her immensely. She chatted all the way to dinner that she had every book in the series, naming each and every one. Susie chuckled softly upon hearing the low moans from those at the front of their procession.

———

The box rested in her lap. Susie stared at it. She cleared her mind from all distractions, and fortunately there hadn't really been any today. Dinner went smoothly, evening Story Time was a success, and the Munchkins had gone off to Dreamland without a hitch.

All that was left to make her day complete was to open this box.

"Nana said when I was ready, I would know. How will I know? Ashara said that if I focus, I will open it. Focus how? On what?"

Her fingers lightly caressed the ornate carvings, tracing the unicorn, the flowers and the filigree scrollwork. That triggered something familiar. She traced over it again.

"What is it?" she asked her memory. "Why are you so familiar?" she asked Nana's puzzle box.

Suddenly she knew. She pulled the pendant out from under her shirt. "It's the same pattern!" she shouted for joy as she compared the two patterns. "Yes; this is it. I know it!"

"Okay, now what?" she asked, standing to her feet.

She began to pace around the room, holding the pendant in her hand. Gently her fingers caressed it as she paced. "Think," she told herself. "Think!" "What did Nana tell me?"

Her mind searched for the memory. She grinned. She knew.

Nana had told her to: "Never take it off. It is a talisman, an amulet of protection. It will reveal many truths to you at the proper time."

She giggled and danced around the room. The pendant is the key to opening the box. She was so excited. After her third victory dance around the room, Susie dropped onto the sofa beside the box, picked it up and began examining it again. There was no key hole; nothing to even suggest one. She felt all along the edges of the box. Nothing. She looked on the bottom of the box. Again, nothing.

"Think!" she ordered herself. "How would I disguise a way to use this pendant to open this box?"

With a light and gentle touch, Susie moved her fingers over the wood. Slowly she touched each and every carving. She stopped. She began to laugh. "Oh, how clever. How very, very clever."

The eye of the unicorn was actually a keyhole. Carefully she inserted the pendant, turned it counter-clock wise and heard a distinctive click. Eureka! The box was now open.

Victory is sweet.

Chapter 40

NANA'S MESSAGE

With trepidation, anticipation, curiosity and elation building within her, Susie raised the lid of the puzzle box. Its cedar lining gently infused the air around her with its pleasant scent. She found several items that were familiar; some were not.

First she found the little satin pillow on which her pendant had been presented to her. She removed it and set it on the table. Next she found the small box that had held her cloisonné brooch, and placed it on the table next to the satin pillow.

Another similar box had Simon's name written in it. She opened the box, marveling at the counterpart to her brooch. It was a ring, made of a metal which she had never seen. It felt cold to the touch, and its ghostly, pale color was nearly translucent. A thin, round disc served as a platform for a small, icy blue diamond. The diamond was perfectly round; no sharp edges, no edges at all. Without any visible means to hold it there, the diamond sat, perfectly centered, on top of the disc. Susie looked to see if there was any trace of a glue, but saw none.

"Perhaps it's an industrial glue and only requires the tiniest amount," she pondered. But in looking down through the clarity of the stone, there was no glue to be seen, only the metal disc beneath the stone.

Susie closed the ring box and moved to the next item. It, too, had Simon's name written on it. She opened it and smiled. It was a pendant just like hers. She closed the lid and set it aside.

At the very bottom of the puzzle box lay a large, bulky envelope that bore her name, written in Nana's hand. For a moment she sat very still, staring at the envelope. Tears began to sting her eyes as she realized that these were Nana's last words to her, placed in this box for safe keeping for just this moment.

Gingerly Susie retrieved the envelope, holding it in front of her. She wept as she gazed upon it, her tears flowing down her face in little ribbons of salty water. Gently she pressed the envelope against her lips, and then against her heart before placing it in her lap. Breathing slowly in and slowly out several times, Susie quelled the churning emotions within her heart, enabling her tears to cease their flow.

With an unwavering resolve, she opened the envelope and removed the folded stationery. Susie couldn't help but chuckle fondly at its thickness. Nana was always one for words; she had such a dramatic flair, and an uncanny ability to speak or write with such flowery abandon.

Unfolding the letter, she began to read:

My dearest, precious Susie,

The day of your twelfth birthday approaches. I know this because I know you. I know that you will not give up until you have opened the puzzle box. And I know you well enough to know that you will do so before your twelfth birthday as I have told you many times that you must do. It is good that you have done so.

This is an amazing and exciting time in your life. It will be filled with all manner of new, exhilarating experiences that will leave you breathless at times. You are about to enter a whole new world, literally and figuratively. I know you have experienced some new things at Glen Hollow, enabling you to see and hear that which others cannot.

By now, you should be seeing and speaking with Tahlranel. If you should decide to follow the heritage of your lineage, your birthright, you will meet an Angel named Ashara. I am laughing, dear Susie, as I write this because, knowing you as I do, more than likely you have managed to find a way to force the meeting ahead of schedule.

There is so much I need to tell you to prepare you for what is about to happen. I will start by telling you a little about our family heritage. As you are aware, we all have this unique birthmark. It identifies who we are, our lineage. There are others that have different birthmarks, denoting their lineage.

Our lineage bears the mark of the angel's lips, representative of speaking the Truth of the Almighty One. His Truth, His Word, is our Power, and His sword is the Sword of Truth. It is our Sword as well.

We are part of a group known as Guardians. There are different types of Guardians, and they each have a specific purpose. Our lineage is part of the warrior Guardians. And yes, dear Susie, warrior does mean what it implies; to stand and do battle. What you will learn is that the battle is not yours, but is the Almighty's. If you listen to His voice, if you follow His directive, the battle is won.

Teaching our children about our heritage is usually done at an early age, generally starting about three, and begins with the most basic of lessons. By the time they reach their twelfth birthday, they are fully cognizant, fully aware, of what is truly real, and are ready to begin the training phase. On their twelfth birthday, they receive the Visitation, after which they must choose whether or not to walk the warrior path. If they do not choose the warrior path, all learning, all knowledge and all memoires of it are removed; they live in blissful ignorance. If they do choose the warrior path, training begins. Training is different for each one, depending largely on one's own innate abilities and spiritual strength. It can last many months or many years.

Your mother did not want this path for you or for Simon. She wanted to spare you both all that goes with it. She wanted you both to live as most people do, happily unaware of the real world. Part of me wanted to shield you both as well, even though I knew it would not be possible. You have been seeing the others from the time you were born, very rare and very much an indication of your inherent abilities. I knew this to be true and told your mother. She did not want to hear it, for it served to show how unusual are the gifts that you possess. Your abilities and spiritual strength grew exponentially with each passing day. It became increasingly difficult to explain away some of the things you did or said, although she did try.

It was her hope that if you didn't know the Truth, the dark forces would leave you alone because you would not be involved in the battle. She forgot that the choice was not hers to make; it is yours and only yours. She also forgot that the Almighty One chooses whom He will choose; and the one He chooses, He fully equips. In her spirit she knew this to be true; but in her heart as a mother, she chose to forget, allowing her mother's heart to rule instead of her spirit.

When your parents died, the force of your anger and grief was so great that it not only blocked out your ability to see and hear the others, but your memory of them as well. You also shattered every window, every breakable item, in a radius of three hundred yards. You didn't intend to do it; it just happened. And it happened because you had no training to help you handle your abilities.

Because your defenses were so strong, it was decided that it was paramount to allow you to bring down your own barrier when you were ready. I did my best to teach you how to think, to understand situations and circumstances, to resolve and solve problems rationally and logically. I told you stories through our Story Time in order to help you to reach the decision to remove your barrier.

Several times I thought you were just about ready, but you never seemed to be able to take that final step. Just so you know, the stories I told you are real. They happened just as I told you. I was the warrior that went to all of those places at the direction of, and obedience to, the Almighty One. There were many other battles, but I could not share those even in story form because you were not ready in any way to hear those stories. I would have loved to have shared those with you, as well as those of your mother's and also of my daughter's, your grandmother. Perhaps, as part of your training, Ashara will share those with you and those of our ancestor's.

It is my fervent hope that you will follow in our footsteps and walk the warrior path, utilizing fully your gifts and your spiritual strength. But whatever choice you make, I am, and always will be, most proud of you.

As to Glen Hollow, Ashara chose Glen Hollow as the place that will best serve your needs and that of Simon's. If you remember, I arranged with Mrs. Crenshaw for you to contact her upon my passing. What you did not know was that I also arranged for her to see to it that you both are placed at Glen Hollow, even though she ardently tried to convince me a traditional family would be a better choice. Under any other circumstance, I would have agreed with her. I could not tell her why it needed to be Glen Hollow, nor can you.

You can never tell anyone of the things that you have already learned, nor of the things that you will learn. It is only for the line of the Guardians. That is just one of the minor sacrifices we make. There will be many other sacrifices, and some will be very difficult to make. But you can do it, and you will do it. I have every faith and confidence in you, for I know you.

On your twelfth birthday, you must wear the cloisonné brooch I gave to you on your tenth birthday. Always remember to wear it on your birthday and only on your birthday. I cannot stress this enough. Please do not forget. The only time you will cease to wear it will be when you pass it on to your first-born daughter on her tenth birthday. Please do not forget.

And on your twelfth birthday, you must be waiting at a window before dawn. Visitation always comes just before sunrise begins, when the light has faintly begun to pierce the darkness but well before the sun can be seen on the horizon. You will know immediately when the Visitation has begun, trust me on this. More than that I cannot tell you.

Much will be explained to you on that day. You will be given three days to make your decision. If you choose to follow the path of our lineage, your birthright, your training will commence. It will be more difficult for you, my precious, little one, because you did not receive the proper preparation. But I know the strength that you possess. I know your heart. I know your spirit. And I know that whatever you set your mind to accomplish, you will accomplish.

If you should decide not to follow the path of our lineage, that is okay, Susie dear. There is nothing wrong with that choice. Whatever memories you have of this path, whatever you have learned thus far will be removed. You will still live a full, rewarding and wonderful life.

I will always be proud of you and love you whatever choice you make. This is also true of your parents and grandparents. We all look forward to the day when we will be reunited.

Should you choose to follow in our footsteps, Ashara will help you when the time is right to begin to teach Simon what he needs to know. Upon his tenth birthday, please give to him the ring that is in the puzzle box. Instruct him that he is to wear it on his birthday and only on his birthdays. He will do this every year until he passes it on to his first-born son upon that child's tenth birthday. Also give to him the pendant that is identical to yours. Instruct him as I did with you: "Never take it off. It is a talisman, an amulet of protection. It will reveal many truths to you at the proper time."

The week before he turns twelve, you will give him the puzzle box to open. Do not tell him how to open it. Do not show him how to open it. Do not give him any hints on how to open it. He is to open it alone. He must do so on his own accord if he wants to read his letter. Place his envelope on top of yours when you return your letter to the puzzle box.

I am so very proud of you, Susie. I always will be. I love you, and I will be watching over you.

Love Always,

Nana

Pressing the pages against her heart, she closed her eyes. Her tears began to flow as the mental barrier she had constructed so long ago came crashing down in its entirety. Now she fully remembered her past. She remembered what happened the day she was told her parents died, the morning after the accident.

Nana was right; her anger and her grief were so intense, she railed against everything. That violent force created such a percussive wave that it destroyed anything breakable in its vicinity, causing a tremendously loud sonic boom to be heard. Everyone assumed it had been the fault of a jet, flying high enough to remain unseen, although news reports had claimed that the military and the commercial airport had denied any such plane was flying overhead at the time. It was eventually written off by everyone as just one of those little mysteries of life.

Quietly Susie sat, allowing the memories to reintegrate. She laughed softly, remembering the first time she toddled after a pixie. She was barely seven months old, and had only been walking a week. The pixie was stunned that Susie could see her, and thought it a coincidence at first. She tested Susie, darting this way and that, up and down and finally coming to rest upon a flower, still veiled. Susie had giggled, and reached her hand out to the pixie.

The pixie curtsied, flew to Susie's cheek and kissed her. Hovering next to Susie's ear, she whispered, "We have waited a long time for you, little one. We will guard you well until the appointed day." The pixie darted in front of Susie, waved and left.

One by one the memories were restored. One by one she relived those early years. So very precious were those memories to her now. Tears rolled as she vowed, "I will never again forget."

Susie exhaled a deep breath and wiped away her tears. Carefully she folded Nana's message and returned it to the envelope. She removed Simon's envelope from inside of her envelope and placed her envelope on the bottom of the puzzle box. Gently she laid Simon's envelope on top of hers, ready for the day he opened the puzzle box. One by one Susie returned the other items to the puzzle box and closed the lid. She heard the lock click and smiled.

She sighed, a happy, little sigh. Nothing was hidden any longer. Now she knew the Truth, and it no longer frightened her. She knew who, and what, she is. Many questions were yet to be answered, but she knew they would be.

There were now the strangest sensations coursing through her; more acute was sound, and smell and sight, more clear now was the invisible world to her. She could see and hear that which most corporal beings could not.

She tested her newly resurfaced gifts by returning the puzzle box to its place on the shelf by simply picturing it there.

"'Thank you, Nana," she whispered; "for everything."

Laughing joyously, she rose from the couch and left her sanctuary, returning to her Dorm.

Chapter 41

AULD LANG SYNE

Susie awoke. She felt more alive now than ever before. A robust sense of energy streamed through her, filling her and infusing her with vitality and a keen awareness of everything around her. Heightened sensory perceptions permeated her with amazing abilities. She could hear the birds chirping outside. The more she concentrated on them, the more she precisely could discern their location. Looking out her window, she could see them in their nests, far beyond the meadow. Somehow the distance melted away, and it was as if they were just outside her window.

Her mind shifted to Juls. Susie could actually hear the music Juls was listening to as she practiced. She laughed. Inwardly Susie giggled as she thought, 'Oh, I'm going to have fun picking on her for that selection.'

Gazing up into the sky as the pre-dawn was just beginning to break, Susie observed the marvel of all of the colors of the light spectrum previously unseen by her. She sighed happily, enjoying the spectacle. As the faintest hint of light began to stream across the horizon, Susie beheld a scene far greater than that of the light spectrum – the sky, the earth, filled with celestial beings. Witnessing the angels singing their morning worship brought tears to her eyes. The sight was awesome; but the sound was so incredible, mere words could not describe it.

"Nothing on earth compares; nothing on earth even remotely comes close to that wondrous sound," Susie whispered. Closing her eyes, she joined in their song of praise, thanking the Almighty One for all that He has done, is doing and will do.

Opening her eyes, she smiled. A sense of completeness blanketed her. All of this had been hidden from her by her own doing. 'Never again,' she thought.

"Good morning, Susie."

"Good morning, Tahlranel." Susie turned to greet him with a grin as wide as her face.

"I see you have opened the puzzle box and are restored," he stated.

Susie's laugh was light-hearted. "Yes," she affirmed; "and it's wonderful." She crossed over to him, hugged him and rested her head against him. She sighed. "I wish I hadn't blocked it."

"Wishing will not change what was. It is better if you learn, and not repeat it," he replied.

Chuckling, Susie pushed back, giving him 'the look'. "Like I don't know that? Obviously, I've learned," she replied in a playful tone.

"There is always that hope," he responded with a smile. "Now, I am certain once you have thought about it, you will know that you cannot speak to Juls regarding her choice of practice music. That would lead to questions you cannot answer, causing potential problems."

"How did you ...," Susie began and stopped.

He smiled and responded to her unvoiced question. "Yes, I know. However, you will need to learn how to temper your abilities, how to control them, for your own sake and that of others."

Susie gave him a dubious look.

His words were kindly spoken as he continued, "I know that it is all new to you, and you are rejoicing in what you are experiencing. This is good. But you must also learn not to invade the minds of others on a whim or as a lark. Had you been cognizant of who you are from the beginning, this would not be an issue today. No matter; we cannot change what was, but we can work on what is."

He smiled. "Your task today is to not allow the thoughts of others to be heard or seen by you."

"And how do I do that?"

With an amused smile, he answered, "By ignoring the sights and sounds that are from their minds and their souls."

He could see from her expression that she did not understand. "Consider you are watching a movie, and someone speaks to you. You can still see and hear the movie, but not comprehend what is happening or the dialogue because you are concentrating on what the person is saying to you. It is the same principle, but it does require practice."

Susie laughed. "Well, I should be able to get a lot of practice here."

Nodding, Tahlranel agreed and vanished.

The girls were all in cheerful moods, and Megan was especially chatty and playful this morning. After several alternating rounds of 'Tickle Monster' and 'Itsy Bitsy Spider', she finally decided it was time for their 'good morning' group hug. Her pronouncement might have had more to do with the fact that Juls, Kat and Dani were threatening to exclude both Megan and Susie if they didn't hurry.

Megan bounced off her bed, resembling a trapeze artist, and ran into the hallway. Susie quickly joined them, and they shared their group hug before hurriedly getting ready for the day.

It hadn't been as difficult as Tahlranel had made it seem. So far, it had been relatively easy, although Susie was tempted a time or two. However, she discovered she was soon put to the test upon entering the Dining Hall. Having a greater number of people around proved to be a little more difficult, giving credence to Tahlranel's words. With some effort, she managed to succeed. It wasn't until Miss Fiona entered that Susie's poise faltered a little.

Just prior to Miss Fiona's arrival, Susie was being inundated with constant and persistent pleas from Simon and Timmy to listen to their ideas about a 'Train Town Welcome Party'. They wanted everyone at the manor to attend, and wanted her to tell them how to do that. They peppered her with questions about what day and time would be best for the party, what decorations there should be and if their ideas were good in that department. They listed every conceivable snack as being the food fare and wanted to know her thoughts concerning their ideas. Finally they began pleading that she tell them how to ask Mrs. Coppersmith to provide the treats. Translation: they wanted her to ask Mrs. Coppersmith to prepare the food, and for her to plan the party with Mrs. Coppersmith. They both had reached the whining and wheedling stage, their voices taking on that near screeching quality. She was just beginning her answer when she caught a glimpse of Miss Fiona as she entered.

The most beautiful, ethereal creature walked into the Dining Hall, moving as if she was floating on air. The lighting shimmered on her pale skin, casting the effect of Miss Fiona having been sprinkled with gold dust. Her thick hair, with its long, spiraling curls, glimmered as she walked, creating an aura of a river of golden fire. Softly her sea green eyes glowed with an eerily, pulsating quality.

Susie was stunned, but what startled her the most was what happened next. Glancing mischievously at Susie, Miss Fiona winked. And when she did, she unfurled her gossamer wings, iridescent and sparkling as if covered in glitter. She flapped them a couple of times, then smiled impishly as she tucked them against her body.

Susie choked; Kat began pounding her on her back, asking if she was okay. Several others, adults and children, offered their assistance. Susie declined, shaking her head and assuring everyone she's fine. Quickly Juls picked up Susie's glass of milk and handed it to her, insisting that she drink in order to help soothe her throat. Susie complied, desperate to shift the focus of everyone's attention elsewhere.

"You look like you've seen a ghost," Kat teased.

Susie shot her a warning look.

Kat just grinned.

Now that Susie's emergency was no longer an emergency, Simon and Timmy returned to their mission. Susie compromised, telling them that she would go with them when they were ready to ask Mrs. Coppersmith to plan the party with the two of them, reminding them that it is their party and not hers. That was acceptable to them, and their focus changed from Susie to their party plans. With a vivacious and flamboyant manner, Megan announced she wanted to help. She was immensely vexed, developing a serious pout when they declined her benevolent and gracious offer.

Very casually, Susie reminded the boys of Megan's extensive party planning experience by lavishing praise on Megan for such wonderful parties she has had. Megan laughed and her spirits rose, delighting in the praise and the attention. Susie further mentioned that if the boys were smart, they would allow her to help because it is a lot of work to plan a party. Simon and Timmy held a fast pow-wow, whispering furiously to each other. They began giggling, then proudly announced that Megan could be their helper. Susie chuckled, watching the three of them praising each other for their good ideas.

Susie stole a glance at Miss Fiona. Instantly her wings unfurled, and she wiggled them slightly before tucking them in once again. Turning her head slightly, she winked at Susie before returning to her conversation with Grammy.

Susie inhaled deeply, softly and then slowly exhaled. 'So it's true,' she thought; 'Miss Fiona is a fairy. What other surprises are there?'

Looking away from Miss Fiona, she noticed Kat was staring at her, a puzzled expression prominent on her face. "What is it?" she whispered, leaning sideways toward Susie.

Susie shook her head. "Nothing; I'm a little tired, that's all." She gave Kat a reassuring smile, but it was obvious from Kat's expression that Kat was not fooled by her explanation.

Kat's eyes narrowed slightly, and she said, "We'll talk later."

Susie shrugged, giving a fast glance around the table. None of the other children had noticed anything. However, the adult tables were a different story; Miss Pritchett and Kevin both were watching her, keenly aware that something was happening.

———

Kitchen duty was fun this morning. In Mrs. Coppersmith's absence, Miss Elsa began a round of songs and Miss Taryn joined in, alternating selections with her. Most of the songs Susie didn't know and was pleasantly surprised that even Miss Taryn took the time to teach her the songs. They had a great time, laughing and teasing as they worked.

Mrs. Coppersmith arrived about thirty minutes into their song fest and was in an exceptionally good mood, even complementing Miss Taryn on several occasions. The Munchkins had approached her immediately after breakfast, and did so without Susie. They ran to Mrs. Coppersmith, competing as to who would be the one to ask her first. She was thrilled, listening to their excited ideas until she finally told them that such a grand party as the 'Train Town Welcome Party' would require some extensive planning. She made an appointment with them right after naptime to discuss the particulars. Their little egos just soared.

Entering the kitchen, humming and singing, her face glowed with joy. As Mrs. Coppersmith bounced and soft-tapped her way next to Taryn, she announced she would need assistance in planning and preparing for the

'Train Town Welcome Party'. With a festive tone, she asked Taryn if she would be so kind as to oblige.

A surprised Miss Taryn froze momentarily before a little smile emerged. Nodding, she quickly agreed.

"Good," Mrs. Coppersmith said, giving Taryn a hug; "I'll be needing you to sit in with me on the planning session this afternoon with them."

Tears stung her eyes as Taryn hugged Mrs. Coppersmith. "I'd love to," she said.

Grinning, Mrs. Coppersmith told her, "It won't be easy. We're going to pull out all the stops like we used to do. Remember?"

Taryn laughed. "Oh, I remember."

"Make sure you have your sketch pad and pencils ready. You'll need to make some quick designs to show them what we're talking about. You have to take into account that they're little ones, so we have to explain in ways they can understand."

Taryn's eyes lit with a passionate fire. "I won't disappoint you."

"Of that I have no doubt," Mrs. Coppersmith responded affectionately, patting Taryn's cheek.

"Come help me check supplies, Elsa," Mrs. Coppersmith stated as she hurried to the storerooms.

"Yes, ma'am," Miss Elsa responded, quickly folding her drying towel and laid it on the table. She smiled at Miss Taryn and said, "You are so lucky. It'll be a lot fun."

"I know; I can't wait. It's been such a long time since we had parties like this," Miss Taryn elatedly agreed.

"Elsa! What's keeping you?" Mrs. Coppersmith bellowed, her voice carrying well the considerable distance from the storage pantries and into the kitchen.

Miss Elsa grinned. "I believe that's my cue," she told Susie and Miss Taryn. Quickly she headed toward the doors that led to the various storage pantry rooms. "On my way," she called out to Mrs. Coppersmith.

Susie had been grinning the whole time, thrilled that Miss Taryn was actually changing. Her premise was a little optimistic, and very much premature.

Miss Taryn gave her a haughty glare as she tossed the towel onto the table. Glancing at the clock, she coldly stated, "You can finish putting away the dishes. I have better things to do."

She turned and strode out of the kitchen, leaving Susie alone.

———

Susie had searched for Miss Fiona after kitchen duty but couldn't find her. She had tried everywhere and was sorely tempted to use her abilities, but decided not to break her word to Tahlranel. Lunch time was coming soon enough, and she'd make certain to talk with her afterwards.

Deciding a quick nap was in order, Susie entered the Dorm and collapsed onto her bed, snuggling under the warm and comfy bedding. Within minutes, Kat jumped onto her bed and sat cross-legged.

"Now tell me what was going on at breakfast," she demanded. "What did you see?"

"Can we do this later? I really need a nap," Susie countered.

"No," Kat replied forcefully. "Tell me what you saw."

While staring at Kat, a counter move occurred. Susie crawled out from under her covers and joined Kat, sitting cross-legged as Kat was. "I tell you what," she began the compromise; "if you tell me what you saw the other day, I'll tell you what I saw this morning."

Kat crossed her arms, scowling at Susie. "That's not fair."

"Sure it is," Susie affirmed. "We both have information the other wants. You share, and I'll share."

"You go first," Kat grinned.

"Nope, you go first because I had already asked you," Susie reminded her.

"A technicality," Kat protested.

Susie laughed. "Maybe so; but if you want to know, you have to tell me first."

Kat grinned playfully. "How will you know if I'm telling you the truth?"

Susie smiled serenely. "I'll know. Kat. I can see the Truth."

For the briefest of moments, Kat looked baffled. With a shrug, she smiled. "Okay, you win."

Giving a heavy sigh, she said, "I hope you believe me; you should by now. Okay, here goes. There were a couple of pixies ... I promise, I'm telling the truth ... there were a couple of pixies just dancing around, doing their little, happy dances, giggling and laughing, turning aerial somersaults and flying all over that side of the Dining Hall. I kept scowling at them because I wanted them to go away. Pixies can't shield themselves for very long. It takes a lot of their energy. It's different with angels and fairies; they can remain invisible forever if they choose. Anyway, can you imagine what would have happened if everyone suddenly saw them? They'd all go crazy and panic."

Kat shrugged, furrowing her brow as she added, "You know how people are."

Susie nodded, contemplating what Kat had just told her. "Have the pixies always done that?"

"No," Kat replied, mulling it through. "It's only been recent that they've started coming here. They're here pretty much every day now. Lots of them are coming. I've tried to talk to them, but they won't talk to me. They just giggle like crazy, and leave for a while." She laughed. "They are really happy about something."

Kat's expression changed as she looked at Susie. "Hey; they started coming right after you and Simon arrived. It's you! You're the reason they're here, and why they're so happy. Why is that?"

Surprised that Kat's power of deduction and observation was far greater than she had anticipated, Susie shrugged and looked down at her hands. Kat was wading into areas that Susie wasn't certain she could share. She heard Tahlranel speak to her mind, telling her that she can confirm what Kat already has experience with, namely the fairies, pixies and angels.

Susie smiled. "I don't know why. Maybe it's a coincidence, maybe not. Next time you see one, tell me; and we'll both try to talk with it. Deal?"

Kat nodded, "Deal. Now your turn," she responded.

"Okay, you may find this hard to believe, but it's true," Susie begin, hesitantly. Lowering her voice to a whisper, she confided; "Miss Fiona is a fairy. Honest. I saw her wings, and she glowed. And she knows that I know."

Kat burst out laughing, fell back and began rolling from side to side. This is not the reaction that Susie had expected.

Finally Kat sat up, still chucking, and shaking her head. "You are such a goof," she giggled. "Is that all? I already knew that."

Astonished, Susie asked, "You did? Since when?"

"Since the first time I saw her," she laughed. "Man, you're a little slow on the uptake sometimes, Susie. What am I going to do with you?" she teased.

Susie laughed, teasing back, "I don't know. Maybe you need to start educating me."

Kat nodded. "Maybe I do. Hmm, where to start, where to start? I'll have to think about that, and get back to you," she said, jumping off the bed.

Strolling to the doorway, Kat paused when she reached it. "I do believe we need to meet after everyone has gone to bed. Can't afford to have anyone know what we know," she intoned with a perky grin, her eyes twinkling mischievously.

"I guess not, Susie agreed wholeheartedly; "just tell me where and when."

"I'll let you know," she giggled as she left.

Miss Fiona and Miss Ginger were absent from lunch, having gone into Foxboro Station for supplies. Kevin had been conscripted to drive, and Sam tagged along to keep him company while the ladies shopped. Susie was a little disappointed, but she knew that at some point she'd be able to talk to Miss Fiona. She had a lot of questions, and Miss Fiona surely had the answers.

Miss Pritchett had caught Susie as she entered the Dining Hall, inquiring if she was feeling better. Susie seemed confused, so Miss Pritchett recounted Susie's choking episode from that morning. Smiling as benignly as possible, Susie assured her nothing was wrong. However, Susie wasn't at all certain that Miss Pritchett believed her explanation, given that Susie had a hard time not looking at Miss Pritchett's scar now that she knew the truth. And considering everything else she has learned, Susie was certain Miss Pritchett could read her face well enough to know that Susie was hiding something. Susie sure hoped that the first thing Kenatae taught her was how to hide her thoughts and expressions; otherwise, she would always be in a predicament around here.

When lunch was finally over, Susie took the naptime opportunity of the Munchkins to heart. As they veered into the Rec Room for their naptime, she entered the Dorm and quickly dove under her covers.

———

Luckily, Susie awakened in time for Story Time. She bolted upright, glanced at the clock and was relieved to see she still had fifteen minutes. The nap had done her some good, but the tired feeling persisted. She promised herself that tonight she would get a good night's sleep. No expeditions, no hunting; just sleep.

Jose chose a cute story, one that depicted a young farm boy who had found a baby lamb, lost from his mother. Its illustrations were extraordinary in detail and in its bright colors. The story was a wonderfully written tale, heart-warming and with a very upbeat, happily-ever-after ending. The Munchkins adored it; and so did the others, truth be told.

———

Susie stole a few glances at Miss Fiona during dinner and was relieved that she didn't notice any of them. Kat, on the other hand, did. The first time, Kat just grinned; but after Susie's fifth covert attempt, Kat frowned, giving Susie an 'are you crazy' look. Susie ceased her efforts at being a spy and concentrated on the conversation, currently fixated on the Munchkin's 'Train Town Welcome Party'. The enthusiasm they displayed was hilarious; their voices would raise an octave or two, squeaking as they rushed to tell everything they knew about the plans. Not to be outdone by each other, their voices became louder and louder, histrionically increasing as they each sought to be heard, and heard first.

Noticing Miss Pritchett was reaching for the bell, Susie told them to hush before she rang it. Their eyes widened in dismay, terrified at what the ringing of the bell might mean. In midsentence they ceased chattering, slinking down in their chairs, hoping to hide from any impending punishment.

None was forthcoming, although Miss Pritchett did state that she was very happy the children chose to cease using their outside voices, and promptly thanked them. They began giggling and shushing each other, keeping as low a profile as they could. Mr. Sean spoke, instructing them to sit properly in their chairs, followed by a reminder to give a proper response to Miss Pritchett's thank you.

Three little heads popped up like gophers in a field, sing-songing in unison, "You're welcome, Miss Pritchett."

Everyone burst out laughing, the Munchkins loudest of all.

———

During the bedtime tuck-in rituals, first with the boys and then with Megan, Susie was privy to another round of their party planning ideas. Because they were so excited about the 'Train Town Welcome Party', they were squirming and wiggling, giggling and laughing even more so than usual. Susie had patiently listened to every detail, time and again. She had lauded them repeatedly for their party planning skills, and that it would absolutely be the best party ever, bar none.

All had confessed it really wasn't them; it was Miss Taryn and Mrs. Coppersmith. The boys graciously deigned to admit that Megan was also a little helpful. Megan, of course, included the boys in her round of accolades without hesitating, telling Susie that they really had some neat ideas, even if they were boys. After their "confessions", they would launch into another round of party details.

When Susie asked what day the party would be, they proudly told her it would be on Saturday afternoon so that Reverend Tillman could come. She had praised them for being so kind as to include the Reverend. Again they giggled and snickered, telling her it was Mrs. Coppersmith's idea, but that they thought it was a good one.

Miss Ginger had to cut short Susie's time with the boys, as Miss Cora subsequently did with her time with Megan.

Quietly slipping into her room, Susie got ready for bed and slid under the covers without turning on the light. Within seconds, she had fallen fast asleep.

———

"New Year's Eve! Tomorrow is my birthday," Susie whispered excitedly as she jumped out of bed. No one had mentioned if there were any New Year's Eve celebrations at Glen Hollow, so she decided she would ask. If not, she would ask if she and the other children could have a movie night as a way to celebrate.

Quickly she made her wake-up rounds and spent a little extra time with Megan, much to Megan's absolute delight if the high-pitched laughter and squeals were any indication of her sublime happiness. They did a fast "good-morning" group hug before scurrying away to get ready.

On their trek to breakfast, Susie asked Miss Cora if Glen Hollow celebrated New Year's Eve.

Miss Cora responded with a jubilant, "Oh yes, most definitely. Right after dinner, all of you children get your baths and into your jammies, slippers and robes so that it's easier to put you to bed if you're asleep come midnight. Then we all gather in the Parlor. We share stories, sing songs and play all kinds of games. And Mrs. Coppersmith makes some really good treats. At midnight, everyone sings 'Auld Lang Syne'. We toast the New Year, and drink a glass of sparkling apple cider. For those that don't like it, there's hot chocolate."

"Sounds like fun," Susie commented appreciatively.

"It is. Oh, I almost forgot," she added as an afterthought. "We have a tradition that we also do. Paper and pencil are given to everyone. We write on the piece of paper our troubles, our worries, and then fold that paper. Everyone puts their paper into the wire roasting basket. Just seconds before midnight, the basket is placed into the fire, and all our troubles and worries disappear in a puff of smoke. We're ready to start the New Year with minds clear, and hope for better things to come. Isn't that a great tradition?"

"Does it work?" Susie asked, grinning.

"Of course, if you want it to," Miss Cora softly spoke. "It's symbolic. Obviously neither the fire nor the smoke actually remove troubles or worries, but you can change your attitude, your outlook. Sometimes that is enough to improve your life. That is what the tradition means; clearing out the old, bad, negative thoughts and, with the New Year, allowing hope and good thoughts to enter. Understand?"

Susie nodded. "Yes, I do. It's a good idea. I like it."

Miss Cora laughed merrily. "I'm so glad you approve, Susie," she commented, linking arms with Susie; and together they entered the Dining Hall, laughing and teasing each other.

———

After morning kitchen duty, Susie made her way up to her sanctuary. The Munchkins were in another planning meeting with Mrs. Coppersmith and Miss Taryn. For some reason, it was now "top-secret", and no one was allowed to have any of the details. Dani and Kat had decided to assist Miss Hilda with the laundry (very strange); and Juls was practicing, no surprise there. Jose and Aaron were playing a game of chess; the winner would play against Jared, who was currently in a practice session with Kevin.

Susie entered and quickly built a fire in the fireplace. It was so cold; the weather forecast was for the temperature to drop to below zero by late afternoon. At this rate, the snow would never melt. On the plus side, she thought, it can't snow when it's this cold. She laughed at herself. "That's exactly what Nana used to do," she mused aloud. "She always found the positive in every situation."

Pulling Nana's afghan from the chair, she cocooned herself in it and sat on the hearth, waiting for the fire to catch and warm the room. She reflected about the reminder Miss Pritchett had given during lunch regarding the New Year's Eve celebration scheduled for after bath time. She had explained, as Miss Cora had done with her, the Evermore family tradition. The impending festivities created a stir of excitement among everyone, but especially among the children. After all, it was the only night they were allowed to stay up late. And they were going to participate in a tradition that Miss Pritchett had said her family had done for hundreds of years, and that they were now part of that family.

It is a good thing, Susie decided. It will help them all bond as a family, one of the many ways they did this for each other and for the children. She smiled and leaned against the wall of the stone fireplace. Within just a few minutes, she was roasting and quickly moved away from the fire. She draped Nana's afghan across the back of the chair, sighing as she looked around the room.

She felt content. 'Strange,' she contemplated; 'I have no apprehension about tomorrow.'

Chuckling at the oddity of her being concerned about the lack of concern, she slowly strolled across the room to the windows. Curling up in the center window seat, she watched the old oak tree. Its outer branches, where they are thinnest and smallest, barely swayed in the light breeze that was blowing.

'Truly a marvelous tree,' she thought.

"You've weathered just about everything nature can do, and still you stand. You have a few scars and rough patches, but that gives you character," she whispered, smiling at the old behemoth. "I'm so glad you've made it. Please don't ever stop."

She rose and began walking toward the fire. She stopped and came back to the window. Pressing her nose up against it, she said with a giggle, "When Simon tries to climb you this spring, and he will, please don't let him fall."

It seemed as if the gentle giant heard her for one lone branch, facing her window, began to sway, moving up and down as if agreeing with her request. She laughed and laughed, telling it "thank you" as she returned to Nana's chair.

She spent the rest of the afternoon passing the time reminiscing days gone by.

———

It was Dani's turn to choose a story, and she chose a story that her mother had read to her many times when she was younger. And to be certain that it was read today, she brought her own copy just in case the Library didn't have one. The story was "The Ugly Duckling."

Susie grinned. She had always loved it, too.

———

Dinner time came and went. Most of the children were too excited to eat, Susie included. Eagerly they all rushed to take their baths and get ready for bed prior to trouping downstairs to the Parlor for the festivities.

In the Parlor they found tables laden with all manner of snacks and drinks. There were bowls and platters of popcorn, potato chips, corn chips, pizza bites, sausage biscuits, ham biscuits, plain biscuits, several jams and preserves, a variety of nuts, raisins, dried fruit slices, and even peanut butter and jelly sandwiches. For sweet treats, Mrs. Coppersmith had provided several types of cupcakes. And to quench one's thirst, there was water, milk, coffee, hot spiced cider and hot chocolate. Several bottles of sparkling cider were being iced in a large metal tub. To Susie, it was truly a wonder that Mrs. Coppersmith and her small staff could do so much. And the greatest wonder was that they never seemed to tire of it. They actually seemed to enjoy doing it.

She didn't have much time to ponder the why of it; Simon had launched himself at her, squeezing the life out of her. He was quickly joined by Timmy, and followed within seconds by Megan. Like a pack of the proverbial hyenas, their giggling and laughing drowned out her pleas to be careful, that she was about to fall. Susie lost her balance; and they toppled over, landing on the carpet with a thud, Susie on the bottom.

Everyone rushed over, frightened that they were injured. They weren't. The Munchkins roared with laughter, squealing, "Do it again! Do it again!" Susie couldn't help but laugh, too, since everyone was all right. Most everyone did chuckle; it was a funny thing to see – after they knew no one was hurt.

Mr. Sean had been first on the scene, and bested Mr. Henry by just seconds. After verifying that everyone was okay, both men did point out to Megan, Timmy and Simon that they could have hurt Susie or even themselves. In a firm tone Mr. Sean strongly suggested that they be more careful in the future.

Three angelic faces solemnly swore they would - but how long they will retain that tidbit of instruction is anyone's guess. Within seconds they were wrestling. Their excited laughing and giggling infused the room with a carefree spirit; and most everyone laughed along with them, watching their exuberant behavior.

As soon as everyone had arrived, Miss Pritchett asked for their attention. It took several attempts to be heard over the talking and laughter. Once quiet was established, the first order of business was for everyone to find a seat somewhere. Quickly Miss Ginger, Miss Cora, Miss Elsa, Miss Fiona and Miss Thelma gave paper and pencil to each person. Miss Pritchett encouraged everyone to write down a care or concern, and afterward fold the paper.

Simon wanted to know what exactly is a care or a concern because he wasn't sure if he had any. Everyone laughed, including Miss Pritchett.

"Well, Simon," Miss Pritchett answered; "I hope you don't. I'm sure all the adults here feel as I do, and would very much love it if we take such good care of all of you that you don't have any worries, or cares or concerns. However, it can be anything that troubles you, such as losing your favorite toy, or thunderstorms, or falling out of trees, or being afraid of the dark ..."

"Or spiders," Simon added, gleefully looking at Susie.

"Or losing your hair," Mr. Henry added jovially.

"Or losing your teeth," Grammy chimed in, laughing loudly.

"Or losing your mind," Mrs. Coppersmith bantered, laughing cheerfully.

Everyone was laughing by this time, nudging each other and teasing as to who had what cares or concerns of the ones just mentioned.

"How true," Miss Pritchett agreed heartily to the suggestions made. "Do you think you get the idea now, Simon?"

He vigorously nodded his head.

Susie assisted Simon with his "care" paper, Aaron assisted Timmy while Juls assisted Megan. The Munchkins folded their papers, holding on to them until the cast iron, wire roasting basket was held out to them. With great aplomb, Simon stood and forcefully dropped his into the basket.

"Good-by and good riddance," he ceremoniously told it. Everyone laughed, amused at the expression of his sentiment, one that they shared but had not voiced.

Mr. Sean placed the roasting basket by the fireplace, waiting for the midnight ritual.

Games were first on the celebration list, and they began with 'Grapevine'. It was comical! It was so amazing to see how one sentence could become so distorted by the time it reached the end of the line.

Simon, Megan and Timmy especially enjoyed playing 'Grapevine'. Susie couldn't help but wonder if what Simon had repeated in her ear was actually what Timmy had whispered to him. She had a sneaking suspicion that they had changed the message intentionally for dramatic effect. But then, based on the number of pranksters in the room, any one of them could have done the same.

After several rounds of 'Grapevine', they played 'Duck, Duck, Goose' which was followed by a few rounds of 'A Tisket, A Tasket; A Green and Yellow Basket'. Everyone enjoyed these, including the adults.

Next came the quieter games, such as 'Go Fish', 'Uno' and 'Old Maid', although none were what you could actually call quiet in reality. There was a great deal of laughter, of teasing and of bragging.

Last came the time to share a story; each person in turn would share a favorite memory. As on Christmas Day, the adults sat on the couches while the children sat on the carpet. Well, most of the children did. It was eleven o'clock, and several of the children had already fallen asleep. Megan, Timmy and Simon, being the first to do so, were already deep in Dreamland.

Megan had curled up on Miss Pritchett initially, but had wiggled down to where her head was in Miss Pritchett's lap, her torso across Mrs. Coppersmith and her feet were in Miss Hilda's lap. Timmy had begun by cuddling up in Grammy's lap. Slowly he had descended until his head was in her lap, his torso lay across Miss Bettye and his feet were in Mr. Sean's lap. Simon, of course, had inched his way into Susie's lap, beginning his sojourn by first leaning against her. Then he curled up beside her, resting his head against her. Slowly he progressed until his head was in her lap. Finally he wormed his way into her lap, curling up into a ball and resting his head against her chest.

After fifteen minutes, Susie's back was beginning to ache so she tried to shift him back to the floor. That didn't work, even in his sleep he clung to her. She gave up, deciding to let him be. Periodically she would try to shift her position enough to relieve her back, but the throbbing continued.

After several minutes of watching her struggle, Mr. Henry knelt down beside her and whispered, "Let me take him. It'll be all right."

Looking into his eyes, Susie could see the love and compassion he had for them. He smiled reassuringly. Susie nodded.

Mr. Henry easily scooped Simon up into his arms and carried him to the couch. Miss Thelma grinned, her face glowing with joy as she reached up for Simon. Mr. Henry eased down beside her, placing Simon's head in her lap, stretching him across his own lap and placing Simon's feet into Jason's lap. Everyone chuckled softly, amazed that Simon never stirred, sleeping through the entire move.

Miss Cora quietly rose and removed a stack of lap quilts from a cedar chest. Gently she laid one over each of the little ones, ensuring their extended stay in Dreamland. Having successfully done so, she handed one of the lap quilts to each of the older children before covering Dani and Jose, who had fallen asleep on the carpet. Miss Fiona followed behind her, handing out pillows. Gently she slid one under Dani and then Jose, both sound asleep. When she gave one to Susie, she winked. Susie smiled.

Susie enjoyed the sharing of memories. It was a great way to learn about everyone, and it was interesting. One by one, the older children began yawing, their heads drooping just a little. One by one, they began falling asleep until every last one of them had entered into Dreamland.

The next thing Susie knew, she was being awakened along with the other children. The adults chuckled as their confused faces finally awakened enough to realize what was happening.

"It's almost midnight," the adults kept chanting. "Come on, wake up. We're going to burn the papers in just a minute."

They yawned and stretched, rubbing their faces and their eyes, and yawned some more. Miss Elsa, Miss Taryn and Miss Fiona carried the glasses of sparkling cider on trays, distributing them to those who wanted a glass. They allowed the children to take a sip to see if they did; there were no takers. Right behind them, Mrs. Coppersmith brought mugs of her special hot cocoa with mini-marshmallows. Eagerly the children accepted the mugs of hot cocoa as fast as she could distribute them.

They were ready, just waiting for the clock to strike midnight. Ten seconds to go, and they began the countdown as Mr. Sean set the roasting basket onto the fire. The care and concern papers burst into flame and were quickly consumed, gone by the time they had counted to zero. Everyone clapped and cheered the vanquishing of the cares and concerns. Susie had to admit that it did feel good, even if it was only symbolic. She smiled happily at Miss Cora; Miss Cora winked and returned her smile.

The antique grandfather clock began striking the midnight hour. They all yelled "Happy New Year!"

Miss Cora softly began to sing 'Auld Lang Syne' and everyone joined in, most singing the melody and a few singing harmony. It was wonderful; a feeling of elation spread through Susie and the others as the past was now the past, and all things were new and possible with the dawn of a new year.

Susie watched the faces of each person, adults and children. Her spirit soared when she realized that they all were bonding as a family, even Miss Taryn and Mr. Dale. There was a flicker within their souls that she could see. She smiled – 'there is hope,' Susie concluded.

When the song was done, they lifted their glasses and mugs to each other and toasted, saying, "Happy New Year. May all your hopes and dreams come true, and may God carry you in the palm of His Hand until you reach Heaven's shore."

Everyone finished their chosen beverages amid streams of laughter, good-natured bantering and hugs 'good-night'. The children were among the first to head upstairs, escorted by Grammy, Miss Cora, JT, Miss Ginger and Allan Roy.

It didn't take any time at all for the children to dive into bed, falling fast asleep. It had been a long day; but it had also been a good day, a very good day.

Even better, it was now a new day and a new year, filled with hope and with the promise of better things yet to come.

Chapter 42

THE VISITATION

It was bitterly cold, this the first day of January; and rightly so since it was half past four in the morning. Frost had formed lacy patterns of ice on the window thick enough in some places to obscure vision. The subzero Artic front that had been forecast had stalled over the mountains, granting them a reprieve albeit a temporary one. In its place, a massive cloud system covered the area, bringing with it large amounts of frozen moisture.

Snow had fallen heavily during the night, adding greatly to the deep piles of packed snow from the previous days. At some point the falling precipitation had turned from snow into sleet and followed by ice, encasing the mounds of snow and creating the illusion of a world made of sparkling diamond dust. Ice cycles cascaded down from the roof, resembling large mountains turned upside down. The trees were weighted down, first with a heavy layer of snow followed by a thick sheet of ice.

From the window, high up in the attic room, Susie quietly watched as a family of deer exited the woods, remaining close to the forest edge. They entered from the north, far from the oak tree that stood near the front of the meadow. "Simon's tree," she mused, for he had 'claimed' it as his own ever since they arrived at Glen Hollow. She sat very still in her window perch, fearing that even the slightest movement might be seen by them and would cause them to flee back to the safety of the forest.

She watched as the male deer cautiously made his way a hundred yards or so into the meadow, now deeply covered in snow and ice. Every so often he would pause and sniff the air. He was so big, nearly twice the size of those at the petting zoo in Stonebridge where Nana had taken them last summer. Susie wondered how his head stayed upright with the immense size and weight of his antlers. When satisfied all was safe, papa deer turned his head and called to the doe trailing him. She ventured forward, trusting his instinct, yet vigilant in her own right.

Whenever she came to her sanctuary in the earlier morning hours, Susie would see them. Sometimes she was certain they had seen her, for they looked directly at her. Yet they didn't run. And so it was this morning; the papa deer looked at her, turned toward the momma deer, and then they both looked up at her. Two fawns cautiously edged their way from the darkness at the forest edge and stood next to their parents.

Susie held her breath for what seemed an eternity as her eyes were held in a spiritual bond with the deer family. In that instant, Susie felt as if they had accepted her just as she accepted them. The papa deer raised his head skyward and made a soft sound; the deer family turned away and casually went about their daily business, foraging for food. The buck and the doe broke through the ice and snow with their hooves, revealing the winter grass hidden underneath. The fawns quickly came, devouring whatever their parents provided.

Slowly releasing her breath, Susie smiled as it created a fog that covered the window glass. She closed her eyes and leaned her head against the window pane. Its icy coldness stung her face as she pressed against it. Little by little it numbed her skin until she no longer felt its needle-like sensation. This is *her* special place, she mused; it is the one place she could be alone. Here she could think and sort through things; or just sit here, quiet, without thought, and enjoy the scenery.

Opening her eyes, Susie gazed upon the deer family and smiled – she liked to think that they knew she was here and accepted her into their family.

She sighed. "That's silly," she chided herself; "they'd probably run from me if I were down there."

In an instant the realization came; smiling, she chuckled softly. 'No, they wouldn't run,' she mused to herself. 'Not now, anyway. Now that I remember who I am, and what I can do. I know I can talk with them, and they won't be afraid of me.'

She focused her thoughts on the male deer; she could see and feel his apprehension. It was the same with his mate; she too was pensive. The fawns, not so much. They were hungry; they were all so hungry. Susie's heart cried for them. Her unguarded emotions put into motion that which her heart desired, to feed them. Spontaneously the earth gently warmed quite a large area of the pasture, dissolving away the ice and snow. The fresh grass was fully exposed, giving plenty of food to the deer. Within minutes they were joined by other deer, and even some rabbits came to the feast.

Shocked at what happened, Susie just stared; then she laughed. "Awesome," she whispered.

The joy was short lived; she realized what she had done wasn't appropriate. It would lead to an awful lot of questions and an investigation, which would be fruitless, but would still draw attention to that which must remain hidden.

She sighed and muttered; "I'm sure I'll be told not to do that again, but it was an accident."

Her hand slowly reached up, gently cradling the pendant that Nana had presented to her on her tenth birthday. She felt a little sad as she remembered that day. She missed Nana; she missed her parents, too. Susie raised the silver filigree pendant up to her lips and kissed it lightly. Still cradling the pendant in her hand, her fingers glided to the unicorn brooch that she had pinned just over her heart, the way Nana had done two years ago. Gently she touched the brooch, feeling the raised outline of each figure.

"I'm wearing them, Nana; just like you told me," she whispered, saying a little prayer that somehow Nana would know.

The ebony night sky suddenly was lit with a bright infusion of light, pouring through Susie's window and momentarily blinding her. Startled, she bolted upright. While shielding her eyes with her hands as much as possible, she looked out the window. For a brief, few seconds the meadow was brighter than the mid-day sun. The light disappeared as quickly as it had arrived, leaving the meadow with only the diffused light of the moon filtering through the thick, winter clouds.

Susie blinked several times, attempting to regain her vision. Her eyes slowly adjusted, and she could once again clearly see the meadow. The deer and rabbits were gone, frightened away by the strange light.

As her eyes scanned the meadow, her gaze fell upon the old oak tree. It was precisely at that moment she saw it. There, standing under the massive oak tree, was a tall, white horse. Her first thought was that Lacy had somehow managed to get out of the barn. Quickly she realized it couldn't be Lacy for this horse was much taller and far more muscular. And, she realized, although Lacy would have a whitish appearance, this magnificent looking horse was the whitest white, giving it a radiant effect in the soft, diffused light of the moon.

No wind was blowing, yet the silky strands of its incredibly long mane and tail appeared to gently sway, as if floating on air currents unseen.

"Beautiful," Susie whispered. "What a beautiful horse."

"No, wait!" she exclaimed, pressing up against the window for a better view. "It's not a horse – it's … it's a ….a unicorn!" she uttered in astonishment.

Rearing high up on his hind legs, the unicorn began to paw at the air with his front legs. His strokes were strong and fluid, resembling that of a marathon swimmer with all the grace and eloquence of a dancer. He held the pose for several minutes before returning to his normal stance.

She watched as it began to paw at the ground, a sense of urgency conveyed in that action as if calling her to come. Then it stopped. The majestic creature looked directly at her, his eyes locked onto hers. Ever so slowly it began to toss its head, its luxurious mane flowing like silken strands with each and every movement.

Gaping at the creature, Susie sat transfixed, barely able to breathe, too stunned to even think. She didn't move; she didn't blink. Part of her was afraid it was an optical illusion which would disappear if she made any sort of movement. Part of her wanted it very much to be real; and that part was at war with itself, fearful of what it would mean competing against the excitement of all that it could mean.

Her heart raced, her mind whirled with questions. Susie held her breath. 'Is it real? Am I dreaming? Is it an illusion?' her mind asked.

As if in response, the unicorn began to softly whinny to her. Suddenly she understood the sounds he made. She could actually hear in her mind him calling her by name, telling her to come.

"This is it!" she shouted ecstatically. "This is the Visitation! Oh … my … gosh! The book! The Unicorn book! Nana's song! The Unicorn statue! It's all true!"

Keeping eye contact with him, Susie rose to her feet. Once again the creature gave a toss of his head. Somehow Susie knew it to mean she had to decide and decide now. Decision made, Susie told him to wait for her; she'd be right there.

She ran down the attic room stairs, closing the door but didn't take the time to lock it. Racing down the corridor, she took the foyer stairs in threes, jumping from the seventh stair down to the ground. Her mind recalled the many times she had chided Simon for running and for skipping stairs. She couldn't help but laugh at the irony. Susie rushed to the front door and unlocked it. No small feat; the cast–iron bolt was as big and as heavy as the hinges appeared to be. But she finally managed to get it to slide, enabling her to open the door. It groaned and creaked in rebellion as she pulled it open. Her heart seemingly stopped beating as panic arose in her, fearful that the entire household would be awakened by the ghastly sounds it made.

Slipping outside, Susie half expected to see an empty meadow though she was hopeful the unicorn would be there waiting for her. To her delight, he was. Quickly she closed the door, grimacing at the groaning noises and the loud click it made as it fastened.

Without reservation, Susie ran as fast as she could to the meadow, ignoring the freezing cold air of the winter night and the deep ice and snow through which she trudged. Her pajamas, robe and slippers provided little if any warmth, but that didn't matter to her. Spurring her on was the need to know. She had to see it, to touch it, to know with absolute certainty it is real.

There he is, just ahead – not more than a hundred yards away, yet it seems as if it is a million miles. She slowed her pace. Her breaths had become shallow and fast, partly from the frigid cold and partly from the adrenaline rushing through her veins. Her heart was pounding hard, jolting with each contraction. Every pulse beat thundered in her ears like the crashing of ocean waves against a rocky shore.

Now she was within thirty feet. He is still there. He is still watching her, focused on her as intently as she is on him. Slowly she advanced toward the creature, holding her breath and praying that it wasn't an illusion, a mere figment of her imagination. She exhaled and paused briefly, allowing her breathing to return to some semblance of normalcy before she approached the majestic being.

Gazing into its deep blue eyes, Susie felt a calmness, a serenity flow through her like a warm, soothing bath. Susie noticed that he had maintained eye contact with her from the moment she stepped outside; never moving, just watching and waiting for her.

She had arrived now, standing within a yard or two of this wondrous creature. She was enamored by his beauty and grace, the magnitude and strength of this noble creature. All the while his focus had been on her; he never wavered. His eyes remained securely joined with hers by some type of force, like an invisible tether holding them, connecting them, one to the other.

Moving and feeling as if she had entered a world of dreams where time and space have no meaning, Susie gradually reached for him, extending her hand toward him in a gesture of friendship. Gently nodding his head three times in rapid succession, the Unicorn stepped forward, closing the distance between them to mere inches.

Slowly he lowered his head until their eyes met, placing his forehead against hers. Overwhelming images of love and of compassion, of peace and of tranquility, of mercy and of grace, of faith and of hope, of honor and of strength, of loyalty and of trust, of friendship and of companionship, of knowledge and of wisdom, of truth and of understanding, of righteousness and of holiness flowed through her being, filling her soul and her spirit, imbuing her with a sense of power far greater than she could ever have imagined.

In an instant, it was gone – he had severed the connection. Susie began to cry, grieving the loss of such a wondrous conduit to the Divine. Instinctively her hand began to stroke his neck, his mane, as her thoughts slowly turned away from mourning and into thanksgiving. Smiling at the Unicorn, she realized that if she never felt that conduit again, she was truly grateful that she had been given the opportunity to experience it at least once.

Then the Unicorn spoke, his words clearly and firmly placed into her mind. "I am a servant of the Almighty One. I am Levtahorel, the Purveyor of Truth. I have been sent to you. You are of the Guardians. Your lineage is that of the warrior path. I am here to show you things that you do not know, that you may clearly see and understand the path that is before you. In three days you must choose which path you will follow. Should you not choose the warrior path, it will not be opened to you again. Do you understand?"

Susie nodded, answering softly, "Yes."

"Are you willing to see?" he asked.

Again she responded, "Yes."

"Are you ready?" he inquired.

"Yes," Susie answered with a little stronger conviction in her tone.

"Come up here," he said.

Instantly Susie was transported from the ground and was sitting on the back of the Unicorn. Her laughter was light-hearted and carefree, with as much abandon as that of a toddler discovering for the first time the feel of soft, plush grass.

"That is a small thing in comparison to what the Almighty One can do," the Unicorn told her.

In what seemed but only a second, the meadow disappeared in a flash of brilliant light, and they were high above the earth. What lay before them now was a place overgrown with vines, weeds and brambles. Barely visible beneath the overgrowth was a small, circular structure, classical in style. What little she could see were of twelve columns similar to the columns of the pergola. Large mantle pieces resting on top of the columns connected them together, creating an open forum in the interior of the circular structure. Its layout was similar to that of a small amphitheater.

The Unicorn told her, "It has been over fifty years since the sacred place was tended. You will restore this place in time for the spring celebration."

Puzzled as to how she would ever find this place much less restore it, Susie cast a dubious glance at the Unicorn. "I'll do my best," she responded.

Without any apparent movement, their location changed again; they were now hovering far above a mountain. Below them was a clearing, surrounded by forest on three sides and a wall of granite on the other. A small stream trickled out from between a crevice, collecting into a rock basin which had been carved by the water itself over the course of time. Spilling over the basin, it became a small brook, weaving its way through the meadow before descending down the mountain and into the lush valley at the base of the mountain. Halfway between the crevice and the center of the clearing was a massive boulder, flat-topped and rising a few feet out of the ground. It was as if nature had made a table. Someone had placed a circle of white stones in the center of the clearing. It appeared to be a firepit.

'Where are we?' Susie thought.

"Spirit Mountain," he answered; "a sacred place. You will soon learn of it from Kenatae. He knows much of the old ways and has much to teach you. The Stone of Protection must be returned."

Her mind questioned, wondering how he knew what she was thinking. Instantly she realized how foolish that thought was.

The Unicorn laughed, delighted that understanding was beginning to open in her mind. Like that of a blossom opening when light touches it, so too was her mind.

"I know your thoughts, little one," he told her. "You cannot hide them from me. Should you choose the warrior path, you will learn to harness the power of Life and of Light, and will be taught how to use your abilities to do this. When you learn this, you will be able to read my thoughts without my having to place them in your mind."

"Who will teach me to do this?" she asked him, using only her thoughts. It seemed silly to speak when he didn't need her vocalization to hear her.

He nodded his head, approving of her change in approach. "There will be many that teach you over the course of your training, each with their own level of understanding. The one who will oversee your training is Ashara. It is she who will come to you for your decision on the third day."

"When will my training start?" she asked.

"Soon," he answered.

They left Spirit Mountain, instantly transported in a stream of light. Looking down, she saw The Falls of the Anicaw River. Remembering the Icori legend of the Spirit-Witch, she wondered if that is why he brought her here.

"Yes," he affirmed. "Now look deeper. Use your abilities and look beyond what your physical eyes can see."

Susie focused her attention on the Anicaw, looking past what her eyes alone could see. Surprised and delighted, she saw the individual water drops that form the River; deeper still, she could see the atoms of each drop of water. Looking even deeper, she now beheld that which corporeal eyes cannot see, the water sprites.

Far beneath the river bed, in a deep, watery chasm, she saw them. They were shimmering, translucent creatures, their movement smooth and fluid – just like flowing water. Softly they glowed with a bright, iridescent light that sparkled as if millions of tiny fireflies were living in a web of light. The light each one radiated merged together into a gauzy curtain, flowing into a ring of light around them and rose upward into a dome, encasing them in the translucent blue light.

In the center of this ring was a darkness, darker than the darkest, moonless, starless night. A horrible, vile creature would rail against their light, attempting to push the light away, testing the boundaries and the strength of their light. Each time it would scream and howl, slinking back into the darkness as if mortally wounded. Every time the water sprites remained steadfast at their post, never wavering.

The creature tried again. Only this time, it looked up at her, locking eyes with Susie and sneered. Its flaming eyes and horrendous fangs were clearly visible and terrifying to behold.

Startled, Susie gasped, turned away and buried her face into the mane of the Unicorn.

"Do not be afraid," he told her. "She is bound. She cannot harm you."

"Is this the spirit-witch of the Icori legend?" she asked as a shiver ran through her.

"Yes," he confirmed. "Evil seeks to release her. Many dark ones are coming, and those that walk the dark path are also coming. They will try to release her. You must be ready when that day arrives. You must be vigilant in order to stop her release."

"When will this happen?" she asked nervously.

"Time is irrelevant. You will be ready if you diligently train," he assured her.

Without any apparent movement, they had now returned to the meadow at Glen Hollow, and were once again under the old oak tree. No sooner had he alighted than she found herself instantly transported to the ground.

"When will I see you again?" she asked as she gently stroked his mane.

"Probably you will not. The Almighty One determines where I am sent," he responded.

"Please don't go," Susie implored him. "I have so many questions."

He affectionately nudged her, then placed his forehead against hers. Immediately she felt a calming wave of love, of compassion and of peace as it flowed through her, soothing her and quieting her fears.

"I know," he spoke gently. "Hear me, little one. Listen closely to my words and understand. Should you decide to follow the warrior path, all your questions will be answered. Should you decide not to follow this path, then all your memories, all your knowledge, all your understanding will be removed. Your abilities will be masked for your protection as well as for the protection of others. Do you understand?"

Susie nodded. "Yes, I do." The thought of never seeing him again saddened her greatly. Throwing her arms around him, she wept.

"Do not cry, little one," he spoke softly; "All is well, come what may."

He gave her a nod of reassurance and nuzzled her cheek. She smiled at him through her tears and gently kissed his nose.

And then he was gone. The starburst took him away; she was alone under the mighty oak tree, standing in the meadow at Glen Hollow. Darkness prevailed save only for the faint light of the moon dimly penetrating through the heavy blanket of winter clouds.

As she returned to the manor, suddenly Susie was aware that she hadn't been cold while she was with the Unicorn. Now that he was gone, the icy blast of air chilled her to the bone. Traversing as quickly as she could through the ice and snow, she shivered all the way to the manor.

The warmth of the manor dispelled any lingering chill, dissipating the shivers, quelling the shaking and quieting the chattering of her teeth. She ran up the stairs, to her Dorm and to her bed. Sliding under the inviting warmth of her bedding, she glanced at her clock. It was still 5:05.

'I'm back at the same time I left. How is that possible?' she asked herself.

She laughed at the silliness of such a question. Time and space had no relevance in the real world. As she snuggled down, she said a brief prayer of thanks to God for all His many blessings. Yawning, she dropped into a deep sleep.

Chapter 43

ALL IS WELL, COME WHAT MAY

Opening her eyes, Susie felt well rested, replenished even. This had not been the norm for her the past few weeks, and it was strange considering she hadn't had much sleep during the night. After the New Year's celebration, she'd barely had four hours of sleep before rising. And she'd had less than an hour after returning from the Visitation. She breathed in deeply, slowly, and held it for a moment prior to exhaling. Raising her arms overhead, she stretched, arching her back and pushing her head deeper into her pillow. In a deliberate, slow motion, she moved her arms alternating them up and down and stretching further with each upward movement. On the last cycle upward, she held her right arm in place as the left rose to meet it, maintaining that stretch for a few seconds more before relaxing.

The clock revealed only twenty minutes before time to wake the girls. Closing her eyes, Susie snuggled back down, enjoying her warm, comfortable bed. It felt good just to lay still, she tried to keep her mind clear, her thoughts at bay. Unfortunately, her mind would not cooperate; it would not be silent or still. Whirling through her mind were thoughts of all that has happened since she arrived at Glen Hollow, nearly four weeks ago.

Images and memories resurfaced of her escapades and discoveries: The "Histories" volumes, the series of books by Helga Gretchen Von Richter - how she found them and of her first foray into the Inner Realm (although she didn't realize it at the time); the voices she's heard, the music, the wind chimes, the scent of lilac, the woman in white, the awesome portraits of Angel and Gabriel, the beautiful and gentle Lacy, the Chapel, and the amazing Dolphin fountain and the Unicorn statue. She remembered how she found the passageways, how they led her to the Hidden Room and ultimately to the Inner Sanctum. She thought about all the secrets she has learned so far about the Evermore family and about Miss Pritchett.

Nini's words slowly floated to the surface of her memories, reminding Susie of what Nini had said, all that she had said. The recollection caused

Susie to be torn between being exhilarated and being anxious. At times it felt as if the weight of the whole world was bearing down on her – until Susie remembered that Nini had also told her that she'd be holding Susie up in prayer. That knowledge comforted her for she knew Nini was a prayer warrior. Nini had said that Susie was here to fight a great evil that was coming. The very thought struck an intense, petrifying terror deep in her soul. How could she be expected to fight a great evil? And if she didn't, surely someone else would, she rationalized.

She thought about Kenatae, about what he had said; and she smiled. Although she had cause to be concerned and apprehensive (after all, Nana always said that fools rush in where angels fear to tread), she couldn't help but be happy in that Nayatowah are real; and she was especially thrilled that Nayatowah allowed the three of them to pet it, something that had never before happened. She grinned as she thought, 'That must be a good sign.'

Her mind recalled the incident of their unexpected and uninvited arrival into the Inner Realm, and of their subsequent rescue by Ashara. She laughed softly as she remembered the reaction the tigers had to the names of her mother and her grandmother, but most especially of their reaction to Nana's name. She sighed deeply, remembering what Ashara had said to her when they were alone after Ashara had sent the others back to bed. 'Another will be chosen', Susie recalled Ashara telling her if Susie declined the warrior path.

"Who?" Susie whispered; "and where is this person now?"

Her mind shifted to Nana's message, and she cried softly. So much Nana couldn't tell her, couldn't share with her because she was so unwilling to hear. It grieved her so deeply to realize how much sorrow and worry she must have caused Nana. "I'm sorry, Nana," her contrite words were spoken in a hushed tone.

As her mind focused on the positive message from Nana, her tears ceased flowing, first ebbing to an occasional trickle until finally subsiding altogether. Nana's message was one of love, of trust, of faithfulness and of hope. Nana loved her and was proud of her, period. Whatever her decision. Nana hoped that Susie would follow in their footsteps, had every confidence that Susie would do so; but Nana would not coerce her to choose the warrior path.

Closing her eyes, Susie shook her head slowly. Her mind whirled around the idea of this so-called "choice". She was free to choose, that's what they all said. If she chose to follow the warrior path, so much of her life would change and that frightened her. If she didn't choose it, then her life would be ordinary as it had been prior to Glen Hollow; and she wouldn't remember any of this. As Nana said, she would grow up here and live a full and happy life. Tempting, so very tempting.

An idea slowly slithered into her mind – if she chooses the warrior path, her dream with Molly to have their own fashion house could not be. Susie burst into tears, pulling her pillow over her face and curling into a ball. "Nana said we have to make sacrifices to walk the warrior path, but this is too much," she cried, weeping bitterly into her pillow.

Little by little her tears dwindled as her mind shifted its focus again. She thought about the Unicorn, Levtahorel, what he had shown her and what he had said. How could she be expected to find that place? She had no idea where to look, who to ask or how it could be found. Even more insane - how could she be expected to restore it? She didn't know anything about such things.

"And then there's that evil, vile creature," Susie further contemplated; "she saw me. She's probably already told her demon friends about me. Won't they come after me if I decide to choose the warrior path? Mommy thought they'd leave me alone if I wasn't on the warrior path, but Nana thought Mommy was wrong. If I don't choose the warrior path, will that awful thing be released? Won't someone else be sent to stop it? If she's released, what happens to everyone here? Will they be hurt? I don't know what to think," she sighed, frustration rising.

Thoughts of Kenatae and Spirit Mountain blazed forefront in her mind, creating a sad smile on her lips. Levtahorel told her Kenatae would teach her. Obviously he wouldn't if she didn't choose the warrior path. All her memories would be gone, and Ashara would tell him no. Not that she would know anything about it; her memories would be gone. Her mind latched onto something else that Levtahorel had said – 'the Stone of Protection must be returned'. He didn't say she had to return it, just that it had to be returned. But why show her the Mountain and tell her if she wasn't the one to return it? Maybe she was just to see to it by sending someone else. She smiled and sighed; that idea was far more pleasing than the alternative.

Her mind flashed back, recalling in vivid detail when Levtahorel placed his forehead against hers, allowing her connection to the Divine through his spirit. Tears flowed as she realized that she would not remember that wondrous encounter either should she choose not to follow her lineage and walk the warrior path. And just like Nana and Ashara, he told her she must choose. In three days, she must choose.

'It's so unfair,' she cried silently, covering her face with her hands. 'How can I choose? There isn't a perfect choice. If I don't choose the warrior path, I lose forever everything I've learned, everything I've experienced and everything I know. And if I don't choose it, that might even cause harm to everyone here. If I do choose it, I have to give up all my dreams and plans, and so does Molly. And I'll have to face so much I don't know; and terrible, evil things will constantly try to kill me. How am I supposed to choose? ... How am I supposed to choose?'

Wiping away her tears, she sat up and looked around her. Susie smiled happily as she watched Juls practicing and the other girls sleeping so soundly, so peacefully. She focused on Simon and Timmy and began to softly laugh. Both had their bedtime buddies clutched tightly against their bodies, fast asleep with big smiles on their faces. Susie smiled affectionately as she watched Aaron and Jose sleeping peacefully while Jared performed his morning Tai Chi.

Closing her eyes, Susie listened. She could hear the singing of the birds and the rhythmic beating of their wings as they flew, seeking food. She could hear the chattering of the squirrels and chipmunks deep in the forest. She laughed, softly listening to the sounds of the bunnies as they scampered across the snow and ice covering the meadow. She listened to the sounds of the deer as they foraged for food and their calls, warning of potential danger or that all is clear.

A heavy sigh escaped as she wondered what she should do.

"Tahlranel, are you here?" she whispered.

No response.

"Tahlranel, please; I need to talk with you. Please, please come talk with me?" she pleaded as tears filled her eyes, spilling onto her face. "Please?" she implored.

Still no response.

"It's not fair," she cried out to him. "Please answer my questions. I need to know what will happen if I don't choose the warrior path. And I need to know what will happen if I do. Please, please come talk with me?" she begged. "Don't leave me alone. Please don't leave me alone."

No response.

Unknown to Susie, Tahlranel was there and so was Ashara. His heart melted, and he asked Ashara to allow him to speak with her. Ashara denied his request, reminding him that Susie has everything she needs to make her choice. She smiled at Tahlranel, telling him that he could comfort her, easing her heart ache as she determines the path she will choose.

Tahlranel smiled. Instantly he sat beside Susie, wrapping his arms around her and whispering words of comfort and strength to her.

Susie sighed deeply, feeling the tension leave her body. She dried her eyes. Slowly she breathed in deeply and just as slowly she released it, repeating the process twice more. She felt better, stronger.

Quietly she reflected; "It boils down to this: if I choose the warrior path, my life will dramatically change. Some good, some not so good. If I don't choose the warrior path, my life will go on without any knowledge of the other path."

The alarm sounded; Susie rose, turning it off before slowly walking toward the doorway. "You can't miss what you don't know," she reasoned. She sighed. "I have three days to decide. Lucky me."

———

The girls bounded out of bed fairly easily this morning. Megan was very excited, her bright, blue eyes just sparkled. She laughed and giggled, wiggled and squirmed, thoroughly enjoying their routine of 'Itsy Bitsy Spider' and 'Tickle Monster'.

After their "good morning" group hug, Megan insisted (hands on hips, foot stomp and pretty, little pout style-insisted) that she needed a second one; her day was just not going to start right if she didn't have it. How could anyone refuse? With smiles and laughter, they gave her the second group hug, this time a little more enthusiastically. They toppled over, ending up on the floor and rolling with laughter.

All the way to breakfast Megan held Susie's hand, skipping along beside her and chatting all about Hazey and Mazey. Apparently, they were "in quite a pickle" (as Megan phrased it), and she didn't know how to help them. She wanted Susie to come talk to them after breakfast. Susie smiled, trying her best not to laugh, reminding Megan that she had kitchen duty right after breakfast. Susie lightly squeezed Megan's hand and told her she'd be glad to have a little chat with them after kitchen duty. Megan's frown became a joyous grin; she profusely thanked Susie for being such a good friend to Hazey and Mazey. Susie just laughed.

She and Megan were the last to arrive at the Dining Hall. Megan tended to dawdle which was why Miss Cora usually escorted her. Megan, however, had latched onto Susie this morning and was adamant that she walk with Susie. Miss Cora did not object.

As they entered, Susie was absolutely stunned. Everyone yelled, "Happy Birthday, Susie!" amid brightly colored, rainbow confetti falling down on her from its perch over the door.

Megan jumped up and down, clapping her hands, and giggling with delight. "We surprised you; we surprised you," she squealed.

Simon and Timmy came running to her, throwing their arms around her in a united, big bear hug. They were closely followed by the other children who all demanded a turn at giving Susie a birthday hug. The adults also streamed over, hugging her and wishing her a happy birthday before returning to their seats.

The Munchkins escorted Susie to their table, chattering nonstop. Simon couldn't wait to spill the beans, telling her that the top-secret party plans they had been doing were for Susie's birthday surprise. Not to be left out of the confession, Megan and Timmy quickly gave their interpretations of the plans and of what was to come, the three of them trying to be heard over each other.

A sharp, piercing whistle was heard, bringing an end to their energetic explanations.

Miss Pritchett rose from her chair, thanking Mr. Sean for restoring order. She asked everyone to bow their heads for the Blessing. Miss Pritchett asked the Blessing, ending it with thanking God for the New Year, for new beginnings and for all of the wonderful things the New Year will bring. Susie felt that same stirring in her heart as when Nana prayed, and a smile of contentment slowly emerged.

Mrs. Coppersmith had made a bountiful feast for breakfast. However, in celebration of Susie's birthday, the pancakes were Susie's favorite – nut and harvest grain. For dessert (a big surprise to everyone), she had prepared chocolate pancakes with warm raspberry syrup, whipped cream and berries on top. Now these were not your ordinary chocolate pancakes made with plain batter and chocolate chips in the batter. These were a special creation that Mrs. Coppersmith made just for Susie's birthday - a dark chocolate, fluffy buttermilk batter with chunks of chocolate chips and whole raspberries. It was like eating a big, fluffy chocolate-raspberry cake, and was an instant hit with everyone.

As a bonus, Miss Pritchett announced that chores for the children were suspended for the day; the theater room was open, and all of the G-rated movies were preloaded should the children want to watch movies today. This resulted in an explosion of claps, whistles and a variety of cheers from the children and from several of the adults. Motioning for quiet, she laughed, telling them not to forget to be on time for Lunch or for Dinner. She rang the bell and breakfast was officially over.

———

It seemed really odd not to have kitchen duty, but Mrs. Coppersmith insisted that Susie enjoy her day. Even more odd was that she really missed kitchen duty. Well, maybe not the duty part so much, but Susie did miss the fun of working with Mrs. Coppersmith, Miss Elsa, Miss Fiona - and even Miss Taryn, when she was in a good mood.

Susie, the other children and several of the adults had hurried to the Media Room right after breakfast. Although she could think of a hundred things that she could be doing (and probably should be doing), she gave in readily enough upon seeing the delighted and happy faces of the Munchkins. They romped and danced all the way to the Media Room, so happy they were spending the entire day with Susie.

As they entered the Media Room, a slight disagreement broke out between Megan, Timmy and Simon as to who would be the first to sit in Susie's lap. When she told them that unless they could find a way to agree, no one would sit in her lap. All three faces froze in panic. Quickly they began generously offering each other the coveted position of being first. After several minutes, they had an agreement as to who would be first, who would be second and who would be third. They also reached an agreement as to how long each lap sitting should be.

To prevent arguments regarding what was viewed and in what order, Miss Ginger had each of the children draw numbers from out of a bowl. Miraculously, Timmy, Megan and Simon had the top three spots. Fortunately, the selection of cartoon movies that interested them were about forty minutes each.

Here she sat, Simon currently in her lap with Megan on one side and Timmy on the other. They did indeed take turns sitting in her lap, lasting about fifteen minutes each. Currently they were watching one of Megan's favorite cartoons, having already seen Timmy's favorite. Simon's choice was next, followed by Jose's favorite, which was a full cartoon movie. By the time it ended, it would be time for lunch, after which the Munchkins would be down for their nap. Then the process would repeat itself until dinner.

They all voted to suspend Story Time in favor of movies since Story Time was every day, and they usually had movie night once a month and with only one movie. Susie didn't mind; she really wasn't in the mood to tell any stories anyway. Of course, she didn't tell them that; she just smiled and said that they made good sense.

And so, here she sat, enjoying the movies, but that was just the smallest part of it. She discovered that what she enjoyed most of all was the comradery she felt with all of the other children, the uniting and bonding as a family.

———

The day was now done, the Munchkins were in bed, and she was trying to decide whether to go to bed early or read. She had decided not to go to her sanctuary; she wanted a little distance, a little perspective away from it.

Susie had also decided not to give Simon's photo scrapbook to him just yet. Giving it to him as a present would hurt the other children's feelings, making them feel left out, especially Megan and Timmy. She decided that she would first add the pictures from Christmas and New Year's Eve before she gives it to him. It also occurred to her a few minutes ago that she could make one each for Megan and Timmy, leaving enough room for any old photos that they may have. She decided she would ask Miss Pritchett in the morning about Megan's family, and Grammy about Timmy's.

'Definitely, read,' she told herself. She had found a new book by one of her favorite authors. It was the latest in the mystery series. The young sleuth was in Scotland, visiting distant cousins while researching her family's genealogy. She stumbled upon an ancient document that would rattle the family to its core. Many had sought the document for countless generations, finally deciding it was just another highland myth. But those who didn't want it to surface would stop at nothing to keep it hidden or destroy it, and anyone who knew its contents.

"Lights out, birthday girl," Miss Cora told her with a cheerful smile. "I hope you had a really, good day."

Susie smiled. "I did."

"Good," she responded tenderly; "I'm so glad. What are you reading?"

Susie placed her bookmark on her page and handed the book to Miss Cora. "It's the newest one. I found it in the Library last week."

"Ooh, I love her books. May I read it after you've finished?" she asked.

Susie grinned. "Sure."

"Thanks," Miss Cora smiled, returning the book to Susie. Giving Susie a hug, she said with affection, "Good night, Susie."

"Good night, Miss Cora," Susie replied.

Susie crawled into bed. After her usual litany, she asked for a good night's sleep, one in which she would sleep all night through, and wake up well rested.

Morning came; Susie was delighted that it was the sound of her alarm clock waking her, and not some weird noise or anything else abnormal. She felt good; no, she decided, she felt great.

She quickly stretched, waking up her muscles and looked out her window. It was a beautiful morning. The pre-dawn light was just beginning to filter through the darkness, the birds were beginning to sing, and there wasn't a cloud in the sky. It was a great day, absolutely a perfect morning.

Humming, she made her usual morning routine, complete with Megan Time and with their 'good morning' group hug. She wondered if perhaps Dani and Megan had been right; it did seem as if their mornings and days went better now that they had group hugs.

'Could be a coincidence,' she considered. Shaking her head, she chuckled; 'Nah; it's the hugs.'

The day had gone well; everything was back to normal. She had morning kitchen duty again. The Munchkins were preoccupied with getting the buildings and set pieces of Train Town finished; most especially, though, they were engrossed with the final preparations for the 'Train Town Welcome Party' tomorrow afternoon. Juls was practicing ballet while Jared was practicing martial arts with Kevin. Dani and Kat were working on a project of their own, in which they had elicited the help of Jose and Aaron. There was a considerable amount of whispering between them at breakfast, lunch and during dinner. Whenever anyone would inquire as to what they were planning, they would do their best to feign ignorance.

She laughed as she read her journal entry. She finished recording the day's events and sighed. The thought wove through her mind that Ashara would change her journal entries as well if she didn't choose the warrior path. Nothing would remain of what she knows now.

"Tahlranel, where are you?" she asked softly. "Why aren't you here?" Her face displayed the intense loneliness and sorrow that she felt.

Unseen, Ashara shook her head, telling Tahlranel that he must remain veiled.

"Why?" he asked her.

"You know why," she answered. "I know this is difficult for you since she is your first charge who is part of the Guardian paths." She smiled reassuringly at him. "She has all she needs to make her decision."

"But she hasn't made it," he reminded her.

"True," Ashara replied.

"And if she doesn't choose?" he pressed.

"Then she has chosen," she gently explained; "for in not choosing, she has chosen not to walk the warrior path."

"But if her questions are answered, then she would choose and choose the warrior path," he countered.

Ashara's smile was a patient one. "Would she? And if she did yield to your influence, perhaps that is the wrong decision for her. You must trust that the Almighty One will enable her to make the decision that is right for her, according to His purpose and to His plan."

Tahlranel nodded, yielding to the knowledge and wisdom of his superior.

Ashara laid her hand upon his shoulder, strengthening him and comforting him. "Go and comfort her," she softly told him and left.

Tahlranel sat beside Susie in the window seat. He placed his hand on her shoulder and whispered words of comfort.

Susie sat quietly, reflecting again on all the many things that had happened just since her arrival at Glen Hollow. She thought about all the stories that Nana had told now that she knows they are real. She chuckled, remembering the many times she had wished that they were real.

"I guess you should be careful what you wish for," she laughed, amused at the irony.

She thought about Nana, Nini, Kenatae, the Nayatowah, Ashara, Levtahorel, Gorza, and that awful, evil creature currently bound by the water sprites. She thought about each and every one of the people here, what might happen to them if she did, or if she didn't, choose the warrior path. She thought about her abilities, growing stronger with each passing day. It seemed as if for each and every variable, there were dozens springing from every one.

"How can I plan? How can I possibly decide?" she asked pragmatically. "I don't have enough information. I need more answers."

'Funny,' she thought, realizing a change in her emotional state had occurred; 'it doesn't bother me as much as it did yesterday."

Sighing, she said aloud, "I don't know. Maybe I'm looking at this the wrong way. Maybe I need a new perspective."

Veiled, Ashara returned, smiling at Tahlranel. "You see; she has just taken the first step toward making a decision."

"So, she will choose the warrior path," he commented, encouraged.

Ashara laughed. "I do not know what she will choose. I do know that she is no longer overwhelmed by the thought of having to make the decision. That is the first step. She will make her decision soon."

Tahlranel smiled. "You were right," he admitted; "she can and must make the decision on her own."

"Yes," Ashara affirmed. She smiled tenderly at Susie and left.

———

Saturday morning had arrived, and Susie awoke with a song in her heart. She felt exhilarated. She leapt out of bed long before the alarm rang, joyous and feeling as if she were walking on air. In awe, Susie watched the emergence of the earliest rays of light, just before the advent of dawn. She saw the music of the light, of the earth and of the air. She heard the worship of the angels and witnessed the marvelous worship of all creation to the Creator. She danced and spun around her room, worshiping in her spirit together with them. Their song kept repeating in her mind, 'O Lord, O Lord, how majestic is Your Name in all the earth' as she danced and worshiped.

All too soon she had to leave and wake the girls; but the song remained in her heart, and she hummed it as she awakened each one. Her time with Megan seemed more precious this morning than it ever had, as did their 'good morning' group hug. Susie noticed that all of the girls were in high spirits, laughing and giggling, teasing and playful. It was good.

Breakfast was fun; everyone was in such a great mood. Miss Fiona was teasing Dale, trying to draw him out of his shell. It appeared to be working. Susie had never seen him genuinely smile, nor could she ever remember hearing him laugh. He actually had a nice smile and a pleasant laugh.

Susie watched Miss Fiona for a while, wondering why she hadn't been able to catch her alone. Every time she tried, someone would show up or Miss Fiona was called away. She desperately wanted to talk to her; she knew Miss Fiona was aware that Susie knew she was a fairy. Susie also knew that it was Miss Fiona in that portrait of Miss Pritchett as a toddler. She had so many questions and was certain that Miss Fiona could answer some, if not all. She was beginning to suspect that Miss Fiona was avoiding her.

'Like Tahlranel,' she thought. She hadn't seen him since the Visitation.

Breakfast ended and kitchen duty beckoned. Miss Taryn was in a really good mood, launching them all in a rambunctious version of 'Manic Monday', followed by 'Girls Just Want to Have Fun', followed by 'Mama Mia' and then 'Dancing Queen'. These were quickly followed by Miss Cora's choices of 'Man! I Feel Like a Woman' and 'That Don't Impress Me Much'. Mrs. Coppersmith then launched 'Purple People Eater', followed by a rousing rendition of 'Old Time Rock and Roll' (of course) to conclude their song fest.

After kitchen duty, Susie slipped upstairs to her sanctuary. She built a cozy fire, enjoying its warmth. After several minutes of contemplation, Susie decided to spend the remainder of the morning reading her journal entries, beginning with the day they arrived at Glen Hollow.

———

Lunch time found everyone eagerly anticipating the 'Train Town Welcome Party', set for later that afternoon. Story Time was cancelled due to the party, and that was okay with Susie. The Munchkins (with the help of many others) had worked very hard building Train Town, and also in preparing for the 'Train Town Welcome Party'. Their voices had reached a fevered pitch, revealing that nap time would be a misnomer today. Periodically one of the adults would remind them to use their inside voices, decreasing the decibel level temporarily but not for any length of time. Their excitement seemed to be contagious though, helping to infuse them all with a delightful sense of anticipation.

After lunch, Susie decided to visit the Chapel, the Dolphin fountain and the Unicorn statue. She began with the Dolphin fountain, then proceeded to the Unicorn statue. She still marveled at the talent that created these works. Her eyes misted a little as she gazed upon the Unicorn statue, drinking in every nuance of its sculpted form. Tenderly her hand caressed the granite mane and neck as a melancholy smile formed upon her lips.

"You look exactly like Levtahorel," she whispered to the silent creation. "Did the artist know him? Is that why you look so real?"

Last she went to the Chapel. Susie walked to each of the stained glass windows, admiring them for their beauty. She no longer wondered why the scenes depicted what they did; she knew. She sat quietly in the same pew as she had with Kat on Christmas Eve, allowing her mind to replay the event as if watching a movie. A tender smile graced her face as she softly laughed. Kat was amazing, truly amazing. Without being told why it was important that Susie remember, Kat accepted the angel's instruction and did so. She chuckled with affection remembering Kat's distress when Susie had gone into a panic mode. For all Kat's air of hostility and aloofness, she had a tender heart, one as good as gold.

Her mind wandered to the services held, especially the one just before Christmas. She laughed, remembering the songs chosen by children. She grinned, thinking how nice it was that neither the Reverend nor the adults were upset by the goofy choices – in fact, they seemed to enjoy those songs as much as the children did. A peaceful calm settled over Susie as she revisited the message given by the Reverend: true Peace and everlasting Love. An inner light caused her countenance to glow, creating a sparkle in her eyes.

Susie rose and left the Chapel. Returning to the manor, she quickly put away her outdoor clothing. Walking toward the Library, she paused at young Elizabeth's portrait for a moment before proceeding to portraits of Gabriel and Angel. Smiling fondly, she whispered a greeting to them, gently patting their necks.

Entering the Library, she strolled to the East section. Her smile broadened into a full grin when she saw the fire cheerily blazing. Someone had built a grand fire, complete with cinnamon sticks tossed into it for its heavenly scent as it burns.

She ran her hand along the short bookcase where she had found the first of Helga's books, softly laughing at the memories those books evoke.

Approaching the oak cabinet, she smiled and stood in front of it, recalling how the cabinet had caught her eye that very first time. Laughing with a soft chuckle, she remembered the effort it took to find the key that opened the cabinet. A soft sigh escaped as the memory of when she first opened the 'Histories' volume came to mind, and how she was enchanted by its beauty. A sad smile shrouded her expression as she recalled the history pages she had read, especially that of Josephine's. Her mind flashed to the letter from Edgar Allan Poe and of Josephine's journal entry, both recounting the tragic event of the death of Annabel Lee in 1824 due to pneumonia. The questions still persisted in her mind regarding both Miss Pritchett's page and the lack of one for Dara. She wondered if she would ever find the answers.

Instantly the thought leapt into her mind, 'Never, if you don't choose the warrior path.'

Shaking her head as if to dispel the thought, Susie turned to leave. As she did so, her eyes cast across the carved squares along the wainscotting. She chuckled, recalling how she took refuge in the hidden alcove from the Dani and Kat; and how, in this East section, she had heard Miss Fiona talking with someone unknown to Glen Hollow. Was it Ashara, Susie wondered. She sighed, turned and left the Library.

Next Susie made a stop at the Music Hall, remembering the day she slipped in here and played. How wonderful it had felt. She remembered the Recital that Juls had written and directed, a marvelous production.

'How truly gifted a dancer she is,' Susie mused silently; 'and instead of showcasing her own gift, she chose to write a program that would showcase the others, and focus on the meaning for the Recital.'

"Juls has come a long way," she whispered aloud.

Leaving the Music Hall, Susie crossed the corridor and entered the Parlor. The good memories flooded her, causing tears to flow down her cheeks as the scenes played in front of her. It felt as if she had stepped into them, invisible but there. It was as if time itself is a loop that is continuously circling; one only need know where to wade into it to relive the moments as they actually happen.

Quickly she turned and exited the Parlor, taking the circular stairs all the way to her sanctuary. She opened the secret door and ran to the Hidden Room, opening its door and entering. Surveying the room, she remembered every detail of its discovery, of the East Wing rooms she had explored and of the Inner Sanctum.

Susie stood in front of the painting that guarded The Secret of Glen Hollow, hiding the way to the Inner Sanctum. Now she knew the woman portrayed is the angel Ashara, the white tiger is Roktur, the Unicorn is Levtahorel, and the white wolf is Nayatowah. She sighed. She had learned so much in such a short time; but in comparison to what she didn't know, it was merely a single drop of water in a vast ocean.

Staring at the image of Ashara, she pleaded, "Why can't you tell me what I need to know? Why the silence? Why is Tahlranel gone?"

Susie waited, but no answer was forthcoming. With a heavy heart, she turned away, striding quickly out of the Hidden Room and making her way back toward her attic room. She entered the stairwell by the rock wall and descended rapidly. Running to the door of the secret floor, she hurriedly opened it. Darting into the room, she ran to the portrait of the toddler, Miss Pritchett.

Throwing back its dust cover, she looked at it again: absorbing every detail, every brush stroke. It was Miss Fiona depicted as the face of the butterfly; the face of the firefly was Miss Annie from the Diner. No doubt about it. Susie was amazed at how fast she could assimilate things now, and was astounded at how much her physical strength and agility had also increased. It wasn't just her mental and spiritual gifts that were rapidly developing, her physical body was also doing so in direct correlation, one to the other. Dropping the cover down over the portrait, Susie turned and ran back to the door, closing it behind her.

Running as quickly as she could, she reached the stairwell in no time at all, then hastily ascended the stairs. Susie darted into her attic room and closed the secret door.

Walking with an aura of unfettered determination, Susie strode to the fireplace. Opening the secret hiding place, her fingers carefully removed Miss Murielle's journal and also her letter to her daughter when Miss Pritchett was just a little girl. She carried them to the table beside Nana's chair before settling herself in the chair. Susie read them again. When she finished, Susie returned them to their hiding place.

With a slow, unwavering stride, Susie walked over to the bookcases, reached up and removed Nana's puzzle box from the shelf, placing it on the table. She opened it, removed Nana's message and read it again. Carefully she returned the message to its envelope, placing it under the envelope addressed to Simon. After closing the lid, she set the puzzle box back on the shelf. Susie returned to Nana's chair and sat quietly, watching the fire.

The afternoon had passed quickly. It was now a quarter to three; the party was to begin at three. Susie rose, extinguished the embers and made her way to the Rec Room.

———

The party was awesome, incredibly so. Miss Taryn truly had a flair, a talent, nay a gift for decorating. In each corner of the room there were brightly colored balloons, held together to form swag banners. Connecting the balloon banners were twisted crepe paper streamers of red, yellow and blue. Just below the balloon banners were construction paper trains, in bright colors, running all around the circumference of the room on bright red, construction paper train tracks. Curled paper streamers, in every color of the rainbow, hung down from the ceiling. A bright, red ribbon was wrapped around the train table, sporting a gigantic red bow on one side. A pair of cardboard "scissors", at least three feet tall, stood point down and was leaning against the train table.

Mrs. Coppersmith had several finger foods available for munching such as pizza bites, pigs-in-a-blanket, pimento cheese sandwiches, peanut butter and jelly crust-less triangles, potato chips, corn chips and cheese puffs. To satisfy a sweet tooth, there was a choice of strawberry cupcakes, mini pecan pies and apple turnovers. The thirst quenchers were coffee, apple juice and fruit punch.

The ribbon-cutting was done by the Munchkins, each one taking a turn holding the "scissors" and making a "cut" on the ribbon. Mr. Sean made the final cut (with a real pair of scissors), severing the ribbon and thus officially opening Train Town. As co-mayors, Megan, Timmy and Simon each gave a short, prepared speech. It was obvious that the person who assisted them in creating their speeches was Mr. Henry; he silently mouthed the words along with them. When they finished, the boys bowed while Megan curtsied; and everyone clapped and cheered.

Their little faces just beamed with exhilaration, their eyes sparkling as they pranced and danced around the room, giggling and laughing. Mr. Sean called them to come push the button to start the trains, and they eagerly ran to him. He had made a special red button, one big enough that all three little fingers could touch and push it at the same time. Inwardly Susie laughed; how well he knew them.

It was fun watching the trains; however, Susie thought it was more fun watching the antics of Simon, Megan and Timmy. The expressions on their faces were comical and adorable.

At four-thirty, Mr. Sean officially ended the party, allowing Mrs. Coppersmith and helpers to take the remaining food and drinks back to the kitchen and begin the preparations for dinner.

Simon was still engrossed with Train Town, so Susie decided to go upstairs and read her book. As she entered the second floor landing, she heard music coming from the East wing. It was the same tune as before. Pausing at the top of the stairs, she searched each direction. All corridors were empty.

Sprinting along the balcony, Susie arrived within minutes at the East wing door. She listened. It was still playing, softer now, but still playing. It ceased. It was so quiet. Pressing her ear against the door, she listened. There was a faint sound, but it wasn't music. Susie kept listening, straining to hear. She wasn't certain, but she thought it was laughter, like that of a small child. Now it was gone. Susie waited and waited, but neither the music nor the laughter returned.

"What is it?" she asked the door. "What is going on?"

No answer.

Turning, she sprinted back down the balcony, to the South wing and all the way to her bedroom. She had better things to do than play 'cat and mouse' or 'hide and go seek'.

Grabbing the book from her desk, she jumped onto her bed and settled against the headboard. She began reading.

———

Simon was a little petulant that Susie had not remained after the party and played Train Town with them. Although she explained to him that she wanted to finish reading her book, he still pouted. Megan forgave Susie as did Timmy, both declaring that it was okay with them. Dinner was nearly over when Simon, with a big, dramatic sigh, finally conceded, granting her his forgiveness. She laughed, thanked him and gave him a kiss.

"Puh-lease," he said as he feigned displeasure.

Timmy and Megan both vigorously protested that she didn't give them a kiss, so Susie quickly rectified her error, asking them to forgive her. Of course they did, hugging her fiercely. Simon, feeling left out, decided he also needed a hug and protested that he had not been given one. Susie gladly gave him his hug.

Order was now restored in their universe; within seconds the diminutive trio was back to giggling and laughing, planning all sorts of escapades for Train Town and its residents. Currently they had Binky, Jr, and Rocko as full-time residents, and Hazey and Mazey as part-time residents. Susie enjoyed watching their planning sessions as much as anyone. It was funny, an amazing kind of funny, to watch their minds work.

After Dinner, everyone gathered in the Parlor for Story Time. Looking at all the expectant faces, seeing their excited anticipation, Susie chuckled lightly. 'If only they knew,' she thought. However, it was not to be, and she knew it.

"Which one are you going to tell tonight?" Simon asked, bouncing on his pillow.

Timmy and Megan thought it looked like fun and also began bouncing, trying to outperform Simon's bounces and each other's. Unfortunately, Miss Ginger put a stop to it. Their eyes flashed with mischievous gleams as they pushed their pillows together, casting a quick, backward glance at Miss Ginger to see if she was watching. She was, but they didn't know it. She had slightly turned her face away to prevent them from seeing her laugh.

Susie bit her tongue to keep from laughing. The last thing she wanted to do was to encourage any further antics. Grinning, she answered Simon's question. "I thought tonight I would start one of Nana's super, special stories," she said.

"I know; I know!" Simon yelled, jumping up and down.

"No, Simon," she corrected him with a smile; "I'm pretty sure you don't know this one. You were only about two years old the last time Nana told it."

His brow furrowed as he began a pout. "Tell one I know," he insisted.

"Why, Simon? Don't you want to be as excited and surprised, and have as much fun as everyone else?" she asked.

He hadn't thought about it in that light before. He absolutely wanted to have as much fun as everyone else. Problem solved; decision made. "Okay," he readily agreed, dropping back down onto his pillow next to Timmy.

Megan and Timmy were already sprawled out onto their tummies, chins firmly planted into the palms of their hands as their elbows dug deep into their plush pillows. Now that Simon had settled himself, they were ready to begin.

"A long, time ago, in a land far away from here," Susie began telling the story just like Nana had done for her so many times.

———

Tuck-in time with Simon and Timmy was its normal routine, full of secrets shared, kisses and hugs. Reverend Tillman, apparently, had as much fun playing Train Town with them as they had with him. He regaled them with stories about the days of old and promised to take them on a real, old-timey train ride as soon as Miss Pritchett, or Mr. Sean or Mr. Henry brings them to Micah's Landing. He had told them in great detail about the train station, the switchman box, the engine, and especially the dining car and the caboose. He said they would get their own whistle, just like a real conductor. Curious, she asked if they knew what a conductor was, and was pleasantly surprised that they did know. Her reaction tickled them, and they launched into naming all of the jobs, and what they were. She was impressed.

Tapping her watch, this was Miss Ginger's third reminder trip. Susie kissed both boys, put their bedtime buddies in bed with them and told them both "good-night". Sweetly, they chorused back to her "good-night, Susie".

With great haste, she dashed down the corridor to her Dorm and to the not-so-patiently waiting Megan. Miss Cora told her to keep it short because it was already eight forty-five. Susie apologized, promising to keep it short.

Megan was not happy, crossed her arms and pouted. She promptly informed Susie that it wasn't fair that the boys get a longer tuck-in time than she does. Susie tried convincing her that, since there is two of them, it really isn't longer. Megan scowled. Susie chuckled as an idea blossomed.

"Megan, every morning you and I have about fifteen minutes together. After that, we have 'good morning' group hug time. The boys don't get that special time with me, just you. Is that fair to them? Should we stop having our special morning time so that you all have the same amount of time with me?"

Megan quickly shook her head. "No, that's okay. We'll keep our morning time, and they can have more than me at bedtime," she graciously offered.

"Good," Susie agreed. "I like our morning time, too."

Susie listened as Megan ran quickly through her secrets that couldn't wait, her plans for tomorrow, and her prayers. Susie gave her a hug and a kiss, tucked her in and told her "good-night".

Megan so sweetly looked up at Susie, her bright, blue eyes sparkling with joy. "I love you, Susie," she said; "good-night."

Tears began to well in her eyes as Susie leaned down and kissed Megan's forehead. "I love you too, Megan. Sleep well."

Susie turned and left before her tears could fall.

———

Susie couldn't sleep. She was restless, too many things pressing on her mind. Tossing back her covers, she got out bed and hurriedly dressed. It was nine forty-five. She was going to her sanctuary, using the new passage she discovered. With lightning speed, Susie hurriedly dressed, layering several layers of warm clothing.

Quietly she crept through the Dorm. Slowly she opened the door, peering out into the corridor. It was empty. Slipping out the door, she closed it gently and headed toward the laundry room. She changed her mind, deciding on the Chapel instead.

Entering the circular stairwell, she descended rapidly, pausing just out of sight on the fifth step up from the first floor landing. She peeked down into the corridor; all clear, but then it should be this time of night. Susie dropped down and ran to the Cloak Room, quickly donning her outdoor clothing. Slowly she opened the door and peered out into the corridor; again the coast was clear. She ran as fast as she could to the back door.

Bracing herself mentally for the night air, she pulled the door open, exiting into the pergola. No amount of mental preparation could truly fortify one for the intensity of just how harsh and piercing the winter air is. Within seconds of leaving the warm manor, she was shivering and shaking; and her teeth began chattering. Moving as quickly as possible, she headed for the Chapel.

Once inside the vestibule, her body heat returned to normal, relieving her of the quakes, shakes and chattering. Entering the Sanctuary, she felt the peace return; calmness and tranquility were once again hers. Slipping into the first bench she came to, she removed her coat, hat, scarf and gloves prior to taking a seat.

Closing her eyes, she absorbed the harmony, the peace and the tranquility of this place. She listened, really listened. She could hear sounds of worship. She opened her eyes; she was alone, yet she could sense the presence of another. She smiled, grinning from ear to ear. 'Tahlranel is here,' she thought.

She laughed, realizing that Tahlranel had not left her. He was remaining veiled. Why, she didn't know. And why she could now hear him, even veiled, she didn't know. But she thought it was interesting, even intriguing.

Susie softly laughed. The Reverend was coming. She could feel his presence, hear him and see him in her mind's eye.

"Susie, are you all right?" he asked, concern registering in his voice.

Smiling, she turned to face him. "I'm fine, Reverend; come sit with me," she pleasantly invited.

"I don't want to disturb you," he spoke with a gentle tone and kind smile.

"You're not. Please join me," she insisted.

The elderly man sat beside her as she scooted over to make room for him.

"Why are you here so late?" she asked, a little curious.

His smile was full of joy, and his eyes were filled with compassion and understanding as he gazed upon her. "I come here every Saturday evening before I go to bed." He winked. "I like to come to His house to tell Him good-night whenever I can."

Susie laughed and laughed. "That's funny," she told him.

"Why?" he asked, amused and a little perplexed at her declaration.

With a soft laugh, she answered; "Because God is everywhere. He hears you whether you're in the manor or in here."

The Reverend grinned and nodded his head. "Very true," he agreed. His eyes twinkled with amusement as he continued, "But I like to think of it this way: If someone calls me on the phone to tell me good-night, that's great; but if they can come to my house to tell me, that's even better. So I come to His house when I can and tell Him good-night."

Susie smiled happily. "I like that," she said softly.

He laughed lightly, nudging her shoulder with his own. "I thought you might."

They sat together in silence for quite a while. In here, time seemed to have a way of ceasing to exist, as if this place, this Chapel, was in a world all its own.

He spoke, his voice soft and kind, "Anything in particular bring you here?"

With only just the briefest motion, Susie shrugged her shoulders. "A lot of things," she replied, trying hard to keep her voice emotionless.

"Trying to solve the mysteries of the universe, I suppose," he said teasingly.

Startled, Susie turned and looked at him, unsure of how to respond.

He saw so much in her eyes, reminding him of someone he knew long ago – Miss Pritchett's mother, Murielle.

He patted Susie's hand as he compassionately told her, "Don't worry, child. You do not need to say what is troubling you. He already knows. And that is enough. I will keep you in my prayers. Would you like me to pray with you now?"

Susie nodded.

He prayed; and, oh how strong, was his spirit. He truly was a man of great faith, a mighty prayer warrior. He finished his prayer and smiled at her.

"Thanks, Reverend," she said with a huge grin, hugging him. "Thank you so much."

"You're welcome, child. Go in peace," he responded.

Standing, Susie quickly put on her outer wear and headed for the door. "Good night, Reverend," she called back to him.

"Good night, Susie."

Susie left, quickly returning to her Dorm.

Reverend Tillman rose with considerable effort, slowly walked to the altar and sank to his knees. He didn't know what troubled Susie, but he had seen many times that same look in Murielle's eyes and on her face.

She would come to him for prayer, telling him she just needed him to pray. He would do so, allowing the Spirit of God to determine what she needed and how to answer her prayer. Always she would tell him later that his prayer for her was answered; but she would never say just what the answer was, nor what the problem had been.

He never asked. As he had told Susie, God already knows what the problem is, and what the answer is. It wasn't necessary for her to confide in him in order for him to pray. All he need do is to ask God for His answer to be sent, believe that He will send it, and it will be done.

He began praying for Susie.

"Susie …. Susie… Su-- -sie-e-e."

Susie groggily opened her eyes. She yawned. 'Was that Megan?' she wondered. She yawned again and looked at her clock. It was one minute after two.

Dragging herself out of bed, Susie headed down the hallway to Megan. Megan was fast asleep. "Whatever," Susie mumbled though a yawn.

Susie returned to her bed. Sliding back under her covers, she closed her eyes and began drifting back to sleep.

"Susie …. Susie… Su-- -sie-e-e."

"What now?" Susie threw back her covers and headed back to Megan. Again, Megan was fast asleep. Or was she? Susie crept quietly across the floor, peering intently at Megan. Fast asleep. It wasn't her.

Shaking her head, Susie trudged back to her own bedroom. Wondering if it could be Kat playing a joke, Susie decided to verify that Kat was in bed and asleep. Her next stop was Dani, and finally Juls. All were fast asleep.

'Maybe I dreamed it,' she thought, shuffling back to her own room. Crawling back in bed and snuggling down, Susie slowly began drifting to sleep.

"Susie …. Susie… Su-- -sie-e-e."

The sound began pulling her out of Dreamland, but not quite.

"Susie …. Susie… Su-- -sie-e-e."

This time, she awoke. She sat still, listening. Susie watched the minutes tick by as the minute hand marked each one. After fifteen minutes and no further sounds, she decided it had to have been a dream. Again Susie slid under her covers, determined to fall asleep and stay asleep. She felt that familiar floating sensation just as twilight sleep begins, ushering you into a deep sleep.

"Susie …. Susie… Su-- -sie-e-e."

There it was again. Susie tried to ignore it. Whichever one of the girls it was, she wasn't going to be fooled into getting up again. Obviously one, or all, were playing this joke and had quite proficiently fooled her into believing they were asleep, which they weren't.

"Susie …. Susie… Su-- -sie-e-e."

She covered her ears with her pillow.

"Susie …. Susie… Su-- -sie-e-e."

Tossing her pillow aside, she bolted upright. "What!?"

"Su-- -sie-e-e."

Susie got out of bed and began looking around. The clock showed it was now two forty.

"Su-- -sie-e-e."

"Who are you?" she whispered. Susie didn't know who or what it was, but she knew it wasn't the girls. Perhaps it was the ethereal friend that has been helping her discover the secrets, or perhaps the woman in white or whoever has been playing the music.

"Su-- -sie-e-e. Come and see."

'It's a test,' she thought; 'it's got to be a test. Ashara wants to see my reaction. That's all it is.'

"Su-- -sie-e-e. Come and see."

Irritated, Susie responded, "Where are you?"

"Su-- -sie-e-e. Outside. Come and see. Come and play with me."

Chills suddenly ran through her; she realized this was not anything she has previously encountered. An ominous feeling now seemed to infiltrate her room, oppressive and alarming. She sensed a presence that was dark, very dark and sinister.

Susie looked out her window. She didn't see anyone. She waited, keeping watch by the window. Nothing. Closing her eyes, she began breathing deeply, centering herself and clearing her mind. Susie opened her eyes. She knew. It was outside. She sensed it. Whatever it was, it was in the meadow just beyond the oak tree.

She focused; she looked. She smiled. 'I see you,' Susie thought.

"Su-- -sie-e-e. Come and play with me."

Susie didn't respond; instead, quietly she slipped out of her room, quickly entering the Common Area. She was testing whatever this is to see if it knew her thoughts, or if it could see her without being present in the same room. She listened regularly and heard nothing. She listened again, deeper, and heard it projecting the sound toward her window. She smiled triumphantly.

'So it is limited,' Susie thought. 'But what is it? Is it a demon, or a vile thing like the spirit-witch or something else?'

"Su-- -sie-e-e. Come and play with me."

'Whatever it is,' Susie realized with growing dread; 'it knows who I am, where I am. And it has come for me.'

"Su-- -sie-e-e. Come and play with me."

'Maybe this really is just a test,' she rationalized, trying to remain calm. 'Maybe if I ignore it, it'll go away. No one else can hear it, just me. If I don't respond, it might get bored,' Susie tried convincing herself.

A thought wove its way through her mind, chilling her to the bone. 'If I do that, it might come after Simon, or Timmy, or Megan or any of the others. It might attack all of them.'

'I can't let that happen. I won't let that happen,' she vowed silently. 'I have to get rid of it; but how? What do I do?'

"Su-- -sie-e-e. Come and play with me." Its voice sounded more confident now, much stronger as if it gained strength by her inaction.

'Where is Tahlranel?' she wondered. 'Where is Ashara?'

Quickly she prayed, asking that Tahlranel and Ashara come to her aid. She prayed for strength, and also to know what to do to get rid of whatever it is that had come calling. Returning to her room, she dressed quickly and quietly, making certain to wear warm clothing.

"Su-- -sie-e-e. Come and play with me." It was now chanting over and over, getting louder and louder with each cycle.

As covertly as she could possibly move with all the layers of clothing she had stacked upon herself, Susie made her way downstairs to the Cloak Room. First she pulled on her boots, then she got into her coat, hat, scarf and gloves. Quietly she made her way to the front door.

Remembering her last rendezvous with this door, Susie focused, telling it to be silent. She did it more in jest than anything, but it worked. The door swung open without making a sound.

"Awesome," Susie whispered. She closed the door behind her, silence continuing to reign.

She stood on the platform, staring at the old oak tree.

"Su-- -sie-e-e. Come and play with me." Its hideous voice now carried a hint of triumph.

Silently Susie thought, 'You are really beginning to annoy me.'

"Su-- -sie-e-e. Come and play with me."

Susie knew exactly where it was; but she pretended not to know, looking all around. Slowly, deliberately she walked down the steps, crossed the driveway and headed into the meadow. Her mind flashed to her first day here – Kat had said the bad ones won't come any closer than the old oak tree out front. 'Good to know,' Susie thought.

"Su-- -sie-e-e. Come and play with me."

She appeared to be aimlessly walking, as if her destination was unknown to her. Anyone watching her would have easily made that assumption. And they would have been wrong. Susie continued her seemingly haphazard approach, as if she was completely lost.

Whatever it was, it was keeping itself veiled. What it didn't know was that Susie could see the disturbed ripples in the air around it. She knew exactly where it was, and when it moved. Each step she took, it took one as well. As she moved toward the meadow, it moved toward her.

She calculated her every step; each one bringing her closer to the old oak tree in a diagonal approach, albeit one that was in zigzag fashion. The annoying creature matched her step for step. Finally she had it where she wanted it. It had broken the barrier. It was no longer veiled, but seemed to not know it. Susie pretended not to notice, though she could see it from out of the corner of her eye. She shivered as tingles ran down her spine, becoming intense shudders. Its gruesome appearance made her heart quiver, and she struggled to maintain her composure.

"Where are you?" she called out to it while still facing away from it.

"Over here. Come and see. Come and play with me." Its voice held a cunning sense to it, like a predator stalking its prey. A feeling Susie didn't at all care to have.

Susie prayed, asking for strength, for knowledge in order to defeat whatever it is. She asked again for Tahlranel and Ashara to come to her aid. Steeling herself, Susie turned and faced it.

"What is your name?" she asked it, summoning all the courage she could.

"You can see me?" it asked surprised and confused. "No, you can't see me," it snarled, refusing to accept the truth.

"By the Power of the Name of the Almighty One, tell me your name," Susie commanded.

It groaned and growled, and then screamed at her before responding, "I am called Dekazhu; I have the strength of ten."

It moved slowly toward her like a snake ready to strike. In a gravely tone it sneered; "I know your name is Susie. I know who you are."

The depth of the insidious undercurrent in its tone caused her heart to flutter, and her knees to slightly buckle as a strong tremor rolled through her body. Forcing her knees to straighten, she stood her ground.

"I command you in the Name of the Almighty One to tell me what you are, and who sent you," she ordered it with as much confidence as she could muster.

Shrieking and howling, it quickly moved away from her as if it had been severely wounded. "I am a demon. Marnok has sent me."

It began a slow, rumbling laugh as it slithered from side to side. "Su---sie-e-e. Come and play with me."

"Enough," she said, irritated at it, and its annoying chant. "Be silent," she ordered.

It laughed again, more treacherous than before. "Su-- -sie-e-e. Come and play with me. I will show you your death. Would you like to see? Come and play with me."

Susie did not respond. A memory flashed, and she recalled the words in the Icori Legend used to defeat the spirit-witch, Shanaroosh.

The demon moved closer toward her, cackling as if it had already won. Its voice was a rasping, guttural sound, and its tone was one of triumph. "Su-- -sie-e-e. I have come for you. You are no more."

In a voice strong with conviction, of purpose and of faith, Susie commanded the demon entity, "In the Name of the Almighty One, Creator and Sustainer of all things, and by the Power of His Holy Name, I command you, Dekazhu, to return to the Abyss."

Shrieking, screaming and piercing groans erupted from the evil spirit, sounds that were far more horrifying than even its gruesome appearance. It writhed and twisted as if in great pain, thrashing and clawing desperately at the air, seeking escape from its fate. And then it was gone.

Susie closed her eyes and sank to her knees, crying and shaking. Her physical, mental and emotion strengths were spent; she dropped hard onto the ice encased snow, the palms of her hands bearing the brunt of her rapid descent. A myriad of emotions washed over her like the waves of an angry sea storming ashore, pulling and pushing, crashing and retreating until they slowly and ultimately dissipate into a calmer tide.

After all the emotions had roiled through her, calm was restored to her spirit. Weakened, she pushed herself back up onto her knees, thanking God for His protection and for sending the demon to the Abyss. She thanked Him for enabling her to stand her ground and not run from the demon, and for protecting all of Glen Hollow from it. Sluggishly she stood to her feet, a little unsteady at first, and wearily began to walk back to the manor.

The splendor of the clear night sky was beginning to darken as a blanket of black clouds began to swiftly move into the area. The beautiful moon and the bright stars were being obscured by the darkness of the thick clouds. It seemed strange to Susie that a winter storm had come out of nowhere; the forecast had been for sunny skies and warmer weather all week.

'No matter,' she thought; 'it will be daybreak soon; and even the dark clouds cannot blot out the worship of the angels, nor of creation's song to the Creator.' Susie looked forward to it.

Susie climbed up the steps; barely able to move, her body was so very tired. She paused at the landing. Slowly and with a heavy heart she looked back at the meadow. Susie couldn't help but wonder why Tahlranel and Ashara did not come, why they had left her all alone.

"I asked for them to come," she whispered. "I believed they would. Why didn't they? Why did they leave me alone?"

Tears filled her eyes, spilling down her face in a hot, salty torrent. The sense of abandonment swelled within her, gripping her heart as she struggled to understand. Susie turned around, immense sorrow and disappointment overwhelming her as she entered the manor.

Veiled were the forces of Light. Ashara, Tahlranel, Roktur, Nayatowah and Levtahorel were there and watching. Had she been in any danger, Ashara would have rescued her and sent the demon to the Abyss.

"Has she chosen?" Roktur asked Ashara.

"I don't know," was her response.

"It appears she has," Tahlranel commented.

"Appearances can be deceiving," Ashara reminded him.

"They are coming," Levtahorel stated, watching the demons surround and fill the air above Glen Hollow, darkening the sky and blotting out the moon and the stars above them.

"Yes, they are," she acknowledged; "and many more will come."

"Why do you think they sent only a foot soldier?" asked Tahlranel.

"It was a test," she answered; "they wanted to know her strength. Now they know."

"Do you think she will choose the warrior path?" Nayatowah asked.

"What I think is irrelevant. We will know soon," she answered her friend with a smile.

Roktur snorted. He smiled. "You believe she will. I know you well, my old friend."

Ashara laughed. "So you do, my old friend; so you do. But it isn't that I believe she will. I have hope that she will."

With conviction, Ashara repeated, "I have hope."

THE END

ABOUT THE AUTHOR

Karen S. Putnam lives with her husband, Philip, and their zany black cat, Shadow, in Cordova, TN. In addition to the Susie and Simon series, she has several other series which are in various states of progress. She currently is working to finish the first book in the vampire saga, after which she will finish the next book in the Susie & Simon series.

Made in the USA
Charleston, SC
14 February 2015